P9-CEI-577

Bellefleur

OTHER BOOKS BY JOYCE CAROL OATES

Bellefleur

Joyce Carol Oates

HR
A Henry Robbins Book

E. P. Dutton   New York

In the tenth chapter of Book IV (Once Upon a Time . . .) references are made to
Benjamin Franklin's "A Narrative of the Late Massacres in Lancaster County of a
Number of Indians, Friends of this Province, by Persons Unknown, with Some
Observations on the Same," in John Bigelow, ed. Works of Benjamin Franklin, Vol. IV,
Federal Edition (New York, 1904), pp. 22–48, passim; and to Benson Lossing,
The Empire State: A Compendious History of the Commonwealth of New York
(Hartford, Conn., 1888), pp. 463–465.

Portions of this novel have appeared in the following publications: "The
Birthday Celebration," in Virginia Quarterly Review; "The Spider, Love," in
TriQuarterly; "Fateful Mismatches," in Ontario Review; "Nightshade," in Story
Quarterly; "The Clavichord" in Confrontation.

For information contact:
Elsevier-Dutton Publishing Co., Inc.
2 Park Avenue, New York, N.Y. 10016

Library of Congress Cataloging in Publication Data
Oates, Joyce Carol,
Bellefleur.
"A Henry Robbins book."   I. Title
PZ4.0122Be [PS3565.A8] 813'.54 79-28193
ISBN: 0-525-06302-1

Published simultaneously in Canada by
Clarke, Irwin & Company Limited, Toronto and Vancouver

Designed by Mary Gale Moyes

10 9 8 7 6 5 4

A limited first edition of this book has been privately printed by The Franklin Library.

In memory of Henry Robbins
(1927–1979)

Time is a child playing a game of draughts;
the kingship is in the hands of a child.

—HERACLITUS

Author's Note

This is a work of the imagination, and must obey, with both humility and audacity, imagination's laws. That time twists and coils and is, now, obliterated, and then again powerfully present; that "dialogue" is in some cases buried in the narrative and in others presented in a conventional manner; that the implausible is granted an authority and honored with a complexity usually reserved for realistic fiction: the author has intended. *Bellefleur* is a region, a state of the soul, and it does exist; and there, sacrosanct, its laws are utterly logical.

—JOYCE CAROL OATES

Contents

Book Three IN THE MOUNTAINS . . .

Book Four ONCE UPON A TIME . . .

Book Five REVENGE

Bellefleur Family Tree

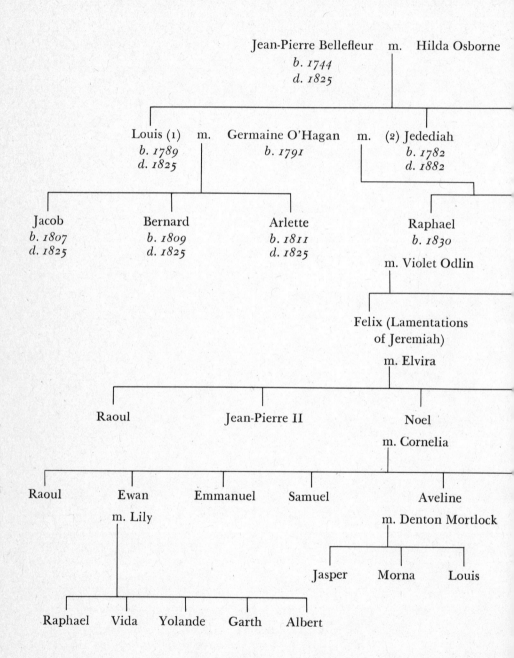

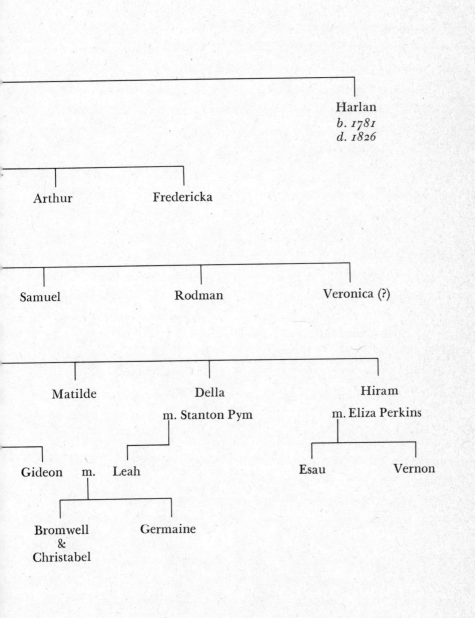

Harlan
b. 1781
d. 1826

Arthur   Fredericka

Samuel   Rodman   Veronica (?)

Matilde   Della   Hiram
m. Stanton Pym   m. Eliza Perkins

Gideon   m.   Leah   Esau   Vernon

Bromwell
&
Christabel   Germaine

Book One
MAHALALEEL

The Arrival
of Mahalaleel

It was many years ago in that dark, chaotic, unfathomable pool of time before Germaine's birth (nearly twelve months before her birth), on a night in late September stirred by innumerable frenzied winds, like spirits contending with one another—now plaintively, now angrily, now with a subtle cellolike delicacy capable of making the flesh rise on one's arms and neck—a night so sulfurous, so restless, so swollen with inarticulate longing that Leah and Gideon Bellefleur in their enormous bed quarreled once again, brought to tears because their love was too ravenous to be contained by their mere mortal bodies; and their groping, careless, anguished words were like strips of raw silk rubbed violently together (for each was convinced that the other did not, *could not*, be equal to his love—Leah doubted that any man was capable of a love so profound it could lie silent, like a forest pond; Gideon doubted that any woman was capable of comprehending the nature of a man's passion, which might tear through him, rendering him broken and exhausted, as vulnerable as a small child): it was on this tumultuous rainlashed night that Mahalaleel came to Bellefleur Manor on the western shore of the great Lake Noir, where he was to stay for nearly five years.

Bellefleur Manor was known locally as Bellefleur Castle, though the family disliked that name: even Raphael Bellefleur, who built the extraordinary house many decades ago, at an estimated cost of more than $1.5 million, partly for his wife Violet and partly as a strategic step in his campaign for political power, grew vexed and embarrassed when he heard the word "castle"—for castles called to mind the Old World, the past, that rotting graveyard Europe (so Raphael frequently said, in his clipped, formal, nasal voice, which sounded as if it might be addressed to a large audience), and when Raphael's grandfather Jean-Pierre Bellefleur was banished from France and repudiated by his own father, the

Duc de Bellefleur, the past simply ceased to exist. "We are all Americans now," Raphael said. "We have no choice but to be Americans now."

The manor was built atop a high, broad, grassy knoll surrounded by white pine and spruce and mountain maple, overlooking Lake Noir and, in the distance, the mist-shrouded Mount Chattaroy, the tallest peak in the Chautauquas. Its grandeur as well as its battlemented towers and walls proclaimed it a castle: English Gothic in general design, with some Moorish influence (for as Raphael studied the plans of innumerable European castles, and as he dismissed one architect after another, the mood of the building naturally altered), a raw rugged sprawling beauty of a kind never seen before in that part of the world. It took a small army of skilled workmen more than seven years to complete, and in that time the name *Bellefleur* became famous throughout the state, drawing much praise and flattery (which soon wearied Raphael, though he felt it his due), and ridicule in the public press (which left Raphael speechless, beyond even rage—for how could any sane, civilized person fail to be stirred by the grandeur of Bellefleur Manor?). *Bellefleur Manor, Bellefleur Castle, Bellefleur's Monument, Bellefleur's Monumental Folly:* so people chattered. But all agreed that the Nautauga Valley had never seen anything like it.

The sixty-four-room building was made of limestone and granite from Bellefleur quarries in Innisfail; from sand pits at Silver Lake, also owned by Raphael Bellefleur, tons of sand were hauled by horse-drawn wagons for the mixing of mortar. The house consisted of three sections, a central wing and two adjoining wings, each three storeys high, and guarded by battlemented towers that rose above them, with a curious massive grace. (These towers were designed to contrast with several smaller and more ornate Moorish turrets rising from the corners of various wall façades.) About the oriel windows and immense archways limestone of a fairly light hue was used, in a spiral ribbon pattern, pleasing to the eye. Most of the roof was covered with heavy imported slate, though there were sections covered with copper, which caught the sunshine brightly at times so that the manor appeared to be in flames: burning, but not consumed. From across Lake Noir, a distance of many miles, the manor took on various surprising colors, eerily beautiful at certain times of the day—dove-gray, pink-gray, mauve, a faint luminous green. The heavy, even funereal effect of the walls and columns and battlements and steep-sloping roofs dissolved across the distance so that Bellefleur Manor looked airy and insubstantial as a rainbow's quivering colors. . . .

Raphael was displeased at the slowness of the construction, and then he was displeased when it was completed. He regretted not having planned for a larger entrance hall, and a somewhat different porte cochere, and a coachman's lodge in darker stone; he would have preferred the walls even thicker than six feet (for he feared fire, which had already destroyed a number of wood-frame mansions in the area); and the loggia on the second floor, with its thick columns between the first and third floors, struck him as ugly. Sixty-four rooms, perhaps, would not be enough: suppose his party should wish to meet at Bellefleur Manor one day? He would need a guest chamber of extraordinary dimensions and beauty (later, the Turquoise Room was added) for visitors of uncommon worth; he would need three gate houses instead of two, and the central gate house should have been larger. So he fretted, and strode about his property, trying to assess what he saw, wondering if it was as beautiful as people said, or as outlandish as his eye suggested. But he could not retreat: he must go forward: and when the last team of horses dragged the last load of materials over the turnpike from Nautauga Falls, when the last pane of imported stained glass was in place, and every piece of antique or custom-made furniture delivered, and every painting and tapestry hung, and the Oriental and Turkish carpets laid, and the parks and gardens and graveled walks prepared; when the last of the rooms was wallpapered with fine imported paper, and large hasps and locks affixed to each of the heavy-gauge steel doors, and the last carpenter—there were Germans, Hungarians, Belgians, Spaniards hired over the years—set into place the last panel, or mahogany newel post, or teakwood floor; when the last white-marble mantelpiece, imported from Italy, was in place, and the last crystal and gold chandelier, and the carvings and mosaics and sculpture and drapery and paneling Raphael had desired were in his possession . . . then he looked about him, pushing his pince-nez sharply against his nose, and sighed in resignation. He had built it: and now he must live in it.

(For Raphael was afflicted from boyhood with the Bellefleur temperament, an unfortunate combination of passion and melancholy: there never was any help for it.)

By the time Mahalaleel came to the manor, however, it was much changed. All but a very few of the staff of thirty-five servants had been dismissed over the decades, and a number of the rooms were closed off, and the wine cellar was badly depleted, and the marble statues in the garden were crudely weather-stained. As the delicate Japanese trees sickened and died they were replaced by sturdier North American trees—oak, cypress, silver birch, ash: some of the most beautiful pieces of furniture had been seriously scarred and battered by children, though they were, of course, traditionally forbidden to play in most of the rooms. The slate roof leaked in a dozen places, the turrets were storm-damaged, weeds grew where an outdoor swimming pool had been planned, the parquetry floor of the entrance hall was badly injured when Noel Bellefleur, as a young man, rode one of his horses into the house, for reasons never explained. Sparrow hawks and pigeons and other birds nested in the open towers (and the stone floors of these crude structures were strewn with the skeletons of tiny creatures); there were termites, mice, even rats, even squirrels and skunks and raccoons and snakes in the house; there were, everywhere, warped doors that would not quite close, and warped windows that could not be forced open. Tulip trees badly damaged by porcupine and starving deer were not adequately treated, nor was a magnificent wych-elm whose topmost limbs had been struck by lightning. The roof of the east wing had been only superficially repaired after a bad spring storm, and on the very night Mahalaleel arrived at the manor the highest chimney of this roof would be damaged. But what was to be done? What could possibly be done? To sell Bellefleur Manor was unthinkable (and perhaps impossible), to acquire another mortgage was out of the question. . . .

Grandfather Noel rode about the property on his aged stallion Fremont, taking notes in a small black ledger, recording the repairs that must be done before another season passed, calculating (though not very accurately) the sums of money required. He was most disturbed about the condition of the cemetery, where the handsome old marble and alabaster and granite markers, and above all Raphael's mausoleum with its fine Corinthian columns, were in shameful condition. To die, and to be buried *there* . . .! And how spiteful the waiting dead would be . . . !

But he did no more than complain perfunctorily to his wife and the others, and his remarks had become so familiar by now that his sons Gideon and Ewan hardly made a courteous pretense of listening, and his daughter Aveline said, "If you would let me run the household, instead of Gideon and Ewan, maybe something could be done. . . ." But the old man was hobbled by inertia, it dragged at his ankles, dragged even at his horse's ankles, and he was apt to pause in the midst of an impassioned speech, and, with an abrupt, resigned gesture of his arm turn away. It cannot be helped, any of this, these evil days that have befallen us, he seemed to be saying, it's the Bellefleur fate, it's our curse, there is no escaping it in this life. . . .

The Bellefleurs had always been distinguished from their neighbors in the Valley, not only by their comparative wealth, and their controversial behavior, but by their remarkable history of misfortune. Fate doled out to them an ordinate amount of good luck but then countered with an inordinate amount of bad luck. Impossible to characterize our family's experience, Vernon Bellefleur thought: are we beset by tragedy, or merely farce?—or melodrama?—or pranks of fate, sheer happenstance, that cannot be deciphered? Even the Bellefleurs' innumerable enemies considered them exceptional people. It was generally thought that the Bellefleur "blood" brought with it a certain capricious melancholy, a propensity for energy and passion that might be countered at any time by a terrifying bleakness, a queer emptiness of vision: so great-uncle Hiram once tried to describe the phenomenon by speaking of the exuberance of water gushing from a pipe . . . and then draining away, swirling away, down a drain . . . sucked by gravity back into the earth. First you are one, he said; and then, suddenly, you are the other. You feel yourself being sucked away . . . your exuberance sucked away . . . and there is nothing, nothing, you can do about it.

Bellefleur women, though troubled by the swelling and ebbing of this mysterious energy themselves, tended to minimize the phenomenon by saying it was a mood, a phase, a humor someone was going through. "Ah, you're in one of your moods, are you," Leah might say lightly to Gideon, as he lay fully clothed on their bed, in his muddy riding boots, his head drooping over the side and his face gone dark with blood and his eyes quite unfocused; and though he would not reply—though he might lie like that, paralyzed, hardly breathing, for hours—it was still only a mood in Leah's estimation. "Where's Gideon?" Leah's mother-in-law Cornelia would surely ask as the family assembled for dinner in the smaller dining room—for the large dining room in the manor's central wing, with its somber, heavy German tables and chairs, its morose Dutch oils, its begrimed ornamental plasterwork and crystal chandeliers in which tiny spiders had spun a galaxy of webs, and its eight-foot-high fireplaces which had acquired over the decades the look and even the smell of open tombs, had not been used for years—and Leah would shrug her magnificent shoulders indifferently and say, "He's given himself up to a mood, Mother." And her mother-in-law would nod wisely and make no further inquiries. After all her eldest son Raoul had long ago given himself up to a mood, a sinister humor, and her brother-in-law Jean-Pierre, imprisoned in Powhatassie at this time, was said to have committed a crime, or crimes, of so ludicrous a magnitude that if he were guilty (and of course he was not: the judge and the jurors, openly prejudiced against the Bellefleur family, had refused to consider his case fairly) it was certainly as a consequence of a demonic black mood, and nothing else. And when great-great-great-grandfather Jedediah retreated to the side of Mount Blanc, there to seek God in His living essence, surely it was a surrender to a curious mood, a treacherous mood . . . one which might have obliterated the entire Bellefleur line at the start. A cousin of grandfather Noel's, in a temper over the family's plans for his life, threw himself into the revolving blades of a thirty-six-inch saw at one of the family's Fort Hanna sawmills, and it was said of him, contemptuously, that he had given himself up to a mood. . . . And Leah herself, who was considered by her husband's immediate family to be almost too self-possessed, had been violently beset by odd quirks of behavior as a girl. (She had had the *oddest* pets, it was said. The *oddest* infatuations.)

It must have been a mood, on that unnaturally warm September night, that provoked her into a quarrel with her husband: it must have been a mood that led her into running downstairs and giving refuge to Mahalaleel at all. She knew, everyone speculated, that Mahalaleel's presence would madden poor Gideon. . . .

And so indeed it came about.

All that day the sky above Lake Noir was lurid with pale orangish-green swaths of light, as if it were sunset, and the sun were setting less than fifty miles away at the very rim of Mount Chattaroy. The mountains to the north were invisible. The air was malevolent. Toward dusk a warm rain began, gently at first, and then rippling with increasing violence across the lake. Then the wind lifted. The unnaturally dark waters of Lake Noir were whipped darker still, waves rose and sprawled forward and rushed wildly to shore, sleek and leaden-gray, with an air of angry impatience. One could hear—one could *almost* hear—their voices.

Young Vernon Bellefleur, walking in the pine woods, wondered if he should take refuge in the old workers' barracks below the cemetery, or run for home. Storms terrified him: he was a great coward. He could hear voices in the winds, crying piteously for help, or simply for attention—from time to time it seemed to him, horribly, that he could recognize a voice. Or did he imagine it, in his abject terror . . . ? His grandfather Jeremiah, swept away in a flash flood, nineteen years ago, in a storm like this—his baby brother Esau who had lived only a few months—his own mother Eliza who had disappeared after kissing him and tucking him in bed for the night—*Goodnight, my sweetheart, goodnight, my little one, my mouse, my sweet baby mouse.* . . . He listened, in terror, and did not dare move.

The child Raphael, watching the storm approach from a closed-off room on the third floor of the east wing, shielded his eyes as the sky was split by lightning. He cried aloud at the surprise of it. For a brutal instant Mount Blanc was illuminated: it had taken on a queer hard mistless flattened quality, like a paper cutout, glaring with light that pulsed from within. Raphael too heard disembodied cries, blown like mere leaves. The Spirits of the Dead. They sought refuge on nights like this but, being sightless, they could not really determine how close they were to the living.

Later that night, before he undressed for bed, Gideon Bellefleur checked windows and doors, seeing with angry resignation how the roof leaked in one room after another, and how ill-fitting the window frames were—but what good did it do, to be angry? The Bellefleurs were rich, they were certainly rich, but they hadn't any money; they hadn't enough money; not enough to repair the manor with the thoroughness it required, and what point was there in small, short-range repairs? Gideon reached out to close a banging shutter, his head bowed, his face contorted, his lips pressed tightly together so that he would not mutter an obscenity. (Leah could not tolerate obscenities from him. Or from any man. *You want to desecrate life,* she cried, *by desecrating the very origins of life: I forbid you to say such ugly things in my presence.* But then she herself frequently swore. When vexed or frustrated she swore, schoolgirl oaths, childish exclamations, *Oh, hell, damn, goddamn!*—which upset Gideon's mother but which struck Gideon himself as irresistibly charming: but then his young wife was so beautiful, so magnificent, how could she fail to be charming no matter what sprang from her lips?) It was at that moment Gideon saw, or believed he saw, something emerge from the darkness at the edge of the lawn two floors below. It moved against the wind with remarkable alacrity and grace, like a gigantic water spider, skittering across the surface of the grass. *My God,* Gideon murmured softly. The thing, thwarted by the high garden wall, hesitated a moment, then made its way along the wall, less gracefully now, groping as if blind.

Gideon leaned out the window, staring. His face, his thick long hair, the upper part of his body were soaked with rain. He would have shouted —shouted something—but his throat was constricted, and anyway the wind was far too loud, and would have blown his words back into the room. Then there was another flash of lightning and Gideon saw that a large slovenly wisteria tree, grown sprawling against the wall, was buffeted about by the wind so that it gave the odd appearance of moving toward the house. But that was all: nothing else was there: his vision had tricked him.

For a while the storm subsided, and everyone went to bed, and then the winds began with renewed force, and it was clear that no one would sleep much that night. Leah and Gideon embraced in their bed, and spoke nervously of things they had agreed not to speak of again—the condition of the house, Leah's mother, Gideon's mother, the fact that Leah wanted another baby and could not, could not, for some reason could not conceive though she was already the mother of twins (five years old at the time, Germaine's sister Christabel and her brother Bromwell); and then they were quarreling; and somehow Leah, sobbing, struck Gideon with her rather large fist, on the left side of his face; and Gideon, stunned at first, and then furious, gripped her shoulders and shook her, *What do you think you're doing, who do you think you're hitting,* and threw her back hard against the headboard of their antique bed (Venetian, eighteenth-century, a canopied intricately carved gondola outfitted with enormous goose-feather and swansdown pillows, one of the silliest of Raphael Bellefleur's acquisitions, Leah's favorite piece of furniture, so wondrously vulgar, so lavish, so absurd—she had rejected the bed her parents-in-law gave them when she came as a bride to the manor, and insisted upon this one after having wandered through the closed-off rooms, knowing precisely what she wanted: for she had played in the manor as a very young girl, one of Gideon's cousins, one of the "poor" Bellefleurs from the other side of the lake). And then she kicked at him, and he threw himself on her, and they grappled, and cursed each other, and grunted, and panted, and as the storm raged outside they made love, not for the first time that night, and ground their damp tearful faces against one another, and murmured *I love you, oh, God how I love you,* and not even the Spirits of the Dead, their forlorn tumultuous heartrending cries, could penetrate their passionate heaving ecstatic labor. . . .

And then it was over, and both were asleep. Gideon swam effortlessly, through what must have been a flood; but he was untouched by uprooted trees, debris, even corpses flung along by the current; his heart swelled with triumph. It seemed that he was hunting the Noir Vulture once again. That enormous white-winged creature with its hunched shoulders and mottled, naked, monkeyish face. . . . Leah sank to the very bottom of sleep, where she was pregnant at once: not only pregnant but nine months' pregnant: her belly swelled and pulsed and fairly pounded with life.

And then, suddenly, she was awake.

Downstairs, at the very front of the house, far away, something was crying to be let in.

She could hear it plainly: it was crying, begging, clawing to be let in.

Leah shook off her warm, heavy, mesmerizing sleep, and was at once drawn up to the surface where the storm still howled, and something begged piteously for entry. Without hesitating she rose naked from bed and slipped on her silk robe—one of the few items of clothing that still remained from her trousseau of six years ago, now badly frayed and a little soiled at the cuffs. Her husband flung an arm toward her and murmured her name in his sleep, querulously, possessively, but she pretended not to hear.

She lit a candle and shielded the flame with her hand and body so that Gideon would not be disturbed, and hurried barefoot out of the room. Once she was in the corridor she could hear the creature quite plainly. It was not a human cry, it had no language, but she understood it at once.

And so Germaine's mother went to open the door to Mahalaleel: naked beneath the white silk robe that fell to her ankles: a tall woman, an exceptionally tall woman, tall and strong and full-bodied, her long legs superbly muscled, her neck columnar, her thick braid of dark, burnished-red hair falling between her shoulder blades, heavily, to the very small of her back: a beautiful giantess upon whose deep-set eyes and long, straight, Roman nose and slightly parted fleshy lips the candlelight swayed and shimmered caressingly.

"Yes?" Leah cried, as she descended the great mahogany staircase. "Who is it? Who is out there?"

She hurried downstairs without glancing at the old tapestries, which hung in spent, faded folds, and the niches in the stone wall where marble busts—of Adonis, Athena, Persephone, Cupid—had been accumulating masks of grime for decades, and now rather resembled mulattoes of indeterminate sex; she passed the curious old Civil War drum on the first-floor landing, which Raphael Bellefleur had had covered with his own skin, after his death, and edged with brass, gold, and mother-of-pearl (poor Grandfather Raphael!—he had anticipated homage for generations, and now not even the idlest of the children took notice of him): she hurried, barefoot, her heels striking the faded crimson carpet heavily, the flickering candle held aloft, tendrils of dark richly-red hair loose about her forehead, her great eyes bright with unaccountable tears.

"Yes? Who is it? Who is it? I am Leah, I am coming to let you in!"

There was such a commotion, what with the clawing and wailing at the door, and Leah's full-throated cry, that the rest of the castle—already awake because of the storm, or sleeping only fitfully—was soon out of bed. In those early years the twins were always sharply attuned to their mother, Christabel especially: now they slipped past Lettie and ran along the first-floor corridor from the nursery, little Bromwell whimpering as he adjusted his wire-frame glasses, Christabel wild-haired and tearful, her nightgown slipping from one small shoulder. "Mother, where are you! Mother! Is it a ghost trying to get in!" And naturally the cousins sprang out of their beds, Lily's and Ewan's noisy children, crowded together as they peered wide-eyed over the banister: and Ewan himself, bear-sized, vexed, his broad face reddened and his graying hair crazy about his head as if the gypsy moth had got into it to spin her amazing cocoon: and aunt Lily trailing along behind, a cashmere shawl over her shoulders and clutched at her sagging breasts, her pale wan face as unfocused as a smeared watercolor, pulling at her husband's arm, "Oh, what are they doing now, oh, stop them, Ewan, is it Gideon, is it Leah, what on earth are they doing *now*—" And at the very head of the stairs Vernon appeared, trembling, his mismatched pajamas hanging from his skinny frame. He could not stop himself from pulling at the straggly white-blond hairs that grew from his chin, for he had very narrowly escaped certain spirits, that afternoon in the forest, he had run desperately home as they chattered and shrieked and clutched at his sleeves, and pinched his ears and aimed tiny burning mocking kisses at his pursed lips, and now it seemed to him that the boldest of the spirits had found him out and would in a moment break down the door and rush up the stairs to claim him. . . . Yet he did not shout at Leah to leave the door unopened, like the others.

Edna the housekeeper was up, her flannel robe straining across her enormous breasts; and the servants Henry and Walton; and the children's tutor Demuth Hodge, whose hair stood up in comic tufts; and at last poor Lettie, who woke to find the twins gone from their beds and a violent wind rocking the house and rain in gusts pitched against the windows, like pebbles thrown by a mad hand. "Bromwell, Christabel, where are you!" she cried. (Though her thoughts—poor Lettie!—were only of their father.) And grandfather Noel appeared in his underclothes, which were shamefully soiled. His yellowish white hair floated about his skull and his foreshortened, beakish face was livid with rage. "Leah! What is this! Why have you thrown the entire household into chaos! I forbid you to open that door, girl! Don't you know what happened in Bushkill's Ferry, haven't any of you *learned*—" He limped badly, for his right foot had been nearly blown away in a mine explosion in the closing days of the War.

And there was aunt Aveline in her quilted satin robe, her hair done up in dozens of curling rags, and her husband Denton close behind with his bland mollusk's face, and their sharp-nosed little girl Morna, and their thirteen-year-old Louis who was grinning stupidly, thinking that one of Uncle Gideon's enemies had come to get him, and wiry little Jasper who broke away from his mother's clutching hand and ran boldly down the stairs after Leah—"Aunt Leah, do you want help! Do you want help opening the door!" And naturally Lily's and Ewan's children ran down too, the girls Vida and Yolande as noisy as Garth and Albert, and only Raphael holding back: for in truth of all the Bellefleurs Raphael was perhaps the most frightened, that tumultuous night of Mahalaleel's arrival. Far away upstairs grandmother Cornelia was muttering angrily to herself as she tried to adjust her wig without a servant's kindly assistance (for the old woman believed that the house had been struck by lightning and was on fire, and she *must* leave her room, and of course her pride would not allow her to be seen by her sons and daughters-in-law and grandchildren and even by her old husband, without her new French wig). Great-grandmother Elvira stirred in her sleep but was unable to wake: the cruel winds pitched her about, she saw clearly the waters of the Nautauga rising (as indeed they did that night, some twenty inches an hour during the worst of the storm), and reasoned angrily once again with her husband Jeremiah *not* to try to save the horses, as he did nineteen years ago; but of course the stubborn old man paid no attention to her though his overalls and even his bushy black beard were soaked, and something very sharp had pierced his boots so that the left boot had filled with blood, and the ugly scar on his forehead, a war wound of which he was foolishly proud, had gone white with apprehension. "Do you want to drown! Do you want to drown and be swept away!" she shouted at him. "Then I won't be responsible for you! I won't be responsible for locating your miserable old carcass and burying it!"—which indeed she was not, as it happened. Uncle Hiram who so frequently walked in his sleep, especially at this point in his life, was, oddly, soundly sleeping in his bed, in his handsome bedroom suite overlooking the garden; he was to know nothing of the commotion, and to express astonishment, the next day, both at the fact of Mahalaleel and at his niece Leah's headstrong behavior. ("But why cannot Gideon control his wife," he was to inquire of his brother Noel, "isn't the boy somewhat *ashamed* of their relationship?") Aunt Veronica did not come downstairs either, though she had been awake, evidently, for hours; she heard the shouts and felt a faint curiosity but remained in her room, fully dressed, a rain cape about her shoulders, simply waiting—waiting out the storm?—waiting.

And then Gideon himself appeared at the top of the staircase, snapping up his trousers. His great muscular chest gleamed with perspiration beneath the matted dark hair; his mouth was an angry red circle inside his beard; his eyes fairly bulged in their sockets. "Leah," he shouted, "what the hell are you doing down there? Whoever wants to get in—let me see to it! *Let me see to it.*"

But of course it was too late. Leah, helped by Jasper and Albert, had unlocked the door and was struggling to swing it open (this particular door, in the old entrance hall at the very center of the manor, was never used now: it was made of solid oak on both sides, and lined with steel to make it fireproof, and must have weighed nearly one hundred pounds:

and of course the hasps and hinges were badly rusted); and quite suddenly it *was* open, blown back furiously against the wall; and rain exploded inward; and there in the immense arched doorway—there, scuttling desperately and ignominiously inside, rushing toward Leah's feet, was a skeletal creature, no more than rat-sized, its dark fur wet, its ribs showing, its silvery-gray whiskers broken, its tail limp and dragging and thin as a shoelace. What an ugly thing! What a begrimed starving contemptible rain-soaked ugly thing!

Gideon hurried down the rest of the stairs, shouting. Why, the thing was a rat: he would kick it to death at once. Ewan's oldest son Garth made a swipe at it with a chair. Jasper clapped his hands and yodeled to frighten it. Grandfather Noel was shouting that it was a trick of some kind, a trick to distract them—they were in danger—there were Varrells crouched outside in the shrubbery—why hadn't anyone thought to bring a gun? The creature, terrified, was cringing behind Leah's legs, its belly flat against the floor. Bromwell said that it was a muskrat and wouldn't harm anyone: could he have it, could he have it as a pet? Gideon shouted that it was a rat, it was diseased and filthy and would have to be killed. Someone thought to close the door—the rain was torrential—but now the poor creature could not escape. Gideon approached it, Leah tried to push him aside, saying, "Let him alone! What does it matter if he's ugly!" and a noisy half-circle of children advanced, stomping, clapping their hands. The creature hissed, retreating; then, seeing it was trapped, it sprang forward and darted between Gideon's legs; then it ran crazily along the wall, colliding with table legs, bumping against grandfather Noel's naked ankles. Everyone was screaming: some in alarm, some in excitement. A rat! A giant rat! Or was it a muskrat! Or an opossum! Or a wildcat! Or a fox cub!

It ran from side to side, its teeth bared, its ears laid back. Leah stooped to catch it. "Here! Come to me! I won't hurt you, poor thing!" she cried. And it hesitated only an instant, and then—seeing Gideon bearing down, his face contorted—it leapt into her arms. But so great was the commotion, so obstreperous the children, that it panicked in her arms and began snarling and scratching and tearing at her with its teeth. "Now! Now! Poor thing!" Leah cried. She held the squirming creature, which was evidently much heavier and more muscular than its skeletal shape indicated, and would not let it leap free, and crooned to it as if to a baby, though she was bleeding from a half-dozen welts on her arms and cheeks. Della, Leah's mother, appeared in the foyer, in a long black gown, her small, nearly bald skull covered by a transparent black nightcap, crying, "Leah! Put that thing down! What on earth are you doing! I say—*put that thing down at once!*" She tried to seize Leah, but Leah jerked away; Gideon tried to wrench the creature from Leah's arms, but she would not surrender it, saying, "Why do you torment the poor thing—why are you so cruel?" She held the squirming creature away from her body but it was still slashing at her, and now there were ugly red welts on her shoulders, and even on one of her white, hard, lovely breasts—the sight of that must have maddened her husband. "Ah, now you're being naughty!" Leah said in a queer exultant voice. "Do you want *me* to punish you?"

"Leah, for God's sake let me get rid of it," Gideon said.

But there was no reasoning with Leah once she fixed her mind on something.

She lifted the creature slowly above her head, so that it could not *quite* reach her with its flailing claws. The muscles of her magnificent shoulders and arms grew taut. Still crooning she managed to calm the creature, and at last to stroke its head. "Poor thing, poor wet cold terrified thing, are you hungry?—would you like to be fed, and sleep by the fire? You can't help your ugliness, can you!"

She lowered it and cradled it in her arms, though it was shivering convulsively. "You're a poor lost thing, like any of us," she whispered.

And that was how Mahalaleel came to Bellefleur Manor: Leah saved him, and took him back to the kitchen where a fire was burning, and gave him food—milk, scrapings from a frying pan, bacon rind, chicken bones—which he nibbled at without much zest, trembling, his eyes darting ratlike in his angular, bony head, his skinny silly tail lying limp on the floor behind him. Then she dried him in a big towel, murmuring, "Now you'll be warm, now you'll be safe, now no one will harm you," ignoring her husband and her mother, who were pleading with her to do something about her wounds. Gideon stared at the welts, at the glistening blood, and his heart sank within him, and his vision went black, and he felt—ah, how bitterly he felt!—his soul close to draining out of his body: for his beautiful young wife, his cousin Leah, the mother of his twin children whom he loved so much he could not bear it, *would not* obey him. All of the Nautauga Valley held him in awe, there was not a man in the region who dared stand up to him, but his own wife—his own wife!—defied him constantly, and what could he do? He loved her, he was sick with despair over her, and would have wrenched the skinny shivering Mahalaleel out of her arms and snapped his neck with one deft gesture if he believed it might have made any difference: which Mahalaleel, gazing at him covertly, through his silvery-white lashes, must surely have sensed.

"Come to bed, Leah," Gideon said wearily.

The others had retreated. The house was now quiet. Even the storm had subsided. Was it near dawn? Leah, stretching, half-closed her eyes with pleasure, her body rippling like a fish's, as if she were oblivious of Gideon. At her feet, on the flagstone hearth, the wretched creature slept at last.

"Come to bed," Gideon said, taking her arm.

She did not resist. With a modest gesture she drew her ripped, bloody robe closed over her breasts, and turned to her husband as if to bury her face in his shoulder.

"You must be very tired," he said.
"*You* must be very tired," she said softly.

And in the morning when Edna went into the kitchen, she took one look at the animal by the fire—she took a single look, and cried aloud, and ran to her mistress. For there slept on the hearth not the starved, contemptible, ratlike wretch of the night before, but an extraordinarily beautiful cat: an enormous long-haired cat with coppery-pink fur, puffed and silky, and an elegant plumelike tail, and stiff, long silvery whiskers that fairly bristled with life. "Mahalaleel," Leah said, naming him at once, snatching at a sound she had never heard before—but somehow it was exactly right, it *was* exactly right—as if an imp had whispered it in her ear. (Later she was told *Mahalaleel* was out of the Bible, and she halfway wondered if the name was appropriate: for Leah was one of the Bellefleurs who prided themselves on their contempt for the Bible.) "Mahalaleel," she whispered, *"aren't* you a beauty. . . ."

The cat stirred luxuriously, and opened its eyes—pellucid, frost-tinged ovals in which black slits appeared to float, languidly—and made a gurgling sound of assent, as if it recognized her. Surely it did recognize her.

"Mahalaleel—?"

Leah knelt before him, lost in wondering. She made a gesture to stroke his head but he stiffened—his marvelous ears moved a small fraction of an inch back—and she hesitated. "Aren't you a beauty after all," Leah whispered, gloating. "Wait till the others see you!"

She commanded Edna to heat milk for him—no, not milk: cream: Mahalaleel must have cream. And fed him herself in a chipped Sèvres bowl. At last he allowed her to touch him, shyly at first, and then with more confidence. (Ah, if this enormous creature should turn on her, as an aged, half-blind hunting dog had once turned on her when she was a noisy little girl!—if he should become enraged suddenly, and rake her with those nails, and tear at her exposed flesh with those fangs! But it was a risk she took eagerly, her blood pulsing with a queer delirious pleasure.) She stroked the thick silky fur of his back, and even rubbed his head behind his ears, and tickled his chin, and pulled out a half-dozen stinging nettles from his fur, and rejoiced at the sudden purring sound, both guttural and crackling, he made deep in his throat. What a beauty! What a marvelous creature! When the rest of the family saw him they would be astonished! He finished the cream, and Leah scrambled to her feet to find him something more—cold roast beef, a cold chicken leg—and he devoured it with a fastidious zest that was a pleasure to see. His immense plume of a tail, in which hairs of myriad colors meshed—bronze, saffron, dove-gray, black, white, silver—rose slowly until it was erect, fairly quivering with delight.

Leah sat a short distance away, the skirt of her robe tucked about her ankles, her arms hugging her knees, staring. Mahalaleel must weigh thirty pounds, she estimated. And he was *not* part bobcat or lynx, he hadn't any mixed blood, he was a purebred, as flawless an aristocrat as the Persian cat Leah had coveted many years ago, belonging to the headmistress at La Tour, where Leah had boarded as a schoolgirl. Girls who by docility or high grades or shrewd maneuvering found themselves favorites of Madame Mullein were allowed to stroke the cat's head on certain occasions: but of course naughty noisy rebellious Leah had never been a favorite. Ah, that bitch Mullein! Leah had wished the woman dead, and indeed she *was* now dead, and now Leah had a cat of her own, a creature quite simply the most beautiful animal she had ever seen. (And of course Leah had adored her horses, especially as a young girl; and she had had, from the age of twelve until nearly nineteen, when she became engaged to Gideon Bellefleur, a most unusual pet—a large satiny-black spider of which she was inordinately, and perversely, fond; and she'd had a sentimental attachment to numerous Bellefleur hounds, and the usual household cats and kittens: but none of these creatures was to mean as much to her as Mahalaleel.)

"Yes, aren't you a beauty, *aren't* you a gift," Leah murmured, hardly able to tear her eyes away from Mahalaleel, who was now washing his paws with quick, deft strokes of his pink tongue, oblivious of her. There was something mesmerizing about his fur: roseate, shining, silky and light as milkweed fluff, and yet astonishingly thick; and how endlessly fascinating, how haunting, the pattern—which she could not *quite* discern—made by those thousands of hairs, each with its own subtle color. From a distance of some feet Mahalaleel looked one color, a frosty pinkish-gray; closer up he looked another shade, laced with bronze. From one angle he appeared to be eerily transparent, as the morning sunshine penetrated his fine, delicate, rather large ears; from another angle, where his long, thick tail and his somewhat outsized feet with their pink-gray pads were in evidence, he looked massive—a creature whose considerable bulk was dense with muscle, though disguised by deceptively pretty, even frivolous fur light as bird's down. But how magnificent! Leah stared and stared.

Hugging her knees, her disheveled braid lying over her right shoulder, she stared at the beast she had named Mahalaleel. He was an omen, quite clearly: an omen of great good fortune. How languidly he washed himself, oblivious of her. . . . Half-consciously she fingered the scratches he had made the night before in his terror. They still hurt, and had now begun to itch. Her fingertips took note, with a curious bemused detachment, of the fine, hard, hairlike ridges of coagulated blood on her forearms, and shoulders, and low on her right cheek, and even on her right breast: ah, the strange pleasure of seeking out those welts, scratching them lightly, teasingly!—the strange pleasure of encountering such very interesting and unexpected textures on her own flesh, where, the previous day, there had been only smooth unmarked skin. And though this beautiful creature had hurt her he had behaved without knowing what he did, and was consequently innocent.

"Mahalaleel? Why have you come to us?" Leah whispered.

The cat continued to wash his paws, and then his ears, and then he stretched and yawned—showing magnificent teeth, ivory-white, so sharp and strong that Leah drew in her breath. Suppose he *should* suddenly attack her . . . ? Suppose he should sink those teeth, sizable as an ocelot's, into her flesh? She leaned forward to pet him again, moving cautiously. With an aristocrat's natural disdain he drew away slightly, and then allowed her to stroke his head. "My beauty, my Mahalaleel," she said.

When the rest of the household saw Mahalaleel they were, of course, astonished. That skinny ratlike creature of the night before, that ugly doomed little beast—! Transformed into *this*.

Grandfather Noel spoke for them all by stammering, "But it doesn't —it doesn't seem *believable*—"

Mahalaleel stretched and turned away, curling into a massive ball on the hearth, ignoring them.

From that day onward the uncanny creature Mahalaleel lived with the Bellefleurs; indeed, he had the run of the castle, and everyone's awed admiration—everyone's, that is, except Gideon's. Gideon could not help but wish from time to time that he *had* broken the creature's neck, on that stormy night. For it seemed (though why it seemed so, no one knew) that everything began on that night. And, once begun, it could not be stopped.

The Pond

Mink Pond, a half-mile north of Bellefleur Cemetery. In a stand of hemlock and mountain maple and ash. In a sun-dappled secret place.

Mink Pond, where Raphael Bellefleur, the twelve-year-old son of Ewan and Lily, played and splashed about and swam, and spent long hours lying on the small raft he had fashioned out of birch logs and wire, staring into the water. Most days it was clear, and he could see to the muddy bottom seven or eight feet below at its deepest.

Mink Pond, a pond so new and so secret that the older Bellefleurs knew nothing about it. If someone asked Raphael where he'd been all morning and he said, in his rapid indistinct murmur, Oh, nowhere—the pond, his grandfather Noel would assume he was talking about a pond just the other side of the old pear orchard. There's plenty of bass there, his grandfather said, and I've seen herds of white-tails browsing there, one time more than thirty-five, I counted them, the biggest old buck with an antler spread of three feet, I swear!—but you know, boy, that pond's a home for snapping turtles too and those buggers are dangerous. He poked Raphael with his forefinger, chuckling. D'you know what a snapping turtle can do to a young boy wading?—or fool enough to swim? And as Raphael blushed red, and yearned to escape (for he was a shy child who rarely raised his voice, and made every effort to avoid the raucous company of the other boys), the old man laughed crudely, pressing his hands against his little potbelly, which strained against his vest and trousers, rocking from side to side. D'you know what one of them hefty old buggers can do, snapping away at nice warm tender meat dangling in front of him?

Mink Pond, which was Raphael's discovery, down behind the graveyard where none of the children played. The day after Mink Creek flooded, wild from melting snow up in the mountains, flooded more than any of the other creeks that flowed into Lake Noir, Raphael tramped out in his rubber boots, blinking against the glare of the sun, his hands stuck in his pockets for warmth though it was April and nearly spring and the terrible winter was said to be over. (Up in the mountains there were great gorges and valleys packed with snow, people said. There were glaciers of such cruel dense silvery-blue ice, jammed in sunless ravines, that perhaps they would never melt and there would be a new Ice Age, and what then? —would the Bellefleurs have to travel about by sleigh, as in the old days, or walk with snowshoes everywhere, like old Jedediah?—would tutors have to live in the manor to instruct the children, or would there be no education at all?) But the snow did melt, and the creeks did go wild, and overflow their banks, and as the warm spring rain fell the ice-locked world of the highest mountains groaned and gave way and turned to water that rushed downhill, fiercely downhill, in hundreds of runs—Laurel Run, Bloody Run, Hare Run, Columbine Run—spilling into rivers and creeks, headed for the lake, and then for lower ground, and, it was said, for the ocean hundreds of miles away, which the children had never seen. Raphael, studying the handsome old globe in the library (it was so large that not even big-armed Ewan could reach all the way around it and touch his fingertips together), could not even find Lake Noir, and grew dizzy at the thought of the ocean's immensity. With something so big, he told his cousin Vernon, you would have to spend your entire life just making your mind equal to it. . . . I don't ever want to see the ocean.

Mink Creek in less turbulent seasons was a wide meandering creek where Bellefleur horses and cattle and sheep watered; though narrower, and steeper, on higher ground, it sprawled in the meadows, turning back lazily on itself in a sequence of *S*'s. It was fairly shallow in parts, and as deep as twelve or fifteen feet in others. Cattail and sedge and alder and willow bushes grew thick and disorderly on its banks. Great bleached-white boulders lay strewn everywhere, tossed down, the children were told, by a giant with a bad temper who lived atop Mount Blanc. But when did that happen, they asked. Oh, a hundred years ago, they were told. But did it *really* happen, they asked. *Really?*—what do you mean, *really?* You see the boulders there, don't you? Go out and judge for yourselves!

Alone Raphael tramped upstream one morning, thinking he would discover the creek's source. His uncle Emmanuel was famous in the Valley (though people laughed at him too: certainly Ewan and Gideon laughed at him) for the fine, fastidiously detailed maps he had made of the mountains, which showed every river, creek, brook, run, pond, and lake; Emmanuel disappeared for long stretches of time, for as many as eight or nine months, and all of the children, or at least all the boys, admired him. It crossed Raphael's mind that he might run away from home, and go to live with his uncle, somewhere up in the mountains. . . . But after less than three miles he gave up, exhausted. The creek bed and much of the bank were a jumble of rock, dislodged shale, fallen trees, rotting logs, and queer writhing pockets and eddies of froth; some of the waterfalls were as high as ten feet, and their spray was chill and blinding. Raphael estimated that he had climbed only a few hundred feet up the mountain but he was badly winded. His face stung where willow branches had slapped it, his ears roared from the falls, wasps buzzed angrily about his head, he had frightened—and been frightened by—a ring-necked snake sunning itself on a log (his brother Garth had once brought home in triumph a twelve-footer, slung about his neck like a muffler), and when he drew off his boots to rub his aching feet he discovered a half-dozen leeches between his toes, fastened to his white skin. Nasty ugly horrible things, sucking his blood. . . . Fixed so *tightly* to his flesh. . . . He nearly panicked at the sight of them, and whimpered aloud like a small child. By the time he returned home his head pounded from the sun and every nerve in his frail body was twitching.

Why did God make bloodsuckers, Raphael asked his older sister Yolande, didn't He know what He was doing?

Yolande, pretty Yolande, delicately scented with a cologne-touched lace handkerchief tucked into her belt, did not even glance at him. She watched her mirrored reflection and continued brushing her long hair, which was brown and blond and auburn, all at once, but which had, to her exasperation, a tendency to separate into ringlets on her shoulders. Don't be a baby, Raphael, she said, absently, you know there's no more a God up in the sky than there's a Devil sitting on a throne in Hell.

At lessons the next morning Raphael asked Demuth Hodge the same question. Mr. Hodge, soon to be dismissed from Bellefleur Manor (and without ever knowing precisely why: he had *believed* he was teaching Latin, Greek, English, mathematics, history, literature, composition, geography, and "basic science," with great success, considering the Bellefleur children's wildly varying skills and interest and patience), mumbled something about not being allowed, in his capacity as tutor, to speak to the children of religious matters. "You must know that your family is divided on the subject—there are those who believe, and those who do not—and neither side will tolerate the other's position. So I am afraid I dare not respond to your question other than to suggest that it is a profound, noble question, which you might spend the rest of your life answering. . . ."

Last of all he went to cousin Vernon, who taught the children, sporadically, "poetry" and "elocution," usually on dark rainy afternoons when his own rambles into the woods were impractical. But Vernon spoke with an ecstatic certainty that disturbed his nephew. I say to you—all things are gods—*all things are God.* The living God is not distinct, my dear confused boy, from His creation.

The creek was dangerous on higher ground, and the lake was rough even on fairly mild days, stirred by underground currents; but Mink Pond was safe. It was safe, it was hidden, it was *his* pond. The other boys had no interest in it. (There were no fish in Mink Pond, only minnows, and not even very many frogs.) Raphael's brothers and cousins and their friends rowed out onto the lake, or rode on horseback down to the Nautauga, where they could fish for pike and largemouth bass and black bullheads and catfish and perch and satinfin shiners and carp. Why the hell would anyone want to hang around that little pond, they asked Raphael. It isn't anything more than a drinking hole.

Mink Pond. Raphael's pond. Where he could hide away for hours, and no one would disturb him. Grandfather Noel spoke of the pond but he clearly didn't know what he was talking about, his memory must have been confused, because the area beyond the pear orchard was just a marshy soggy meadow where red-winged blackbirds and grouse nested; there was no *pond* there at all.

Why does Grandfather keep talking about the pond with the snapping turtles, Raphael asked his father. There aren't any snapping turtles. There isn't any pond where he says.

Your grandfather might be getting things mixed up, Ewan said curtly. He had very little time for the children, even for his favorite, Yolande; he was always hurrying out to check on the tenant farmers, or track down an ailing cow, or drive to Nautauga Falls to meet with someone at the bank. His face was often brick-red with anger he couldn't speak of because it might mean another quarrel with his younger brother Gideon, and all the children were wise enough to shrink aside when he passed, and never to draw his attention to them at meals. He said to Raphael, sternly: Show respect for your grandfather. Don't you ever let me hear you mocking your grandfather.

But I wasn't mocking anyone, Raphael protested.

Mink Pond. Where the very air was gentle with listening. Should he whisper aloud it heard him, it did not question or challenge his words, it was his secret, his alone. He sometimes crouched for hours in the waist-high rushes, watching dragonflies and fisher spiders and whirligig beetles, which were tireless. *That* they existed struck him from time to time as extraordinarily amazing. And *that* he existed in the same world as they . . . His mind drifted free of shore. It skittered across the surface of the water with the insects, or sank slowly to the bottom of the pond, darkening as it sank; but he felt no apprehension with the approach of this darkness, which was so different from the darkness of his room in the manor with its high ceiling and drafty windows and odor of dust and anger. Is there anything in the world you love more than that pond of yours, Raphael's mother Lily asked him, stooping to kiss his warm forehead, not guessing the truth that lay hidden in her words: just as the leopard frogs lay hidden in the grasses at the very edge of the pond, and leapt noisily into the water when he approached.

Yet it happened, one cold October afternoon within a week of Mahalaleel's arrival at the manor, that Raphael nearly drowned in his pond.

Nearly *was* drowned, that is. For he was set upon, as he lay dreaming on his raft, by a boy named Johnny Doan whom he hardly knew.

The Doan boy was fifteen years old, from a family of eight children who lived on a five-acre farm several miles south of the main Bellefleur property, on the outskirts of the little village of Bellefleur (which was hardly more than a railroad depot and a few stores, since the granary had closed down). Many years ago the Doans—women and children as well as men—labored in Raphael Bellefleur's enormous hop fields; indeed, they were brought to the Nautauga Valley for that reason, along with other workers, and housed in barracks-style buildings with tin roofs and only the most rudimentary kind of plumbing, at the edge of the fields. At one time, at Raphael's peak, he employed more than three hundred workers, and drew a crop from over six hundred acres—it was said in the state (not altogether truthfully) that the Bellefleur hop plantation was the largest in the world at that time. Raphael himself took pride in the quality of his hops, which he claimed was far more subtle than that of hops planted on lower ground (in Germany, for instance), and in the discipline with which his foremen treated the workers. I am not here on earth to be loved, he frequently told his wife Violet, but to be respected. And so indeed he was not loved by his workers, or even by his foremen, or managers, or distributors, or associates, or the three or four other extraordinarily wealthy landowners in the Chautauquas—but he was certainly respected.

Hop-growing days in the Valley were long past, but a considerable number of the descendants of the Bellefleur workers were scattered throughout the region. Some worked at the big canning factories in Nautauga Falls and Fort Hanna, where tomatoes, pickles, peas, and various citrus fruits underwent processing; the Bellefleur family owned part of Valley Products, the largest company. Some worked at odd jobs and seasonal labor, and could always rely upon welfare and unemployment insurance in the cities, while a number had done fairly well for themselves, acquiring over the years small farms of their own—though these farms did not generally encompass the richest valley land, which was owned by the Bellefleurs or the Steadmans or the Fuhrs. Some of the descendants of Raphael Bellefleur's workers were now under contract to Noel Bellefleur and his sons, as tenant farmers; or they worked in sawmills and granaries in Innisfail and Fort Hanna; or, like the Doans, they hired themselves out for harvesting, or fruit picking, or day labor of one kind or another (the digging of irrigation ditches, the construction of outbuildings), though Gideon Bellefleur preferred to import workers from the South, or from Canada, or even from one of the Indian reservations, since he had come to the conclusion recently that local labor could not be relied upon. If a worker did not work a full day, he would not receive a full day's wage. *A man who contracts to do a job and doesn't pull his own weight is a common thief,* Gideon often said. The Doans also tried to make a living from their scrubby little farm, growing wheat, corn, sickly-looking soybeans, and raising a small herd of cows. They had no idea of how to keep the topsoil from drying out and blowing away, or perhaps they had no interest in such things, so naturally their farm was turning to dust and in another few years they would be unable to pay their mortgage and the farm and the farm equipment (such as it was) and the house (a two-story shingle-board shanty with a tarpaper roof, and bales of hay dragged untidily up against the cement-block foundation, for warmth over the long winters) would be sold at auction, and the Doans would disappear into one of the cities to the south, perhaps Nautauga Falls, or Port Oriskany, and no one would hear of them again. . . .

Johnny Doan was the third of five boys, and despite the poor diet of fatty meat and starches and refined sugar Mrs. Doan fed them he had grown to the size of a mature man by the age of fifteen. His wide shoulders were always slumped, and he carried his rather small head somewhat forward, so that he appeared to be staring suspiciously into the dirt. He lazed about his father's farm, dull-eyed, weasel-faced, his pale limp hair falling across his forehead, a filthy gray cotton cap with the initials *IH* (International Harvester) loosely set upon his head. Whenever anyone outside the family greeted him he revealed tobacco-stained teeth in a quick, half-mocking smile, but he never replied; it was thought by some that he liked to play dumb, and by others that he was slightly retarded. Of course he had been allowed to quit the county school at the age of thirteen, in order to work for his father.

But he did not work for his father regularly. Nor did his older brothers. They drove about the countryside, when they could afford gas. They took odd jobs, but quit after receiving the first week's wages. In his dirty bib overalls, shirtless, sometimes barefoot, or wearing old mud-splattered boots, Johnny Doan was a familiar figure in the village of Bellefleur; and he was sometimes sighted along country roads some miles from home, simply walking, alone, his hands stuffed in his pockets, his undersized head slightly bowed. Answering a complaint made by the father of a child attending the small public school in Bellefleur, the sheriff of Nautauga County drove out to the Doans' one Sunday afternoon, and spoke with Johnny and his father (about, it was said, Johnny's bullying of younger children), and after that Johnny rarely appeared in the village, though he was seen as frequently as ever walking the country roads, cutting through pastures, squatting by the sides of ditches, utterly alone, companionless, the gray cap perched atop his head, his expression flaccid and content. Hello, Johnny, a friend of Mr. Doan's might call out heartily, d'you want a ride somewhere?—are you going somewhere?—slowing his car or pick-up truck so that Johnny might catch up. But the stained teeth showed themselves in an empty grin, and the blank brown eyes kept themselves blank, and Johnny never condescended to accept a ride. It might have been the case that he hadn't any destination.

One afternoon he threw the pitchfork down in the manure of the puddled barnyard, and walked away. Trotted away. Through his father's scrubby pastureland where outcroppings of rock jarred the eye, through a neighbor's cornfield, where dried stalks rustled with his passage, along a clayey dirt road lifting into the foothills. It was not the child Raphael Bellefleur he intended to injure, and not even the Bellefleur girls he wanted to spy upon—pretty Yolande, pretty Vida!—and Gideon Bellefleur's wife, the one with the red-brown hair and the squarish chin and the high, heavy breasts, yes, *that* one!—nor did he want to encounter the Bellefleur boys, whom he wisely feared. It was the castle he wanted to see. He had seen it several times already, and he wanted to see it again. And the lake. All of the Bellefleur property was posted against trespassers and he wanted to trespass and so he trotted along through fields of wild grass and beggarweed and broom sedge and willow bushes, changing himself into a dog, his tongue lolling, his head carried slightly forward so that his shoulders hunched. It was a bright chilly October day. He came to Mink Creek and followed it downstream for a while, not wanting to get his paws wet; fearing the swift current; excited by the hilly land on the other side. At last he came to a shallow bend, where Bellefleur children had placed large flat stepping-stones, and so he trotted across, and leapt to the other side. He was a long-tailed yellowish creature, part hound and part beagle. His tongue was a moist pink, his gums were a very dark grape. His teeth were stained brown but were still quite sharp.

Bellefleur Cemetery atop a grassy overgrown hill. A wrought-iron fence, badly rusted. A pretentious wrought-iron gate, its bottom spikes stuck in the earth, unmoved for years. He lifted his left hind leg and urinated on the gate, then trotted inside and urinated on the first of the gravestones. Marble, angels, crosses, granite, moss and lichen and a small jungle of ferns. Earthenware crockery set atop graves. The dried carcasses of plants, flowers. He sniffed at a large square marker with a perfectly smooth, gleaming front and rough, irregular edges; but of course he could not read the legend. The long grasses stirred. There were hoarse whispers, there were muffled shouts. He was frightened but would not bolt. His shoulders lifted slightly, his nose sank to the ground, the skin over his prominent ribs rippled, but he would not bolt, the Bellefleurs would not scare him away. Instead he trotted deliberately to what looked like a small house: a temple some fifteen feet high, with four columns, and angels and crosses carved about its border, and another legend in foot-high letters which he could not read and did not wish to read, knowing it said no more than *Bellefleur,* and bragged of someone dead who would be resurrected. Johnny paused for a long minute to inspect a queer stunted figure with the head of a dog—was it a dog?—was the thing an *angel?*—guarding the entrance to the temple. He sniffed at it, and then lifted his hind leg again, and trotted contemptuously on.

Near one of the freshest mounds he kicked over several clay urns, which broke into large startled pieces. He seized a tiny flag, an American flag, in his teeth, and tried to shred it. You see what I can do, he said. You see what the Doans can do. With one of the clay shards he tried to scratch his name on an ebony-black gravestone but the clay wasn't sharp enough. He would need a chisel, and a hammer. . . .

You see what the Doans can do!

But suddenly he was frightened. He didn't know if he had spoken aloud or not. It was difficult for him to determine what was shouted, what was whispered, what was only shaped in his own thoughts, silently, and maybe the Bellefleurs were listening, maybe one of their hired men was patrolling the cemetery and would fire upon him . . . ? The land was forbidden land as everyone knew. It was posted against all trespassers and there was a rumor that the Bellefleur boys shot at intruders with .22's, just for the fun of it; and the county court would never convict them, the sheriff would never even arrest them. . . .

He was frightened and angry too. First the wave of fear, and then a stronger wave of anger. He pushed at one of the old crosses; but he could not dislodge it. It was so *old,* the dates were 1853–1861, they meant nothing to him, really, except that the body beneath the sunken earth must be nothing more than bones, just lying there helpless gazing up at him, nothing more than bones, he giggled, exhilarated, and lifted his leg again to urinate. They said there were spirits but he didn't believe in spirits. He didn't believe in spirits in the daytime, and when the sky was clear.

He prowled about, sniffing, and suddenly his thoughts were on the Bellefleur girls he had seen the week before, on horseback, trotting along the old Military Road. Two young girls, not quite his age, one with long curly wheat-colored hair: he knew their names were Yolande and Vida, and he had wanted to shout at them, *Yolande, Vida, I know who you are!* but of course he had remained hidden. Last May he had spied upon the Fuhr wedding in the village, at the old stone church, and he had seen, in the midst of the milling crowd of gay, well-dressed men and women, Gideon Bellefleur and his wife Leah: Leah, full-bodied and arrogantly beautiful in a turquoise dress, her chignon visible beneath a stylish cartwheel hat, Leah who was taller than most men, much taller than Johnny's father. . . . Johnny drew nearer, staring. No one noticed him, or so it seemed: why would those well-to-do people notice *him:* and so he stared and stared at Leah Bellefleur, who carried a cream-colored parasol which she spun, restlessly, between her gloved fingers. He could hear—he could *almost* hear—the woman's low husky teasing voice. She had drawn slightly away from the others, she and one of the Fuhrs, and they were talking and laughing together in a way that made Johnny's heart contract, for he wanted—he wanted— *Leah,* he might have shouted, *I know who you are! We all know you!* The young man with whom she was speaking was nearly as tall as Gideon. He was fair-haired, beardless, quite handsome, and though he laughed and joked with Leah he was also staring at her with an emotion Johnny could well comprehend. It gave Johnny pleasure to carry the Bellefleur woman's image with him, and to subject it, in the privacy of the night, to certain fitting tortures: tortures with hog-butchering knives, branding irons, and whips (the very whip, an old buggy whip, his father used on Johnny and his brothers, having stolen it from the Bellefleur stable years ago): just what she deserved.

A flicker began to shriek and he resisted the impulse to run wildly out of the cemetery. He *did* trot downhill, now in a hurry to leave, but the fence, the iron fence, the spikes . . . He found an opening and jammed himself through, whimpering, on all fours, his scrawny tail trembling close to his haunches.

He did not believe in spirits, not even in Bellefleur Cemetery. Not during the day.

Now in the near distance the castle floated. Bellefleur Castle. The coppery roofs, the pink-gray towers. Vapor rising from the dark lake. And behind the monstrous house the sky was marbled blue and white, harsh glaring colors.

He paused, staring. He was breathing hard: the shrieking bird had frightened him though he knew better.

Bellefleur Castle. Larger than he remembered. Still, it could be destroyed. It could be burnt. Though it was built of stone it could be burnt, from the inside perhaps. Even if the stone itself would not burn the insides would burn—the fancy woodwork, the carpets, the furnishings.

A bomb might be dropped from high in the air. In a magazine that was nearly all photographs he had seen pictures of flaming cities in black and white, he had seen and admired the helmeted young pilots smiling out of their cockpits, looking his own age. There were the castle, the old stone barns, the garden behind its high secret wall, the curving white-gravel drive lined by trees whose names Johnny did not know. . . . Ah, but nearer him were old wood-frame sheds, used long ago for hop drying, now overcome with trumpet vine and ivy, their roofs nearly rotted through and about to collapse; *those* buildings would burn.

He trotted downhill and found himself approaching the creek again. It had twisted about, and now ran through pastureland; in some places its red-clay banks were more than six feet high, in other places—where cattle came to drink—they sloped down gradually into the water. A *Posted: No Trespassing* sign caught his eye. Though he could not decipher the words, could not have named the individual letters, he understood the message.

"Bellefleur," he whispered.

They could shoot someone like him, if they wished. Out of anger or out of sport. If they wished. If they caught sight of him. There were rumors, ugly tales: wandering dogs shot, fishermen who ignored the posted signs shot at (so Dutch Gerhardt claimed, though he had been fishing Bloody Run high up the mountain, on Bellefleur property, yes, but miles from the house). . . . And then, five or six years ago, when a number of the fruit pickers in the Valley talked of striking, and the young man from downstate who had worked at organizing them and had made so many angry speeches was found badly beaten, blinded in one eye, in a field overlooking the Nautauga River. . . . When Hank Varrell, a friend of Johnny's nineteen-year-old brother Eddy, made a remark about one of the Bellefleur women—a girl from Bushkill's Ferry, a distant relative —it somehow got back to the Bellefleurs, and Gideon himself sought Hank out, and would surely have killed him if other people hadn't been present. . . . Johnny shook himself awake. He had been walking along, staring at the ground. When he looked up he saw the pond: he saw sunshine slanted through hemlocks and the golden leaves of mountain maple, reflected in the pond: and he saw the child on the raft, stretched out on his stomach, one finger dipped in the water. He saw the pond and the child at once.

Dark, fine-looking hair. The Bellefleur profile, recognizable even at a distance of some yards: a long Roman nose, deep-set eyes.

"Bellefleur," Johnny whispered.

Already he staggered from the weight of the rocks. Three or four in his overall pockets, others held clumsily in his arms. He threw the first of them before he called out—but even then he did not speak: the sound was a cry, a jeer, a shriek, mere noise, not quite human.

The boy's head whipped about. His expression showed an utter blankness of astonishment, beyond fear, beyond even surprise. Johnny ran to the edge of the pond, shouting, and threw another rock. The first had missed, the second struck the boy on one shoulder. That Bellefleur face: Johnny would know it anywhere though this particular boy was small-bodied, and his skin had gone dead-white. Bellefleur! How'd you like your face smashed! How'd you like your fucking head held underwater!

The boy cried out, one hand upraised, and it made Johnny want to laugh—did he think he could protect his precious little face?—his face that was small and delicate as a girl's? Johnny splashed into the pond and threw another rock, grunting. It missed the boy, it did not even cause much water to fly up, Johnny felt a flame in his belly and groin, he would kill the little bastard, he would show him and all the Bellefleurs— Another rock, a smaller rock, struck the boy on his forehead and knocked him backward; and immediately a stream of bright red blood appeared; and Johnny hesitated, standing now in water up to his knees. His jaw had begun to tremble. He was panting, his shoulders raised and curiously hunched.

"Bellefleur!" he whispered a third time, leaning forward to spit into the water.

If the boy hadn't begun to cry, if he hadn't begun to gasp and whimper and cry like a baby, Johnny might have shown mercy, but he did cry, and lay so limply on his side, as if someone had really hurt him, that the flame rose again in Johnny's belly, whipping up to the back of his throat. He shouted, throwing another rock, and another, and another —and when he paused, blinking sweat out of his eyes, he saw with amazement that the boy was gone: he must have fallen over the side of the raft, and sunk into the pond.

Johnny stood for a moment, staring. He held the last of the rocks in both hands; he could not think what to do with it. Half consciously he reasoned that if he let it drop, it would splash him. . . . But then his pant legs were wet anyway. . . . But if the boy climbed over the side of the raft he would need it to throw at him. . . . But maybe the boy had drowned. . . . Maybe he *had* killed him. . . .

"Hey. Bellefleur," he said in a low, hoarse voice. He did not speak loudly enough to be heard, even if the boy had surfaced. His voice was cracked and uncertain, as if he had not spoken for some time, and the effort pained him. The back of his throat *was* raw, as if he'd been shouting. "Bellefleur . . . ?"

It might have been a trick. But the boy did not surface. The pond looked fairly deep, its ripples were widening and sprawling out, a few water beetles, terrified by the commotion, were now coming back, and the birds' silence was filled in by a squirrel's furious scolding.

Johnny Doan backed away, and let the rock fall to the ground, and turned to run. He was just a boy, a boy with a flushed face and wet overalls and an old cloth cap on his head. The cap flew off, but he missed it at once, and stooped to pick it up, and jammed it hard on his head, pulling it down over his forehead. So he left no evidence behind. So he ran away from Mink Pond, and made his way out to the Innisfail Road some miles to the west, and arrived back at his father's farm by supper time; and though his jaw trembled faintly and his eyes filled with moisture that was not tears he was drunk with exhilaration, and could not stop grinning.

"*Bellefleur,*" he whispered, wiping his nose with the side of his hand, and giggling softly. "You see what we can do!"

The Bellefleur Curse

According to mountain legend there was a curse on Germaine's family. (But it wasn't merely a local legend: it was freely alluded to in the state capital five hundred miles away, and in Washington, D.C.; and when Bellefleur men fought in the Great War they claimed to encounter soldiers who knew them by name, by reputation, and who shrank away in superstitious dread—You'll bring misfortune on all of us, they were told.)

But no one knew what the curse was.

Or why it was, or who—or what—had pronounced it.

There's a curse on us, Yolande said listlessly on the eve of her running away. There's a curse on us and now I know what it is, she said. But it was to Germaine she spoke, and Germaine was at that time only one year old.

There is no such thing as a curse, Leah said. If we want to hold onto our sanity we have to cleanse ourselves of these ridiculous old superstitions. . . . Don't ever say such things in my presence! (But this was much later. After her pregnancy with Germaine, after the birth of Germaine. As a young girl and even as a married woman Leah had frequently behaved in a superstitious manner, though she would have been angry if anyone in the family had taken note.)

The older Bellefleurs—grandfather Noel, grandmother Cornelia, great-grandmother Elvira, aunt Veronica, uncle Hiram, aunt Matilde, Leah's mother Della, Jean-Pierre, and the rest—and of course all the dead —knew very well that there was a curse; and though as younger men and women they might have excited themselves speculating on the nature of the curse, at the present time they were silent on the subject. You can embody a curse without being able to articulate it, uncle Hiram said not long before his death. Like a silver-haired bat carries the distinguishing marks of his species on his back.

Gideon once said, with a thoughtfulness uncharacteristic of him, that the curse was a terribly simple one: Bellefleur men die interesting deaths. They rarely die in bed.

They never die in bed! Ewan said with a boastful laugh. (For *he* planned not to die—however and whenever he died—in any sort of bed.)

Bellefleur men die absurd deaths, grandmother Della said flatly. (She was thinking, perhaps, of her husband Stanton's death, one Christmas Eve long ago: and of her own father's death; and there was great-grandfather Raphael, who died of natural causes, but had determined by the terms of his will that his body be grotesquely mutilated after his death.) The men die absurd deaths, Della said, and the women are fated to survive them and mourn them.

They don't die absurd deaths, they die necessary deaths, uncle Hiram said pedantically. (For he himself had escaped death innumerable times—in the Great War, and in countless accidents over the years, suffered as a consequence of his sleepwalking affliction, which no physician could cure.) *Everything that transpires in this universe transpires out of necessity, however brutal.*

It was pointed out that great-great-great-grandfather Jedediah, whom everyone considered a saint, died an extraordinarily peaceful death within a few years of his wife Germaine: he simply dropped off to sleep on the eve of his 101st birthday, in the simple bed with the pine posts and the old horsehair mattress he insisted upon, in the servants' wing (his narrow, rather dark room had been intended as a valet's room, but he insisted upon having it—the handsomer, more pretentious rooms made him uneasy); his last words, though cryptic, *The jaws devour, the jaws are devoured,* were nevertheless uttered with a beatific smile. And there was a Bellefleur named Samuel, a son of Raphael's, who disappeared in one of the castle's more spacious rooms—and he too was never found. (He was spirited away in the Turquoise Room, now called the Room of Contamination, and shut off forever from the Bellefleur children who would have loved to explore it.) A long time ago there were whispers that great-aunt Veronica had died, after a lengthy wasting illness, during which her beautiful complexion grew waxen, and her eyes became luminous in their shadowed sockets; but the rumor was obviously absurd because great-aunt Veronica was still living, in superb health, even somewhat plump in recent years, and marvelously youthful for her age. Among the women, Raphael's unhappy wife Violet *did* die an unusual death, it was thought for love: she simply walked into Lake Noir one night when Raphael was away and no one was attending her: and her body was never recovered. And there were, of course, the early, unfortunate deaths—Jean-Pierre and his son Louis, and Louis's three children, and his brother Harlan, about whom so little was known; and Raphael's brother Arthur, the diffident, stubborn Arthur, who died in an attempt to rescue John

Brown; and there were others, innumerable others, most of them children, who died of diseases like scarlet fever and typhoid and pneumonia and smallpox and influenza and whooping cough. . . .

Or was the curse, as Vernon thought, something very simple . . . ?

What is gained will be lost. Land, money, children, God. (But—skinny and agitated and chronically unhappy, with his beard so scant and prematurely grizzled, and his love for Leah never declared, and his black ledgerbooks (taken from old Raphael's desk) filled with sloping smudged scrawls that he claimed was poetry, and would transform the world one day, and expose his family for the tyrants they were—what did cousin Vernon know? So no one listened, or half-listened and waved him away with an impatient wave of the hand. His father Hiram was most impatient of all, for Vernon had turned out *not quite right:* his blood was all his mother's, and she had failed disastrously as a Bellefleur wife, and was best forgotten. After she ran away from the manor, many years ago, Hiram, uncharacteristically silent, and extremely ill-tempered, had fashioned for her a two-foot marker of cheap granite, *Eliza Perkins Bellefleur, May She Rest In Peace,* set down in the corner of the cemetery, on a downward slope, given over to *Queenie, Sebastian, Whitenose, Chinaberry, Sweetheart, Bitsy, Love, Pegs, Mustard, Buttercup, Horace, Baby, Daisy, Bat, Pinktail,* and others: the children's various pets: dogs, cats, a turtle, an unusually large and attractive spider, a raccoon with gentle manners, a gray fox cub that did not live to maturity, and a bobcat cub that experienced the same fate, and even a redback vole, and a near-odorless skunk, and several rabbits, and one snowshoe hare, and at least one handsome ring-necked snake. Of his mother's position in the Bellefleur Cemetery—but of course it was only a *symbolic* position, the woman wasn't actually buried there, she wasn't actually dead—Vernon prudently declined to speak.)

But then perhaps the curse had something to do with silence. For the Bellefleurs, Leah's mother Della often said, would *not* speak of things that demanded utterance. They spent time at foolish activities like fishing and hunting and games (how the Bellefleurs loved games!—games of any kind—cards, jigsaw puzzles, checkers, chess, their own flamboyant variants of checkers and chess, and other games invented by them during the long iron-hard mountain winters; and every variant of hide-and-seek, played with manic enthusiasm in the labyrinthine recesses of the castle —a reckless activity, as it happened upon one occasion that a Bellefleur child, decades back, ran to hide somewhere in the cavernous cellar, and was never found despite days of frantic searching; nor did his poor bones ever turn up) with the abandon of very small children grasping and clutching at things only to throw them immediately aside, as if time were an unfathomable, inexhaustible pool instead of something like old Raphael's once-famous wine cellar, which was quickly depleted in the years following his death and the decline of the Bellefleur fortune. They chatter about inconsequential things, Della said bitterly, and frequently; she lived most of the time across the lake, in a red-brick Georgian house at the very center of the village of Bushkill's Ferry, and though her family could not discern her house across the miles she could discern theirs very easily: indeed, the eye always leapt to Bellefleur Manor on its hill, there was no escaping the castle, even at twilight when the sun's slow slanting orange-red rays illuminated it, and the lake itself began to sink into its uncanny darkness. They chatter about pork roasts and candy apples and antler spreads, Della said, while everything falls in pieces around them. They go tobogganing on Christmas Eve and one of their people is killed and the next day they open their presents as if nothing had happened, and they never speak of it, they *refuse* to speak of it. (But her husband, Stanton Pym, who did indeed die in a tobogganing accident, hardly six months after the marriage, and when poor Della was four months pregnant with Leah, had never been considered *one of their people:* so perhaps Della's charge was unwarranted.)

Then again the curse might have been that the Bellefleurs were so hopelessly, and at times so passionately, divided on all subjects. Germaine's uncle Emmanuel, whom she saw only once in her life, and who appeared in the Valley only rarely, and never predictably, since he professed a violent dislike for what he called "city life" and "overheated rooms" and "women's talk," included on all his maps of the region the original Indian name for the area—Nautauganaggonautaugaunnagaun-gawauggataunagauta—which meant, in essence, for it could not be literally translated, a space-in-which-you-paddle-to-your-side-and-I-paddle-to-mine-and-Death-paddles-between-us. Those silly Indian names, the Bellefleur women said, why couldn't they say directly what they *mean*, like us? Emmanuel's reverence for the Indians and the local Indian culture (which could hardly be said to exist any longer since the treaties of 1787 had banished all Indians from the mountains and the fertile farmland along the river, and a few thousand of them lived in a single reservation north of Paie-des-Sables) was mocked by most of the family, who did not know quite how to interpret it. Emmanuel was, of course, "strange"—but that did not entirely explain his affection for Indians, and his even greater affection for the mountains. He was a throwback to Jedediah, evidently —and perhaps to Jean-Pierre himself, who had degenerated to the point of taking on a full-blooded Iroquois squaw as his mistress, shortly before his death. (But had Emmanuel ever "known" a woman? His brothers Gideon and Ewan loved to discuss this subject, indeed it was one of their few safe subjects, and while Gideon believed firmly that of course Emmanuel *must* have had sexual experience, Ewan liked to add that it mightn't necessarily have been with a woman: whereupon both brothers laughed loudly. Of their oldest brother Raoul, who lived one hundred miles to the south in Kincardine, and whose sexual life was so bizarre, they rarely spoke.) So the Bellefleurs, Emmanuel once said, were always at war: they had the disposition of minks: and he wanted no part of their curse. (But then it was said of Emmanuel that he himself was under a curse or an enchantment, so how could he presume to judge others?)

Long before Germaine's brother Bromwell fled Bellefleur and made his name—*his* name—in the vast shadowy world south of the mountains he liked to pronounce, with his child's unself-conscious authoritative lisp, that a "curse" was unlikely; but if indeed one could chart the undulating pattern of something that resembled a "curse" through generations of the same family, no doubt it could claim some scientific validity: as genetic inheritance, not as superstitious crap. For Bromwell, clerkish and prematurely balding, even as a small child, with his delicate wire-rimmed glasses and his austere pale forehead with its armor of hard, flat bones knit worriedly together, and his small slender fingers that were always twisting about a finely sharpened pencil, had the theatrical flair of selecting the absolutely right wrong word: of awakening his listeners (whose eyes sometimes glazed over, for who can tolerate fifty-minute lectures on the improbable nature of "infinity," or the rather monotonous mating habits of algae, or the earth's subtle gravitational pull on the *sun*—as an analogue, the waspishly brilliant child would quickly make clear, to the theological notion of God's dependence upon his only free-thinking creature Man—who, even among the hard-of-hearing, sweet-faced, pious old widows and grandmothers and aunts of the manor, could tolerate such observations from a child not yet ten years of age?) with a sudden razor-like thrust of vulgarity, which always confirmed his listeners' uneasy judgment that he was not only brilliant (as they halfway suspected Hiram's gangling son Vernon was, despite his eccentricity) but also correct.

So the curse was inherited in the blood; or it was breathed in with the chill, fresh, somewhat acrid piney air; or it was just a way of denying the strident rationalist claim that nothing, absolutely nothing—no God, no design, no destiny—sought to push its facial bones up hard against generations of perishable Bellefleur skin. Moving with a manicured fingernail a carved ebony draught, puckering and pursing his lips over the checkerboard, uncle Hiram liked to murmur that he, fallible as he was, blundering and groping (though in fact he was a shrewd, rather malicious checker player: he would not lose, not even to an ailing child) and half-blind in his right eye from an incident in the War which he refused to discuss (evidently he had left his tent, was sleepwalking his way toward the enemy trenches, when a great explosion of flame destroyed not only that tent and the young soldiers who slept within but some fifty-odd soldiers altogether—and Hiram Bellefleur was untouched save for a bit of fire which darted to his eye), fallible as he was and no more than a competent gamesman, he was nevertheless more astute than the God of creation, whom he contemptuously dismissed as senile: that God "existed" he had no doubt, for he was, surprisingly, one of the "religious" Bellefleurs, but this God was comically limited, and near worn-out, and hadn't the spirit in recent centuries to meddle in the affairs of men. So the "curse" was just chance: and "chance" is just what happens.

At such times Hiram might be playing draughts with Cornelia, or Leah, or one of the children—young Raphael, perhaps, who was so quiet,

so unnaturally quiet, since his near-drowning in the pond (the circumstances of which he chose *not* to explain completely to the family). If
Hiram was playing with one of the women she was likely to wave aside
his fanciful remarks, to which she had probably not listened in any case;
if he was playing with Raphael the child hunched his thin shoulders over
the board, shivering, as if his great-uncle's words chilled him but could
not be refuted.

Yes, Hiram said with sardonic pleasure, the famous Bellefleur curse
is nothing more than *chance*—and chance is nothing more than what
happens! So those of us who aspire to some degree of control, let alone
moral intelligence, cannot be victims of absurd grotesqueries like the rest
of you.

People outside the family, however, even those who lived hundreds of
miles away, in the flatland, and heard only the most oblique, most exaggerated rumors of the Bellefleur clan, never hesitated to speak of the
Bellefleur curse, as if they knew exactly what they were talking about, and
there was no mystery surrounding it at all. The curse on the Bellefleurs,
it was said, was very simple: they were fated to be Bellefleurs, from womb
to grave and beyond.

The Pregnancy

For a number of years Leah halfway thought there was a curse of some kind on *her:* she couldn't seem to have another baby.

Of course she had the twins. And had them within the first year of her marriage, when she was still nineteen. A nineteen-year-old mother of *twins.* (It just isn't like you, Della in her mourning said primly; to do something so—well, *extravagant:* as if you were trying to please *his* side of the family.) She hadn't wanted to marry, she hadn't wanted to have a baby, but if it *had* to be, why, she was rather pleased with the fact of twins. In all the history of the New World Bellefleurs—some seventy-eight births (not all of them, of course, live births; and in the old days many infants died over the long winters)—there had never been a single instance of twins before.

(Aunt Veronica remarked mildly, one night at dinner, playing with her food as she usually did by pushing it about her plate with a ladylike fastidious show of indifference—for she had been brought up in the days when ladies did not exactly *eat* in public, they reserved their grosser appetites for the privacy of their rooms—no matter that their generous figures belied their ascetic pretensions—Aunt Veronica lowered her eyes but sent her remark out in Leah's direction, There were some sort of, I don't know, twins or triplets or maybe more, born to my poor cousin Diana—she married some sweet boy in the Nautauga Light Guard but there must have been bad blood on his side of the family—the Bishops, they were—out of Powhatassie—they were something to do with banking —or had a big resort hotel on the lake, I don't remember—anyway it's long before your time and nobody remembers and nobody probably even remembers poor Diana: but *she* had twins, or triplets, or quadruplets, or whatever you call them, and they were all wizened and joined together in funny ways, a head to a stomach or two stomachs, and they didn't have all their necessary parts or limbs, it was disgusting to see, but very sad too, of course, very tragic, I remember trying to console Diana and she just screamed and screamed and wouldn't let anyone near and wanted to nurse the pathetic little things but of course they were dead, they never even drew breath, and everyone said, Oh, Lord wasn't it a mercy!—and they presented some sort of theological problem too, I can't remember exactly why—how did you baptize them, and how did you bury them— but in the end it must have been solved and I don't know why I even bring the subject up, Leah, it doesn't have a glimmer of a thing to do with *you,* does it?—the twins are so beautiful, and they're absolutely separate, they weren't joined together one bit, they don't even *count* as the other kind of thing at all.)

But after the amazing birth of Bromwell and Christabel nothing happened.

Two babies, a boy and a girl, and both handsome; and both in fine health. And for a year or so Leah was grateful not to be pregnant, since even with nursemaids and servants and Edna to oversee the house she certainly did not want another baby. But then the months passed, and the years, and she *did* want another baby, and nothing happened; nothing at all. One morning as she lay beside her sleeping husband she thought clearly that she would be thirty years old before long, and then she would be thirty-five, and forty, and—and forty-five: and it would be over. The womanly part of her life would be over.

The family insisted upon children, of course. They adored children, or at least the idea, the sentiment, of children. Increase and multiply: go forth and populate the earth: for the earth is there to *be* populated, by Bellefleurs. The Bellefleur line was not to dwindle away as so many New World aristocratic lines had: Raphael, who managed to inflict ten pregnancies on his rather neurasthenic wife Violet, often spoke of the need to have as many children as possible because (and he was quite correct) they could not all be relied upon to survive. He had a dread, an almost superstitious dread, of the Bellefleurs going the way of the Brendels (who had owned as much land in the mountains as Jean-Pierre himself, in the early 1800's, but had lost it all through speculation, and sheer bad judgment, brought on by what Raphael considered a weakening of the intellect as a consequence of too much money and too much luxury: and the men disappeared, or simply refused to marry, or, if married, failed to have sons) and the Bettensons (Raphael was a boy of twelve when Frederich ran mad out into the snow after his lumbering company went bankrupt, and afterward his children all scattered and were never heard of again) and the Wydens (whose "name" survived today only with a black family in Fort Hanna, headed by the light-skinned descendant of one of Wyden's slaves). It was great-grandmother Elvira's belief that her father-in-law did not enjoy his children, in fact did not take much notice of them at all; but he was obsessed with having children, particularly sons, and never quite recovered from the tragic disappointment of his oldest son Samuel (who would have been Germaine's great-uncle had he survived:

though in fact he was believed not to have died, in the usual sense of the word, and still to exist, or at any rate to be present, in the manor, when Bromwell and Christabel were children). The line had come so close to dying out, to being eradicated, back at the very start: when poor Louis and his two sons and daughter were murdered over at Bushkill's Ferry, and the only surviving Bellefleur was a mountain hermit no one had seen for years. And yet, miraculously, it had *not* died out . . . though there was the constant fear that it would, and all the land and fortune, or whatever remained of it, would fall to strangers.

So Leah, despite her brash girlish disdain for such things, fell under the enchantment of the Lake Noir branch of the family, and shrewdly saw that Noel Bellefleur was a fool about pregnant women—even women like herself, of a size and a disposition not conventionally "feminine." And once she was pregnant she found herself subdued; she found herself expressing an interest in the women in the family, and in their activities (quilting, crocheting, embroidering, overseeing the yearly canning, manipulating engagements, arranging for social evenings—a ceaseless round of social evenings, over the winters especially!—and vociferously mourning the dead) that was not hypocritical, or even experimental; she grew softer, and sweeter, and burst into tears easily, and liked nothing better than to curl up in Gideon's arms, and she spent an inordinate amount of time during that first pregnancy sound asleep: sometimes she staggered with exhaustion an hour after waking, and (this, the restless young woman who had raced her handsome sorrel mare at valley competitions, and who had swum halfway across Lake Noir one rainy day in late September as a girl of sixteen, merely on a dare) could barely hold her head up through a meal, and yawned repeatedly, and napped everywhere in the lived-in part of the house and once or twice in parts of the house that were kept unheated, and, most astonishing of all, found it too much trouble to disagree when Gideon or his family spouted nonsense. Pregnant with the twins Leah grew even more beautiful. Her skin was golden, her perfect lips shaped themselves in a perpetual unconscious mesmerizing half-smile, her eyes, though deep-set and somewhat shadowed, took on a queer childlike brightness as if they had just been washed with tears. Even before the triumphant birth of twins her father-in-law had fallen in love with her, and revised (and in public) his doubts about the wisdom of Gideon's marriage to a cousin from across the lake.

(It was not simply that Leah was a first cousin of Gideon's, but that she was a "poor" relative; and not simply that her mother Della bitterly despised the rest of the family; but, decades ago, the entire family—headed at that time by Jeremiah and Elvira, her parents—united to oppose poor Della's infatuation with Stanton Pym on the grounds that this upstart young bank clerk with his fashionable outfits and his imported automobile was a shameless, fantastic, ingenious fortune hunter, and any issue of their union was likely to be flawed—though strapping Leah did not *appear* to be flawed.)

Nevertheless the marriage did take place, and Leah and Gideon obviously adored each other, and Leah quickly became pregnant—but not *too* quickly, for that would have disturbed the older Bellefleurs as much as it would have disturbed Della herself—and gave birth to twins after a lengthy but not inordinately fussy labor; and all was well. For a while. For several years. And then . . . Do you know what I wish, she whispered to Gideon, I wish we would have another baby, do you think I'm silly, do you think the twins are still too small . . . ? And she began to yearn for a baby, to daydream, to invent silly names; even to befriend her sister-in-law Lily, who had of course been living in the manor for years before Leah's own arrival, and who was *somewhat* disdainful (ah, it's mere jealousy! Gideon assured her) of Gideon's bride. Competitive as a girl in her horseback riding and swimming and even in her schoolwork (though she had never been a really good student, her mind was too restless, her imagination too playful) she began to feel, to be, competitive as a woman. As a mother. As a would-be mother. She looked upon Lily with envy, though she did not envy Lily her husband, or her actual children (except for sloe-eyed Raphael with his shy good manners and his obvious admiration for *her*); she coveted her sister-in-law's easy pregnancies. Naturally she did not really want to be a brood mare (as she unforgivably said one night, in Cornelia's presence, uncaring how her words offended her mother-in-law) but she would not have minded, no, she would not at all have minded, just one more baby. Even a girl.

A fever of desire grew in her, and she and Gideon made love passionately, and frequently; sometimes one would feel the other staring, and turn, and see with a pang of desire so strong it was nearly convulsive (and this quite frequently in public, even at large social gatherings in neighbors' homes) the other gazing so rawly, so openly that—that there was nothing to be done except the two of them must stammer excuses, and leave, and hurry away together. They were hardly able to wait until they were safe in the privacy of their suite of rooms before they tore at each other's clothes, and kissed hungrily, and groaned aloud with the violence of their desire. Once they did not make it to the manor, but hurried into the old icehouse at the edge of the lake; another time, returning from a wedding party in Nautauga Falls, Gideon drove his car boldly off the road and across a hilly field until it came to rest, not quite hidden, in a stand of burnt-out hemlock.

Gideon fell ever more deeply in love with his wife over the years. It was indeed like falling—he felt himself sinking, plunging, disappearing —being sucked into a passion for her, for her voracious appetite for him as well as for her glorious body itself, which he had never anticipated as a bridegroom. He fell more and more deeply in love with Leah, and at the same time he rather feared her. During their turbulent courtship he had been halfway fearful of her, but halfway amused as well—she was so *defiantly* virginal, so clear to give her young cousin to know that she disdained love and marriage and sex and above all men and their animal natures; but after their marriage, after the birth of the twins, it seemed to him that the frequent savagery with which she clutched at him spoke of a Leah deeper, more impersonal, more puzzling than any he had guessed at: than any he had married. She seemed to be *a* woman, *any* woman, and not *the* particular young woman he loved.

In the delirium of passion her skin went dead-white, and it seemed to him that her lovely mouth, her lovely eyes, her somewhat flared nostrils were harsh tears in that skin, the mouth especially straining for release. He could not hold her tightly enough. He could not penetrate her deeply enough. Their lovemaking gave off an odor of heat, of merciless pummeling intensity, and though they whispered to each other *Leah* and *Gideon,* and uttered their secret love words, it was not always a certainty that *Leah* and *Gideon* were involved. His taste on her anxious dry lips, her taste on his, the finest hairs of their sweat-slick squirming bodies twined together, and whole patches of skin made suddenly abrasive, raw as sandpaper: what a struggle, what a contest! Simply to keep from drowning was an effort, Gideon sometimes thought ruefully, lying exhausted beside his sleeping wife, whose breath still heaved in sleep, harsh and uneven and troubled, though the subtle rosy flush now tinted her throat and part of her face. He had thought of Leah as a ferocious virgin, in the early days of their marriage, and it had pleased him, in a sense, to pretend alarm at the remarkable strength—the remarkable physical strength—of his young wife; now the very muscularity of her desire, her choked grasping need, the curious fact (which should not have occurred to him, since he loved her so very much and wanted to protect her from all insult, even his own) that she was willing to be . . . shameless: that in the desperate agony of those last minutes of love, when it was evident that she might, she very well might, fail to reach the climax her body so violently demanded, she was willing to beg: groaning his name, half-grunting, not knowing what she said, what crude words forced their way out of her. Leah Pym, his proud young cousin, tall and broad-shouldered and supremely self-confident, knowing the value of her beauty, the value of her magnificent head of thick auburn hair, the value quite simply of her *soul* (which stood somewhat apart from her, detached and arrogant and quick to pass judgment on her as well as on others)—how has it happened, Gideon wondered, with guilty pleasure, that she has been so transformed?

He thought: Is it I, Gideon, who has transformed her?

Long ago as children they had played certain games that left Gideon dry-mouthed and terribly upset. He saw Leah rarely, he was warned against seeking her out, she was Della Pym's daughter—Della who hated them all—and so the opportunities of meeting her, joining in games with her, were few. But he remembered one occasion. At the old brick community center in the village. When he was already too mature for such games, and likely to make trouble. (Ewan had been banished from certain activities years before: he was brash, bullying, the size of a grown man, and the other children feared him.) A game called "The Needle's Eye."

Singing in children's quavering excited voices, marching in a ring, girls and boys alternating, grasping hands, a game that had been played for generations, children circling, hot-faced, their eyes snatching at one another, Leah twelve years of age and a head taller than the other girls, her lovely face flushed as if with windburn, her dark eyes avoiding his. Gideon took his place on the inside of the circle and clasped hands with a Wilde girl from downriver, over the heads of the marching children, and his pulses rang with the familiar witless words he paid no attention to, for he was staring—staring—at his young cousin with the waist-long auburn hair and the small, high breasts that had begun to push against her hand-crocheted blue sweater.

The needle's eye that does supply/ The thread that runs so truly/ It has caught many a smiling lass/ And now it has caught you./ Oh, it has caught one and it has caught two./ It has caught many a smiling lass/ And now it has caught you. Gideon's partner did not want to bring their arched arms down over Leah's balky head, out of jealousy or out of simple fear that Leah might jab her in the ribs, but Gideon forced their arms down, trapping his cousin, and the boys who grasped her hands released them, and there Leah stood, blushing angrily, staring at the floor, as the children sang "The Needle's Eye" through once again, now lustily, with an air of barely restrained violence. Leah was to be kissed. In public. Before everyone's eyes. Leah Pym, her face gone a furious pink, her lower lip protruding, her gaze lowered in shame. *The needle's eye that does supply/ The thread that runs so true. . . .*

Gideon was not accustomed to brooding over the past; he was not accustomed to thinking in this way, perhaps to thinking at all—it wasn't in his nature. But the memory of that asinine game made his eyes fill with tears, and his pulses leapt, for he *was,* still, that sixteen-year-old boy, staring with dry, parted lips at his beautiful cousin, who had not spoken more than a dozen words to him in her life. How he loved her, even then! And how humiliating, how agonizing it was. . . . When he'd moved forward to grasp her shoulders and kiss her (for it was not only his privilege, it was his obligation according to the rules of the game: and though there were adults looking on they would not rush between the children, they would not shout, *Stop! You nasty low-minded creatures!*), she had murmured a low breathy panicked protest and ducked to escape, lowering her head as if involuntarily, and butting poor Gideon's mouth. While the children laughed uproariously Gideon had had to staunch the blood with some fussing old woman's handkerchief. Leah had run out of the hall.

Now he pulled at his wiry black beard, and ran his hands hard over his face, and sighed. Is it I, Gideon, who has transformed her?

If he might take his brother Ewan aside, to speak frankly with him. To inquire. About women: about women who are anxious to have babies. (But it was possible that Ewan, married to that pallid spiritless woman, might not even know what Gideon was talking about. Or might turn it into a crude hilarious joke.) If he might take his father aside. Or his uncle Hiram. Or one of his cousins in the Contracoeur area, which he rarely visited now because of a disagreement that grew out of last year's leasing of some land along the river. . . . And there was his cousin Harry whom he'd always liked, but he too was estranged, it had to do with finances, his father and Hiram, maneuverings Gideon knew very little about.

But the family never spoke openly about serious things. So how might he begin . . . ? Embarrassing enough to speak of illnesses, accidents, debts, financial problems of any kind; risking old Noel's anger and feigned ignorance. The official Bellefleur attitude was one of robust jocularity. Men drinking together, men at the hunting camp. Nothing so important it can't be laughed away. Shouted away. (Across the lake old Jonathan Hecht, a cabinetmaker who had done work for grandmother Elvira decades ago, lay stricken with a "wasting" disorder that was a consequence of old war injuries, and spent most of his time in bed now, set up downstairs in the parlor or, in warm weather, out on the veranda: the old man was obviously dying, at times he was too feeble even to lift a hand in greeting, but when Gideon's father rode over to visit him he spoke cheerfully, even harshly, with an air of subtle accusation, striding to the bed and whipping off his hat, all outdoors bustle, smelling of horse and leather and tobacco, *Well, Jonathan, how the hell are you on this fine morning! Looking better, in my opinion! Feeling better too, eh? Oh, you'll be up and at 'em in no time! Have to hide the little girlies from you, yes? . . . You know, Jonathan, two things would fix you up just fine: a little snort from this-here that I smuggled past your wife, and an hour or two out on the lake with me, just trolling for the hell of it, to see what turns up. A few lungs-full of fresh air'd set you up right, 's no wonder you lay around looking so groggy and slow, what with the smell in this place. . . .*

(The old man's step-granddaughter, Garnet, a shy anemic-looking girl with long straggly blond hair that was all snags and snarls, tried to warn Gideon's father, tried to silence him, but of course he paid no attention. He had come to Bushkill's Ferry on his old stallion Fremont to *cheer that miserable bastard up*, as he'd said, and he wouldn't allow any of the silly Hecht women to dissuade him.)

Nor did Gideon feel that he could talk to Nicholas Fuhr, his friend since childhood, or his other friends in the area—that would have been a violation of his marriage, an act equivalent to infidelity.

So Gideon never spoke to anyone of his uneasiness with his wife, and certainly he could not speak to *her;* not of anything so deeply, so profoundly, intimate. That he, her husband, believed she had become obsessed with . . . with the desire for . . . with desire itself. . . . That he believed she became, at times, almost a little unbalanced. . . . This passion, this grim joyless striving, this contest between them: was it simply for the purpose of having another baby? He could not bring himself to speak to her about such matters, the two of them hadn't a vocabulary to contain such thoughts, Leah would have been irrevocably wounded. They could send each other into roars of laughter with crude imitations of the family—Leah as her sister-in-law Lily, Gideon as Noel or his pompous uncle Hiram—they could even speak frankly of decisions Noel made without consulting Gideon, and they could chide each other when one of them slipped into a mood (it was usually Gideon, these days), but they could not speak of their intimate physical life, their sexual bond, their love. At the very thought of such a trespass Gideon rose hastily and left for the stables, where he might stay for an hour or more, not thinking, not even brooding, simply breathing in the dark odorous hay-and-manure-and-horse comfort that so calmed him. He would *not* speak to her about such things. And anyway he reasoned that once she conceived, once she was again pregnant, the obsession would die.

But then, incredibly, she failed to conceive.

Month followed month and she failed, she failed to conceive, and it was this word she insisted upon—*fail, failed*—this word Gideon had to endure. Sometimes it was a frightened whisper *I keep failing, Gideon;* sometimes it was a curt blunt statement, *We keep failing, Gideon.* Bromwell and Christabel were in superb health. Bromwell walked a few weeks before Christabel, but both learned to talk at about the same time, and everyone exclaimed at the babies' good natures: Aren't you fortunate, Leah! Don't you just *adore* them? "Of course I adore them," Leah might say, distracted. And a few minutes later tell Lettie to take them away. She loved them but they must have represented to her a past accomplishment, some uncanny miraculous coup she'd managed at the age of nineteen; but now she was twenty-six, now she was twenty-seven, soon she would be thirty. . . .

And then the family began making certain remarks. Certain inquiries. Aunt Aveline, grandmother Cornelia, even aunt Matilde, even Della herself. Do you think . . . ? Wouldn't you and Gideon like . . . ? The twins are now five years old, don't you think it might be a good time for . . . ? Once Leah snapped at her mother-in-law, "It isn't as if we haven't *tried,* Mother; we do practically nothing else," and the remark was repeated everywhere, it was thought to be so typical of Leah Pym's "indelicate" nature. But she was so beautiful, with her deep-set blue eyes, which were slate-blue, very dark, and her strong chin, and her perfect wide lips, and her proud bold quivering posture, that of course she was forgiven: at least by the men of the family.

At the same time Lily kept having babies. It must be a simple feat, it must require a simple-minded integrity, Leah thought, eying her sister-in-law with a weak smile that concealed a powerful contempt. Or are there tricks, secret rituals . . . ? Superstitious maneuvers? She woke one morning, a few weeks before Mahalaleel's arrival at the manor, and thought quite clearly—*I don't believe in anything, I am a natural atheist, but suppose I experiment with . . . with certain beliefs.* (Ah, but really she was incapable of "believing"! She laughed at omens, at warnings, at all silly chatter about spirits and the dead and Biblical injunctions that had sprung, she knew full well, out of some old crabbed desert hermit's sexual frustration; she even dismissed, perhaps too impatiently, her mother's self-pitying tale of a "prophetic" dream she'd had on the eve of her young husband's accidental death.) She would experiment, however. She would hypothesize. Of course she could not believe because she was too intelligent, and too skeptical, and had too wild a sense of humor. . . . She half-believed, perhaps. She was a natural atheist but she might half-believe if she put her mind to it.

I don't believe in anything, she thought angrily.

But if I *do* believe . . .

But of course I don't. I can't. Hiding things under pillows, whispering little prayers, calculating when the twins were conceived, what sort of food Gideon and I had eaten that evening . . .

But if I *do* . . .

While making love with Gideon she gripped his buttocks tight and shut her eyes and thought *Now, now, at this very moment, now,* but the words struck her as absurd, and she sank back, helpless, half-sobbing, miserable. She wanted to die. But no: of course she didn't want to die. She wanted to *live.* She wanted to have another baby, and live, and all would be well, and she would never want anything again in her life.

Never anything again in your life?

Never.

Not anything? In your entire life?

In my entire life.

Another baby—and nothing else, in your entire life?

Yes. In my entire life.

So she tried little tricks too silly to mention, and murmured little prayers, but still nothing happened: she was willing to make a fool of herself but nothing happened. She fell into moods of languor and depression in which she halfway wished—and deeply wounded Gideon by saying so—that she hadn't married at all. "I should have entered a convent. I shouldn't have given in to you," she would say at such times, pushing out her fleshy lower lip like a child of twelve. "But you loved me," Gideon protested. "No, I never did, how could I, I knew nothing about love, I was just an ignorant girl," Leah said carelessly. *"You* insisted on marrying. You were such a bully, I gave in out of fear of you, that you'd treat me the way you did that poor tame spider!" "Leah, you're misrepresenting the past," Gideon said, his face darkening with blood. "You know that's a sin. . . ." "A sin! A *sin!* Imagine calling the truth sinful!" And she laughed him away, then burst into tears. Her moods were so capricious, so stormy, it was almost as if she *were* pregnant.

I don't want to be a woman any longer, she thought.

But then: Oh, God, I want to have another baby. Just one more! Just one! I would never ask for anything again in my entire life. It wouldn't even have to be a boy. . . .

She thought it must be a good omen, not only that the great cat

Mahalaleel came to the manor, but that he so clearly favored her. He was partial as well to Vernon and great-grandmother Elvira, who knew how to rub the back of his head with her knuckles, and he would sometimes tolerate pretty Yolande petting him and fussing over him; but he ignored the rest of the household, even the servants who fed him, and once in Leah's earshot he hissed angrily as Gideon stooped to pet his head. "All right, then," Gideon muttered, rising to his full height and resisting the impulse to kick the creature, "go back to hell where you belong."

Because Mahalaleel was so discriminating, it soon became a mark of good fortune if he curled up at someone's feet, or rubbed around someone's legs, making his throaty crackling noise. He had a habit of coming up behind both Leah and Vernon and thrusting his big head beneath their hands importunately, demanding to be petted: it was an extraordinary gesture, and never failed to astonish and delight Leah. "Aren't you bold!" she laughed. "You know exactly what you want and how to get it."

She and her niece Yolande brushed his thick cloudy coat with Leah's own gold-backed hairbrush, and tried to lift him in their arms, laughing at his weight. In the right mood he could tolerate a surprising amount of attention, but he always stiffened when the youngest children approached: Christabel was not welcome, nor were Aveline's noisy children, nor Lily's (except for Yolande and Raphael), and even cautious Bromwell, frowning behind his glasses, wanting only to "observe" and take notes on Mahalaleel. (He had already begun his journal, which was filled with minute observations, and measurements, and even the results of several dissections performed on small rodents.) Immediately after settling in the house Mahalaleel drove away the other tomcats, and made coquettish subordinates of the females; the household's six or seven dogs kept their distance from him. He was allowed to roam nearly anywhere he wished. At first he slept in the kitchen, on the wide warm stone hearth; then he chose a comfortable old leather chair in the room known as Raphael's library; then he spent one night in the first-floor linen closet, sprawled luxuriously on grandmother Cornelia's fine Spanish tablecloth; then he was discovered beneath the red velvet Victorian settee in a little-used drawing room, snoring faintly amid the dust balls. Sometimes he disappeared for an entire day, sometimes for a night; once he was gone three days in a row and Leah was heartbroken, convinced that he had abandoned her. And what a bad-luck sign that would be . . . ! But he reappeared suddenly, in fact at her very heels, making his hoarse guttural sound and butting with his head against her hand.

He made grandfather Noel nervous by coming up silently behind him, and staring with his wide-spaced tawny green eyes as if he were about to speak. He teased the kitchen help for food, and was rather shameless about his tricks: fed by one servant he nevertheless cajoled another into giving him food, and then another: and yet he never exactly mewed like a hungry cat, he never condescended to *beg*. He quickly became something of a household puzzle. How was it possible, the chil-

THE PREGNANCY · 45

dren asked, that Mahalaleel could be sleeping soundly by the fireplace in the parlor, but when you left the room or only turned your head he was gone—simply gone? Albert and Jasper swore they had seen Mahalaleel up a tall pine back of one of the logging roads, a mile and a half away. It was one of those pines with no branches or limbs for a considerable distance—seventy-five feet or more—and there was Mahalaleel perched on the lowest limb, absolutely motionless, his hair gray and indistinct, his enormous tail curved about to cover his paws, his wide staring intelligent face terrible as that of a great horned owl about to swoop down upon its prey. They wondered—how could a cat so large manage to climb that tree?—and was he trapped there, would he need help getting down? They called him but he did no more than glance down at them, as if he'd never seen them before. They tried to shake the tree, without success. "Mahalaleel, you'll starve up there!" they shouted. "Mahalaleel, you'd better come home with us!"

It was getting dark, so the boys ran home, intending to bring a flashlight back and some food with which to tempt him—but as soon as they burst noisily into the kitchen they saw that Mahalaleel was already there, washing his oversized paws daintily on the hearth. When did he come back, they wanted to know. Oh, a few minutes ago, Edna said. But he was trapped up a tree in the woods! He was trapped up a big pine and couldn't get down! they said, astonished.

Mahalaleel was an excellent hunter—the women of the house didn't want to know the number of wood rats he brought in his strong jaws to the kitchen door, nor the size of the rats; Leah was the only one to dare enter the dining room where, one freezing morning, Mahalaleel had produced out of nowhere a massive snowshoe hare which he was greedily devouring—in fact, most of the neck and the back of the head were gone, and raw strings of muscle glittered bloodily in Mahalaleel's teeth as he glanced up with an almost human leer—lying sprawled on the gleaming mahogany table Raphael had had imported from Valencia. "Oh, my God, Mahalaleel!" Leah cried. The sight of the half-eaten rabbit, and her beautiful pet's bloody muzzle, and the greenish frost-tinged eyes in which the black iris was greatly dilated made her feel faint. It was a terrifying sensation, as if she were losing her balance at the edge of a cliff. Yet even at that moment—reeling, half-blind—she wondered if perhaps she might be pregnant. Faintness *was,* after all, a symptom of pregnancy.

It soon became Mahalaleel's custom to follow Leah upstairs in the evening, and to make his bed at the foot of Leah's and Gideon's enormous bed. Gideon was annoyed: what if the creature had fleas? *"You* have fleas," Leah said curtly. "Mahalaleel is absolutely clean." To humor his wife Gideon pretended to admire the cat; he even stroked its arrogant head, and tolerated its disdain. He could not block a sensation of absurd disappointment when it refused to purr for him.

Mahalaleel not only purred luxuriously for Leah, but flopped over onto his back, and allowed his pinkish-gray stomach to be tickled, and made playful kittenlike lunges at Leah with his paws and teeth. If he should forget he was playing, if he should unsheath his claws, and sink his teeth in her flesh—! Gideon lay listlessly against his pillows, watching Leah pretend to attack Mahalaleel, watching the giant cat squirm and gurgle and lash out and flick its plume of a tail, and it crossed his mind more than once that if the cat *should* wound his wife—why then he would batter it to death at once, with his fists if necessary. He hadn't a gun in this room. Or a knife: Leah pretended to abhor such things. But Gideon Bellefleur with his muscular arms and shoulders, his long supple fingers, could very easily kill a creature like Mahalaleel with his hands.

"Be careful, Leah," he said. "You're playing too rough with him."

Leah jerked an arm away. The cat *had* snagged a claw in the sleeve of her silk nightgown, and there *was* a faint red line, hardly more than a hairsbreadth, on her forearm. "Gideon, your voice upsets him," she said irritably. "Must you speak so *loudly* when there are just the three of us in this room . . . ?"

After a short while Mahalaleel was not content with sleeping at the foot of the bed, curled up on the turquoise and cream-colored brocade cover (which he had already soiled somewhat, with his hairs, and dirty feet); during the night he made his way on tiptoe, walking with extreme delicacy for so large a creature, to lie between Leah and Gideon. Gideon was never certain when Mahalaleel made his move, but it was during a period of Gideon's deepest, most intense sleep, so that he was never awakened, and at dawn he would discover himself pushed far to the right side of the bed, crowded out by that damned Mahalaleel.

"Tonight he sleeps in the kitchen," Gideon said.

"He sleeps *here,*" Leah said.

"He belongs in the barn with the other animals!"

"He belongs *here,*" Leah said.

And so they disagreed, and quarreled frequently, but Mahalaleel continued to sleep with them, leaving his multicolored hairs everywhere — even, Gideon might discover to his fury, in his eyelashes, or in his beard. He had to excuse himself from a conference with his father, his uncle Hiram, Ewan, and a bank officer from Nautauga Falls, because something had worked its way in his eye and his eye was watering and tears were streaming down his cheek: of course it turned out to be a cat hair.

He recalled Mahalaleel's appearance, that rainy night. A rat, really. An opossum. With that skinny ugly tail. He *might* have stomped it to death right there in the foyer, and Leah could not have stopped him, and no one would really have blamed him. Now it was too late: now, if Mahalaleel disappeared, Leah would grieve over him. (She wasn't herself these days —hadn't been herself for months—too easily brought to tears, to rage, to a black dispirited mood.) Leah would know of course that Gideon had done it and she would never forgive him.

So Mahalaleel continued to sleep in their bedroom, and at dawn Gideon would wake with a start to see the cat gazing unperturbed at him, no more than six inches away. The creature's eyes were golden-green and flawless, like jewels; there was something fascinating about them. Gideon knew better, he knew that animals hadn't any grasp of their own being, they did not, after all, *create* themselves, yet he could not tear his eyes away from the cat's. The silky fur, soft and rising cloudily, revealing in a single ray of sunshine all sorts of amazing improbable colors—not only an eerie crystalline dove-gray, and an ivory-white, but saffron, and russet, and gold, and even a sort of lavender-green; the subtle misty design hidden in the layers of fur and fluff—vaguely tigerish, rainbow stripes of every variety of width and depth of coloring; the pert, rather snubbed grape-colored nose with its sharply defined nostrils (so sharp they looked, even at close range, as if someone had outlined them in black ink with a fine-tipped pen); the silvery-white whiskers which measured, according to Gideon's son Bromwell, nine inches from tip to tip, and were always straight and bristling with cleanliness; the tip of the tongue, so damp and pink, which often protruded slightly, just a fraction of an inch, between his front teeth in the morning—a sign of lazy contentment, of absolute satisfaction. Gideon's public attitude toward his wife's pet continued to be one of indifference or disdain: he was a horseman, after all, like his father, and had never fussed much over dogs, not even the finest hunting dogs on the estate. So he ignored Mahalaleel downstairs. But sometimes in private he *almost* admired the creature. . . . He stared at its calm unblinking uncanny eyes, and it stared back at him, showing the tip of its tongue, its big knobby oversized feet sometimes beginning a little dance: kneading at the very pillow on which Gideon's head lay: sheathing and unsheathing those great curved claws.

One morning Gideon awoke very early to see Leah sitting up in bed, her long dark hair falling over her shoulders, in untidy strands across her breasts. The cat lay slumbering between them, an enormous patch of warm shadow. Before Gideon could speak Leah reached out to grasp his shoulder, and then his forearm; her grip was surprisingly hard. He dreaded what she might tell him. And yet it turned out to be the best possible news: she was certain, she claimed, that she was pregnant.

"I feel something there. I'm not imagining it, I *feel* something, it isn't even like the other time, it's something quite different—quite distinct. I can *feel* that I'm pregnant. I *know.*"

And so she was pregnant, indeed. And so Germaine came to be born.

Jedediah

Jedediah: 1806. A pilgrimage into the mountains. In his twenty-fourth year. I will be a guide if necessary, he told his angry father, I will live absolutely alone for one full year, he told his skeptical brother, please don't worry about me, don't think about me at all.

Jedediah Bellefleur, the youngest of the three sons of Jean-Pierre and Hilda (who had fled her husband in 1790, and lived now in seclusion with her wealthy elderly parents in Manhattan), relatively slight-bodied for a Bellefleur, particularly for one who wanted to explore the western range by himself. No more than five feet six inches tall in his thick-heeled leather boots. No more than 130 pounds in weight, at the time of his departure. (When he returned—ah, when he returned!—he barely weighed one hundred pounds. But that was much later.) Unlike his brothers Louis and Harlan, and certainly unlike his notorious father, Jedediah was soft-spoken and reserved; his silence was sometimes mistaken for aloofness, even for contempt. He had a narrow triangular face surrounded by sprigs of dark electric hair which was always unruly, as if stirred by inordinately restless thought. Jean-Pierre had forced him to ride as a very small child and in a freakish accident (the normally tractable gelding had been panicked by the smell of blood on someone's clothes: it was November, it was pig-butchering time) he was thrown, and badly hurt, and as a consequence would walk with a slight limp his entire life. If he was bitter—but of course Jedediah was not bitter—if he even contemplated bitterness toward his father, he did not show it: he had learned shrewdly not to show anything of his secret life to his father.

Yet it was not his father Jedediah was leaving; nor was it—he was *certain*—his brother's young wife, about whom his thoughts circled obsessively. If he meant to run away from Germaine he might have gone anywhere, he need not have exposed himself to such hardship. (And in a sense Jedediah hardly saw his sister-in-law now. Hardly "saw" her after the wedding ceremony and the wedding party—held unwisely at the Fort Hanna Inn, a noisy brawling tavern on the river in which Jean-Pierre had invested some of his money, and which was ideally suited for all-night drunken parties from which, early in the evening, tiresomely respectable guests fled, and native Indians—Indian women, that is—might be welcomed in, immune from state and county laws governing their presence in establishments that served alcoholic refreshments; and, some days later, the housewarming party which the young couple bravely gave (for it was not only the groom's father who had gotten so shamefully drunk at the wedding party, and offered to fight the Fort Hanna Inn proprietor who, he said, was cheating him of "thousands of dollars of revenue," but the bride's father as well—an Irishman named Brian O'Hagan who made do in the wilderness by trapping beaver, and speculating in land rumored to be rich in silver and gold along the Nautauga River—"rumored," that is, by the very people who wanted to unload their land) in the handsome log house with its wide veranda and several fieldstone fireplaces the old man was giving them as a wedding gift—after these incidents Jedediah did not really "see" Germaine at all. He carried her image about with him, effortlessly, and helplessly, and at odd unanticipated times—while kneeling in prayer on the floorboards of his bedroom, while struggling to saddle the small-bodied but uncannily strong roan mare he intended to take with him on his pilgrimage, while washing his face at dawn, bringing pools of icy water against his sleep-seared eyes—he might sense her presence, as if she had come up quietly beside him, and was about to lay her hand on his arm.

Germaine O'Hagan was sixteen years old. Louis was twenty-seven. She was no taller than a child, quick and dark and lithe and very pretty, with self-consciously "gracious" movements she had learned from observing ladies at church; when in the presence of the Bellefleurs she stood very straight, her small hands clasped together just below her breasts, her eyes wide and dark and intense. She was not intimidated, though she might have been surprised, by Jean-Pierre's boisterous charm—his exaggerated compliments which always sounded mocking when addressed to women, and which were, indeed, viciously mocking when addressed to his wife; his airy theatrical mannerisms; his spinning out of farfetched "frontier" tales learned in private clubs in Manhattan, and around mahogany tables on Wall Street, in the feverish years of his "rise"; and his careless tactless familiarity with the country's ruling families, and with Washington politicians, generally known as contemptible *but* possessing devilishly admirable traits not unlike those attributed to Jean-Pierre Bellefleur, a duke's son after all, himself. She was not intimidated, not even alarmed, since her *own* father—! Ah, yes, her own father. Who was still trying to sell Jean-Pierre shares along the Nautauga. Who bathed twice a year—in May, and then again in September, before the first frost.

She was pregnant, after less than two months of marriage.

She was pregnant, a girl of sixteen who looked, even close up, like a child of twelve.

Jedediah had been planning to leave for years, he had been dreaming of the mountains, the high lake country, the solitude of balsam and tamarack and yellow birch and spruce and hemlock and tall white pines, some of them as thick as seven feet at the base, of surpassing beauty, and ageless: even before the most public of his father's disgraces (the others, those that had broken his mother, were certainly worse), even before his brother brought home the little O'Hagan girl he claimed from the first he intended to marry—no matter that Jean-Pierre had plans for him, as he had plans for all his sons involving heiresses of Dutch, German, even of French stock, before the newspapers hawked the secrets of "La Compagnie de New York," and even after: and then too, if he wanted simply to flee Louis and Germaine and the heart-stopping fact of their union, the fact that they shared the same bed night after night, now routinely, now without even self-consciousness (though Jedediah could not quite comprehend such an enormity) he might have followed Harlan out west, or settled in to work farmland along the Nautauga, since his father owned thousands of acres of land in the Valley and would have leased or sold it (he would not have given it, at least not until Jedediah married) very reasonably. But it was the north country he turned to. It was the north country he required. To lose himself, to find God. To ascend as a pilgrim, confident that God awaited.

I will be a guide if necessary, he informed his father, who was, at first, speechless with anger: for when the West Indies deal went through he would *need* men he could trust as overseers, who would not be timid about handling the slaves firmly. I will live absolutely alone for one full year, from one June to the next, he told his skeptical brother Louis, who was rather hurt—for he was extremely fond of Jedediah in his bullying negligent way, and it frightened him, initially, to contemplate life with the family so diminished. For *family* meant everything.

(First their mother had fled, after her nervous collapse. After their father had disgraced himself in public—or so it would seem, if one judged the situation not by the old man's casual remarks but by the highly vocal remarks of others: Jean-Pierre Bellefleur's second term as a congressman had ended abruptly, attended by charges of scandal and corruption, but it was never clear exactly what he had done since so many other men were involved, businessmen and politicians alike, what with inadequate laws and governors famously "pliant," as the expression went. After weeks of newspaper exposure of La Compagnie de New York, a shareholding organization for founding a New France in the mountains for titled French families dispossessed of their property by the Revolution, at three dollars an acre (Jean-Pierre and his partners had, of course, paid the state far less after *this* revolution, when great masses of wilderness land originally owned by the British or by British sympathizers reverted back to the government, and state land commissioners were authorized to sell as much of it as possible, in order to populate the north country, and to establish a buffer between the new states and British Canada)—after weeks of secret meetings—the presence of strangers in the Bellefleur household—Jean-Pierre's alternating panic and crude blustering euphoria—somehow it came about that no formal indictments were made. None. Jean-Pierre and his partners and La Compagnie were not even fined. But by then Jean-Pierre's marriage was over: though it could not be said that he missed his wife. And then, years later, Harlan had fled, taking with him a matched team of Andalusian horses, and wearing around his lean middle a money belt stuffed with cash and all that remained of their mother's jewelry.)

And now Jedediah. Young Jedediah, who had always seemed so fearful of life.

"One year!" Louis laughed. "You really think you'll stay up in the mountains *one year!* My friend, you'll be back home by the end of November."

Jedediah did not defend himself. His manner was both humble and arrogant.

"Suppose you stay too long, and the passes fill up with snow?" Louis said. "It will go to fifty-seven degrees below zero up there. You know that, don't you?"

Jedediah made an indeterminate gesture. "But I must withdraw from this world," he said softly.

"Must withdraw from this world!" Louis crowed. "Listen to him talk—sounds like a preacher! Be sure you don't withdraw altogether," he said.

Jedediah tried to explain himself more systematically to Germaine. But the girl's staring tear-filled eyes distracted him.

"I must—I want— You see, my father and his friends— Their plans for cutting down timber— Their plans for building roads and bringing in tenants—"

Germaine stared at him. "Oh, but, Jedediah," she whispered, "what if something happens to you? Up there in the mountains all alone. . ."

"Nothing will happen to me," Jedediah said.

"When the first snowfall comes, what if you can't get out? As Louis said—"

Jedediah had begun to tremble. It alarmed him that he would remember—he would *see*—this young girl's face even after he had fled her. "I want to—I want to withdraw from the world and see if I am worthy of —of—God's love," he said, blushing. His voice shook with a fanatic's frightened audacity.

The girl made a sudden helpless gesture, as if she wished to touch his arm. And Jedediah drew back.

"Nothing will happen to me," he said curtly.

"But if you leave now—if you leave now—you won't be here when the baby comes," Germaine said. "And we thought—Louis and I thought — We *want* you to be the godfather—"

But Jedediah withdrew, and escaped her.

In her young husband's arms she lay sleepless and dazed, and surprisingly bitter, for the first time since their marriage. "He doesn't love us," she whispered. He was running off and leaving them, he was going to risk his life in the mountains, maybe turn into one of those deranged hermits you sometimes hear about: men gone mad from too much solitude. "He doesn't want to be our baby's godfather," Germaine whispered. "He doesn't love us."

Only half-hearing, Louis nuzzled her neck and murmured Now, now, Puss.

"Just when our first baby is coming," Germaine said.

Louis laughed, and tickled her, and buried his warm bearded mouth in her neck. "But he'll be back for the second, and the third, and the fourth," he said.

Germaine did not want to be consoled. Open-eyed, sleepless, she found herself rather angry. It was not like her: but then no one in this household really knew her: they thought she was a sweet docile little girl. And so she was, when it suited her. "He won't be back for any of them," she said. "He is abandoning us."

Like several of her Dublin relatives—her female relatives—little Germaine prided herself on being, from time to time, but always unpredictably, clairvoyant—gifted with second sight. So she knew, she knew. Jedediah would not only not return for the birth of their other children but he would *never* see his nieces and nephews—never in this lifetime.

"Oh, how do you know, Puss!" Louis laughed, rolling his burly weight upon her.

"I *know,*" she said.

"Powers"

Leah with her immense swollen belly. At five months she looked as if she were already nine months pregnant, and the baby might force its way out at any moment. What odd feverish dreams she endured, half-lying on pillows, the muscles of her legs now packed with soft plump flesh, her slender ankles swollen, her eyes rolling back into her head with the violence—the queerness—of her ideas! Were they hers, or the unborn child's? She felt the creature's power, her head aswim with dreams that left her panting and feverish but utterly baffled. She could *feel* the unborn child's spirit but she could not *see* in her mind's eye what it wished of her, what it craved.

I am going to accomplish something, she thought frequently, opening and closing her fists, feeling her nails press against the palms of her hands. The soft pliant eager flesh. . . . I am going to be the instrument, the means by which something is accomplished, Leah thought.

And then again days passed and she thought nothing at all; she was too lazy, too dream-befuddled to think.

Her hair lay loose on her shoulders because it was too much trouble for her to plait and roll it, or even to have one of the girls tend to her. She lay back against her pillows, yawning and sighing. Her puffy hand caressed her midriff, as if she feared nausea and must remain very, very still: for at the oddest, least expected times she was overcome by a spasm of retching that quite unnerved her. Until now she had *never* been sick to her stomach—she prided herself on being one of the healthy Bellefleur women, not one of the sickly self-pitying ones.

Leah holding herself still, very still. As if listening to something no one else could hear.

Leah wild-eyed and sly as if she had just arisen from love, a forbidden love, her mouth fleshier than anyone remembered, curved in a slow secretive smile.

Leah in her drawing room, on the old chaise longue, in a dream-stupor, her lovely eyes heavy-lidded, a teacup about to slip out of her fingers. (One of the children would catch it before it fell; or Vernon would lean forward on his knees, on the carpet, to take it gently out of her hand.) Leah ordering the servants about in her new voice, which was petulant and shrill and rather like her mother's—though when Gideon said so, perhaps unwisely, she angrily denied it. Why, Della did nothing but *whine* the livelong day, wasn't Della famous in the family for her monotonous mournful self-pitying dirge—!

Leah more beautiful than ever, with her healthy high-colored complexion that put the other women to shame (winter bleached their cheeks, gave them a listless dead-white skin), her deep-set eyes that seemed enlarged with pregnancy, a very dark blue, almost black, keen and thick-lashed and usually glittering, as if flooded with tears—tears not of sorrow or pain, but of sheer inchoate emotion. Leah's laughter ringing out gaily, or her robust full-throated girl's voice, or her suddenly warm, faintly disbelieving murmur when she was struck with gratitude (for people—neighbors, friends, family, servants—were always bringing her little gifts, fussing over her, inquiring about the state of her health, staring with an unfeigned and most gratifying *reverence* at the mere size of her). Only her husband was a witness to her body's amazing elasticity, which rather frightened him as the months passed: her lovely pale skin stretched tight across her belly and abdomen, tight, and tighter still with each week, each day, an alabaster-white, astonishing. Whatever was growing inside her was already alarmingly large and would grow even larger, stretching her beautiful skin tight as a drum, *tighter* than a drum, so that Gideon could do no more than murmur words of love and comfort to her, while staring, or consciously not staring, at that remarkable mound where her lap had once been. Had he fathered twins again, or triplets . . . ? Or a creature of unprecedented size, even in a family in which hefty infants were quite common?

"Do you love me," Leah murmured.

"Of course I love you."

"You *don't* love me."

"I'm faint with love for you. But intimidated."

"What?"

"Intimidated."

"What does that mean? Intimidated? Now? Why? *Really?*"

"Not intimidated," Gideon said, stroking her belly, leaning down to kiss it, to press his cheek gently against it, "not intimidated but in awe, somewhat in awe. Surely you can sympathize. . . ."

He pressed his ear gingerly against the tight-stretched skin, and began to hear—but what *did* he hear, that so immobilized him, that drew the irises of his eyes to mere pinpricks?

"Oh, what are you chattering about, I can't hear you, speak up, for God's sake," Leah would cry, seizing him by the hair or his beard, and tugging him up so that he would be forced to look at her face. At such times she might burst unaccountably into tears. "You *don't* love me," she said. "You're terrified of me."

Indeed, she was to grow colossal with her pregnancy so that, in the final month or two, her very features appeared gross: the mouth and the flared nostrils and the eyes visibly enlarged, as if a somewhat ill-fitting mask had been forced upon her. Her lips were often moist, there was spittle in the corners, a certain feverish breathlessness that enhanced her beauty—or was it the curious *power* of her beauty—and made Gideon look away, stricken. She was his height now. Or taller: standing barefoot she could gaze quite levelly into his eyes, smiling her perverse, secretive little smile. And Gideon was of course an exceptionally tall man—even as a boy he had had to stoop somewhat to get through doorways in ordinary houses. She was his height now or a little taller, a young giantess, beautiful and monstrous at the same time, and he *did* love her. And he was terrified of her.

That winter Leah was the uncontested queen of the household. There was no disputing her authority: Lily kept prudently to her part of the manor, though it was ill-heated and shabby, and cautioned her children (who, smitten with Leah, disobeyed her) not to cross her tyrannical sister-in-law's path; Aveline was uncharacteristically silent in her presence, and deferred even to her brother Gideon; aunt Veronica, appearing for a few minutes in the evening, if Leah was still awake, or briefly in Leah's cozy drawing room just before dinner, when the warm flames of the fireplace were reflected in the darkened windows, and the lovely great cat Mahalaleel might be dozing at Leah's feet, would stand silently gazing upon her nephew's young wife, her placid sheep's face showing only a curious impersonal interest—though she gave Leah a number of small, charming gifts that winter, and was to give the infant Germaine an antique rattle that had once belonged to her own mother, and which had considerable sentimental value. Even grandmother Cornelia began to defer to her, and did not answer back when Leah spoke insolently; and great-grandmother Elvira, often too weak to come downstairs for days at a time, was continually asking how Leah was, and sending servants and children back and forth with little messages and admonitions. Della Pym moved back into the manor to be with Leah in the final weeks of the pregnancy, despite her son-in-law's quite explicit lack of enthusiasm, and brought with her Garnet Hecht, who was not exactly a servant but a "girl who helped out" —and even Della, closemouthed and stubborn, was observed backing down before her daughter's demands. And of course all the men of the household were entranced by her. And nearly all the children.

After the fifth month Leah was immobilized much of the time. It was too awkward for her to climb stairs so she began to spend nights in the drawing room that overlooked the garden, half-sitting and half-lying against goosefeather pillows on a handsome old chaise longue. This room, sometimes called Violet's Room by older members of the household (though Violet Bellefleur, Raphael's unhappy wife, had disappeared into Lake Noir many decades ago and would surely never return, and even Noel and Hiram, her oldest grandchildren, could barely remember her), was an exceptionally attractive room, beautifully decorated with crimson silk wallpaper and oak wainscotting and alabaster lamps with white globes, and in one corner was a clavichord built for Violet by a young Hungarian cabinetmaker, a small, delicate-appearing, but quite sturdy instrument made of numerous woods: the jewel of the room though it was cracked on top and no one played it any longer. (Leah had tried; flushed with the excited, audacious complacency of her condition she had actually tried, remembering only dimly, and in fragments, the rudimentary piano lessons she had had at La Tour many years ago, and had resisted sullenly at the time—but her weight was nearly too much for the bench with its slender legs of veneered oak, and in any case her oversized fingers were too clumsy for the delicate walnut keys. She tried to play "Hark the Herald Angels Sing" and the scale of C-major and a nameless boisterous square dance tune but the sounds that came out— tinny, jerky, shrieklike—were embarrassing. In the end she brought her fist down on the keys, which protested faintly, and closed the instrument, and forbade the children to play it, though Yolande's touch was reverent and sensitive and she could *almost* play a recognizable tune.) The carpet was still fairly thick, a mazelike design of crimson, green, creamy-white, and very dark blue; there were numerous old chairs, some of them generously overstuffed, and a horsehair sofa the children loved to bounce on; and an armoire with mother-of-pearl fixtures and a dramatic carving of the Bellefleur coat of arms (a falcon volant, a snake draped about its neck); and a seven-foot fireplace made of fieldstone. Violet's portrait had hung above the mantel for some time, but in recent years had been replaced by a rather dark, badly cracked landscape painting of indeterminate origin, thought to be "Italian Renaissance." About the room were curious things brought in from other parts of the house by the children —a ferocious tiger (thought to resemble Mahalaleel) carved from a whale's tooth, brass prickets with aged candles that would not burn, a queer distorting mirror about three feet high with an ornate ivory-and-jade frame that had been in the drawing room for years, but no one had troubled to hang—so that it was merely propped up against the wall and, because of its odd, oblique angle, sometimes reflected things perversely, or did not reflect them at all. (Once, gorging herself on chocolate-covered cherries and walnuts, and allowing greedy Mahalaleel to lick her sticky fingers, Leah had glanced across to the mirror and was startled to see, framed by sallow ivory and lusterless jade, absolutely nothing at all —neither herself nor Mahalaleel. And when one of Lily's boys, Raphael, leaned forward to accept a chocolate from her, he was reflected only in a vague muddy haze. Another time sweet-faced Vernon, entering the room, was reflected as a narrow, twisted column of light; and once, though Leah and Mahalaleel and the twins were quite normally reflected in the mirror, aunt Veronica, passing before them, was not only not reflected at all but blotted their images out as well, so that only the corner of the room remained.)

There was a parquet-topped table where Leah and the children and Vernon played cards that winter and spring, and the chaise longue—once an extremely beautiful piece of furniture, with carved mahogany legs and a sumptuous gold brocade covering—upon which poor Leah lay with increasing frequency, as the months passed and the child she carried grew larger and distinctly heavier. At first Leah had tried discreetly to hide her swollen belly, especially when friends came to visit—Gideon's closest friend Nicholas Fuhr, who was unmarried, and who had always been—or so Leah thought—halfway in love with her; and Leah's friend from girlhood, Faye Renaud, now married and the mother of several young children herself; and older friends of the Bellefleurs, and neighbors—with shawls, comforters, quilts, and even drowsy Mahalaleel himself, or at any rate his enormous fluffy plume of a tail. She troubled to arrange folds in a decorous fashion, to drape herself in shapeless dark gowns, even to loop strands of pearls about her neck, and to snap on oversized earrings —for, as grandmother Cornelia said, such tricks drew the eye upward. And the sight of her belly *was* disconcerting. (Even Gideon's cousin Vernon, a year or two older than she, and so clearly and painfully infatuated with her—the poor gangling young man liked nothing better than to read poetry to her on those dreary afternoons when the sun set at three o'clock, or failed to appear at all, Blake and Wordsworth and certain of Hamlet's soliloquies, and lengthy, incoherent, passionate poems of his own that put Leah in a comfortable stupor, her great eyes half-closed, her slightly swollen fingers clasped together over her belly as if securing it, one of the twins—usually Christabel—frankly napping nearby: even Vernon with his eager shy smile and his hopeful gaze and the reverent, melodic dipping of his voice as he read, or recited, *God appears and God is light / To those poor souls who dwell in night / But does a human form display / To those who dwell in realms of day,* appeared to be intimidated by the very fact of her, and if she groaned with sudden discomfort, or pressed a hand in alarm to her belly, feeling an instant's terrifying pain, or even made a good-natured allusion to her condition —which *did* make certain routines of life, like washing one's hair, and indeed bathing at all, and going to the bathroom—extremely difficult, poor Vernon would blush at once, and stare at her face with somewhat widened eyes as if to emphasize his *not* looking elsewhere; and smile his childlike perplexed smile, hidden in his beard. Though he was a Bellefleur himself, he never knew when the Bellefleurs were joking, or when they were being deliberately coarse in order to unsettle him, or when they were—as, upon occasion, they certainly were—utterly without guile.)

As the months passed, as the long winter months slowly passed into a cold, drizzly spring, Leah's appetite, never modest, became voracious. Around Christmastime her favorite foods were rum puddings and goat's cheese, and then she developed a near-insatiable craving for mashed apricots, and Valley Products stewed tomatoes, and pepper ham which she ate with her fingers to Cornelia's amazed disgust; and then, as the dead-white skin of her belly tightened over the swelling mass, and her poor ankles and knees grew bloated, and her breasts that had always been fairly small for her frame, and young and hard, grew larger almost daily, and began to ache and leak milk, to Leah's distress, and even her neck thickened so that, though still lovely, and columnar, it must have been the size of Ewan's, she began to devour raw beefsteaks, chewing for long minutes at a time, and grew nauseous at the very sight and odor of the food poor Edna prepared for the rest of the family, even Edna's famous boysenberry cream pie which Leah had always loved; and then, to her husband's surprise—for Leah made much of her disdain for men who drank, or for anyone who showed such a contemptible *weakness*—she habituated herself to glasses of wine in the early afternoon, and two or three bottles of Gideon's and Ewan's favorite dark ale as the day progressed, and some Scotch, and perhaps in the evening, while she played checkers or Parcheesi or gin rummy, some more Scotch (she soon acquired a taste for grandfather Noel's favorite liquor, and he rather liked drinking with her—Leah is the only woman with sense enough to understand a joke, and to laugh at it, he often said, flushed with his success with her: for she *was* a queenly young woman, beautiful despite her size, and bathed in a warm, lightly damp, erotic glow), and then, in the late evening, when even the most stubborn of the children was in bed, she ate chunks of Gorgonzola cheese and drank in large mouthfuls some very old heavy red Burgundy lately discovered in a recess of Raphael's cavernous wine cellar, long since thought depleted, and sipped at Spanish liqueurs, and crème de menthe, and a labelless brandy in which specks of genuine gold floated, and at midnight she fell into a stuporous doze from which no one could have awakened her, not even Gideon, so that she simply remained in Violet's drawing room, and they covered her with quilts, and tended to the fire, and brought a fresh saucer of cream for Mahalaleel, who slept at the foot of the couch on those nights—which were less frequent as spring approached—he chose to remain in the house.

She grew negligent—or was it contemptuous—and thought, Why be ashamed of the way I look? Why not take pride in myself? And so she stopped bothering with pearls and earrings, which only made her nervous anyway, and if she could have pulled her wedding ring off her thickened finger she would have done so, and instead of dark, drab, discreet clothing of the kind her mother always wore (insisted upon wearing, for Della was perpetually "in mourning" for her young husband whom the Bellefleurs had killed), she began to wear, not only for special occasions when the Steadmans or Nicholas Fuhr or Faye Renaud stopped by, but on quite ordinary eventless mornings, brightly colored gowns, some of them floor-length, with wide rakish sleeves, or decorative beads or feathers, or handmade Spanish lace: and sometimes the dresses had open necklines, so that Leah's full ripe astonishing breasts were partway revealed, and Vernon, entering the drawing room hesitantly, carrying his ledger filled with scribblings (he was quite vain, and yet embarrassed about his "scribblings," his poetry, and would read it only to Leah and certain of the children, making sure that Gideon and Ewan and his father Hiram were nowhere near: a rhapsodic singsong invocation of his masters Blake, Wordsworth, Shakespeare, Heraclitus, mixed in with interminable reflections (which poor Leah, whose head swam these days when she did so much as leaf through one of Bromwell's science encyclopedias, or even one of Christabel's simple readers, could make no sense of—it was difficult enough for her to restrain great torso-shuddering yawns as Vernon read in his tremulous, reedy, rather oracular voice, which was his special "poetry voice") on family legend of dubious authenticity: the meaning of the Bellefleur curse; how Samuel Bellefleur was seduced by spirits that dwelled in the very stone walls and foundations of the manor; how Raphael really died; why he had insisted—not only perversely, but uncharacteristically, for throughout his lifetime he had scorned unconventional behavior—that his cadaver be skinned, and the skin tanned, and stretched across a drum; why the house was haunted (and Leah had to admit that it probably *was* haunted, but like the rest of the family she simply stayed out of the most troublesome rooms, and saw to it that the most dangerous room of all was kept locked, even padlocked, against the inquisitive children who *would* nose out any secret, however terrifying) and in what odd ways, throughout the generations, it had been haunted; what Gideon's brother Raoul's fate would be (though in Gideon's presence Vernon would certainly not dare to approach that painful subject); why Abraham Lincoln had chosen to spend his last years in seclusion, on the Bellefleur estate; what had really happened to great-grandfather "Lamentations of Jeremiah"; why his own mother Eliza had disappeared without warning; why the family was doomed unless—but on this point the poetry drifted into an even more puzzling obscurity, and Vernon tended to mumble, and Leah had only the imprecise idea that salvation lay with Vernon or what he represented, and not with the other Bellefleur men or what they represented)—Vernon, alas, touchingly eager for an hour or two with Leah, during the afternoon when all of the men, Leah's husband in particular, could be relied upon to be absent, and only the gentlest, the most civilized of the children—Bromwell, Christabel, Yolande, Raphael —might be present, and fairly engrossed in their books or games, or trying (with minimal success) to interest Mahalaleel in the most comely and spirited of his new brood of kittens, would stare at her bosom, at the smooth, glaring-white tops of her enormous breasts, and freeze where he stood, and stammer a greeting, too stricken even to blush for a minute or two. . . .

But why be ashamed of the way I look, Leah thought angrily, though in fact she *was* somewhat ashamed, or at the very least painfully self-conscious (for she remembered how, as a girl, she had pitilessly scorned the very idea of having a baby, and had vowed that *she* would never find herself in so disgusting a condition); why not take pride in myself as I am.

"Vernon, for Christ's sake," she would say impatiently, reaching out to him, to squeeze his cold, timid, boneless hand, "sit *down,* I've been waiting for you, I've been bored all morning, Gideon's all the way to Port Oriskany and won't even be back tonight, he's negotiating for something so complicated, and so tedious, I didn't even make a show of asking about it—some granaries?—something about the railroad? Oh, your father would know but don't ask him, let's not give a damn about such trivia! Read me what you've written since yesterday. Pour me some ale first, and have some for yourself, and could you pass those nuts—unless the children have gobbled them all up—and sit down, please, right here, right by the fire. Sit *down.*"

And so, bedazzled by her, his knees somewhat weak, Vernon Bellefleur would sit only a few feet from Leah Bellefleur, his breath scanty, his nervous skinny fingers tugging at his beard. And he might begin by reading, in a self-conscious, heightened voice, some lines of Shelley, or Shakespeare, or Heraclitus (*This cosmos none of gods or men made; but it always was and is and shall be: an everlasting fire, kindling in measures and going out in measures*), whom he clearly thought to be brothers of his, and while at times it was all Leah could do (for she *was* a well-mannered young woman, in principle) to resist snorting with laughter at his vanity, at other times she found herself so deeply moved that a tear might trickle fatly down her cheek and her little boy might say, with that disconcertingly clinical edge to his voice, "Mamma, why are you crying?"

"I have no idea," she would say stiffly, wiping her face on her sleeve like one of the children.

Gideon was away, Gideon was so frequently away, on business, on his father's and Hiram's business, and so Vernon came to visit (for handsome Nicholas Fuhr, whom Leah might very well have married—*might* have married, once marriage struck her as inevitable—certainly could not drive over, nor could Ethan Burnside, or Meldram Steadman, out of fear of Gideon's jealousy), Vernon who was not much different from the women, and whom Leah was very fond of, though she sometimes nodded off not only when he was reading to her but when he was speaking to her; and Gideon, if he knew, was not at all jealous. Contemptuous, perhaps. But not jealous.

"Sit down," Leah would say, stifling a yawn, "and read what you've written since yesterday. I've been so dull and heavy-headed and lonely all morning. . . ."

Though Vernon was not yet thirty his brown hair was graying, especially at the temples; and his skimpy beard was nearly all gray. What a pity, Leah thought, that he hasn't a wife—hasn't a wife and never will have one

—since *she* might take him in hand, and trim that beard, and the stiff little hairs in his ears, and see to it that he doesn't wear the same baggy trousers five days running, and that greasy little vest. He needs kisses to liven up his complexion. . . .

Vernon, leafing through the ledger, fumbling with the oversized pages, glanced up at Leah as if—but of course it could not be possible —her stray, whimsical thoughts had the power to communicate themselves to him. He stared at her for a long uneasy moment. *She* blushed, gazing at the young man's thin, sallow face, and his slightly mismatched eyes (one was pale blue, the other pale brown: it was the blue eye that seemed to have the correct vision, and confronted things directly; the brown eye peered off a fraction of an inch to the left), and the tangle of his eyebrows, which were as thick as Gideon's. Vernon had the Bellefleur nose—long, straight, Roman, waxen-pale at the very tip—but in other respects, about the mouth, and about the eyes especially, he must have resembled his mother. His forehead was narrow and high, creased with years of brooding; there were premature lines, like parentheses, framing his mouth; the shape of his face was queerly triangular, since, though his forehead was narrow, his chin was quite small, and looked, from the side, as if it were melting away to nothing. Yet there was something attractive about him, something appealing. Though he was not *manly,* he was certainly nothing like Gideon or Ewan or Nicholas Fuhr, still, Leah thought with sudden conviction, he *was* warmly attractive, as a child or a beast might be attractive, in its very vulnerability. And then there was the young man's shy eagerness, his gentle manners, and the way—once he began to read—he forgot his surroundings and became increasingly passionate, so that his thin, rather reedy voice began to take strength, vibrating with intensity. Leah knew nothing at all about poetry—she had memorized poems at La Tour, for her English and French classes, but even at the time she grasped very little of what she memorized, and forgot it all as soon as the school year was over—but she admired Vernon's obstinate devotion to his craft, especially in the face of ridicule. (Ah, ridicule! What he hadn't had to bear, since he first became infatuated with words—not their meanings, not even their sounds, but their very weight and texture —as a child of nine or ten, poring over the leather-bound "classics" in old Raphael's library.) She could not really resist feeling something of the contempt for Vernon that most of the family felt, since the poor man had failed so miserably, and so frequently, at one after another of the tasks Hiram had set him (the last in the series of failures took place in the Fort Hanna sawmill, where Vernon had had a "managerial" position, but rumor had it that he mingled with his men, even ate lunch with them, and sought them out in taverns after work, where in his quavering hopeful voice he read them incantatory poems in long heavily stressed iambic lines on such subjects as—the very men themselves, sawmill workers with little or no formal education, the sons of impoverished farmers or day laborers or men who had joined the army to fight in the last war and had never returned, men who, in Vernon's feverish imagination, celebrated the "dignity and mystery" of honest physical labor unclouded by thought, uncontaminated by the obsession with personal gain that characterized the property-owning class: all this, this apotheosis of unfurrowed brows, swelling gleaming muscles, the very *nobility* of the Animal-in-Man, declaimed in lengthy and heavily stressed poems the men could not follow, and had no wish to follow—when they wanted only more money from the Bellefleurs, and preferred to deal with Ewan or even the old man himself, who cared nothing for them as men but would not, at least, embarrass and anger them by composing sentimental poems in their honor. And so in the end the Fort Hanna workers jeered poor Vernon out, and might even have roughed him up one night in a riverside tavern if they had not been apprehensive of Ewan's or Gideon's revenge: for the Bellefleurs were famous in exacting vengeance). Since coming to live at the castle as Gideon's wife, Leah had been only peripherally aware of Vernon, and then primarily as Hiram's son. She knew of the comical Fort Hanna episode, though not its humiliating details, and it crossed her mind more than once that perhaps the episode wasn't laughable as everybody (especially Hiram) thought—perhaps it was most unfortunate—even tragic. She wondered: Had Vernon run off somewhere alone and cried? Was he the sort of man who might allow himself to cry?

He was still staring at her, his lips parted in a queer half-smile. She could see a fine film of perspiration on his forehead.

". . . did you ask? If I cried?" he said hesitantly.

"What?"

"I didn't exactly . . . I didn't exactly hear, Leah. You were saying something about . . ."

"I wasn't saying anything," Leah murmured.

"Just now when I sat down, I thought I heard you say . . ."

"But I didn't *say* anything!" Leah cried, her face burning. "I said only *Sit down, sit down and stop squirming around and pour us both some ale,* that's all I said, didn't I?—Christabel?—Raphael? You've been here all the time, you've heard everything I said—"

Vernon's fuzzy blue eye remained fixed on her. It was a *most* unnerving moment. Leah's usual brash confidence failed her, she found herself pleating her skirt, staring down at her nervous fingers. "What's this nonsense about crying!" She laughed. "I never said anything about *crying.*"

"You didn't, that's true," Vernon said slowly, "and yet I . . . I seem to have heard . . . I seem to have heard you . . . your voice. . . . It was very distinct, Leah. But . . . but . . . I *know* you didn't say anything," he finished lamely.

"I certainly didn't. I've just been sitting here, dying of thirst, trying to get comfortable. Raphael, hon, *will* you pass us that bowl of nuts? I'm famished, I feel faint."

Vernon stared down at the black ledger on his knees as if he had never seen it before. He was clearly rattled, and Leah suddenly wished him away. Oh, for God's sake get out of here! Get out of my drawing room! Let me gorge myself on nuts, let me drink ale until I drop off, why the hell are you *sitting* there like a fool! I don't love you, no woman could possibily love you, you're a clown, a scarecrow, you aren't even a *man,* why don't you gather up your asinine verse and *get out of here.*

He jumped to his feet so abruptly that he hadn't time even to grab the ledger.

His expression—stricken, withered, deeply wounded—cut Leah to the heart.

"I—I—I'll leave," he said in a faint, broken voice. "I won't bother you again."

"But, Vernon—"

He backed away, blinking rapidly. Now not even his good eye had the power to keep her in focus.

"But, Vernon, what on earth is wrong— *What* is wrong—" Leah said guiltily.

He backed away, stepping onto the children's checkerboard, so that both Christabel and Raphael exclaimed irritably, and then he nearly staggered into the firescreen, all the while mumbling a disjointed apology, and assuring Leah that he would never bother her again.

"But, Vernon, I never *said* a word," Leah cried.

In her distress she managed to get to her feet, shifting her weight forward. For a moment she swayed as if she were about to fall. But her thick, strong legs held, and by leaning slightly backward she regained her balance. But by this time Vernon had fled to the door.

"Vernon, my dear— Vernon— Oh, I didn't *mean* it, I didn't *say* it—"

But he fled, shutting the door behind him.

Leah began to cry, it was all so unfortunate, such a misunderstanding, she had been unconscionably rude, and to a man who clearly adored her—who adored her, unlike Gideon, without any hope of possessing her—

"Aunt Leah, why are you crying?" Raphael asked, astonished.

Her own little girl was staring at her too. "Mamma—?"

Ah, she was becoming eccentric like the rest! The children would soon be giggling over her, whispering about her behind her back. Yet she could not stop crying. The child in her womb gave one of his little nudges, squeezing her bladder.

"I'm not crying," she said angrily.

When Gideon came home she was to say in the lightest possible voice that she had badly hurt poor Vernon's feelings; but Gideon, exhausted from his trip, and deeply discouraged by the negotiations, mumbled a near-inaudible reply. He was lying flat on his back, fully clothed, one arm over his forehead. Leah was to say, again lightly, that she had had an uncanny experience the night before: she had hurt Vernon's feelings—

"Yes. You said," Gideon murmured.

—had hurt his feelings without saying a word. As if, somehow, her thoughts had had the power to travel to him, to communicate themselves to him. Which was of course impossible.

"Yes. It's impossible," Gideon said, without taking his arm from his face.

It was in early April, when the sky had been overcast for nearly a week, and a harsh percussive rain hardened suddenly into hail, and rang out against the castle's innumerable windows, that Bromwell got to his feet at the conclusion of a gin rummy game, and, taking a small notepad out of his pocket, read off figures and statistics in a rapid voice, so excitedly that Leah could not follow. "Bromwell, what is this?" She laughed.

The other children, who must have known what Bromwell was about, watched Leah closely. Christabel had shoved three or four fingers into her mouth. Raphael, the oldest of the children in the drawing room, stared at his aunt without smiling; his expression was guarded. (For some months now Raphael had been behaving peculiarly. No one could say what precisely was wrong, not even his mother was comfortable enough with him to inquire, and even Ewan was in the habit of staring at him with a barely concealed shudder: for there was *something* uncanny about his stealthy manner, his great dark bruised-looking eyes, his air of gazing at the others as if he were in another element, distant from them, undersea, inaccessible.) Jasper and Morna giggled in the same furtive high-pitched way, which Leah found quite exasperating.

"What is going on?" Leah cried.

"For a while, Mamma, we were certain you were cheating," Bromwell said. Though still a very small child—Christabel had begun now to outgrow him, and he would never catch up—he had the air of an adult man, standing with one forefinger upraised. The thick lenses of his glasses distorted his eyes subtly, and Leah, staring at him, could not have said what color his eyes were; it struck her dizzily that this pompous child was no one she even knew. ". . . must admit that I was of that party, at first. But then I made it a point to observe closely. To observe at each game. Beginning, as I've said—" and here he glanced at the notepad again— "on New Year's Day. So I have a complete record, up to the present time. You must have noticed, Mamma, how often you've been winning games with us?"

"Have I?"

"You've won nearly every game. Gin rummy, checkers, Parcheesi, war. Hasn't it struck you as odd?"

"But I've been playing with *children,* dear."

"That has nothing to do with it, Mamma," Bromwell said emphatically. "I can beat Uncle Hiram at chess three games out of five now."

"You can? Really? But since when, Bromwell?"

"Mamma, don't distract us. The issue is—are you aware, Mamma, that you have powers?"

"That I have—what?"

"*Powers.*"

Leah stared from one child to another. Her little girl had closed her eyes tight and squinched up her face, and Raphael smiled a tiny embarrassed smile. ". . . Powers?" Leah said faintly.

"You direct the cards. No matter who shuffles and deals, no matter how assiduously we try to prevent it—you direct the cards. They fly out to you. I mean, the good cards, the desirable cards."

"Oh, Bromwell, what nonsense!" Leah said.

"But it's true, Mamma."

"It certainly isn't true!"

"Bromwell is right, Aunt Leah," Raphael said softly. "The cards seem to . . . jerk out of my fingers when I deal. Certain cards. If I try to keep them back they cut me, their edges are very sharp. . . ."

"Raphael, that isn't *true*," Leah said, biting her lips. She threw herself back on the couch and clasped her hands over her stomach, as if to hold it in place; though it was quite difficult, she brought her ankles together and pressed her feet hard against the floor. The nasty little children would not get at *her*. "You're just . . . you're just spinning tales. Because you play games poorly, and you think that if someone beats you consistently it's because she is cheating. . . ."

"Not cheating, Mamma," Bromwell said quickly. "No one has accused you of cheating."

"The cards fly to me, you said. . . . Ah, what utter nonsense! What *insulting* nonsense!"

Christabel began to cry, without opening her eyes. "Mamma, don't be *mad*," she said. "Don't be mad."

"My own children accusing me of cheating!" Leah shouted.

Grandmother Cornelia entered the room, her white hair curled and impeccable about her cheerful, malicious, red-withered-apple of a face. Quite clearly she had been eavesdropping in the corridor. "What's this, Leah, dear? What's this?"

"The children say that I cheat, because I win all the games," Leah said contemptuously. Her skin fairly glowed with indignation: the firelight cast bronze and gold upon it, so that even the near-invisible white lines about her enormous eyes were illuminated. "They accuse me of influencing the cards."

"And the checkers too, Aunt Leah," Morna said daringly. "And the dice."

"But it isn't cheating, Mamma," Bromwell said. He tried to take her hand but she drew away, and then slapped at him. "Mamma, please, you're so emotional, didn't I explain it all? My statistics, and the odds against your winning, which are incredibly multiplied with each new game —*and yet you continue to win.* Look, I've made up a graph. It's possibly a little too complicated but I felt the need to superimpose graphs of the others' games too, and the ratio of your winning to their losing in terms of points, and all of it in relationship to the frequency of playing itself—

see, Mamma? It's all perfectly objective, there's no room for prejudice or emotion, really! No one is accusing you of—"

Grandmother Cornelia took the notepad from the child's fingers and peered at it through her bifocals. ". . . accusing Leah of cheating . . . ?" she muttered.

Leah snatched the notepad away and threw it into the fire.

"Why, Leah!" Grandmother Cornelia said. "Of all the rude behavior . . ."

"I could wish you all in hell," Leah said, clutching at her belly, tears now streaming down her plump cheeks. "I could wish the nasty lot of you in this very fireplace, in these very flames!"

"Mamma, no!" Bromwell shouted.

"Mamma, no! Mamma, no!" Leah said in a mocking voice.

"But no one has accused you of—"

"You don't love me," she said, weeping freely. "Not you or your father or anyone. You don't love me, you're jealous of the baby, you know he's going to be so beautiful, so strong, he won't have weak eyes and he won't be disloyal to his mother—"

Lily appeared, poking her head through the doorway. And behind her was Aveline, in a woollen dressing gown. And there was Della, awakened from her afternoon nap, her gunmetal-gray hair lying flat and thin on her head. "Is it her time? Is she having contractions?" Della asked. Leah could not determine if her mother was annoyed, or merely excited.

"Oh, go to hell, the lot of you!" Leah screamed.

She shut her eyes tight, and rocked on the chaise longue, gripping her belly, gripping the child in her womb, who quivered with life—with wild, elastic life—and in that instant she saw, behind her eyelids, the orangish-green flames of hell that licked joyously at everything within their reach. Yes. To hell. No. Not yet. *Yes.* I hate them all. . . . But no. No. No.

And when she opened her eyes there they were, still: Della and Cornelia and Aveline and Lily and the children, staring at her, unharmed.

The River

Thousands of feet up in the mountains the Nautauga River begins, beyond Mount Blanc, beyond Mount Beulah, above Tahawaus Pass in the northwestern range, in a nameless glacier lake scooped smoothly out of granite, no more than forty feet at its widest.

Here, the river springs down out of the lake, five feet wide, only a few inches deep, transparent, plummeting wildly, falling downward, always downward, crashing and breaking across heaped-up boulders, catching the sunlight and fracturing it into a million dizzying bits of light, always rushing impatiently downward. Mile after mile it falls, year after year, joined by smaller streams—some of them little more than rivulets trickling snakelike across slabs of rock—a spider's web of tributaries that, drawn powerfully together, become a torrential river, a true river, crashing over ridges of rock, falling many feet, giving off icy steam and spray and a deafening thunderous roar that can be heard for miles. At one point the river rushes through a steep canyon, and changes color: suddenly it is magenta, russet, orange-red: and always its roar is deafening: and always it gives off clouds of mist that drift heavily upward, so that waterfalls appear to fall from midair, suspended between the canyon walls.

When Jedediah came to the edge of the cliff, limping with exhaustion, his horse stumbling beside him, he felt for a terrifying instant the enormity of his mistake—the enormity of all human error—but the thunderous sound rose to engulf him, making his skull and teeth vibrate, and his vision misted over, and his thoughts were swept away.

"My God— My Lord and my God—" he whispered.

But his words were swept away.

It was late afternoon. Shapes tinged with orange danced on the farther cliff, graceful and splotched with sun. Jedediah wiped his face, drew his sleeve roughly across his eyes. Ghosts, demons, spirits of the mountains? For four days he had heard their whispers, their dovelike cooing, their lewd cries, and he had told himself that he heard nothing. But there *were* shapes on the other side of the river, dancing in the rainbow-wet light. They were iridescent, they quivered with joy.

From somewhere higher up the mountain a rock plunged, unloosing a small avalanche of rocks and pebbles and dirt. Jedediah gripped his horse's reins tight. Moisture gleamed on his face like droplets of perspiration. . . . Then the avalanche was over. The loose stones had fallen hundreds of feet down into the river and had sunk without a sound.

In his saddlebag, along with his bedding and other light provisions, he had a leather-bound Bible that had belonged to his mother. In it, in the Gospels, he might read of the casting-out of devils; he might read once again of the powers promised to those who believed in the Lord Jesus Christ, and who sought to come unto the Father by way of Him. But for the moment he could not move. He stood, gripping his horse's reins, staring across the river at the queer stunted pines that appeared to be growing out of solid rock. A near-invisible rainbow arched above them.

The mountain's voices, the mountain's music. . . . From time to time it was alarmingly clear. But there was nothing human about it, perhaps because, at this height, nothing *could* remain human: Mount Blanc was more than fourteen thousand feet high, Jedediah must have climbed to a height of at least six thousand feet, without quite knowing what he had done. There was no other direction for him except upward.

The rainbow quivered, almost visible. Jedediah stared at it, shading his eyes. Perhaps it was not there. Perhaps the high thin air had begun to affect his brain. The wailing of the spirits—but of course there *were* no spirits—was not self-pitying or heavyhearted, nor did it seem to be addressed particularly to *him.* It was all about him, on all sides. Though he trembled with cold he was not frightened, for he knew, he knew very well, that there were no spirits in the mountains, not even in the highest and most remote of the mountains, it was simply the river's torrential roar and the high altitude that made him dizzy, and caused his thoughts to come falteringly, like little pinches.

That day, he had been walking for ten hours. His legs ached, the heel of his right foot throbbed with pain, yet he felt elated: despite the invisible creatures beckoning to him on the farther shore, tempting him to believe in them, he felt quite jubilant.

"My name is Jedediah," he cried suddenly, cupping his hands to his mouth. How forceful his voice was, how young and raw and yearning! "My name is Jedediah—will you allow me to enter your world?"

Great Horned Owl

In the spring of 1809, after the last snowfall in early June, Louis Bellefleur set out to find his brother Jedediah, who had been gone three years. He could not accept it, that Jedediah had become a recluse, one of those eccentric mountain hermits about whom so many stories were told (told and retold and embellished and pondered over, in country stores, in taverns, in depots, in trading posts, in the offices of coalyards and granaries where, in winter, their stocking feet brought up close against the red-warm curving bottoms of wrought-iron stoves, men gathered to talk and sip cheap mash whiskey—for there was always a crock of whiskey nearby, even on the counters of general stores, and a ladle for customers who could not be bothered with glasses—and repeat stories they'd heard months or even years and decades previously, laced with hilarity, or malice, or envy, or simple frank astonishment at the pathways others' lives took). Louis knew approximately where Jedediah was camped, since a half-dozen men had met with him up beyond Mount Beulah, and two or three had actually talked with him and handed over to him the letters and provisions and small gifts (a handknit sweater, woollen socks and mittens, a fur-lined hat, all Germaine's work) Louis had sent. These hunters and trappers, eccentric men themselves who might disappear for months at a time, brought back conflicting reports of Jedediah Bellefleur, which left Louis greatly disturbed. One trapper swore that Jedediah's beard fell to his knees and that he looked like a man in his sixties; another claimed that Jedediah had shot at him as he approached his cabin, and screamed that he was a spy or a devil, and that he should go back to Hell where he belonged. Another report had Jedediah lean and muscular and bare-chested and dark as an Indian, not especially friendly, or interested in news of his father or brother or sister-in-law, or even his two very young nephews (which hurt Louis's feelings tremendously: Jedediah *must* be interested in his nephews!), but quietly hospitable, willing to share his supper of rabbit stew and potatoes with his visitors, provided they said grace with him, on their knees, for what seemed like a very long stretch of time. Still another report, which Louis and Jean-Pierre both discounted at once, had Jedediah living with a full-blooded Iroquois squaw. . . .

When Louis located his brother's shantylike cabin—built on a wide rocky ridge on the side of Mount Blanc, some hundred or more feet above a narrow, noisy river, and facing Mount Beulah some miles to the east— it did not surprise him, though it rather discouraged him, that Jedediah was not there. Not only not there, but he had, evidently, run off only a few minutes before: a fire was burning in a tiny crude fireplace dug into the earthen floor, an old leather-bound Bible Louis recognized as having belonged to their mother was lying opened on a stoollike table, some greasy potatoes, still warm, lay on a flat wooden plate—for Louis, per- haps?—who *was* famished from the hike, but mildly nauseated by the odor of the cabin; and in any case he had brought along his own provi- sions, smoked ham and cheese and Germaine's whole-wheat bread. "Jedediah? It's Louis—" So he stood in the doorway of the cabin, crouch- ing, shading his eyes, calling for long minutes at a time, though he knew that Jedediah knew who he was, and had deliberately fled, and was at this very moment (Louis could almost *feel* it) watching him from higher up the mountain or from across the river. "Jedediah! Hello! It's me, it's Louis! It's no one to harm you! Jedediah! Hello! It's your brother Louis! It's your *brother*—" He shouted until his throat was raw, and tears of despair and rage stung his eyes. That sly little *bastard,* he thought. To make me yell like a fool. To make me *care.*

Louis examined carefully the hard-packed dirt floor of the cabin, but found nothing. He then examined his brother's bed (a plain cornhusk mattress, no longer fresh, bumpy and uneven and stale-smelling and probably bug-ridden, and covered with a heavy, soiled brown blanket that looked like a horse blanket, complete with leather straps and buckles), and the Bible with its worn leather binding and its thin, gilt-edged pages and the small fussy Gothic type that looked so familiar but which annoyed Louis, the very sight of which annoyed Louis (had Jedediah, his own brother, become a religious fanatic?—had he hidden himself up in the mountains like one of those Old Testament prophets who hid themselves in the desert, maddened with God, touched by God's fire, ruined forever for the world of man?)—though he forced himself to glance at the opened pages, in case they held a message he must decipher. (The Bible was open to Psalms 91–97. *He that dwelleth in the secret place of the most High shall abide under the shadow of the Almighty. I will say of the Lord, He is my refuge and my fortress: my God; in Him will I trust. . . . He shall cover thee with his feathers, and under his wings shalt thou trust.*)

He went outside and called again. There was a faint echo, and an- other. "Jedediah? Jedediah? It's your brother. . . ." He walked about the rocky clearing, careful not to lose his balance. Jedediah had built the cabin here, evidently, so that he could look out upon Mount Beulah—one of the highest peaks in the Chautauquas, and topped at all times with snow. A beautiful site but impractical. Windy on even this June morning. Dizzying. Blinding. A hundred feet below was the river, which bore little resemblance to the wide, brown-tinted stream of the Valley; the sound of its rapids was thunderous. Louis squatted at the cliff's edge and stared down. Crashing water, wild white spray, boulders and petrified logs and pockets of scummy froth. The granite beneath his feet vibrated. His teeth and skull began to vibrate.

"Jedediah? Please . . ."

Jedediah was watching him. He knew, he could feel it; but he could not determine where Jedediah was. Behind him . . . in front of him . . . slightly above him . . . to the right, or to the left . . .

"Jedediah? I've come to bring you news. I haven't come to do you harm. Do you hear? Jedediah? I haven't come to do you harm but only to say hello, to shake your hand, to see if you're well, to bring you news. . . . How are you? You're alone, eh? Did you trade off your horse?"

He turned suddenly, to stare up beyond the cabin. But there were only tall massed trees. Pines and hemlock and mountain maple. Stirred by the wind. But unmoving, really; utterly empty.

"Jedediah? I know you're nearby, I know you're listening. Look—" And here, for some reason, he tore off his red neck scarf and waved it frantically. "I *know* you're watching. At this very moment you're watching."

Strange, that his younger brother should fear him. Jedediah, so far as he knew, had always liked him; at any rate he had always *obeyed* him, more or less, just as he had obeyed the old man. A quiet, small-framed, docile young man. With that narrow squeezed face, rather homely, self-conscious, weak. Something of a coward. And stubborn too, in his quiet way. Limping since the riding accident when he'd been six or seven; self-conscious because of the limp, which was pronounced when he was tired. Poor child. Poor little bastard. . . . But now he had outfoxed Louis by running away after Louis had hiked two days and a morning to find him.

"Jedediah!" Louis shouted, cupping his hands to his mouth.

He was a thickset, porcine young man, a week from his thirtieth birthday. His jaw was broad, his nose rather long and full, with dark flaring nostrils; his red-brown beard was clipped short and blunt. When he shouted his eyes bulged and veins in his forehead and neck grew prominent.

He straightened; his knees had begun to ache. With fastidious, self-conscious movements he retied the red scarf about his neck. (Germaine had made the scarf. Which Jedediah might guess, if he was watching closely.) As if conversing quite ordinarily with his invisible brother he said, "Well, the news back home is mostly all good. I can't complain. In my last letter—which I know you got, Jedediah, I *know* you got—though you couldn't be troubled to reply, not even to let us know that you're in one piece or not—let alone to congratulate us: there's not just little Jacob now, he's already two and growing every day, getting into everything, there's Bernard, just three months old, the apple of his mamma's eye and quite a howler, there's the baby Bernard too, as well as Jacob—and you haven't seen either of them, let alone be their godfather—but I'm *not* here to chew you out, I didn't climb fifty miles up into these goddamn mountains for *that.* . . . Well, in my last letter I told you about Germaine and the babies and the addition to the house, and did I tell you about Pappa and his friends and the Cockagne Club—they bought into a steamboat, one of those gambling boats—floating casino—and of course there's plenty of drinking, and women too—and the Methodists in the Valley are up in arms—they're taking some petition or something to the governor —but Pappa isn't worried, why *should* he be worried—he's buying into a spa at White Sulphur Springs, and maybe into a coach line to connect it with Powhatassie too, but I don't know the details yet—it depends upon a loan and you know Pappa never talks about his business until it's settled and no one can cheat him—"

Louis's throat ached from the effort of speaking in order to be heard over the river. He paused, conscious of his brother watching him. But *where* was he, in what direction . . . ? Jedediah might be crouched behind one of those immense boulders farther up the mountain; a sudden movement and a landslide might start, and Louis could be killed. Then again Jedediah might even have climbed a tree. "Don't you even care about Pappa, Jed?" Louis said softly. "Pappa and Germaine and Jacob and Bernard. . . . Germaine says you won't see your family again alive, you won't see your little nephews, she told me to beg you to come back . . . but she said it would be useless. . . . But if I could actually see you, if I could reason with you, I can't believe that it would be useless."

As soon as he paused the great silence returned. It seemed to roll in upon him from all sides, but especially from the river's deep canyon and the immensity of Mount Blanc. My brother has gone mute in his solitude, Louis thought. He has gone mad. But it was annoyance Louis felt, and he could not keep it out of his voice: "Don't you even care about Pappa, Jed? Your own father? He's getting to be an old man—he'll be sixty-five, I think, sometime this year though I'm not really supposed to know—don't you even *care?*—he's aging no matter how he disguises it, and he misses you; he says every day how he misses you. The message he sent with me was just—he misses you, and wants you back. He isn't angry. He really isn't angry. For one thing there's the Cockagne Club taking up so much of his time, and he's spending a lot on clothes again, and has his hair dressed and dyed whenever he's in the city, and he's been outfitted with new teeth—they gleam like ivory, maybe they *are* ivory— Germaine says they don't suit him but how can anyone speak to Pappa, especially about something so intimate?—you know how sensitive he is, how proud—"

Again he fell silent, beaten back and defeated by the river's noise; and by the oppressive silence of the mountains. He was unaccustomed to being in the wilderness by himself: if he went hunting or fishing, which he did fairly often, he was always in the midst of a lively company of men his own age. They were serious about hunting, and Louis considered himself one of the finest hunters, one of the very finest marksmen, in the mountains; but they were also serious about drink and food and one another's company. The solitude of the mountains, the queer unnerving relentless beauty . . . which was a kind of ugliness . . . baffled him. That his young brother should hide away here was an alarming riddle. Don't you know you're a Bellefleur! Louis wanted to shout in disgust. You can't just hide away from blood ties, from your obligations. . . .

"I've come so far, I'm exhausted, I want only to see you and embrace you, I am your brother," Louis said, looking helplessly around, turning, his arms outstretched, his face reddening with anger he dared not show. If only he *might* clasp hold of Jedediah's skinny hand, if only he *might* seize him . . . why then perhaps he wouldn't let him go: he'd bring him back to Lake Noir tied and trussed if necessary. "Jed? Can you hear me? Are you watching? You don't mean to be so cruel as to let me make a fool of myself like this, after so many hours of hiking, and I'm getting a little short-winded, I guess—Germaine thought it was dangerous of me to go alone but, you know, I wanted to be alone—out of respect for you—out of love for you—I could have come with a few other men, and even some dogs, that kind of thing, you know, and we could have sniffed you out pretty easily, and tracked you down, and in fact Pappa has had that idea from the first, a few weeks after you left—he interpreted your going away as an insult to him, you know—which it *is*, really—in a way—it's an insult to all of us— You know Germaine wanted you to be Jacob's godfather, and then she wanted to name the new baby after you, because she said maybe you'd want to return and see him, but I said no, under no circumstances, he's already been gone three years when he promised to return in one, he doesn't respect and honor his blood ties, he doesn't love any of us—not even his father. And you know there are obligations, Jedediah, that come with Pappa's land and investments. We are doing quite well, and next year should be the most exciting year yet, with the White Sulphur Springs hotel, and the coach line, and if that scheme for a railroad actually goes through, or even some halfway decent roads—why, we'll be able to clear half the timber in the mountains, clear it and get it to market, Pappa owns thousands and thousands of acres of good timber but he hasn't had much luck yet in getting it out—just those little operations around the lake, and they're mainly played out now, just stumps and scrub trees and witchhobble, worthless land, he can't even sell it to some fool settlers because it would be too hard to clear, and he had some bad luck, a fire over toward Innisfail, thousands and thousands of trees he was planning to cut down— He needs you to help him, Jedediah; he *needs* both his sons; he told me he's disinherited Harlan, and if you don't come back and don't show any respect or love or common humanity he will certainly disinherit you— Are you listening? Goddamn you, are you listening?''

Louis was suddenly conscious of his brother watching him, from the rear of the little cabin, no, it was from above the cabin, in the air; in a tree. He stooped to pick up his shotgun. (He had taken off his backpack, and laid it and the gun down near the cabin door, as soon as he arrived in the clearing.) His face pounded thickly with blood. He hurried forward, the gun raised, one eye half-shut. Ah, yes! There! A movement in the lower limbs of one of the tall pines! But it was only a bird. A great bird.

Louis stared, his pulses beating. Perched haughtily on a limb, gazing without expression down at him, was an owl—a great horned owl—one of the largest Louis had ever seen. From the ground it looked as if it might measure thirty or more inches in height, and its face, its squat neckless head, was colossal. The stiffly erect ear tufts, the strong clawed feet grasping the limb, the great staring eyes fixed in their sockets and outlined boldly in white and black, as if with a painter's brush. . . . The stillness of the creature as it gazed upon him with its intelligent, somewhat skeptical yellowish eyes in which the black iris floated; the alarming arrogant beauty of the thing. . . .

Panting, Louis raised the gun higher and sighted the owl and made to pull one of the triggers. The owl did not move. It stared calmly at him, with Jedediah's eyes: or was it simply Jedediah's expression about the eyes: and the fairly small beak that looked like a human nose: and the *knowingness* of the thing, that recognized him, knew why he had come, had been listening intently to his secret thoughts, with that tranquil godly contemptuous look that had, of course, been Jedediah's all along, even as a boy. Jedediah stared at him out of the owl. The owl was Jedediah. Which was why it showed no fear, why not even its softest, finest belly feathers rippled in the wind, and its tawny pitiless eyes did not blink. Louis struggled to hold the barrel of the gun aloft. But it was very heavy. He panted, he grunted, trying to pull one of the triggers. But his finger was numb. His finger was frozen. The right side of his face, and even part of his neck, had gone numb—frozen. And his right eyelid was suddenly heavy, paralyzed, unmovable.

"Jedediah . . .?" he whispered.

The Uncanny
Premonition
Out of the Womb

The Bellefleur curse, it was sometimes thought, had to do with gambling.

A Bellefleur is a man, certain detractors said, not altogether fairly, who cannot resist a bet—no matter what the circumstances are, or how unfortunate the consequences.

For instance, there was the time (in the early morning hours, after the festivities of Raoul's wedding party) when the men made bets on a race across the southern tip of Lake Noir, Olden Pond, and all of Silver Lake: a night cruise of more than forty miles, with three difficult carries, more than six miles of dangerous current—all to be doubled before dawn. The winning canoe would share a thousand dollars between them and all that remained of the champagne in the manor. And so they raced—Noel Bellefleur and Ethan Burnside, Ewan Bellefleur and Claude Fuhr, Gideon Bellefleur and Nicholas Fuhr, Harry Renaud and Floyd Jensen. Though it was mid-July the first lake was veiled with a bone-chilling fog. And the water lilies and rushes in Olden Pond were far more numerous, and thicker, than anyone remembered. And the stream plunging down into Silver Lake was so violent that two of the canoes—Ewan's, Harry's—overturned.

And so they raced, without the women's knowledge. Through the mist, along the old pathways nearly impassable with witchhobble, taking turns shouldering their canoes, keeping up a good-natured drunken banter. If their arms ached, if their knees threatened to buckle, if they were fairly delirious with exhaustion when they returned (Ewan and Claude won, by at least a quarter-mile; next came Noel's canoe; and then Gideon's; and last of all Harry's and Floyd's) of course they did not say. And for years afterward they would brag of the night's reckless race, though they tried, delicately, to make as little allusion to poor Raoul as possible; it became one of their tales—the summer night Ewan and Claude beat the others over to Silver Lake and back.

Then there was the time, many years ago, when the men grouped themselves into two parties, and took on two remote ponds in the Mount Chattaroy area, where deer came to feed in great numbers (as tame as sheep, they were, so that a canoe could come up to within yards of even the most skittish doe) and on the very stroke of noon of July 31 (the leaders of both parties made certain that their pocket watches were synchronized, so that the "stroke" of noon would not be anticipated by one or the other) the slaughter began. The men allowed themselves a mere hour to float, since they hadn't much need of venison, and in any case it would be too burdensome to tote both boats and baskets of meat out to the road from such remote ponds; whichever party killed the most deer was acclaimed the winner, and shared a considerable purse. (When there were wealthy hunters involved, friends of Raphael's or, at a later time, Noel's, the Bellefleurs naturally met and raised their bets; when the parties were comprised primarily of local landowners, the Bellefleurs courteously tempered their enthusiasm. One day long ago, when Gideon's grandfather Jeremiah was himself a boy of about seventeen, it was said that $10,000 changed hands, to be divided among six men, including Raphael, who had organized the sport though he hadn't much interest, so it was said, in hunting or deer or "sport" at all. . . . The number of slaughtered deer varied: in some versions it was eighteen, in others as high as forty. But since not even the bucks' heads were toted back it must have been difficult to estimate with any accuracy.)

And there was the time, when Gideon was a boy of fifteen, and he and Nicholas and Ewan and Raoul were allowed to accompany their fathers to a horse race in Kincardine, and afterward, at an inn, the men gambled with the inn's proprietor and certain of his customers that they could distinguish not only the make of liquor served them in unidentified glasses, but its proof; they challenged the Kincardine men to a contest in which the blends were broken down, and the years given, and even (Noel was especially adroit at this, having practiced so assiduously) the place of origin. As soon as Noel Bellefleur sniffed his first drink, and sipped it, and set it down calmly on the bar and announced: "Ninety proof. Sixty-five point five percent rye at five years old, twenty-five percent bourbon at six years old, the rest some good sour spirits . . . most likely from Hennicutt County, Kentucky; yes, Hennicutt County, on account of their kegs being all center-cut maple, and impossible to miss—" why, the Kincardine men naturally wanted to withdraw their bets, but it was too late.

And there were times, many times, when a fair amount of money changed hands around poker tables, at all-night sessions. At Bellefleur Manor; at the White Sulphur Springs Inn which was, for a while, the most famous watering place in the mountains, and drew numerous Southern plantation owners and their families; at the rambling wood-frame Innisfail Lodge, before it caught fire and burned to the ground ("But it was, of course, heavily insured," men said simply, meaning no criticism of the Bellefleur owners); in private camps and homes. Poker, billiards, iceboat racing. For a while, glider-racing. (But a disastrous accident, resulting in the deaths of two young men, one of them a cousin-twice-removed of Noel's, put an end to these contests.) Money changed hands with great alacrity and excitement. Money, and occasionally horses, and even land. If the women knew (and all the women disapproved, some of them—like Cornelia and Della—most angrily) they said very little; for what was to be done . . . ? The Bellefleur men were rich, they had a passion for gambling, they were famous in the mountains for their reckless, inventive challenges, and for their courtesy and grace in defeat (which was infrequent enough: for they were amazingly lucky), what was to be done to prevent them from their play . . . ? After all, they controlled the fortune.

Horse racing was far more public, of course. Most of the betting was public. Men rode their own horses, they were acquainted with nearly everyone involved, the races (at the Powhatassie fairgrounds, at the Derby track, across the state in Port Oriskany where competition was most severe) were events of great local significance; and so it would have been thought rather eccentric if an owner did not naturally bet on himself. The women still disapproved, but less vehemently. Upon occasion they even allowed themselves to be caught up in the fever of the races: for betting on horses wasn't an idle pastime, like betting on the April morning when ice-locked Lake Noir would finally crack, or betting on who might wrestle whom to the dirty floor of a riverside tavern, or who could shoot a shot glass off the head of a retarded boy who worked for some tavern keeper—it had to do with an owner's pride in his horse and in his own performance. It had to do with pride in one's blood, in one's *name*.

Gideon was astounded by his wife's suggestion.

"But why now?" he said.

Leah gazed at him thoughtfully, her eyes half-closed. She was sitting in an oblong of sunshine, near the old sundial at the very center of the garden. Though she was no longer quite as beautiful as she had been— it was mid-July, the baby was due at any time, her eyes were ringed with fatigue and her skin had lost its superb glowing health, and she wasn't able to carry the extraordinary weight of the unborn child with nearly as much style as previously—she had had Garnet Hecht help her fashion her hair in the heavily ornate manner in which she'd worn it as a bride (copied from an inept but charming portrait of Raphael Bellefleur's beautiful young English wife Violet: the back hair arranged in a glossy chignon, two distinct bands of hair tied tightly with a velvet ribbon, its ends hanging down loose; a narrow braid over the crown of the head; and, in addition to *that,* wavy bangs brushed low over her strong, intelligent, somewhat crinkled forehead) and she was wearing a white crocheted shawl over a gown of coarse, knobby material, ochre mixed with green, which Gideon had never seen before. As a consequence of a disagreement that had taken place between them several days ago—Gideon had not liked Leah's retort to an innocent-seeming question of his mother's about the condition of Bromwell's health—Gideon faced his wife with his hands self-consciously on his hips, his knees slightly bent in horsey fashion, his eyes narrowed.

"Because . . ." Leah said slowly. "*Because* . . ."

Her darkened, hollowed eyes gave to her tired face something of the glimmer of a death's-head: but she had looked, in the last weeks of her pregnancy with the twins, very much like this, and Gideon steadfastly refused to become alarmed. His manner was guarded, his jaw rigid. He had not broken down during their quarrel, he had not burst into helpless, enraged tears, wanting both to pummel the woman and to embrace her, and so the crisis seemed to him past, and he *would* not succumb. He preferred today's slow, dreamy, drawling voice to her usual nervous, strident voice, though it seemed to him extraordinarily arrogant of her to have sent poor frightened Garnet Hecht (all elbows and skinny legs and flyaway hair, her pretty face distorted when she merely gazed upon Gideon, with whom, as Leah so mockingly said, even in Garnet's presence, she was piteously in love) to summon him into the garden to speak with her—as if she were royalty, and he one of her subjects. She sat on a cushion on one of Raphael's thronelike granite chairs, beside the rusted, useless sundial (which, shadowless, gave no time), both arms resting lightly on the mound in her lap, which always seemed about to move, to shift its position, her pale swollen legs clumsily outstretched, her swollen feet in brocade slippers Cornelia herself had made for her; she sat there, immobile, imperious, monumental in her very weight, gazing at her husband with her head tilted back, so that her eyes were hooded and she seemed to be peering at him from a distance. A month-old kitten, gray-and-white-striped, hardly more than a potbellied ball of fluff with big ears and a pert erect tail, played with the hem of her skirt and had even begun to tear the material; but Leah did not notice.

Gideon waited. His knees were really trembling, slightly; imperceptibly; he had come close to breaking down several days ago, he had wanted very badly to bury himself in her, sobbing, demanding—demanding that she return to him, as she'd been: his fierce virginal bride whose very soul, like her lean, hard, skittish body, had been tightly closed against him so that he had had to conquer it, and conquer it, and again conquer it; and she had dissolved into tears of love for him; for *him.* But now . . . Now the woman was so wonderfully, so arrogantly, pregnant, what need had she for him?—what need had she for a husband? Other people only distracted her from her ceaseless brooding, her obsessive concern with her body and its urges and sensations. Months ago Leah had confessed to Gideon, in a puzzled voice, groping for the correct words, that nothing was so real to her now as certain flashes of sensation—tastes, colors, even odors, vague impulses and premonitions—which she interpreted as the baby's continuous dreaming, deep in *her* body. (Our son, Leah said, our son's dreaming that pulls me down into it, the way an undertow might pull you down into the lake even when the surface of the water appears to be calm. . . .)

"Because," Leah said, the skin about her eyes crinkling, "it seems to me necessary."

She had summoned him to her, when she knew—she must have known—that he and Hiram were leaving that morning for New York; she had summoned him to her to suggest that he place a number of bets, with different parties, on himself and his stallion, for next Sunday's race at Powhatassie.

"Necessary?"

"I can't explain."

They had not made love for many months. Only dimly, sadly, could Gideon remember: but then it was wisest not to remember. She had expelled him from her bed out of a nervous, and certainly premature caution. (Dr. Jensen himself had assured Gideon that lovemaking, at least of a gentle sort, would not be at all injurious to the unborn child, up until the very last month or two. But that had been before the child had grown to so prodigious a size.) Even as an adult, as the father of children, Gideon could not *quite* determine how a man might deal with a woman whom he could not make love to, and consequently disarm; for it seemed to him that a woman, even a relatively plain, unassertive woman, had all the advantage . . . all the power. He could not have said what this power was, where it presides, how precisely it might touch a man, but he knew its sinister strength.

"You've never taken much interest in my horses before," Gideon said stiffly. "You've always disapproved, like your insufferable mother, of such things as gambling. And now you seem to be giving me permission . . ."

Leah glanced down at the kitten, which had begun to attack her ankle; with an effort, fairly grunting, she stooped over to seize it by the scruff of its neck. In midair the tiny creature kicked and bleated. Gideon, staring at the kitten, at his wife, struck by her magnificent russet hair, which gleamed in the intense sunshine, was rocked with an emotion he could not comprehend. He loved her, he was helpless in the face of his love for her, yet this emotion seemed to encompass and swallow up even love. Like other Bellefleur men before him, like Jean-Pierre himself many decades before, Gideon looked upon a face so incontestably not his own, so distant from anything he might have dreamt, that he experienced it simply as fate.

"You don't love me," he whispered.

Leah did not hear. She dropped the kitten from a height of twelve inches or so and it immediately lay down and rolled over, showing its rounded, palely fuzzy stomach. It kicked frantically, pawing the air, though Leah's hand was safely out of reach. ". . . before I was even born," Leah said. "Your side of the family. Your father most of all. *Don't deny it.*"

She was alluding to her own father's death, one Christmas Eve many years ago. He had been killed in a tobogganing accident—it *had* been an accident—on one of the treacherous hills north of Mink Creek. Gideon made a gesture of impatience. They had discussed this incident many times and had come to the conclusion, which Gideon hadn't at all forced, that Leah's mother had imagined it all—a conspiracy against her young husband, a deliberate capsizing of the toboggan, Stanton Pym thrown against a tree and killed outright.

". . . that night, don't deny it. And the bets were collected," Leah said. "At the very funeral they were collected."

"I really doubt that," Gideon said, his face burning.

"Ask my mother. Ask your own mother."

"None of this has anything to do with *me,*" Gideon said. "I was a child of three or four at the time."

"There was a great deal of betting on the toboggan race and perhaps on other matters too, that night," Leah said. "And the bets were collected, at my father's funeral."

"You speak with such authority, but you really don't know," Gideon said uneasily. "You have only your mother's word. . . ."

"Your side of the family has always gambled. It's in your blood, it's part of your fate. And so . . . And so it occurred to me, the other night, that the Powhatassie race might be an important event in our lives."

"Did it!" Gideon said. But his mockery was so light, so diffident, that Leah did not detect it. "It occurred to you the other *night . . . ?*"

"What time is it?" Leah said, frowning. She turned stoutly to look at the sundial but it showed only a sliver of a shadow, a very pale gray. "I don't have my watch. . . . You and Hiram are leaving now, aren't you?"

"Why did this suddenly occur to you, after so many years?" Gideon said. He was still standing some yards from her; he had not come closer; quite deliberately he was keeping his distance. He could well imagine the fragrance of her gleaming red hair, and her body's close secret sweetness. "You've always disapproved," he murmured. "In fact you begged me not to race, when we were first married. . . . You were afraid I might be injured."

"I've talked with Hiram," Leah said. "You should be leaving now."

Gideon did not hear. He said, in the same low voice, "You *were* afraid I might be injured . . . ?"

Leah's gaze shifted. For a brief moment she said nothing.

"Ah, but you *weren't* hurt, were you! All those years. . . . And before we were married. . . . The ice-racing, the diving, the swimming, canoeing at night, wrestling, boxing, all the dangerous things . . . the ridiculous things. . . . Things young men do. . . . You *weren't* hurt," she said faintly. "And you won't be."

"And I thought you and Della disapproved of the betting too. The principle of betting. Isn't it dishonest, isn't it sinful . . ."

"I don't believe in sin," Leah said curtly.

"I thought you were so fiercely moral, about dishonesty."

"About telling lies. About being mean, and narrow-minded, and selfish. As for gambling—it isn't very different from ordinary business investing, as Uncle Hiram has explained. I don't think I quite understood before."

"But now you understand."

"I . . . I . . . I understand many things," she said slowly.

The oblong patch of sunshine had grown wider, and more intense. Gideon stared, squinting at Leah. There was something she had said that disturbed him, but he could not grasp what it was; the very sight of her, the groping and yet magisterial tone of her voice, had begun to mesmerize him. ". . . many things?" he said.

"His dreams. *His* plans for us," she whispered.

"His . . . ?"

She crossed her fleshy arms over her belly, protectively, rocking slightly forward.

"You must leave. You'll be late for the train," she said. "Come here, kiss me goodbye, you haven't kissed me for so long. . . ."

In that moment her mood changed. And Gideon was unlocked. And came to her, dropping on one knee, his arms encircling her, rather roughly, his lips pressed against hers, at first timidly, then greedily, as he felt her strong arms close about him. Ah, how lovely it was to kiss her! Simply to kiss her! Her wide fleshy lips seemed to sting, her darting tongue made him dizzy, the weight of her body, the impulsive tightening of her arms, nearly caused him to lose his balance and topple into her lap. She was so large, so magnificent. She could draw him into her, and swallow him up, and he would shut his eyes forever, in bliss, in surrender.

After all, Gideon thought brokenly, I am the father. *I* am the *father.*

Horses

It was on a nameless chestnut gelding of no great beauty or grace, but with a normally tractable disposition, short-headed, blunt-nosed, with a single white stocking on his left forefoot—won at cards with British officers not three weeks before the Golden Hill riot in January—that Jean-Pierre Bellefleur, looking, with his smart three-cornered hat of black velvet, and his costly new leather boots, somewhat older than his twenty-six years, first saw Sarah Ann Chatham: at that time a girl of no more than eleven or twelve, small-featured, snub-nosed, with a lightly freckled oval face of disquieting beauty, and pale golden silky hair, and a bearing that was at once childlike and imperious; and . . . and even before the girl laughed and pointed at him (his mount, alarmed by an approaching stagecoach, was rising on his hind legs and whinnying pite-ously, and Jean-Pierre began to shout in French), showing her babyish teeth, pulling free of the hefty red-faced Englishwoman beside her (a nursemaid, a governess?—she was too ugly to be a relative)—even before Jean-Pierre, sitting in the cold brownish-yellow muck, had the opportu-nity to stare fully at her, he had fallen in love. . . . For the rest of his life he would recall not only the incredible shock of the cold, the muck, the graceless fall itself, and not only the beautiful, elated child's cry in the instant before the servant hurried her along (for she had responded to Jean-Pierre's accident as if it were an antic meant only to amuse, and only to amuse *her*), but the queer indecipherable joy of the moment—a joy that arose out of an absolute certainty—a sense that his fate was now com-plete, his life itself complete, laid out invisibly before him but laid out nevertheless, and awaiting his acknowledgment. He was in love. Pitched to the street, the object of amused derision (for others, too, were laugh-ing openly: that he was so clearly French was naturally part of the joke), his dandyish clothes ruined; he was in love. All that, as a boy, he had been told and read of the New World—that native Indians of astonishing classical proportions lived here, and went nude even in winter, in forests of prodigious beauty and beside streams visibly crowded with salmon and trout (one had only to dip a hand-net in the water to capture them); that there were undefined, unimaginable monsters, some as tall as fifteen feet, that lived freely in the mountains, and made sporadic raids on the settlements, carrying off even adult men as prey; that there were, in certain areas, diamonds and rubies and sapphires and great blocks of jade in the soil, and silver and gold deposits of a lushness never seen before on earth; that there were fortunes to be made in a six-months' space of time, and *never any regrets*—all these marvels paled beside the snub-nosed impetuousness of a girl he did not even know, at this time, was the youngest daughter of an ailing customs commissioner in New York, an officer of the Crown who, within the year, would evacuate his family home to England, and leave Jean-Pierre bereft forever.

(Of course there were other horses. Innumerable horses. Even an albino—of nearly as high a quality as Gideon's famous Jupiter, decades later, with the same pinkish skin and white hooves, fifteen hands two inches in height, thirty-two inches from girth to ground, a dazzling snow-white horse that, seen, could not always be believed; even the matched Andalusians his malicious son Harlan was to steal from him one windy night. In the period of prosperity that came before, and led into, his catastrophic term in Washington as a congressman, Jean-Pierre began a rhapsodic memoir of his experiences with horses, *The Art of the Equestrian,* which, though never completed, was to appear in serial form in the small upstate newspaper he would acquire in the early 1800's. There were other horses, many horses, just as there would be many women—a flood of women, in fact: but it was the nameless chestnut gelding he would recall, with ferocity and love: his first mount of the New World, the earliest of his innumerable prizes!)

Pepper, the young black gelding who threw Jedediah, and then stumbled backward over the screaming child, snapping his leg just below the knee, was another "good-natured" horse. After the accident Jedediah's mother insisted that he be sold, or given away; but Jean-Pierre refused. It was hardly the horse's fault, he said, that some contemptible fool in blood-stinking overalls and boots came too close . . . and it was hardly the horse's fault that his boy hadn't enough sense to grab onto a saddle horn. When, after the bone was set, and after, slowly, it mended, Jedediah still limped, it was often the case that his father asked him impatiently what was wrong. "Are you trying to reproach me?" he said. "You can walk correctly if you *try.* " Eventually the horse was sold when Jean-Pierre needed money quickly, and most of his property was tied up in complicated legal arrangements. But he was to remain in Jedediah's imagination, in the dimmest, least fathomable region of his mind's eye, for the rest of his life: a gigantic whinnying creature, utterly black, both wraith-like and portentous as stone, rising on his hind legs, careening backward, bringing down the incredible irrevocable *fact* of his weight on a child's bare knee. In the delirium brought about by his solitude Jedediah would wake speechless from dream-visions in which the horse appeared—not as Pepper, not as one of his father's horses, not even as a horse, but as an aspect of God Himself.

Then there was an ugly scrappy creature of uneasily mixed blood—Arabian, Belgian, saddle horse—Louis's stallion Bonaparte, later called Old Bones. He was named not for the megalomaniac emperor but for his older brother Joseph who, traveling incognito as the mellifluous Count de Survilliers, acquired through Jean-Pierre's Compagnie de New York some 160,260 acres of uninhabitable and unfarmable wilderness land under the mistaken impression that, as part of New France, it would prove a reasonable and even idyllic retreat for the defeated emperor himself, once he escaped Saint Helena. (Unfortunately, Napoleon was closely guarded on Saint Helena and his escape was never a possibility. And the 160,260 acres *were* uninhabitable, despite Jean-Pierre Bellefleur's hearty enthusiasm, and his dreams of roads, railroads, and even canals to come.) The elder Bonaparte was wall-eyed, and so was Louis's stallion. But while the horse was, even in his prime, graceless and temperamental, he was also resilient, shrewd, and courageous, and as stubborn as his master. Perhaps to antagonize his father Louis liked to say that he wasn't a horseman—wasn't an *equestrian*—and ridiculed the cult of breeding Thoroughbreds. He had read in a newspaper that in the long run, over a period of many years and many races, Thoroughbreds did not make all that much *profit* for their owners.

It was the roan stallion Bonaparte Louis was riding that April afternoon in 1822 when he pursued the noisy hooting mob out of the settlement on the south shore of Lake Noir (not to be called Bellefleur for some years)—the mob, the laughing, frightened justice of the peace, and the doomed Indian boy himself (tied by a length of barbed wire to the saddle horn of a man named Rabin, an old Indian trader, and forced to run alongside Rabin's horse). Louis shouted to the men that they might have the wrong person, they'd better let the boy stand trial, they'd better call in the sheriff and have an investigation—and one of the Varrells, a man Louis's own age and approximate size, but with sharply slanted cheekbones and dead-black straight hair, reached over, swaying drunk in his saddle, and struck Bonaparte's neck with his fist. He shouted at Louis to get the hell home. The stallion whinnied in alarm and danced away, his great eyes rolling, but he did not rear back; and Louis, though astonished that anyone would have the audacity to strike out at him, was nevertheless clear-headed enough to do nothing more than settle his horse, and to resist returning the blow while he and Varrell were both on horseback. For he wanted, after all, to save the boy's life. . . .

It was on a smooth-gaited, high-headed Costeña mare that Harlan Bellefleur appeared after years of absence, come home to revenge his family's massacre: townspeople in Nautauga Falls eyed the remarkable horse, with its arched, muscular neck, its abundant gray mane, its dance-like gait—and most of all its handsomely attired rider, who wore lemon-yellow gloves and a floppy-brimmed hat of soft black wool—and murmured that they had never seen anything quite like it; it was something "foreign." (Indeed the horse was Peruvian, sleek, dun colored, with bright, large, expressive eyes set wide in its head, and small ears, and a muzzle that was almost delicate. Harlan himself by this time looked more Spanish than French, and it was only when he leaned from his saddle to inquire courteously about directions to Lake Noir—or did he ask, bluntly, as some witnesses claimed, where he might find the Varrells?—that he seemed, by way of his somewhat nasal inflections, a native of the region: in fact, a Bellefleur. After his death the mare was confiscated by local authorities and disappeared only to turn up, a few months later, in the Tennessee stable of the notorious Reverend Hardy M. Cryer, soon to be Andrew Jackson's "turf adviser.")

Raphael Bellefleur professed to admire horses, and indeed he owned several fine Thoroughbreds, and nodded sagely in the company of his many horse-minded associates; but in fact he could barely tell one horse from another, an Arabian from a Morgan, a Standardbred from a Percheron. All that raw, blunt *physicality* paralyzed his imagination; he liked to think in terms of dollars, tons multiplied by dollars divided by costs. Before politics became a disorder of the nerves for him, and he felt some interest in, if not actual affection for, his magnificent estate, he was often seen in an elegant English two-seater, riding about the graveled lanes, always impeccably dressed despite the reddish dust that arose in capricious clouds, and the pitiless summer sun (which, even in the mountains, could turn the fine thin air to a quivering 105 degrees on windless afternoons). His horses were all English Thoroughbreds, for it was quite true, as the rumor went, that Raphael Bellefleur scorned the French, and professed not to understand a word of his grandfather's tongue; hadn't he, for instance, sailed to London to acquire an anemic pigeon-breasted English girl by the name of Violet Odlin, and wasn't he attempting to furnish his improbable castle in the style in which he imagined English country squires furnished their castles? His chief groom bragged in town that one of their stallions was descended from Bull Rock himself—Bull Rock being, as horse lovers knew, the first English Thoroughbred import, brought to the Virginia colony in 1730; and even Raphael's lesser horses were prizes. But he hadn't any time for racing, or shows; and all forms of hunting repulsed him; so the stallions were exercised mainly by the stablehands, and after his death, when the Bellefleur fortune declined sharply, and poor Lamentations of Jeremiah took over the estate, what remained of the horses were sold off one by one. . . .

During her first years in America, when she was still a reasonably young bride, before her ten pregnancies overtook her, and something very like the black mood of the Bellefleurs poisoned her system, Violet herself was frequently seen in the two-seater, or in her husband's ebonized, gilt-trimmed coach, driven by a liveried black man in a scarlet and gold fez, *not* a slave, but a freed man originally from the Ivory Coast, lithe and graceful even with a whip, and possessed of a "magical" way with horses. He drove Bellefleur's wife to visit friends, other men's wives, in mock castles and baronial mansions in the Valley (for these were the days, in the 1850's and '60's, of heady prosperity in certain areas of the North), and observers were struck by the aristocratic beauty of the matched Thoroughbreds—their fastidiously groomed coats a very dark brown, gleaming with fragrant imported oils, their manes brushed and, upon occasion, braided—and, carried along by the strength of their superb legs, the wan, washed-out, halfway apologetic, halfway cringing beauty of the woman in the carriage with the heraldic embossed Bellefleur insignia on its doors: "There is Lady Violet," the more reverent murmured, possibly knowing that Violet Odlin was nothing more than Mrs. Raphael Bellefleur, but sensing her husband's heroic pretensions—her husband's, not her own. For Violet, the brim of an enormous veiled and beflowered hat usually slanted across her fine-boned face, had very few pretensions. And in the end she had none at all.

The Bellefleurs' oldest son Samuel—who was to say shortly before his tragic disappearance, though the remark has been attributed, over the years, to various members of the family—*Time is clocks, not a clock: you can't do more than try to contain it, like carrying water in a sieve*—was given, for his twentieth birthday, one of his father's finest English Thoroughbreds, a deep-chested, rather angular, leggy bay named Herod. Young Samuel, his father's pride, was an officer in the Chautauqua Light Guard, and his Bellefleur handsomeness—the strong chin, the bone-straight nose, the deep-set eyes—was shown to great advantage in the Guard's dress uniform (which, as represented even in fading, coppery-pale daguerreotypes that could not do justice to its heroic colors—the towering ermine hat, the smart white jacket, the green trousers with their dazzling white stripe, the skin-tight white gloves, the scarlet ornamentation about the sword's deep sheath—was to strike later generations of irreverent, unsentimental Bellefleur children as merely ludicrous), and mounted on stately Herod he looked, it must be said, the quintessence of New World aristocracy; who could fail to comprehend, and even to sympathize with, his father's deep pride in him . . . ? Samuel Bellefleur was the envy of his fellow officers, and even of his superiors. (Ah, his fellow officers! All of them were, like Samuel, the sons of well-to-do landowners; they and the male members of their families were enchanted with fine-bred horses, military processions, ceremonial occasions, sabers, muskets, the latest in weaponry and military strategy, and the need to rebuke, to punish, in fact to bring to its knees, the traitorous Confederacy. They were also powerfully moved by military music: "The Star-Spangled Banner," "Buchanan's Union Grand March," "The Tars from Tripoly," "Brother Soldiers All Hail!" brought quick tears to their eyes, and caused their hearts to swell with the instinct, the almost physical need, to march into battle. They would all, with the exception of Samuel Bellefleur, ride off to war in 1861, and while not each was to be killed in action not one escaped grievous suffering; nor did their handsome steeds survive more than a few months.)

Felix (later renamed by his possibly deranged father Lamentations of Jeremiah) loved, as a boy, his pony Barbary, a Shetland with large expressive gray eyes, a marvelous gray-and-white dappled coat, and long thick hair that, brushed hard, seemed to give out galaxies of light from within; as a child of five or six he was to be seen carried about the Bellefleur estate, on the newly laid pinkish seashell-and-gravel drives, in a pony cart originally made (so the rumor went, and it sprang from Raphael's neighbors) for a Prussian prince. Sometimes his driver was the aloof Ivory Coast black in his fez and braided jacket, sometimes a mere local boy, the son of a hop-field foreman who, dressed uncomfortably in black, and carrying a lightweight whip more suitable for a woman's hand, sat stiffly erect and refused to speak to his shy, hopeful little charge, who had no friends, and not even any brothers, really, since Samuel, years older, paid no attention to him, and Rodman, his senior by two years, chose to assert his precarious authority by bullying Felix. The hop-field foreman's son was driving the elegant little canopied cart on that August morning when the kidnapping took place, and when—after the boy was found in a ditch, his skull crushed—it became clear that he had disobeyed Raphael Bellefleur's instructions and driven out toward the river, where Raphael's growing paranoia told him, correctly as it turned out, thieves and kidnappers *did* await (for the history of the Valley aristocrats was not a placid one: forbidden to hunt and fish on territory that had once seemed quite clearly their own, or no one's, accused of poaching and trespassing if they strayed off their own small farms, Chautauquans began to exact revenge in small sinister ways, by starting fires, destroying dams, poisoning cattle, and in large flamboyant ways, by picking off their wealthy neighbors as they were driven here and there in their custom-made carriages—the marksmanship of the Chautauquans being legendary), after it was obvious that the boy had brought not only his own misfortune on himself, but the greater misfortune of the kidnapping of Felix Bellefleur, Raphael said before witnesses: "If the little beast had been alive when they found him, *I* would have kicked in his miserable skull. . . ." Felix was to turn up, unharmed, some three weeks later, in New Orleans; by then he had already begun to affect a shy, gentle Southern drawl. He could give no account of his kidnapper or kidnappers, and it was possibly his placid indifference to his father's three weeks of grief, rather than the fact of the kidnapping itself, that led Raphael to rename and even rebaptize him Lamentations of Jeremiah. But what of Barbary, the child clamored. Where is Barbary . . . ? The docile little Shetland was never to be found, though the pony cart, overturned, had been almost immediately discovered in a nearby stand of pines. "Where is Barbary? What did you do with Barbary? I want Barbary!" the child wept, turning away not only from his father but from his distraught mother as well.

Of Jeremiah's eventual offspring, of his three surviving sons, only the energetic, restless Noel took to horses, and bragged of himself, in later years especially, as a fool about a good horse: if the management of the estate hadn't taken up so much of his time (for his father, even in his fifties, became increasingly negligent and half-minded) Noel would certainly have traveled about the country, and even to Mexico and South America, searching out horses to add to the Bellefleur stables. He would have bred real racing horses—would have hired professional jockeys— would have bought into tracks like Havre de Grace and Bennings and Belmont Park itself. His brother Hiram, educated in the classics at Princeton, and as a young adult wonderfully obsessed with "the world," as he put it, of finance, had no interest in horses whatsoever—hadn't even any awareness of their comeliness, or their ineffable scent, or their magical *presence* (which so comforted, during difficult times, both Noel and his son Gideon—more than once father and son discovered, faintly embarrassed, that the other had also made his way into the darkened stable, simply to stand with his arm around a horse's obliging neck, his cheek pressed against a horse's dry, scratchy mane that smelled of marvels: sun, heat, open fields, open roads along which one might gallop forever, raising clouds of dust behind him.). As for Noel's older brother Jean-Pierre II— he had professed, for a time, the interest in handsome horses customary to young gentlemen of his class, but he was a poor rider, he never cared to groom his own horses, he used the riding crop ineptly, and was, as a young boy, always being thrown, or brushed off by low-hanging tree branches toward which his malicious mounts would race; he had given up horses by the time he was thirty. (Which was, at his trial for first-degree murder, the defense's strongest point. For the only witness to the escape of the murderer claimed that Jean-Pierre had ridden off on a dark horse with three white stockings and a close-cropped mane and tail—a horse that *was,* indeed, in the Bellefleur stable—unless of course the witness had deliberately lied—unless the entire trial, perhaps even the murder of the eleven men (among whom only two were Varrells, and those with local reputations that were for the most part insignificant) had been contrived merely to hound, to embarrass, to shame, to humiliate, and to destroy the Bellefleur family. The witness was the saloonkeeper's garrulous, mean-spirited wife, who had for some reason Jean-Pierre could not explain taken a violent dislike to him from the first; and naturally in the confusion of that night, the interruption of the card games, the over- turned tables and chairs, the shouts that lifted to screams and then to shrieks, the very indescribable *reality* of that tragic night at Innisfail— naturally she had fixed her mind on Jean-Pierre as the murderer, and the defense's attorney, excellent though he was, superbly gifted in the art of cross-examination and of addressing both the jury and the judge with an air of intelligent complicity that could not fail, given his elegance, to flatter, was simply unable to dislodge her from her "story." The mur- derer was Jean-Pierre Bellefleur and he had ridden off on a horse with three white stockings and a close-cropped mane and tail, a black horse, or a very dark brown horse; and he had ridden, the wretched old woman claimed defiantly, as skillfully as anyone she'd ever seen: like the very devil himself.)

Germaine's mother Leah, then Leah Pym, loved horses as a girl, and would have raced her sprightly, spirited sorrel mare in fairground competitions with both boys and girls, had she been allowed; but of course girls were barred from such competitions. They might race with one another, but their victories hardly mattered, and drew little interest. For a while at La Tour, bewitched perhaps by the predilections of other, wealthier girls, Leah took part in stately shows, demonstrating her mastery of her horse, and her horse's reluctant mastery of certain difficult, dancelike maneuvers. Fetlocks clipped, her smooth-gleaming hide only a degree or two lighter than Leah's thick russet hair, every part of her washed by Leah herself, and brushed with a dandy brush, and polished (with a linen cloth!) until she shone, her mane clipped and braided with red ribbons that fluttered fetchingly in the breeze and mimicked the graceful undulations of the ends of the green velvet ribbon that hung down from Leah's chignon, the supple little mare executed all the proper responses to the commandments given her—"Go Large," "Circle," "Volte," "Half Volte and Change," "Half Pass"—and performed with precision, if not always enthusiasm, rather like Leah herself. The mare's name, Leah was to remember, years later, when, sated with adulthood and wealth and the ceaseless maneuvers these demanded, and nostalgic with longing for a girlhood she had in fact detested (ah, Della's decades of mourning, her dry droll humorless remarks about men, about Bellefleur men especially! —her pretense of impoverishment when, as everyone knew, her brother Noel gave them all the money they needed, and not only paid Leah's exorbitant tuition at La Tour (where he had *not* sent his own daughter Aveline, saying—quite correctly—that she simply wasn't intelligent enough for the school), and her show-horse expenses, but refrained, as a gentleman, from saying anything at all when Leah abruptly quit one morning, in the middle of a French grammar quiz, and returned to Bushkill's Ferry with a single piece of luggage . . .) was *Angel.*

Gideon's stallion Jupiter was famous throughout the state. An albino bred to race!—to carry a man of Gideon's size easily and gracefully! Jupiter was a remarkably tall horse, some eighteen hands, and his coat was ivory rather than white, and his smooth-rippling mane and tail were so striking, and his head, his eyes, his ears, his profile were so uncannily beautiful—he had to be seen, people claimed, to be believed. A graceful giant of a horse. Spirited, obviously very strong, possibly even headstrong (for Gideon had to use his knees to control his mount, who was always shivering and shuddering, and yearning to leap forward, to run free with or without his master on his back), possibly even dangerous. (It was rumored, falsely, that Jupiter had killed his previous owner. Or a stablehand at the Bellefleurs'. Or had tried to kill Gideon himself.) When Gideon first appeared at local competitions with his albino stallion a murmur always arose from the crowd at the very sight of him. Young Gideon Bellefleur with his thick, brushlike dark hair and his dark beard, his prominent cheekbones, his strong nose, his skin that was always tanned, but a warm, honeyish tan, not at all swarthy or Indian-burnt; not at all coarse. Young Gideon Bellefleur who was so handsome, so aloof and yet courteous, and remarkably graceful for a man of his size and build: and was it true, people asked, that the Bellefleurs were still millionaires?—or was it true that they were nearly penniless, and had mortgaged the castle twice over, and would soon be forced to declare bankruptcy? They stared hard at Gideon, and felt both envy and resentment of that envy, and yet a curious wild affection as well, for he was—he and Jupiter and the pride they so blatantly took in each other—somehow more real, more wonderfully, incontestably *real* than the other men and their mounts. Even had he lost—and he did not, of course, lose—they would have stared at him with the same fixed, fascinated gaze, something in them calling out to him, yearning for a glance of recognition from him, from the haughty Bellefleur in him, which of course he would never give —was quite incapable of giving. Gideon Bellefleur. And his legendary albino, Jupiter. . . .

Nevertheless, Gideon was to sell the stallion immediately after the Powhatassie race, and he would have sold all the horses in the Bellefleur stable if old Noel hadn't stopped him.

The Whirlwind

On that summer afternoon many years ago, several weeks before Germaine's birth, a record number of spectators came to the fairgrounds at Powhatassie, to see Gideon Bellefleur ride his white stallion Jupiter against six other Valley horses, including Marcus, the three-year-old golden chestnut stallion owned by Nicholas Fuhr. Though Jupiter was the favorite to win the four-mile heat, it was rumored that his age—six years—was beginning to tell; it was rumored that he had done poorly in secret workouts on the Bellefleur track, and that the shrewdest bets were now being placed on Marcus. Of the other horses only one was promising—a beautiful dapple-gray mare with English and Arabic blood, about fifteen-four hands, eleven hundred pounds, far smaller and slighter than the Bellefleur and Fuhr stallions. She was owned by a farmer and horseman named Van Ranst, from the eastern corner of the Valley, a stranger to the Bellefleurs (and one who would go on to breed horses for competition not only at tracks throughout the state, but at Belmont Park, and in Kentucky, and Texas, and even in Jamaica, Cuba, and the Virgin Islands); her name was Angel (and when she learned this fact Leah, who had bet far more on Jupiter than anyone, even Hiram himself, knew, felt a thrill of despair).

A fair clear summer day. More than forty thousand persons were jammed on the course, which had been designed to accommodate little more than half that number; the Bellefleurs, with the exception of Gideon (who had no time to contemplate such nonsense) were inordinately pleased, since fairgrounds officials announced a record turnout and the record turnout was surely in Gideon's honor. By this time Jupiter's fame was no longer limited to the Nautauga Valley and the Chautauqua mountain region. There was talk hundreds of miles away of a magnificent ivory-white stallion that, despite his size and muscular frame, could run a four-mile heat in 7:36, manned not by a light-boned jockey but by his owner, one of the young Bellefleurs, himself a figure of mild regional notoriety. To see the albino stallion run was to allow oneself to be bewitched: for the creature was so dazzling-white, a white more intense than white, and even his great pounding hooves were white (and always kept spotless), and his long silky mane and tail, as soft as a child's hair —and, it was said, the skill of his master was such that horse and man appeared, on the track, a single striving creature, wondrous to behold. It was not only women who gazed upon horse and rider with an adulation so intense as to verge on alarm.

"You love their eyes on you, don't tell *me!*" Leah cried half bitterly.

Gideon, brushing his thick hair, bent slightly at the knees so that he could stare at his reflection in the mirror, declined to reply.

"They're mad about you. They crave you. Last July, that pathetic creature from downriver—do you remember—and she was actually *engaged*—and to one of the young men at Nautauga Trust—pushing her way through to you like that, her hair in her eyes, her face smudged: to offer herself to you so openly! As if I, your wife, didn't exist."

"You exaggerate," Gideon mumbled. "It wasn't like that."

"She'd been drinking. She was desperate. I might have taken pity on her if she hadn't practically pushed me aside . . ."

"*Would* you have taken pity on her, really, Leah?"

"As a woman I could sympathize with her derangement."

"It was Jupiter she wanted, not me."

"Then certainly I could sympathize!"

Gideon's shoulders shook, as if he were stricken with silent laughter.

Driving to Powhatassie husband and wife were seated side by side, but did not touch; nor did they speak. There was talk of the purse— $20,000—which was the highest in the state; there was talk of unofficial betting; of the threat that reformers would picket the fairgrounds, and that one of the area's leading evangelical ministers would preach against horse racing from a hay wagon, as crowds began to arrive—a rumor that was to prove unfounded, though the Powhatassie race would be, to future reformers, the most natural instance of what was wrong with such events, where the Devil had the freedom to mingle with spectators, to corrupt them with sickly dreams of instant wealth, and to excite them with the promise of capricious violence. There was talk too of Nicholas Fuhr and Marcus, who would certainly give Gideon a run for his money. . . . There was talk in the limousine of many things, but Gideon and Leah sat in silence, staring before them, Gideon's hands resting uneasily on his knees, Leah's crossed arms resting on her immense stomach.

Hiram, acting as Leah's agent, had employed a certain bookmaker out of Derby to act as *his* agent; and a rather large bet was made in his name, on Jupiter. But since Jupiter was the odds-on favorite, a dismaying amount of money must be risked, many dollars to bring in a single dollar. "If we lose . . ." Hiram said thoughtfully, pressing his glasses against the bridge of his nose. "We won't lose," Leah said. "We can't lose." "But if, if, simply for the sake of speculation, *if,*" Hiram said, "if we lose, my girl, how can we tell the others . . . ?" "We won't tell the others, why should we tell the others," Leah said quickly, "we can't possibly lose—haven't I made that clear to you? I *know.*" "You know, you've seen?" Hiram asked doubtfully. "I know, yes," Leah said passionately. "I've seen."

And then through another agent who was to suspect, but not to know, her identity, Leah made a sizable bet of her own. She hadn't the cash to cover it, naturally—she hadn't any money of her own, and no property at all—but she had a pearl necklace, and a sapphire ring edged with diamonds, and a canvas sack of Georgian silver stolen from the recesses of a kitchen closet, and a pair of eighteenth-century Dutch Delft vases by Matheus van Boegart, stolen from one of the third-floor rooms; and a medieval anlace, a two-edged dagger with an immense jeweled handle, come across by accident in a trunk stuffed with dresses, women's shoes, and religious trinkets. While making the transaction Leah wore one of Violet Bellefleur's old hats, a yellowed gauzy rather poignant thing the size of a wagon wheel; it stank of mothballs and age, and the veil, drawn down becomingly to Leah's strong chin, gave her face the eerie anonymity of a statue's. "This bet," the agent said, sniffing out of nervousness, "this bet is a serious matter. I want you to know, if you don't" —perhaps he sensed, beneath her calm, a glacial terror neither she nor the child in the womb comprehended—"that such a sum of money is a serious matter." "I understand," Leah said softly. Like a maiden, like a very young girl, the sort of girl, in fact, she'd never been, she gave herself over to the agent's penciled calculations, and accepted from him, without a murmur of protest, the fact that her winning—that is, her husband's winning—would be so much less than her losing. The one would be magnificent, the other catastrophic.

Because of the reserve between them Leah did not dare ask, nor would she have wanted to ask, the sum of money Gideon himself was betting. But through a judicious interrogation of Ewan she gathered that the sum was fairly modest—it would bring in only about $12,500—no more than $15,000. "But doesn't he expect to win!" Leah cried involuntarily, staring at her brother-in-law. She and Ewan rarely *looked* at each other: it might have been that Ewan's bearish figure, his unruly graying hair, his brick-red skin, parodied certain inclinations in her husband, who was a far more attractive man; it might have been that Leah, for Ewan, was so much more his natural mate—big-boned, arrogant, fleshy, voluptuous—than his own wife, he dared not contemplate her even speculatively. "Of course he expects to win, we always expect to win and we *do* win," Ewan said, with an offended dignity that rather charmed Leah (for she was, like Della, inclined to believe that the Lake Noir Bellefleurs were essentially barbaric), "but there's always the possibility, after all, that we won't." "But I deny that possibility," Leah said. Her breath had become labored. If Ewan noticed, he might have attributed it to her condition. "It isn't a possibility at all," she said. "He can't lose. Jupiter can't lose." "I agree," Ewan said, nodding, as one might nod to a distraught person, or a very small child whose babbling *almost* makes sense. "Oh, yes, I agree. I wouldn't be a Bellefleur if I didn't agree," he said. "But still." "But still?" Leah cried angrily. "But *still,*" Ewan said. Leah contemplated him for a long moment, her slate-blue eyes narrowed, their focus so intense she might have appeared, to poor bewildered Ewan, somewhat cross-eyed. Then she said, finally, shaking her head, "He cannot lose. I know. I would stake everything I own on it—my life, even—even the life of this child."

Once, as children of perhaps eight or nine, Gideon and his friend Nicholas were tramping through the woods on the Bellefleur estate, when, quite suddenly, in a hairsbreadth of an instant, they found themselves facing, across a narrow stream, a full-grown black bear. The creature appeared to be staring at them, its head inclined to one side; and then, after a long moment, it turned and moved indifferently away, back into the woods. With its poor eyesight, perhaps it *hadn't* exactly seen them . . . and they were downwind from it. . . . Both children had begun to tremble badly. Gideon, the taller of the two, glanced at Nicholas, and burst into laughter. "You look so funny," he said, wiping at his mouth. "Your lips are white." "*Your* lips are white, goddamn you," Nicholas said. Throughout their boyhood the bear remained at the periphery of their vision, even after, in fact, they had seen other bears, and even hunted them: the glimmering white on the creature's chest, the blunt cagey head, the perked-up ears that were like a dog's, the stance of the thing itself, which was like a dog's, uneasily raised on his hind legs. "*You* look funny," Nicholas said, giving Gideon a shove; and quite naturally Gideon shoved him back. Their bowels contracted with fear. Their pulses rang. "A black bear won't attack," they told each other, "there wasn't any danger, d'you see how it walked away?—it didn't want any trouble from *us.*" One of the mythologies of their boyhood was established.

And when they were both fourteen, and hunting with their fathers and older brothers, in the foothills south of Mount Blanc, they came upon, from different angles, a solitary white-tailed buck browsing in a drowned-out field, and both their shots rang out at once—and both their shots struck the deer, which gave a single whistling snort of incredulity and anger, before it turned, and sprang, and fell to its knees, bleeding wildly from two great gaping wounds in its chest. They had struck the deer!—both their shots! One shot from each gun, and each had struck its target! In the very first instant the young Gideon may have felt a pang of resentment at the fact of Nicholas—the fact that they would be forced to share the giddy triumph of their first kill—and he sensed his friend's resentment of *him;* but in a matter of minutes, as the boys ran splashing through the flooded field, hooting and shouting crazily, they were reconciled to each other, and perhaps even secretly pleased. ("Nicholas is my closest friend," Gideon told his father when, one Christmas, it seemed that he was spending too much time at the Fuhrs', and not enough at home. "But friendship never takes precedence over family," his father said.)

The black bear of their childhood had contemplated them with that uncanny solemnity that belongs to nature, and had appeared to judge them—to judge them as insignificant. It had simply turned and trotted away. But the white-tailed buck—ah, the magnificent buck with its thirty-inch antler spread!—the buck was another story, the story of Gideon's and Nicholas's first significant kill. And it was one they were to tell often.

Nicholas Fuhr, now thirty years old, still unmarried, still with as wild a reputation in the Valley as he'd ever had (having eclipsed Gideon years ago, after Gideon's marriage), was a handsome, beardless young man, nearly Gideon's height, with curly wheat-colored hair and slightly sloped broad shoulders, and a habit, which endeared him to his friends, of throwing his head back when he laughed, and of laughing in great appreciative explosive outbursts. His people were comfortably prosperous farmers; like their neighbors the Bellefleurs they had once made a small fortune selling timber in great quantities, and they had even—like the Bellefleurs, in the mid-nineteenth century—mined iron ore, out of broad but rather shallow deposits in the foothills. The Fuhrs had settled in the region some decades before Jean-Pierre crossed the Atlantic, and they had sold the colony the iron ore that was eventually fashioned into the famous chain of 1757 that was stretched across the Nautauga at its narrowest point, at Fort Hanna, in order to block passage of French ships. ("A chain across the river!—I don't believe it," Gideon would say as a boy, as he and Nicholas hiked along the bluff above the Nautauga. Sometimes it had seemed to him that amazing things had been done so easily in the past, long before his or even his father's birth—that there was a magical quickness, a magical fluidity, between the imagining of a feat and its execution. And hadn't there been dangerous Iroquois everywhere, and frequent sorties by Algonquins from the north, not these sour, defeated half-breeds who ran down pregnant does, and had fished the trout streams nearly dry, and might still be found, from time to time, on Sunday mornings in Bellefleur or Contracoeur, lying in a drunken stupor in the center of the street, their clothing vomit-stained, their faces scarcely human? Hadn't there been gigantic black panthers, and gray wolves so reckless with hunger they might rush into a clearing and make off with small children; hadn't there been many more coyotes and bobcats and black bears, and tall creatures no one had exactly seen, bearlike, and yet half-human? All that remained of that time were the swamp vultures, or the Noir vultures (sometimes called the Bellefleur vultures, but not in the presence of a Bellefleur) and these were retreating, it was said, deeper into the swamp north of the lake; not one had been sighted for years.)

Before the race Gideon shook hands with Nicholas, whom he had not seen in months; the men stared at each other, and smiled self-consciously, and talked, for a few minutes, of inconsequential matters—it had been for years a matter of hilarious ribaldry between them, that Nicholas's cousin-twice-removed Denton Mortlock should have married Gideon's priggish older sister Aveline; as adolescents, frequently aflame with filthy, outrageous visions, they had mocked and jeered and tried to imagine scenes of sexual activity between the two phlegmatic stoutish persons—but then Aveline *did* have three children, and what, precisely, might that mean? So Gideon murmured something about the Mortlocks, who were already assembled in the Bellefleur box at the homestretch; and Nicholas murmured, almost too quickly, a coarse jest; and Gideon laughed; and suddenly there was nothing to say. At another time Nicholas would certainly have inquired after Leah, with whom he was, it was sentimentally believed, half in love; but the tension of the race was building, one could very nearly feel it in the air, and anyway, these past few months, hadn't Leah seemed—hadn't she presented herself, deliberately, when Nicholas came to visit—rather strange?—rather too flagrantly, lewdly pregnant?—so that poor Nicholas, who had dreamt innumerable times of Leah Pym's body, felt faint in her presence, and even somewhat nauseated; and his dreams now of her were jarring. At another time Nicholas would certainly have inquired after Gideon's father and mother, and Ewan, and the twins, and the rest, but today he was distracted, he seemed uncharacteristically nervous, as if he'd felt, in his friend's hard handshake, how very much Gideon needed him to lose.

Gideon stroked Marcus's neck thoughtfully. He had always been very fond of the stallion—he'd wanted, a year ago, to buy him from Nicholas —and now it seemed to him that the horse was somewhat taller, and more muscular in the flanks, than Gideon remembered. A comely golden chestnut with a large asymmetrical star on his forehead, and three of his legs white past the knee. Marcus shivered beneath Gideon's hand and turned to nuzzle him. But Gideon knew he must be careful.

Backing away he said, with a ritual salute of farewell: "Maybe you'll want to sell him, when the race is over." And smiled to show that his words were meant in jest.

Nicholas snorted with laughter. His gray eyes caught Gideon's, and crinkled with excessive mirth. "Maybe you won't be able to afford him," he half-shouted.

And so the friends parted. And so, in that way, with Nicholas's familiar face somewhat distorted, and his hand raised in a playful warning fist that mocked Gideon's own gesture of farewell, Gideon would remember Nicholas. . . .

The horses were saddled. "Bring out your horses!" rang through the warm air. During the brief parade to the post spectators began to shout "Jupiter to win!" or "Marcus to win!" or (perhaps because the odds were so attractive) "Angel to win!" The sky was still clear. The early mild breeze had died away. People stood, and strained to see Gideon Bellefleur on his gigantic ivory-white stallion, and Nicholas Fuhr on his brown-bronze stallion; and the slender dapple-gray mare ridden by a boy who looked no older than eighteen, and who smiled nervously at the crowd's roaring; and the other horses—each of them quivering with energy. One minute to the start of the race. Thirty seconds. And the drum tapped. And Leah, seated between the twins and grandmother Cornelia in the Bellefleur box (for Della, of course, had refused to come, she had stared for a long painful moment at Leah and said harshly, I know something of what you've done, Leah, you and Hiram, and that poor fool Gideon as well, I *know* what you've done and I know what you deserve), her arms folded tightly on her belly, watched impassively as Marcus, on the rail, shot forward at once. But then Marcus was quick, Marcus had always been quick. Close behind him was the gray mare, in a strategic position; and then Jupiter; and the others.

Leah watched, expressionless. She remained seated while the others leapt to their feet. Marcus, and Angel . . . and Jupiter (who looked, in the hallucinatory brightness of the track, beneath his rider's considerable weight, by far the oldest of the horses) . . . and, close behind Jupiter, gaining on him, a red bay whose very dark mane and tail flew wildly, and whose impatient rider, crouched unnaturally forward in his saddle, beat at him lightly and rapidly with his whip.

For the first mile Marcus remained in the lead, and the graceful little mare seemed at any moment to be preparing to overtake him, and Jupiter and the red bay contested each other for third place, and the others trailed behind; and the shouting of the spectators died down, only to rise again, with a sound of hysteria. Leah half-closed her eyes. And *there* she saw the Bellefleur horse, her horse, and *her* husband, flying into the lead, silky mane and tail rippling in the bright air. We cannot lose, she thought calmly. The child in the womb had assured her. Had allowed her to see into the future; to know. We cannot lose, she instructed herself. The future has already occurred.

She opened her eyes, dazed, to the crowd's tumult, and saw that now the red bay was in third place, and the great white horse, obviously straining, was in fourth place . . . and the feisty little mare had overtaken Marcus himself. (Jupiter, of course, had stamina. Could outlast the others. But Marcus too was a strong horse, and had never run so well as today, hurtling from the post into first place like that—what thoughts must be flooding Nicholas's mind! It was not possible that he should even *wish* to outrun Gideon.) The twins were standing on their seats, even Cornelia was standing, muttering to herself. Ewan's children fairly bawled. Come on! Come on! Come on! Leah winced—whether from the noise or a sudden tinge of pain in her belly—and thought, the Bellefleurs must have dignity, everyone will be watching. But even grandfather Noel was shouting and waving his fists. His old man's puckered face was flushed, wormlike veins stood out on his forehead, he had never looked so *furious* in Leah's memory. The stylish white linen suit the family had talked him into wearing, with its polka-dot vest, and the matching tie, now hung rumpled on him as if, in the span of these very few minutes, he had sweated away a number of pounds. We cannot lose, Leah wanted to assure him, so you must take care—you must not strain yourself—your son *cannot* disappoint you.

As they swung into the near turn for the final mile Jupiter made his move. As Leah had known he would. Jupiter, Gideon, the Bellefleurs, Leah, the child-to-be-born. Spectators began to scream. The mare had kept her lead heroically, and from time to time the boy glanced over his shoulder to see how close Marcus was—and he was very close—and the mare was lightly whipped so that she might spurt forward. The red bay in third place. Jupiter maneuvering to get around him. Gideon crouched low over the stallion's magnificent neck and had no need to use his crop. Leah stared, stared, at the horses' pounding hooves. So very many of them. Flying manes, tails, flying legs, such superb beasts, it hardly mattered which of them won, they were all superb, all beautiful. But Gideon must win. Jupiter must win. An aureole about them, shimmering light, moisture, infinitesimal rainbows caught within it, despite their speed. The white rail. Infinite white rail. The white stallion, which seemed now enormous: even its shadow, flying along the track, was gigantic. Leah swallowed, tasting dust. The air was very dusty. Her eyes were pulled upward and she saw that the sky had turned dark. Quite suddenly it had turned dark. From behind one immense swollen purplish-black cloud a tiny white sun peeked, as if in jest.

And then the whirlwind. The dust spiral. Suddenly, on the track, in the homestretch. Dancing forward to meet the horses. It must have been ten or twelve feet in height. Undulating. Snaking. Yet it appeared to be in no hurry. *Yet* it did dance swiftly forward. . . . Now Jupiter was rapidly gaining, Jupiter had stolen the rail on the turn, the red bay was suddenly dropping behind, exhausted, no matter that its impatient rider had begun to beat a tattoo on him; and it did seem—or might the queer brightness of the air, that single shaft of piercing white light, have distorted everything?—that Jupiter and his rider were not only accelerating their speed but gaining in size, so that even sturdy Marcus looked like a pony, nobly and futilely galloping through the dust? Leah's lips parted. She might have been about to cry out. Not to her husband but to Nicholas. Nicholas on the golden chestnut, straining forward, his head already dipping oddly; Nicholas whom she loved; whom she loved as a brother; as her husband's dear friend; as a man she *might* possibly have . . . in another lifetime . . . if . . . Now the mare, distressed by the whirlwind, had begun to falter, had already lost her stride. The whirlwind moved most gracefully toward her. At her. Into her. Blinded, she shook her head; she must have whinnied in terror; and swung suddenly sideways, toward the rail; and crashed into it; and horse and rider fell. The crowd was screaming. Leah realized she had pressed her hands against her ears. Her lips were dry, coated with dust. Her eyes watered. Dazed, she glanced around to see that the air was filled with dust. It *was* dust. The tiny white sun illuminated each of the dust motes as they knocked about like fireflies or Ping Pong balls, gaily, giddily. Christabel had begun to cough. Grandmother Cornelia was breathing in shuddering gasps through a white lace handkerchief. Ah, what is happening! Is *this* what must happen! Leah thought, rising slowly to her feet, blinking her great burning eyes rapidly.

The race was nearly over. Spectators were coughing, and shouting, and waving their arms frantically. In the homestretch Nicholas, his head bowed, one gloved hand rubbing at his eyes, began to shout at Marcus, and then to use his whip. But the horse was exhausted, and the whirlwind now danced close about him as if teasing him; and Jupiter was rapidly gaining, running as if he had awakened from a dream, untroubled by the whirlwind and the dust that now blanketed the track in all directions. Leah's cheeks were streaked with tears. Jupiter *would* push into the lead. Jupiter *would* win. . . . But Nicholas used his whip harder, as if suddenly desperate, and Marcus, though beginning to stagger, tried to thrust himself forward by great springs from his hindquarters; despite the taunting dust spiral he managed for a moment to actually quicken his pace, with a frantic spring—and another!—as his golden-bronze sides heaved, slick with sweat, and his eyes rolled white and foam flew from his gaping mouth. Jupiter, now beside him, showed no sign of fatigue, nor did he appear to notice the dust spiral, which had grown now to a height of perhaps fifteen feet, and was dancing along with the horses to the finish line. Leah, standing, her feet far apart in order to balance her weight, found that she was gripping the railing with both hands, and that her knuckles had gone dead-white, the bones showing through the skin. Gideon, she prayed. Nicholas. It *was* the case that the albino horse was considerably larger than the chestnut. As he began to pull past Marcus, his extraordinarily dark shadow flying along beneath and beside him, the smaller horse began to tremble quite visibly. Nicholas's hand rubbed at his eyes. Horse and rider screamed as a dust tentacle leapt out at them suddenly, plunging into the horse's eyes, writhing snakelike about his legs. Marcus swerved to the side, and Gideon with great skill reined Jupiter clear, and then, quite suddenly, Marcus tripped—fell—pitched forward—threw his rider over his head and onto the track—and Jupiter pounded past without an instant's hesitation.

So Gideon Bellefleur on his ivory-white stallion Jupiter won the Powhatassie race. And won (it was rumored throughout the region) a considerable amount of money. For the Bellefleurs, being Bellefleurs, and addicted to gambling, had wagered heavily on the race; it was whispered that they had made innumerable bets, under fictitious names, and that they cleared, on that remarkable day, a small fortune—though of course no one in the family would ever speak of such things. If a neighbor, meeting Noel Bellefleur in town, or riding his own, rather rangy stallion Fremont along the road, called out to him—You folks did pretty well the other day, eh?—Noel might affect a look of frowning bewilderment, and mutter something about the purse—that it would keep the horses in oats for another season, and his sons in whiskey.

Gideon was rumored to have offered the entire purse, $20,000, to the Fuhr family. But of course the Fuhrs refused it—for why should they accept Bellefleur money, and under such circumstances? I don't want it, I don't deserve it, it's a bitter thing, Gideon said tonelessly, but why should the Fuhrs listen? Why even should the Bellefleurs listen? At the wake Nicholas's father turned away from Gideon though he knew very well—he must have known—that Gideon had had nothing to do, really, with his son's death. (Marcus had died at once, of a broken neck; but Nicholas had died after a day and a night of agony, his chest massively crushed, each of his arms and legs broken. . . . The mare Angel was dead as well: she had been so cruelly injured, her owner had had no choice but to shoot her between the eyes. But her rider, though badly hurt, and possibly crippled for life, was fortunately in no danger of dying.)

Gideon had had nothing to do with Nicholas's death, but the Fuhrs did not want to see him again, or even to hear his name. They did not want Bellefleur pity or Bellefleur tears, or, at the funeral home, lavish floral displays—lilies, white iris—sent by the Bellefleurs. Of course Gideon had not *caused* the accident, of course he could not be reasonably *blamed*, and even the most bitterly distraught of the Fuhrs knew it—surely everyone knew it!—but still they did not want to hear *his* protestations, his grief, they did not want to see his tear-reddened eyes or smell his whiskey-sweet breath.

And they certainly did not want his money.

Nocturne

When, after more than ten months in the womb, and after a seventy-two-hour labor of such violent pain and remorseless, convulsive heaving, that Leah, stoic throughout the pregnancy, and unwilling to speak aloud of her dread, was reduced to a thrashing screaming animal whose cries rang out, through the opened windows, to permeate the darkness, and were said to be heard across the lake (so that there was, for Gideon, nowhere to hide, and not even a drunken stupor could save him)—when, after the ordeal of a labor so colossal that there would never be, for Leah, words to contain it (and it was her private theory that the labor itself hadn't begun that oppressively hot August evening after dinner when most of the family were down at the lake, and only the grim-faced silent Della, in her tiresome mourning, attended her; it had really begun that Sunday at Powhatassie, after the finish of the race, after Nicholas was carried on a stretcher off the track—not known yet to be so irreparably injured, but unconscious nevertheless, and bleeding—and she was stricken by a lightning-bolt of pain intense enough to darken her vision, as if not only her eyes but her entire body, her entire vision, had gone blind), and in her incoherent bawling she cried out not only for her mother to help her, and for poor Gideon (whom she had banished days earlier from her bedside—she couldn't bear, she claimed, to witness *his* hapless suffering, since her own was terrible enough: "Get away! Get out of here! I can't stand it! I won't have you here! You're really a coward, you're really a baby yourself, go on out of here, go play poker with your friends, go get drunk, you love to get drunk, you've been drunk for the past month! Go away from my bedside, go on *out* of here!" she cried, her broad face streaked with perspiration that seemed already to have worn little rivulets into her flesh, no matter how often Della or Cornelia wiped it away), but God Himself, in Whom she had never believed: God Whom she had, even as a small girl, cheerfully mocked (at times even to her mother's face, for it was *always* a delight to upset Della); when after the stench of blood in the room, and the first sight of the infant's head between Leah's smeared thighs, caused not only aunt Veronica to fall down in a dead faint but Dr. Jensen himself (and Jensen had been so marvelous when the twins were born, talking to Leah constantly, even, at the crucial moment, pressing on her abdomen and breathing with her, sharply and deeply and rhythmically, with her, as if his lungs had the power to inform hers—as in fact they did: the birth, after a ten-hours' labor, had gone miraculously well)—when all this had transpired, and Leah's poor wracked body was free of whatever had inhabited it, Cornelia spoke first, saying, "It should be suffocated at once," and great-grand-mother Elvira said, "It could be taken away—taken to Nautauga Falls— left on the doorstep of an orphanage—" and Della, having elbowed the other women aside, ignoring her daughter's wailing (for Leah, in her delirium, *wanted* the creature), said simply: "I'll take care of it. I know what to do."

If Leah was a lush, plump, darkly red multifoliate rose, spoiled by years of careful nurturing in fertile, manure-rich soil, then Garnet Hecht was a straggly wild rose, one of those stunted, anemic, but still pretty blos-soms whose petals are, almost at once, blown; such wild roses are usually white, or pale pink, and their pistils are frail and powdery as a moth's wings; even their thorns are meekly dull beneath one's exploratory thumb.

Still, Gideon thought, running, Garnet's tiny hand grasped hard in his (how light it was!—her bones were as thin as a sparrow's), still, such roses *are* pretty once you actually examine them.

"Gideon, oh, stop—Gideon, please—Gideon—"

But she could not catch her breath, he pulled her along so quickly, through the woods beside the lake, late at night, only the three-quarter moon (which was the color of curdled milk, angrily glaring) and a scatter-ing of stars as witnesses. They were running together through the pine woods just to the north of the manor; underfoot were needles upon which their feet slipped, and Garnet cried out in breathless alarm. "Oh, Gideon, please—I didn't mean—I'm so afraid—Gideon—"

The pine trees were perfectly straight. Perfectly black, in silhouette. Ahead was the uncanny dark of Lake Noir, in which the moon—even this bright, pulsating moon—was reflected only dimly; and no stars were reflected at all.

Behind them, far behind them, a woman's wail arose; and Gideon ran faster. He was panting hard. He was wordless. Poor Garnet staggered after him, her thin arm outstretched, her childlike hand grasped tightly in his, sobbing, not daring to slacken her pace.

"Oh, but Gideon—I didn't mean—please—"

It was Della Pym who had sent Garnet to Gideon, with something to eat—cold sliced turkey, and ham, and half a loaf of that thick whole-wheat bread he loved, and some date-nut bread as well—for after Leah's labor began he had gone upstairs to the third floor, over into the east wing, where he had been sleeping, off and on, since the Powhatassie race, with only a bottle of bourbon to keep him company, and his Springfield rifle (with which, from the window, he shot hawks and crows out of the sky— or had been shooting them before the wise birds learned to avoid that wing of the house). He had been sleeping on the floor, on a filthy old carpet, in his clothes, and his mother claimed—not quite truthfully—that he hadn't washed or shaved or rinsed his mouth since Nicholas's funeral. If Leah would not comfort him (and she would *not,* his weakness disgusted and frightened her), why then he would allow no one to comfort him, let them rap on the door, or pound, let them murmur his name or pronounce it, as Noel did, sharply and briskly—*Gideon, what the hell are you doing to yourself! Gideon, open this door at once!*

Garnet, trembling, climbed the stairs to the third floor, and crept along the shadowy hallway, a candle in one hand, the silver tray heaped with food, and covered by a white linen napkin, in the other. Because she knew she would be struck dumb when he confronted her (*if* he confronted her, for he hadn't unlocked the door even for Cornelia, these past few days) she whispered ahead of time: Oh, I love you. Gideon Bellefleur. I love you. I love you. I have loved you since the first day I set eyes on you. . . . And, yes, it was on your white stallion, you were riding your white stallion, through the main street of Bellefleur, and you never saw me staring, you never glanced my way. . . . You never glanced to the right or the left, riding through the village like a prince. It was on your white stallion I first saw you, and I loved you at once, and I will always love you, no matter that you never glance at me, or even know my name. . . .

Drunk and grinning a lopsided grin, and smelling of a man's sweat, Gideon *had* opened the door; and leaned against the doorway staring at her. I didn't think I had really heard anyone knocking, he said. You didn't rap very hard, did you. You aren't very strong, are you.

He snatched the tray from her and threw the napkin aside and began to eat. Ravenously, like an animal; like a wolf. Garnet stared at him, her face burning. He tore at the meat with his head inclined to the side, like a wolf. His strong stony-white teeth gleamed in the tremulous candlelight.

She had thought she would faint—a terrible dizziness arose in her— but she had not fainted. She stood rooted to one spot, staring at Gideon Bellefleur. Oh, I love you, she whispered in secret.

"It can't be allowed to live—"
    "It—they—must be put out of their misery—"
    "Don't let Leah see! Is she awake?"

Voices ballooning around the bed. Great tall teetering figures.

The taste of blood, of salt, of orange-burning fire, drawing all sensation to the tongue. . . .

Leah had given birth and lay back in a delirium.

They were gasping. Whispering. What a tragedy! What could they do! Aunt Veronica, bringing a water-filled basin to the bedside, saw what lay squirming there and with a soft faint Oh! sank forward, in a dead faint. And Floyd Jensen, sleepless for most of the seventy-two hours, stared at the creature for a long, long moment—not one baby (and a giant baby at that) but two babies: then again not *two* babies (which would have been quite within the normal order of things) but one and a half: a single melon-sized head, two scrawny shoulders, and at the torso something hideous that resembled, in Jensen's feverish imagination just before he fainted, part of another embryo—

The creature had only two arms, two tiny fists, which it flailed angrily. And of course it was bawling.

"Don't let it wake poor Leah! Oh, what should we do—"

"It should be put out of its misery—suffocated at once—"

"But it's living, it's *alive*—"

"Is she waking up? No? Hold her still—"

"It should be put out of its misery!"

"Might we take it to the city? Where no one—no one would *know?* An orphanage, a hospital—the steps of the cathedral at Winterthur—"

Grandmother Della in her soiled black dressing gown, her scalp showing in pink slats through her thinning yellow-white hair, her eyes unusually bright, all but shouldered Cornelia aside. *Cornelia,* her brother's silly chit of a wife! She stepped forward masterfully, just as she had stepped forward, years before, at the astonishing birth of Bromwell and Christabel, and raised both squirming infants aloft, to clear their lungs, give them a shake, get them wailing—for wasn't she, after all, no matter how she disapproved of the girl and of the girl's bully of a husband, the grandmother?—the mother's mother? This creature was far heavier than the twins. But she raised it aloft. And, staring frankly, with a curious half-repulsed half-satisfied little smile, she said: "Just look at it! Shameless! You can see it's meant to be a girl but that other part sticking out—just look!—why, those things are hanging halfway to its ankles, I never saw anything like it—"

Leah lay weakened and delirious on the blood- and sweat-soaked sheets. Murmuring: Mother, Gideon, dear God. Mother. Gideon. Oh, please God, dear God. Help. . . . Give me my baby.

Through the window a curdled-milk moon. No night sounds at all: not even crickets: Leah's screams had silenced everything.

The baby shrieked. Kicking, fighting. For breath. For life. Two somewhat abbreviated legs, and part of an abdomen, and rubbery-red slippery male genitalia, possibly oversized—it was difficult, with all the commotion, for Della to estimate—growing out of the abdomen of what appeared to be a perfectly well-formed, though somewhat large, baby girl. *Her* legs were longer and appeared to be normal, and her tiny hairless vagina was a healthy purplish-pink, the size of Della's smallest fingernail, between the thrashing legs.

"*I* know what to do," Della said loudly.

Gideon's hands, acting of their own accord, tore the girl's clothing away. And then his own. If he could have torn her skin away as well, he might have done so: how greedily, how desperately, his fingers plucked! He wanted nothing between them, not a breath, not a thought.

She strained apart from him but he forced himself, his great weight, onto her; and then into her; half-angrily he ground his mouth against hers and felt her hard childish teeth, resisting. Somewhere, far away, a scream sounded—or was it a loon's wail—but Gideon, plunged so far into this girl whose name he didn't recall, heard nothing.

. . . Gazing at him with lovesick moonstruck eyes. Her words trailing off into the air, in his presence. Long thin hands, bony fingers, the nail bitten back to the quick, a habit that excited his disgust. Leah mocked. Of course Leah mocked. The girl was silly . . . yet the surprise of her in the corridor, the sudden alignment of eyes and hair and pert little chin that made her beautiful to his sleep-dazed eyes . . . the shy soapish odor of her . . . that tiny hand grasped so tightly in his. . . . She wept, she sobbed of love. Love. He did not hear. He no longer knew where he was. In the pine forest above the lake, on the needle-strewn cold ground? Something that was not the girl drew him down violently, as if the earth had cracked open and it was into the very earth itself he plunged: weightless, bodiless, helpless. Falling. Deeper. The desire to crush, to annihilate. To smother those cries. Plunging. Tearing.

A demon poked at him with its hot sharp tongue, breathing boldly into his face. The tongue in his ear. So moist, so agitated! He could not control himself. The girl in a daze murmured, Love, love, oh, I love you, murmured a name that must have been his, but he did not hear: and then gripped his back, which had gathered itself into bunches of muscles, rising, arched, furious, as Leah herself might have gripped it, once *did* grip it, long ago.

"Oh, Gideon, I love you—"

Grunting, Della carried the squirming thing to the walnut cabinet at the far end of the room, ignoring her daughter's cries, and pushed aside a silly Chinese porcelain boar's-head tureen—the costly junk her family had accumulated, she would have liked to make a pyre and burn it all! —and flopped the baby down. And, keeping her back discreetly to the others, blocking Leah's view if, risen on her elbows, she should actually be watching, with one, two, *three* skillful chops of the knife, solved the problem once and for all.

She turned to face the room. Drawing her first full breath in many minutes she said, triumphantly: "Now it's what it was meant to be, what God intended. Now it's one, and not two; now it's a she and not a he. I've had enough of *he,* I don't want anything more to do with *he,* here's what I think—" and with a sudden majestic swipe of her arm she knocked the bloody mutilated parts, what remained of the little legs, and the little penis and testicles and scrotum, onto the floor—"what I think of *he!*"

Book Two

THE WALLED GARDEN

The Vial of Poison

Germaine's grandfather Noel Bellefleur carried with him, in secret, for more than fifty years, a vial of about two inches in length, encrusted with tiny cheap-cut rubies and diamonds (or perhaps they were colored glass and rhinestones), filled with cyanide. No one knew of the vial of poison: not even Noel's wife, not even his mother. He carried it with him at all times, except when he slept, and even then it was never more than a few yeards away, hidden in a drawer. When, in later years, he and Cornelia no longer shared a bed, and occasionally—on account of his harsh snoring, Cornelia claimed—did not even share a room, he began to keep the vial beneath his pillow. For safekeeping, he thought. Waking in the night after a disturbing dream, or after no dream at all, he would reach under his pillow anxiously and there it was—the tiny object, stone-studded, its roughness pleasurable to his fingertips, warmed by his presence.

From time to time he unscrewed the minuscule cap, and sniffed at the contents, his eyes hooded. The poison smelled wonderfully astringent. As quick, as surprising, as mothballs or ammonia or skunk: odors he halfway liked, in their mild forms. He might even shake the white crystals out on a surface and examine them. Did poison, even so marvelously effective a poison, lose its miraculous power to kill, after a period of time . . . ? Though there were innumerable reference books in his grandfather's library which he might have consulted, though he might even have inquired, casually, of his grandson Bromwell (who, at this time, when Germaine was only an infant, had acquired a remarkable library himself, and never exactly with anyone's permission: the child simply ordered whatever he liked—a complete set of the *World Book,* volumes on biology, astronomy, chemistry, physics, mathematics, even a telescope kit that came in a large packing case to the depot in Bellefleur, where Gideon went, mystified, to pay $400 for whatever it was his headstrong little boy had ordered *now*), and though he might certainly have asked Dr. Jensen, who dropped by frequently at the house, to check on Leah and her new baby girl, he said nothing to anyone—the poison was his secret, sacred to him, unutterable. From time to time he simply changed the vial's contents, filling it with "fresh" cyanide.

Noel Bellefleur in his old age had the shrewd, rather raffish appearance of an osprey surfacing from brackish water, a squirming fish in its beak. There was something blurred and soiled about him. His nose had a slight knob in it, his cheeks were relatively unwrinkled but very shiny, the scar from an old war wound gleamed boldly on his forehead like a third eye: an eye more clearly defined than his own eyes, which, behind the lenses of his glasses, were gauzy, unfocused, as if set in water. He limped badly, and with what appeared to be a deliberate awkwardness. He wore shapeless outfits at home—trousers that drooped on his somewhat shriveled haunches, and white shirts that, not tucked into his belt, were allowed to billow out, roomy as nightshirts or a servant's smock. Even when he appeared in public his linen was never very clean. Germaine was to think of him as birdlike, indeed—a hook-beaked bird in an untidy nest. One would not have been surprised to see feathers and down clinging to him. When he troubled to shave, which was infrequently, he did a poor job of it, and sometimes appeared in the breakfast room bleeding from a half-dozen tiny nicks, indifferent to, sometimes angered by, his family's protestations. Once every several months a barber was driven to the manor from Nautauga Falls, to tend to both Noel and his elderly mother Elvira (who received the man in the privacy of her room). If Noel was a thin, watchful, rakish old bird, his wife Cornelia was a plumped-out guinea hen, still an uncommonly attractive woman with small, pretty hands and feet, and snow-white hair that was perfectly and stiffly groomed at all times.

Like birds the two pecked at each other, from time to time, impatiently, irritably, but without violence. If Cornelia had known of the secret vial she would have exclaimed: "That crazy old fool is doing it to spite me—he wants to humiliate *me.* He'll swallow cyanide and leave me behind and everyone will point me out: that's the woman whose husband committed suicide to escape her!"

But in fact Noel had acquired the precious little object when, as a boy of seventeen, he had suffered, perhaps even more painfully than Hiram and Jean-Pierre, his father's protracted humiliation: the decline of the family's fortune, the selling-off of land, the dismantling of old Raphael's railroad (the wonderful little cars, even the ties, were sold for scrap metal! —and the furnishings, which no one wanted, were stored in one of the unused hop barns, where rain soon destroyed them), the desperate attempt to make quick money by raising foxes. . . . "What now, what next," Hiram muttered, with a sigh like a thud, and Noel, unable to spend *all* his time with his horses, began to lie about the house, a skinny, loose-jointed boy, listless, overtaken by a Bellefleur malaise as severe as any, feeling too weak, too miserable, to raise a finger. In those days Jean-Pierre, named appropriately for old Jean-Pierre, was his mother's darling, spoiled and capricious and very good-looking, with dark curls and dark, cunning, puppyish eyes, and he was somehow able, despite the Bellefleurs' financial problems, to spend a great deal of time playing cards in the Falls, and in certain notorious riverfront taverns: twenty years old to Noel's seventeen, he would nevertheless (being guileless, and infinitely good-natured) have brought his younger brother along on his expeditions, in order to snap him out of his "mood"; but Noel always refused. He did acquire from Jean-Pierre, however, who had won it at poker, the bejeweled little vial. "It's for smelling salts or something," Jean-Pierre said, tossing it to Noel. "Maybe opium. *I* don't have any use for it."

"Cyanide," Noel said at once.

"What?" asked Jean-Pierre, smiling. *"What* did you say?"

He hid the little vial away and showed it to no one. Once it was filled with poison it acquired a peculiar life or spirit of its own—quite as if it were another Bellefleur, another member of the family—but at the same time it was indisputably *his.* Suicide, Noel thought dreamily, as a boy in his late teens and then in his early twenties, ravaged by lurid violent fantasies of sex which of course he could not control, suicide, just the thought of it, the thought of escape, why is it so luxurious . . . ?

Often he fingered the vial, safely hidden in his trouser pocket. While enduring conversations in the drawing room with his female cousins and aunts, or sitting through interminable dinners. Suicide, the thought of it, the luxurious thought of it, why did he smile so suddenly, his delight raying across his face? For of course he never intended to use the cyanide. Never. But the *thought* of it, the *feel* of the vial, were most satisfying.

(In the family there were legends of odd "suicides." Noel's grandmother, for instance, who drowned in Lake Noir . . . and his own father, perhaps, Lamentations of Jeremiah, who insisted upon going out in a murderous storm though everyone in the family tried to stop him: wasn't that a kind of suicide, really? Strangest of all was the contrived death, the "assassination" of President Lincoln, an intimate friend of grandfather Raphael's—or so family legend would have it, and Noel, being skeptical, *did* have his doubts. But it was generally believed in the family that Lincoln had arranged for his own "assassination," so that he could retire from the world of politics and strife and domestic pain, and live out the remainder of his days as a special guest at Bellefleur Manor. The poor man had come to abhor his life with its public and private burdens, and its very real crimes (so many thousands of men killed in the war, which no notion of political justice could ever absolve, and hundreds of civilians imprisoned in Indiana and elsewhere, without due process of law—simply at *his* imperial command). Lincoln had, it was said, so despaired of life that he wanted only to tear a hole in the earth's side and plunge through and lose himself forever. . . . And so, by means of a plot Noel had never quite understood, which was completely financed by Raphael Bellefleur and perhaps even imagined by him, the public Lincoln had been "assassinated" so that the private Lincoln might live. Of all the forms of suicide, Noel thought, *that* had the most style.)

At the funeral for the poor Fuhr boy, killed in that freak accident, Noel, possibly the most intoxicated mourner present (though his own son Gideon was well fortified by whiskey—it was just that, Noel thought resentfully, Gideon was *young,* and could hold his alcohol with as much control as Noel had once had), fingered in secret the precious vial, and gave himself up to thoughts of death.

Death. How suddenly it might come when you didn't want it. How reluctantly it came when you did. Nicholas Fuhr was dead: he'd survived any number of riding accidents, and fistfights, and God knew what else: but suddenly he was dead, his poor body broken. There were a number of men Noel had wished dead in his time—the Varrells, of course, before they were murdered (and the blame placed wrongly on Jean-Pierre); one or two rivals for Cornelia's hand; his nation's wicked enemies in the war. But he had never killed anyone. Not even as a soldier. He would not have wished to actually kill anyone, to actually bring about a death, and it troubled him that perhaps, when the time came (and when might it come? —he was an old man now, his eyesight was failing, the lake salmon were fished out, Fremont was getting wobbly) he would be incapable of taking the cyanide he had hugged to himself for so many decades. . . . Odd, how his grandfather Raphael had continued living. An embittered old man. Still wealthy, but a failure: a failure at politics, a failure as a husband, and (so he thought, and said) a failure as a father. He certainly wanted to die, living in near-seclusion all those years, only his Honored Guest (some comradely political failure he'd picked up on his campaigning, some party hack he had, for reasons no one knew, become indebted to: the rumor, absurd of course, was that the bearded old man was Abraham Lincoln!) to keep him company, along with his books and journals. He *must* have wanted to die, Noel thought, yet he hadn't had the courage, or the bitterness, to kill himself.

He, Noel, would have the courage. When the time came.

But now he sipped whiskey, and brooded over the past, and found it too much trouble to bestir himself even to comfort Gideon, who badly needed comforting, like an overgrown child; he had told Gideon several times that the accident at Powhatassie wasn't his fault, it certainly wasn't his fault, he must forget it, or if he couldn't forget it (Nicholas, after all, had been Gideon's closest friend) he should try to extricate himself from it, in his memory—and above all he shouldn't feel guilty for having won the race, which he and Jupiter deserved to win; or for winning all that money. (Not that Noel really knew how much money had been won. He half-suspected that Hiram had cleared a great deal, in secret; and he had a vague idea that Leah herself had done well. *He* had won a modest amount, only $6,000.) But he let Gideon go, and paid no attention to his wife's querulous remarks, sipping whiskey, chewing on his cigars, rubbing the kittens' heads roughly, and tickling their balloon-fat little bellies, thinking of the past, of all that had gone wrong: not only did things *go wrong,* Noel thought, bemused, they went into knots and snarls, tortuous as the eye-dismaying designs on one of his sister Matilde's crazy quilts. (Which *were* crazy. All interwoven interlocked dizzying colors. Too much for his brain to absorb. Ah, his sisters Matilde and Della! It pained him to think of them. Perhaps he would not think of them. Della blamed him, unfairly, for her husband's accidental death, and was not above whispering *Murderer* at him, nearly three decades later; she even blamed him— and this was a measure of the old woman's bullheadedness—for the fact that Gideon and Leah had fallen in love, and insisted upon marrying though they *were* cousins. And Matilde. Perfectly lucid in conversation, good-natured and even good-humored whenever he visited her, but obviously insane—for why, otherwise, would the woman live up there north of the lake, in an old hunting lodge in what remained of a fifty-acre camp Raphael had built for wealthy guests (one of them was the Supreme Court Justice Stephen Field, who managed to hold his position, and his power, for more than three tumultuous decades; another was the industrialist Hayes Whittier, who exerted so much control over the Republican Party, and whose son—twenty-one years old, but with the physique of a ten-year-old—was dying of consumption: so it was Raphael's idea that the north woods, *his* north woods, might save the boy)—why on earth would Matilde keep so stubbornly to herself, eccentric as any old mountain hermit, refusing his and Hiram's money, growing her own vegetables and raising a few scrawny chickens, making a spectacle of herself in the village —in the village that bore her own family's distinguished name!—by buying up rags and old clothes, and selling those crazy quilts, and occasionally eggs, home-baked bread, and vegetables? He would *not* think of her.)

Ah, but should he allow himself to think of Jean-Pierre?—at whose trial (in fact trials, since the first resulted in a hung jury) he had not merely fingered but actually grasped the poison vial, wondering if he should use it himself if Jean-Pierre was found guilty, or whether he should slip it to his brother. . . . But Jean-Pierre was too cowardly to take cyanide, just as he was too cowardly to have murdered ten or eleven men; he would have. burst into tears, and possibly told their mother. And shame, anger, rage, had fueled Noel after the conviction, so that he hadn't *wanted* to die, not even to escape the ignominy bruited about everywhere in the newspapers, and chuckled over by the Bellefleurs' many enemies, who did not care that justice was being mocked so long as the Bellefleurs were wounded. He had not wanted to die but the little vial—its very existence, the fact of its promise—comforted him a great deal.

Then there was his oldest son Raoul, managing one of the family's sawmills down in Kincardine, who, caught up in a peculiar marriage, or in a peculiar ménage (Noel really knew little about the situation, he shut the women up when they began to speak of it, detesting gossip not his own) never—*never*—came home to visit. Not even during Cornelia's illness a few years ago. Not even when Noel himself was laid low with intestinal flu one winter, and sweated off eighteen pounds. "That boy doesn't love us," Noel said bitterly. "He has his own troubles," Cornelia said. "He doesn't *love* us or he'd come visit," Noel said. *"And that's all."*

Jean-Pierre, his good-looking dandyish brother; now in prison for life plus ninety-nine years plus ninety-nine years plus ninety-nine years. . . . And his oldest son Raoul, whom he'd thought, in his vanity, had so closely resembled *him*. . . . And Della who hated him, and Matilde who had no need of him (stout, winesap-apple-cheeked, chasing a clucking chicken out of the kitchen so that Noel could have a seat, smiling politely and answering his questions: How was she getting along, did she need firewood, did she need provisions, did she need money?—did she need *him?*) And Cornelia who baited him, who did not respect him as a woman should respect her husband. (Their marriage had gone off course on their honeymoon. In fact on their wedding night. Though they had made their wedding journey plans in secret, and had told only a few family members, nevertheless Noel's friends and drinking cronies caught up with them at the White Sulphur Springs Inn where they were spending the night, and treated them to a raucous "horning"—a serenade of bells, tin pans, firecrackers, and horns of various kinds, and many ribald shouts and shrieks; and Noel, following mountain custom, very cheerfully following mountain custom, had of course invited the drunken party in for more drinks, and cigars, and even a few games of poker. Next morning he'd been astonished to learn that his bride was *miffed.*) And there was his father, Lamentations of Jeremiah, who had worn himself out trying to recoup the family's losses, never outliving *his* father's disappointment in him, and that cruel jeering name, administered with such deliberation. Poor Jeremiah had been swept away in the Great Flood almost twenty years ago, and his body had never been recovered, never given a decent burial. . . .

The living and the dead. Braided together. Woven together. An immense tapestry taking in centuries. Noel began drinking the day of Nicholas's death, and continued drinking into the autumn, making a pig of himself by the fireplace, spilling whiskey and tobacco and ashes down his front. . . . The living and the dead. Centuries. A tapestry. Or was it one of Matilde's ingenious quilts that looked crazy to the eye but (if you allowed her to explain, to point out the connections) made a kind of dizzying sense . . . ? He mourned his lost father, and his imprisoned brother, and even his unnamed son who had died at the age of three days, long ago; he mourned Hiram's pretty young wife Eliza; and his oldest son Raoul; and the others. The others. Too many to enumerate. He'd had a disagreement with Claude Fuhr a while back and their friendship of decades had ended in a shouting match and neither had apologized and perhaps Noel *should* have made the first move because he, being a Bellefleur, possessed more charity. . . . But he had not apologized, and now they were blaming Gideon for Nicholas's death, and everything went wrong, tied itself into ugly knots and snarls only a quick swig from the bejeweled vial could solve.

After the excitement of the new baby, the women discovered Noel there by the fireplace and, for a brief while, fussed over him. Even Cornelia. ("Don't you want to see your new granddaughter, old man? She's quite a sight!") Even Veronica, who usually paid no attention to him. (It was generally thought that Veronica was one of Noel's sisters. But in fact she was an aunt. Years older than Noel though she looked remarkably young—with her full, plump face unmarked by character lines, her somewhat coarse, ruddy cheeks, her smallish, close-set, placid hazel eyes, and her hair—so honey-warm a brown, it must have been dyed, and very expertly dyed at that: Noel once tried to figure out the woman's age but his brain resisted and he simply poured himself another drink.) Even Lily, who was ordinarily jealous of Leah, came round to cheer him up by saying he should see the new baby—he should see her at once, she was growing so fast—she wouldn't be a *baby* much longer.

He growled that they should leave him alone. *To every thing there is a season, and a time to every purpose under the heaven: a time to be born, and a time to die. . . . A time to kill and a time to heal; a time to break down, and a time to build up. . . . A time to laugh, and a time to weep.*

Nevertheless, one day, he peeked through the open door of Leah's boudoir and saw . . . and saw Leah in a green silk dressing gown, one breast exposed, full and waxen-white, the nipple, elongated, an astonishing pink-brown; he saw one of the servant girls lifting a baby into her arms; he saw, transfixed, the baby (which *was* a healthy-sized baby, kicking and flailing its arms robustly) start to nurse, its blind, greedy little mouth grabbing at the nipple. He stood, staring, his hands in his pockets, and his knees turned to water, and his glasses misted over. Oh, dear God, he thought.

Leah, boldly, called him in. Why stand there gaping? Hadn't he ever seen a baby before?—a baby nursing before?

"Isn't she hungry this morning!" Leah said. She shuddered, she laughed. There was a curious elated, gloating sound to her voice which excited Noel. "Ah, just look at that! *Isn't* she a beauty!"

The small hands made clenching, grabbing motions. The eyes were half-shut with pleasure; and then opened wide with agitation—a deep, clear green—as if there were some danger the breast might be taken away.

"Such a little pig, isn't she!" Leah laughed.

"A very . . . a very healthy baby . . ." Noel said faintly.

"Well, she's big enough. And getting bigger every day."

Noel wiped and polished his glasses. And sat, timid as a suitor, on Leah's couch. His daughter-in-law had never looked more beautiful—her complexion was whitely-hot, as if with concentration; her blue eyes shone in triumph; her lips were full and moist. A considerable quantity of milk had dribbled down the front of her silk gown, and its odor was so warm, so stale, so sweet, that Noel grew dizzy. Ah, if only *he* could nurse at Leah's breasts!

Why had he hidden away all these weeks, brooding over things he couldn't change, spitting into the fireplace like an old man?

That afternoon, he stayed until Leah chased him out. And returned the next morning, and stayed and stayed. He did not know whether he should envy Gideon or not—there was something courteous, something almost too formal, about Gideon and Leah now: they no longer quarreled in front of the family, or slapped at each other; they no longer squeezed each other's hands, or whispered in each other's ears, or kissed noisily. Gideon had trimmed his beard and mustache, and made a show of behaving, after those terrible black weeks following Nicholas's death, like a gentleman; and Leah addressed him with a small cool discreet smile. In the early days of their marriage Cornelia had been scandalized, the way the two of them "pawed" each other in public. . . . But those days appeared to be past.

Still, Noel *did* envy his son. Because Gideon was this woman's husband, after all. Her husband, and the father of that beautiful baby.

Leah had always turned aside when stories of the family were told, and she had always professed boredom when the subject of the Bellefleur "fortune" was brought up, as it so frequently was. But now, suddenly, she wanted to hear everything, everything Noel could tell her, going back to the original Jean-Pierre . . . the youngest son of the Duc de Bellefleur . . . banished from his homeland by Louis XV for his "radical ideas" about individual rights . . . arriving penniless in New York and yet, within years, evidently rich enough to acquire, in the 1770's, some 2,889,500 acres of wilderness land for seven and a half pence an acre. . . . It delighted Leah to learn that this extraordinary man had wanted at one time to control the northeastern border of what had newly become known as the United States of America (which meant the control of waterways as well, and commerce with Montreal and Quebec); and that he had even drawn up plans—how seriously, Leah wondered!—for breaking his wilderness kingdom away from the rest of the state, and even from the new nation, in order to establish a sovereignty of his own. It was to have been called Nautauga, and it would have had close diplomatic and commercial ties with French Canada.

"Ah—Nautauga," Leah whispered. "Of course. Nautauga. How simple. . . . Almost three million acres, all *his*. Nautauga."

The only likeness of Jean-Pierre Bellefleur the family had was a poor engraving that had been the frontispiece of *The Almanack of Riches,* a paperbound book published in 1813 by Jean-Pierre and a printer friend, in shameless imitation of Ben Franklin's *Almanack:* in the shadowy reproduction a bright pair of eyes gleamed, and the brows hulked dark and ponderous and shrewd. A handsome man, bewigged, with a very black dandyish beard. That long thin noble Bellefleur nose. Middle-aged, perhaps. Not old. Leah studied the picture, holding it up to the light. A handsome man, yes; and there *was* something noble about him.

"Tell me everything you know about him," Leah commanded her elders. Then, after a pause, bravely: "Even the circumstances of his death."

So the days passed. Autumn plunged, as it must, into winter; the sun described a laconic parenthesis in the sky, and disappeared as early as 3:00 P.M.; and sometimes there was no sun at all. Yet Noel Bellefleur was never happier.

What's that silly little melody you are always humming, Cornelia asked him suspiciously, why are you smiling to yourself?

Aveline said, Is Pappa sneaking whiskey in the mornings now?

Leah, the cause of his chattery good spirits, pretended to notice nothing unusual at all. (Her husband's strong-willed father *had* always been one of the liveliest of the Bellefleurs.) He talked to her for hours, tireless. And if he said, "But, Leah, I must be boring you—I must be wearing you out with this old dead history," she always protested vehemently. How could he *think* of such a thing, boring her with facts about the Bellefleur family . . . !

Old Jean-Pierre, that outrageous man. Nautauga in its earliest years. The old house across the lake at Bushkill's Ferry. (In which the tragedy had taken place: but Noel did not wish to dwell upon *that*.) Jean-Pierre's empire, his tumultuous years as a congressman, his partnerships in resort hotels, steamboats, coach lines, taverns; *The Almanack of Riches* (which, despite its derivative nature, went through three hundred printings!); the scheme to bring Napoleon to the Chautauquas; the old Cockagne Club; the timber-razing projects; the Arctic elk manure scandal; the innumerable women or tales of women. . . . Noel chattered away happily. His own children had never cared to hear these tales, except for the story—necessarily abbreviated—of the Bushkill's Ferry massacre; and so it was something of a miracle that young Leah Pym, the most beautiful bride ever brought to live in Bellefleur Manor, should show such an intense, such an *insatiable* interest. Noel fairly glowed with pleasure. One of Leah's questions could start him off for an hour or more. It frequently seemed, on those long lazy lamp-lit winter afternoons, that Jean-Pierre Bellefleur, the old man himself, was in the room with them, standing with his back to the fire, leaning against the mantel, puffing on a foul-smelling pipe and shaking with merriment. . . .

One noon Noel gathered together a party of children for a drive across Lake Noir in his horse-drawn sleigh. The ice was solid—wonderfully solid —frozen now to a depth of twenty or more inches. (The ice of Lake Noir! —a phenomenon taken for granted by local residents, but well worth the attention given it by curious visitors: How is it possible, strangers wondered, that ice, which is after all merely water, should possess the shading and even the texture of onyx, and that it should refuse to melt in the warm breezes of April, retaining its solid state well past the time when ice-locked ponds and lakes on far higher ground had cracked . . . ? Examined in chips or drops Lake Noir did not have a dark or even a shadowy cast; it appeared to be "normal"; and when young Bromwell studied it carefully beneath his microscope he could find nothing exceptional about it. But in bulk it was peculiarly lightless, and seemed to reflect or radiate a blackish sheen, like that of ravens' feathers. It was one of the family legends that the Bellefleur dead, though officially buried in the cemetery, really went to live in Lake Noir, in its murky depths, and could sometimes be sighted beneath the ice, standing upside down with their feet against the ice, by one who was himself fated soon to die. But the children believed this tale only when they wanted to frighten themselves.)

Racing across the ice, several of the grandchildren—Christabel, Louis, Vida—bundled up beside him, beneath a wool-and-feather-lined quilt, Noel had a sudden idea: he reached in his pocket for the vial of poison: and there it was, there as always it was. But it no longer gave comfort. It no longer seemed important. Poison? A quick death? Suicide? But why? (So Noel imagined his daughter-in-law interrogating him, the color high in her cheeks, her magnificent eyes glowing.)

You—a Bellefleur? Taking comfort from the cowardly thought of *suicide?*

His first impulse was to throw it away; but of course the ice was solid, the vial might be discovered. So he put it back in his pocket. Since they were going to visit poor Jonathan Hecht this afternoon (Jonathan's condition had worsened, he wasn't expected to live beyond the New Year) it occurred to Noel that he should leave the vial with his old friend. Ah yes! —with Jonathan.

"That poor old man," Noel thought, his heart swelling charitably.

The Vision

High above the mist-shrouded river. In the many-faceted light, quivering with moisture, that breaks off the mountain. (The name of the mountain? Jedediah has forgotten. Only with an effort can he grasp that things—even so vast, so uncharted—have been given *names.*)

In his wanderings he keeps that mountain in view. It is one of the few snow-covered peaks in the Chautauquas, which are said to be old mountains, eroded by millennia. In a dream he learned that the mountain is a sacred mountain, presided over by spirits that, like angels, are not human; nor are they, exactly, God. They have to do with God. But are not God. Not exactly. . . . He keeps that mountain peak in view. Sometimes he stands motionless and stares at it, observing how, as the minutes pass, or perhaps they are hours, passing silently, seamlessly, the "white" cap shifts and blurs in the sun, as if preening before him. It trembles, writhes, shakes itself.

God?

But God hides within His creation.

In certain lights the mist turns to flame. His breath is sucked from him, his eyes fill with involuntary tears. Ah, that the entire world could so easily turn to flame!—except for God's fastidious mercy. Which holds the sun back. Which measures what man can bear.

Jedediah contemplating "Jedediah." It seems that he inhabits a body. Uses it to walk about in. The eyes—*his* eyes—are evidently the means by which he draws God to him. When he read the Bible, in those days before the spirits' humming and singing and their coy, sweet whispers ("Jedediah? Jedediah? Come to us!") distracted him, it was evidently the case that God, though a spirit, was to be evoked through the print of a book: through verse after verse of that old leather-bound book. *Hear my prayer, O Lord,* Jedediah whispered, *and let my cry come unto thee. Hide not thy face*

from me. . . . For my days are consumed like smoke, and my bones are burned.
. . . My heart is smitten, and withered like grass. His eyes smarted in the smoke
from his tiny fire, his voice was hoarse with longing. Still, he did not raise
his voice; he did not beg; certainly he did not command his Lord. Very
softly he whispered, *Keep not thou silence, O God: hold not thy peace, and be not
still, O God.*

It would be many weeks, Jedediah reasoned calmly, before God
might reveal Himself.

One of the mountain spirits slipped giggling beneath the covers and, in
a gesture both childlike and depraved, ran her thin cold fingers up and
down his thighs.

Jedediah turned at once to embrace her. Hard. Hard. Though they
were pressed together in the dark, though his ravenous mouth was
against hers, he could see her quite distinctly.

He groaned with the surprise of her. Of it.

Strange, in his father's house, in his brother's household, he had
seen only a small warm pretty face. Hair, eyes, shoulders. Shyly expressive hands. He had looked at her often enough, covertly, but he had never
seen her.

Now he saw her vividly. Piercingly.

With his very skin he saw her.

The mole beside her left eye, the delicate vein on her forehead. The
tiny, white, almost invisible lines about her mouth, which was a girl's
mouth. He had not remembered that her limp, curly hair was so fine,
feathery-fine, and that it stirred with his breath as he grew near.

Germaine?

She smiled. Revealing slightly grayish teeth that were charmingly
crooked. The incisors were a fraction of an inch longer than the front
teeth so that her smile gave her the quick, fey, shy, somewhat wicked look
of a woodland creature—a wolverine, a fox. And what color were her
eyes? Brown? Gray-brown? Hazel flecked with gold? At the moment
when his hard, eager, desperate flesh entered hers—when the soft, warm
resistance of her body suddenly gave way—her eyelids fluttered and her
eyes rolled white in their deep-set sockets.

Germaine, he groaned.

And afterward he woke, his heart pounding so violently that he
feared he might be having a seizure: with both hands he pressed against
his chest, against his tumbling heart. His lips were too numb to shape a
prayer.

Then he saw what had happened, what the spirit had teased him into
doing, and he woke fully, humiliated, angered. As his heartbeat slowed
and his breathing returned to normal her image faded swiftly. He realized
with spiteful pleasure that he had forgotten her name. As he had forgotten the name of the mountain, and the name of the river that plunged
below him, so thunderous he no longer heard it.

Her small hectic face? Faded, erased. The quick daring movements of her hands? Gone.

She was his brother's wife, his brother's child-wife. A girl of sixteen, imagine, married to that bullying ignorant fool! He remembered Louis's name clearly, of course, but he did not remember *hers*. . . . Begging him to stay until the baby was born. Don't you want to see your little nephew? —aren't you going to be his godfather? A certain flirtatious, nervous lilt to her voice, so that he would not *really* think she was begging.

Now he never thought of her. He never thought of any of them.

Except, at unanticipated times, at moments when his soul felt unaccountably weak, watery as gruel, he found himself gazing upon his father through his eyelashes; his head bowed; his manner supplicant. *There,* the man who was his father. The man whom God had employed to bring him into the world. Into time. Into suffering. Into sin. What did it mean, Jedediah wondered, stooping to rub his ankle which throbbed painfully at such times (for all his money, Jean-Pierre Bellefleur had a reputation for miserliness, and perhaps it was true—he refused to take his son back to Manhattan, to an "overpriced" butcher, and turned him over, after the accident, to a drinking companion of his, a Dr. Magjar, who had drifted down across the border from Quebec and who spoke only a few words in English, and spoke them poorly: Jean-Pierre's logic being that no great skill was needed to set a few bones)—what did it mean, what did God intend, that out of that man's loins he, Jedediah, should have sprung?

The shock, the disgust, of that first trip to the north country. Two weeks of hunting, fishing, canoeing. Indians. Iroquois. Imagine, an Iroquois guide! And Iroquois children. Your own age. And lakes, and mountains, a wilderness as far as the eye can see . . . !

Harlan and Louis and Jedediah, then a very young child. Their mother, of course, remained behind in their twelve-room town house, and Jean-Pierre did not mention her once during the two weeks. Instead, at the lakeside camps, at the riverside inns and taverns, there were other women, astonishingly friendly, noisy, gay: women who tilted their heads back and roared with laughter. One of them, no younger than Jedediah's mother, and far less attractive, ran her fingers roughly through Jedediah's hair and told him he had his father's beautiful dark eyes, Satan's eyes. She had smelled of perspiration, like a man.

Jean-Pierre, his voice slurred with drink, his eyelids drooping. Hugging the boys. Jedediah and Louis, but Harlan wrenched free; and then Louis pushed away. Hugging Jedediah, who could not move. If you fall in love too young, Jean-Pierre said shrilly, you will always be alone. Her name was Sarah. Her name . . . but it wouldn't mean anything to you . . . it wouldn't mean anything now. . . . If you fall in love too young and nothing comes of it you will always be alone for the rest of your life. So you might as well open the doors. Bring the crowd in. One, two, a dozen, two dozen, what the hell, what does it matter. . . .

Jedediah had wanted to shrug himself free of his father's embrace, but he had not dared to move.

His father, his father's voice. In the cabin with him. He felt the danger of that voice's intimacy.

Suppose his father hunted him down. Made out a warrant for his arrest. Or paid a gang of men to bring him back. (Slung over a horse, wrists and ankles bound. A deer carcass. A gutted deer.) In the first year of his solitude he had thought God would reveal Himself at any moment . . . but his only surprises, his only visitations, were from men: trappers, hunters, men like himself who wandered the mountains, some of them known to him from his life *down below,* most of them strangers. Every few weeks one or two of them might approach his cabin, calling his name. (For *they* knew *him.*) Except in the deep of winter, when the fifteen-foot snowbanks protected him, these unwelcome visitors would interrupt his solitude so often that it sometimes seemed (but of course he was imagining it, he really knew better) that his father and his brother were employing them, not merely to bring letters and provisions and unwanted gifts, but to destroy his peace. In that first year . . . or was it more than a year . . . letters were thrust boldly into his unwilling hands . . . and the request was even made that he write out a reply . . . a few words, a few lines . . . to be brought back home. Of course he always refused. Sometimes in anger, sometimes in alarm. Write out a reply! But why, and to whom? He had given them up. He had surrendered himself to God.

Nevertheless he skimmed the letters, holding them at arm's length. For perhaps God might address him through another's voice. Through his brother's scribbling, with its misspellings and its frequent exclamation points. ("Wait till you see your little nephews, growing so fast!—and the town is growing too—Papa bought into a coachline, and a ferry, and one or two other things that will come as quite a surprise!! He asks after you & sends his love. . . .") But he never read the letters carefully, his eye darted about in panic, and in the end he usually folded them and burned them, so as not to risk the temptation of reading them at another time. And he was right to do so, as he discovered one morning when he *did* examine a sheet of paper that was only scorched around the edges: for it turned out that his father now spent most of his time at White Sulphur Springs, at something called Chattaroy Hall, where wealthy southerners came to summer, bringing with them their daughters, their marriageable daughters, and Jedediah was of an age when he must marry, and take up the responsibilities of an adult, and if he could see one or two of these lovely girls—who couldn't hear enough about *him,* who already adored him for living alone in the mountains—

Elsewhere was the commandment to *Love & Honor Yr. Father.*

One night, feverish, the skin of his forehead, cheeks, and upper chest actually burning, Jedediah stumbled out into the dark, into the rain, and turned his astonished face upward, convinced that someone had called

his name. God? Was it God? Calling his name above the noise of the river,
and the hard pounding rain?

He had been ill for several days. His bowels had sickened, turning
to water; a fine gray mist passed before his eyes. He slept and woke and
slept again, sometimes waking in a convulsive shiver, sometimes with a
snort like a deer's snort—his throat was so dry, so parched.

God? The God of Abraham, Isaac, and Jacob? The God of Wrath and
of infinite majesty?

A God of fist-sized raindrops. Falling from the sky. How odd, how
very odd, the beautiful way in which they fell: so weighted, so heavy! He
gaped up into the sky. There was no sky, there was nothing to see, only
the immense glistening raindrops, striking him with the force of pebbles.
He had lived his entire life so far, Jedediah thought dizzily, without
worshipping the God of Rain. Without standing bareheaded, utterly submissive, supplicant, virginal as a young bride, his face turned up to the
hammer-force that fell from God.

Calm. Silence. Silence within the deafening roar. Silence within the
tumult of his veins, the chatter inside his skull.

God? Now? In this hour?

One hour was all hours, one raindrop all raindrops. God in each, in
all, icy-hard, piercing. It was very cold. But there was no wind. But it was
summer. Wasn't it summer? The first summer after the summer of his
leavetaking . . . or perhaps the second summer . . . the second, or the
third. . . . One summer was all summers, just as one raindrop was all
raindrops, and he had only to stand there, bareheaded, bare-chested, a
supplicant, meek before God, opened to God's love.

The beautiful drumming rain! The ceaseless rain! Egg-sized, fist-
sized drops of rain! Mesmerizing. Blinding. (For he could not even see
the edge of the bank, he could barely see the doorway of the cabin behind
him.)

The burning sensation was gone. Now he shivered, in gratitude. Rain
ran down his forehead, his cheeks, his chest, it ran down his body in
caressing chilling streams, not many drops but one single drop, a vast
benevolent soothing flood.

God? he whispered softly.

And then for some reason he turned to look back, and saw, there,
in the doorway of his cabin, the very mountain spirit who had teased and
tormented him, and led him into sin: she was holding her arms out to him,
though not blatantly, not boldly: her small oval face was pale, and utterly
familiar, and her voice, though loud enough to be heard over the roar,
was gentle. *You will have to come back, Jedediah. To me.*

The Spider, Love

From approximately the age of thirteen and a half, until she was eighteen, and Gideon Bellefleur so valiantly courted and won her, Germaine's mother kept as a pet a spider of remarkable size and beauty, which she called *Love*.

"Ah, isn't it a handsome thing, just *look* at it," Leah would say, as it quivered in its spittle-glistening web (and the web itself was a masterpiece, Leah would have liked to draw it in pen-and-ink, in all its exquisite detail), or scuttled about the walls and ceiling of her room (upon which it frequently left, at first to the distress of her roommate at La Tour, and La Tour's headmistress, Madame Mullein, and then to the angry distress of her mother, a translucent film or slime that, though almost imperceptible at first, gradually darkened to form ineradicable tracks), or crept affectionately up her arm to her shoulder where it nuzzled, blackly silky and bold, against her neck. "It's just the gentlest thing, aren't you? It wouldn't do any harm to *anyone.*"

Which Leah knew wasn't altogether true. For Love did bite if irritated, and Leah's fingers were covered with angry little stings about the size of mosquito bites, which grew red with her impatient scratching; and if she didn't feed it immediately in the morning—dead flies and other insects, even dead spiders; bread crumbs; cookie crumbs; milk and sugar and tiny bits of meat, offered with a tweezers—it would sometimes leap down from its web and sting her sharply on the back of the hand. If anyone was present (and there were girls at La Tour, her age or younger, who, fascinated and disgusted by Love, crept into Leah's room very early, before chapel, to watch the handsome spider at his breakfast) Leah did no more than draw in her breath sharply, and cry "Oh!—aren't you naughty!—can't you wait a *moment?*" and suck at the tiny wound, giggling, her eyes shining as they darted over her silent, staring audience of girls in floor-length nightgowns and woollen robes, their hair, long as Leah's, unbraided for the night and falling loose past their thin shoulders. "He gets ravenously hungry during the night, because it's so long for him," Leah explained.

Quite frequently one of the girls, lingering behind after the others had left, would ask Leah shyly if she might feed Love sometime. Or have him perch on her finger, or her shoulder, as he did so jauntily with Leah when the mood struck him. "I wouldn't hurt him, I wouldn't crush him or anything," the girls promised, when Love was still fairly small—penny-sized, with a modest little belly; and then as the weeks passed, and Love greedily devoured the dozen little meals Leah offered him daily, and grew —grew to the size of a roach, then to the size of a hummingbird—the girls said, shivering, hugging themselves, "I wouldn't be afraid of him—I wouldn't drop him, or knock him away—I wouldn't *scream*, Leah, please!"

Though Leah always accepted food the girls brought, and was partic-ularly pleased to receive walnut fudge (since it was not only one of Love's favorite foods but one of Leah's, and Della never—*never*—sent fudge to La Tour), she always refused to allow the girls to participate in the ritual of feeding Love. He was *her* discovery, *her* pet. There had never been anything like him in the history of La Tour Academy for Girls, and there never would be, and Leah was so unhappy there, so lonely and restless and angry, and yet spitefully proud of herself (for she *was* a Bellefleur: she belonged to the Bellefleur family and as far as anyone knew she belonged to the *wealthy* Bellefleurs), that she refused not only most of the girls' timid requests for Love, but their timid, inarticulate, groping over-tures for friendship as well. And then too there was the possibility, the very real possibility, that Love would sting a girl so hard that she would betray Leah and run to Madame Mullein. Or might Love even (and this thought rarely crossed Leah's mind, it was so hideous) quickly grow to prefer another girl, another girl's trembling finger, her soft freckled arm, the warm fragrant scent of her hair . . . ?

Leah's roommate Faye Renaud was a child of about average size, and consequently much shorter than Leah, with unruly frizzy hair, and nonde-script features, and a slight stammer that sometimes exasperated Leah (who, even when intimidated by a teacher or one of the older girls, spoke out quickly and boldly, for no one was going to get the better of *her*), and sometimes charmed her: Faye was Leah's closest friend at the school, her only friend really, and the girls sometimes liked to pretend that they were sisters. But even when Faye begged for a chance to pet Love's fine satiny-black hair ("I won't tell the other girls, Leah, please!" she whis-pered) Leah thought it wisest to refuse.

"Love is a wild creature, after all," Leah said, with dignity.

Very late one night, when all the lights were out, shut off by a master switch operated by the headmistress, Leah, sleepless, homesick for the mountains, for the very *feel* of the Chautauqua air, and the odor of brackish Lake Noir, homesick even (though she would certainly not admit it) for her mother, imagined she heard something beneath her bed. Heard it, or felt it. Sensed it somehow. . . . As a small child she had frightened herself with the thought of nasty ugly creatures hiding beneath her bed. They were vaguely aquatic, yet dark, darkly sluggish, like eels writhing in mud; they were possessed of a queer half-human slyness, though they were also, and this is what terrified her, hardly more than black shapes. They were keenly aware of *her,* of every move she made in bed, and so it was necessary for her to lie perfectly still, her arms rigid at her sides and her breath as shallow as possible.

But she had outgrown these silly creatures. The only thing beneath *her* bed, Leah thought, was dust balls.

And so, while Faye slept a few yards away, Leah lay at the very edge of her bed and reached under. She groped about quite boldly. Of course there was nothing! What could there be! Her fingers closed about a slipper and tossed it aside. And encountered a ball of dust. (Leah was often scolded for her "failure to observe the rules of cleanliness"—for even her clothes, and even her hands and feet and neck, were not always as clean as they might be.) And encountered, then, something else . . . at the very first like a dust ball, it was so soft, so fine, so filmy . . . and then it was firmer . . . and it tickled . . . ah, it was moving! moving! . . . and then it stung her.

She was so surprised, she did not even yank her arm out; she simply moved it a few inches away. And lay there, frozen, her eyes opened wide in the dark.

And then, after a few seconds, she felt the softness again . . . she felt the tickling again . . . as the thing crawled over her hand. She lay motionless, waiting. It was going to sting. She knew it was going to sting. That piercing needlelike thrust. . . . But it simply remained there, on the back of her hand. A mouse? A baby mouse? Leah had, of course, seen innumerable baby mice, and it always distressed her when the cats tormented them, when they ran about blindly, squealing, squeaking for life; even baby rats were darling creatures. But a mouse beneath her bed? Mice in the room? Rats?

She drew her hand cautiously away. Where was that slipper. . . . If she acted quickly enough perhaps she could crush the thing before it escaped. . . .

But with remarkable alacrity, and a kind of grace that seemed almost human, the thing leapt back onto her hand and began to make its way, slowly, as if aware of her apprehension, up her arm . . . very slowly up her arm . . . its delicate legs brushing against the delicate hairs of her arm. . . . Staring at the faintly moonlit ceiling Leah lay paralyzed, and thought, as the creature fumbled a little by the crook of her arm, that it would now fall off: it couldn't get a toehold: it would fall off and she would scramble out of bed, on the other side of the bed, and scream for help. But the creature did not fall off. It simply turned, and made its way up to her shoulder, at the same slow, deliberate pace, as if it were fully conscious of her, and able to read her thoughts.

Leah did not dare move. Odd, that her heart continued to beat calmly, that she did not fly into a panic. She was an unusually strong-willed, even stoic child, and felt contempt for the "ladylike" girls at the academy, but there had been times—once, when Angel reared back from a copperhead, and again when a boy, younger than Leah, started inexplicably to sink, to drown, while swimming in Lake Noir—when she had lapsed into a state of sheer brainless panic. And she had a bad temper: she was a *most* moody, mercurial child: sometimes, Della shouted, she was possessed of a demon, and only a good exhaustive beating would cure her. But that night as Love crept delicately along the smooth skin of her upper arm, to pause at her shoulder, its thin legs poised like a dancer's, its keen sharp eyes fixed intelligently upon her, Leah did not panic, did not babble out for help, though she wanted, ah, how very much she *wanted,* to cry "Faye, help me! Faye, do something! Get a shoe, get a boot, hit it, please, crush it, *please!*"—she did not succumb to the terror she felt, but lay motionless, hardly breathing.

And in the morning, at dawn, when the room finally grew light enough for her to see (for the feathery weight on her shoulder, so close to her ear, though unmoving, apparently unthreatening, did not allow her to sleep: she even began to imagine she could hear it breathing), she turned her head slowly, her eyes narrowed, her lower lip caught hard in her teeth—and there it was: there, the handsome spider: hardly more than spider-sized at the time, but remarkably sleek, with tiny beadlike eyes, and hair of burnished black, so fine, so thick, as to resemble fur.

"Why, you're a *spider,*" Leah whispered in amazement.

Love, a secret from Faye for a brief while, and from the other girls for several weeks, grew rapidly. His favorite foods were bits of other insects mashed around in sugar-milk, and very tiny bits of meat. (A silver-dollar-sized piece of fatty beef, smuggled upstairs in a napkin from the dining hall, would keep Love engrossed for days.) From the very first Love was keenly sensitive to his mistress's moods, and if she was tearful he would rub against her ankle, like a cat, and scuttle up her to nuzzle against her neck and cheek; if she was nervous he would crawl rapidly about the walls, spinning out abortive webs, the strands of which fell loose, swaying, responsive to the slightest movement of the air. When Leah was in high spirits Love kept his distance, with an almost resentful dignity: he spun his fascinating web in a high corner of the room and perched in its center, watching her, censorious, immobile, offended. At such times Leah would clap her hands and call him, her cheeks flushed, her eyes gleaming with the *wildness* of it—that she, Leah Pym, had a spider for a pet!—a sleek handsome black hairy-legged yellow-beady-eyed *spider* for a pet.

"Come here! Now you come *here!*" she cried, bringing her palms smartly together. "Don't you want to be fed all day? Don't you give a damn? You, Love! You pay *attention* to me!"

But Love would not be commanded, nor could he be wooed. He came to his mistress only when the spirit moved him: sometimes surprising her by leaping from the wall onto her head and burrowing into her hair (on Sundays and on Wednesday evenings when dining was "formal," Leah and Faye prepared each other's hair, sometimes with enthusiasm, sometimes impatiently: Leah's dress-up hairdo was quite elaborate, involving not only a heavy chignon but several brands and braids of hair wound about her head, and full, fluffy, wavy bangs that nearly obscured her eyebrows: and it was invariably into *that* charmingly pretentious hair arrangement that the mischievous Love insinuated himself, a minute or two before the bell rang to summon the girls downstairs), and, more frequently, scuttling up her stockinged leg to her underpants of cotton wool and burrowing inside *them* and crawling, flattened, sly, across the swell of her stomach, while she squealed and slapped at him and jumped about the room trying to dislodge him—knocking over her desk chair, the tea things, the water basin, poor Faye's potted fern, the stack of kindling wood beside the little fireplace. And there were times—especially after she had returned to Bushkill's Ferry, and home, and Love was much larger, having grown to the size of a sparrow—when Love sensed that her mind was elsewhere as she fed or stroked him, and, in a sudden ill-natured frenzy, stung her most cruelly on the back of the hand, or the breast, or even her cheek. Leah's scream, her shock, her sudden childish tears, *somewhat* placated him at such moments. "Oh, that hurt, that hurt, why did you do that, oh, you did that deliberately, you *calculated* that, don't you love me?—haven't I been good to you? Do you want me to take you out to the woods and turn you loose? Don't you *love* me?" Leah whispered.

The beautiful young Leah Pym and her gigantic black spider, incorrectly said to be a black widow spider, became quite notorious in the Valley. Very few people had actually seen the spider, and fewer yet had seen it perched upon her shoulder like a tamed bird, or nestled in her hair; but everyone had an opinion about it.

When the girl first returned from the academy at La Tour—appearing, unannounced, at her mother's door, tearful and weakened and alarmingly thin (for she had lost a considerable amount of weight, having succumbed to a terrible melancholia that not even contempt for her classmates and her teachers and the headmistress could dissipate) it was said that she had contracted some deathly illness, down in the flatland. (La Tour was one hundred or more miles to the south, a fairly prosperous commercial city of moderate size, on the Hennicutt River; mountain people claimed that the air in such low-lying places was foul, and that they had actual difficulty breathing it, through their nostrils especially, because it was so unpleasantly thick-textured.) It was whispered that she had had a disastrous love affair—with one of her teachers?—but were there men teachers at the Academy?—ah, but then perhaps poor Leah had been victimized by a *woman!*—and it was no wonder that Della, imperious closemouthed Della Pym, refused to discuss the situation. Word spread that the girl had behaved very oddly during her last weeks at the school: she had stopped eating; tore pages out of her diary and textbooks, and burned them; gave away clothing because it no longer fit her, being too loose; gave away jewelry; even a lovely mink hat that had been a present from her uncle Noel, about which she had always been rather vain. She had refused to go to chapel. Or to her classes. She had "pined away" for Bushkill's Ferry, for Lake Noir, for the mountains. She had lost all interest in her sorrel mare, and was to leave Angel behind at the academy stable, when she left so abruptly. Strangest of all, the girl had a most unusual pet. . . .

This daughter of Della Pym's, Della's only child, born some five months after her father's death, was known generally to be willful and vain and bad-tempered, though Della certainly had not spoiled her. One of Gideon Bellefleur's earliest, fondest memories of his beautiful cousin had to do with a violent temper tantrum she threw at the age of three: something so maddened her that she stamped and kicked and threw herself about, and savagely ripped the front of her white satin dress with its Flemish lace collar and cuffs, and had to be carried out sobbing by one of the adults. Upon another occasion she sulked at the wedding of a cousin in Innisfail, and drank glass after glass of champagne, and challenged certain of her boy cousins to a wrestling match (which they wisely declined), and, gaily intoxicated, her long billowing skirts hoisted to midthigh, she waded in a brook and splashed about and refused to come back when her mother called her. She was then no more than eleven years old, but her hips had already begun to fill out, and her small breasts had a distinctly womanly fullness and softness to them, that made Gideon and his brothers quite uneasy. The incident ended abruptly when Leah stumbled back to shore, wet and breathless and white-faced, weeping, for reasons no one could comprehend, "I don't want to! I don't want to!" What it was the child did not want, no one knew, nor could she explain. "*I don't want to!*" she sobbed, tears streaking her rounded cheeks; and Gideon, then a boy of fifteen, could do no more than stare.

(Odd, that Della and Leah came so frequently to Bellefleur celebrations. It seemed they were *always* underfoot, and Leah was even bold enough, once or twice, to bring her hairy little pet along. Though Della detested her wealthy relatives she always accepted their invitations to weddings and christenings and holiday gatherings because she felt that they did *not* really want her and were counting on her refusal—and why should she give them that pleasure? "For my sake, Leah, behave like a young lady," she always said; but when, inevitably, Leah behaved quite badly, she never seriously scolded her afterward. "You've got *their* blood in you, after all," she would say apathetically.)

Leah was sixteen years old when, diving from a granite cliff into Lake Noir, and swimming, through a chilly September rain, halfway across the choppy lake, she caused her cousin Gideon to fall irrevocably in love with her. He halfway knew he had been falling in love with her for years, by degrees, and that astonishing sight—the husky, strapping, deeply tanned girl in the green one-piece bathing suit, diving without hesitation into the water some fifteen or twenty feet below, every muscle beautifully coordinated—was nothing more than a final blow. Leah swam as strongly as Gideon himself, her heavy dark hair wound about her head like a helmet, her face pale and stubborn with effort. He had wanted—but had been unable—to run off the cliff and splash down beside her. He had *wanted* to pursue her and overtake her and turn it all into a boisterous joke. But he hadn't moved, he had simply stood there, staring, watching that body sleek and forceful in the water as an eel's, in the grip of an emotion in which love and desire were so inextricably braided that he was left quite literally breathless.

(Much later, when Noel closeted himself with his son, and pleaded and reasoned and shouted with him, and even dared to lay hands on him, Gideon's only response was a baffled, sulky, "Well, I don't *want* to want her, not only is she a cousin of mine but she's a daughter of that insufferable old bitch! What do you think, Pappa, do you *think* I want any of this?")

As a fairly young girl Leah attracted suitors, some of them, like Francis Renaud and Harrison McNievan, a decade or more older than she; and of course there were a number of boys Gideon's age who were very interested in her. But all were intimidated by the spider Love. There were tales—not, in fact, very exaggerated—of the girl's wanton cruelty in allowing Love to clamber across a visitor's shoulders, and even to sting upon occasion. (You would have thought, people murmured, that the Pym girl would have respect for poor Harrison—with his arm crippled from the War, not to mention all the land he inherited!) At the age of seventeen and eighteen Leah enjoyed a perverse popularity in the region, despite her frequent and quite open disdain of men, and her skittish, even priggish behavior when she was alone with a man. It might have been her very nervousness she wished to disguise, by outlandish requests (she commanded Lyle Burnside to fetch a silk scarf of hers that had blown— or had she allowed it to blow?—down a steep cliff along the Military Road) and girlish pranks edged with malice (she agreed to meet Nicholas Fuhr on Sugarloaf Hill one summer day, and sent a fat, somewhat retarded half-breed girl instead) and sudden, inexplicable outbursts of temper (at a wake—of all places!—she turned to Ewan Bellefleur, who had been eying her with an unsubtle smile, and accused him of being wicked, of gambling and wasting money, of being unfaithful to his fiancée (whom at that time Leah had never met: she knew only that Ewan was marrying into a Derby family of surprisingly modest wealth), and of having fathered illegitimate children—an attack that amazed Ewan, not because it touched upon anything he might be in a position to deny, but because it was so unprovoked: hadn't his look of frank, appreciative interest in his cousin at all *flattered* her?).

"That's Della's work," Ewan was told. "The woman wants to poison her daughter against all men, but especially against Bellefleur men."

The ugliest—or was it the most amusing?—episode involved a young man named Baldwin Meade, who was rumored to be related, distantly, to the Varrell family, once numerous in the Valley, before the notorious feud with the Bellefleurs in the 1820's killed off so many on both sides. It might have been that Leah was attracted to Baldwin Meade *because* of this connection, for what would infuriate her wealthy relatives more than a liaison with one of their enemies?—even if the feud was long dead, and hardly more than a source of embarrassment to all. (Though this was not exactly true. Ewan and Gideon and Raoul had sworn, as boys, to revenge themselves if and when the occasion arose: for, rejecting the state's claim that Jean-Pierre Bellefleur II had murdered two Varrells that night at Innisfail, along with nine other men, they calculated that six Bellefleurs had been killed to a mere three or four Varrells, which seemed to them monstrously unjust.)

If Baldwin Meade was related to the Varrell family he certainly did not emphasize the fact, nor did he resemble them in the slightest: they had been swarthy, thick-chested, of no more than moderate height, with hirsute bodies, and beards that grew halfway up their faces; and it goes without saying that the Varrells, the Bellefleurs' old enemies, were uneducated, crude, brutish, and inarticulate. ("Why, you look as if you'd just joined the human race a few weeks ago," Harlan Bellefleur was heard to exclaim, in actual surprise, even as he raised his Mexican handgun to blow half the man's face away; witnesses were struck by Harlan's graceful manner, the way in which he *hesitated* before he pulled the trigger, as if the very idea, the very thought, that the man cowering before him wasn't altogether human, held a profound significance he must contemplate—though not at the moment.) By contrast Baldwin Meade was tall, slender, clean-shaven, a cheerful if indiscriminate talker, and though his manners were about average for the mountains he was certainly not coarse, and took care never to use profanity or barnyard colloquialisms in the presence of those women designated as ladies. How, exactly, he behaved on that Fourth of July night, what sort of things he said to Leah, what sort of things he wished to do, or actually *did,* to Leah, no one knew: for the girl would never tell, and one could hardly bring the subject up with her mother.

Returning home from the band concert and the fireworks display in Nautauga Park, in a two-seater drawn by a roan gelding, driving in the dark along the Bellefleur Road, Leah and her twenty-six-year-old suitor must have quarreled somewhere between the intersection of that road and the Military Road, and the village of Bellefleur itself, for it was only a few hundred yards away from the old iron forges (once owned by the Fuhrs), near the crest of a very long, steep hill, that the young man was found the following morning. Not dead, but nearly so: delirious and raving and crying for his mother: his right arm and the right side of his face grotesquely swollen, watermelon-sized. Leah had driven the carriage back to Bushkill's Ferry and had been considerate enough (for she always respected the needs of animals, even though horses no longer interested her) to unharness and feed and drench the gelding, and to stable him in the Pym's old barn; she made no secret of the fact that the carriage was on her mother's property, and left it in plain view, in the cinder drive, for any curious neighbor to see. But she never explained the incident, she shrugged and laughed and waved her arm, saying that people "exaggerated," and if they really wanted to know why didn't they ask silly Baldwin Meade himself? It was claimed by the men who brought Meade in, and by Dr. Jensen, who tended to him, that the poor boy had been copperhead-bit in three places, and it was extremely fortunate for him that he was found as early as he was, for by noon he would certainly have died. Copperhead-bit! people said. They pulled thoughtfully at their lips, they smiled slyly. *Copperhead!* Not likely.

When Gideon Bellefleur first visited Leah as a suitor, and not as a boy, or a boy cousin, he was humiliated and outraged by the fact that Leah, in an open-necked polka-dot sundress, her lovely hair all curling-iron ringlets and spit curls and waves clearly meant to emphasize not only her beauty but her arrogant confidence in that beauty, nevertheless received him in a dingy, musty side parlor of the old Pym house; and the enormous black spider was perched on her shoulder, on her very skin.

She fixed her very dark blue eyes upon him with an almost mocking concentration as he spoke, but it seemed quite clear to Gideon, who blushed and stammered, that she was not really listening to his words. (Indeed, she was thinking, as she stared at her handsome cousin, with his thick dark hair that rose from his forehead like a brush, and his squarish jaw, and his eyes that were so prominent, almost bulging with—with what?—energy?—excitement?—that any other girl would fall in love with him, possibly in a matter of minutes, but that she was *not* such a girl. And she thought, lazily stroking Love's hairy back, in order to placate him (for he seemed unusually agitated, she could feel his tiny heart beating), that though it might be amusing to appear to fall in love with Gideon Bellefleur, since it would outrage not only the Lake Noir Bellefleurs but, most of all, Della herself, such an antic might bring with it consequences she could not foresee. Gideon's reputation was not so wicked as Ewan's, but he was a gambler, and it was common knowledge that he and Nicholas and one or two other young men frequently raced their horses on outlaw tracks, and involved themselves with sluttish women back in the mountains, and over in Derby and Port Oriskany; and he had been very cruel to an acquaintance of Faye Renaud's, the daughter of a Unitarian minister who had presumed, on the basis of two or three innocent outings, always in the company of others, that Gideon Bellefleur would soon be engaged to *her*. Still, there was the quite appealing fact that Gideon lived in the castle, and Della loathed the castle, and frequently made a show—a silly show, in Leah's opinion—of actually shielding her eyes from it, on exceptionally clear days when its eerie sprawling coppery-pink shape appeared to float above the lake, far closer than, in fact, it was. And Leah was curious about the castle, for she'd seen, over the years, only the grounds, and the walled garden, and two or three of the larger downstairs rooms, which were really public rooms, open to any Bellefleur guest. She *wanted* —ah, how badly she wanted!—she could not resist wanting, despite Della's warnings—to see every room, every cubbyhole, every secret passageway, every corner of that monstrosity. Gazing at Gideon her eyes misted over as she saw the two of them, Gideon leading her by the hand, descending the stone steps into the vaultlike cellar . . . where strands of cobweb would brush against their eager faces, and mice would scamper away in corners, and the air would smell of damp, of mildew, of rot, of pitch-black darkness itself, a darkness ten times black . . . and Gideon's flashlight would dart about . . . and he would grip her hand hard if she stumbled . . . and if she began to tremble with the cold he would turn to her, and . . .).

Gideon broke off in the middle of a sentence and said roughly that he didn't want to bore her; he'd better be going. He had wanted to ask her to accompany him to Carolyn Fuhr's wedding but she was clearly not interested. . . . "You keep petting that thing on your shoulder," he said. "That ugly thing on your shoulder."

Leah blushed, and brought Love into her lap, where she stroked his back and sides, and tickled his fat little belly, or bellies, with her forefinger. She and Gideon stared at each other for a full minute, and then she said, blushing even more deeply, "He isn't ugly! How dare you say such a thing!"

Gideon got to his feet, with the graceful dignity of which he was sometimes capable, and made a mocking little bow with his head, and simply walked out of the parlor and out of the house and down the brick walk.

But at their second meeting he was again insulted, for this time not only was Love present (though not in his mistress's lap or on her shoulder, but quivering at the center of a five-foot web spun out so recently, in a high corner of the room, that it glistened wetly, and possessed an almost icy, crystalline beauty—quivered, Gideon saw with disgust, as he greedily devoured bits of food placed in the web for him), but Della— Della with her cheerless bustle, her long black skirts that looked (as Cornelia said) as if they were fashioned out of feedbags!—Della with her dried-up prunish shrewd face, and her small head that seemed to be made of ill-fitting plates of bone, and her wasp's smile, and her obvious gloating dislike of *him!*—was in and out of the room, bringing the young couple tea and stale chunks of carrot cake, and inquiring after Gideon's family with a feigned courtesy, and sympathetic little moues when she heard that Noel had been laid up with the grippe, and Hiram had injured himself sleepwalking again, and the deer and porcupines were eating up everything in sight. Leah appeared to be somewhat more congenial on that afternoon, but it was difficult to tell: her dimpled smile, her calm level lovely dizzying stare, her erect posture, her strong hands clasped at her knees, her murmured assents: what, really, did they mean? Was she trying to signal Gideon, when Della's back was turned?—or was she perversely trying to signal Della, while Gideon looked blankly on? And the huge ugly creature in the web, devouring *his* bits of carrot cake, and fairly shuddering with the ecstasy of eating. . . .

After less than an hour Gideon left the Pyms', his face burning with frustration. He had managed to extract from his cousin a vague promise (retracted the very next day, by messenger) that she would accompany him to a lawn party at the home of the former senator, a man named Washington Payne; but he had the uncanny, maddening idea that she was not really *listening,* that she was not *aware* of him at all.

And so he did not see her for several weeks, and scrupulously avoided thinking of her, and got into a fairly vicious fight with his brother Ewan when Ewan taunted him crudely about her, and spent as much time as possible with his horses. (His favorite horse at that time was the stallion Rensselaer, descended from old Raphael's English Thoroughbreds, a grandson, many times removed, of Bull Run himself.) But of course his mind dwelt on her; his very senses, it seemed, swerved upon her at the slightest provocation. A girl's uplifted voice, the odor of must and damp, the sight of cobwebs in the dew-glistening grass. . . . Children splashing about at the shallow end of the lake. . . . A polka-dot dress worn by his own, rather plain sister Aveline. . . .

One night he rode Rensselaer over to Bushkill's Ferry, to the Pyms' old red-brick house, and, his nerves perfectly steady, his audacity fortified by no more than two or three swallows of good mash whiskey, he calculated, from the ground, which room was his cousin's, and climbed an oak tree with long, slovenly, overhanging branches, and managed, his gloved hands moving deftly and quickly, not only to get the ill-fitting window open but to open it without making any noise; and he climbed inside, and found himself, indeed, in his cousin's room (a spacious, attractive room, but far messier than he had anticipated), only a few yards away from his sleeping cousin, whose wild dark hair cascaded across her pillows, and whose moist, pouting lips were slightly parted. But judicious Gideon Bellefleur did no more than glance at the sleeping girl. He went at once to the immense, elaborate cobweb that stretched from floor to ceiling, and, without giving himself time to think, without giving himself time to feel the trepidation he might reasonably have felt, simply reached out to grab the spider: a thick, weighty black shadow hovering in the web, its yellow eyes open, its many legs already beginning to thrash. Another man might have killed Love with a gun, or even a rifle; another man might have used a sharp hunting knife; but Gideon made no concession to the hideousness of the creature other than his gloves—fine, soft, beautifully fitting leather gloves with suede ornamentation, custom-made to accommodate his large hands.

The thing made a high shrieking noise, not unlike a bat, and stabbed repeatedly at him with its mouth (which contained teeth, or teethlike, and very sharp, serrations in its jaw), and kicked wildly at him with its many legs (which, though scrawny, were really quite elastically strong), and thrashed about so violently that Gideon nearly lost his balance and stumbled backward. He had not calculated exactly how to kill it—strangling was impossible, it hadn't a neck—but in the excitement of the moment his gloved hands acted as if by instinct, as if, in the dim Bellefleur past, they had killed many a Love, just by holding it fast, gripping it fast, and squeezing. . . .

Despite the struggle Love put up, despite the spider's remarkable size, the episode lasted no more than two or three minutes. By then of course Leah was awake. And had lit the kerosene lamp on her bedside table. And was sitting up in bed, the covers held tightly over her breasts, her hair in heavy darkly-red curtains, frizzled at its ends with alarm, on either side of her beautiful pale face. When Gideon, panting, finally turned to her, and with a magnificent disdainful gesture let drop what remained of Love on the very end of her bed, on a folded-back cotton quilt, Leah stared at him sullenly and said, in a voice so soft he had to stoop to hear, "*Now* look what you've done, Gideon."

The Nameless Child

He was excited because he could see that the pond had changed greatly since last autumn. Everywhere, on all sides, there was new life. Cattails. Water willow. Burr reeds. An uneven line of tiny alder sprung out of nowhere—out of the marshy soil. He was excited, tramping about in his boots, his woollen shirt sleeves rolled up to his elbows the way Ewan often rolled *his* sleeves up. But within a few minutes he grew breathless, and had to stand very still. It was the muck that exhausted him, pulling at his boots, sucking down as he struggled to walk at the very edge of the pond where the mud was softest.

Do you remember, Raphael whispered. Do you know who I am . . . ?

The pond had changed. There were water lilies in bloom, and dragonflies hovering in the air. A rich wet odor. He couldn't breathe it deeply enough. That winter he had been sick, he'd been sick more than once, the last time with bronchitis and a high fever (so that March passed in a hot delirium, like a rapid shallow stream in which nothing is distinct except the swift movement, the passage, itself), and so it sometimes hurt him to breathe sharply; but the smell of the pond was so rich and dark and good he felt comforted.

Mink Pond. *His* pond. *His* secret.

The shouts of his brothers and cousins rang out, some distance away. At the creek, most likely. Playing at war, playing at shooting one another, crouching behind boulders, poking their heads out incautiously, stretching their mouths to jeer. He had let them run ahead of him, he had adroitly eluded them, and now they had no idea where he was, and would never think of him, would let him alone. . . . Do you remember who I am, Raphael said without moving his lips.

How odd, how surprising, the unanticipated growth of the pond. Of course it was deeper than last August, and larger by some six or ten feet all around, because of the thaw, and the cascades of water that plummeted down from the mountains. But it had grown in other ways. There were more cattails, more reeds, innumerable foot-high water willow; and the creamy-white lilies; and horsetails and marsh marigold and pennywort and spike rushes. Many insects. Dizzy with the sunshine. The wet warmth. Dragonflies, diving beetles, water striders. Frogs. As Raphael approached the edge of the pond one frog after another leapt into the water. The water was clear enough for him to watch their quick deft progress as they swam away from him, toward the darker, deeper water at the center of the pond.

His brothers' and his cousins' shouts. Girls' voices as well. And, cutting through their raucous noise, which had the power to annoy but not to disturb him, the terrible, jarring sound of a chain saw. (The giant elms and oaks near the manor were being cut back, after the winter's damage. There was evidently money for that now. And for repairs on the slate roof, which had been leaking badly for so many years.)

Then the chain saw was silent, and the pond's sound—which was not a voice, not even a whisper, but an almost inaudible lapping or bubbling murmur—rose to encompass him. It was soothing like music, like music without words. Though the pond could not speak and could not, perhaps, exactly *remember,* it was allowing Raphael to know that his presence was sensed.

His official name—which he had been shown once or twice, on documents with gold seals and the Bellefleur coat of arms in red and black wax —was Raphael Lucien Bellefleur II. Within the family he was Raphael. A few of the children called him Rafe. (Though most of the time they called him nothing—they did not concern themselves with him.) Alone in his sickbed when even the tiresome hired nurse was out of the room he had no name at all; nor did he have a name by the pond. He slipped into invisibility, nameless.

Sick, his eyes rolling back in his head, he had calmed himself thinking of his pond. Of course it was frozen over—frozen over and packed with heavy snow—seven or eight feet of snow—and if he had been allowed, as of course he wasn't, to go out on showshoes with the other boys, he might not have known where the pond was, even: though he should have remembered the configuration of hemlock and mountain maple and ash down behind the cemetery. In those brief dark winter days the pond was hidden from sight but Raphael, pretending drowsiness even when his mother and his favorite sister Yolande were with him, saw on the insides of his reddened eyelids the pond of last autumn, defiantly visible, its surface winking like scales in the sun. His pond. Where the Doan boy had tried to kill him. *His* pond. Which had taken him in, even the outlandish surprise of him, a yelping thrashing drowning child, a terrible coward, plunging and sinking in the water (which had turned muddy as if with disgust), clumsy as a heifer.

He had comforted himself with the pond. It seemed to him that he could bring his temperature down simply by approaching the pond, walking in it, past his ankles, past his knees, past his groin. . . . The soft featureless black mud took him in, but did not draw him off balance. The pellucid water, though agitated by his clumsiness, did not turn cloudy.

Sometimes he woke from a small dream and shook his head in surprise, that so much time had passed. The dream might have begun in midafternoon; but when he opened his eyes it might be dusk. Aunt Leah's cat Mahalaleel frequently slept at the foot of his bed, and it was remarkable how long the cat could sleep. He sometimes twitched, and shuddered, and made kittenlike mewing sounds, and his great ears trembled, and his large knobby paws kneaded the quilt; but he slept deeply and profoundly and even if Raphael moved his legs or adjusted his pillows Mahalaleel did not wake. That's because a cat dreams so hard, the nurse told him. They dream of—oh, all kinds of things—I suppose it's pictures mainly—and they do a lot of running. You can tell.

It was good luck, Raphael knew, that Mahalaleel came up to his room, to sleep on his bed on those dark winter afternoons. Morna said that a cat might creep into a baby's room and jump right into the cradle and suck the baby's breath away, so the cat shouldn't be allowed in Leah's room with the new baby, or even in Raphael's room, because he slept so much. Yolande said that was idiotic: Cousin Morna repeated the stupid things Aunt Aveline told her: *of course* Mahalaleel was good luck, because of his beautiful eyes, and his beautiful fur. But when Raphael leaned down to pet the cat he sometimes made a vexed little sound, deep in his throat, that showed he didn't want to be touched at that moment.

Bronchitis and a high fever, running for four days. Dr. Jensen, and the woman with the carrot-colored hair, hired out of a Nautauga Falls hospital, and brought up to the castle with a surprising number of boxes (she liked, she said, to have her own things about her—she'd thought that Bellefleur Castle would be cold and damp and frightening, judged from the outside), the expense immaterial. (Raphael overheard the adults conferring. *The expense,* Gideon told Ewan, *is immaterial.*) When she believed Raphael was asleep the woman actually got down on her knees and prayed, whispering: Dear God, don't let this boy die on me, don't let him die, I know You wouldn't play such a cruel trick on me. . . .

Of course he hadn't died. With a thrill of contempt he thought of how far he was from dying: how, walking into the pond, he had felt the cool buoyancy, the springiness, of the water which would never *allow* him to drown.

That day, something had struck him on the forehead with a terrible, incalculable force, and he had fallen off the raft and into the water, so quickly, so suddenly, it was as if the world had heaved itself sideways and sloughed him off, insubstantial, feathery, as a burr. He must have shouted, he must have cried out—he heard a child's astonished scream —but there was no time to think, to see, as the dark water rose over his mouth, his nose, his wide staring eyes. What was happening could not be happening and yet: and yet, even in the water, thrashing about helplessly in the water, he was struck by another rock that crashed down upon him from high in the air, and the dark mud at the bottom of the pond rose up to him. His body struggled. His arms, his legs. He was gasping for air where no air existed, where there was only water, water and mud, still he sobbed, swallowing and choking, raw and desperate and wild and doomed he sobbed, for Raphael knew he was drowning even when he no longer knew that he was Raphael who would drown; he reasoned clearly with a part of his mind which was curiously detached from the ugly thrashing about (as if floating in midair some distance away, but sightless, having no eyes with which to see) that the Doan boy had come here to kill him, to deliberately kill him—that he *would* kill him, and no one would ever know.

But he hadn't been killed. He hadn't drowned.

Squatting at the edge of the pond on this wet sunshine-rich day, his lungs grateful for all the air they could draw in, however sharp, however chilly, it might be, Raphael found himself staring at a small school of very small fish a few feet away. Very tiny fish!—darting, dipping, suddenly reversing direction, and then again reversing direction, so close to him now that he could have reached out, and scooped them up in the palm of his hand. Pickerel . . . ? He did not move, staring at them. Such tiny creatures, near-transparent, hardly longer than the nail of his smallest finger. . . .

He had been saved by entering their element, by learning to breathe in the water: suddenly lithe and slippery as a fish, wriggling away from the deadly surface, away from the hazy ceiling of light through which more rocks plunged, like gigantic murderous raindrops: he swam under the raft, and clutched at it with fingers that were immediately emboldened and strong enough to hold him in place. And then there was silence. A vast profound silence. Through which, gradually, the pond's voice, the pond's subtle rhythmic murmurous voice, rose. He had not drowned, he had not even lost consciousness despite the wound to his head. But he was no longer awake. He was no longer Raphael Lucien Bellefleur II. He remained there, beneath the raft (slatted with hazy light, for the logs were fitted very clumsily together), his lungs cautious in their new element, his lips tightly pursed together, waiting, not waiting, in a trance of such calm, such delectable bliss, in which minnows of light and a deeper blanketing dark contended, that when the danger was past—when the danger was long past—he roused himself reluctantly, and swam out from under the raft.

He had had no time to scream *Help me,* and indeed his voice was choked by the water, by the pond's surprisingly dense, stubborn substance, and yet the pond had helped him: perhaps even before Raphael himself had known the magnitude of the danger he was in. The pond had embraced him, had buoyed him up, had given him shelter, had allowed him to breathe even in those clouds of faint swirling mud. It had hidden him, it had protected him. It had saved his life.

How unreal, how *uninteresting* was the world to which he returned, an incalculable period of time later . . . ! Shaking his wet hair out of his face as he stumbled to shore, wiping at his eyes, gasping for breath. His body was ungainly, staggering beneath the renewed weight of the world that must be borne, a column of air stretching upward, into the featureless sky, and at the same time pressing down heavily upon his head and frail shoulders.

An effort, to lift his feet. To make his way back home.

Where they would cry out with alarm at the sight of him, and ask him what had happened. . . . (An accidental fall, his forehead striking a rock, his clothing soaked.)

Unreal, uninteresting, that world. The castle. The Bellefleurs. His people.

Raphael Lucien Bellefleur II.

The world stretched away in every direction and the pond, his pond, was at its center. But he could tell no one about this: nor could he tell them about the Doan boy pitching rocks: they would make a fuss, they would stir the air with their emotion, their anger. Perhaps they would even want to take revenge upon the boy. The pond had saved Raphael, it had hidden him, had borne him aloft when danger was past, and so he must not want revenge: he was fated not to die and so it should not matter —it *did* not matter—what violence another human being had committed against him.

The tiny fish had disappeared into the shadow of some floating pond weed (which, too, was new to Raphael's eyes), and now, on the opposite shore, a marsh wren had poked its head shyly through the rushes. Raphael, motionless, clasped his arms around his knees.

He waited. He had the rest of his life.

The Walled Garden

It was in the lush ruins of the old garden, behind the mossy fifteen-foot granite walls, that Leah learned from Germaine what the nature of her task must be.

"What do you want of me? What is *wanted* of me?" Leah asked, excited.

The baby stared at her, with those remarkable eyes. And clenched and unclenched her little fists.

"Yes, Germaine? Yes? What?"

Leah leaned over the gondola-cradle, hardly daring to breathe. At these times the baby's powers were such that Leah could feel a heartbeat not her own, a wild demanding pulse not her own, throbbing inside her body. It was almost as though the baby had not yet been born, but remained, still, in her womb, drawing nourishment from her and yet giving her nourishment as well, pumping blood into every part of her.

"Yes? Germaine? What do you want of me? Has it anything to do with—with the house, the family, the fortune, the land?" Leah whispered.

When no one was around the baby girl stared quite directly at her. Leah felt almost faint, staring into those eyes. The baby's lips moved too but no words emerged: only gurgling bubbling sounds, and high-pitched shrieks, which Leah could not decipher.

"Yes? What do you want of me? Oh, yes—please—I won't be afraid—" Leah begged.

Visitors appeared, and Germaine became a baby again; oversized, to be sure, but not exceptional. She wheezed, she bawled, she wet her diapers, she kicked her summer blanket off, like any temperamental infant. So that Leah became a mother again, quite eagerly she took on the role, changing diapers, rocking the cradle, accepting the fulsome compliments she knew Germaine detested (ah, how fast your little girl is growing! why, it's hard to believe she's grown so much since—has it been only a week?). She held the baby in her arms, staggering beneath the surprising weight, for which she was never prepared, and blushing, laughing with pride, ah, yes she *is* growing, she has a prodigious appetite, she sucks up more milk than the twins combined and still she's hungry for more!

Then the visitors left, the chatter faded, and Leah sent the servant girls away too, so that she and her daughter could be alone. And she would say, almost timidly, peering over the side of the immense cradle: "Did I make a fool out of myself with them? Did I embarrass you? Should I have sent them away at once—?"

It was on an unnaturally warm day in May that, half-dozing, her arm slung across the baby in the cradle, Leah realized what her task would be.

And how simple, how clear!—how lucid, Germaine's wish!

The family must regain all the land they had lost since the time of Jean-Pierre Bellefleur. Not only must they regain all the land—a considerable empire!—but they must labor to prove the innocence of Jean-Pierre Bellefleur II as well.

"Ah, of course!" Leah cried, astounded. "Of course."

She rose to her feet, greatly moved. Her heart swung back and forth like a pendulum.

"Why—of course."

The baby watched her closely. The small brilliant eyes did not blink.

"How could I have been so slow, so stupid," Leah murmured, "not to have understood until now. . . . The Bellefleur name: the Bellefleur empire. As it once was. As it should be, today. And poor Jean-Pierre— an innocent man rotting away in the Powhatassie prison—*how* could my family have forgotten him all these years!"

She was to be accused of reckless, improvident thinking by her mother-in-law Cornelia, and by her own mother, and even, it was said, by her husband; but in fact she had brooded over the situation of the Bellefleurs for some time, even before the birth of Germaine. How had it come about, by what sort of mismanagement and bad luck, that the Bellefleurs, who had once owned one-third of the mountain region, and thousands of acres in the Valley, had lost so much? How had it come about, by what devilish conspiracies of their enemies (and in certain cases it was probable that their "friends" had joined forces with their enemies to cheat them), and outright, blatant maneuvering, that they had been forced to sell great parcels of land, hundreds of acres at once . . . ? It wasn't simply the Jean-Pierre case that had gone so badly in court: Leah learned from Elvira that a number of small cases had gone against the Bellefleurs, having to do with property boundaries and mineral rights and laborers' compensation. While at one point local judges were likely to find *for* the Bellefleurs even when, perhaps, they were not exactly in the right (Leah admitted that the original Jean-Pierre had been involved in questionable doings, and even Raphael, the most scrupulous of businessmen, the most deliberate of gentlemen, had evidently overstepped his rights upon occasion) as the decades passed the Bellefleurs slipped out of favor, somehow lost their hold, suffered rather than profited by their exaggerated reputation (but what was the Bellefleur "reputation," exactly?—now that Leah lived in the castle, now that she truly *was* a Bellefleur, she could not recall what outsiders said). Judge after judge had found against them; juries were even less reliable (being open to bribes and intimidation by the Bellefleurs' enemies); after the astonishing verdict of guilty was handed down to Jean-Pierre II, and his two subsequent appeals rejected, it was commonly said in the family that no Bellefleur could expect justice in this part of the world. At the age of eighteen Hiram was sent off to Princeton, to get a good liberal arts education, then to enter law school so that he might, someday, be elected or appointed to the bench, and help to make right the outrageous situation his family had to endure—but nothing came of it, Hiram professed to be bored by the law, could not force himself to study (he much preferred speculating, on paper, and acquired prodigious fortunes by way of phantom investments in the stock market), and simply returned to help run the estate; and that was that. The Bellefleurs no longer had powerful friends and acquaintances in the government. The governor, for instance, was a man no one in the family knew —and this was the man, Leah exclaimed, who could pardon Jean-Pierre if he wished, at any time! The governor had such rights, and in the days of Raphael Bellefleur they would certainly have been employed in the family's favor; but now everything was changed. "We should place one of our own people in the governor's mansion," Leah said boldly. "We should have a senator. We should regain all that land—why, if you look at one of Raphael's old maps, it's enough to make you burst into tears, what we've been cheated of! They want to take *everything* from us." (And here she sometimes unrolled one of the four-foot-long parchment maps, covered with spidery lines and notations, which she had come across in an old trunk otherwise given over to someone's soiled cavalry uniforms —absurd ermine hat, green trousers, scarlet aiguillettes, boots, buckles, stained white gloves—during those queer elated restless weeks of Germaine's early infancy when Leah carried her baby about everywhere despite the baby's weight, prowling the castle late at night, humming and singing to quiet the baby (who was capable from the very first of astonishing cries and paroxysms of rage), her own footsteps springy, exuberant, triumphant, as if given spirit by Germaine's ceaseless vitality, which wore out everyone else.) "And if we placed someone in the governor's mansion, there would be no problem about getting a pardon for Uncle Jean-Pierre," she would say.

The maps, the old maps, surveyors' maps mainly: what a kingdom they had encompassed! It was indeed, as Leah said, enough to make one burst into tears. She was able to stir grandfather Noel to emotion, and to make the otherwise skeptical and lethargic Hiram angry, by pointing out with a pencil or an old quill pen (rummaged from Raphael's desk) all that they *had* owned at one time, and what was taken from them, piece by piece, parcel by parcel, the very best land in some cases, along the river, and mineral-rich holdings in the Mount Kittery area: it was a tale both Noel and Hiram knew well, but to have it pointed out to them was another matter, by Gideon's excited, ferocious young wife, who did not hesitate to interrupt them in midsentence when they attempted feebly to explain the circumstances behind one or another of the forced sales, most of which had taken place in Jeremiah's time; and it *was* another matter to see, as Leah quickly sketched in for them to see, how the original holdings, those two million acres, were broken down into jigsaw-puzzle parts that *could* be unified again.

"Here, and here, and here, and along here," Leah murmured, tracing imaginary lines, squinting as she bent over the stiff paper, which she frequently had to lift away from her baby's greedy clutching hands ("Ah, that little pest, she's into *everything,* wants to put *everything* in her mouth!" Leah exclaimed), as the men pressed near. "This area here, you see?—it's now owned by the McNievans—and along the river here, isn't this the Gromwell Quarry—and this triangular section here, from White Sulphur Springs to Silver Lake—do we know who owns it?—you can see how easily all this could be brought together again, the way it really should be. The land is all one, it belongs in one section, there's something unnatural and insulting about the way it's broken up, don't you agree?"

She was so beautiful in her fever of righteousness, and her slate-blue eyes shone so magnificently, how could the men respond except by saying, "Yes, yes, we agree, *yes,* you're absolutely right."

The garden, the walled garden. A sunny hazy jumble of kisses and warm embraces, scoldings, vermilion flowers, yellow and white butterflies, maple seeds flying in the heat of May. A rich blue sky in which giant faces hovered. Isn't she a beautiful baby! Isn't she big! Intoxicating odors: bananas and cream, raspberry jam, chocolate cake, lemon squeezed into tea. Honey-and-milk, greedily sucked.

Something mashed on a spoon. The spoon's metallic taste, and its hardness. A sudden rage, like an explosion: kicking, shrieking, the food thrown away.

Doesn't she have a mind of her own, Leah laughed, wiping the hem of her dress with a napkin.

The walled garden, those warm spring days. Weather-stained remains of statuary imported from Italy by great-great-grandfather Raphael: a startled and chagrined Hebe, the size of a mortal woman, her hooded eyes downcast and her slender arms weakly shielding her body; a crouching marble Cupid with bulging eyes and a sweet leering smile and wings whose curly feathers had been fashioned, with great care, by an anonymous sculptor enamored of detail; a comely Adonis whose right cheek was discolored, as if by inky tears, and whose base was overgrown with briars. (And of course the baby stumbled into the briars, despite Leah's sharp eye. And of course there were heart-stopping wails heard everywhere, so that several of the children, playing by the lake, ran back to see who was being murdered.)

The walled garden where Leah contemplated her maps, drinking coffee for hours, nibbling at pastries, rocking Germaine in her lap and humming to her. A constant sound, a constant music, punctuated by others' voices—Christabel (who wanted to hold the baby, who begged to be allowed to feed the baby, even to change her diapers) and Bromwell (who, until Leah put a stop to it suddenly, had been weighing and measuring and minutely examining his baby sister day by day, and experimenting with her ability to focus her eyes, to grasp at objects, to recognize people, to smile, to respond to simple queries and games and stimuli —heat, sound, color, tickling, pinching—of various degrees of intensity: he was keeping a fastidious record of the baby's growth for scientific purposes, he protested, angry with his mother for her ignorant proprietary attitude which was, he said, characteristic of peasants) and grandmother Cornelia (who spent a great deal of time simply staring at the baby but who was reluctant to hold her, even to touch her, even to be a witness to her diaper-changing or bath—"Those green eyes just look *through* me," she murmured, "*through* me and *through* me, and never come to an end"), and cousin Vernon (whose straggly ticklish beard and singsong voice as he recited his poetry elicited immediate smiles from the baby) and Noel and Hiram and Lily and Aveline and Garnet Hecht (who frequently helped out with Germaine when Leah was in the mood—and she was not always in the mood—to tolerate the girl's cringing manner) and the other children, the many other children. . . . Of course Gideon appeared from time to time: towerlike, colossal, imperious: with the right (which none of the other men seemed to have, not even grandfather Noel) to seize Germaine in his hands and toss her up into the sky so that squeals and shrieks rang out everywhere in the garden. And there were strangers' voices, strangers' faces, too many to count.

Only aunt Veronica did not appear in the garden. For she was in perpetual mourning, it was said, and allowed herself to emerge from her suite of rooms only at night, and then of course the baby was put to bed.

Sunshine, bumblebees, mourning doves pecking eagerly at crumbs, scattering into the air when Germaine approached, waving her arms. The big cat Mahalaleel flopping onto the grass and rolling over onto his back, so that Leah or one of the children might rub his stomach. (How quickly one of his invisible nails could catch in someone's skin!—it was always an accident, and there was always a tiny drop of blood.) Dragonflies, crickets, rabbits startled out from bushes, garter snakes, black-capped chickadees. The remains of a box-hedge maze, in which the children ran wild, pretending to be lost. There was a dying monkey tree someone had shipped back from South America, and a Russian olive, no longer flourishing, planted, according to family tradition, by aunt Veronica's lost love. There was a gigantic cedar of Lebanon with more than thirty limbs, each the size of a tree of ordinary proportions. There were, at the rear of the garden, wych-elms, silver firs, white spruce. And ivy and climbing roses that grew where they would, choking out other plants.

The garden, where Leah scribbled drafts of letters, bent over an old lap desk she'd found in an attic: to attorneys, to judges, to the governor of the state. Scribbled her letters, or dictated to Garnet Hecht. (By way of Elvira she learned that Jean-Pierre had been fearful for months that something terrible would happen to him—he hadn't any enemies of his own but the family had enemies, and it was well known that the Varrell brothers had planned some sort of attack; by way of Jean-Pierre's brothers Noel and Hiram she learned in some detail of the judges' prejudices—the first judge, Phineas Petrie, who had handed down the sentence of life plus ninety-nine years plus ninety-nine years plus ninety-nine years plus ninety-nine years plus ninety-nine years plus ninety-nine years plus ninety-nine years plus ninety-nine years plus ninety-nine years plus ninety-nine years in a voice, witnesses claimed, of unctuous cruelty, had a history of disliking the Bellefleurs because, decades earlier, a young Petrie soldier and a young Bellefleur soldier had gone off together on the Big Horn Expedition of 1876, the Petrie boy under the command of Lieutenant-Colonel Custer and the Bellefleur boy under the command of General Terry, and one had perished and the other had survived; the judge who heard the first appeal, Osborne Lane, had been rejected by a beautiful young woman who later became involved with Samuel Bellefleur, and so naturally he detested the very name Bellefleur; and the judge who heard the second appeal, and who dismissed it so rudely, was an old political rival of Senator Washington Payne's—the senator having been financed generously by Bellefleur money, or so rumor had it.) Leah read off her letters to the children, and sometimes stopped in midsentence, and crumpled the stiff sheets of stationery and threw them to the ground. "I am the only one who cares any longer," she said angrily. "The rest have given up! They should be ashamed of themselves, *Bellefleurs* who have *given up!*"

It was in the garden, half-dozing in the slanted honey-warm sunshine, that Leah recalled Germaine's birth: no more than an hour of labor, and then the miracle of the baby, put into her arms, nursing vigorously at once; and Gideon at her bedside gripping her hand. You were the easiest of all, Leah murmured. You were no trouble at all. Why I hardly *bled.* . . .

Now there was a mossy stripe on her belly. And her belly, her waist, her thighs, were flaccid. And her breasts drooped. But she was losing weight gradually, already her ankles and calves were back to normal, and her face showed only a few lines of strain. How good you look, Leah, people said. And to Gideon: How beautiful your wife looks. . . . (And Gideon smiled stiffly and thanked them, for what else could he do?)

The garden, the hum of insects. Mealtimes, naps. Kittens rolling and tumbling underfoot. A game of peek-a-boo around the sundial, around the lonely towering statue of Hebe. Under the low-hanging branches of the cedar of Lebanon. (Where, one morning, they discovered a partly devoured opossum Mahalaleel had dragged over the garden wall.) Leah ripping open envelopes, letting them fall to the terrace floor. Leah calling impatiently for one of the servants. Leah bumping her nose against the baby's pug nose, or wiping the baby's mouth, or sauntering about with the baby on her hip, listing to one side. Leah shaking the rattle—of carved hardwood, with coral and silver ornamentation—that was aunt Veronica's present to Germaine. Or blowing up a red balloon and allowing it to streak away, fluttering, falling to the grass as Germaine squealed. Leah hauling Germaine up, out of the brittle dead leaves in the old fountain, her voice ringing, Now what have you done, for God's sake, do you want to blind yourself?—as the baby cried.

It was in the garden one May morning, when Gideon was leaving for a five-day trip to the Midwest, in connection with a number of horses he was selling, that Leah first brought up the subject of his uncle Jean-Pierre, who must be released from prison, and the necessity of regaining all the land—*all* the land—the Bellefleurs had lost. Gideon was bent over the baby's cradle, one forefinger gripped by the baby's surprisingly strong fingers; he made a grunting sound that might have been an assent.

"Then you'll help me? Gideon?" Leah said.

She moved to slide her arm around his waist, then hesitated. Gideon was staring at his daughter's greeny-hazel eyes, that so powerfully seized him: that seemed almost to grip him, to fix him where he stood. He had never quite comprehended the fact of the twins, the fact that *he* had fathered Christabel and Bromwell, and it was beyond him, it was dismayingly beyond him, that *this* baby was his as well. Of course it was all ordinary, even routine, he had even helped choose her name, everyone had behaved matter-of-factly about the birth (he knew of course about the difficult labor, he knew nothing about the birth itself), these things happened all the time, it was better to let the mind skate lightly over them, not to puzzle or brood. . . . When he pulled his finger away the baby's grip tightened.

"Ah, she's strong! She's wonderful, she's so quick!" Gideon laughed. "She's *strong.*"

"You'll help me?" Leah said.

Straightening, Gideon brushed his hair back from his forehead with both his hands, in a brusque movement, and smiled toward Leah without exactly looking at her. "Of course," he said, "whatever you want."

"Whatever I want . . . ?" Leah said, sliding her arm around his waist.

"Whatever, whatever, whatever," Gideon said, backing away.

Bloody Run

On the bluff above Lake Noir where wild lilac grew in the midst of second-growth pines, beside the foot-wide Bloody Run (in early June still fed by melting snow on higher ground, and plunging with an eerie guttural music down the bluff's granite outcroppings, in a half-dozen frothy cascades, to the dark water ninety feet below), on the very earth where once, on other June evenings, others, other Bellefleurs, love-sickened or love-obsessed or loveless, stood to gaze across the lake's moody planes to the forest on the far shore and the crescent of Silver Lake in the distance, luminescent even when the moon was smothered by cloud—on the very soil, tufted with wild grass and saxifrage and clover, where Jean-Pierre Bellefleur in his middle years stood dreaming of a girl, a girl's face, he had not seen for three decades, and Hepatica Bellefleur first succumbed to the embrace of that swarthy bearded man, now nameless, who courted her with such vigor and eventually won her, to the misfortune of both, and Violet Odlin Bellefleur, pregnant for what was probably the tenth time (there were so many brief pregnancies, so many miscarriages, and several infants dead at birth or surviving only a few days, she had not only lost count but considered it part of her obligation as a wife and as a dutiful obedient Christian to withhold from any activity so conscious as counting), walked in the moonlight, restless, murmuring aloud, occasionally punctuating the low-throated noise of Bloody Run by peals of girlish laughter, as she rehearsed not the vigorous rejection of Hayes Whittier's proposal to her, which was so inevitable, so ineludible, she need not have groped after the words, but the acceptance which she knew she would not give (no matter that her rejection would destroy for the second time her husband's hopes for the governorship, and perhaps his spirit as well—Violet *was* a virtuous wife, incapable of imagining herself otherwise), and Veronica Bellefleur strolled in secret with that

Swedish nobleman who called himself Ragnar Norst and who explained
away his dusky complexion and his dark liquid thick-lashed eyes by alluding merrily to some "Persian" blood on his mother's side of the family,
and Ewan Bellefleur lay vigorously upon one or another of his anonymous girls, in the heat, the near-maniacal obsessive heat of his precocious
and prolonged adolescence, which was quite a serious matter to Ewan
most of the time and to his innumerable hapless girls all of the time, and
Vernon Bellefleur wandered and was to continue to wander, a book in
one back pocket, papers inked with ideas for poems, stray words that
struck him as musical, first lines of love sonnets—in whose convoluted
syntax his cousin Gideon's wife was to emerge as one *Lara,* the supreme
and unearthly love of the poet's life, the only reason for the poet's life
—in his other pockets or in hand, growing moist in hand, as insomnia and
dread of sleep compelled him to climb up along Bloody Run though he
was quickly breathless, and beggarlice and burdocks stuck to his trouser
legs, and his heart contracted with the knowledge that all that he did was
futile, and Yolande, unknown to him, was to walk, in the sunshine, half-
dreaming of—of who?—of what?—sometimes the seductive image of her
reverie possessed a face, a man's face, her uncle Gideon's?—or the face
of a stranger?—or that of a young man from a cattle farm on the Innisfail
Road whom she rarely saw; and sometimes the image wasn't a man's face
at all but her own, uncannily transformed, shining with unexpected
ethereal beauty like that of a May poplar (supreme in its golden-green-
radiant glory for a few days, before the other trees come into leaf), not
only shining but somehow magnified, her face spread out semitranspar-
ent against the lake, the forest, the sky itself, arching over *her* as she
paused intoxicated with the promise of—the heady rich seductive promise of—of whatever it was—whatever it would turn out to be, that image
worthy of Yolande Bellefleur's devotion: here the lovers pressed mutely
together, ground themselves helplessly together, clutching each other,
whimpering, *Don't move, don't move,* for if nothing happens, if nothing
actually happens and no seed is released then Gideon hasn't been unfaithful, not precisely: and there will be no consequences.

One June night, beside Bloody Run, on the hill above Lake Noir, and
not for the first time in this secret place: Gideon and Garnet locked
together, their straining bodies joined, wed, implacably fused together:
Gideon whispering *Don't move* like a prayer.

His eyes shut tight. Entering her, not breathing. Ah, the slightest
move! The slightest error! She lies very still, gripping him. Breasts
pressed flat against his chest. Unmoving, unprotesting. They must avoid
the slightest friction. . . . He has forbidden her to say that she loves him,
it is a wild little snarl of a song he doesn't want to hear, any more than
he wants to see her pale rose-petal of a face, bruised and torn and
befuddled by the mere size of him, and what he must perform. *Don't move,*
he whimpers. Their heads are a few feet from Bloody Run but already
they are unaware of the rivulet's gurgling. They are unaware of the lake

below, or the sky above, which is dissolving slowly in a rather chill ecstasy of moonlight. Naturally there will be consequences but the lovers are locked too fiercely together to comprehend even that they are locked together, that they belong in two separate bodies and that there is danger, grave danger, in what they are doing, impaled upon the moment, the present moment, the past and future forgotten: everything else forgotten.

Every part of his immense body, every cell, quivering, about to discharge itself. They must remain motionless and innocent as the dead. As figures on the tombs of the dead. Breathing slowed, slowed. A preternatural calm. They must. *Don't,* he murmurs, his eyeballs aching, his hands fumbling to hold her still. (He feels her prominent pelvis bones against his thumbs.) That skinny little thing Garnet, who would be able to love such a skinny thing, isn't she pathetic, of course I'm fond of her and she is pretty but isn't she pathetic, so in love with *you.* . . . But then all the women are in love with Gideon Bellefleur aren't they. . . .

Stop, Gideon whispers.

He is so large, so swollen, so tense with this piercing, terrible pleasure, which wants only to shout madly and dispel the night, that the girl's neck and backbone might easily snap; so he must hold himself as rigid as possible, his knees trembling with the unnatural effort, an icy sweat broken across his forehead and back. In his mind's eye he sees, jumbled together with a dozen other things, two horseshoes where his jaws should be, pressing, pressing together with awful violence. *Stop. Wait. Don't.* His ribs are steel bands that have begun to quiver so finely, so minutely, that they are in danger of shattering: it is almost intolerable that the girl's stunned fingers should grope against them. His neck is a rod, his penis is a rod: his lungs contract with infinite cunning for if they swell suddenly all is lost: his eyes, held fast behind his glaring lids, have begun to bulge and are in danger of starting out of his head. His penis is a rod, an anguished rod, pushing slowly into the girl, pushing her down into the grass, into the earth, moment by moment, beat by beat. There is no stopping it. There is no stopping. But he whispers, *Stop* through his gritted teeth.

The needle's eye, the needle's eye, tiny voices sing, mixed in with the sound of the tumbling little brook, and Garnet, hearing them, instinctively draws in her breath, and tightens her grip—her slender arms across his back, her surprisingly strong legs against his. The needle's eye has caught many a smiling lass and now . . . and now it has caught you. . . . At the wedding, at the very altar, she had nudged against him and given him a look that made him feel faint, whispering, You don't love me: you've had so many women! You don't love me! In the dazzling white gown of moiré silk, hundreds of pearls sewn to it, her veil more delicate than the crystalline stars of Lake Noir's deep ice, so quivering with life that the rich powerful beats of her heart were visible in her eyes, she simply stared at him: and her wide beautiful mouth relaxed, but almost imperceptibly, so that he knew he was saved. She ran recklessly to the edge of the cliff and dove off, her body plunging downward so gracefully, so perfectly, that it seemed she must be willing it: and he wanted to run after and throw himself into the water beside her, but he could not move. The needle's eye, the needle's eye . . . Her head, a colt's head, came up to bump his jaw. And there was laughter. You don't love me, you are such a bully, the voice rang out, teasing him almost to a pitch of madness, I will never forgive you for what you did to Love, I will never forget, laughing shrilly as he tried to undress her and she wriggled away to run heavy-footed about the bedroom of the hotel suite, and he gave chase, his laughter frightened, an unfamiliar laughter, his arms clumsily out-stretched, and then she was slapping at him, harder than she should have slapped, and her skin was hot to the touch, and her eyes glared feverishly, and she kissed him full on the lips, sucking and biting, and then reared back, and pushed him with the heel of her palm, and looked at him for the first time, her face distended with exaggerated revulsion—Oh, just look at you, just look, grizzly! Baboon! Look at the hair, the frizz, on you, oh, my God *look,* her voice rose gaily, wildly, and a coarse bark of startled laughter escaped from her, How can you!—how is it possible!—I didn't marry a baboon, did I! Gideon, stricken, ashamed, did not at first run after her but tried to say—what was it he tried to say—stammering, mumbling, his overheated face going hotter still with the impact of his bride's disgust—tried to say that she must have seen him swimming, hadn't she—he couldn't help himself—the hair on his chest, and on his belly—he couldn't help it—he was sorry—but she must have seen him swimming, hadn't she, and other men as well— Rain like demons' merry insubstantial faces pressed against the bedroom window, Gideon halfway thought in his confusion that people in the hotel knew about them and had somehow climbed up to stare, or were they his friends, his brothers and cousins, come to mock him, while Leah in a distant corner of the room crouched, her body rosy with candlelight, gleaming as if it were, like his, covered with a fine oily film of perspiration, and then she burst into tears, and he hurried to her and embraced her, surprised at how small she was, in his arms, and how passionately she pressed her face against his chest Oh I love you, Gideon, I love you I love you—

Don't move, Gideon says faintly.

Don't don't don't move.

The girl, exhausted, sobbing, lies motionless beneath him, but can-not relax her grip on him, in terror of the voices so close to her head in the wild grass, and the presence that sprawls beside them, Don't stop, go on, what the hell are you doing, you two, do you think I don't know about this, do you think I haven't been spying all these months, go ahead, go right ahead, what a pair of idiots, what a pair of contemptible idiots, Leah laughing angrily, jubilantly, a straw or a blade of grass between her teeth so that she can tickle poor Gideon, drawing the invisible blade from his ear to his lips and back again, tickling, tickling, poking the blade into his ear, drawing it down along his vein-taut neck, along his shoulder, slick with sweat, Do you think I don't know everything that goes on in my house, do you think I haven't seen you two looking at each other or whispering together, what a pair of idiots, drawing the teasing blade across his back, along his backbone, and then suddenly, without warning, her warm moist bold hand falls upon his back, rubs his backbone, rubs at the very base of his spine, at that small knob at the base of his spine, rubbing with such robust lewd energy that Gideon is at once plunged— catapulted—into a delirium from which, out of which, he can never hope to return, though even in his final paroxysm he begs *No please don't stop wait no no—*

The Poet

      Germaine's great-uncle Vernon, the poet, prematurely grizzly, sweet-faced, with the mismatched eyes that so delighted her (Vernon loved to squat before her, closing one eye and then the other, the blue eye, the brown eye, the blue eye, as the child gasped and muttered and waved her fists, sometimes shutting both *her* eyes in the excitement of the game, squealing with laughter that grew wilder as the game accelerated and the brown eye, the blue eye, the brown eye, the blue eye opened and shut more and more rapidly, until tears streamed down Vernon's cheeks and were lost in his beard) was said, openly, with that Bellefleur "frankness" that caused so much grief, to be a disappointment to the family and especially to his father: not simply because he was evidently incapable of adding up a column of figures (something Bromwell had mastered at the age of two), or intelligently following family discussions on the perpetual subject of interest rates, debts, loans, mortgages, tenant farmers, investments, and the market prices of various Bellefleur commodities, and not even because as a slope-shouldered, absentminded, apologetic bachelor whose face resembled (as his niece Yolande affectionately said) a hunk of aged cheese, and whose shapeless clothes, so rarely changed, gave off an unfortunate odor of onions, stale sweat, solitude, befuddlement, rotting fruit (he thrust apple and pear cores into his pockets, orange rinds, banana skins, even half-eaten tomatoes, for he usually ate while on one of his walks, composing poetry in his head and then scribbling it down on slips of paper which he also thrust into his pockets, often not quite conscious of what he did), and— but how might it be expressed?—simple *oddness,* he was unlikely to marry into a prominent or prosperous family, and in fact unlikely to marry at all; but because of his essence, his soul, his very *being.*

Of course the family did not use these words. They used other words, and frequently.

"Remember that you're a Bellefleur," Hiram told Vernon irritably, when he set out on one of his rambles (sometimes he went no farther than the cemetery, or the village; sometimes he hiked all around Lake Noir and turned up in Bushkill's Ferry where, despite his extreme shyness (in public, even at times in the presence of his own family, he suffered a perpetual blush as if his somewhat roughened skin were windblown) he offered to recite his most recent poems in the general store or at the feed mill or even at one of the taverns (where men who worked for the Bellefleurs were likely to gather); sometimes his poetic inspiration (which he explained as "God dictating") was so complete that he lost track of his surroundings and wound up along a wild stretch of the Nautauga, or up in the foothills in bad weather; once he disappeared for seventeen days and had to be hunted down by hounds, lying weak with malnutrition and a "storm" of poetry in the ruins of a trapper's hut some forty miles northeast of Lake Noir in the shadow of Mount Chattaroy). "Remember that you're a Bellefleur, please don't bring embarrassment on us, don't give our enemies reason to ridicule us," Hiram said. "As if they don't have reason enough already."

"We don't have enemies, Father," Vernon said softly.

"I will have Henry follow you, if you like. On foot or on horseback. And then if you get lost, or injure yourself . . ."

"Who are our enemies, Father?" Vernon said. Though he faced his father boldly he could not prevent his eyes from squinting; and this was a mannerism that particularly annoyed Hiram. "It doesn't seem to me . . ."

"Our enemies," Hiram said, "are perfectly visible."

"Yes—?"

"They're everywhere, don't be an idiot. That *pretense* of yours of being halfwitted, a poetic genius touched by God—!"

"I'm not a poetic genius," Vernon said, his face going brick-red. "You know perfectly well that I have only begun, I am in my apprenticeship, I have many, many years to go. . . . Father, please don't distort everything! It's true that I am a poet and that God has touched me . . . God dwells *in* me . . . and I, I . . . I have dedicated myself to poetry . . . which is the language God uses in speaking to man . . . one soul addressing another. . . . You must know how I am groping and blundering, how I despair of creating anything worthy of God, or even of being heard by my fellow man, what a perpetual mystery poetry is to me: is it a way of coming home, a way of coming back to one's lost home? Sometimes I understand so clearly, in a dream, or when I'm half-awake, or, this morning, feeding Germaine in the garden, when she stuck all her fingers in her mouth and spat out her mashed apricots in my face and shook all over with laughter at the *look* of me, and I found myself staring right into her eyes, and laughing too, because . . . because . . . some barrier had been crossed, some wall between our souls had been . . . It's as if there is an envelope between us, a membrane, nearly transparent, do you see, Father, between your soul and mine, as we stand here talking, and mere words will not penetrate it . . . though we try, God knows we try . . . but . . . but sometimes a gesture, an action, a certain *way* of speaking . . . a way of speaking which is music or poetry . . . which can't be willed, or learned . . . though it can *halfway* be learned. . . . Sometimes, Father, do you see," he said, his words tumbling over one another slapdash and desperate, and his eyes narrowed nearly to slits in the face of Hiram's stony silence, "do you see. . . . It . . . it can. . . . Poetry. . . . I mean our souls. . . . Or was I talking about God, God speaking in us . . . in some of us. . . . There is a place, Father, there is a home, but it isn't here, but it isn't lost either and we shouldn't despair, poetry is a way of getting back, of coming home. . . ."

Hiram had turned partway aside, so that *his* injured eye, his clouded eye, faced Vernon. After a long moment he said, in an uncharacteristically patient voice, "But there is a home, Vernon. Our home. Here. Right here. Exactly—precisely—*here.* You are a Bellefleur despite the misfortune of your mother's blood, and you live here, you feed upon us, this is your home, your birthright, your responsibility—and no amount of that high-toned babble can alter what I say. You are a Bellefleur—"

"I am not a Bellefleur," Vernon whispered.

"—and I ask you only not to bring more ridicule on our name."

"I am not a Bellefleur except by accident," Vernon said.

Hiram stood quietly. If he was upset he gave no indication: he did no more than tug at his cuffs. (Every day, even in the depths of winter when the castle was snowbound, Hiram dressed impeccably: in custom-made suits, in dazzling white shirts which he sometimes changed by midafternoon, and again by dinner; he wore a variety of vests, some of them colorful; and always his watch and chain; and gold or jeweled cuff links. Though he had suffered all of his life from a curious sort of malady —sleepwalking—he gave every impression of being not only in excellent health, but of being in supreme control of himself.)

"I fail to understand what it is you're saying, Vernon," Hiram said softly.

"I don't want to antagonize you, Father, but I must—I must make it clear—I am not a *Bellefleur,* I am only myself, Vernon, my essence is Vernon and not Bellefleur, I belong to God, I *am* God, God dwells in me, I mean to say—I mean that God speaks through me—not always—of course—but in my poetry—when my poetry is successful— Do you see, Father," he said, so nervous, so excited, that flecks of saliva appeared on his pale lips, "the poet knows that he is water poured into water, he *knows* that he is finite and mortal and may drown at any time, in God, and that it's a risk to summon forth God's voice—but the poet must accept that risk—he must take the chance of drowning in God—or whatever it is— I mean the poetry, the voice—the, the rhythm— And then he isn't whoever people say he is, he doesn't have a name, he doesn't *belong* to anyone except that voice—and they cannot claim him—they dare not claim him—"

Hiram turned suddenly, and struck Vernon across the mouth.

It happened so quickly, so unexpectedly, that neither quite comprehended what had happened for several seconds.

"I—I—I say only," Vernon gasped, backing away, his hand pressed against his bleeding lip, "I say only that—that—that—man's true home is elsewhere, I don't dwell in this castle of pride and vanity, amid all these —these hideous possessions—I am not your son to order about—I am not your possession—I am Vernon and not Bellefleur—I am Vernon and not—"

Like his son Hiram had a pink flushed face, and now it grew even pinker. With a gesture of familiar, resigned disgust, he simply waved his son out of the room.

"You're mad," he said. "Go drown yourself."

"I am Vernon only and not Bellefleur and you dare not claim me as Bellefleur," Vernon said, weeping, crouched in the doorway like a little old man; "you drove my mother from me with your *Bellefleur* cruelty, and you buried me alive with your *Bellefleur* insanity, and now you—and now — But you will not triumph— None of you will triumph— I know that you and the others are plotting something—you and Leah—even Leah—Leah whom you've corrupted with your talk of money, land, money, power, money, money— Even Leah! Even Leah!"

Hiram waved him away with a magician's calm disdain. His hands, like Vernon's, were long and soft; but his nails were meticulously filed. "What do you know, my boy, of *Leah,*" he murmured.

Paie-des-Sables

On two midsummer nights in succession, camped by remote, nameless lakes somewhere south of Mount Kittery, Gideon and his brother Ewan underwent a peculiar joint experience—shameful, ugly, inexplicable, and above all distressing—which no one in the family was ever to learn about, and which the brothers themselves, almost as soon as they returned to Bellefleur Manor, were to forget.

They had been weeklong guests at the enormous mountain camp of W. D. Meldrom, the State Commissioner of Conservation. (The Bellefleurs had been friends and business associates of the Meldroms for many years, going back to the lively days when Raphael Bellefleur gave so copiously to his fellow Republicans' campaign funds; there had been a marriage or two between the families, not brilliant, but satisfactory to both sides, and great-grandmother Elvira's brothers had, for some years, worked with the Meldroms on their logging operations in the northeastern-most corner of the state.) It was Gideon's and Ewan's mutual argument, put to Commissioner Meldrom discreetly but persistently, as they fished for bass, with light tackle, disguising their boredom (for there was no drinking at the Meldrom camp, and the lake was so richly stocked that with nothing more than a safety pin and a bit of worm—so Gideon contemptuously said—the clumsiest fisherman could catch, half-hour by half-hour, all the squirming wriggling ferocious three- and four-pound bass he might want), careful never to speak too emphatically, and never to allude to the Bellefleurs' and the Meldroms' arrangements in the past, that the current state law guaranteeing that the thousands upon thousands of acres of land owned by the state would be "forever wild" was impractical: wasn't timber a crop like any other, shouldn't it be harvested like any other?—weren't those forests owned by intelligent and farseeing lumbermen like the Bellefleurs far healthier than the "wild" forests, which were vulnerable to beetles, locusts, diseases of all kinds, and fires sparked by lightning, and windstorms? Under the current state law, passed by a legislature swamped and intimidated by conservationists' special pleading decades ago, after the Great War, it was even the case that diseased and decaying trees, even trees felled by storms, could not be removed from the forests; they were to remain where they had fallen, regardless of the hazard, and the waste, and the fact that privately owned woods (like those owned by the Bellefleurs and the Meldroms) were cut back carefully, in order to produce mixed hardwoods and conifers, of varying ages, with open spaces and trails, and as little witchhobble as possible. . . . What the brothers wanted were "managed cutting" privileges from the state, on the very land (though they certainly did not press this point) their family had once owned.

Timber *is* a crop, and it *should* be harvested like any other, Meldrom said slowly, but over so prolonged a period of time, and with so many interruptions (Gideon and Ewan were quickly bored with the commissioner's family, and with his other guests, most of whom were elderly and hard of hearing, and they found the three-hour dinners in the elegant "log" lodge, attended by innumerable servants, insufferable), that it seemed he must surely be saying something else too.

"The old bastard wants a kickback, obviously," Gideon said.

"You think . . . ? But didn't he make such a stink, a few years back, about Jarald and his gang, in the Game Commission . . . ?"

"The problem is, how to determine what he'd accept, what wouldn't insult him, but at the same time . . . at the same time, obviously, we have to think of ourselves, of how much we can afford," Gideon said, yawning. Frequent yawns were, for Gideon, a way of both expressing and restraining anger; he sometimes yawned five or six times in a row, until his jaw cracked and tears spilled out of his eyes.

The brothers were sitting sprawled on a plump-cushioned rattan sofa before a birch fire, drinking bourbon they had prudently brought from home, in the main room of their cabin—an eight-room Swiss chalet made of peeled and varnished logs, and decorated with a curious mixture of expensive imported furniture, custom-made "rustic" furniture done by cabinetmakers in the area, and backwoods things: chandeliers fashioned out of elk horns, tables made of similar horns and gun stocks, ashtrays that had once been hooves, pillows and wall hangings and rugs made of the skins of bears, panthers, bobcats, beaver. They were sitting in their underwear and stocking feet, staring listlessly into the fire.

"Hiram," Ewan said finally.

"Oh, of course Hiram! . . . But Father sent *us* up here."

"We could discuss it with Hiram anyway. Father wouldn't have to know."

"Hiram would tell him."

"Well, what do you think—? How much?"

Gideon drained his glass. "I'm not thinking anything. I don't *think* about certain things."

"It's like a poker game," Ewan said uneasily.

"But it's no fun," Gideon said.

The brothers sat for a while in silence. Gideon waited for Ewan to swing the subject around to their wives, as he so frequently did—not so that he might speak, stumblingly, of his increasing difficulties with Lily (who wanted to move out of the manor and live, as she put it, anywhere else), but so that he might query Gideon about Leah, in whom he was *too* interested; but when Ewan finally spoke it was to say, simply: "Shit."

And so they left the Meldrom camp before dawn of the next day, telling the servant assigned to them that they had been called back to Bellefleur by messenger. There was an emergency at home, one of their children was sick, would he please explain to Mr. Meldrom, and give him their apologies? It was unlikely that Meldrom would believe them but they didn't care. "The hell with Meldrom." Gideon laughed.

Without needing to confer (for as soon as Ewan mentioned poker the night before, both brothers knew what they would wind up doing) they drove to Paie-des-Sables, where, at Goodheart's Lodge, there was in fact a poker game going, and the brothers were immediately welcomed into it.

Details of the subsequent seventy-two hours were unclear, and afterward neither Gideon nor Ewan quite remembered when, or even how, they lost not only all the cash they had brought with them, but their watches, their belts, and their beautiful leather boots, and their car (a plum-colored Pierce-Arrow with pale gray upholstery, bought and jointly owned by the brothers that spring, when Gideon finally overcame his revulsion for the money—for what he knew of the money—he had won at the Powhatassie race). In the early hours of the game Gideon was doing quite well; and Ewan not at all badly; but as time passed, as players left the table and other players appeared, one of them Goodheart's grandfather (an aged, querulous, crafty, fig-faced half-breed, said to be part Algonquin, part Iroquois, and part Irish, with an absolutely toothless mouth and a vocabulary of no more than a dozen English words and a history—which neither Gideon nor Ewan took seriously, knowing how Indians confused dates or lied—of having been arrested for poaching on Bellefleur territory *in the time of Jean-Pierre Bellefleur*), and as the brothers drank what remained of their own bourbon and then kept pace, drink by drink, with their new friends, paying for most of the rounds, elated and boyish and noisy, and vastly relieved, as Gideon said, to be in the kind of poker game they could handle . . . somehow, somehow it happened, without their really gauging the extent of their losses, that they lost everything they had brought to Paie-des-Sables that was worth losing. And there was some question about Goodheart's honoring their IOU.

Gideon angrily shuffled and reshuffled the deck, demanding that another game begin at once. Ewan sat slumped in his chair, ashen-faced, scratching at his beard with dirty blunt fingers. It was another morning, fine and misty, raining intermittently; the floor of the tavern, made of rough-sawn wood, was littered with bottles, cigarette and cigar butts, tissues, napkins, crumpled-up cellophane wrappers, partly eaten sandwiches. Goodheart's grandfather reappeared (he had slipped away the night before with $600 of Gideon's money and $360 of Ewan's, thanking the brothers profusely for their "kindness" and grinning a toothless grin that was meant, evidently, to be imploring) and Goodheart and the other men conferred with him, speaking in an Indian dialect that was mainly harsh throaty consonants, unintelligible to Gideon and Ewan. They stood some distance away at the bar, chattering, glancing at the brothers and even cupping their hands instinctively to their mouths in a crude, childish gesture of secrecy—as if Gideon or Ewan had the slightest notion of what their words meant.

"Those fools," Gideon said, shuffling the deck. "That old bastard. *Him.* I want another chance at him."

"They don't want our IOU," Ewan said groggily.

"The half-breed bastards, they've *got* to accept it."

"They don't want it, I can tell, the old son of a bitch is telling them not to take it. . . ."

"We'll buy this goddamn fucking place out from under them," Gideon said. "Buy it and raze it. Run them off. Chase them back to the reservation."

"They're afraid of us."

"Why the hell should they be afraid of us!" Gideon shouted, bringing his fist down on the table. "An IOU from a Bellefleur is worth more than cash from anybody else!"

". . . cheated. But I didn't actually see," Ewan said.

"The hell they did, *I* would have seen," Gideon said.

Ewan brought his shot glass thoughtfully to his mouth, and clicked it against his teeth. "Maybe we should go home. Come back some other time."

"I'm offering these half-breeds an IOU for a thousand dollars and they'd better honor it or I'll come back here and burn the place down, I'll rip off their fucking ears, I'll scalp them, the sons of bitches, it's an insult, they can't insult our name like that, I'm not going to sit still for that kind of thing," Gideon said. He even made a move to rise, letting the cards fall onto the table; but some force, like a hand pressing against his forehead, held him back. He sat down again, heavily. ". . . that kind of thing. Fucking insult."

"They're afraid of us. They think we might—"

"Think we might win everything back we lost, the buggers. I want that Pierce-Arrow back. I *want* it back and I'm going to get it, listen to those fools babble away, look at that old Indian crook, you'd think he was some sort of priest or medicine man or something, I want another chance at him, I want that car back, otherwise," he said, rubbing roughly at his eyes, "otherwise there will be nothing left. . . . And you know who will give us both hell. . . ."

"Lily hadn't better give *me* hell," Ewan said loudly. "She's tried that once or twice already and she knows what happens. . . . Drove me wild, got me so I wasn't able to see, shaking her until her teeth rattled. . . ."

"You bastards had better sit down with us! You had better honor that IOU, and sit down, and get this goddamn game going!" Gideon shouted.

But it looked as if there would be no game.

But then it looked as if there might possibly be a game: if the Bellefleurs would settle for a somewhat different arrangement.

Gideon and Ewan conferred, and came to the conclusion—a disgruntled conclusion—that they would accept the altered terms of the game: they would be given credit for $500, but the other players would put up, not cash, but two fine horses, complete with saddles, blankets, and camping equipment. (For how otherwise would the Bellefleurs get home?—they were many, many miles from home.)

And so a new game was begun, and this time Goodheart's grandfather was not so clever, and within an hour Gideon and Ewan had lost not a penny of their $500, and had in fact won the horses, the saddles, and the camping equipment, which consisted of a large but badly frayed and soiled canvas tent and two canvas sleeping bags, similarly soiled, and reeking of odors the Bellefleurs preferred not to interpret. The horses were swaybacked and knobby-kneed, a pair of geldings with stained teeth, but they looked, to Gideon's bloodshot eye, halfway reliable; they would get Ewan and himself home; or anyway close to home. The surprise amidst the winnings was a very young girl, Little Goldie, who was said to be of mixed blood, and whose husbandless mother had run away a few nights earlier with a Canadian trapper.

From the first it was clear that something was wrong, alarmingly wrong: for how could so blond and pale-skinned a child, with such fair blue eyes, and such an upturned nose, and so gracefully *Caucasian* an air be a half-breed? Gideon grumbled that they might as well take her, she couldn't hope for much of a life in the Indian village, and one more child wouldn't matter to the Bellefleurs; she was about Christabel's age anyway; and Leah would probably be delighted. Ewan grumbled that the castle was overflowing with children already, sometimes it seemed to him that there were more children running up and down stairs, and playing hide-and-seek in the cellar and in the stables and barns, and rummaging about in rooms that were out of bounds, and causing a general commotion, than any of the adults could actually account for. . . . Who was going to feed all these children, Ewan wanted to know. And now that Leah had had a new baby Lily was whining and nagging to have another baby herself: where would it all end?

"Poor thing, she isn't destined to any happiness up here in the mountains," Gideon said. "So I don't see, Ewan, that we have any choice."

Standing in the mud behind Goodheart's Lodge, staring at the twin nags and the child, who stared back at them impassively, the brothers were suddenly sober. The rain had taken on a chill that would drop to freezing by sundown, though it was late July.

"All right, then," Ewan said angrily. "Whose will she be? Yours?"

"Ours," said Gideon.

So far as they could learn Little Goldie had no last name, or could not remember it. She spoke in harsh, thick consonants, her head bowed, her small chin pressed against her throat. A fine, soft, pale skin, lightly freckled as if dusted with pollen; waist-length blond hair that, though unwashed and hanging in greasy snarls, was nevertheless disquietingly beautiful.

The brothers stared at her. There was something about her pert oval face, her snubbed nose, her bright brown eyes . . . Her manner that was at the same time diffident and imperious, frightened and sullen . . .

A beautiful child. But only, after all, a child.

They set out in the rain from Paie-des-Sables, Gideon in the lead with Little Goldie perched before him, shivering beneath a waterproof cape held over her head like a hood. When they stopped to make camp, shortly before sundown, at nine in the evening, the rain had turned to snow flurries. "You'll be warm, you can wrap yourself in this blanket," Gideon said. "And they've given us plenty to eat." (Stringy smoked ham, several loaves of dark bread, odd-shaped hunks of goat's cheese, and a half-dozen cans of pork and beans. Goodheart had slipped a carton of eggs into Ewan's saddlebag at the last minute, but most of the eggs were broken when they unpacked.)

Gideon and Ewan were too weary to talk with Little Goldie, who lay curled in her blanket by the fire, staring sightlessly into it; they hadn't the spirit even to talk with each other. They passed a bottle back and forth in silence, and Gideon's mind swung loose: he saw again Meldrom Lake from the window of the Swiss chalet and regretted violently that he had left; he saw again his host and his host's guests in their boats, fishing for bass, and this time it seemed to him that one of the younger guests, a blond, bearded man who had made little effort to speak with Gideon or Ewan, had not only the profile but the manner, the inimitable air, of Nicholas Fuhr. Gideon shuddered. He wanted to protest, but could not speak. In the meager fire there danced certain obsessive figures: Leah with her grotesque swollen belly and her balloonlike legs, Gideon's son Bromwell with his wire-rimmed glasses and his prim, priggish, old-mannish expression, Gideon's mistress Garnet who reached out for him with her scrawny arms, her mouth shaped into an anguished, silent, maddening *O* of desire. (Leave me alone, Gideon whispered. I don't love you. I can't love anyone but Leah.) Dwarfing the others suddenly was the new baby Germaine, her cheeks pudgy and flushed with the delicate pastel coloring of a peach, her eyes uncannily bright. It occurred to Gideon that he had dreamt of Germaine at Meldrom's camp, the night before he and

Ewan slipped away, and that she had something to do with their escape. How strange! He must ask Ewan if *he* had dreamt of her too—

His head jerked up suddenly. There was a commotion nearby. He had fallen asleep by the fire, his forehead on his knees, and he woke to a hellish sight—his brother Ewan crouched atop Little Goldie, grinding himself into her, one big hand covering her mouth and nose so that she was unable to cry out. Gideon screamed for him to stop. He jumped to his feet and grabbed his brother by the hair and wrenched him away from the child.

"Ewan, Ewan, what have you done?" Gideon said. "Dear Christ— what have you *done?*"

But Ewan was too groggy, too confused, even to defend himself. He simply crawled away, half-undressed, and hid beneath his sleeping bag like a guilty child. And Little Goldie, though sobbing, the whites of her eyes showing crescent-thin beneath her eyelids, was too exhausted to respond to Gideon's questions. She was asleep again within half a minute, and Gideon, gazing upon her, thought it must be for the best—even if Ewan had injured her, even if she were bleeding, a few hours' deep sleep would give her strength.

That was the first night. On the second night, camped beside a small, compact glacier lake, Gideon stationed himself between Little Goldie and Ewan (who had been silent for most of the day, meekly contrite), and again he sat gazing into the fire where there danced demonic figures: his wife, his children, his mistress, his father, his mother, Nicholas Fuhr on his prancing stallion, Goodheart's grandfather with his wrinkled fig of a face and his eyes beadily wise.... A female figure beckoned to him lewdly. Its pale hair fell untidily to its waist; its small breasts were exposed, showing tiny, hard, perfect nipples. Though his bones ached from the ride along the mountain trails and from the damp, cold air, though he did not *want* to be drawn to her, Gideon nevertheless crawled on his knees to the figure ... which turned out to be much more wiry and combative than he had imagined.... Eyes shut, head ringing with an urgency that was more anger than lust, Gideon groped to silence the screams, pressing the palm of his hand hard over a mouth and part of a nose. *Be quiet. Be quiet or I'll hold your head underwater.*

He was wakened by his brother's incredulous shouts. Ewan had hold of him by the hair, and was wrenching him off Little Goldie, who struck at him with her tiny fists and babbled in a language he could not comprehend. "Gideon, for God's sake! *Gideon,*" Ewan said, dragging him backward. He tripped and fell, and Ewan fell also, and they lay for a while in the mud, breathing heavily, not looking at each other. Then Ewan whispered: "My God, Gideon. *You.*"

He began to sob. His chest and throat were wracked with sobs. What he must do: stumble to his feet and run to the lake and throw himself in the clear, freezing water, and let his clothes soak and grow heavy until he sank, until his body was dragged to the bottom of the lake, and his thick shaggy hair and beard were weighed down, and his eyes bulged sight-lessly, and no one knew where he lay, and no one knew his name, and his place in the family cemetery lay vacant forevermore. . . . He *must* stumble to his feet and run down to the lake, no matter how his brother tried to dissuade him. . . .

But instead he fell asleep.

And woke before dawn, to see Ewan just returning from the lake where he had splashed water onto his face and chest.

"Good morning, Gideon," Ewan said in a queer elated voice.

They looked at the child, bunched up in her soiled blanket, her freckled face wan and pale, almost nacreous, yet eerily charming—a snub-nosed doll's face, innocent as Christabel's. Her thin breath, drawn irregu-larly through her strawberry-pink lips, made a faint rasping sound. She slept deeply and placidly as an infant, and it was entirely possible that she would remember nothing.

"Still," Ewan said reluctantly, "we should drown her."

Gideon rubbed his face with both hands, and yawned so violently that his jaws cracked. A loon was calling on the lake, invisible, answered at once by another loon. The odor of fresh pine pervaded everything. Gideon's bones were sore, his head ached from the ugly raw dreams that had careened through it, his eyes wanted to roll back into his skull, recoiling from the sight of the wretched child; yet he felt a prick of elation. "We should, yes," he said.

Ewan remained standing, his feet apart, his flannel shirt unbuttoned to the waist; and Gideon remained sitting, his knees now drawn up to his chest. When he returned to the manor, he thought dreamily, after having been gone so very, very long, he would order a steaming hot bath drawn for himself, and he would take a bottle of rum into the bath with him, and one or two of his father's Cuban cigars.

Little Goldie was sleeping by the burnt-out fire, a strand of snarled, greasy hair fallen across her forehead.

"But, being Bellefleurs," Ewan said, sighing, "we won't."

"We can't," Gideon said quickly.

He managed to get to his feet, pulling up on Ewan's arm. How quickly he'd aged! He felt older and shakier than Noel. . . . Ewan was watching him closely, his eyes threaded with blood. For a long groggy minute the brothers could think of nothing to say to each other. Birds had begun to chatter: redwings, sparrows, thrushes. Something scuttled in the underbrush a few yards away. One of the swaybacked horses raised his head and neighed uneasily, and Little Goldie twitched inside her blanket, but did not wake.

"Yes. I mean no. We *can't*," Ewan said, expelling all his breath.

The Holy Mountain

On his tremulous bony knees on a granite ledge maliciously ridged with razorlike shards of ice, his hands clasped tightly together, his head atop its long, very long slender neck drifting upward to the polar cap of the holy mountain Mount Blanc, his teary eyes half-shut against the wind that blasted out of a turquoise-blue sky, all clarity and innocence, he heard, beyond the shrill percussive rhythms of his own voice (which, so rarely raised, so rarely heard aloud except in impatient helpless moments when he quarreled with the mountain spirit who impertinently and unmercifully inhabited his clearing, if not always actually his cabin, in the guise of his brother's young wife—for without Jedediah's conscious choice he had begun, one night, to reply to the spirit's flirtatious queries, and then to respond, sometimes with exasperation and rage, to its outlandish proposals: they should both strip naked and dive into the dark plunging water below!—they should howl and tear at each other and roll about the clearing, beneath the full moon!)—kneeling on his granite ledge, his head bowed, his voice ringing out as it did every morning as the sun rose, perhaps aiding the sun in its reluctant rising, he heard, half a heartbeat after each of his words, each syllable of his defiant words, an echo, a faint mocking near-inaudible echo in a voice utterly unknown to him: and immediately went silent.

He waited, opening his eyes cautiously.

In recent months, or was it recent years, Jedediah's hearing had become increasingly acute. He could hear the cries of incredulous pain, needle-thin cries of pain, from the hemlocks cut down miles away, on lower ground: a piteous thing, he'd had to stop his ears with bits of rag, for the trees were not even dragged away, they were skinned in the forest where they lay and then left to suffer, their life's consciousness easing from them slowly, as perhaps it eased into them slowly, and while their

butchers took no heed, heard no sound at all, Jedediah was unable not
to hear. His sharpened senses picked up the cries of small birds torn apart
in midair by hawks, and rabbits seized by owls, and raccoons set upon by
wolves; one especially frantic screaming brought him out of his cabin on
a winter morning to see, far away, across the chasm, a thrashing furry
creature the size of a fox hauled away in the talons of a gigantic bird—
it had a naked red-skinned head but a heronlike beak, its feathers were
evidently white, tipped with black as if with tar, its tail was long and
pronged, extraordinarily long—an amazing predator Jedediah had never
seen before and could not identify.

He knelt, his head inclined to one side, his beard—which had evidently grown long again—he had trimmed it only the other day—brushing coarsely against his bare shoulder.

Silence.

God?

Silence.

. . . Therefore I say unto you, Take no thought for your life, what ye shall eat,
or what ye shall drink; nor yet for your body, what ye shall put on. Is not the life
more than meat, and the body more than raiment? Behold the fowls of the air.
. . . Consider the lilies of the field. . . . Therefore take no thought, saying What shall
we eat? or, What shall we drink? or, Wherewithal shall we be clothed? . . . But seek
ye first the kingdom of God, and His righteousness; and all these things shall be added
unto you. Take therefore no thought for the morrow: for the morrow shall take thought
for the things of itself. Sufficient unto the day . . .

Again the echo. Faint, blithe, jeering. He *heard* it with a terrible
clarity though his own voice did not weaken.

Slowly he got to his feet, straightening himself with an effort. (His
right knee ached nearly all the time now. He could not remember when
it had begun: only the other morning, yet it had been with him always.)
He shielded his eyes and looked from side to side, as far as his gaze would
hook, down into the ravine that leapt with shadow and sunlight and
boiling white foam, down the boulder-strewn hill to the pine forest; and
up, slowly, reverently, to the very top of Mount Blanc. That timber died
away as the mountain rose toward God, that snow and ice covered its very
summit, seemed to Jedediah testimony of the mountain's holiness. He
could stare and stare across the windswept miles to the mountain until
his eyes ached and his vision weakened, and feel that he had only begun
to pay it homage. For wasn't it likely that so sacred a place dispelled all
evil. . . . Wasn't it likely that Satan himself would cower before that brute
glacial magnificence . . . ?

Once Jedediah had stood on his ravine ledge, shielding his eyes as
he watched a sparrow hawk gliding and dipping downward, and a shot
rang out—and a bullet passed close by his head. He had thrown himself
on the rock at once. Without thinking—without having the time to think
—he threw himself down, and lay flat for a very long time; and then,
cautiously, his numbed lips shaping *Dear God, have mercy, dear God have*

mercy, don't allow me to die before You have shown me Your face . . . don't make of my pilgrimage to Your kingdom a mockery, and my love for You a clumsy joke, terminated so abruptly by a meaningless accident, his arms and legs outspread, he had managed to crawl backward from the cliff, and to barricade himself in his cabin. (By that time he had strengthened the shantylike structure with heavier birch logs, and weatherproofed the roof; he had laid down floorboards; he had set two panes of glass in his windows, which were no more than a foot square; and he had built himself a sturdy oak door with an iron latch.) In the cabin he lay on his cornshuck bed, too weak for an indefinite period of time even to continue his prayer; and then he must have slept, for when he woke it was night and he was entirely alone and God allowed him to know that the danger had passed, and he was once more alone on the mountain, and no one would injure him; and his heart filled with elation like a child's elation, when he learns that he is not to be punished, after all, but gathered in his mother's arms, into her warm forgiving bosom.

The next morning, quivering with his own defiance, Jedediah strode out to the cliff's edge—and saw, after a few minutes, that he *was* entirely alone, and that God had not misled him. From that day onward no one had ever shot at him again.

From time to time, however, he did suffer intrusions. It seemed to him that the intruders—trappers, hunters primarily—followed close upon one another's heels, and that he had little time to himself to bask in the mountain's holy solitude, and to feel himself refined into a pair of eyes only—a pair of eyes and a self that was so thin, so pure, it possessed the brittleness of a sheet of translucent ice—as God intended. (For why otherwise had God called Jedediah Bellefleur up into the mountains, except to purify him of the heat of creation?—the frenzy of lust, the madness of groveling about in the flesh, bodies writhing upon bodies in a futile attempt to annihilate their aloneness? Why otherwise than to save him from his brothers' fate, and his father's repulsive fate, sinking ever more hopelessly into the quagmire of the senses? For though his brother Louis was married, and God was said to look with favor upon husband and wife, and to consider them one flesh in holy union, Jedediah knew very well that God recoiled with distaste from the baser instincts, and dwelled in His inviolable magnificence high atop Mount Blanc where no living thing could survive.)

Jedediah lived on lower ground, however. And so human beings interrupted his peace. If he heard them coming he naturally hid, but what could he do if they took him by surprise! Once the mountain spirit that amused itself by taking the shape of, and mimicking the voice of, Louis's child-bride was teasing him with one silly fanciful thing after another— in a high-pitched disingenuous girl's voice chiding him for having trapped a raccoon for food, such a pretty creature, such an adorable face, and so very nearly tame—and so very *fatty!*—ugh, how could he eat such meat!—how could *he,* prim passionless monkish Jedediah, bring himself to eat such meat!—and he had been so distracted, so anxious lest he succumb to the spirit's torment and begin to answer back (which, sadly, he often did—and nothing delighted the mountain spirits more than to trick a human being into conversing with them *as if they existed*), that he had not heard or even seen an outlandish little party of visitors: a group of some six or seven girls, about the age of his sister-in-law (whose name he had forgotten, but he remembered that she was sixteen and *very* young for her age), dressed in woollen shorts that fell just to the knee, and heavy-knit socks, and hiking boots of a kind Jedediah had never seen before, and enormous bulky-knit jackets in a variety of bright colors. The girls' cheeks were apple-red; they were out of breath because of the altitude, but obviously in excellent health; their braided hair bristled with exuberance. Jedediah disguised his surprise and dismay, and put aside his hoe (for it was a warm June day, one of the first warm days of the year, and he was going to set down a garden, potatoes mainly, despite the thin pebbly inhospitable soil), and offered the little party water, tinned meat, dried fruit, chunks of black bread grown stale and hard but nevertheless edible if soaked in gruel—all that he had, in fact—for the girls *had* come a great distance, and it might be said that they were his guests so long as they remained on the mountain. But the leader of the hiking party thanked him, and accepted only water, which the girls drank with evident delight, passing Jedediah's battered tin cup from hand to hand, and giggling at him over the rim. They might have been sisters, they so resembled one another: bright dark eyes, dark brown bangs that fell low over their foreheads, cherry-red lips.

For some reason he did not want them gone quickly. When hunters and trappers and even Mack Henofer dropped by, it was obvious from Jedediah's curt, brusque manner and his near-muteness and the way he stared stonily at the ground that he wanted them gone as quickly as possible—he found that he could breathe only with difficulty in their presence—he *detested* it that these crude men should presume to offer him whiskey and tobacco as if they pitied him. (And of course Mack Henofer, who brought him unwanted supplies and letters and gifts and news from back home, and who even offered him bits of gossip about Jean-Pierre that were considered, on lower ground, marvelously scandalous, could never quite comprehend Jedediah's disdain.) But he halfway regretted it when the girls, after resting no more than ten minutes, went on their way again, thanking him in unison, and breaking into song as they hiked away without once glancing back. (Jedediah's keen ears picked up their song even as they trudged out of sight. He thought it wonderfully charming, if simple-minded, and wondered if it was a popular tune of the day down below:

> *I'll be no submissive wife*
> *No, not I; no, not I*
> *I'll not be a slave for life*
> *No, not I; no, not I*

Think you on our wedding day
That I said, as others say
Love and honor and obey
Love and honor and obey

No no no no no no
No no no, not I

I to dullness don't incline
No, not I; no, not I
Go to bed at half-past nine
No, not I; no, not I

No no no no no no
No no no, not I.)

He was hurt to discover that they hadn't drunk the water he had offered them—they had done no more than pass the tin cup around, raising it to their lips, and pretending to drink. For days afterward he heard their singsong voices, wafted back to him by the mountain winds, *no no no no no no, no no no not I.*

Another visitor who had also taken him by surprise (the mountain spirit had been laughing warmly at him for picking weevils out of his oatmeal one by one, and setting them free—why didn't he simply dump all the oatmeal down into the river, why didn't he, come to think of it, drag everything out of his cabin, all his supplies, and his bedding, and even the little stool he had put together with such difficulty, and toss it all over the side!—what a lark!—and how *good* he would feel afterward! —for didn't Christ say give up all you have and follow Me!) was a very tall man in his early thirties, perhaps, with silvery brown hair that fell to his wide shoulders, and tanned, leathery skin that appeared to glint with tiny crystals of salt, and a long straight beak of a nose, and long eyes in which the iris floated rather like a tadpole, with a tadpole's minuscule curl of a tail. A remarkable man, more than a head taller than Jedediah, and obviously very strong—he carried a knapsack and camping equipment as if they weighed next to nothing—but gentle, soft-spoken, excessively courteous. He accepted a bowl of mushroom-milk soup from Jedediah, and warmed himself at Jedediah's hearth, but seemed more interested in querying Jedediah about the region: for he was a cartographer by profession, and was involved in an ambitious project that would take many years to complete, the fastidious mapping of the region traversed by the Nautaugamaggonautaugaunagaungawauggataunauta. So, taking notes in pencil, he interrogated Jedediah about streams and runs and trickles, and lakes on higher ground, and ponds no matter how small, and mountain trails long ago grown over since the first explorers had passed. He spread out his elaborate parchment maps for Jedediah to examine; he was clearly proud of them, and anxious lest they get too close to the fire, or Jedediah happen to touch them by accident. "Nothing matters so much as learning the precise contours of the earth on which we live," he told Jedediah in his soft, calm voice. "That is our way of learning God." It pleased Jedediah, but rather puzzled him, that the tall man should show no curiosity at all about *him.*

And then there was Mack Henofer. Too frequently—every six or seven months, or was it once a year—there was Mack Henofer, always when Jedediah least expected him. He was a trapper who lived on the eastern slope of Mount Blanc, alone as Jedediah was alone, but clearly not self-sufficient: for he went eagerly to the settlement at distant Contracoeur, where he traded his pelts for cash, and then to the towns to the south, to Fort Hanna and Innisfail and even to faraway Nautauga Falls, which Jedediah only dimly remembered. It was said of Henofer that he had come to the New World as an alternative to prison in Newgate, and that he had left Manhattan Island for the north country as an alternative, quickly chosen, to conscription in the army; he had left the Lake Noir region, again quickly, as an alternative to marriage. Jedediah knew little about him, and never inquired after him except to express the hope, in a rushed courteous murmur, that Henofer was in good health. He was certainly a spy of Jean-Pierre's, and may even have wished to cajole Jedediah into attending to a number of his trap lines, but Jedediah could tolerate him for brief periods of time, and never showed his anger.

(How often Henofer arrived, how frequently was he underfoot! One day in the mountains is all days, all days are one, a single seamless fluid passing of the sun across the sky, moment by moment, quickly, as one breathes, now it is daybreak, now it is the tide of noon, now it is midafternoon, now the sun begins to sprawl as it sinks, now it is dusk—no more than a few moments—now it is night: and one sinks into the oblivion of sleep, into the same dark the sun has penetrated. The days passed so rapidly and there was Henofer, once again, grinning apologetically at Jedediah, showing his blackened teeth and sometimes the tip of his red tongue which Jedediah imagined, but knew he only imagined, to be subtly forked. He was *always* hallooing for Jedediah from the clearing, he was *always* making himself at home in the cabin, content to wait for days until Jedediah returned.)

Thick-chested, with spindly legs, and a moth-eaten woollen cap pulled low on his forehead in all weathers, Henofer was an emissary of Jean-Pierre's but—as he made repeatedly clear—he considered himself a friend of Jedediah's first. "Both of us have come to live in the mountains to get away from those—" and here he sometimes groped for the correct words, or spat out a shocking obscenity—"and we have to be loyal to each other. That's all there is to say." Yet it wasn't, for once his tongue was loosed he could talk for hours, gobbling up all the food poor Jedediah felt obliged to offer him (which frequently included the delicious dried apricots and raspberry, marmalade, and strawberry preserves Louis's wife had just sent, and strips of salt-dried beef, and nuggets of caramel

candy), telling him all the unwanted gossip, items not likely to have found
their way into the letter Louis had sent (for Louis wrote to Jedediah
faithfully, though it had been a very long time since Jedediah had troubled to reply). The settlement at Lake Noir was growing rapidly, according to Henofer, and there were boundary disputes and duels; men killed
in tavern fights; trouble with Indians and half-breeds; lynchings of Indians and half-breeds; a rowdy poor-white family named Varrell who lived
in the foothills but were moving one by one into the settlement; envy and
resentment at the way Jean-Pierre and Louis were buying up land and
fencing it off; and resentment too at certain of Jean-Pierre's schemes—
he had recently made a fair amount of money by selling a number of
wagonloads of something he called Arctic elk manure, to downriver farmers who had settled on poor soil, and needed their land rejuvenated by
a "high-nitrogen" substance. . . . And Henofer even presented Jedediah
with tiny perfumed envelopes in which his sister-in-law had slipped, for
what reason Jedediah could not fathom, babies' curls. The first curl was
pale brown, the second a very light blond, the third dark brown. So there
were, now, three babies. Louis and his wife had had three babies. And
Jedediah had two nephews and a niece—Jacob and Bernard and—what
was the girl's name—Arlette?—Arlette. Of course they must be beautiful
children. Of course Jedediah was happy. It was all God's wish, wasn't it,
God's plan. But *why* did Louis's wife send Jedediah those silly little curls?
He did not know how to respond and so he made no response at all; he
threw the curls into the fire.

Dear God, he prayed, *please grant me my own life. My wholeness in Thee.
My salvation. My freedom from them . . . from her.*

And then Henofer would leave, finally, having nothing more to say,
and Jedediah frequently wept with the sheer bliss of aloneness. For he
knew that God would not show His face to him unless he was utterly
alone.

He called out, and waited, trembling, to hear the echo.

But there was no sound except the river. The river, and the birds'
stray shrill senseless cries.

Is someone there, he called, cupping his hands to his mouth; but there
was no reply. . . . *Why do you torment me,* he called, more softly, *why do you
mock me when I utter God's word. . . .*

Yet there was only silence, and even the mountain spirit who so
merrily plagued him was absent. He was entirely alone. He knew himself
alone. Yet if he spoke in God's word, if he raised his voice to utter Christ's
teaching, in a voice of brass, he knew the mocking echo would return: he
knew that whoever tormented him would begin again. *Why do you mock me,
why do you hate me,* Jedediah whispered, standing on his windy ravine and
casting his gaze about as far as it would go, *who are you . . . ? Are you someone
sent by my father, or someone in the hire of Satan, or someone I have inadvertently
wronged during my life down below . . . ?*

Nothing, no sound. No movement in the sky that arched above Mount Blanc except the ceaseless motion of the clouds, and the quick darting flight of a sparrow hawk, intent on prey too small for Jedediah's eye to perceive.

In the Nursery

At the age of seventeen, when he fell so tumultuously in love with the Bellefleurs' adopted daughter Little Goldie, Garth was nearly as tall and as broad-shouldered as his bearish father Ewan, and possessed of an even more irascible temper: when friends forcibly restrained him from accepting the malicious bet of a daredevil diver at the Nautauga Falls fairground one summer when Garth was fourteen (the daredevil, Flaming Pete McSweet, dove into a ten-foot canvas tank from a one-hundred-foot tower that swayed in even the mild breezes of August, to the awe and delight of his hushed audience, and though it was his practice to plunge through the air livid with orange-red flames he was willing to allow the brash Garth Bellefleur to dive without setting himself on fire—and odds, in Garth's favor should he win, were a very generous fifty to one) he turned on them wildly, beating one into unconsciousness, dislocating another's jaw, seizing another in his massive arms and picking him up from the ground and squeezing until the boy (who was hardly frail himself) shrieked for him to stop. When Ewan found out about the incident—the bet rather than Garth's assault on his friends—he was furious, and dragged the boy out into one of the empty hop-curing barns, shouting that he had nearly made an ass of himself, he had nearly allowed some son-of-a-bitch con man to trick him into breaking his neck, and in public to boot, and that if he was so thick-skulled, so stupid, he had better stay home where the women could watch him. Garth's chagrin, and his awe of his father, made him cringe before Ewan's rage, and meekly accept some half-dozen whiplashes on his back, buttocks, and thighs. He even wept, alone in the barn afterward; or at any rate he was wracked with loud, hoarse, tearless sobs that left him exhausted and weak as an infant.

Because Leah did not want Germaine to move into the nursery yet (she wasn't a year old despite her size, and the rapidity of her maturation, and Leah frequently worried over her—she had an unreasonable fear that the baby might die suddenly in her sleep), and it was discovered one day that Christabel and Bromwell were really too big for the nursery (and no longer got along: Bromwell claimed that he couldn't tolerate his twin, she was so slow-witted, so ordinary, and it rather offended him that she was several inches taller than he and could now bully him whenever she wished), the nursery was free for Little Goldie when Gideon and Ewan brought her home; and she was settled in there at once. There she had her choice of several charming little beds, each with its good horsehair mattress and its canopy; she could choose among the exciting clutter of hundreds of toys—dolls, stuffed animals, games, puzzles, crayons, paints, child-sized drums and bugles and cymbals, several rocking horses, a five-foot high Viennese merry-go-round with three handsome steeds. But standing in the doorway of the nursery Little Goldie was heard to say, in her hoarse, guttural murmur, "This isn't my place."

They pretended not to hear, and fussed over her all the more. Both Leah and Lily claimed that she was a gorgeous little child: so undernourished, so mistreated! Grandmother Cornelia was slower to come around: it had been a considerable shock for her when Gideon and Ewan (who had been missing for nineteen days) simply tramped in her breakfast room and said bluntly: "We've brought home an orphan, Mother, we had no choice." Her sons were bedraggled and mud-splattered and clearly exhausted, and Cornelia had to stare at Gideon for several long seconds before she was certain he *was* Gideon—his beard was so grizzled, his eyes so bloodshot. . . . An orphan! A little girl dressed in rags, her face filthy, her hair hanging in greasy strands! The resigned violence with which she scratched her head was a clear indication that she had lice, and there was something disturbing—sullen, or merely mischievous—about the set of her eyes and her thin arched eyebrows. Cornelia managed to say, "Why so you have," though she felt as if she might faint. She had been lying majestically on her chaise longue, swathed in a billowing silk gown, feeding bits of a cherry croissant to one of the kittens, and Gideon and Ewan had strode ahead of the servants, pulling that strange little child between them, tracking mud everywhere. "Why . . . why, so you have," Cornelia murmured, staring at the girl. For several weeks she was to say to Edna (not to any of her family, who would have hooted her down out of uneasiness as much as simple disbelief) that Little Goldie was an elf-child, not a real child at all. Or perhaps she *was* a half-breed.

But in the end grandmother Cornelia declared her a beautiful child —a little angel—and claimed that Gideon and Ewan had done the proper thing in bringing her home with them. "We're Bellefleurs, after all," she said. "We can take in any number of abandoned children."

Little Goldie struck the skeptical Garth as *strange* rather than *beautiful.* (And, anyway, what did *beautiful* mean . . . ?)

Demuth Hodge had been dismissed long ago, sent away by a taciturn

Ewan with six months' wages and no explanations (one theory was that Leah had been furious because Demuth allegedly "disciplined" Christabel and Morna by rapping their bottoms with a ruler, after they slipped some overripe and easily squashed boysenberries into the pocket of his old tweed coat; another theory was that Bromwell had contemptuously denounced the young man—his knowledge of higher mathematics, Bromwell declared, was sheer fraud). Though the family had advertised everywhere for a replacement, both in the United States and abroad, no applicant appeared whose *vita* and person pleased everyone; so the Bellefleurs were without a tutor. Since they were reluctant to send the children away to school, especially the younger children, they had no choice but to attempt to educate them at home. Hiram gave instructions every morning from 9:00 A.M. until noon in arithmetic, algebra, classical mythology, and world geography; Vernon instructed them, two or three unscheduled afternoons a week, in composition, literature, and "elocution" (which mainly involved the passionate reading of poets dear to him, aloud, to a small giggling audience always on the brink of mutiny). But Bromwell volunteered to tutor the new child, perhaps because, at first, she excited his curiosity: she seemed to have come from so distant a land, so remote a territory, that her very humanity was suspect. How odd, how coarse, her words . . . ! Was it some Indian dialect she tried to speak, or a language of her own, utterly private? It might be a challenge, a scientific challenge, Bromwell thought, to teach the child how to be human . . . how to become human, through the English language.

But he soon grew impatient. "Repeat after me," he said, and again, "Repeat after me, *please,*" and *"Are* you listening? *Do* you comprehend?" Garth and Albert and Jasper hung about in the doorway of the nursery, snickering. They rather resented Little Goldie. *Another* child . . . ! Another comely child, drawing the adults' attention. . . . Garth called out suggestions of his own, which were ignored. He thought it especially comic that Little Goldie could barely hold a pen—she was always splashing ink on herself and Bromwell. How clumsy, for a girl . . . ! It was only when Bromwell pushed his glasses up onto his forehead and rubbed his eyes in a weary, adult gesture, and said in his sharp curt voice, "Maybe you *are* a half-breed, or anyway a halfwit: in either case we may as well abandon lessons," that Garth felt a rush of sudden, irresistible emotion—not the hilarity that reduced Albert and Jasper to shrieking hyenas, but rage —rage so violent that he had to be restrained from throwing the terrified Bromwell out the window to which he had carried him, snarling: "You little bastard! You wise-ass little bastard! Now you see how you like it! Now you see how hard you land! *Now—*"

Garth would have defined it as resentment he continued to feel as the weeks passed, had he been given—as he was not—to brooding over his own emotions: resentment and a dull baffled aching anger and a sense of something obscurely *not right.* Garth had always been a fairly close-mouthed boy, though inordinately noisy and lively; he had walked home one winter afternoon from bobsledding, after a spill in which no one was evidently hurt, holding his hand close against his side, saying nothing to the other children, though the smallest finger of his right hand had been nearly severed (and was to be sewn back on by a remarkably quick-witted Leah, even as the doctor was sought) and there was of course an alarming loss of blood. He would never *say* what was wrong, if he was growing angry, or why he was growing angry—it was his habit merely to erupt into passion. Even when Yolande (with whom he shared certain secrets against their parents and the other adults) asked him what was wrong, was he slipping into a black mood, he muttered only, "Go to hell with you, you nosy damn bitch."

In the nursery were things Garth had played with as a child, and outgrown—the rocking horses, the merry-go-round, the stuffed animals —though he could only dimly remember them, and their very sight filled him with an inexplicable inchoate anger. He watched the strange child move among them, as silent as he, lifting and setting down toys as if she too were recognizing them, but did not quite know what to do with them. Several of the girls—Christabel and Vida and of course Yolande, who could not resist anything stray and mysterious—played with Little Goldie, making friends by degrees, helping her with her lessons now that Bromwell was banished from the nursery (and it was the case, rather oddly, that Gideon took Garth's side in the outburst, and would have walloped Bromwell's behind if the child hadn't burst into tears), and with her ABC sampler, which she was doing in rich purples, golds, and greens, exactly like the old, tattered sampler on the wall, framed and behind glass, that had once been done by someone named Arlette Bellefleur—ABC's, numerals up to ten, and the statement I AM ARLETTE BELLEFLEUR BORN 1811 —though of course the sampler on the wall was badly faded. No one thought it puzzling that Garth, who was always out of doors, even in bad weather, lingered about the nursery with the girls, quick to offer to repair their dollhouse (which must have been, Yolande said, one hundred years old, and termite-ridden) when the swinging wall fell off its hinges, and to help them move furniture about (they aped the restless Leah who liked nothing so much as to spend a rainy afternoon ordering the servants to rearrange the furniture, and struggling impatiently with pieces herself)— the teetering whatnot shelf made of empty spools of thread, painted Chinese red, and filled with dolls' china and tiny glass birds and animals and eggs, which Garth carried without effort, and in a wonderfully graceful way, so that nothing toppled off and broke; the child-sized horsehair sofa that was a replica of one of the parlor sofas; the heavy music box, which must have been three feet deep and five feet long, the size of a child's casket, said to have been made in Switzerland though it was equipped with American rolls. When Yolande thanked him spiritedly, as if she were proud—especially before Little Goldie—of how considerate her older brother could be, Garth blushed and could not think of anything to say. He knew only that the strange little girl with the solemn freckled face and the waist-long white-blond hair was staring at him intently.

So he fled the nursery, and spent a week or so outdoors—working on the farm, accompanying Ewan and Hiram on a business trip to the Falls. And then he reappeared one stormy afternoon when the temperature dropped thirty degrees in an hour, and asked if they wouldn't like him to build a fire in the little fireplace—? By this time Goldie was clearly more at home, and seemed happy to see him. She laughed often, though she would not always explain her merriment; she hugged Yolande when Yolande guided her clumsy hands so that she could thread an especially fine needle; she offered Garth a doll's cup of the rank catnip tea the girls had brewed. One of the women had taken the time to set her hair in ringlets, and she looked as sweet, as demure, as improbably pious as the pencil drawings on the nursery walls of numerous Bellefleurs as children (these insipid drawings, done by more than one artist, portrayed Raoul, Emmanuel, Ewan, Gideon, and even Noel, Matilde, Jean-Pierre II, Della, and Hiram, and one or two unidentified children, in identical poses: their hands clasped in prayer, their eyes cast beseechingly heavenward); but even then Garth did not comprehend how he loved her.

He cranked the music box for the girls, and willingly changed the heavy copper rolls, though it embarrassed him to be forced to admit— as Bromwell would not have been forced—that he hadn't any idea of how the mechanism worked. "It just goes like this, this thing in here," he said, growing warm as Little Goldie along with Christabel and Yolande pressed near. The music box hadn't been one of the pastimes Garth had cared for, when *he* had slept in the nursery, and even now he found its smooth gleaming oak sides and its fussy etched-glass lid discomforting. It might so easily break down and how on earth would he repair it?

One of the rolls gave out, at various speeds, English minuets and rondos and dainty tinkling tunes, another bellowed hymns accompanied by a wheezing organ, still another—Garth's favorite—sang "The Battle Hymn of the Republic" and "General Harrison's Grand March" and the "St. Louis Light Guard Polka and Schottisch." Garth grew to like the music, or at any rate to like Little Goldie's solemn, awed interest in it, and though the other girls rapidly lost interest and drifted away, and Yolande began to be absent from the nursery for days at a time, Garth never grew tired of turning the brass crank. On their honeymoon, in fact on their wedding night, the "St. Louis Light Guard Polka and Schottisch" was to attain a wildly ecstatic beauty.

Because he had never been in love before Garth had no idea, nor might anyone have thought to explain to him (for he *was* naturally moody, and often turned away with a snarl when approached) why he was stricken with insomnia, why he lost his appetite, why he wanted only to be by himself—in the cemetery, up at Bloody Run, riding his horse along Mink Creek—or why, perversely, he wanted never to be alone, but with Little Goldie. He bloodied his cousin Louis's lip when Louis inadvertently bumped into him, and then again he ran out barefoot in the rain, late one night, to waylay his uncle Hiram who, sleepwalking, had managed to open the two or three doors locked for his protection, and who was stumbling open-eyed, his arms feebly extended, in the direction of the Bellefleurs' dock on Lake Noir: and Garth did this with a peculiar abashed courtesy. (He had, in the past, been sent after Hiram, and had never been able to resist grabbing the pompous old fool's arm roughly, and shaking him awake, though he was instructed not to do so.) He turned on Mahalaleel when Mahalaleel leapt up from nowhere onto the wrought-iron table in the garden where some of the family was lunching, and nearly made off with a turkey drumstick, though the rash action resulted in a badly lacerated forearm, and everyone chided him: he shouldn't have tried to *hurt* Mahalaleel, he should only have tried to retrieve the drumstick. And then again he was patient with Vida, and told the boys not to follow Raphael out to his pond but to leave him alone, what did it matter, what the hell did it matter, if Raphael wanted to be by himself every day? His blood pounded with a sudden impulsive fury, and then subsided; and he felt sometimes like weeping; and he *did* suffer from insomnia for the first time in his life. (Previously Garth had been certain that people who claimed to lie awake all night were lying. They must be lying, for how on earth did they keep their eyelids from closing as his did, within seconds after he lay his head on the pillow?)

One night, sleepless, he wandered the second-floor corridor in the direction of the nursery, and happened to see great-aunt Veronica gliding along, noiselessly, ahead of him, her feet evidently bare, and very pale, her long thick gunmetal-gray hair loose on her shoulders, her dark robe (for she wore mourning, like Della, even at night) billowing about her— and he thought it odd that Veronica should pause at the nursery door, and stand with her head inclined to it for several long seconds, and then open the door and step inside. Odd, and disturbing, though he couldn't have said precisely why—for wasn't it the prerogative, even the duty, of the women in the house to check on the younger children from time to time? But he followed Veronica into the darkened nursery and saw, by moonlight, how she bent over the sleeping Little Goldie, and how stiff her back went when she heard or sensed his presence. She turned to him readily, however, as if not very surprised, and, her forefinger to her lips, pushed him back out into the candlelit corridor, and said, her eyes nearly shut as if she were winking: "What a charming little sister Ewan and Gideon brought home for you. . . . She's *very* attractive, isn't she?"

But it was only after several distressing weeks, at dusk of a blustery August day, when, in Little Goldie's presence, he first began to comprehend the nature of his affliction. Vida and Christabel and Morna and Little Goldie had served him "tea" in the nursery, using miniature cups and saucers, and everyone was sillier than usual because it wasn't tea they sipped but sweet cream sherry one of the girls had stolen from downstairs (Bellefleur children, throughout the generations, always stole sweet sherries and liqueurs from downstairs, and were rarely caught, even by adults who had done the same thing as children in the same house), when they began to giggle at the pencil drawings on the walls which looked, in Christabel's reiterated phrase, like horses' asses. There was Ewan as a little boy! So funny, rolling his eyes upward! And grandfather Noel of all people! And Hiram, hardly more than a baby! Oh, why were their lips so dark, as if they were wearing lipstick, and why did the girls have such grotesque hairdos! And their eyes *shone* like angels' eyes. The most angelic, the most alarmingly beautiful, of the portraits was that of Garth's uncle Gideon, who must have been about Little Goldie's age at the time of the drawing. Christabel giggled and giggled at it, until her cheeks were wet with tears. "Just look at Daddy! Just *look* at Daddy!" she cried. But Little Goldie, suddenly sober, ran to the wall, and stood on her tiptoes to examine the portrait. Garth saw how her expression changed; how raptly she stared up at the striking child inside the ornate gold frame. Little Goldie mumbled something that sounded like, "That's him, is it," and Garth's insides contracted violently with a poison he knew at once —though how could he have known, being so inexperienced?—was jealousy. He gripped the tiny teacup so hard its handle shattered.

The Hound

In a full-bodied white blouse and a long cornflower-blue cotton skirt, wearing her new straw hat with the wide pink velvet ribbon that fell in two streamers down her back, Yolande Bellefleur left the graveled path of the park and, seeing that no one watched, climbed over a split-rail fence with no more than two quick deft movements that hardly showed the white of her petticoats. . . . There was no one to observe the fact that she was slipping off into the forbidden woods north of the cemetery, alone; there was no one to see how becomingly the pink streamers fell against her curly wheat-colored hair. One moment she was on the path, walking without haste: the next moment she had disappeared into the stand of hemlock and mountain maples that bounded the park at this end.

She was fifteen years old and very pretty and she was on her way— ah, no one would have guessed!—though *why* on an ordinary weekday morning would she be wearing so fetching an outfit, and her brand-new (it was hardly a week old) straw hat rather than her old straw hat?—on her way—so she mouthed the words, shivering—to meet her lover. Yolande Bellefleur was on her way to meet her lover.

The woods, the forbidden woods! The forbidden Bellefleur woods!

Sunless and preternaturally silent and yet enchantingly beautiful: or was it simply the peace of the forest that was so beautiful? Those who strolled idly through the woods found themselves saying less and less, for words, in this dark still inhuman place, rang hollow; tasted suddenly meager on the tongue; lost their meaning. Peace, tranquillity, silence, the soft bed of pine needles always underfoot, springy, spongy, seductive, lulling. . . . One lowered his voice in this place, and soon stopped talking altogether. For what value had mere *words,* here?

Still, she shaped her words aloud, though shyly (for the forest had already begun to intimidate her): "Yolande Bellefleur is on her way to meet her lover. . . ."

Nine-thirty in the morning. A fresh clear windless day. She had wakened early, stirred by the memory of Saturday's prolonged delirium: the Steadman wedding upriver at the Steadman estate, Irma Steadman married at the age of seventeen, Yolande one of eight bridesmaids. . . . Irma Steadman, her friend, standing there beside her bridegroom, in that long full gown with its layers of Spanish lace, and the veil that had been her grandmother's, her small sweet face radiant (for there was no other word); the young man beside her in his bridegroom's outfit, with the silk-embroidered buttonholes and the ruffled cuffs and the sprig of orange blossom in his lapel, and the smart gleaming patent leather shoes. . . . Yolande's gown was made of moiré silk, buttercup yellow, and her shoes matched the bride's: made of fine white kid with small high heels and tiny pearl buttons. Ah, she had *loved* it. Loved them. Loved the entire day.

Her side began to ache, from walking so fast, she was out of breath and the straw hat had been knocked askew. How deep the woods were, how eerily beautiful. . . . Children might play at the edge of the forest but girls Yolande's age were cautioned not to walk in it, not even in twos or threes, and certainly not alone. If Lily knew—! If grandmother Cornelia knew—! "Oh, for God's sake what do you think will happen to me," Yolande snorted, "do you think I'll be *raped*, for God's sake!" Lily stared at her as if she'd never heard anything so astonishing. She missed the opportunity, even, to be angry: just stood there staring at her brash arrogant daughter. "Well, Mother, I mean . . . I mean, for God's sake," Yolande murmured weakly. "You know very well that nothing can happen to me in our own woods."

Tales of girls alone in the forest many years ago: someone named Hepatica, a distant aunt or cousin, who had walked alone in this very woods, evidently, and had met . . . or been confronted by . . . by whom, by what? Yolande did not recall. There were hints that something had happened or almost happened to aunt Veronica, long ago (but it would have to be *long* ago, Yolande giggled, for poor thick-waisted homely aunt Veronica was hardly the type of woman to drive men into a frenzy of lust), and something had almost happened to Aveline as well. . . . Cautionary tales, frankly silly tales that Yolande only pretended to listen to: she *knew* very well how foolish the older women were being. Yolande this, Yolande that. Yolande, don't run, you must learn to walk like a lady, and when entering a room you should . . . you should not . . . you should . . . . Never cross your knees, don't cross your arms either, you don't want to flatten your bosom but you certainly don't want to make it prominent by crossing your arms beneath. . . . *Are* you listening? Where is your mind? Yolande!

A white-and-brown hare bounded away in terror so extreme she halfway thought it must be playful or mocking. Why run from *her*, what possible harm might *she* do? "Oh, you silly bunny! Silly dear darling bunny. . . ." There were deer in the Bellefleur woods, hidden from sight; and owls and foxes and raccoons and pheasants; there might be bears— though probably not so close to the house; there might be (and here Yolande swallowed hard, for she hadn't thought of this earlier, she never thought of such ugly distressing things) snakes . . . long thick squirming hideous snakes. . . . (Hadn't Garth brought home, the summer before, a twelve-footer?—draped about his neck, its head bashed in, is warm glinting coral-brown skin looking supple as if it still breathed?) But snakes, she knew, felt the vibrations of footsteps, and fled . . . even the poisonous snakes fled . . . most of the time. Snakes do not *want* to confront human beings, it was said.

Once there had been panthers and wolves in this very forest, but they had been killed off, or driven out. From time to time the Noir Vulture appeared, a bold vicious predator that could lift creatures the size of foxes and fawns into the air, and tear them apart as it flew, ripping and stabbing with its long thin beak: but the Noir Vulture was nearly extinct, and Yolande had certainly never caught a glimpse of one; even her brothers had never seen one. "Oh, very likely there isn't such a thing," Yolande murmured aloud, "very likely they've just made it up to scare us. . . ."

Another panicked crashing through the underbrush. This was a somewhat larger creature, and Yolande's heart leapt as if it wanted to burst free of her body. Ah—what a commotion! But there was nothing to fear. A pity that the forest creatures lived in such terror, bounding away from Yolande Bellefleur in her pretty blue skirt and her smart straw hat, as if they imagined she was a hunter. . . . Her heart was still pounding. It shared in the creature's frenzied panic, and wanted to fly free of her ribs and escape into the forest.

Yolande stood motionless, until the attack of panic subsided. Overhead was a small patch of sky, straight overhead, no more than a few inches in circumference: it looked like a faint blue ball poised on the topmost branches of the pines. "Well—if it rains I won't get wet," Yolande said aloud. "The rain couldn't penetrate all *that.*"

She came upon a glade of long, bent-over grass, where coarse chicory grew, and another blue flower she couldn't resist picking and entwining in the band of her hat—were they dayflowers?—and now she looked very pert and pretty indeed; and where was her lover?

The glade would have been, she saw, an appropriate meeting place.

There was no one to observe her kicking off her shoes, and dancing three steps in one direction, and three steps in another. . . . And she began to sing, to hum, even to whistle, snapping her fingers, even lifting her skirts for a little impish kick that showed her petticoats. In the city last June she'd seen a music hall show, she'd marveled at the dancers' white satin outfits, their high-piled black hair that gleamed like tar, their garishly made-up faces, their—but what was it!—their *style*. One or two of the girls had seemed not much older than Yolande herself. She might have sneaked backstage, she might have knocked at a dressing-room door to inquire timidly how one became a dancer or a singer . . . ? Or an actress . . . ?

A pity her lover was late. A pity he couldn't hear Yolande singing the rousing "When the Boys Come Home" with which the music hall program had ended: the girls high-stepping, in white boots, with red-white-and-blue streamers across their breasts, and high fur hats that might have been made of ermine.

Then she broke off, since she'd forgotten the words. It was such an old song. What did she want with an old song. She took off her hat and sailed it onto the grass and, shaking her hair vigorously, gave her lips that poutish smile Aunt Leah used so frequently, while her eyes—but ah! her eyes were so much more *powerful* than Yolande's—widened mischievously. Even when she sang to the darling new baby, even then her face was so, so . . . but Yolande's face was narrower, smaller . . . her lips weren't so full . . . perhaps she only made herself ridiculous, imitating her aunt? And then she did not even like Leah. Decidedly, she did not like Leah. She wanted to snatch that baby out of Leah's arms and sing to it in her own voice, in her own way,

> *Sleep, baby, sleep,*
> *Thy father watches the sheep,*
> *Thy mother shakes the dreamland tree,*
> *And down falls a little dream on thee. . . .*

Her voice was husky, wispy, melancholy. She wondered—could it be trained? The lighthearted dancing-about songs called forth a high girlish voice, and made her want to dance energetically about; but the lullaby called forth a different voice. Which was nicer, Yolande wondered; which would her lover prefer. . . . ?

She sang the lullaby again, rocking an imaginary baby in her arms. A single tear rolled down her cheek. Her blue eyes glittered and her lips trembled with an emotion she could not disguise; but there was no one to observe.

Or was there someone nearby . . . ?

She broke off the lullaby and glanced around with a half-smile on her lips, for it *was* possible that . . .

"Who's there?" she called out gaily.

A mild wind blew through the topmost branches of the pines so that the cones stirred and winked.

She danced about in circles until she was breathless, and then threw herself down on the sun-warmed grass, and closed her eyes, and felt within seconds how her lover approached her, crouching over her, the hairs of his mustache drawing near. . . . Ah, what if his kiss tickled! "Doesn't such a thing tickle," she had asked Irma, and both girls had collapsed in a fit of giggling, burying their overheated faces in the pillows of Irma's bed.

But she must not giggle now. She wasn't a child. The moment was sacred. Her lover (whose eyes were very dark and moist, whose mustache was small, trim, neat, and gave off an odor of wax) was simply bending over to kiss her, as lovers do, as men do, it is really quite commonplace, it is not at all unusual, nothing frightening. . . . But it *might* tickle.

She had expected another lover, a young man whose family owned a large farm on the Innisfail Road, ah, what was his name, how strange, how very strange, she was losing his name, though it was a name she murmured to herself a dozen times each day, what *was* that young man's name . . . She was expecting, perhaps, her uncle Gideon: sometimes just as she sank into sleep his lips brushed against hers: they were often in a sleigh hitched to Jupiter, flying across an ice-bound Lake Noir beneath a full moon, Gideon in the remarkable fur coat—made of muskrat pelts as darkly lustrous as mink—he had had fashioned for himself some years back, as a playful match to Leah's ankle-length Russian sable. His expression was stern, he did not smile, in fact he looked through her as he usually did around the house, and yet—suddenly—wonderfully—he leaned over to her and brushed his lips against hers—

She shivered. Her eyes were not simply closed, but shut tight. Her lover *was* leaning over her. His eyelashes curved upward, his skin was a faint olive color, he gave off an air of profound, slack melancholy, he was no one she had ever seen before.

"Mother," Yolande would ask Lily that very day, "doesn't a kiss tickle, now tell me the truth!"

She began giggling and could not stop. Her eyes flew open, there was no one above her, she sat up, flushed, giggling so that her shoulders shook. . . . At a carnival in Powhatassie some years ago she and her friends had gone to the very exhibit their parents had forbidden them to see, the Exotic Wonders of the New World, and what sights!—what sad fraudulent sights! Dodo, the bird-faced boy with his absurd plaster beak and his slightly crossed eyes, pretending to screech while beneath the platform (Yolande claimed she could practically *see* it) some fool sawed away at a fiddle. Myra the Elephant Girl, really a middle-aged woman, lardy and obese, with grotesquely swollen blue-veined legs and feet the size of hams in cloth slippers. The Whipsnake Man, whose skin glinted all over with silver-gray-blue scales: even between his toes, as he solemnly revealed to his audience. A frizzy redheaded beanpole with a concave chest and legs and arms so skinny the joints looked enlarged many times, a squat toad-like creature with Tartar eyes whose specialty was scooping up insects (but were they *really* insects, as one of Yolande's friends whispered, maybe they were just *raisins*) on his rather broad tongue, a grizzled old drunk pretending to be legless (Ambrose the Veteran of Three Wars). . . . What nasty ugly things! And most of them were frauds, obviously. (You don't want to waste twenty-five cents on anything like that because, for one thing, it's all fake, Ewan had told the children.) Most ludicrous of all was a thing in a foot-high jar, the Hermaphrodite Baby, a creature with a single head and torso, and only two spindly arms, but burdened with an extra set of legs and private parts that grew out of its stomach. . . . The girls backed away from the exhibit, one or two even shielded their eyes with their fingers, but Yolande, poking them, said, "Oh, that's some stupid little old *rubber doll* they stuck in there—!" as they ran giggling out into the sunshine.

The attack of giggling passed. She felt suddenly tired. It was time to return home before anyone missed her.

"All right then for you, if you're not coming," she said sullenly. "Next time *I* won't come."

So she headed back to the house, walking quickly, her gaze fixed on the mossy needle-strewn ground. The forest had darkened, the air was pine-sharp but melancholy, it seemed later in the day, perhaps she would be late for lunch . . . ? Though she knew the way home very well, and prided herself on her sense of direction, somehow she took a wrong turn, and passed a fallen, badly decomposed white pine she remembered having seen some fifteen or twenty minutes before. "Oh, hell, *now* what a silly goose you are," she muttered. So she strode off in the right direction, her head down, the straw hat clamped to her head (for it was being knocked off repeatedly by low-hanging branches that sprang out when she least expected it, and several times a malicious branch nearly poked her in the eye), and after a maddeningly long while she emerged from the forest . . . but she was at the edge of the cemetery instead of the park . . . so once again she must have turned herself around without knowing it.

"Oh, *what* is the matter, how can I be so . . ."

Her face went red as if she suspected someone was watching, and laughing at her distress. There was nothing to do under the circumstances but indicate that she fully realized how silly she was: imagine, getting lost in her own woods, winding up in the cemetery instead of near the house! But at least she was no longer lost. If she took the long way around, and followed Mink Creek to the lake, she would have no difficulty getting home; though she would probably miss lunch.

She climbed the hill to the cemetery, and as she swung her legs over the fence (which badly needed repairing—you'd think with all the purchases and fuss of the past few months, Leah in command, throwing money about, someone would have suggested that the *cemetery* be looked into) she was certain—she *was* certain—that someone watched her.

It might have been great-grandmother Elvira prowling about the graves with her watering-can and clippers, or it might have been aunt Della, or even grandfather Noel; it might have been some of the younger children, though they were forbidden to play here; possibly the gardener, or one of the groundsmen, though everyone complained that these men had gotten so lazy over the years, they not only didn't do all their duties but didn't exactly know what they were. . . . But no one called out to her, no one greeted her. "Why, Yolande! What are *you* doing here . . . ?"

Slowly and self-consciously Yolande climbed the hill, noting with a pang of guilt the gravestones in this older section of the cemetery, tilted and weather-streaked. The babies' markers were especially sad: they were so small, so flat: and there were so *many* of them. (There were so many Bellefleurs. More dead than living. Far more dead than living—obviously! —though Yolande had never thought of it before.) She could hear them whispering meanly as she passed: Who is that silly goose of a girl, who is she to think so well of herself?—imagine, being vain, with her snarly hair all cockleburrs, and her skirt grass-stained, and that fancy straw hat dented at the crown—and she *isn't* pretty if you study her profile, her nose is too long and her chin is too sharp—

"I'm sorry," Yolande whimpered.

Up on the path she paused to catch her breath. It was a handsome path—pink cockleshells mixed with white gravel—but crabgrass and wild barley had poked through and were taking over. "I don't know why, I really don't know why, it isn't better kept up here," Yolande murmured. "But I promise I'll speak with them. There seems to be more money now, maybe it's only a matter of time until they get around to *here*. . . . No, I really don't know why, but you shouldn't blame me!"

Some distance away a figure stepped from behind a tree, where he must have been pressed flat, to behind one of the large tombs: but no, it was a shadow, it must have been a shadow, that tree was so narrow no one could have hidden behind it. Yolande circled the tomb, her heart pounding, and saw that no one *was* there.

"Well—that's silly! I call that absolutely silly," she said.

The dead were stirring to consciousness of her. She felt their vexation, their sleepy cranky curiosity: Who is *she?* Which one of us is *she?* When she had been very little the family had driven out to the cemetery more frequently, every Sunday in good weather, to trim the grass around certain graves, to plant annuals—geraniums, marigolds—and Yolande and the other children were given special tasks: Yolande remembered having to pick aphids off roses, wonderful big-blossoming white and red and yellow roses. (But where were the roses now?—only a few straggly climbers, overgrown, their petals tiny and anemic.) Dandelion, crabgrass, barley, wild oats, bittersweet nightshade with its small red berries. Goldenrod, of course—especially along the fence—growing as tall as five feet. Barnyard grass, gone to seed, beginning to burn out. The more recent graves were still in fairly good condition, but even here the geraniums were drying away, the clay pots were cracked or overturned, the frequent American flags, stuck into the ground, were faded and frayed: "Oh, I don't know why," Yolande whispered, "but you shouldn't blame *me!* I promise I will come back tomorrow and tidy things up. Not today, I feel so tired today, but tomorrow. I won't even start with people I know like Uncle Laurence and Great-aunt Adah, I'll begin with the very oldest corner, with the babies, I'll put flowers by the babies' graves first of all, the poor things don't even have any names to be called by. . . ."

A sound behind her, like a chuckle. She turned at once, blinking. No one. Nothing.

A pair of nuthatches fluttered into view, and began pecking at a sycamore. Though Yolande knew it must have been the birds she said, nevertheless, in a hoarse brave voice: "Albert, is that you? Albert? Or Jasper? *Garth?*"

She was not going to run out of the cemetery, she walked along without haste, pausing at the great mausoleum near the front entrance. It was overgrown with English ivy and the colored marble eyes of the four attendant angels had grown dim, but it was still an impressive structure. Fifteen feet high, with graceful Corinthian columns, made of white Italian marble . . . designed by and made to order for great-great-grandfather Raphael. . . . Yolande had been told the name of the queer jackel-headed god that guarded the tomb, but she could not remember it now. He had grown smaller over the years but his rude grin had become even more lascivious. "Are you some sort of angel," Yolande whispered. "I'm glad I won't have to be buried in here, with *you* out front."

Actually, there was room in Raphael's mausoleum. There was a great deal of room. How ironic it was, how angry it must have made the old man, that no one lay in there but Raphael himself!—and then (so it was said) only part of *him*. (For there was a family tale, which Yolande had never believed for five minutes, that the Civil War cavalry drum kept on one of the landings of the unused central staircase was fashioned out of great-great-grandfather Raphael's skin! A clause in the crazy old man's will had insisted that his heirs have him properly skinned, and the skin treated, and made into a drum to be used daily to call the family to dinner or what not. . . . Such wild fanciful things like this that Yolande tried to keep secret from her girl friends, for fear they would think her as peculiar as her family.) But part of Raphael was buried inside, at least. Perhaps he sensed her nearness, and would have liked to speak to her . . . or was he in a perpetual black mood since none of his plans had worked out . . . ?

"I'm sorry," Yolande said. "I hope the rats haven't gotten inside here, then what would you do?" She pressed her forehead against the marble, and felt how pleasantly cool it was. (She had a headache suddenly, and the marble soothed it; or did the touch of the marble cause the headache, which came so abruptly . . . ?) "Someone should clean this for you. The birds have made such a mess in all this fancy carving, it's a good thing you can't see it! And it wasn't a good idea, maybe, to give the angels *colored* eyes, it makes them look . . . it makes them look a little demented, like they're about to spring into the air and flap away."

Old Raphael's plans hadn't worked out, Yolande knew. He had wanted to be governor of the state . . . or senator . . . he had had, even, ambitions for higher office: Vice President, President. President of the United States! And of course his millions of dollars weren't enough, he had always wanted more, he had wanted to be the first *billionaire* in this part of the world. You *had* to admire him, Yolande supposed. But she was just as glad he'd died many decades before her birth. There were already enough Bellefleurs for her to contend with.

Great-grandmother Elvira had said once that no one had ever been so unfortunate as her father-in-law Raphael: everyone around him disappeared into thin air! So there was no one to house in the costly mausoleum after all.

(*His* parents Jedediah and Germaine had already been buried, of course, and their grave marked with a handsome eight-foot granite stone; he could not unearth them and rebury them in the new mausoleum. And he did not care to unearth the Bellefleurs buried far across the lake, at the edge of Bushkill's Ferry—the Bellefleurs who had been murdered in their beds, before his birth. That sordid incident angered him not just because members of his family had been killed, and killed by malicious cowards in the dead of night, but because—because there was an incontestable shame in it. However you interpreted the massacre it was the case that the murdered Bellefleurs had been *bested.*)

How sad, Yolande thought, circling the mausoleum. Even if he had been a difficult man (and which Bellefleur men *weren't* difficult?) he deserved to be buried with his loved ones close by. But it was a fact that he was alone: his wife had disappeared into Lake Noir, and her body was never recovered; his favorite son Samuel had disappeared in the very heart of the castle; and his youngest son Lamentations of Jeremiah was to be swept away in a terrible storm, only a few years before Yolande's birth.

"Oh!" Yolande cried. Suddenly, she felt the old man's spite, emanating from the grave. A piercing needle-sharp pain ran right through her forehead. "Oh, how *nasty.*"

She hurried away and saw, through pain-quickened tears, the figure of a tall gangling boy in overalls and a gray cap a short distance away. Her first reaction was simple relief: so there was someone real, after all, and not a spirit! Then, seeing the boy's derisive lopsided grin, and half-recognizing him, she hesitated, and tried to call out, "Who are you, what are you doing in—" but the words wouldn't come.

He ducked away and hid behind a tombstone. That he would do such a thing—hiding from her even as she stared at him—was such a mockery, such a peculiar prank, Yolande felt almost faint. "Oh, but I know who you are," she whispered, her fingers fumbling at the gold chain she wore around her neck, searching out the little gold cross. "Your name is . . . You live on . . . Your father is my father's . . . How dare you hide on me!"

One of the trespassers who so plagued grandfather Noel, one of the poachers, maybe, or someone fishing Mink Creek hoping none of the Bellefleurs would discover him. "I could have you arrested," Yolande whispered. "You know you're not supposed to be here, any of you."

Despite her jarring heartbeat she was not frightened; she was *not* going to be frightened on her own soil. And with the Bellefleur dead all around her as witnesses. But still she thought it most prudent to head for the front gate. For of course he wouldn't follow her. He wouldn't dare follow her. Even now he was hunched down behind that tombstone like an idiot, pretending she hadn't seen him; pretending she didn't know he was there. Oh, maybe he *was* retarded, there were so many of them in the area. . . .

(Those tenants farmers and their broods of children! Illiterate louts. Savages. The men drank and beat their wives and children, the mothers drank and beat their children, the children ran wild—wouldn't go to school though the Bellefleurs, nearly single-handedly, paid for the school and the books and the teacher's salary—ran wild and set fires and injured one another, and what on earth could you do about it? The ugliest tales were told: the Varrells and the Doans and the McIntyres and the Gittings: a boy named Hank Varrell had doused someone's collie with gasoline and set him afire because the other boy hadn't believed him when he lied about some job or other he'd been promised in the city, and what was worse (so Garth said, Garth had been the one to tell Yolande about the incident) was that the sheriff hadn't even been called, because people out there were afraid Varrell might set a human being on fire next time.)

So Yolande left the cemetery, and descended the hill to the creek, walking at a normal pace. She was not frightened, she was not going to allow herself to be frightened; the boy would only laugh at her; she *wasn't* frightened. (Though the stitch in her side had returned. And her head still ached.) She followed the fishermen's path alongside the creek, knowing the strange boy would not pursue her.

"Why, if I told Papa about this . . . or Grandpa . . . or even Garth . . . Why, Garth and his friends, or Uncle Gideon, or . . ."

She did not want to look back, for fear he was watching her, but she couldn't help herself: and there *was* something following her though it didn't look like the boy or even a person . . . unless it was a person crawling along through the high grass. . . .

Yolande swallowed. She felt faint. Perhaps if she ran back into the forest and hid, perhaps if she shut her eyes tight, her lover would find her, her true lover would discover her and save her and carry her back home. . . . But, ah!—it wasn't a person, it was a dog. Only a dog.

She crossed a marshy meadow, holding her skirt and petticoats off the ground (how muddy and nasty everything was!—her shoes were ruined) and saw in the corner of her eye the dog trotting parallel with her.

"You go away back home!" she cried. "You know you don't belong here!"

If only her lover would appear: he would clap his hands vigorously and frighten the dog away. And sliding his arm across her shoulders he would walk her back to the house. . . .

"Shoo! Go away! Go home where you belong!" Yolande cried.

It wasn't a dog she recognized. A hound with a mud-splattered yellowish hide, and a tail that had never been trimmed. Even at this distance Yolande could see it had the mange. Odd, how it contemplated her as it trotted along; its expression was almost human.

"You heard me—we don't allow stray dogs on our property," Yolande said, beginning to sob.

The creature paused, lifted one hind leg, and in response to her words urinated on a clump of weed flowers.

"Oh, aren't you nasty. . . . Dogs are so nasty . . ." Yolande whispered.

She turned and walked faster and believed she could see, a mile or so away, the towers of the castle, the towers of her home. She would be there in a little while and they would take care of her and the hound wouldn't dare follow her, any more than the boy had dared follow her, and she would tell her father and Uncle Gideon about what had happened, and *then* . . . The yellow dog trotted beside her, now at a distance, now uncomfortably close, growling and nipping at her heels, and then falling back, half-cringing, staring at her with his dark moist eyes. He was *seeing* her, he was *thinking* about her. . . . Yolande tried to keep from sobbing. Because if she once gave in, she couldn't stop. But her hat was gone: her hat had been knocked off and was lost and she didn't dare look for it: so the sobs began. The dog, keeping pace with her, its tongue lolling, drew its lips back from its stained teeth in a look of studied derision.

The Room of Contamination

On the third floor of the northwest wing of Bellefleur
Manor, overlooking the immense muscular grace of the cedar of Lebanon, and, in the distance, the mist-shrouded slopes of Mount Chattaroy,
was the extraordinary room known at first as the Turquoise Room—for,
some years after the completion of the castle, when it was believed (erroneously, as it turned out) that the Baron and Baroness von Richthofen
were to be monthlong guests of Raphael Bellefleur, this part of the
northwest wing was redone as a combination guest room and drawing
room, in a most elegant fashion: on one wall was a large plate-glass
mirror, approximately six by ten feet, enclosed in a bower supported by
two pairs of highly ornate columns from Pisa, of Italian Renaissance
design; fronting the mirror was a latticed grillwork giving a delicate,
somewhat precious floral effect with vines and small wine-dark roses;
descending from the vaulted ceiling were three dragon-ornamented
chandeliers, in gold and crystal; above the fireplace were four oak-
sculpted figures, of indeterminate age and gender, swathed in long voluptuous gowns; the floor was marble, and always chilly; there were, on the
walls, paintings attributed to Montecelli, Thomas Faed, and Jan Antho-
nisz van Ravestyn; and the furniture and ornamentation were finished
predominately in turquoise and gold. It was rumored that more than
$150,000 had gone into the Turquoise Room alone but the exact figures
were never known except to Raphael Bellefleur, who of course spoke to
no one about financial matters, not even his brother, or his eldest son.
(It was characteristic of Raphael's studied generosity that, in 1861, he
would hire to take his place in the 14th Regiment of the Seventh Corps
of the Union Army of the Potomac not one but two bounty soldiers, and
that though he contracted to pay them a fairly small, fixed price, he in fact
paid them far more, on the condition that they tell no one—no one at all

—exactly how much he was paying. And since one of the soldiers died almost immediately, in Missouri, and the other was to die at Antietam, under McClellan, the extent of Raphael's largess was never known.) The Turquoise Room was probably the most beautiful room in the manor but within a few years it was closed off from the rest of the house, its great tulipwood door locked forever, and it came to be known—in whispers, predominately among the servants—as the Room of Contamination.

For more than seventy-five years the door has been locked, Vernon told Germaine, walking with her in the garden, pointing to the windows on the third floor, beneath a particularly rain-rotted pinnacled roof: and the door will always remain locked.

The little girl, not plump so much as sturdy, solid, strong, peered up at the bay windows with their heavy mullions and tracery, and did not ask why, as if she knew the answer very well.

(The other children, overhearing, naturally asked why, and Vernon told them the room was accursed, it was contaminated, no one must ever be allowed to set foot in it again: for something terrible had happened to their great-great-uncle Samuel Bellefleur in that room, when he was still a young man in his twenties. And naturally the children asked what had happened to him; even Little Goldie, who was customarily silent in Vernon's presence, as if his very warmth, his unstudied affection, intimidated her, joined the chorus asking what? why? were there ghosts? was he murdered? what was *in* the terrible room?)

Even when the unfortunate Lamentations of Jeremiah was hounded by his late father's creditors into auctioning off paintings, statuary, and other luxurious furnishings, a mere three years after Raphael's death, the Room of Contamination was not unlocked. Had Jeremiah wanted it open, Elvira would not have consented, for she had agreed to marry into the Bellefleurs only upon the condition that (for rumors spread so wildly in the north country!) certain rooms in the castle never be opened, and certain misfortunes never be dwelt upon; and even if Elvira had given her consent, no servants would have been willing to cross the threshold. . . . The room was not simply haunted, it was *contaminated.* To breathe its air was to risk madness and death, and even dissolution. (Ah, but one midsummer night, overly stimulated by the public fireworks display the Bellefleurs had put on along the southern shore of the lake, Gideon and Nicholas Fuhr, then in their late teens, rode back to the manor alone with the intention of prying open the door. The fireworks display had been magnificent, spectators for many miles around had come to stare, reduced to awed silence by the ingenious kaleidoscopic explosions, the "Eruption of Mount Vesuvius," the "Battle of the *Monitor* and the *Merrimac,*" "God punishing the cities of the plain"—and for some reason it occurred to the boys that they would never again have such an opportunity to explore the Room of Contamination. Of course they did not believe that the room was really "contaminated"; they knew very well that the old tales of ghosts and spirits were absurd; so there was hardly any risk in what they did, apart from the risk of punishment should they be caught. But when, with two crowbars, a screwdriver, and spike and a mallet, they tried to open the door (beautifully carved in rococo fashion and finished in gold and turquoise), they felt almost immediately the queerest sense of . . . of languor . . . languor and vertigo . . . as if they were at the bottom of the ocean, barely able to lift their arms, barely able to keep their heads from nodding. . . . There was such a pressure on every square inch of their bodies, even on their eyeballs, that each found it too difficult to speak, to explain to the other that he was weak . . . or ill . . . or dizzy . . . or suddenly frightened. After no more than ten minutes Gideon dropped his instruments and stumbled away, and Nicholas crawled after him, and neither boy was to mention the episode to each other, ever again.)

Young Samuel Bellefleur had deeply gratified his father by graduating with honors from West Point, and by having been promoted, at the age of twenty-six, to the rank of first lieutenant in the Chautauqua Light Guard. Though photographs showed a conventionally handsome boyish young man with deep-set Bellefleur eyes and a small prim mustache and something both impetuous and smug in the set of his jaw, it was said that no one—no man—in the entire north country was so attractive. He possessed a remarkable grace and composure, whether riding in procession on his English bay, Herod, in the splendor of his full-dress uniform, with the chin strap of the towering ermine helmet cutting deep into his flesh, and his white-gloved hand casually on his saber; or dancing at one or another of the lavish balls that were so popular in the fifties, among the landowners in the Valley; or debating certain lively issues of the day with his father and his father's friends—the Paine decision of 1852, for instance, which freed a group of eight slaves brought to New York for reshipment to Texas, and caused great distress among the slave-owning states and great delight elsewhere—in Raphael's handsome drawing room. His fair brown hair was charmingly wavy, his voice was usually well modulated and gentle, his manners were gracious if somewhat self-conscious, and he put to shame his loutish brothers Rodman and Felix (or Jeremiah, as Raphael insisted he be called) simply by the way he entered a room, approached his mother, raised her limp hand to his lips and bowed over it, his heels smartly but inconspicuously together. In secret he scorned the passivity, the weakness, the "holy" patience of Violet Odlin Bellefleur, and did no more than pretend, with minimal effort, to believe the High Church claptrap she evidently believed; he was really not much more respectful of Raphael's "beliefs"—which he saw, not altogether fairly, as hypocritical—though he was certainly respectful of Raphael's behavior, and of Raphael's considerable financial success. "To hear the old man talk in public," Samuel said to his closest friends, officers in the Light Guard like himself, "you'd think he wanted a monopoly on lumbering in the mountains only to further God's work on earth, and to be in a position to bolster up the new party, wouldn't you!"—the new party being, at that time, the Republican Party. But in Raphael's presence he always behaved with dignified respect, and made a show of listening—or perhaps he actually *did* listen—when his father launched into one of his long, convoluted, grimly persuasive monologues about the graft, corruption, and outright wickedness in the Democratic Party, the Luciferian dimensions of Stephen Douglas, and the need to bear in mind at all times Hobbes's admonition that men require a common power to keep them in awe, for otherwise they will be plunged into war: *outright* war. (In secret, of course, they are locked in a perpetual though unacknowledged war, of which economic struggle is but one manifestation.)

Samuel was frequently embarrassed by the intensity of his father's sentiments; *he* much preferred horse racing, card games, hunting and fishing, dancing and parties, and of course excited speculation on the future (for surely the future involved war?), and who might marry whom. Though no one in the family ever mentioned the Bellefleurs' tragic past (that massacre in Bushkill's Ferry!—Samuel detested the victims as well as the murderers, and wondered if his friends murmured behind his back and expected *him* to pursue that old shameful feud), Samuel was as conscious of it as his brothers, and resolved that the future of the Bellefleurs would be as pure as the past was despoiled; and if, or when, *he* died, he would die with dignity, his saber in his hand. He would certainly not be surprised in his bed. . . .

A year or two before Samuel's experience in the Turquoise Room, he was engaged to the youngest daughter of Hans Dietrich, whose fortune and castellated mansion on the Nautauga River, if not his land (he owned only ten thousand acres, though they consisted of fertile valley farmland and a thick pine and spruce forest he would not allow to be thinned) rivaled those of Raphael Bellefleur himself. Dietrich made his initial money in wheat, and ventured, with minimal success, into hops at about the same time Raphael Bellefleur conceived of the scheme of creating the world's largest hop-growing plantation (though the scheme was not to be realized until after 1865); he became increasingly reckless with his investments, since in general they did so well, and made him so outlandishly rich. Consequently he paid no attention when Raphael (who had certainly hesitated before speaking out, knowing it an imprudent maneuver in the unacknowledged war of which Hobbes wrote so persuasively) came to Dietrich Castle one day to warn him against entering into a partnership with a man named Jay Gould, about whom Raphael had heard paradoxical and disturbing things. . . . So it seemed quite fitting, even to his friends, when Dietrich lost his fortune, and rather than file for bankruptcy and allow his numerous enemies to gloat over his shame, and even to prowl about his castle on auction day, he wandered off alone in his beloved woodlands above the Alder River to die in one of those "white mist" storms that can last for a week without lifting. The engagement, naturally, was broken off, though Samuel was halfway tempted— for he *did* think highly of the girl, despite knowing her only superficially

—he *did* love her—to insist upon the wedding in the face of his father's and even the Dietriches' opposition: but in the end nothing came of it. The engagement was broken, the family moved away, the castle's furnishings were sold at auction for a fraction of their price and the castle itself (a pretentious monstrosity, the Bellefleurs thought, modeled after a medieval Rhennish fortress, with rugged stonework that gave it a pockmarked appearance, and a ludicrous number of turrets, towers, battlements, balconies, and windows of all fanciful distracting shapes: diamond, square, rectanglar, elliptical) was eventually sold to a Dutchman who had made his fortune in bricks, in Manhattan, and who wanted to retire to the north country, where fish and wild game were so famously plentiful. . . . (At the time of Germaine's birth all that remained of Dietrich Castle was the central, squarish, four-storeyed tower, rising battle-worn and pockmarked out of a field of rubble.) For many years, however, people as far away as Contracoeur and Paie-des-Sables reported seeing Dietrich wandering in snowstorms, stumbling and groping about in the lurid white mist, at times a gigantic figure, even fatter than Dietrich had been in life, at other times lank and shriveled, and always shy—*he* fled from *them,* the legend went. But Samuel knew such tales were sheer rubbish, like the rumors he absorbed rather than overheard about his parents, and brushed them away with an airy cavalier gesture.

He would never have had his curious initial experience in the Turquoise Room, and the tragedy that followed would never have taken place, had it not been for a set of circumstances nearly too complex (so Vernon said, though perhaps he didn't exactly know all that had happened) to transcribe. But Samuel's uncle Arthur was back from the Kansas Territory filled with incoherent but impassioned praise for a man who had, evidently, along with several of his own sons, hacked five proslavers to death at Pottawatomie Creek. The man's name was John Brown, already one of the most famous of the free-soil agitators, and Arthur Bellefleur—until only a few years previously a shy, stammering, portly youth with an inclination toward the ministry, as some have an inclination toward respiratory ailments, until, one evening at a church hall in Rockland when he heard Brown, in person, speak of the evil of slavery and the necessity for man to wreak God's vengeance on the slavers, he had become transformed—"converted"—Arthur, still stammering, though no longer shy, a deerskin outfit stretched tight across his penguin shape, his hands and saliva flying about, seemed to be reasoning with—was in fact reasoning with—his brother Raphael to give him not only the use of the coachman's lodge and a number of the guest chambers of the manor for an unspecified amount of time (indeed, some of Brown's soldiers— though not Brown himself—were already there, in the kitchen, eating and drinking ravenously all that Violet had directed should be offered them: ten or twelve bearded and disheveled men, three of them husky brutish runaway slaves with skins of an unimagined blackness), and not only a generous amount of money in support of the cause (for Brown, Old

Osawatomie, though in hiding and rumored to be wounded, would soon return to initiate a series of guerrilla raids of slaveholding settlements, and he was calling for at least two hundred rifles), and not *only* some five or ten or fifty or two hundred acres of wilderness land so that Brown could, when he wished, establish a rival nation, a "second government" with a population center to rival that of Washington, D.C., as the struggle against the abomination, slavery, grew in ferocity—but also (and here Samuel had to marvel at his uncle's audacity) Raphael Bellefleur's personal blessing.

"John Brown has said, and you must know it to be true, that the slaveholders have forfeited their right to live," Arthur said. *"You can't deny the truth of that statement."*

"You're asking me to condone murder," Raphael said in a queer drawling voice. He seemed disoriented, as if he and not his brother had just rushed in out of the night.

From boyhood on Samuel and his brothers had been accustomed to hearing their father discuss politics with his friends and political associates, primarily upstate Whigs, and there were numerous occasions when the discussions became animated, and boisterous, and almost—though never quite—violent; and there had been a dismaying interlude of several weeks when their aunt Fredericka, Raphael's sister, then thirty-six years old, had pleaded without success for the entire family's conversion to her new religion—"True Inspiration," it was called by its small number of followers, headed at that time by a maniac German named Christian Metz —or, at the very least, financial support for the sect's community five hundred miles to the west at Eben-Ezer ("Hitherto the Lord has helped us"). ("You are blind to the truth that stares you in the face, that shouts at you to listen, poor sinner, and rejoice that the scales have at last fallen from your eyes!" Fredericka wept, daring to put her hands on her brother —who was so appalled by the disorder of her hair and dress, and by the fact that she would actually *touch* him, he had not the presence of mind to thrust her away.) So the boys were accustomed to lengthy debates, some more spirited than others, some more susceptible to absurd rhetorical displays than others. But the intensity of the quarrel between Arthur and Raphael was alarmingly different.

"You dare not deny the truth of what we say!" Arthur shouted.

"Brown is a murderer!" Raphael shouted.

"We are at war, in war there is no murder!"

"Brown is a maniac and a murderer!"

"I tell you, we are at war! You are the maniac—the murderer—to deny it!"

Samuel knew that his father believed, as he himself did, and most people did, that the Negroes were sons of Ham, and accursed; they didn't feel pain or exhaustion or despair like the white race, not even like Raphael's Irish laborers, and they certainly did not possess "souls"— though it was clear they were more highly developed than horses and dogs. Exactly what they were, what they represented, how responsible for their own damnation they were, was debatable; and under ordinary circumstances, with a rational opponent, Raphael would have enjoyed a debate. But Arthur had clearly been touched by madness himself. The Old Man had, he said, put a hand on his shoulder and declared him a lieutenant colonel in the army to overturn slavery, and tears had poured down his cheeks, and he had known at that moment *why he lived.*

Politically Raphael Bellefleur opposed slavery because he opposed the Democrats; privately he knew the system to be an enviable one—it answered the only important moral requirement that might reasonably be asked of an economic strategy: it worked. (And wasn't it the case, he asked Arthur, on the very night of Arthur's arrival, that some stocks of men are clearly bred for labor in the fields, and others for *thinking;* wasn't it the case—ah, so obviously!—that some creatures are born to be slaves, and others to rule?) God did not create all men equal, even in heaven there is a division of labor, a hierarchy, and if one didn't believe in heaven, or in God (though Arthur evidently did) then one must acknowledge that nature herself insisted upon the dominion of men over beasts, and the dominion of some men over others—for how, otherwise, had slavery ever come about? "Free the black man and leave him to his own devices, and he'll soon have his own slaves," Raphael said angrily. And flailed about, groping and stammering, quoting Thucydides on the Peloponnesian War (". . . it is a general necessary law of nature to rule wherever one can"). And Arthur, trembling, ignored his words as if they were too contemptible to be acknowledged, and said: *"What John Brown is doing is nothing less than the greatest service any man can render to God at the present time."*

From somewhere Samuel's once-meek uncle, a comical little figure with his penguin's body and his penguinlike manner of holding his short arms out from his body stiffly, as if he didn't know quite what to do with them, had learned to speak in a low, level, forceful, dramatic way, and to fix his eyes fiercely upon his listener; he had learned, Samuel couldn't help but see, a soldier's courage. It was of course ridiculous that he should claim to believe—that any white man should claim with a straight face to believe—that the black race not only should be raised to the level of the white race, but *would* be raised, and within a generation. It was ridiculous too that God should so frequently be invoked in what was a political matter. Nevertheless Samuel admired Arthur's strength of conviction, and even his fanatical energy. Why, he was willing to die for the insurrectionist cause . . . !

So when Raphael turned to his eldest son and asked, with a dry, sardonic dignity, his eyes half-shut behind the shining lenses of his pince-nez, what *his* opinion on the subject was, Samuel's heart swelled with a not-altogether sincere rush of sympathy, and he said: "They may have justice on their side, Father." Seeing Raphael's queer pinched look he paused, and then went on, with an almost boyish pleasure at the gravity of the moment, "Or at least history."

Consequently it came about . . . and how immediately it came about, with what passion, must be an indication (so Vernon believed) of Raphael Bellefleur's derangement, or imbalance, as early as the mid-fifties . . . that with a furious mock-servility Raphael changed his mind about driving the scruffy little gang of "soldiers" away, and made a show of insisting to Arthur that they remain in the manor as his guests, his personal guests: two or three of them might even wish (unless Arthur wished?) to reside in the Turquoise Room.

The swiftness with which Arthur's expression altered—his mist-gray dilated eyes at once narrowing, his grimace softening to a malicious smile —showed how keenly sensitive he was to his older brother's game, and so at once *he* agreed: why, yes, certainly, it was only appropriate, no need to hesitate, the Negroes would be given that room, for who else—including Arthur himself?—had a better right to it?

Exactly, Raphael said. And, still turned to his son, and still not looking at him, he directed Samuel to make the arrangements: inform the housekeeper, inform Violet, go to the kitchen and introduce himself to the "soldiers," perform all the tasks that a gracious host would perform since, unfortunately, the head of the family felt indisposed and would now be retiring for the night. . . .

"Father," Samuel said, lurching to his feet, "you aren't serious!"

"I am as serious as you have been," Raphael said.

So the three runaway slaves were chambered for the night in the Turquoise Room, whose splendors were so astonishing, so inestimable, that it was quite probable the poor men did not even register the honor bestowed upon them—or they might have thought that each room in the castle was as luxurious. Whether they slept well, or uneasily; whether they were gratified by Raphael's generosity, or baffled by it, or suspicious; whether they sensed the crude joke behind their host's action—no one knew—but they asked Arthur if they might be housed elsewhere, the following day. And so they were moved to the coachman's lodge. (And within a week Arthur and the men were gone—"word had come," Arthur said mysteriously, of a change in plans; even the establishment of a second capital would have to wait.)

The Turquoise Room was aired, and scrubbed, and polished, and a number of its furnishings removed (some to be vigorously cleaned with kerosene, and given to the servants; some to be burned outright), and Raphael inspected it and saw that it was as beautiful as ever; it *was* a splendid room, worth every penny it had cost. Then it was shut up again, and not reopened until Senator Wesley Tidd came to visit, in order to discuss the logistics of a partnership with Raphael Bellefleur in an iron-ore mining operation in Kittery. (Out of the Kittery mines was to come the iron that sheathed the *Monitor* in the war—as well as iron for any number of other military equipment. Two hundred thousand tons were to be extracted from the Bellefleur mines annually, during the peak years, before the mines wore out.)

Evidently Senator Tidd spent a restless night in the Turquoise Room, for in the morning he seemed drawn and tired, and apologized for "not being himself." His head ached, his eyes watered, his stomach was upset, he had suffered unpleasant dreams. . . . Almost timidly (for though the Senator was a thoroughly unscrupulous man he had impeccable social manners) he asked Raphael if perhaps . . . if perhaps he could be moved to another room? He was not accustomed to making such requests, but he *had* endured a particularly difficult night, and though the room was beautiful—even more astonishing than legend would have it—he feared it had been ruined for him on this visit.

And then again, some months later, when Hayes Whittier was a houseguest, he was discovered strolling about the park's graveled walks well before dawn. When Raphael questioned him he answered evasively, saying only that he hadn't slept well; he supposed it was indigestion. Later in the day he too requested another room. . . . His manner was sober, even grave. "What was the nature of your dissatisfaction with the room?" Raphael asked. "I was not dissatisfied with the room," Hayes said at once. "But you spent an unusual night?" Raphael asked. "Ah, yes," Hayes said, his voice dropping, his gaze fleeing Raphael's, "a somewhat unusual night." "Was there . . . any sort of odor?" Raphael asked hesitantly. Hayes did not reply; but he did not appear to be casting his mind about for a proper reply; he was simply staring at the ground. "Was there," Raphael asked, "any sort of . . . of presence? I mean, could you . . . Could one . . . Could one *sense* a presence that might be called foreign, or . . ." Hayes hunched his shoulders in a way he had, and ran his forefinger over the bump at the bridge of his nose. When rising to speak in support of Secretary of War Cameron, some years later, he was to make the same gesture, and to speak in the same slow, distracted, profoundly melancholy voice. "There were a number of presences," he said, staring at the gravel underfoot, "and . . . and, yes, yes, I suppose you might characterize them as *foreign.*"

Though the filigree and *objets d'art*—and that enormous intimidating mirror—would constrain them to some extent, and there could be, naturally, no young women present (as there frequently were, near the end of the evening, when the men met at the officers' club), Samuel and several of his friends from the Light Guard decided to spend their poker night in the Turquoise Room, in order to investigate it.

For two or three hours their boyish high spirits must have had a subduing, or soothing, effect upon the "presences"—for nothing much happened that might be considered uncommon, though cards slapped down were frequently overturned, or blown off the table by an imperceptible breeze, and the wine the men sipped—a very dry white Portuguese wine from Raphael's cellar—seemed to go at once to their heads, as if it were pure alcohol. Then, despite Samuel's hearty insistence that nothing was wrong, that they had to resist the seductive power of their own imaginations, it soon became evident that invisible creatures were in the room with them: the game was more and more interrupted, a glass lifted to someone's lips by itself and wine spilled, gold coins spun and rolled about, a ghost breath rippled Samuel's hair playfully. There were heavy indentations in chair cushions, the impress of someone's generous buttocks. The mirror grew cloudy and indistinct. Diamond-shaped crystals on one of the chandeliers began to rattle. There was an odor of flesh— not altogether clean—and yet not altogether unpleasant: the odor of perspiration that has dried, mixed with the odor of soil, sunshine, vegetation, unlaundered clothes. Most distressing, however, was the undercurrent of voices, lifting now and then into laughter of a somewhat jeering type. And though Samuel insisted, now rather boisterously, that his friends were imagining everything—they were silly as young girls, routed by spooks and imps!—what fools!—what *cowards*—one by one the young men made their excuses, feebly and nervously, and went home. When the last of his friends rose to leave, swaying unsteadily, Samuel seized what remained of the deck of cards and threw it petulantly down, cursing him; he staggered to his feet, turning his back on his friend, his arms crossed and his shoulders hunched in an attitude of childish fury, and when he raised his eyes he found that he was facing the mirror, staring into the mirror, and that, beyond the filmy glass surface, his friend was not reflected—the room itself was only dimly reflected—and his own image was transparent as a jellyfish's.

He turned, and his friend was still there, chattering, his hand extended for Samuel to shake. If the young man caught in that instant Samuel's own astonishment he gave no indication: quite simply he was escaping, and there was nothing Samuel could do to restrain him.

So he left, and Samuel remained in the room, at first angered by— by whatever it was—by the queer bodiless agitation of air—by the murmurous voices—and the laughter that rose in jagged little peaks—and the *odor.* He drank from a wine bottle, staggering about the room. Why didn't they show themselves, were they afraid of *him,* who were they to intrude on a private card game, to interfere—who were they to trespass in Bellefleur Manor? He saw, reflected in the mirror, a dark figure pass close behind him; but when he turned no one was there. Coward, he whispered.

The gold minute hand on the alabaster clock above the mantel began to move backward. Samuel stared at it, the bottle lifted to his lips. He was angry, he wasn't frightened, quite deliberately he swallowed a few large mouthfuls as he watched the clock hand, though the wine had begun to dribble down his chin. Then he threw the bottle from him and rushed to the clock and stopped the hand, and moved it forward again. There was a slight resistance but he overcame it; and in his zeal moved the hand round and round and round, so that he lost track of the time. . . . Two in the morning, perhaps. Two-thirty. No more than three.

Now when he turned he saw in the mirror a mist-shrouded group of people, all of them black: and detaching itself from the group, with a peculiar airy grace—peculiar because it was so *solid*—was the figure of a woman. Samuel stared, standing motionless. In his distraction he began to dig at the tartar on his front teeth, a habit he believed he had cured himself of years before.

A black woman—a Negress—but not a slave—evidently not a slave —with wide thick grape-colored lips—tobacco-colored skin—a broad, somewhat flat nose, with prominent nostrils—hair that frizzed with static electricity—strong shoulders—muscular shoulders—a thick but long neck—long-lashed eyes—very dark eyes—eyes that fixed him in a mocking stare. He stood immobile, waiting for her to speak—what if she called him by name, what if she claimed him!—his thumbnail now jammed between two of his lower teeth.

A Negress, an African—with what defiantly, hideously African features! Samuel stared and stared, for he had never seen a black woman before, never at such close range, and though the mirror was cloudy, and the outlines of the woman's body bled away into the shadows, she was somehow enlarged, magnified, and subtly distorted, as if she were an image detaching itself from its surface and covering Samuel's eye—a dream-image adhering to the surface of his amazed unresisting eye. But she was so ugly! She *was* ugly, despite her beauty. A mature woman, ten or more years older than Samuel, with heavy breasts that appeared to be hanging loose inside a shapeless sweat-stained garment, and tense cords in her neck, and stained teeth. One of her lower teeth was even missing. . . . Ugly, obscene. Still she held him with that bold stare, as if his expression of alarm and disgust amused her. She *was* ugly, she *was* obscene, he wanted only to turn and run from her, and slam the door behind him, and lock it. . . . But instead he remained immobile, a strand of wavy hair fallen over his forehead, his shirt collar askew, the front of his vest wine-stained, his legs slightly bent at the knee as if their strength were draining from them; and the thumb pressed against his teeth.

But you have no *right* to be here, he whispered.

From that night onward Samuel Bellefleur was not himself—it was said of him, repeatedly, even by persons who had not previously known him well, that he "wasn't himself." Seated at dinner he smiled vacantly, and pushed food about his plate, and replied when spoken to so languidly, so indifferently, that Violet burst into tears more than once, and had to be escorted from the room. He was not discourteous: he made a show of being courteous: but his every word, his every gesture, even the most subtle movement of his brow, communicated a perverse and possibly even malicious contempt.

They could smell the woman on him—they could sense his erotic gravity—a sensuousness so powerful, so heavy, that it held down his soul like an enormous rock, and would not allow it to float to the surface of ordinary discourse.

Raphael was embarrassed, and then angry; and then baffled (for *how* could his son be indulging in a wicked liaison, when he no longer left the manor?); and, in the end, frightened. He had not expected his son to be celibate, he certainly knew of slightly scandalous doings among the officers of the Light Guard, and so long as Violet did not know—or did not acknowledge that she knew—it hardly mattered. But he had not expected anything so rankly obvious as this: and there was, at all times, even in the breakfast room, that incontestable rich ripe overripe fairly reeking *odor* that emanated from Samuel, stirred by his every movement, wafted about in the most innocent of atmospheres. And yet the boy bathed—certainly he bathed—he bathed at least once a day.

Samuel stayed away from the family for longer and longer periods of time, and though Raphael was grateful that he wasn't, at least, leading a dissolute life on one of the gambling boats, or piling up debts in the Falls like other young men in his circle—the boy *was*, after all, sequestered away in the Turquoise Room with the two or three newspapers Raphael subscribed to, and the almanac for the year, and even the Holy Bible!—still he could not refuse to acknowledge his son's increasing estrangement, and the fact that what stared coldly at him out of Samuel's eyes was no longer exactly his son. "Are you not feeling well, Samuel," Raphael murmured, touching the boy's arm, and after a space of several seconds the boy would draw away, slowly, and smile that haughty indifferent smile, and say in a husky voice, "I am feeling *exceptionally* well, Father."

His linen was changed less often. His collars were unbuttoned. He declined to come downstairs when his friends called, and gave as an excuse for missing drill, and for missing the sessions with Herod that had once consumed so much of his time, a drawling mumble about feeling "sluggish." After weeping in Raphael's arms Violet suddenly grew angry, and spoke in a rapid low voice of the "slut" who was ruining her boy: it wasn't anyone on the household staff, she was certain, she was *certain*, she didn't think it could be one of the female laborers, for how could he smuggle the creature up to the third floor day after day?—but he did have a woman, of course he had a woman, a filthy wicked slattern who wanted only to destroy Raphael's heir! (Violet's frenzy, as well as the remarkable words she used, embarrassed her husband to the point of stupeaction: he had never imagined his wife knew such words, let alone of the reality they indicated.)

There were times when, emerging from the Turquoise Room, Samuel actually staggered, and his handsome face—more handsome than ever, it seemed—was oily with sweat. His skin might be feverish to the touch, his lips parched and raw. His mustache, untrimmed, bristled in all directions, and must have tickled; Violet once picked a tiny kinky hair off his lip—and thereby incurred her son's startled displeasure. "Don't touch me, Mother," he said, recoiling. But at least, at that moment, he looked her fully in the face.

Of course they investigated the room in his absence, at least in the first weeks when he allowed them in, but they found nothing—only the scattered newspapers, a cushion out of place, finger smears on the mirror, the minute hand of the clock slightly bent, and the clock no longer ticking. The odor of unwashed flesh, the odor—hardly more subtle—of fleshly delirium was sometimes faint, sometimes overpoweringly strong, so that Violet, hardly able to breathe, commanded the servants to throw open all the windows. How hideous, that smell! How obscene! And yet there was nothing to attach it to: the Turquoise Room was as extraordinarily beautiful as ever, as magnificent as ever, a room fit for royalty.

The only time Samuel showed much interest in his parents' increasing alarm—and then the interest was rather mild—was when Raphael pointed out that he'd been hidden away in the room for eleven hours straight; and Samuel, opening his blood-threaded eyes wide, said that that couldn't be the case—he'd been in there only an hour or so—wasn't it still morning? Raphael explained, trembling, that it was by no means morning. Samuel had been in that room all day, and did he intend to sleep in there again tonight . . . ? What was he *doing* in that room! Samuel began to gnaw at his thumbnail. He frowned, looked through his father, seemed to be making rapid calculations. Finally he said with a wry shrug of his shoulders that "time was different there."

He was absent for longer periods of time, for days at a stretch, and when he did appear at the dinner table he yawned, ran his hand lazily through his hair, let his food grow cold on his plate. He ate so little, he should have been wasting away: but in fact he was as solid as ever, and there was even the beginning of a slight paunch high above his belt. When Violet demanded to know what he was doing in the Turquoise Room he blinked at her as if not knowing what she meant, and said in a hollow, husky voice, "Just reading, Mother, what do you . . . what do you think?" and his slack lips drooped into a negligent smile. He disappeared for three days, and then for four; when they forced open the lock to the Turquoise Room he was nowhere to be seen. But then he appeared downstairs that very evening, and showed surprise once again that he'd been away so long. According to his calculations he'd gone upstairs to read the newspapers and had been there about two hours, but according to *their* calculations he had been gone for four days.

"I think I understand," he said slowly, again with that dull loose smile. "Time is clocks, not a clock. Not your clock. You can't do anything more with time than try to contain it, like carrying water in a sieve. . . ."

And so, finally, he disappeared into the Turquoise Room. He entered it one evening after dinner, and never came out; he simply disappeared. The windows were not only closed but locked from the inside. There were secret passageways out of two or three other rooms in the castle (one of them Raphael's study) but there was no secret passageway out of the Turquoise Room. The boy had simply disappeared. He no longer existed. There was no trace, no farewell note, there had been no significant final remark: Samuel Bellefleur had simply ceased to exist.

One night some months later, Raphael, still grieving for his son, cut short his meeting with a group of Republicans in a city five hundred miles away, and returned to the castle, and ran upstairs to the Turquoise Room (which was now kept locked, since it was so clearly haunted), and, with his gold-knobbed cane, smashed the enormous mirror. Shards of glass flew everywhere, shards of all sizes, icicle-shaped, pebble-shaped, some small as needles, driving themselves into Raphael's flesh. He continued to strike the mirror, however, again and again, gripping his cane with both hands, sobbing and shouting unintelligibly. They had taken his son! They had taken his beloved son from him!

When he was finished only a few slivers of mirror remained on the wall. What faced him—held up, still, by the exquisite Italian columns—was nothing more than the mirror's plain oak backing, mere wood, two-dimensional, reflecting nothing, containing no beauty, badly hacked by the spasmodic blows of his cane.

Tirpitz

On her many travels—to Nautauga Falls, to the state capital, to Port Oriskany, to faraway Vanderpoel—Leah always took Germaine, no matter that the little girl would have preferred to remain at home, playing in the walled garden with Vernon or Christabel or the others; no matter that Gideon objected. "I can't travel without her," Leah said. "She's my heart—my soul. I *can't* leave her behind." "Then stay home yourself," Gideon said. And Leah stared at him, stared him down. "You don't need to make these trips," Gideon said, faltering. "It's just something you are deluding yourself with. . . . We don't *need* you to make these appeals for us."

Leah, knowing how the falsity of his words must strike him, knowing that he couldn't fail to hear, for all his hypocrisy, their tinniness, saw no reason to reply. She simply rang for one of the servants, to help her pack.

There was the matter of Jean-Pierre II unjustly imprisoned in Powhatassie, and Leah's initial petitions denied; there was the matter of locating a partner (one with, as Hiram expressed it, "unlimited resources") for certain mining operations east of Contracoeur, now that the scheme for managed cutting privileges in the pine forests had fallen through (and though Leah never explicitly spoke of the brothers' ignoble failure with Meldrom neither Gideon nor Ewan was allowed to forget it: Leah would say only *"Now* we must shift our plan of attack," *"Now* we must begin again at zero"); there was the need to check up on Bellefleur property, much of it operating at a loss, or with very slender profits; there was the matter of keeping up social contacts (which Leah, like Cornelia, called "thinking of our friends")—for the day wasn't distant when the many Bellefleur girls (Yolande, Vida, Morna, even Christabel, and now even Little Goldie) would be of marriageable age; and for a while, though she couldn't have been sincere about it, there was the matter of finding a suitable husband for poor Garnet Hecht (who had surprised everyone, or nearly everyone, by having a baby: a darling little girl with dark curly hair and dark button eyes who hadn't at this point any name, since Garnet was too listless to name her, yet too weakly stubborn to acquiesce in one of the names Leah suggested). So Leah was busy, marvelously busy, no sooner back at Bellefleur Manor and soaking in a hot bath than she was planning another trip, another mode of attack. Attorneys were hired, and then dismissed, for being incapable of "understanding what I say, when I don't say it," as Leah explained; there were brokers, bank officials, bookkeepers, accountants, tax lawyers, men whose names turned up like mica in a spaded garden as Leah talked excitedly at the dinner table of her plans, and then were covered over again and forgotten; there were of course Bellefleurs in other cities, frequently with other names (Zundert, Sandusky, Medick, Cinquefoil, Filaree), who should—or should not —be cultivated, depending on their usefulness; there were so many politicians—from Governor Grounsel and his Lieutenant-Governor Horehound down through unelected party hacks who might have impressed Leah with their claim of knowing what *really* went on—that no one in the family, not even Hiram, could keep them straight. What this promiscuous assortment of men had in common was Leah: she believed they might be useful, or might at least put her in contact with others who *would* be useful.

Early on, Leah had won over grandfather Noel and uncle Hiram: they were clearly besotted with her, and thought it quite reasonable—even "pragmatic," in Hiram's words—that the old Bellefleur estate of 1780 might be regained, by judicious maneuverings. It would take time, it would require ingenuity and cunning, and secrecy (for if Bellefleur enemies suspected the family's plan they would leap in and buy up the land simply out of spite); it would certainly require diligence and tact (and unfortunately the Bellefleurs had a reputation, generations old, of tactlessness); and *charm.* So if anyone objected to Leah's schemes Noel and Hiram defended them, and great-grandmother Elvira soon joined in (for, as she neared her hundredth birthday, she was visited with increasingly apocalyptic dreams: floods, fires, lightning storms that illuminated the heavens: premonitions that something extraordinary was to happen to the family); and even Cornelia, who customarily opposed her daughter-in-law as a matter of principle, appeared to see some merit in certain aspects of the plan . . . for the grandchildren *would* be of marriageable age soon, the boys as well as the girls, and she *hoped* . . . ah, how fervently she *hoped* . . . that the new generation would choose more discreetly than the old. Gideon quarreled with Leah in the privacy of their suite, and maintained a sullen courtesy elsewhere, and Ewan sometimes vigorously challenged her (he was especially antipathetic to the scheme of securing a retrial or an outright pardon for Jean-Pierre II: Why not let the old boy spend the rest of his days in peace at Powhatassie, by now he's adjusted, he must have a circle of comrades, he receives a monthly allowance from

Father for little treats and niceties, doesn't he—why not let him remain there, and not stir up trouble again?); but when he helped see her off, climbing into the old Packard touring car that fairly sagged beneath the weight of her luggage, turning to wave a goodbye kiss at whoever was assembled on the marble steps, Leah in her smart magenta traveling cloak with the matching kid shoes, her white gloves buttoned at the wrist, the filmy white aigrette bobbing on her slope-brimmed cream-colored hat, her rich glowing exultant face turned to him (and now, nearly a year after Germaine's birth, she had lost the extra weight she'd carried, and even the tiny pinch of flesh beneath her chin, so like Germaine's baby fat, had disappeared)—why, he could not stop himself from grinning, she was so *handsome* a woman, of course she would succeed! If any Bellefleur succeeded in this century, it would be Leah.

Through a helpful acquaintance in the attorney-general's office Leah met a charming middle-aged man named Vervain, a furrier, who showed some interest in the possibility of entering into a partnership with the Bellefleurs, though he knew nothing about mining; but it soon developed that Vervain hadn't the sort of capital Leah required. (And he was too well protected by his female relatives, as a rich widower, to be a possibility for poor Garnet, who *might* have appealed to him . . . a husbandless spiritless frail little mutt of a girl, halfway attractive if glimpsed in the right light, who somehow—no one knew how—no one could *guess* how—had had a darling little baby a few weeks ago.) But it was in the company of Vervain, who escorted both Leah and Germaine to the World's Exposition at Vanderpoel, that Leah met P. T. Tirpitz, the banker and philanthropist, renowned throughout the state for his charitable donations of parks, lakes, renovated mansions, and immense sums of cash to worthwhile institutions (among them the Church of Christ, Scientist, to which he may have belonged). Long ago, it was thought, Tirpitz's father had lent an undisclosed sum of money to Raphael Bellefleur, but Leah didn't know if the transaction had taken place before the worst period of Raphael's career—in short, she didn't know if it had been fully repaid. It was a measure of Tirpitz's gallantry that he made no allusion to past dealings with the Bellefleurs, and affected only a dim but flattering notion of their grandeur, and their significance in what he called "the magnificent history of our nation."

Though he must have been an elderly man at this time—smallish, bald, with odd planes and layers of bone in his skull that made Leah think of her mother, and a tooth chipped in an inverted *V*, which gave him a boyish puckish disingenuous look—he appeared as robust as a man in his mid-fifties, or even younger. On one of their strolls through the Exposition grounds he insisted upon carrying Germaine, who had gotten tired, and it quite impressed Leah—who was, all her life, to be impressed by such obvious demonstrations of strength even when she had long outgrown their usefulness, and could see them, clearly, as nothing more than sentimental vestiges of a too-lively girlhood—remember, for instance, the daring midnight climb of her cousin Gideon into her bedroom where he fought and murdered *Love!*—it impressed her just the same, that the man's legendary wealth, and the rumors of his association with a church she thought nothing if not comical, had not weakened him. His muscles were small but hard, and he staggered only a little under the hefty child's weight. "You really don't need to carry Germaine, Mr. Tirpitz," Leah said, her smile gracious behind the filmy gauze of her veil. "I *need* to do nothing," Tirpitz replied. But he winked at Leah to soften the effect of his words.

(She was to learn later that Tirpitz, *for the past fifty years,* had exercised every morning: sit-ups, push-ups, barbells, leg weights. "The body is an instrument by which we can approach God," Tirpitz said. "It is the *only* instrument.")

He took her to dinner, and arranged for one of his most trusted servants to stay at Leah's hotel with Germaine (even so, Leah worried: she had become, since the birth of this extraordinary child, an almost fussy mother who felt vaguely that something was missing from her own body, an arm or a leg or at least a finger, when her child was out of the room: and then Germaine seemed to *aid* her so, simply by gazing at her and smiling); he took her to the sailboat races on the Eden River, and to the opera, and to the private reception that followed the presentation of a medal to the visiting Emperor of Trapopogonia by Governor Grounsel on the third night of the Exposition (the emperor, whose kingdom was east of Afghanistan, disappointed Leah by resembling Hiram, and by speaking an almost accentless English—though she was naturally flattered by his warmly appreciative remarks to her); he arranged for the three of them to explore the Exposition early Sunday morning, before it was open to the public, pointing out exhibits that were of more than ordinary interest (engines; rockets; calculating machines; the City of the Future with its moving sidewalks and robot-servants and controlled temperatures and handsome manikin-people; the Hospital of the Future where blood, sperm, tissues, bones, and every organ—including the brain —would be stored, and would be available for patients), and ending the tour with the Tirpitz Pavilion, which was of course his own, and which both Leah and Germaine loved best: a five-acre jumble of marvels that included painted and bejeweled baby elephants; a white marble fountain with hundreds of tiers that sent out spray in a dizzying variety of forms; a killer whale named Beppo in a green-tinted transparent tank; a small mountain of orchids of the most extraordinary subtlety and beauty; Egyptian and Mesopotamian statuary; the Zodiac, in diamonds, fixed to a black velvet covering; a life-sized and amazingly lifelike Abraham Lincoln who intoned, in a grave, gentle, but forceful voice "The Emancipation Proclamation" innumerable times a day; carnivorous plants from the Amazon region that, with their yard-wide petals and the steel-spring trap of their jaws, ate and digested not only insects but mice and birds fed to them by attendants. . . . And there was more, much more, so much more that

Leah's head swam, and she felt the drunkenness of euphoria without
having tasted (for it wasn't yet noon) a single drop of alcohol.

"Mr. Tirpitz," Leah said, laying her white-gloved hand on his arm,
"what is the theme of your pavilion?—what is the connection between all
these wonderful things?"

"Can't you guess, Mrs. Bellefleur?"

"Guess! Can't I guess! Oh, I'm no good at guessing, Mr. Tirpitz, my
children are far sharper, if only Bromwell were here—you'd *adore* Bromwell, I think—*I'm* no good at guessing. What is the connection?"

"But, Mrs. Bellefleur," Tirpitz said, smiling so that the inverted *V* on
his chipped tooth showed, *"surely* you can guess."

Yet she could not. So Tirpitz turned to Germaine, and squatted
before her, and asked if *she* could guess; and the child—hardly more than
a baby, with the baby fat still plumping out her cheeks—stared at the old
man with her tawny green-bronze eyes, as if gazing into his very soul, and
said in a small, shy, but unfaltering voice: "Yes. I can."

Tirpitz laughed. He straightened, with some awkwardness (for the
small of his back ached), and at once changed the subject, grasping both
Leah and Germaine by the hand, leading them on, for now it was nearly
time for the Exposition to open to the public, and they must escape
before the hordes descended.

"I find it very hard to breathe in the air of crowds, don't you," he
said.

The evening before Leah was scheduled to return to Bellefleur Manor
she was invited to Tirpitz's private suite on the nineteenth floor of the
Vanderpoel Hotel, where, Tirpitz promised, they would discuss the Bellefleurs' financial situation. Quite by accident—it really was an accident,
he insisted—he knew a little about the geology of the Chautauqua region,
and the iron ore and titanium deposits east of Contracoeur (titanium!—
Leah had never heard the word before), and would like very much to
discuss the plans for several mining operations Leah had mentioned.
Leah had been almost girlishly pleased by his tone, and did not mind his
flirtatiousness ("Ah, but I dread to ask *how* much money you and this
charming daughter of yours want!" he said, and Leah said quickly, "Not
what we want but what we *need,* Mr. Tirpitz," and he said, "For the
maintenance of that enormous estate in the mountains, and to finance
your husband's expensive tastes in horses?" and Leah said, "He's sold all
his horses, and the estate maintains itself—it almost maintains itself," and
he said, "But do I dare believe that, dear Mrs. Bellefleur!") and his
paternal habit of seizing her hand and rubbing it briskly between his own.
(As if Leah's strong, blunt-fingered, overheated hand needed warming!)
She did not mind, even, the old man's smell—an indefinable odor, crisply
acerbic as the air of an attic which pigeons have befouled for decades, and
then again dry and tough as old parchment; and then again (when he first

greeted her, when he had just left his rooms) oily-sweet from the French cologne he dabbed liberally on himself.

So she prepared to meet him in his suite on the nineteenth floor of the Vanderpoel, dressing herself in her most charming outfit (which Tirpitz had already seen once, but Leah couldn't help that)—an oatmeal-colored silk dress with a many-layered skirt, a black velvet hat upon whose fashionably sloped brim three blood-red multifoliate roses bobbed, long black gloves with simulated black pearl buttons, high-heeled leather shoes she had ordered made a half-size too small (for she was vain about her large hands and feet, and took no comfort from Gideon's insistence, in the early days of their marriage, that a woman of her statuesque proportions would look *peculiar* with smaller hands and feet); and she carried her silk parasol, which matched the dress. It upset her, even so, to leave the baby behind—though Mr. Tirpitz had sent over the same servant, a middle-aged Scots woman with a happy disposition and a special love, as she said, for baby girls; she halfway wondered if Mr. Tirpitz would mind if she brought Germaine with her. . . . Odd, it was odd, Leah thought, kissing Germaine goodnight, how much she depended upon this child: how little she concerned herself with the others (she had to make an effort to recall, precisely, the twins—though Christabel and Bromwell were hardly twins now), as if, when gazing at Germaine, she forgot the others entirely . . . and her husband as well . . . and all the Bellefleurs. She seemed to draw energy from the baby, much as the baby had drawn energy from *her,* sucking the warm rich sweet milk from her breasts with a sensual rapacity that had been rather wonderful while it lasted. . . .

"Goodnight! Be good, dear, and go to sleep at once! Oh, I *love* you," Leah whispered, hugging the baby, and not minding that in her excitement the baby grabbed at the cloth roses, and nearly tore one off the hat. "I'll be back by midnight."

Germaine kicked, and fussed, and threatened to cry; but Leah was firm. *"Go to sleep at once."*

On her way out Leah heard Germaine starting to cry, but she paid no attention, and took the stairs down to the street floor, being too impatient for an elevator, and walked the several blocks to the Vanderpoel. There, a silent black man in uniform took her up in a cagelike elevator to Mr. Tirpitz's suite (this particular elevator had only one stop, the nineteenth floor), and another servant, also in livery, but Oriental rather than black, let Leah into the parlor. She exclaimed aloud—there were orchids everywhere—vases and vases of orchids—white orchids, lavender orchids, orchids of a subtle creamy-blue shade—she had never seen anything so beautiful.

She was seated in a comfortably overstuffed chair, and the young Oriental man brought her a drink on a silver tray, which he put down on a table before her. Leah snatched up the drink at once and took a sip. Bourbon, so far as she could tell it was good bourbon, though she wasn't a connoisseur like most of the Bellefleurs; but it was precisely what her nerves required.

The servant disappeared. She was left to herself. She waited, gazing at the orchids, wondering if Mr. Tirpitz owned an orchid plantation—but surely he did—surely he owned a great many things. Not long ago uncle Hiram had spoken of Tirpitz, had mentioned the name in some connection or other, with reverence, Leah believed, but she could not recall exactly. How amazed Hiram and the others would be when she returned with Tirpitz's support for the Contracoeur mines!—how amazed and envious and jealous Gideon would be—

(Gideon. But she would not think of Gideon. She rarely thought of Gideon, and never when she hoped to enjoy herself.)

She sat, and drank the bourbon, and waited, and after some fifteen minutes of waiting she began to get restless, and happened to see—but had the Oriental boy mentioned it, in his shy cold murmur?—an envelope on the silver tray. *Mrs. Bellefleur* was scrawled in red ink on its front. She snatched it up at once and tore it open. And read these words, which had been scrawled in the same dark red ink, in the same loose hand:

> Leah dearest, we are one of a Kind arent we,
> I know you *inside-out* & know you know me,
> if you step into the next room I will make you
> very happy I believe, & ser sear certianly
> you will make *me* very happy & will return I
> promise to the barbarian Bellefleurs in great
> TRIUMPH!!!!!

Leah let the card slip through her fingers, whimpering with the surprise—the shock—the distress of it. She got to her feet, and fumbled to set down the glass; and then brought it up to her lips again and swallowed a large mouthful of bourbon. Her face flamed. She finished the drink. Let the glass fall. Started for the door, almost tripping in her long skirt. Paused. You filthy old son of a bitch, she whispered, you buzzard, I could pick you clean, I could suck the marrow from your bones. . . . She set her hat straight on her head. Stood there, gazing into a mirror, wondering at the red-faced angry woman she saw there. The bastard, she whispered. I will tell Gideon.

She thought of Jean-Pierre imprisoned, for a crime—for crimes—he did not commit, and the townspeople gloating over it; she saw the magnificent wilderness kingdom taken from her family, piece by piece, tract by tract, over the centuries. If Germaine were here . . . If Germaine were here it would be so simple to hug the child to her, to weep into the child's neck. Where have you come from, who are you, why were you sent, what must I do. . . . There were times when, embracing Germaine, and gazing into her eyes, Leah saw, somehow *saw*—as if it were a dream of the previous night she was able, only now, to summon to consciousness— what must be done.

The hotel room was empty except for the overstuffed furniture and the orchids. Everything was silent; street noises did not rise so high. There was Jean-Pierre, now an elderly man, pining away in a prison cell . . . there was the hideous massacre at Bushkill's Ferry . . . the humiliation of the public auction when Noel and Hiram were boys . . . the loss of the land, piece by piece, like jigsaw puzzle parts, over the years. How *real* that was, all of that! And how unreal Leah Pym suddenly felt.

She paused, halfway to the door. Looked back to the glass lying on the carpet, and the card, that rectangular piece of white cardboard, lying beside it. Swallowed, pressed both hands against her burning cheeks, stared. If I could see into the future, she thought in dismay, I would know exactly what I must do. . . .

The Birthday Celebration

The day Yolande ran away from home, never to return
—*never* to return to Bellefleur Manor—was also the day of Germaine's
first birthday.

But was there any connection between the two events . . . ?

On that dry, warm, relentlessly sunny August day, when no breeze
blew across Lake Noir, or down from the mountains, there was to be a
large birthday party in the late afternoon, to which Leah had impulsively
invited all the young children in the area, and their mothers—all the
children from reasonably good families, that is. (And she invited the
Renauds, whom she rarely saw now, and the Steadmans and the Burn-
sides, and even wrote out an invitation to the Fuhrs which, when she
reread it, struck her as humiliatingly meek: so she discarded it.) In her
enthusiasm over seeking out financial and political support for the family
Leah had quite neglected people close to home; she had not even thought
of them for months. *Please come to help us celebrate the first birthday of our
darling Germaine,* she wrote gaily.

At teatime there would be a huge square chocolate cake with pink
frosting and GERMAINE 1 YEAR OLD in creamy vanilla letters, and an entire
table and a stone bench heaped with presents, out back on the terrace;
there would be paper hats and noisemakers and surprise treats for the
younger children, and champagne for everyone else, and even musical
entertainment (Vernon planned to play his flute, while Yolande and Vida
danced, costumed in long dresses and veils and feather boas dragged out
of one of the trunks in the attic); and Jasper was to lead his young Irish
setter through the complicated tricks he had taught the dog over the
summer. . . . *We hope to have a marvelous time and we hope you can join us!*

But Yolande and Christabel planned a smaller birthday celebration,
in one of the children's secret places on the bank of Mink Creek (the

Bellefleur children, in every generation, had "secret" places—in passageways, in nooks and crannies and cupboards and cubbyholes, in haylofts, beneath the floorboards of abandoned barns, behind evergreens, behind boulders, up trees, on roofs, in ice-tunnels (in winter), in manor towers whose floors were strewn with the skeletons of birds and bats and mice, in the old "Roman bath" their elders presumed was safely boarded up); they had nagged Edna into allowing them to bake and frost some cupcakes, and they had stolen from the kitchen larder a half-dozen ripe peaches and some sweet black cherries and a pound of rum-flavored chocolates from Holland. Yolande slipped into her pocket some pink candles for the cupcakes, and a box of kitchen matches from Edna's stove. What a lark it would be, with no adults—with no Leah—hovering near!

So at midmorning they took Germaine out to play in the garden as usual, but they soon crept away through the gate at the rear, each of them holding her by the hand. They would hurry to Mink Creek, to a pretty little cove a short distance from the lake, where the creek emptied into the lake, and there—seated on pine logs, protected from the sun by low-hanging willow branches—they would have their own private birthday celebration, and no one would know. (A noisy gang of boys—Garth and Albert and Jasper and Louis, and a visiting cousin from Derby, Dave Cinquefoil—were swimming off the Bellefleur dock, but they couldn't see the girls; and Leah and Lily and Aveline and grandmother Cornelia were being fitted for their fall clothes, by a dressmaker and her assistant from the Falls, so they would be occupied all morning.)

"This is a special day, Germaine," Yolande said, stooping to kiss the child. "It's your first birthday and it will never come again. . . . Do you know, a year ago you weren't born yet! And when you were born you were just a baby, a helpless little baby, nothing like you are now!"

Germaine had grown into a sturdy toddler, large for her age—very pretty—with red-brown curls and a small snubbed nose and those amazing green-bronze eyes, whose fabled luminosity varied: in the candlelit shadows of Leah's bedchamber they frequently glowed with a discomforting intensity, but in the ordinary glare of midmorning sun they appeared no more striking than Yolande's and Christabel's eyes (for Yolande and Christabel were also extremely attractive). Germaine was a baby, still, and yet more than a baby. She was intermittently and unpredictably precocious: she knew many words, but would not always say them. Then again she could be a terrible infant in a matter of seconds, mewling and bawling and kicking and thrashing about. It was observed widely that she behaved well when Leah was not present, but no one dared tell Leah that. Yolande was of the opinion that *she* could be Germaine's mother, and that Germaine would be far better off. ("Your mother is always fussing over Germaine, she's always kissing and hugging and talking to her, talking some kind of private baby talk, she's always *looking* at her—that would drive me wild!" Yolande told Christabel. "She doesn't look at *me,*" Christabel said weakly.)

Germaine was also given to queer prolonged spells of "knowingness"—when her gaze deepened but seemed unfocused, and her baby's face shifted into impassivity. At such times there was a stubborn Bellefleur set to her pursed lips; she would not respond to kisses, queries, love pinches, or even little slaps. She disturbed the servants by coming up silently behind them. She discomforted one of the dogs by staring into his eyes. Sometimes she left off playing, and was to be seen perched up on the white wrought-iron chair that was usually Leah's, in the garden, with her elbow on the table and her chin in her hand, her expression still and sad and prematurely melancholy. In the nursery one morning she astonished Irene by babbling excitedly, "Bird—bird— Bird—" and pointing to the window, not five seconds before a small bird—it must have been a warbler—slammed into it and fell, its neck broken, down into the shrubbery. Once Garth hitched up the old pony cart to the last pony on the estate, a gentle, rather lazy Shetland with faded brown markings, and watched over Germaine and Little Goldie as they rode squealing with delight around the weedy track; and he claimed that the baby put her hands to her ears and shut her eyes tight a few seconds *before* the pony trotted over a rock that flew up into the cart's axle and nearly overturned it. . . . (On the eve of her birthday Germaine was reluctant to be put to bed, and behaved quite disgracefully in her bath. Leah, her face flaming, was forced to shake the child and cry, No, you don't, no, you're bad, you're deliberately and shamelessly bad and you know better and I won't tolerate it!—and bundle her off, still kicking, to bed. She thrashed about, she threw her pillow out of the crib, she wailed, and held her breath, and choked and sputtered and spat, and threw a tantrum lying down, as Leah watched, biting her lip, but making no move to interfere—for she *wouldn't* be manipulated—and then finally, after an interminable period, Germaine grew tired, and the wails were sobs, and the sobs faint petulant gasps, and suddenly her eyes were closed, and she slept. But within an hour she was awake again, screaming more violently than ever, and when Leah rushed to her she was sitting up in bed, her skin clammy, her pajamas soaked with sweat, babbling about fire—she clutched at Leah and fixed her with those great staring eyes, and babbled about fire—in a voice so terror-stricken that Leah's heart nearly failed. She comforted the baby, and changed her, and brought her to bed in the big bed (for Gideon was away on business that night, he hoped to return by teatime the following day), and after Germaine fell asleep Leah put on a dressing gown and wandered about the manor, too frightened to sleep, convinced that there *might* be a fire—there had been fires enough in the old days —and that Germaine had smelled the smoke or in some way seen the fire —or had foreseen it— But of course there was nothing. And when Leah returned to her bed at 4:00 A.M. she found her daughter sleeping deeply and placidly as any one-year-old.

The girls were in their secret cove only a half-hour when they were joined by twin ginger kittens, about seven weeks old, but unusually long-bodied, who came mewing through the grass, and were greeted with cries of delight: the kittens were petted, hugged, kissed, fed cupcake crumbs, and allowed to go through the frenzied motions of nursing against Yolande's neck ("Oh, how they tickle! Aren't they silly! Just look—the way they knead their paws and shut their eyes and purr, sucking at nothing at all!" she cried), and finally to drop off to sleep in Yolande's and Christabel's laps.

And then the boy appeared.

No, first he threw a rock—a large rock that splashed in the creek only a few feet from where Christabel sat.

The girls screamed, and then Yolande shouted, "Damn you, go to hell!" thinking it was one of the Bellefleur boys. But it was a stranger: the boy in overalls with the cloth cap on his head: and he had the same jeering moronic grin as he came splashing along the creek, bringing his feet down with exaggerated force.

He jumped up on the bank, and seized one of the kittens. Holding it against his chest he petted it roughly, and puckered his lips, and said *Kitty, nice kitty, kitty-kitty-kitty,* in a high-pitched voice meant to mimic Yolande's.

"You put that kitten down! That's our kitten!" Yolande said.

The boy ignored her. His expression was flaccid and self-contained, as if he were alone. "Don't you scare that kitten," Yolande said faintly.

Christabel had scrambled farther up the bank, hugging herself; Germaine was sitting in the grass, a messy half-eaten peach in her hand. Yolande got slowly to her feet, staring at the boy. She was very frightened. But angry too. "You don't have any *right* to be here," she whispered.

The boy looked at her for the first time. His eyes were small, mud-brown, moist. On his forehead were premature lines, which deepened with mock concern.

"*You* got no right to be here," he said.

He reached up to tug the cap down more tightly on his forehead, still holding the kitten against his chest. It had begun to struggle wildly.

Then Christabel asked nervously if he'd like something to eat—a cupcake, or a peach—would he like some candies—and the boy turned from Yolande to Christabel, his expression still impassive. "Candies," he said, approaching Christabel, his mouth opening, his ugly tongue protruding like a dog's, so that she understood he wanted the chocolates put in his mouth. Which she did, with a thin little giggle. The boy chewed two candies, frowning, then spat them out—spat them into the creek without bothering to lean over, so that the mess dribbled on his trouser legs.

". . . kinda shit is that . . . trying to poison me . . ." he muttered.

"Those are good candies! Those are from Holland!" Yolande cried.

He took hold of Christabel by the hair and pulled her to the creek bank and pushed her off, and she fell splashing in two or three feet of water. "You want to come swimming too?" he asked Yolande. "You and the baby? Eh? Take off your clothes and come swimming too?"

"Don't you dare come near me," Yolande said.

He stared at her, and smiled slowly, revealing his tobacco-stained teeth. Yolande saw that he was Garth's age but that something was wrong, something was terribly wrong with him. "You want to take off your clothes, eh? And get in the creek with me? All of us, eh? Come on! Hurry up! I know your name, missy," he said softly. "It's Yolande."

"Go home," Yolande said, her voice shaking. "You shouldn't be here, you'll get into trouble. If you go home now we won't tell . . ."

"*You* get out of here," the boy said to Christabel, who was trying not to cry, "and take the baby with you. Go on—get! I don't want no crowd here."

"Please," Yolande said, "leave us alone. . . ."

"We're going swimming! You and me! Gonna take off our clothes and go swimming!"

Germaine had begun to make faint sounds, whimpering, gasping, as she pushed herself backward on the grass. The boy, peering at her, stood very still for a long moment, the kitten crushed against his chest, and then said, "Get her out of here! I don't want no baby here! I don't want no bawling baby here!"

Yolande picked Germaine up to comfort her, and Christabel hurried to crouch behind them. Her bare legs streamed water and her teeth had begun to chatter.

"D'you hear what I said, *you!*—you there!" the boy said to Christabel. "Take that baby and get the hell out of here! I don't want no goddamn bawling baby here! Or I'm going to do this to all of you," he said, making a sudden gesture as if he were twisting the kitten's head off. When the girls screamed he grinned at them, and showed that the kitten was untouched, but made the gesture again, his hand cupped about its head—and again the girls screamed, and Germaine began to shriek. He laughed at their distress, but a moment later was irritated by it, and said, raising his voice to be heard over the baby's terrified wails, "You're making me mad! You don't want to make me mad! Yolande Bellefleur, you don't want to make Johnny mad 'cause I know your name and I know how to get you—*Yolande Bellefleur, Yolande Bellefleur*—you want something nice to stuff your pussy with? Better shut up that baby—"

But the baby continued to cry. And Christabel, crouched behind Yolande, had to press her hand against her mouth to keep from sobbing.

"I can't stand no bawling," the boy said. "Y'want me to do *this* to you all—" Again he made the twisting gesture; but this time he did twist the kitten's head. It made a single hideous ear-piercing cry and must have slashed his hands with its claws, for he swore, and threw it out into the creek as lightly as he might have thrown a stone: it sank into the swift-flowing current in the center, a small hurtling scrap of orange, sinking immediately from sight. It had all taken place so quickly the girls could not grasp what had happened. This terrible boy *had* wrung the kitten's neck, he *had* thrown it into the creek. . . . And what was he saying about the baby, taking the baby away, what did he want with Yolande. . . . !

"We could go swimming. Or we could go over there," the boy said, indicating with a jerk of his head an abandoned barn on a rise nearby. "Just you and me, Yolande. I don't want none of them others. . . . Y'want me to twist all your heads off? Eh? Better stop bawling!"

Clearly he too was frightened. His young voice rose and fell with anguish, with daring, with an inarticulate rage; in his impatience he danced about, stomping, bringing the heel of his boot down hard near the girls' feet, as if he were teasing a dog. He touched Yolande's hair. His fingers closed in her hair. A kind of radiance broke across his face—his ugly smile faded—he simply stared at her. After a long moment he said, in a low, broken voice: ". . . that barn over there . . . just you and me . . . just for a few minutes. . . . Yolande. . . . Yolande Bellefleur. . . . Just for a few minutes. . . ."

"Barn! What barn! Where is there a barn . . ." Yolande whispered. The boy pointed.

She laughed, turning, shading her eyes. There *was* a barn nearby. One of the old hop-curing barns. It was badly rotted now, on the brink of collapse: moss of a bright lurid green grew on the sagging roof; even a few tiny maples nested there. "Oh, *there. . . . That . . .*" Yolande said.

He tugged at her hair. Hard. Then a little harder. He did his angry dance-step again, nudging Yolande's foot. And nudging her with his knee. Like a puppet she did not resist: she did not even cry out when his fingers yanked her hair.

"Y'want me to come back here sometime, at night, I could come back at night, and wring all your heads off, all the goddamn fucking Bellefleur heads, wring 'em off and throw 'em in the creek," the boy said softly, bumping against Yolande. "Y'want me to . . ."

"No," said Yolande. "No. It's all right. I'll go with you."

"You'll go with me?"

"Christabel," said Yolande, in an unnaturally high voice, "take the baby home. Take the baby home and stay there. It's all right. I'll go with him. It's all right. . . . Honey, please stop crying. It's the best way, doing what he says. Then everything will be all right. Do you understand?"

She understood. She seemed to understand. Though Germaine was clearly too heavy for her, she even tried to carry her for a few yards; then she lowered the baby to the ground and walked her along. Smiling, her face wet with tears, Christabel waved goodbye to Yolande and the boy. And Yolande waved back. The boy was standing close beside her, his fist still closed in her hair. He was very tall. He had pulled the cap down so tightly on his forehead that his head looked too small for his body. Christabel was to remember that cap—it was gray, with a faded initial—black, or deep red—and its visor was frayed. She was to remember the boy's queer twitching grin and his moist eyes and the agitation of the air about them, as if they were standing on a violently rocking surface. And Yolande's posture, so stiffly erect. And her calmness. Could it be possible

—her calmness! Jaws set rigid so that *her* teeth would not chatter, eyes opened wide in a doll's paralyzed stare—

"Goodbye! I'll be along in a while! Take care of Germaine! Stop her crying! It's all right! *It's all right!*" Yolande shouted.

Of course Christabel ran for help, dragging the baby along. She ran to the lake, where the boys had been swimming; now most of them were on the dock, partly dressed. Garth was the first to hear her screaming.

It seemed that someone had hurt Yolande—or was with her now—trying to throw her in the creek?—drown her? Or were they in one of the barns—?

The boys ran along the creek, found no one at the cove, climbed the hill to the barn, and discovered, there, Yolande and the boy—Yolande's dress was ripped from her shoulders, her small white breasts were exposed, her face was contorted, she shouted *Stop him! Help me! Help me!* She pushed her way free of the boy, who cowered back, his face sagging with astonishment: he stared at Garth and Albert and Jasper and the others as if he could not believe what he saw. Garth recognized him as one of the Doans—the son of one of the Bellefleurs' tenant farmers—and stooped at once to pick up a sizable rock. *Don't let him out! Kill him! Kill him!* Yolande was screaming. Though Garth would not have required her help she seized his arm, tore at him, pushed him forward, even struck his shoulder with her fist. *Oh, kill him!* she screamed, her snarled hair in her face, *Don't let him live!*

Which is what happened.

Within ten minutes the barn was in flames. One of the boys tossed a lighted match, and the barn exploded in flames. (But which of the boys did it? Jasper claimed to have seen his brother Louis strike a match, Louis denied it but claimed to have seen Garth, Garth was certain he'd seen Dave, but Dave, turning his pockets inside out, claimed that he never carried matches in his trouser pockets, only his shirt pocket, and his shirt was back on the dock: *he* halfway thought he'd seen Albert throw the match.)

They bombarded the Doan boy with rocks, yelling and hooting, two of them at the doorway of the barn, the others at the windows, pelting him with rocks (some of them so heavy they could barely be thrown) and stones and pebbles and chunks of dried mud and cow manure, and even branches, and old rusted parts from farm machinery, anything they could get their hands on, anything that might have weight enough to give pain. Yolande, in a frenzy, the bodice of her dress still hanging torn about her hips, ran from window to window, throwing rocks, screaming in a voice no one had ever heard before. *Oh, kill him! The filthy thing! The filthy thing! He doesn't deserve to live!*

Bleeding from the forehead and cheek, whimpering, the Doan boy instinctively ran to a corner, and crouched there, his hands protecting his neck, his entire body shaking; but Garth, leaning in a window, was able to bring something down on his back directly—something rusty and pointed—and a stream of blood leapt out and soaked through his coveralls. And then, within seconds, the barn was in flames. It was odd, it was very odd, afterward a number of the boys considered how odd it was, that they hadn't run into the barn after him—for some reason they had stayed outside—they had contented themselves with attacking him at a distance —as if they had known it might be dangerous to follow him into the barn.

The boy tried to escape from the burning barn, on his hands and knees, in the very doorway of the barn he crawled, and they pelted him with rocks, jeering and hooting, and he fell back, disappeared, and walls of flame hid him from view; and the very air crackled with heat; and from out of nowhere (unless the creature had been sleeping up in the loft, and had hidden there during the stoning) there appeared, again in the doorway, a skinny yellow hound, maddened with terror, its fur licked with flames, a mutt none of the boys had ever seen before, obviously a stray, and quite spontaneously they stoned it, and drove it back, and they could see it bounding, in flames, from side to side, and they could hear its pain-crazed cries for some minutes—until at last it was silent.

They backed away from the burning barn, suddenly exhausted.

"That dog," said Yolande tonelessly. "Where did that dog come from. . . ."

The fire burnt noisily, great billowing clouds of smoke rose into the air, and the orangish flames towered above the tallest of the trees.

"I didn't see any dog," one of the boys said.

"There was a dog. A dog in there. That was a dog. . . ."

"I saw a dog. I don't know where the hell it came from."

They backed away, panting, wiping their faces. In all the vast landscape there was nothing so mesmerizing, so eerily beautiful, as the flaming barn.

"The stupid dog, to be in there with *him*," one of the boys muttered. ". . . deserved it."

"I didn't see any dog," another boy said.

"Oh, he was in there, all right," another said. "He's still in there."

Book Three

IN THE MOUNTAINS ...

In Motion

In that twelve-foot-high granite tower three storeys above the garden (which, in the autumn, was noisy with the labor of workers) Bromwell chattered absentmindedly to his baby sister, not showing the queer half-painful excitement he felt when she so avidly, so eagerly, aped his words and even his gestures (as if, at the age of fourteen months, she were already greedy for knowledge—for *his* knowledge—and her very hunger stimulated a hunger in himself): and many years later as he rose from his seat, unconsciously pressing his somewhat bent wire-rimmed glasses against the bridge of his nose, hearing enumerated, in an English quaintly and brusquely accented, the dimensions of his "prodigious" (an adjective from the popular press, one Bromwell would have scorned had he even known of it) achievements in the young field of molecular astronomy, he was to see again, and to hear again, for a fraction of a fraction of a wondrous second, the night sky cold as a knife blade above Bellefleur Manor, and his own high-pitched rambling voice. Cassiopeia, Canis Major, Andromeda. And there is Sirius. (And the baby would repeat, almost accurately, *Sirius.*) But only in our language, Germaine. And only in our galaxy. And only from this position in our galaxy. Do you understand? Yes? No? Of course you don't understand because no one does. And here: Ursa Major. (*Ursa Major,* said the child, her eyes and hands grabbing at the air.)

In that crude tower above the garden (whose stained, crumbling statuary was being hauled away, heaped in the back of a truck, at last—what an eyesore that crowd was, Leah exclaimed, what a *graveyard*) Bromwell, surprisingly, "watched" his baby sister; and competed with Christabel for the opportunity. "But he's no fun, he doesn't play with her, he never takes her outside, even," Christabel said angrily; "it's always that damn old telescope of his, and those skeletons, and butterflies, and twaddle he's fished out of books—do you even know what it *smells* like up there, Mamma? Why don't you go and investigate!"

Leah, of course, had no time for such things. And since the day when Jasper and Louis broke into Bromwell's laboratory to release the muskrats, mourning doves, grasshoppers, frogs, and garter snakes he'd been keeping there for experimental purposes (his old laboratory on the second floor, that is, years ago), Bromwell made certain, through an elaborate system of locks, wires, and levers, and a secret "eye" in the steel-bound oak door, that no one could intrude, whether to vandalize or merely investigate. "Your son is growing increasingly eccentric," aunt Aveline told her brother Gideon, of whom she had once been extremely fond. "Don't you and Leah *care* that he hides himself away from everyone, that he's experimenting on live creatures, and mixing chemicals, and looking through that microscope all hours of the night?" Gideon, who had taken to ignoring most of his family now, with the exception of his brother Ewan, shrugged one shoulder in passing and said, "Telescope. Not microscope. You half-literate bitch."

Though Bromwell was ill at ease in the presence of the other children, he chattered away companionably with Germaine, despite—or perhaps because of—the difference in their ages. He enjoyed bringing her up to the third floor, to the tower on the northwestern corner he had had one of the servants help him weatherproof with strips of old asbestos siding they had found in an untidy heap in one of the barns; he enjoyed watching her walk in her quick, halting, *thought-absorbed* manner, her pudgy arms extended like a sleepwalker's, her eyes glittering with that peculiar ravenous yearning, as if she knew (as Bromwell surely did) that the visible universe was filled with wonders greatly nourishing to the soul —if only the soul opens itself, unresisting.

The mystery of the world, one of Bromwell's early masters said, is its comprehensibility.

So Bromwell puttered about, sketching in pencil the trajectories of certain planets and comets and runaway stars; making notations in his neat, rigorous, spidery little hand; describing flagelliform orbits that crossed and recrossed the familiar solar system with a whimsicality of their own. (From which Bromwell learned, as the years slowly passed, audacity as well as humility.) Though Germaine was hardly more than a baby, and certainly too young to understand, he was buoyed along by her very presence, and by the greediness of her listening, and spoke aloud any number of things as they came to mind: How can the rest of *them* remain satisfied with what the eye can seize, unmagnified! How can they live so crudely! Never asking the most obvious questions, *Are the past and the future contained in the sky, is there a "single moment" throughout all the galaxies, will it be possible someday to measure God (when the proper instruments are available), why does God delight in motion, is God contained not only in the Universe as it exists at this moment, but in its past and future as well . . . ?* Never asking, *Where does the Universe end, when did it begin, if it's an island what surrounds it, if it began 20 billion years ago what preceded those 20 billion years, is it dead or is it alive, is it alive and pulsing, do its components mate with one another, can I contain them all in my mind . . . ?*

A dust grain turned infinitesimally in the sunshine and revealed to Bromwell's astonished eye a miniature galaxy, diamond-faceted. It might have been the glittering eye of a fly, magnified innumerable times; or the great sun itself, diminished. At such times he began to breathe lightly and shallowly, and his frail body quaked. (Indeed, throughout childhood Bromwell was subject to shivering fits, even when the temperature was mild. Your son is too high-strung, he's too easily excited, members of the family told Leah and Gideon, disapprovingly; he isn't much of a *boy,* is he.) He was hardly three years old before it became evident that his eyes were weak and he needed glasses, rather to his parents' shame. (For they, of course, had perfect vision. *Their* handsome eyes would never require corrective lenses.) One winter, he and his somewhat older cousin Raphael traded a cold back and forth, like pups or kittens in a single litter, greatly worrying their mothers (for what if, in those days before snowmobiles and helicopters, when the castle was snowbound a month or more every winter, one of the children came down suddenly with pneumonia?)—for both had the look of children fated to die young, without protest. Gideon said roughly of his son that he'd outlive all of them; there was no need for the women to fuss. "He just wants answers to his questions," Gideon said. "Give him answers to his questions and he won't need any medicine." But there wasn't a Bellefleur, unfortunately, not even cousin Vernon, who could give Bromwell the answers he required.

(In secret, in his tower, fastidiously polishing the lens of his telescope as he talked to Germaine, Bromwell pushed to the very periphery of his mind the subject of family. The subject of *Bellefleur.* His imagination simply went dead, his prim little mouth settled into an ironic twist. Family and blood and family feeling and pride. And responsibility, and obligations, and honor. And history. Bellefleur history. The New World Bellefleurs were founded, you know, back in the 1770's, when your great-great-great-great-grandfather, Jean-Pierre, settled in the north country. . . . How impatient Bromwell was with such palaver, even as a small child! He wriggled with embarrassment, hearing grandfather Noel drunkenly reminisce, listening to great-grandmother Elvira recall Christmas celebrations, horse-drawn sleigh races on Lake Noir, weddings (at which memorable things invariably happened) between people long dead, of whom no one had heard for decades, about whom no one cared. Even more embarrassing were his own mother's strident claims: *Bellefleur* this, *Bellefleur* that, where's your ambition, where's your sense of loyalty, where's your pride? Bromwell once fidgeted so in her presence that she took hold of him by the shoulders of his jacket to give him a little shake, and *he* shook himself free, wily and graceful as one of the cats, by wriggling out of the jacket and bounding away, leaving Leah with the bodiless jacket in her hands. . . . Why, Bromwell, what are you doing, what are you thinking of ! she had cried, astonished. Are you disobeying *me?*

His embarrassment shaded gradually into contempt, and his contempt into a profound, listless melancholy, for he could not escape *Bellefleur* without escaping history itself; he might belong, then, to a world, but he could never belong to a nation. And then again *Bellefleur* was passion: passions of all kinds. He had no need to spy on his parents to comprehend the nature of the bond between them. (For didn't he observe, frequently enough, in nature, such "bonds"—male and female mating, and mating, and again mating, their striving bodies locked mechanically together, one usually mounted upon another's rear?—didn't he hear, all too often, smutty tales of stud horses, bulls, hogs, roosters? —and he had been oddly disturbed by the men's overloud laughter when someone told of a Steadman ram that had broken into a penned-off flock of ewes and impregnated, within five or six hours, more than one hundred of them. . . . If sex was a fascinating subject to the other boys it was a rather chilling subject to Bromwell, who approached it as he would approach all things, clinically and fastidiously, with the aid of books acquired through the mail. What was sex? What were the sexes? What did "sexual attraction" mean? He read of certain creatures—quahogs, whatever they were—who begin life as males, and who turn into females in order to mate; he puzzled over other creatures who had the ability to change sex within a matter of minutes, male to female to male again, in order to mate; and then there were the hermaphrodites who, possessing both male and female organs, might mate at any time . . . and in some cases continuously, for the life of the organism. There was a microscopic creature, at home in the warmth of human blood, in which the female lived encased within the male, in perpetual copulation: if Nature held no resistance, the extraordinary thing—it was a fluke, aptly named—would populate the world. The sexual eccentricities of oysters and sea hares and fish in general were not really eccentric, nor was it a matter of alarm that so much sperm was "wasted"—over one hundred million sperms in the ejaculation of the human male, fifty times more in the stallion, eighty-five billion in a single ejaculation of a boar!—for each of these evidently wished to populate the world with its own kind. When Bromwell stumbled upon his uncle Ewan straining and heaving and grunting with one of the laundresses in a closed-off downstairs room, or when he happened to see, quite by accident, through his telescope, his own father cupping a young woman's head in his hand, and bringing it roughly to his big-pored face (this on a hill above the lake, a mile away), or when his cousins showed him the pronged bone of a raccoon's penis (they had trapped the creature down by the creek and castrated it), asking him if he had any books that would explain such a strange thing—or was it, in the raccoon, normal?—Bromwell told himself once again that the details of sex were of no significance, for wasn't life on this planet clearly a matter of a metabolic current, unstoppable, a fluid, indefinable energy flowing violently through all things from the sea worm to the stallion to Gideon Bellefleur? Why, then, take *Bellefleur* as central in nature? He much preferred the stars.)

I began by hiding in Nature, Bromwell was to write in his memoir, decades later, *but Nature is a river that carries you swiftly along. . . . Soon your world is everywhere, and there's no need to hide, and you can't even remember what you were fleeing.*

Alone among the Bellefleurs his baby sister intrigued him.

Leah had forbidden him to experiment with Germaine, but in private he did exactly as he wished. He examined her thoroughly, taking note (though he had no theory to explain it) of the curious scar tissue on her upper abdomen, an irregular oval of about three inches in diameter; he tested her eyesight (and was sadly pleased to discover that it was far, far keener than his own); he tested her hearing, weighed her, made pencil diagrams of her hands and feet, kept a fastidious record of her growth (which he seemed to know beforehand would be prodigious—as his assuredly was not); spoke with her as he might have spoken to an intelligent adult, enunciating his words carefully, giving her time to repeat them after him, *moon, sun, star, constellation, Cassiopeia, Canis Major, Andromeda, Sirius, Ursa Major, Milky Way, galaxy, universe, God. . . .* "You learn fast, don't you," he said in satisfaction. "Not like the rest of them."

He was pious and methodical in his experiments, and there was always an air of reverence about him—a child who appeared to be, at least at a distance, a somewhat undersized ten, in a knee-length white laboratory coat, his hair cropped short and shaved up the back, his thick-lensed glasses fitting snugly on his nose as if he'd been born with them—even when what he did was illicit, and would have enraged his mother. Forbidden to dissect animals he nevertheless continued to dissect them, though his interest in biology was quickly ebbing, as his interest in the stars blossomed; forbidden to experiment with what he called his sister's "powers" he nevertheless experimented with them, sometimes allowing into his tower, as a control, sweet Little Goldie (who represented, to Bromwell, the "average" intelligence) and even the hoydenish, rapidly growing Christabel (subdued for weeks after the curious and unexplained incident of the barn fire out by Mink Creek, but naturally somewhat restless, and impatient, and likely to taunt her twin if he surrendered, even for a moment, the natural power his superior intelligence allowed him: but Bromwell needed her since she represented the "slightly above average" intelligence) since she had been born of the same parents as Germaine, and presumably shared genetic inclinations. He oversaw three-hand casino among the girls, though Christabel and Little Goldie thought it ridiculous, to be playing cards with a baby!—and noted how frequently Germaine won, or would have won had she known how best to play the cards she received. He had Little Goldie sit across the room and stare without blinking at full-color illustrations in his *Elements of*

Biology, and he queried Germaine, patiently, about what she "saw" Little Goldie seeing; or he instructed Little Goldie to run somewhere and stare for five full minutes at a distinctive, sizable object (a water tower, a tree, one of the new cars) while Germaine, in the tower, twitched and whimpered (and frequently soiled her diapers) and tried to say what Little Goldie saw. Her fists paddled, her chin was wet with baby spit, she stammered, and squirmed, and caused the very floor of the room to vibrate with the intensity of her emotion—and much of the time (according to Bromwell's calculations 87 percent of the time) she really did "see" what the other child saw. And after Germaine pointed excitedly, one morning, at an empty beaker on a windowsill, not more than five seconds before the beaker was blown off and shattered on the floor, Bromwell instructed her to push off the sill, by her own "powers," a similar beaker —and would have kept the poor child there for hours (for *he* had the reptilian patience of an adult to whom time possesses no value except in proportion to what it might reveal, what meager nugget of truth it might suddenly cast up) had not she reverted, after the first hour, to infanthood, and began screaming and thrashing about so violently that he feared the entire household would rush up his private stairs and break open the locks to his private tower. And then Germaine, whom he needed, upon whom he was so curiously dependent, would be taken from him forever. . . . And of course he would be soundly whipped by one or the other or both of his parents.

"Don't cry! It's all right. It's all right," he mumbled, embarrassed.

It was one of his schemes that, by leading Germaine through a labyrinth of possibilities, reading off the names of villages and towns and cities and rivers and mountains, perhaps even moving her hand about on a large map spread across the floor, perhaps even blindfolding her, he might discover the whereabouts of his missing cousin Yolande (missing now for several weeks) . . . and what a coup that would be, how seriously, then, the family must take him, after the failure of numerous search parties and the family's private detectives! But at the very sound of the word *Yolande* Germaine became agitated and would not cooperate.

"Maybe you should limit yourself to experimenting with your mice and birds," Christabel said, looking about the messy tower with her hands on her hips. "Cutting up that poor puppy . . . I remember that poor puppy. . . . Maybe you should let me take Germaine downstairs. She'd rather play with *me,* wouldn't you, Germaine?"

"That puppy was born dead," Bromwell said quietly. "It was the runt of the litter, it was born dead, it would only have been buried, I did not inflict pain upon it, I did not cause its death. . . ."

"Then you should have buried it, you shouldn't have picked around in its poor little chest," Christabel said. "Come on, Germaine, honey! It's too noisy in the garden, they're bulldozing in the garden, maybe we could go down to the lake. . . . Or do you want to stay with *him?* He isn't tormenting you?"

Germaine stared up at her, wordless.

Christabel was now more than a head taller than Bromwell, and much more solidly built. Her face was tanned and strong-boned; her breasts had begun to develop; her legs were lengthening. She carried into the tower an airy flyaway slapdash good humor that exasperated her brother. "Oh, do you really want to stay with *him!* But what—what—" She gestured carelessly and overturned Bromwell's cardboard map of the solar system, as poor Bromwell reached weakly forward. "—what *good* does it do?"

Might there be, Bromwell wondered aloud, staring deeply into his baby sister's eyes, fairly drowning in that tawny-green fathomless gaze, a universe simultaneous with this universe in which a world like ours is propelled about its orbit, now at the aphelion, now at the perihelion, and again at the aphelion, century after century, a shadow-world, a mirror-world, in which, even now, I stand with my hands pressed between my knees, bending over a child said to be my sister, gazing into her eyes, wondering aloud. . . . Might there be, there, exact replicas of everything we have here, and would never *see,* here, without the reality of that other universe, the lead backing of our mirror . . .? And then of course why would there be merely one universe simultaneous with this? Why not a dozen, three hundred, several thousand, several billion? Begun in a terrible explosion and now flying away from one another, flying faster at every moment, each identical with the others; linked by the identity of material (dust, sand, crystals, organic compounds of all kinds) and "life" itself. . . . And might there not be, granted the identity of these innumerable worlds, a way of slipping from one to another. . . .

Germaine held his gaze. She gave him no affirmation, she did not rebuke him.

Bromwell woke from his mild trance to hear a horn sounding nearby. Bellefleur noise, Bellefleur "emergencies"—a day could not pass without the excitement of a laborer's injuries, or good news from Leah (back from one of her trips), or a fight among the children, or a visit from friends or business associates or relatives; or perhaps it was simply someone tapping at the horn of the new Stutz-Bearcat, for the pleasure of making noise. "Ah, well," Bromwell sighed. "Our universe began with an explosion of immeasurable violence . . . so it's natural for the human species to *rest,* so to speak, in violence . . . that is to say, *in motion.*"

Haunted Things

The cherrywood-and-veneered-oak clavichord Raphael had ordered built for his wife, Violet, with its walnut keys and ivory, gold, and jet ornamentation: an instrument of astounding beauty which no one (not even Yolande, who had taken several years of piano) could play. It was not that the keys stuck, or failed to sound; or even that the clavichord was out of tune. But anyone who sat before it to play was disturbed by its quivering air of hostility: for it did not *want* to be played, it did not *want* to make music. Or perhaps it was simply the Bellefleurs it detested. "We should sell this thing, or give it away, or at least store it in another part of the house," Leah once said, in the days when she tried to play the musical instruments she found in the manor. "It sounds so awful. It sounds so *spiteful.*" But her mother-in-law merely closed the keyboard, and said: "Leah, dear, this is Violet's clavichord. It's too beautiful to move out of this room." And so it was, and so it remained.

Damp mischievous kisses floating in the air, planted firmly against lips at unpredictable times: once as Lamentations of Jeremiah was drifting off to sleep in the rolled-up featherbed Elvira had allowed him (she had shoved him out of their bed, insisted he sleep on the floor, forbade him to seek out another room since the rest of the family would know they had quarreled), so that, startled, wildly elated, he erroneously believed his wife had forgiven him, and was inviting him back not only to her warm bed but to her warm embrace; another time as the thirty-year-old Cornelia, locked in Raphael's gloomy library with her stepbrother from Oneida, who was a Presbyterian minister, spread out before her on a desk the scribbled notes she'd taken, usually late at night, accusing the Bellefleurs—these terrible people she had, in all innocence, married into—of unspeakable insults and lapses of taste and crudenesses not to be believed: not a single kiss but many, grinding and sucking playfully all about her face and shoulders and bosom, so that the poor distraught woman went into hysterics and fainted; still another time as Vernon, walking on the promontory above the lake, in a lovesick trance, his arms crossed behind his back, his head bowed, tried out impassioned singsong lines *O Lara my love, O Lara my soul, how can you wallow in another's arms, how can you deny my spirit's chaste love* . . . and would have fallen into the lake fifty feet below, had not the kisses, angry and hissing and stinging as bees (and at first poor Vernon believed they *were* bees) awakened him.

Sixteen-year-old Della's sapphire ring, a birthday gift from her grandparents, disappeared from her finger one night only to reappear, days later, in a brown hen's egg cracked open by the wife of one of the farm laborers, in their wood-frame bungalow at the edge of Noir Swamp. And there was the matter of Whitenose, young Noel's bay gelding (whom Noel had acquired from a stud farm with all the cash he'd saved from birthdays and Christmases, and had broken—with great courage and stubbornness—himself), who so very clearly saw and shied away from and occasionally reared back from invisible creatures of a menacing nature, that Noel could not reasonably discipline him; the inexplicable soughing noises in certain rooms of the manor, as if winds were blowing through invisible cornfields; an odor of fish, rank and irremovable, on the fifteenth-century French embroidered altar frontal Raphael had acquired on one of his rare trips to Europe, and considered—for hadn't it cost a great deal, at auction in London?—exquisitely beautiful; and of course there was the matter (which, outside the family, became the inspiration for many a cruel, spirited gibe in opposition newspapers throughout the state) of the "phantom" voters in certain areas of Nautauga, Eden, Clawson, Calla, and Juniper counties who had turned out in the hundreds to defeat (by a narrow margin) Raphael Bellefleur's third and last bid for political office. . . .

Jedediah, long ago, was so beleaguered by mountain spirits (and mountain spirits are the most capricious) that he soon accommodated himself to their presence, and spoke to them with the half-impatient, half-affectionate concern one might give to troublesome children; but he was still susceptible to vivid, alarming, entirely *convincing* dreams that would have him sinfully bedded with his brother's young wife, and these caused him unremitting distress. (Which he was to feel well into his 101st year.) And Louis's wife Germaine, miles away, down in Bushkill's Ferry, was susceptible to annoying ticklish dreams that had dimly to do with her brother-in-law (whom she hadn't seen for many years, and whom she did not really remember), and which caused her, one night, to unwisely call out *Jedediah!*—thereby waking Louis, who shook the poor woman until her eyes threatened to pop out of their sockets. Felix—that is, Lamentations of Jeremiah—was to complain throughout his life that he was tormented more by "real" things than by spirits, and that he alone among the Bellefleurs was singled out for *absolute* defeat: he had said, after the

bloodbath of the fox cannibalism, that he'd half-known on the very eve
of the event that something terrible was going to happen, that he and his
partner would lose all they had invested in the vicious little creatures, but
(for such was Jeremiah's apathy) he had felt only resignation—for what
could one do to thwart a fate that began so many years ago, when his own
father had, if not disowned him, unbaptized him? *You talk of haunted things,*
Jeremiah had said sadly, *but what of those of us who know themselves haunted
things—haunted things in human form?*

And there was Yolande who appeared, evidently, at the very same
moment in the dreams of a number of the slumbering Bellefleurs—Garth
and Raphael and Vida and Christabel and Vernon and Noel and Cornelia
and Gideon and Leah and (so it was believed, since she woke babbling
a name that resembled *Yolande*) Germaine, and of course Ewan and Lily:
Yolande in a long dark dress with loose sleeves, a sort of robe, her arms
at her sides, her head flung back so that her lovely wheat-colored hair
tumbled down her back, her expression sorrowful but not contrite, not
at all contrite, so that her father, the next morning, brought his enormous
fist down hard on the breakfast table, cracking the glass, and said; "She
has run off with a man, I know it! And just to spite me! And it's obvious
she is still alive!"

Tiny drops of blood, in the children's milk and in the cream bowl,
for days after the cedar of Lebanon was felled by chain saws one shrieking
afternoon (for though the tree was more than one hundred years old, and
of course very attractive, and *of course* it had a sentimental value to the
older Bellefleurs, the landscape architect Leah had hired from Vanderpoel insisted it must come down since it took up too much space in the
garden and would have to be propped up anyway with unsightly boards),
and a sense of agitation throughout the house, as if the giant tree's spirit,
pain-maddened, were running loose: a most unpleasant episode that did
not really end until, some weeks later, the November storm evidently
swept the spirit away. But that was hardly a blessing, since the storm was
to bring with it a worse problem.

And there were, of course, innumerable other vexing things, more
and less mysterious, haunted closets and baths and mirrors and drawers,
and even a corner of Aveline's boudoir, and the dust-coated drum made
of Raphael's skin that sometimes made light tapping sounds as if invisible
fingers were drumming on it restlessly, and the lavender silk parasol,
badly faded and frayed, said to have belonged to Violet, that rolled of its
own accord across the floor, as if angrily kicked—but how seriously were
they to be taken? For, after all, as Hiram frequently said, with his
bemused skeptical smile, *These absurd spirits batten on* our *credulity. If we
stopped believing in them, if, together, unified for once, the entire family stopped
believing . . . why, then, they would be powerless!*

Cassandra

One chilly sunny day in early November Leah acquired another baby—another girl of questionable parentage—for the Bellefleurs.

It was a long, ambitious day, which began with a visit to the Gromwell property on the far side of Silver Lake. Though Leah had of course seen the property before, and claimed to have made a thorough study of its financial situation (which was quite poor—the quarry had been losing money steadily for the past six years), she insisted on being driven over in the new Rolls-Royce limousine, accompanied by Germaine and Hiram, and a young woman just hired to help with Germaine (her name was Lissa: she had been hired to replace Irene, as Irene had been hired to replace Lettie). It was a gusty day, and despite Hiram's disapproval (he was *always* fussing and clucking and disapproving of Leah's whims, like an aging husband) Leah had bundled her little girl up for winter and taken her along. The child loved rides, she loved to perch atop her mother's lap and point and chatter and ask questions, which Leah answered patiently. It was very important, Leah believed, for a child to learn as much as possible—to see as much as possible—even at a very early age.

"And the important thing is, Germaine," Leah said, as they were driven through the gate, "that we own this. All this. This is a sandstone quarry—I'll have to ask Bromwell to explain to us, exactly what sandstone is—and it takes in sixty-five acres, all the way to the Sulphur Springs Road, and we own it now. The papers were signed just last Friday and now it's *ours.*"

They were driven about the property, along rutted lanes, for nearly half an hour; at one point Leah insisted upon getting out and climbing halfway down into a pit, poor Hiram, stumbling beneath Germaine's weight, in tow. ". . . not much to look at," Hiram said irritably. "You'll have a hard time explaining this purchase to Mr. T."

"Nothing I do calls for an explanation," Leah said sharply, turning her fur collar up. "I'm not a child."

She unlocked the manager's office and went inside, bringing Germaine with her. The place was not so dirty as she had feared. An old pulltop desk, its pigeonholes crammed with yellowed papers, a tacked-down strip of linoleum tile, an army cot, pillowless, with a soiled blanket tossed over it. . . .

"Well, Germaine," she said heartily, "here we are! *You* wanted this."

Germaine did no more than glance at her.

"The Gromwell Quarry. We have acquired the Gromwell Quarry," Leah said. "And now—? Well, Germaine, are you pleased? Did I do well?"

Germaine began to chatter, as if she were a small child, and Leah, not knowing whether to be vexed or amused, waved her away. She ran and leapt and stumbled about the room, greatly excited, while Leah contemplated the situation. It had cost far more than she had anticipated, but the Gromwell Quarry was now theirs; and soon they would acquire another tract of land, adjacent to this; and then another; and another; until the original holdings were united once again. Perhaps it would take most of her lifetime, Leah thought, and Germaine herself would have to complete the task. Then again, perhaps it would only take a few years, with her luck. There was no doubt about it, Leah had "luck"; she was possessed by it; she could make no mistakes.

Germaine had clambered on top of the desk, rowdy and naughty as any little child, and was threatening to jump—and perhaps *would* have jumped, had Lissa not hurried into the room to grab her.

"Oh, silly Lissa!" Leah said, laughing. "You behave as if Germaine might hurt herself! But you should know, my girl, that *this* child is blessed."

On the way back to Bellefleur Manor they stopped at Della's house, since Leah had not seen her mother for some time, and both she and Hiram felt an obligation to look in upon poor Jonathan Hecht (who was, unfortunately, asleep or in a kind of coma during their visit, so that he hadn't any awareness of Leah and Hiram peeking in at him: how ill and jaundiced he looked, and how shrunken his eyes had become!—*it's remarkable,* Leah whispered to Hiram, *that he has lived so long*); and she was curious, too, about Garnet Hecht's baby girl. "But what a strange name, *Cassandra,*" Leah said, poking a finger at the baby, which the baby promptly seized, gurgling and smiling happily, if rather cross-sightedly, "however did poor Garnet hit upon *that?*"

"The name was my choice," Della said.

"But wasn't it some barbarian princess or someone," Leah laughed, keeping her voice low so that Garnet (who was in and out of the little nursery, flushed, muttering to herself, all in a flurry over Leah's and Hiram's unannounced visit), "someone who was mute, or was she murdered—or both? Or did she foretell the future, and no one would listen, and she was murdered anyway?"

"The odd bits and pieces of things you remember from La Tour," Della said contemptuously. "It might have been better, as I thought all along, for you to have stayed home. Since you *did* end up someone's wife, after all. And what good has that expensive education done you?"

"Now, Della," Hiram said quickly, "you didn't pay for it. It didn't come out of *your* allowance."

"And you've never let me forget it, have you! You and Noel," Della said, waving rather rudely at her brother.

So the visit began awkwardly, and Leah was forced to make cheerful conversation, speaking of anything that flew into her head. Despite her mother's sour mood, and the faint stench that wafted across the width of the house from Jonathan Hecht's sickroom, and Garnet's annoying fluttery manner (the silly creature was too distracted to do anything more than mumble *Thank you, Mrs. Bellefleur* when Leah handed her a gift for the baby, she set it down on a cabinet without opening it, a darling crocheted sweater Germaine had outgrown so quickly it was good as new), and despite the chill she'd had out at the quarry, Leah was in excellent spirits. Cassandra was a beautiful if somewhat undersized baby (and *were* her eyes crossed, or was Leah imagining it?), and there was nothing so delightful as leaning over the crib of an infant once again. . . . Those dark curls! That damp little smile! Delightful too was the way Germaine was talking to the baby, cooing and burbling in baby language.

"Cassandra is a handsome baby," Leah said, "and she seems to be very healthy, Garnet, aren't you pleased . . . ? She *was* a few weeks premature, wasn't she?"

"I don't know, I really don't remember," Garnet said, blushing painfully. "I . . . I wasn't well. . . . Afterward, for a while, I had a fever. . . . My memory of that time isn't very good."

"It was an ordeal, a baby so premature," Della said. "Of course you had a difficult time. But you're fine now, and so is Cassandra."

"Do you think so, Mrs. Pym?" Garnet said uncertainly.

"Oh, of course," Leah said, taking both her hands. (Such tiny, limp, cold-fish sort of hands! It was no wonder, Leah thought, the girl couldn't find a husband.) "You've always been rather thin, you know, I don't think you look much different than before, and your hair is lovely, if maybe you did something with it up here, on your forehead, otherwise it tends to fall in your eyes . . . and your eyes are lovely, Garnet, you shouldn't hide them . . . you shouldn't always be looking *down*. But you feel well? You've recovered?"

"I . . . I think so, Mrs. Bellefleur," Garnet said slowly.

And then she was off again, imagining she heard the teakettle. She put Leah in mind of nothing so much as a startled rabbit. "Why in Christ's name is she always running," Leah whispered to Della. "It must make you nervous, you always claimed *I* made you nervous. . . ."

"Garnet is a good girl," Della said stiffly. "She has suffered."

"Oh—suffered! We've all suffered," Leah said. She checked to see that Germaine was not hurting Cassandra—she was leaning over the crib trying to "kiss" her—and went to a nearby mirror to remove her hat. ". . . but I've been negligent, you know, I seem to have forgotten all about Garnet," she said, "and the poor thing obviously needs help. Since the father of the baby is nowhere to be found. . . . She *would* make some man an excellent wife, don't you think? We should have married her off before this. What a pity! And what a surprise! Sweet little Garnet Hecht, getting herself pregnant like that, and so skinny she didn't even show until the seventh month . . . isn't she *sly,* really. . . . Of course it was just one time, I'm sure: some farmboy who took advantage of her: or maybe someone from the village. Has she told you, yet, who it was? Or is she still hysterical about the subject? . . . As if we were going to interrogate her!"

"No one is going to interrogate her," Della said.

"Certainly no one is going to interrogate her," Leah said, removing the last of her hatpins. "Her tragic little love affair is her own business entirely. And it isn't as if she were a Bellefleur. . . . Of course she's a cousin of mine, a distant cousin . . . she *is,* isn't she? . . . But then everyone is related to everyone else around here, and it means very little. I wish she would trust me, though. She never looks me in the eye, she never seems to be listening, exactly. It's always been like that between us and I can't imagine why."

Leah was amused to see in the mirror, as she turned, her mother and Hiram exchanging an enigmatic glance.

"She is a very brave young woman," Della said, folding her hands in her apron in a gesture that maddened Leah, it was so falsely meek, so hypocritically subservient. "I doubt that you're capable of comprehending all that Garnet has gone through."

"My pregnancy with Germaine was far worse," Leah said. "Ten months—more than ten months! And *her* baby was born early—"

"It *is* a very sweet baby," Hiram said, clearing his throat. "Now don't you hurt it, Germaine. You don't want to play so rough—"

"Germaine, stop that, come over here," Leah said. "You're not a little baby any longer and you can't climb into that crib—why, you'd crush the poor thing! She isn't an *it,* Uncle Hiram, she's a *she.* You ought to know better," she said, nudging him in the ribs.

"Yes, yes, of course, a *she,* the baby is . . . the baby is a *she,*" Hiram said, folding his arms behind his back. He moved a few feet away, to stare gloomily into Della's meager fire, where damp birch logs were burning with an acrid eye-stinging stench. He was a ruddy-faced portly man, handsome in profile, with waxed mustaches that gave off a synthetic odor, and one somewhat clouded eye. Always fastidiously dressed, with his gold watch chain across his vest, and his gold-and-ivory cuff links, he looked as incongruous in Della's shabby parlor as Leah. It amused Leah to see how uneasy Della and Hiram—sister and brother—were in each other's company. The curse of the Bellefleurs, she thought, was either to be uncommonly close (though that was a rarity these days) or estranged for life.

The silence between them grew embarrassing, so Leah chattered: about the Gromwell Quarry, about their plans for buying Chautauqua Fruits to join with Valley Products, about the mining operations at Contracoeur . . .

"Contracoeur!" Della said. "I didn't realize we owned land there."

"We've owned mineral rights there since 1873," Leah said.

"But what sort of mineral rights?"

"What do you mean, Mamma, *what sort—?*" Leah laughed. "Mineral rights are mineral rights. It's a highly complicated operation, however, and we need mining engineers, in fact Gideon is meeting with someone in Port Oriskany right now. He's been working very hard on this, hasn't he, Uncle Hiram? He's been trying very hard."

"Is he alone?" Della asked.

"No, Ewan is with him. And Jasper. It's remarkable how quickly Jasper is learning," Leah said, fumbling in her purse. "I wish Bromwell would take an interest in such things. . . . But of course he's still quite young, there's still time, I don't intend to push any of my children into anything. Don't you think that's wise, Mamma?"

Leah may have meant this ironically—for certainly Della had wanted to push *her* years ago, at least away from the Bellefleurs—but the moment passed. Della said softly, "And how is Gideon, Leah?"

"*How* is Gideon? Why, he's perfectly fine as always, he never changes," Leah said, shaking a cigarillo out of a package. It was the first time she had smoked one of these things in her mother's presence, and it rather pleased her—pleased and excited her—that Della was staring in undisguised alarm. But Leah chose to take no notice of her mother, and went on chattering in a bright amiable voice about the mining engineering firm in Port Oriskany, and the alterations she was planning in the house, and the renovations in the garden. "Of course we must move along slowly. There's the expense, for one thing, and Grandmother Elvira is naturally upset, and it *is* disorienting. But you'll be pleased to learn, Mamma, that I've had most of those ugly old statues hauled away. And wasn't it peculiar, Uncle Hiram, how parts of statues were found back in the woods—arms and legs and even heads—dragged back in the woods, or down to the lake, evidently by wild animals! The children kept finding parts for weeks, the younger children were always being frightened. . . ."

"Gideon's well, you say? And he's in Port Oriskany right now?" Della asked.

"Mamma, I just now *told* you," Leah laughed, picking a bit of tobacco off her tongue. "My husband is in superb health as always, and asks to be remembered to you. He's been working very hard lately. . . ."

"I see," Della said. She glanced over her shoulder, toward the doorway; but Garnet was not yet in sight. "Occasionally we hear rumors. In Bushkill's Ferry."

"Yes," Leah said, "Bushkill's Ferry always did hear rumors about Bellefleur."

"But as long as Gideon is well, and working hard . . ."

"Of course he's well," Leah said irritably.

". . . and then rumors have to be discounted," Della said, "especially when they show evidence of envy or spite."

"Did you hear about Yolande? Was that one of the things people were gossiping about?"

"One of the things, yes."

"Ewan and Lily have about given up on her," Leah said with a sigh. "It's obvious that she has run away and wants to stay away. . . . There was a fire in one of the barns, did you know? And she ran away that night. According to Lily all she took was a change of clothing and some jewelry and twenty dollars in cash, and—and this is touching, Mamma—a lock of Germaine's hair. She actually crept into the nursery and cut off a curl, just a tiny one. . . . Poor Yolande, I *can't* imagine why she ran away, why she hates her family so, can you? There was a fire in one of the barns, one of the unused barns, but I don't imagine Yolande had anything to do with it. The children are so secretive, though. It's very strange. Bromwell hadn't anything to do with it, of course, but I think Christabel did; but she won't talk about it. Imagine—a child Christabel's age, having secrets from her own mother!"

"Does that surprise you, Leah, really?" Della asked with a dry little twist of a smile.

"Oh, *Mamma,*" Leah said, walking away.

She wandered into the sitting room, where the heavy velvet drapes were kept drawn; she felt quite agitated suddenly. There was something she wanted but she didn't know what it was. Something she wanted badly, and *would* have. But how would she acquire it? . . . She found herself staring at the old horsehair sofa with its scalloped back. And the matching chair in which her young cousin Gideon had sat. Staring at her. Staring at her and at *Love,* perched vigilantly on her shoulder. A wave of nostalgia swept over Leah and she felt, for a moment, close to tears.

O Love . . .

In the shantylike office building at the quarry she had been half-dreaming on her feet, but she couldn't recall the nature of her dream. How odd it was, how very odd, and unlike her. . . . As her body lost all interest in sexual feeling her mind labored to take it up, frequently out of a sense of obscure obligation, as a distracted Catholic might run his rosary beads through his fingers, and even move his lips in blank prayers, while his mind was empty. So Leah imagined illicit lovers in that smelly little building, lying on that inadequate cot, gasping and clutching at each other. *O Love. How I love you.* . . . And then Germaine had nearly toppled to the floor, and Leah had awakened from her trance.

She woke from her trance now and put all thoughts of Gideon and that beautiful spider *Love* out of her mind (for hadn't *Love* been killed long ago, reduced to black glutinous pulp no larger than her fist?), and strode back into the parlor where Garnet, her hands trembling, was about to serve tea. Seeing Leah she stepped backward, her thin foolish face stretched in a hopeful smile. "Mrs. Bellefleur . . . ?" she said, blinking. "Would you care for some . . ."

Leah bent over the cradle, and picked up Cassandra with such care, the baby hardly gurgled. A thick red-brown coil of hair had come loose on the back of her neck. "I think I'd like to bring Cassandra back with me to the manor," Leah said. "She'd have better care, you know. There would be more children to keep her company."

Garnet stared at her, speechless. All the poor thing could do was nervously pleat her apron in her fingers!

"I *said,*" Leah murmured, her face flushed, "that I'd like to bring Cassandra back with me. At least for a while. You don't object—?"

"Leah—" Della said.

"Garnet, you don't object?"

Garnet stood behind the tea tray, staring, struck dumb. It was as much as Leah could do to brush her gaze across the skinny little thing without bursting into angry laughter. "She'd have *much* better treatment with me," Leah said. "You know that."

No one spoke. The fire blazed up fitfully, then died away. Perhaps the flue wasn't completely open—the room was filling with damp eye-searing smoke. Leah hummed into the baby's joyous face, but Garnet and Della and Hiram stood mute. And then Germaine began chattering: something about *baby, baby,* something about *home, coming home:* and Leah glanced briefly up at Garnet (still pleating her apron in her bony fingers) and knew that she had won. And was not at all surprised.

"The Innisfail Butcher"

Though Germaine's great-uncle Jean-Pierre Bellefleur II enjoyed the dubious honor of having his likeness sketched many more times than any other Bellefleur (even his grandfather Raphael, the surly butt of so many newspaper caricatures), and reproduced not only throughout the state but throughout the nation and Canada, and even (so a Bellefleur cousin discovered to his horror and chagrin when, opening the *Times* as he breakfasted in a Mayfair hotel, his eye snagged upon an ugly little headline that had to do with "mass murder" in the States—and saw, above the headline, an incongruously detailed, and even rather handsome, pencil sketch of the thirty-two-year-old "Innisfail Butcher") in England and France as well, and though the less vicious of these likenesses were actually kept, for a while, by the Bellefleur who was always most fond of Jean-Pierre, his aunt Veronica, in a scrapbook bound in white kid, the only representations of Jean-Pierre that were eventually allowed to remain in the manor were the charming pencil sketch on the nursery wall, and a pencil-and-charcoal sketch, equally charming, but perhaps even more romantic, made of young Jean-Pierre just before his embarkation for Europe at the age of twenty-four, for his abbreviated Grand Tour. (His mother was later to blame his father, most unfairly, for the fact that Jean-Pierre's trip abroad was truncated, and the poor young gentleman forced to return home before his education in culture was complete: He would not have drifted into a life of cardplaying and other forms of idleness, he would not have succumbed to the blandishments of his false friend from Missouri, he would not have been in the notorious Innisfail House on that fateful night, and would not subsequently have suffered his tragic fate, had Jeremiah been more judicious in his management of the farm, had he been more *clear-sighted* about the market for wheat . . . ! *The sins of the fathers,* Elvira raged in her grief, *are visited upon the heads of the sons, and the sons are ground underfoot.*)

The sketch on the nursery wall, preserved nicely in a tortoiseshell frame, and rarely subjected to more than an idle glance on the part of the children, showed a sweet-faced child of indeterminate age (the artist must have been unevenly skilled, for all the children's lips looked alike, being feminine and rather bee-stung, while their Bellefleur noses varied, and their eyes—touched up with tiny white dots—looked in some cases preternaturally adult, in other cases so piously soft they threatened to melt into the coarse-grained paper): he might have been five, or seven, or eight: captured in prayer, his cheekbones prominent, his small but striking eyes cast upward above his fervently clasped hands and a near-imperceptible (or did Leah imagine it, having studied the drawing for so long) smirk. Hung for decades between a square-jawed Matilde and a fairly dour Noel, Jean-Pierre II most resembled his nephew Raoul; the only Bellefleur of either sex who was arguably more "beautiful" than Jean-Pierre was Gideon.

The second drawing, taken down from the wall by one Bellefleur, hung again by another, taken down again and again hung, in different parts of the manor, at different stages of the luckless man's career in court —and kept, finally, when Germaine was a child, in Leah's boudoir— showed a handsome, rather foppish young gentleman with curled mustaches and hooklike curls on either side of his narrow forehead, his eyes fixed upon the viewer in an expression of tenderness, sincerity, and grave feeling. "The Innisfail Butcher," indeed—! One could not fail to be moved by the sweet set of his mouth, or the nobility of his slightly uplifted chin. This was the young man who was welcome in the finest drawing rooms and clubs in Manhattan, during the period when the Bellefleurs maintained a modest but attractive town house just off Washington Square; it was said of him by one Manhattan heiress (admittedly, her father's fortune was not immense) that she had never heard any young man of her acquaintance speak so *sensitively* about music. And during that single season when Veronica Bellefleur took her favorite nephew to the theater, and to the races, and to her friends' homes in the city and out on Long Island, when it had seemed not only probable but inevitable that he would make a "brilliant" match, he had behaved, according to all witnesses, with exquisite tact, modesty, grace, and charm at all times. If he had a temper, if he occasionally drank too much (and to the very end of his days as a free man, Jean-Pierre seemed incapable of calculating the effect of alcohol on his brain, though he had a great deal of practice), or flew into a tantrum over a creased collar or a mislaid cuff link or butter served too hard to spread, no one knew except the Bellefleurs and their servants. The only public trait about him that might be characterized as somewhat odd, which his Manhattan acquaintances remarked upon years later, at the time of the trial, was that he frequently joked about the "doom" of his name. Since no one there knew the first Jean-Pierre's fate, and since Jean-Pierre II had little to gain from discussing it in any detail, he would only say, with tantalizing melancholy, that his great-great-grandfather had died a noble but extremely painful death in the War of

1812. Surely you are not superstitious, young women said, sometimes touching his arm lightly in the emotion of the moment, when they were not quite aware of what they did, surely you don't believe that a mere *name* can have any effect upon your life . . . ? Of course not, Jean-Pierre would wittily reply, not a mere *name:* but what of *myself?*

It was not true that Jean-Pierre had not begun his career of cardplaying before the European trip, as Elvira liked to claim; but his activities at that time, as a young man in his early twenties, with aristocratic habits and pretensions, were fairly innocuous, undistinguished from those of most of his contemporaries among the well-to-do landowners in the Valley. He became a serious cardplayer in Europe when, marooned in a Swiss inn during a week of torrential rains, he acquired certain skills—they were not quite tricks—from a fellow tourist, a grandfatherly Englishman from Warwickshire, grandmother Violet's home. (But Jean-Pierre's friend claimed never to have heard of the Odlins.) Before that Jean-Pierre had gamely traveled about from country to country, with oscillating enthusiasm, and varying degrees of head and chest colds, being taken by train or carriage through Belgium, Holland, the Rhineland, Northern Italy, Baden-Baden, the South of France, Paris, Rome, the Algarve, Athens, Southern Italy, Luxembourg (a dizzying jumble whose names he could not keep straight, though he made every effort to record them in his diary, and to send postal cards back home giving his impressions—usually quite brief—of each place, and its art treasures, and "natives"), alone for the most part, and humbly dependent upon English-speaking hotel people and guides; but he was fortunate enough to make a few acquaintances, all of them Americans, and one of them a somewhat older San Franciscoan with whom he rode about on the delightful Brussels streetcars most of one day, in a kind of boyish bliss, shamelessly indulging in his nostalgia for their native land. (Jean-Pierre spent several days in the company of Mr. Newman, who had made a fortune in leather back home, and who was courteous enough to murmur that, yes, indeed yes, he had heard of the Bellefleur family by way of his associates in New York City. They had much the same tastes in art: either a piece of sculpture or a painting struck them at once, or it never did; they were bored with madonnas, and religious subjects in general; the notion of patina alternately amused and bewildered them. If something is merely old, *must* it be good? One fine October day they spent an hour or more admiring, from different angles, the impressive Gothic tower of the Hôtel de Ville, and wondered if it might be possible to duplicate it back in the States: Mr. Newman knew exactly the place for it, on a Nob Hill avenue; Jean-Pierre argued for the Fifth Avenue in Manhattan. Their somewhat forced intimacy came to an abrupt end when, in all innocence, Jean-Pierre suggested that the two of them visit a sumptuous brothel not far from their lodgings, and Mr. Newman drew away in silent consternation, clearly too shocked even to protest. (But how peculiar, Jean-Pierre thought, the man admitted to being thirty-six years old, a bachelor, in every respects "normal" enough!))

After that Europe seemed to deteriorate, almost daily, hotel suites were invariably disappointing, guides were clearly out to cheat him, "art treasures" began to repeat themselves (or had he, poor Jean-Pierre wondered, made a fatal error and reversed his journey, so that he was traversing the very countries he had imagined he was finished with forever?). Trains were delayed, or did not arrive at all. Bridges were washed out. There was a typhoid scare, and an influenza scare. (Jean-Pierre himself experienced a gonorrhea scare of fourteen hours, which left him shaken and chaste for many days.) While waiting out an incessant rain that everyone connected with the inn in which Jean-Pierre was trapped claimed was most unusual, he at least learned, from a similarly disenchanted Englishman named Fairlie, how to be *extremely* clever at poker, and even at bridge—a talent that was to serve him well in the Powhatassie State Correctional Facility.

And then his itinerary was cut short when an expected bank draft did not arrive, and an unexpected telegram of craven apology from his father *did,* and he returned home with far more relief than he showed (he made it a point of *showing,* to his family, extreme indignation—hinting that he had been invited to dine at one of the "oldest houses in Europe" just when the fateful telegram was delivered); and he settled in to apply himself to learning how to manage the complicated Bellefleur estate . . . though it was of course too complicated to be learned by anyone other than a financial wizard (Jean-Pierre's idea of a financial wizard was his brother Hiram, who had failed to be admitted to law school—who had, in fact, left Princeton without his bachelor's degree) . . . and what good did it do, he queried often, to *know* what course to take when the market fell or soared according to its own whims, and there were unscrupulous men manipulating it, and a man's fortune had little to do with his intelligence, or his moral worth? (For certainly no one was a finer, more tediously "moral" man than his father, yet no one in the Valley had failed, in recent years, so ignominiously as Lamentations of Jeremiah with his "fox farm." Even the Varrell trash could laugh at them now, Elvira said.)

Jean-Pierre made sporadic journeys to Port Oriskany and Vanderpoel, sometimes not even giving as an excuse the matter of "family affairs"; he made infrequent trips to New York (for the tall narrow town house at Washington Square South had been sold years before); he began to make a great many trips to Nautauga Falls, Fort Hanna, and other rather rough river towns, and Innisfail—Innisfail, some eighteen miles from Bellefleur Manor as the crow flies, but considerably longer (at least thirty-five miles) if one took the usual route, the Innisfail and the Old Military roads, and then the unpaved Bellefleur Road up to the lake, as anyone but an Indian or a madman (so Jean-Pierre's attorney was to claim, foolishly) would do. And as for riding a horse through the pitch-black night, along an unfamiliar and dangerous terrain . . . when the rider is unskilled, and even fearful of horses . . .

The night of the multiple murders at Innisfail House, the largest and probably the most disreputable of the taverns in the area, Jean-Pierre claimed to have shared a carriage with several passengers, including his new acquaintance from Missouri, Wolfe Quincy, on the trip from Nautauga Falls to Innisfail. He claimed to have gotten a ride back—back, that is, to the village of Bellefleur—with a peddler whose mule-drawn wagon was heaped with all sorts of goods, but who specialized in barbed wire. (The peddler was never found, unfortunately. The driver of the carriage claimed not to remember Jean-Pierre on that particular trip, though he'd seen him previously, on other trips; nor did the other passengers remember him. But Jean-Pierre's fervent story was never to waver.) What precisely happened at Innisfail House between the hours of midnight and two-thirty Jean-Pierre Bellefleur simply did not know. *He simply did not know.*

Eleven men were murdered, one after another. Several were shot at close range, several others were stabbed, and their throats viciously slashed; two who died of bullet wounds were also subjected to throat-slashings. How it happened—how a single murderer was able to do so much, so superhumanly much—no one knew. There *must* have been time for a number of the men to defend themselves, yet it seemed that they did not defend themselves; even Wolfe Quincy died without putting up much of a struggle. (That it was unlikely Jean-Pierre was responsible for the killings was underscored by the fact that his friend Quincy was among the victims. Jean-Pierre was extremely fond of Quincy, and dependent upon him as well, for Quincy could hold his liquor far better than Jean-Pierre, and when they were involved in ambitious all-night games he watched over Jean-Pierre with an almost maternal solicitude. He was a broad-bellied, good-natured man of about forty, originally from Massachusetts, lately from Missouri, an excellent drinking and gambling companion whose only fault was a tendency toward boasting of his exploits in the War: how many men he'd killed, how many horses he had stolen, how many bullets he had survived (and judging from the scars he proudly showed the squeamish Jean-Pierre, there were at least half a dozen). Quincy was the last man, *the last human being on earth,* Jean-Pierre's attorney claimed, Jean-Pierre would want dead.)

Which sounded, in the antiquated courtroom with its faint dry echo, not quite right.

Jean-Pierre was found guilty of murder in the first degree, despite his innocence, and sentenced by Judge Phineas Petrie to life plus ninety-nine years . . . plus ninety-nine years repeated ten times. Evidence was no more than circumstantial; the only witness—the tavern-keeper's malicious wife —admitted that she was nearly fainting with terror when she saw, from an upstairs window, a single rider galloping away into the night, along a narrow trail leading into the foothills. She could not *see* the figure, could not of course *identify* the murderer, but she claimed that "of course" it was Jean-Pierre Bellefleur who had, within her hearing, loudly and drunkenly threatened lives in the past, and had had to be ejected from the tavern more than once, because of his wicked temper. All this was slanderous, of course. And Jean-Pierre protested. He had left Innisfail House before midnight and was home by three in the morning. Because he was so exhausted he had slept in a hayloft . . . he hadn't wanted to disturb his family . . . perhaps he *was* somewhat drunk . . . the events of the night were badly confused. He knew only one thing: that he was innocent of the heinous charge brought against him. And that the "Innisfail Butcher" —how quickly the newspapers had hit upon that vile epithet, and how widely Jean-Pierre's lean, anxious, hawkish face was known throughout the state!—remained a free man, given license to murder again, while he, Jean-Pierre, a victim of grotesque circumstances, was condemned.

The tavern-keeper's wife simply repeated her imbecilic story. The rider on the horse headed in the direction of Lake Noir, by way of the foothills; the dark horse with three white stockings and a close-cropped mane and tail; Jean-Pierre Bellefleur's belligerence and general rowdiness. He was like a child, the woman said, wiping at her eyes. A child pretending to be an adult man, and fooling people into accepting him as such. . . . But also like the Devil. When he drank, he was like the Devil. He just went wild, he had to be dragged out onto the veranda by his friend from Missouri, slapped around and maybe splashed with cold water; and even then he wasn't always all right. (But when Jean-Pierre's attorney, cross-examining the woman, asked her with a droll twist of his mouth why she and her husband allowed such a "devil" into their establishment, she could only stammer: "But—you see—so many of them are—so many of the men—They're *all* like that more or less—" A ripple of laughter ran through the packed courtroom.)

Nevertheless, he was found guilty. By twelve jurors who had seemed, at first, to be just and upright and unprejudiced men. (Though of course no one in the Valley could be "unprejudiced" about a Bellefleur.) It is said that jurors, filing back into court with a verdict of Guilty, do not look at the defendant; but the jurors at Jean-Pierre's trial certainly looked at him. They eyed him, studied him, stared quite frankly at him as if they were in the presence of a venomous but fascinating insect.

. . . And how do you find the defendant?

. . . We find the defendant Guilty as charged.

Guilty!

Guilty as charged!

When of course he was innocent, and could do nothing more than scream and tear at the sheriff's men who were restraining him. No! You can't! I won't let you! I'm innocent! The murderer is at large! The murderer is among you! *I am not the murderer!*

If only the tavern-keeper's spiteful wife had been killed along with the others: then there would have been no witness. But in the pandemonium the woman was overlooked.

If only . . .

For a while he could not be certain he had heard correctly. What did the words mean, *Guilty as charged . . . ?*

Perhaps when the prosecuting attorney had queried him about the old feud of the 1820's—whether he felt any "ill-will," whether he had ever craved "revenge"—he should have answered more carefully, more thoughtfully, instead of uttering, through tight pursed lips: "No."

(For there were, among the eleven dead, two Varrell men. One in his mid-fifties, the other about Jean-Pierre's age. It was his claim that he hadn't known they were Varrells, which was somewhat unlikely; for, as the tavern-keeper's slanderous wife pointed out, everyone knew everyone else in the Valley. And Bellefleurs and Varrells always knew one another.)

He could only repeat his story: leaving the tavern early, getting a ride with the peddler, sleeping in the hayloft because he didn't want to disturb his family. (His father Jeremiah suffered from insomnia, his mother Elvira suffered from "nerves.") When the sheriff and his men came to arrest him at dawn, dragging him out of the barn and knocking him about until his nose bled onto his filthy, already bloodied shirt, he couldn't imagine why they were there; he couldn't make sense of anything they said. They must have had a warrant for his arrest but he didn't remember seeing any warrant.

Ah, if he had stayed a companion to Mr. Newman, if they had followed through on their scheme to duplicate the tower of the Hôtel de Ville in the States! How profoundly and beautifully *innocent* their partnership would have been!

But through an excess of boyish enthusiasm he had irrevocably offended the older man, and now his life was ruined. He was only thirty-two years old and his life was ruined. The Lake Noir district had been notorious in the past for lynchings, murders, arson, and theft, and continual harassment of Indians; but there had never been anything quite so lurid as the "Innisfail Butcher" with his handsome, boyish, *aggrieved* face. He was in all the newspapers, out to the West Coast, the "Innisfail Butcher" who had murdered eleven men and claimed not to remember anything, claimed to be innocent, absolutely innocent: and how *certain* he was! The newspapers naturally resurrected old stories about the Bellefleur-Varrell feud though Jean-Pierre had made clear, in open court, repeatedly, that he hadn't even been aware that two Varrell men were in the tavern that night. . . . But no one believed him, and his young life was ruined.

For a stunned moment he could not believe the sentence old Judge Petrie had passed. Life plus ninety-nine years plus ninety-nine years plus . . . Individuals in the courtroom burst into applause. (For it was felt throughout the community that a death by hanging—a death that would involve, at the most, ten minutes of agony—was far too merciful for Jean-Pierre.) "But I am innocent, Your Honor," Jean-Pierre whispered. And then as the sheriff's men tugged at him he began to shout: "I tell you I am innocent! The murderer is still at large! *The murderer is among you!*"

So Jean-Pierre Bellefleur II, the grandson of the millionaire Raphael Bellefleur (who came so close—so heartbreakingly close—to political prominence), was incarcerated in the infamous state penitentiary at Powhatassie, there to serve a sentence of life plus 990 years.

He fainted at the sight of its massive walls—fainted and had to be slapped back into consciousness—whimpering, still, that he was innocent, he was innocent of the charges brought against him, a terrible mistake had been made— Yes, yes, the guards chuckled, that's what you all say.

The Powhatassie State Correctional Facility housed, at the time of Jean-Pierre's incarceration, about 1,500 men, in a space originally designed for 900. Prisoners customarily fainted or screamed at the sight of its great stone walls, which were slightly over thirty feet high and stretched, so it seemed, for miles, marked at regular intervals by six-sided turrets topped with Gothic cupolas, in which guards armed with carbines and rifles spent their days. The prison, modeled after medieval French prison-castles that had exerted a curious spell, for some reason, on the architect hired by the state to design the facility, was built on a rugged promontory overlooking the dour Powhatassie River, at the very spot at which, according to legend, the water had run red with the blood of Bay Colony pioneers who had ventured too far west and were massacred by Mohawk Indians. Built in the late 1700's, the prison was in visible decline (everywhere walls were crumbling, exposing rusted iron rods), but possessed, still, the ugly nobility of a medieval fortress; and its huge dining hall, with columns, arches, and heavy wrought-iron grillwork on its windows, reminded poor Jean-Pierre of nothing so much as his grandfather's pretensions. There was a curious *religious* aura to the horrific place.

He seemed to know beforehand that his appeals—made to the State Supreme Court, and argued faultlessly—were doomed, for he sank almost immediately into a state of apathy, and maintained a Bellefleur detachment from his surroundings that infuriated, at first, his fellow inmates, and certain of the guards. That his first cell was five feet by eight, that the "toilet" was a hole, uncovered, that the food was inedible (indeed, it was indefinable), that he was issued unlaundered clothes several sizes too big for his graceful frame, that his mattress was filthy and infested with bedbugs, and the single cotton blanket issued to him stiff with filth and dried blood—that there were cockroaches and footlong rats everywhere—and the majority of his fellow prisoners were evidently ill, physically or mentally, and sat on their cots or the floor, or walked about, with the spirit of zombies—that since a riot five or six years ago in which seven guards were killed and twelve inmates "committed suicide" the guards were exceptionally cruel: none of this stirred him.

For some time the only emotion he felt was a deep shame—shame that he had been the cause of his family's fresh humiliation—that it would be many, many years before the Bellefleurs regained their dignity. (As his

brother Noel said, weeping with exasperation, the fact that he was innocent somehow made it all the more intolerable. . . . When Harlan was
arrested, after all, he *had* been guilty, and very publicly guilty, of several
murders, and every word of his, every gesture, must have been enhanced
by the noble melancholy of his predicament. He had killed, he had exacted revenge as, indeed, he was forced to—and then he had died. In
every respect he had acted heroically. By contrast poor wretched Jean-
Pierre, who was *innocent,* was ignominious as a trapped muskrat: his fate
was merely outrageous.)

To anyone who would listen, to guards who greeted him with a
routine, unmotivated elbow in the chest, Jean-Pierre spoke quietly of his
innocence. His manner was courteous and reasonable. He had long given
up shouting. If a penitentiary is a place of penitence, he said, and if an
innocent man is wrongly incarcerated, *how* can he do penance . . . ?
Isn't the very foundation of the penitentiary undermined by such injustice . . . ? The considerable sums of money Jean-Pierre received each
month (which he was later to increase through poker and bridge games
in which, occasionally, guards would participate) allowed him to purchase
cigarettes, candy, sugar (no sugar was provided by the institution, and
cold oatmeal, alternately watery and glutinous—and sometimes dotted
with the remains of weevils—was served every morning, every single
morning), and other small favors, and naturally he tipped his guards, as
he would tip any servant not in his own hire, so the rough treatment
gradually stopped; but it was to be some time—in fact, years—before
Jean-Pierre would acquire a more spacious cell, for him and his body-
guard-companion (there was to be a series of such young men over the
decades, some fifteen or twenty in all: each would be injured or killed by
his successor, another husky young ambitious prisoner eager to serve
Jean-Pierre Bellefleur II). But it took time for Jean-Pierre to acquire this
sort of power, especially because his manner was so subdued, his voice
so hollow and seemingly apathetic, and his insistence upon his innocence
—which, as the guards remarked, was universal—detracted from his natural distinction. So when he reiterated his plea, his listless comical logic,
If a penitentiary is a place of penance, and if an innocent man is wrongly incarcerated
. . . more than one guard burst into rude laughter, and butted him all the
more cruelly in the chest.

(Later, a friendly prisoner warned Jean-Pierre against "talking
crazy." Because if he talked crazy, no matter how quietly, how politely,
he might be diagnosed as crazy. And if he was diagnosed as crazy—by a
state psychiatrist who visited the prison on alternate Thursdays, in the
afternoon, and made judgments and prescribed medicine from his office,
going by scribbled reports handed him by prison officials—he would be
sent across the yard to the Sheeler Ward; and that would be the end of
him. The Sheeler Ward! Jean-Pierre had heard of it: it was named for Dr.
Wystan Sheeler, a physician who had taken interest in the mentally ill in
the last quarter of the nineteenth century, and had prescribed a radical,

and sometimes successful, method of dealing with "madness" through sympathetic immersion in the patient's delusions. Family gossip had it that Dr. Sheeler had attended Raphael Bellefleur for a while, and even lived at the castle. . . . But the Sheeler Ward, which comprised an entire building made of concrete blocks, was simply the hole into which troublesome prisoners—whether "sane" or "insane"—were thrown, and once committed to the ward there was little likelihood that a man would get out. Some years ago a gang of prisoners there had seized a guard, and one of them had torn out his throat with his teeth; and though the prisoners involved in the uprising were, of course, beaten to death by guards, there was still a tradition of punishment in that ward. There was no sanitation, individual cells were no longer used, everyone was kept in a single dormitory room, a vast warehouse of a room, which was unheated, and said to be littered with unspeakable filth. Since the uprising no guard would venture down onto the floor: from time to time they patrolled the ward from a catwalk, and it was from this catwalk that cafeteria workers (gagging, their faces averted, their eyes shut) dumped food once a day, for the men to scramble for. There were men in that ward, Jean-Pierre was told, who were in the tertiary stages of syphilis, quite literally rotting; there was every kind of sickness; and when a man died—which was of course frequent, since the other prisoners were quite vicious—it might be several days before prison officials hauled away the corpse. So, Jean-Pierre's companion said quietly, you don't want them to send you *there*.)

"I can't believe that the family has given up on this man," Leah said. "I can't believe you've done so *little.*"

They tried to explain to her about the appeals, and the many thousands of dollars spent; one or two attempted bribes—that is, gifts—which were unfortunately offered to the wrong officials; and of course other family difficulties; and Jean-Pierre's apathetic manner. He had, for instance, never applied for parole. Not once in thirty-three years. While at first he seemed mildly happy to see visitors he soon changed, and frequently refused to enter the visiting room; once, while Noel presented an earnest, enthusiastic case for the probability of his verdict being overturned by the Supreme Court, he leaned forward slowly and spat against the glass partition that separated them. Never in his life, Noel said afterward, had he been so *thunderstruck.*

"The poor man must have fallen into despair," Leah said. "Everything I've heard about Powhatassie has been vile, incredibly degrading, it's a place for *animals,* not human beings. . . . Perhaps he's ill? Does anyone know? Cornelia says he has never answered his mail, and he's never answered my letters; but then of course he doesn't know me. I don't suppose he even knows Gideon. Does he *remember* any of you? When is the last time anyone has visited him?"

They could not remember, exactly. Noel believed he had visited

Jean-Pierre for the last time some thirty-two years ago (the Sunday of the spitting incident, in fact); Hiram believed he had tried to see him more recently—perhaps twenty-five years ago—but wasn't certain whether Jean-Pierre had condescended to appear in the visitors' room. (A hideous place, all concrete and wire mesh and armed guards, and such a din!— for the prisoners and their visitors had to shout at one another, and there were usually upward of fifty people in the room, all shouting helplessly at the same time. And, Hiram said with an angry flushed face, he was once beside a backwoods woman come to visit her husband, sentenced to Powhatassie for life: the pathetic woman was weeping and moaning, and had no more shame than to unbutton her dress to show her lardy, sagging breasts to her husband.) Their mother had visited him for the last time approximately twenty years ago; when she returned home she went at once to her bedchamber, where she remained, weeping, for several days. Aunt Veronica had never gone, since she left her rooms only after sundown, and visiting hours were from two to five; Della had gone once or twice, and Matilde only a few times. (It was thought that Matilde's reclusiveness began at the time of Jean-Pierre's trial. She turned away all suitors, frequently dressed in men's clothing (but not *nice* men's clothing, Cornelia said; farmhand sort of clothing), spent more and more time out at the old camp, and finally moved there permanently, pretending that a life of raising hens, growing vegetables, and making quilts, samplers, and silly little "artistic" things like carvings was any sort of life for a Bellefleur.) Lamentations of Jeremiah had visited his son as often as Jean-Pierre would allow, which wasn't often because, to perpetrate Elvira's myth, he liked to claim that the telegram summoning him home had ruined his life—he *had* been nearly engaged to an Italian *marchesa* whose family dated back to the twelfth century, and Jeremiah's latest financial debacle had brought the whole house of cards tumbling down. And then of course Jeremiah had died in the Great Flood of twenty years back. So Jean-Pierre hadn't had a visitor from the outside world in twenty years.

"I will visit him," Leah said. "My little girl and I will visit him."

"Oh, but you couldn't take a *child,*" Cornelia cried.

And Hiram said, twisting the ends of his mustache nervously, "The one thing, dear, you know, that's been a kind of stumbling block . . . or perhaps there are two . . . or many. . . . Well, to be frank: his story about the peddler, a peddler allegedly driving a mule-drawn wagon along the Innisfail Road at night . . . in the pitch-black . . . a peddler never glimpsed before or since . . . the story is, isn't it? . . . somewhat strained. And there was the matter of Folderol covered with sweaty scum, and her ankles badly scratched, and her hooves all muddy. . . ."

"Folderol—?" Leah cried, staring at him. "What in heaven's name are you talking about, Uncle?"

"Folderol was the name of—"

"But you just don't *want* to help him, do you!" Leah said, pressing her hands to her cheeks as if they were burning. "You think that the ignominy has been lived down simply because people have forgotten. But they *haven't* forgotten—not really! Suppose Christabel, for instance, fell in love with a—a Schaff, or a Horehound—or one of those old Vander-poel families—I mean with the son of one of those families—do you think they would countenance a match with a *Bellefleur,* as things stand?"

"We must think ahead," Leah said, shaking a cigarillo out of a package. "Didn't Raphael once say—it isn't possible to think *too far* ahead—"

"Christabel *is* maturing rapidly," Cornelia murmured.

Noel threw up his hands in angry despair. "But if you visit my brother, dear, what precisely will you talk about? It isn't as if you know him, after all. I doubt that I would recognize him myself. We tried so often to press him into applying for parole, and in the end he was really quite abusive; in fact I had the distinct impression that he'd settled in, at Powhatassie, as he never had out *here.* The men are allowed to play cards, you know, and according to the warden (at that time—I'm afraid I don't know the current warden) there was always a game going out in the yard, or in the recreation hall, and Jean-Pierre had taught the other men a dozen kinds of poker, and gin rummy, and casino, and euchre, and even bridge— We had hoped he might at least apply for parole, despite Judge Petrie's admonition to the state, but he never did; perhaps he didn't want to risk another humiliation, then again perhaps he didn't want to risk being freed."

"I don't want a parole," Leah said impatiently. "I want a pardon."

"A pardon?"

"From the governor. A pardon. Exoneration."

"A *pardon?* For Jean-Pierre?"

At that very moment Germaine ran into the room and clambered up on Leah's lap. She had something very exciting to tell her mother—something about one of the cats being treed by a Minorca rooster—but Leah quieted her, and brushed her hair back from her overheated forehead. Perhaps to give the older Bellefleurs time to recover (for Leah, despite her impetuousness, was keenly sensitive to others' feelings) she turned her attentions to her daughter, wetting a forefinger to wipe away some dirt, kissing the child's flushed cheek. "Aren't you a pretty girl," Leah whispered. "Aren't you *blessed.*"

And finally, after a long silence, Cornelia said weakly: "But at least don't take Germaine, dear."

The Elopement

One fine autumn morning when the last of the leaves—
the golden maples—were blazing with light, and the sky was so coldly
pellucid a turquoise-blue that it resembled stained glass, Garth and Little
Goldie ran off together, in Garth's new Buick, leaving behind only a
scribbled note (in Little Goldie's childlike hand) slipped under Ewan's
and Lily's door: *Gone to get marri'd.* They sped southward, crossing the
borders of several states, until, breathless, they arrived in one that would
marry them within three days; and so they were married. Because of the
circumstances of their surprise elopement they had time to heap in the
rumble seat of the Buick only a few of Little Goldie's dresses (she had so
many—for her new-adopted family was very generous with new things as
well as cast-off but still perfectly wearable things—it would have been
impossible to choose: so she and Garth merely grabbed an armful out of
the closet), the single suit of Garth's he found tolerable to wear, for brief
periods (it was made of brown mohair-and-cotton, with a modest lapel
and many brass buttons; its trousers were too short but in other respects
attractive), and the old Swiss music box from the nursery. They had also
taken a half-dozen items from the Great Hall whose value they couldn't
have guessed; instinct guided them as blindly toward a rare sixteenth-
century German bell metal mortar and pestle as toward a crystal knick-
knack from Victoria's England, or a "snowstorm" paperweight of unde-
termined origin. Raiding a few rooms during the very early hours of the
night, whispering and giggling, on tiptoe, barefoot, they accumulated
about $2,300 in loose cash taken, in such irregular amounts, from the
pockets of coats and jackets, from out of drawers, from between the pages
of books (in Raphael's library they found a great deal, though some of
it was in currency that "looked funny"—so they left it behind), and even

from piggy banks, that the money was never to be missed. And of course Garth had some money of his own.

The previous day, something very peculiar had happened between Garth and his uncle Gideon, which was never to be satisfactorily explained.

It seemed that several of the children—Little Goldie, Christabel, Morna—were in the old garden room, playing with the twin ginger kittens everyone adored (though they were not kittens any longer, really, being about five months old now, with long slender bodies and very white whiskers, and unusually large feet), when Mahalaleel, the kittens' father, appeared suddenly at one of the windows, mewing to be let inside. In an uncannily human gesture he brought one paw slowly down against the glass, unsheathing his claws, and the children looked around, startled. (For Mahalaleel had been gone from the manor for nearly two weeks, and Leah had about given up on him.)

So the children let him inside, and were delighted at his interest in the kittens, whom he began to groom with all the assiduity of a mother cat. In the posture of a sphinx he reclined before them, gripping them both between his front legs, washing now one, now the other, with his rough pink tongue, his eyes half-shut with pleasure. And the kittens (who *did* appear to be kittens again, suddenly diminished beside their magnificent fluffy-haired father) pressed against him, purring loudly. Little Goldie had not seen Mahalaleel close up. She knelt to watch him wash the kittens, her brown eyes fixed upon him with a curious intensity. How beautiful Mahalaleel was, though tiny cockleburrs were sticking to his fur —how silky, how luxurious, with the roseate highlights of his thick coat, and the pattern, so intricate as to be almost vertiginous, of its myriad colors: gray and pinkish-gray and orange-and-bronze and frosted black! And his pale green eyes with their black, somewhat dilated centers. . . . Little Goldie murmured that she had never seen a cat like Mahalaleel. She leaned closer, staring. Her long hair fell slowly forward, framing her small face.

"Do you think I could pet him?" she said.

"Oh, no, I wouldn't—he doesn't know you yet," Christabel said.

"Oh, go ahead, he's *friendly,*" impish Morna said.

So Little Goldie quite innocently reached out to touch Mahalaleel. And whether because the creature was genuinely startled by the movement of her hand, or whether because he imagined she meant harm to the kittens—or whether he was simply outraged that a stranger should presume to stroke *his* head—he snarled and lashed out at her. And in that single instant he scratched the poor child's forearm quite badly—the tender inside of the arm, near the elbow. Blood sprang out from four distinct slashes and ran quickly down her arm to drip onto the floor.

"Oh! Oh, look what he *did!*" Little Goldie cried in astonishment.

She was more surprised than frightened, but the other girls screamed for help (Christabel in particular, since the sight of blood terrified her), and they were fortunate enough to attract the attention of one of the adults—Gideon—who was just passing by. He hurried inside, saw what had happened, clapped his hands angrily to frighten the hissing Mahalaleel away—Mahalaleel and the kittens as well—and dropped to his knees to examine Little Goldie's wound. "Now don't cry, you'll be all right," he murmured, wrapping a handkerchief around her arm, soaking up the bright blood. "You *shouldn't* have gotten near that bastard of a cat. But you'll be all right: these are only scratches."

It must have been the case that Garth was also nearby, perhaps dawdling in the corridor; because he too heard the girls' screams, and ran into the room less than a minute after his uncle. He came to a stop abruptly, staring at Gideon and Little Goldie, who were both kneeling on the tessellated floor. The girls told him what had happened—how naughty Mahalaleel had been—but he did not seem to hear. "What happened," he asked in a queer strangled voice, "what *happened* to her—"

Gideon glanced around at him, and said, "Go get Lissa, will you, and say there's been a little accident—one of the cats has scratched Little Goldie—we need bandages, and some disinfectant—"

"What *happened,* what are you *doing,"* Garth said.

He towered above them, six feet tall, his jaw suddenly slack, his long thick arms hanging loose. Gideon repeated what he had said, but Garth heard nothing; he was simply staring at them.

"For Christ's sake, Garth—" Gideon began: but Garth suddenly seized him and wrenched him away from Little Goldie, and threw himself on top of him, shouting incoherently. His fists rose and fell, he kneed his uncle in the chest, tried to close his fingers around his throat. It all happened so quickly that the girls stared in amazement, too surprised even to call for help for several seconds. What *was* happening! Had Garth suddenly gone mad!

The two men rolled over and over, colliding with the legs of a chair, knocking the chair against the wall. Someone ran to the doorway. There were shouts and more screams. Gideon shoved Garth away with his knee, but Garth, his face a bright hideous red, managed to throw himself down again, his fingers outstretched. He was babbling that he would kill his uncle—that nothing was going to stop him.

Somehow they struggled to their feet. Gideon's nose was bleeding freely, there was blood—his, or Garth's—smeared on Garth's face and shirt; their chests rose and fell convulsively. Though people were yelling for them to stop they did not hear. They were staring at each other, circling each other. Garth's mother hurried into the room, with grandmother Cornelia close behind. "Oh, what are you doing!" the women screamed. "Oh, stop! *Garth!* Stop!"

Garth rushed his uncle, who caught him in his arms, and, grunting like animals, the two of them staggered backward, crashing through the French doors (so that glass flew and there were more terrified screams).

Then both fell backward against a low balcony railing; and over the railing, and into the rose garden six feet below. The fall did not appear to hurt either of them—perhaps they did not notice it—for their struggle increased in intensity.

Noel came limping over, in his work clothes, shouting for them to stop. He carried a hoe and was accompanied by the farm overseer, and several hired hands, who gaped stupidly at Garth and Gideon. But the fighting men (for Garth *was* a man, nearly as heavy as his uncle) paid no attention.

Now Gideon was on top, slamming his fist into Garth's face; now Garth was on top, shrieking, trying again to close his fingers (which were bleeding) around his uncle's throat. They rolled over and over in the desiccated rosebushes, unheedful of the thorns and the innumerable scratches on their faces and hands that had begun to bleed. From an upstairs window aunt Aveline shrieked: "Turn the fire extinguishers on them! Quickly! Quickly before one of them is murdered!" Vernon appeared, his straggly beard blowing, and made the mistake of approaching them—and suddenly he was propelled violently backward, the book he was carrying thrown out of his hand. (He fell in one of the open trenches, where a new pipe was in the process of being laid, and badly sprained his ankle. But in the excitement no one noticed.) Several Bellefleur dogs ran over, barking hysterically.

"Oh, where is Ewan," Lily cried, leaning over the railing, "where is Ewan—Ewan is the only one who can stop them—"

But Ewan was nowhere to be found. (He had taken one of the pick-up trucks into the village.) Nor was Leah home: she and Germaine were in Vanderpoel for the weekend. Hiram appeared, shaking his cane, shouting for order; order, or he would call the sheriff; but naturally the men paid no attention, and would even have knocked him to the ground as they rolled in his direction, had he not danced quickly aside.

"Help me, you idiots," Noel cried to his workers, and though he boldly seized Gideon by the hair they did not dare come near: and he soon lost his grip on his son. *He* was panting convulsively: he stumbled backward, his hand pressed against his chest. (So Cornelia cried, "You, down there, take care of that foolish old man! Don't let him *near* those two!") The dogs barked and yipped and whined, circling the men, their ears laid back.

On the balcony, stepping on the shattered glass, Little Goldie stared at the struggling men, her small fist pressed against her mouth. Her pale arched eyebrows were brought sharply together, in a look of horror; her skin had gone white, so that her innumerable pale freckles appeared to darken; her blond hair was all atangle. It might have been noted, from the rose garden especially, that she was, in that stance, particularly beautiful—a prematurely adult young girl, with small, hard breasts, a tiny waist, slender hips and legs. "Oh no oh no oh *no,*" she whimpered; but the men took no heed of her either.

Garth lay back, panting, and Gideon stumbled to his feet, dripping blood from his nose. For five or six seconds they rested: and then Gideon ran at his nephew, and the two of them again scuffled, and the women screamed. Albert appeared. And young Jasper. Hiram was trying to break up the fight by prodding the men with his cane, but to no avail; both were oblivious of his timid blows. Jasper and Albert tried to grab hold of Garth, futilely; Noel tried again to seize his son by the hair, but one of Garth's wild fists caught him in the mouth. (And cracked the poor man's dentures.) A shoe flew loose—it was Gideon's—and shreds of Garth's shirt —and skeins of blood.

"Stop! You must stop! I command you to stop!" Grandmother Cornelia shouted, her wig askew.

In the end, however, they stopped only because—instinctively, unconsciously—they felt it was time to stop. Garth crawled away, sobbing; Gideon remained on his side, propped up by one elbow. It might have been the case, since Garth was the one to crawl away, that he had been defeated (and so most of the witnesses argued), but Gideon's blood-streaked face showed no triumph.

But what was the fight about?—what on earth had happened?

Garth hid away in his room, and wouldn't answer; Gideon, though looking a bloody wreck, and so exhausted he could hardly walk, staggered to his Aston-Martin and drove away, ignoring the shouts of incredulity that were raised behind him.

How did it begin?—weren't Garth and his uncle usually on good terms?—didn't they *like* each other?—what had gone wrong?—why did they suddenly want to kill each other?

So the family asked; but no answers were forthcoming.

Great-Grandmother Elvira's Hundredth Birthday Celebration

On the day before great-grandmother Elvira's hundredth birthday, in honor of which a large celebration had been planned by the family, it was observed by Leah and others that Germaine was uncommonly nervous, and even rather cranky—the usually happy little girl refused to be drawn into the others' excitement (most of the children, and many of the adults, were in a near-frenzy of excitement over the party— for not since Raphael Bellefleur's time had so ambitious a social event been planned at Bellefleur Manor); she kept to herself in the nursery, or in her mother's boudoir, or in Violet's drawing room, staring anxiously out the window, with a concentration that seemed adult, at the November sky (which was perfectly cloudless); she was so distracted that a footstep behind her or a gentle "Germaine . . . ?" or one of her favorite kittens, flying across the floor, was enough to frighten her into a little scream. Leah sought her out and knelt before her, framing her face, gazing into her evasive eyes. "What is wrong, dear? Don't you feel well?" she asked. But the little girl answered disjointedly, squirming out of her mother's embrace. The sky tasted muddy, she said. Muddy-black. There were eels in it. The cellar smelled: rubber and skunk and something burnt on the stove. Tiny spiders were crawling up her legs and stinging. . . .

"She must be coming down with something," grandmother Cornelia said, approaching the child but not touching her. "Just look at her eyes. . . ."

"Germaine," Leah said, trying to hug her, "there certainly aren't spiders crawling up your legs! You know better! Those are just goosebumps, you're cold, you can't seem to stop shivering, can you . . . ? Are you getting sick? Is it your stomach? Please tell me, dear."

But she pushed Leah away and ran to the window, pressing her cheek against the pane so that she could peer up, anxiously. Her forehead was furrowed and her lips, which were unusually pale, were drawn back from her baby teeth in an ugly grimace.

"She's such a strange child," Cornelia whispered, shuddering.

". . . Are you coming down with a cold, Germaine? Please tell me. At least *look* at me. There's nothing up *there* to look at!" Leah cried. She caught hold of Germaine again, and again framed her face, this time holding it rather roughly between her hands. "I don't want you to babble such nonsense. Do you hear? Not in front of me and certainly not in front of anyone else. And *certainly* not tomorrow when our guests arrive. Eels in the sky, skunks in the cellar, spiders, what *nonsense!*"

"You'll be frightening her, Leah," Cornelia said.

But Leah paid no attention to her mother-in-law. She was staring into her daughter's face, holding her squirming head still. The eyes were dilated, the skin was pale and clammy, there was an aura of—of what?— something dank, wet, sour, brackish about the child. After a long moment Leah said, "Something is going to go wrong, isn't it. Something is going to go wrong after all my work. . . ." But then, with a little cry of disgust, "But you don't always know. You don't *always* know."

She pushed Germaine away and straightened, and said to her mother-in-law in a vexed, tearful voice, "She doesn't *always* know, does she!"

The party to celebrate great-grandmother Elvira's hundredth birthday was to have been, at first, a family party: and then Leah hit upon the idea of inviting Bellefleurs from other regions, and even other states (Cornelia and Aveline were drawn into her enthusiasm, each supplying lists of names, in some cases of Bellefleurs no one had seen for decades, in such distant places as New Mexico, British Columbia, and Alaska, and even Brazil): and then Hiram hit upon the idea of inviting people from outside the family, since it had been so long since the manor had been open to a number of important, influential guests: and naturally Leah responded to his suggestion with zeal. *Meldroms . . . Zunderts . . . Schaffs . . . Medicks . . . Sanduskys . . . Faines . . . Scroons . . . Dodders . . . Pyes . . . Fiddlenecks . . . Bonesets . . . Walpoles . . . Cinquefoils . . . Filarees . . . Crockets . . . Mobbs . . . Pikes . . . Braggs . . . Hallecks . . . Whipples . . . Pepperells . . . Cokers . . . Yarrows . . . Milfoils . . . Fuhrs* (though of course they probably would not even acknowledge the invitation) . . . *Vervains . . . Rudbecks . . . Governor Grounsel and his family . . . Lieutenant-Governor Horehound and his family . . . Attorney General Sloan and his family . . . Senator Tucke . . . Congressman Sledge . . . the Caswells and the Abbots and the Ritchies and . . . and perhaps even Mr. Tirpitz* (though it was unlikely that he would come). . . .

Leah hired a male calligrapher to write out the invitations, which were sent out on oyster-white cards with the Bellefleur coat of arms embossed in silver on them; if the celebration is to be held, she declared, everything should be done perfectly. A Vanderpoel caterer was retained. More domestic help was hired. Since guests were coming from so far away they would have to spend the night, or even several nights: so the castle's innumerable guest chambers would have to be aired and cleaned and polished and perhaps even repainted and in some cases fumigated. Furniture would have to be reupholstered. Rugs would have to be cleaned. Old stained varnish would have to be scraped off, and new varnish applied. More china must be bought; and more crystal; and silverware. Paintings, statues, frescoes, tapestries, and other ornamental objects would have to be cleaned and switched around from room to room. (How odd, how very odd, Leah thought, studying for the first time certain of the things Raphael Bellefleur had acquired, presumably by way of dealers and buyers in Europe. She wondered if he had actually looked at them before he had them hung: for what could one possibly make of these copies of Tintoretto, Veronese, Caravaggio, Bosch, Michelangelo, Botticelli, Rosso . . . ? There were enormous cracked oils and ten-by-fifteen faded tapestries and frescoes and altarpieces of *The Rape of Europa, The Triumph of Bacchus, The Triumph of Silenus, Venus and Adonis, Venus and Mars, Deucalion and Pyrrha, Danae, The Marriage of the Virgin, The Annunciation, Cupid Carving His Bow, Diana and Acteon, Jupiter and Io, Susannah and the Elders,* there were Olympian feasts and battles and orgies, in which lecherous satyrs leered, and thick-buttocked "graces" clutched wisps of diaphanous clothing comically inadequate to cover their nakedness, and gods with ludicrously tiny phalluses were being stripped by *putti* who were really dwarves with comically foreshortened legs and bulging foreheads. . . . On one wall of Leah's and Gideon's own bedchamber was an immense time-darkened oil depicting Leda and the Swan, in which Leda was an obscenely plump maiden with a dazed expression, reclining upon a much-rumpled couch, and staving off, with a feeble arm, a stunted but ferocious swan with a phallic neck so meticulously rendered it must have been a joke. . . . Leah stared at these things, shining a flashlight on them, feeling lightheaded, and occasionally even nauseous, wondering if she was imagining their satirical *bizarrerie;* wondering if Raphael had intended to purchase such grotesque art, or whether the poor man, for all his money, had been hoodwinked. They would have to come down someday. But there was no time, now, to replace them with other works of art; nor would there be enough money.) She even wanted to open the Turquoise Room, about which she had heard so much, but was dissuaded, not by the other Bellefleurs' pleas, but by the extraordinary sensation that coursed through her when she laid her hand upon the doorknob. . . . (But someone had nailed the door shut, in addition to locking it. Nailed it shut with six-inch spikes. "A pretty sight, in the corridor for any guest to see!" she said.)

A week before Elvira's birthday Leah realized that the estate must *smell.* It was a farm, there were farm animals, how could it not smell? So, over Noel's weak protests, she arranged for an entire herd of Holsteins, what remained of the horses, and a number of hogs and sheep to be shifted by truck to other parts of the estate. (The family had just acquired, at rather a bargain, some seven hundred acres of fairly good land along the Nautauga River, adjacent to the land once farmed, and poorly farmed at that, by the tenant farmer Doan and his idle family.) "I don't see any reason to advertise the fact that we are *farmers,*" Leah said. "And anyway we aren't, really—most of our income comes from other sources."

Domestic help began to arrive, and were housed in the old coachman's lodge: cooks, butlers, maids, groundsmen, even a lampman, even several page boys (who were Hiram's idea: he remembered liveried page boys from his youth, or claimed he did, and had always associated them with the aristocracy). Three seamstresses; two hairdressers; a "floral artist"; a Hungarian gypsy band from Port Oriskany; a string quartet specializing in nineteenth-century Romantic music. A team of electricians came to arrange strings of brightly burning electric lights indoors and out, strung along the battlements and from tower to tower, so that they would be visible for many miles, across the entire width of Lake Noir. "How lovely," Leah murmured. "How lovely everything is. . . ." Two truckloads of flowers were delivered: roses, gloxinias, lilies of the valley, carnations, orchids. Leah and Cornelia and Aveline helped arrange them, in every part of the house; a great basket of orchids was brought to Elvira's suite where the old woman, wearing a wrinkled floor-length houserobe, and pretending to be somewhat peeved by all the attention, claimed there was no logical place for them. "Cut flowers are a shameful waste," she said. "We have more flowers than we know what to do with in the summer."

"But this isn't summer, Mother Elvira!" Cornelia said lightly.

"I'm not even certain it *is* my birthday, this week."

"Of course it's your birthday!"

". . . or that I'm really the age you say," the old woman murmured, shivering in her gown. "Bellefleurs always exaggerate."

A pity, Leah thought, gazing at great-grandmother Elvira, that her husband wasn't still alive; or that no one of her generation had survived. How lonely it must be, to have outlived everyone. . . . Elvira was said to have been an extremely beautiful young woman when she became betrothed to the luckless Lamentations of Jeremiah, more than eight decades previously; and with her fine white hair, her unusually soft complexion, and her slender, almost girlish frame she was still an attractive woman. She might have been sixty-five years old, or seventy. Hardly more than eighty. Ah, but one hundred . . . ! It seemed impossible. *She,* Leah, would never grow so old.

"Why are you staring at me, miss?" Elvira said sharply.

Leah blushed. She realized that the old woman had forgotten her name.

"I was thinking—I was thinking—"

"Yes?"

"That this will be a birthday for us all to remember, and to cherish," Leah said weakly.

"Yes, I don't doubt *that.*" Great-grandmother Elvira laughed.

Leah spent a sleepless night, her mind reeling with last-minute plans. So many guests had accepted invitations. . . . So much food had been delivered. . . . (Several truckloads of choice beef and lamb; Cornish game hens; red snapper, sole, salmon, and sea bass; crabmeat and lobster.) There was a hideous tapestry in one of the third-floor guest rooms that she *must* take down, after all: it showed a naked potbellied drunken Silenus on a swaybacked ass, being led in a riotous procession of nymphs, satyrs, and fat little cupids. Quite possibly the ugliest thing she had ever seen. . . . And what if Germaine were ill, in the morning? And what if Gideon disappeared as he had threatened? (But he wouldn't dare betray the family.) And suppose old Elvira stubbornly refused to come downstairs, to open her presents. . . .

Near dawn Leah had a confused waking dream. She was back at the Powhatassie penitentiary (which she had visited twelve days earlier), being led once again through the five locked gates, one after another after another, in her fox coat and her black silk shantung suit. She tried not to notice the high granite walls, the crumbling concrete, the stench. . . . In the high-vaulted visitors' room she was led to an elderly man said to be her uncle Jean-Pierre Bellefleur II. Silvery-haired, diminutive, with small rheumy colorless eyes; his skin dry and flaking, and dead-white; thin lips stretched in a mock-courteous smile; a hump, small but prominent, between his shoulders. As she approached he raised his eyes to her and his gaze pierced her like a blade: for it was obvious that he was a Bellefleur. Even in his ill-fitting gray-blue prison uniform he was a Bellefleur, one of her people. . . .

"Uncle Jean-Pierre! At last! Oh, at last! I'm so grateful to be allowed to see you!" she cried.

The courtly old man (who looked far older than Noel or Hiram) acknowledged her words with a slight nod of his head.

She sat on the very edge of her uncomfortable chair, and began to speak. There was so much to say! So much to explain! She was Leah Pym, his sister Della's daughter; she was his nephew Gideon's wife; she had come to bring him hope. After so many years, after so many years of the vilest injustice. . . .

As she talked, more and more rapidly, the silver-haired old gentleman merely gazed at her. From time to time he nodded, but without conviction.

He had been falsely accused and falsely found guilty, but his case had not been forgotten, and she and her attorneys were in the process of reviewing it, and soon, very soon, they might have encouraging news. . . .

Around them, other visitors and prisoners were shouting at one another. There was a considerable din. A heavyset young woman beside Leah merely stared at her husband, through the scratched glass partition, and the two of them wept. Ah, Leah thought with a thrill of terror, how awful!

The skin of her uncle's face was like an aged palimpsest. His eyes, close-set and watery, struck her as very beautiful. We haven't forgotten you, we haven't betrayed you, Leah said, speaking more and more quickly, her own eyes filling with tears. It *amazed* her, that she should be facing, after so long, her uncle Jean-Pierre: that after having refused to see her for so many months, he should suddenly have relented. His expression was slightly mocking; yet wise; kind; good. She could see that he had suffered. She could see that he half-pitied her, for her idealism. He thought she was a fool—perhaps. A silly goose of a girl. But she would show him! She wouldn't give up so easily as the others had.

Because I know you are innocent, she whispered.

His lips twitched in a smile. He raised one liver-spotted hand, and drew it slowly beneath his nose.

. . . I know, I know you are innocent, she said.

The visitors' room was a great concrete cavern lurid with voices and echoes. Somewhere, far away, rain pelted against windows. But the windows were opaque. Leah, squinting, could not see the sky—could not see where the angry rain struck.

"The Innisfail Butcher!" This gentle broken-spirited old man with the kindly pitying eyes and the dry wrinkled skin that seemed to lie against his bones in layers, like the skin of an onion. . . .

Leah talked and talked. Perhaps he heard. Perhaps he understood. At any rate he did not try to dissuade her. He said only two things during the course of their ninety-minute visit, and Leah, though straining, could not hear them precisely. The first sounded like *If old Raphael gets in office I think he might pardon me.* Leah, surprised, managed to smile faintly, and to explain that there was a man named Grounsel in the governor's office —and that she and her attorneys had already begun petitioning him. The second remark of Jean-Pierre's was made in response to Leah's spirited statement, that she wished—ah, how she wished!—Jean-Pierre might be a free man by the time of his mother's birthday; it would be, he must know, his poor mother's hundredth birthday. The old man, gazing at her with his mild rheumy eyes, frowned for a moment, and said what sounded like *My mother—do I have a mother—*

The rain interrupted them, slamming against the windows.

And Leah awoke, her heart pounding—and it *was* raining—the morning of the birthday celebration, and pouring rain—vicious pouring rain.

Toward 9:00 AM. the rain stopped, and the sky appeared to open. But how queer, how alarming it looked—as if, Leah thought, one were gazing into a bottomless chasm. But the rain *had* stopped.

The Bellefleur women hurried about the house, giving orders to the help, frequently contradicting one another. Leah wanted *The Triumph of Silenus* taken down at once from the guest room reserved for W. D. Meldrom, but Cornelia insisted that it remain: wasn't it one of the treasures of the estate, an oil attributed to Caravaggio? Aveline wanted most of the furniture in the main drawing room moved about, so that the atmosphere was less casual; she preferred, she said, the original formality of the house, before Leah had gone changing everything around. Della, who had been pressed into a visit, who had, as she said, far more important things to do at home, found fault with the gloxinia plants. They were already dying: sent up from the Falls at such absurd expense, and already dying . . . ! Lily followed the maids about, uncharacteristically critical, stooping to sniff at cushions (she was convinced—it had become one of her obsessions, since the party was planned—that the manor's many kittens had fouled these wonderful old pieces of furniture), ordering floors repolished, sighting strands of cobweb floating from the high, shadowy, vaulted ceilings. It was imperative, she kept saying, that they not make fools of themselves.

The sky continued to lighten, though it was not exactly clear. Warmer and warmer the day became. A hazy sun glared through vast caverns of cloud: ah, how very hot the manor was! The windows must be opened. It was mid-November, there had already been a considerable snowfall, but it had melted, and now the temperature was rising as if it were midsummer: 50°, 53°, 57°, 59° . . .

Leah burst into tears when she saw that one of the children, evidently accompanied by a dog, had tracked mud onto a silk-and-wool carpet that had just been cleaned. And what time was it? The first of the guests—on the specially reserved Bellefleur coach on the train from downstate—would be arriving in about six hours.

The sky darkened suddenly. And suddenly there was a tremendous wind, which blew up out of nowhere. Running to the windows, the Bellefleurs saw to their astonishment that the sky had turned boiling-black: and, in the distance, Mount Chattaroy and Mount Blanc were ringed with clouds that appeared to be on fire.

Then there was a blinding flash of light, followed immediately by a crack of thunder so loud that several of the children screamed in terror, and the dogs set up a howl. Lightning! Lightning must have struck!

They ran about shutting windows. But in some cases it was already too late—the wind was too strong, torrents of rain had soaked everything, one could hardly push the windows closed; and there was the danger of lightning. (It *had* struck nearby—fortunately only a giant oak in the park, which had been struck many times in the past.)

So the Great Storm began: which was to rival in violence and damage the Great Storm of twenty years previously: when all of the low-lying areas were flooded, and so many people lost their lives, and even the dead were washed out of their graves.

The winds were of hurricane force. Sometimes the air was sulfurous and warm—sometimes it was quite cold, bringing walls of ice that struck the windows like bullets, and in many cases cracked them. Trees were felled. Sheets of rain pounded against the gravel walks and drives, turning them to mud. In his tower Bromwell observed, through a telescope, how Mink Creek had already risen: and its waters had turned an unrecognizable clayey-orange.

"Our guests—our party—Grandmother Elvira's birthday—"

"But this *cannot* happen—"

"Why is the sun so bright—"

"Is it a hurricane? Is it the end of the world?"

"Get one of the men to stop that water coming in under the door—"

"Ah, look at Mount Chattaroy!"

"Is it a volcano? Is that fire?"

"What will happen to our wonderful party!"

The sky shifted from side to side as if it were alive. A sickly greenish-orange. And then a livid magenta. Clotted clouds raced from horizon to horizon. The rain lightened; and then suddenly increased; again it fell in sheets, with such malevolence the entire house trembled. There had never been anything like it! The Great Flood of twenty years back had been less violent, and shrouded in mist, so that one couldn't actually *see* what was happening. No, there had never been anything like this. . . .

The winds continued to blow, and the rain continued to fall, hour upon hour. Power lines to the manor were blown down, and though it was midday candles had to be lit; but even the candles were in danger of being blown out by capricious fingers of air. Devilish spirits raced up and down the curving staircases, loosed by the storm, frenzied as hysterical children. And the children—the children *were* hysterical: some of them were so frightened they had run away to hide, others were leaning out of windows and shouting ("Come on, come on, what are you waiting for, come *on,* you can't get us, come on and try!" feverish Christabel screamed from out a nursery window). Leah huddled in a corner of the kitchen with Germaine, trying to comfort her (though it was really herself she was comforting), and then, every few minutes, restless, infuriated, she jumped to her feet and ran out to see—to see—if perhaps the storm wasn't lessening?—and the party might be salvaged after all?

"I could curse God for this! For this vile trick!" she shouted.

Hiram, who had dressed that morning for the party, and was wearing an elegantly tailored suit of the finest lightweight wool, with a very white and very starched shirt, and gold-and-ivory cuff links, and his usual gold watch chain, turned sharply to her, and raised his voice to be heard over the drumlike tolling of the wind: "Leah. How *can* you. If one of the children heard you—! Such superstitious rot, you know very well there isn't any God, and if there is the poor thing is too feeble to have managed *this.*"

Nevertheless Leah ran about like a madwoman, peering out one window and then another, as if she believed the storm might alter from one angle of perception to another, saying to anyone who would listen, "It's a trick. A vile trick. Because we're Bellefleurs. Because they want to stop us—*He* wants to stop us—and He isn't going to!"

Ewan and Gideon came in (for they had been—incredibly—out in the storm) to report that the Nautauga River was rising a foot an hour; and that most of the roads were washed out; the Fort Hanna bridge was said to be washed out; there had been a train derailment at Kincardine. And already three people were reported missing. . . .

"You're pleased about this, aren't you!" Leah screamed. "The two of you! *Aren't you!"*

. . . and Garth and Little Goldie, who had planned to return from their honeymoon in time for the party, must be caught in the storm somewhere to the south. . . .

"Oh, I hate you all! I hate this! I won't stand for this! It was Elvira's hundredth birthday and it won't come again and all my work—my weeks and weeks of work—my guests—I won't stand for this, do you hear!" poor Leah screamed. In her frenzy she ran to Gideon and began pounding his chest and face, but he caught her wrists, and calmed her, and led her back into the kitchen (which was the only warm place in the drafty old house) where he instructed Edna to make a rum toddy for her. And he stayed with her until her sobbing quieted, and she pressed her tear-lashed face against his neck, and fell into a kind of stupor, murmuring *I wanted only to do well, I wanted only to help, God has been cruel, I will never forgive Him. . . .*

In the end the storm was to be somewhat less severe than the Great Flood of twenty years previously; but it was still a hellish thing, and took away the lives of some twenty-three people in the Lake Noir area alone, and caused damage of upward of several million dollars. The roads *were* washed out, many of the bridges damaged past repair; trains were derailed and train beds torn away; Lake Noir and the Nautauga River and Mink Creek and innumerable nameless creeks and runs and ditches flooded, propelling debris along: baby buggies, chairs, laundry that had been hung out to dry, lampshades, parts of automobiles, loose boards, doors, window frames, the corpses of chickens, cows, horses, snakes, muskrats, raccoons, and parts of these corpses; and parts of what were evidently human corpses (for the cemeteries once again flooded, and relief workers were to be astonished and sickened by the sight of badly decomposed corpses dangling from roofs, from trees, jammed against silos and corncribs and abandoned cars, washed up against the foundations of homes, in various stages of decay: some aged and leathery, some fresh, soggy, pale; and all of them pathetically naked); and spiders—some of them gigantic, with bristling black hairs—ran about everywhere, washed out of their hiding places and frantic with terror.

Flood damage was comparatively minor at Bellefleur because the house was on somewhat higher ground. But even there the fruit orchards and gardens stood in a foot of muddy water, and the handsome pink gravel of the walks and drives was washed into the lawn, and the newly planted trees and shrubs in Leah's walled garden were uprooted; and it was a terrible sight, the drowned creatures everywhere—not only wild animals but some of the household cats and dogs, and many of the game fowl, and a pet black goat belonging to one of the boys. A number of Bellefleur workers had to evacuate their cottages and the low barracks-type building at the edge of the swamp; they were moved by truck to temporary quarters in the village, at the Bellefleurs' expense, and of course the Bellefleurs volunteered to pay for their food and clothing, and to reimburse them for their losses in the flood. Elsewhere, on other Bellefleur-owned property, there was considerable damage, the most grievous being the loss of an entire herd of Holsteins, drowned when a creek overflowed. The creatures had been penned up, rather stupidly, on low ground.

At the castle the cellar was flooded (the cellar was *always* flooded, even in minor rainstorms); many windows were broken; slate was torn from the roof and flung for hundreds of yards. Every chimney was damaged, every ceiling was water-stained. When the Bellefleurs, at the height of the storm, at last remembered great-grandmother Elvira, and hurried up to her room, they found the poor old woman in her rocking chair, in a virtual rain that fell from the ceiling. She had pulled her black cashmere shawl up over her head, and though she was shivering, she did not seem especially pleased to see them. She'd sent her maid away hours ago, she said, because she wanted to enjoy the storm in private; and so she *had* enjoyed it, despite the dripping ceiling and the terrible cold. She had particularly liked, she said, the lightning flashes over the lake.

She seemed to have forgotten, or perhaps did not care to mention, the fact that it was her hundredth birthday, and that a great celebration had been planned: which of course would not now take place.

So the storm passed by, leaving damage and heartbreak in its wake, and next morning the Bellefleurs looked out to see a transformed world: ponds everywhere, great puddles of water that, reflecting the sky, looked like glassy lead, fallen trees, small mountains of debris that would have to be cleared away. The men—Gideon, Ewan, even Vernon, even grand-father Noel—made their way by foot down to the village, to help with the flood relief; Cornelia talked of "opening the castle doors" to the home-less. In the end, however, the only flood victim who was taken in was an elderly man discovered by one of the boys over in the barnyard—jammed against the stone foundation of the stable. At first, the boy said, he naturally thought it was a corpse: but it *wasn't* a corpse: the poor old man was alive!

So they brought him in, carrying him, since he was too exhausted to walk, and Dr. Jensen was summoned, and he was laid, half-unconscious, in one of the downstairs maids' rooms. A *very* elderly man—with a livid scar on his forehead—toothless—his cheeks sunken—his skin cancellate, as if it had been soaked for some time—his ragged clothing in shreds—his arms and legs hardly more than sticks, he was so thin. Though his pulse beat was weak it *was* a pulse beat, and he was able, with difficulty, and with much dribbling, to drink some broth Cornelia gave him. Ah, how pathetic! He spoke incoherently—did not seem to know his name, or where he had come from—or what had happened—that there had been a terrible storm, and that he had been caught in it. You are safe now, they told him. Try to sleep. We've called a doctor. Nothing can happen to you now.

When the men returned they looked in upon him, and there he was, propped up against pillows, blinking dazedly at them, his toothless mouth shifting into a hesitant smile. A miracle, they said, that he hadn't been drowned. (And he was such a very *old* man, and so very frail.)

But he was safe now. And he could stay with them as long as he needed. "This is Bellefleur Manor," Noel said, standing at his bedside. "You're welcome to stay here as long as you like, until your people come to claim you. You *don't* remember your name . . . ?"

The old man blinked and shook his head no, uncertainly. His cheekbones were so sharp they seemed about to push through his veined skin.

In the late afternoon great-grandmother Elvira came downstairs to see him, followed by her cat, a white-and-bluish-gray female, and when she came to the foot of his bed she fumbled in her pocket, and took out her spectacles. She peered at the old man through her glasses, rather rudely. He was just waking from a light doze, and he peered at her, smiling his uncertain smile. The cat leapt up onto the bed, making a querulous mewing sound; it began to knead its paws against the old man's thigh. For some minutes great-grandmother Elvira and the elderly man stared at each other. And then Elvira took off her spectacles, and thrust them back in her pocket, and mumbled, ". . . old fool." And she gathered up Minerva and left the room without another word.

In the Mountains,
in Those Days . . .

In the mountains, in those days, there was always music. A music composed of many voices.

High above the mist-shrouded river. In the thin cold many-faceted light. Ice, was it?—or sunshine? Or the teasing mountain spirits (which *must* have to do with God, since they live on the Holy Mountain where the Devil dare not appear)?

Many voices, plaintive and alluring and combative and taunting and lovely, achingly lovely, so very very lovely one's soul is drawn out . . . drawn out like a thread, a hair . . . fine, thin, about to break. . . .

God? Jedediah cried in his ecstasy. Is this God?

But not God, for God remained hidden.

In the mountains, in those days, there was always music.

Catching at one's soul. Seductive, yearning, frail as girls' voices in the distance. . . . But not God. For God remained hidden. Coy and stubborn and hidden. Oblivious of Jedediah's impassioned plea. *Make haste, O God, to deliver me; make haste to help me, O Lord. Let them be ashamed and confounded that seek after my soul: let them be turned backward, and put to confusion, that desire my hurt.* (For his father's spies prowled the Holy Mountain, despite the danger of God's wrath. Defiling the clear bright cold sky, the snowcap easing downward, downward, one day soon to swallow up the entire world in its frigid cleansing purity. . . . He saw them. If he did not see them, he heard them. Their mocking voices, "echoing" his most secret, most silent prayers.)

God's blessing is not always to be distinguished from His wrath. Consequently Jedediah did not know—should he fall to his knees in gratitude to God, that he could hear (and sometimes even feel) the presence of his enemies?—or should he beg God to diminish the power (now grown extraordinary, and frequently painful) of his senses, particularly his sense of hearing?

O give thanks unto the Lord; call upon His name: make known His deeds among the people. Sing unto Him, sing psalms unto Him: talk ye of all His wondrous works. Seek the Lord, and His strength: seek His face evermore.

In those days there was always music but perhaps it was not *always* God's music. The voices, for instance. Quarreling and chattering and teasing. God won't show His face, whyever should He!—to a comical wretch like you! (So the dark-eyed girl giggled, lifting the lid off a pot of rabbit stew and flinging it against the wall. And why? Just for meanness. For deviltry.)

Keep not thou silence, O God: hold not thy peace, and be not still, O God.

A voice, lightly jeering: Keep not thou silence, O God: hold not thy peace. . . . But with a false, wicked emphasis: Keep not *thou* silence, O God: *hold* not thy peace, and be *not still,* O God. . . . (As if the spirits were mocking someone of very limited intelligence. Halfwitted or retarded. Brain-damaged. Senile.)

In the mountains, in those days, the gigantic white bird with the naked red-skinned head appeared frequently, as if in response to a thoughtless utterance of Jedediah's. (For just as he could hear so keenly, so could other creatures hear keenly. If he stepped on a twig all of the mountain was alerted. If one of his monstrous coughing attacks overcame him all of the mountain region heard.) A silent gliding bird. Its shadow, deceptively light, scudding across the stony ground. And then, suddenly overhead, its hideous shrieking: so that Jedediah's heart nearly leapt out of his chest: and it was all he could do, to beat the creature away with the hardwood cudgel he carried with him everywhere.

Pray God, beg God, plead with *God,* Louis's wife teased, pinching at his ribs, and what sails along but that nasty old *bird.*

The bird gave off a terrible stench—it must have been its breath, fetid as if its very bowels were rotten.

Behold the fowls of the air.

Seek ye first the kingdom of God.

The spirits brushed near, nearer than the bird dared, and pretended to take his side. God isn't listening, God is busy down in the flatland, God has betrayed you. Throw that silly old Bible down into the river!

(Ah, but it was one of the surprises of Jedediah's life, that the Bible *was* lying some twenty or thirty yards down the cliff. . . . He could not believe it but there it was: someone had thrown it there: and it took him the better part of a morning, and cost him many cruel welts and scratches, to retrieve it. Even so, several pages were ripped away, and many pages were damaged. His bowels writhed with disgust and anger, and could he have laid hands on that bright-eyed spirit, what might he have done to her! I would show no mercy, he whispered, weeping, because you deserve no mercy.)

But the outrageous incident had the effect, at least, of loosening his bowels. For poor Jedediah, though he prayed God for relief, suffered cruelly from constipation.

In the winter especially. In the winter, certainly.

He had built a crude little outhouse in a thicket some distance from the cabin, hidden from the cabin. Bodily functions had always disquieted him. Not-to-be-thought-of, so he commonly silenced certain thoughts. Except when the pain overtook him deep in the pit of his belly and he was bent nearly double and even the spirits, aghast, fled his torment.

The outhouse, of skinned pine; and a sturdier chimney; and a pretty little piece of stained glass, about a foot square, in a window facing east (sent up by way of Henofer, along with other unwanted things—a bright turquoise blue with beige and red lines—silly, vain, breakable—but undeniably pretty—and, he supposed, harmless: a gift from his brother's wife down below); a shallow well halfway down the mountain into which spring water ran for several months of the year.

"You're going to stay here forever, are you?" Henofer laughed, rubbing his cracked hands briskly and looking about. "Just like me! *Just like me!*"

Henofer and his letters, supplies, gossip, news of the War. (To which Jedediah only vaguely listened. For what did God care of the paltry doings of men—their lust for territory, for goods, for dominion over the high seas? Saliva flew from Henofer's lips as he spoke passionately of the surrender of Fort Mackinaw. An allied force of British and Indians had captured it. And there was Fort Dearborn: captured by Indians: and most of the garrison *including women and children* had been slaughtered. By a general order issued from the War Department the state militia were arranged in two divisions and eight brigades, and thousands of men would soon see battle. The war was necessary; at the same time Henofer did not quite understand its background; nor did he (and naturally Jedediah did not ask, being too courteous) intend to enlist. He was supplying hides to Alexander Macomb and doing quite well. *Quite* well. Did Jedediah know who Alexander Macomb was? Formerly a partner of John Jacob Astor who was worth (so rumor had it) $10,000,000; could Jedediah comprehend what $10,000,000 was? No? Yes? Of course Macomb was not as wealthy but he was a rich man and perhaps it would interest Jedediah to know that his father Jean-Pierre had had some dealings with Macomb not long ago. There was trouble of some kind: and one of Macomb's trading posts, out near Kittery, had been burnt to the ground. "Lightning was the cause," Henofer said, laughing, wiping his eyes. But then some months later the Innisfail Lodge, which Jean-Pierre had owned, was burnt to the ground as well. However . . . the Innisfail Lodge was said to have been substantially insured. But of course Jedediah knew nothing of such things . . . ?)

So he chattered, pulling his filthy woollen cap down low on his forehead. He chewed tobacco and spat onto Jedediah's hearth. Edgy, restless, he could hardly remain seated on the stump before the fire, but kept pulling at his cap and his beard, and looking around the cabin—staring and assessing and memorizing—in preparation for his report to the Bellefleurs down below. For of course he was a paid spy. And of course he knew that Jedediah must have known.

Nevertheless Jedediah remained courteous, for God dwelled with him; or at any rate the promise, the hope, of God dwelled with him. He was a Christian man, humble and soft-spoken and willing to turn the other cheek if necessary. He could not be stirred to anger by Henofer's slovenly presence, or even by the obscene anecdotes he rattled off (a half-breed Mohawk woman raped by a small gang of Bushkill's Ferry men, out by the lumber mill, and turned loose in the snow, naked and bleeding and out of her mind: the Varrells had their fun *there,* Henofer said, wiping his eyes), or boisterous farfetched tales of the war, which were sometimes meant to inspire mirth and sometimes patriotism. In Sackett's Harbor, it seemed, five British ships with eighty-two guns began an assault against the *Oneida.* . . . After two hours of firing it was found that most of the shots on both sides had fallen short. Finally a thirty-two-pound ball was fired by the British, and struck the earth harmlessly, ploughing a deep furrow; and a sergeant picked it up and ran to his captain saying, "I've been playing ball with the redcoats. See if the British can catch back again." And the ball was fitted into the American cannon, and fired back at the enemy, with such force that it struck the stern of the flagship of the attacking squadron, raking her completely, and sending splinters high into the air. . . . Fourteen men were killed outright and eighteen were wounded. And so the enemy retreated while a band on shore played, "Yankee Doodle." What, Henofer asked passionately, did Jedediah think of *that?*

Henofer would not be seeing Jedediah again until the following April. Which was a very long time away. Yet it came quickly: all too quickly. And Henofer returned, cheerful and garrulous as always, with more war news to which Jedediah did not listen. Or perhaps it wasn't the following April but the very next week. Or the previous April. At any rate there was his halloo in the clearing, and his grizzled pitted face with the gap-toothed grin. (No matter that he must have known Jedediah was sabotaging his traps—springing some, opening others to take away the dead or dying or grievously wounded creatures to throw them down into the oblivion of the river.) It might have been the previous April, the April before the pane of stained glass was brought to Jedediah.

Time pleated and rippled. Since God dwelt above time, Jedediah took no heed of time. When he glanced back at his life—his life as Jedediah Amos Bellefleur—he saw how minute that life was, how quickly the mountains with their thousands of lakes swallowed it up.

Henofer disappeared, grumbling at Jedediah's silence. He took his revenge by lurking in the woods for days afterward, spying and taking notes. As a prank he left a wolf's skull behind—hardly more than the jawbone, really—on Jedediah's granite ledge, facing the Holy Mountain. Why he had done it Jedediah would never know.

Perhaps God had used Henofer to send a message . . . ?

Jedediah contemplated the thing, which was bleached white, and oddly beautiful. He saw himself snatch it up and throw it off the edge of the mountain—but, later in the day, it was on the stone hearth before his fireplace.

Are you testing me? Jedediah whispered.

Outside the cabin spirits hummed in their nervous high-pitched manner. Jedediah was able to ignore them, as he ignored the girl's fingers poking and prodding inside his trousers.

God? Are you testing me? Are you watching? he called aloud.

The jaws, the clean white-bleached jaws. Ravenous appetite: God's.

Jedediah woke, startled. He had been dreaming of an angry man, a man shouting and waving his fists at God. But the man was himself: *he* had been shouting.

To do penance he slept outside for several nights, naked, on the granite ledge. Beneath the freezing winking stars. He brought the jawbone with him because it was a sign, it had to do with his sinfulness, though he did not understand it. *Why am I here, what have I done, how have I displeased You?* he pleaded. But there was no reply. The jawbone was silent.

Fateful Mismatches

When snow fell from the cavernous sky in angry swirls day upon day, and the sun but feebly rose at midmorning, and the castle —the world itself—was locked in ice that would never melt, then the children slept two or three in a bed, swathed in layers of clothing, with long fluffy angora socks pulled up to their knees; then there were, throughout the day, cups of steaming hot chocolate with marshmallows that, half-melted, stuck wonderfully to the roof of the mouth; afternoons of sledding followed by long lazy hours before the fireplace, listening to stories. What is the curse on the family, one of the children might ask, not for the first time, and the answer might be—depending upon who was there—that there was no curse, such talk was silly; or it might be that the nature of the curse was such (perhaps the nature of all curses is such?) that those who are burdened with it cannot speak of it. Just so, uncle Hiram liked to say, sadly fondling the tips of his mustache (which smelled so strongly of wax!), just so do creatures in nature carry the distinguishing, and sometimes magnificently unique, marks of their species and their sex, without ever seeing them: they pass through their entire lives without *seeing* themselves.

If uncle Hiram was morose and oblique, others—grandmother Cornelia, for instance, and aunt Aveline, and cousin Vernon, and sometimes even (when his breath smelled sweet with bourbon, and his poor misshapen foot ached so that, stretched out luxuriously before the huge fieldstone fireplace in the parlor, the second-warmest room in the house, he pulled off his shoe and massaged the foot and pushed it daringly close to the fire) grandfather Noel—were surprisingly generous with their words, and seemed to be drawn, perhaps by the high-leaping crackling flames of the birch logs, into disturbing labyrinthian tales the children perhaps should not have been told: wouldn't have been told, surely, by daylight. But only if no other adult were present. Now don't tell anyone about this, now this is a secret and *not to be repeated*—so the very best of the stories began.

The stories, it seemed, always had to do with "fateful mismatches." (This was the quaint term employed by the older women—they must have inherited from their mothers and grandmothers. But Yolande quite liked it. *Fateful mismatches*—! Do you think, when we grow up, she whispered to Christabel, giggling and shivering, do you think that might happen to us?) While most Bellefleur marriages were certainly excellent ones, and husband and wife supremely suited for each other, and no one would dare question their love, or the wisdom of their parents in consenting to the marriage, or, in many cases, arranging for it—still—*still* there were, from time to time, however infrequently, *fateful mismatches.*

Isn't it strange, people said, that the Bellefleur stories are all about love going wrong?—when of course, most of the time, ninety-nine times out of a hundred, things go perfectly well!

Noel laughed behind clouds of foul pipe smoke. . . . Yes indeed, he said, most of the time things go perfectly well. I've noticed that.

It was Yolande herself, at the precocious age of nine, who said, after having heard a fascinating (and convoluted: for it was necessarily expurgated for the ears of children) story about her father's oldest brother Raoul, her uncle Raoul whom she had never once seen, who clearly lived in one of the strangest imaginable households, and lived in it happily enough—it was pretty little Yolande who exclaimed; "The curse on us is that we can't love right!"

She was immediately hushed up. And cautioned never to say such a bizarre thing again, or even to think it. The very idea! Bellefleurs, after all, prided themselves on the depth and passion and longevity of their love. But to her brother Raphael she whispered, half in fear, "Oh, but what if it's the truth—what if it's the truth—and none of us can love right!" Her distress was such, one could not have said whether it was spontaneous or acquired; for even as a young child Yolande had been fond of exaggeration.

The trouble was, the tragedy was, no one cared to hear about the wonderful marriages. Wife and husband bound together for life, and happily; or at any rate not unhappily; who cared? In the midst of the children's very world, for instance, there was the example of Garth and Little Goldie: forgiven almost at once for their recklessness in eloping, given a handsome little stone-and-stucco cottage on several acres of wooded land in Bellefleur Village, and the promise of as much financial support as Garth wished—though Garth, newly self-confident, and freed for the first time in memory of his waspish ill-temper, declared that he would earn every penny of the salary the family paid him for his help in managing the farms. There they were, two young people in love, handsome Garth and lovely Little Goldie, and everything had turned out well; but what was there to say about them?

By contrast, there was a great deal to say about love gone wrong.

And disagreements too. The children were awed by their elders quarreling among themselves, about who had loved whom most, or first, or why a love affair had gone wrong, whether it had been poisoned from within or without, whether it was part of the curse or just a bad accident. . . . Whether a love had been "tragic" or just plain "shameful . . ."

Everyone knew of the Onondagan Indian woman with whom Jean-Pierre lived for several years, and with whom he died, in Bushkill's Ferry (her name was Antoinette—she had been baptized Catholic, and named for Marie Antoinette whose son, the Dauphin—King Louis XVII—was commonly believed to have escaped to the Chautauqua mountains); the match was considered a wicked one, though not half so wicked as it would have been had the old man actually *married* the woman. But few people knew of the much more shameful liaison Jean-Pierre began at the time of his wedding to poor Hilda Osborne, many years previously. He may have just returned from his honeymoon at the time (a two-month trip through the South, culminating with a grand ball in the newlyweds' honor at Chapell Hall in Charlottesville, Virginia), or he may in fact have begun the liaison while still an engaged man: but the shame of it was, he took as a mistress a coarse lumber-camp follower named Lucille who had lived with a succession of men in the Lake Noir area, and so alternated his attentions between this woman in the country and his lawful wife Hilda in Manhattan (where they lived, supported by the Osbornes' generosity, in the palatial brownstone originally built by George Washington's aide "Baron de Steuben," and lavishly remodeled by the Osbornes), that the two women—so different in quality, in temperament, in beauty, in worth! —were made pregnant by him within the same week. Lucille—"Brown Lucy"—remained a shadowy, enigmatic figure—perhaps "Lucille" was not even her name—and it wasn't known at what point in Jean-Pierre's ambitious career he jettisoned the woman. As late as 1795, when Hilda first attempted to file for divorce, he was said to have been involved with a north country woman, presumably Lucille; there were children now— three or four, at least, all sons—but how (so Jean-Pierre as well as his sympathetic friends asked, laughing), *how* could one be certain whose sons were whose, when a woman of such promiscuous morals as this "Brown Lucy" was involved—! By the time Jean-Pierre ran for Congress in 1797 the woman had been dropped from his life, for pragmatic reasons. (And then, as he explained, when drunk, to anyone who would listen, even to his son Louis and his daughter-in-law Germaine, *he hadn't loved her any more than he had loved the other one, his wife:* both women were desperate stratagems to keep him from throwing himself in the river or slashing his throat because the only woman he'd ever loved was lost to him when he was still a young man. . . .)

Of Harlan Bellefleur's women little was known—he was said to have been involved, for a brief while, with the widow of a saloonkeeper somewhere in Ohio, and was said to have had, in unclear succession, not only a full-blooded Chippewa "wife" but a Haitian "wife" as well; and in the crumpled papers found on his person, after his death, there was a scribbled message for his "sole heir" in New Orleans, about whom no one knew anything—except that, as an officer of sorts alongside Jean and Pierre Laffite, in Andrew Jackson's militia (made up of sailors, backwoods riflemen, Creoles, Santo Domingan Negroes, and Baratarian pirates), he had had occasion to spend some time in New Orleans in late 1814 and the early weeks of 1815. But it was doubtful, as Louis's grieving widow said, that *Harlan* had left a "legitimate" widow, still less a "legitimate" heir.

Then there was Raphael, who sailed to England in order to acquire the right sort of wife: and returned with the frail young woman (eighteen at the time, to Raphael's thirty-one) Violet Odlin, whose neurasthenia deepened with each pregnancy (there were ten in all—though only three live births). Perhaps the marriage was a good one. No one knew, since Raphael and Violet rarely exchanged a word in public; in fact, after some eight or nine years of marriage they were rarely seen together except at the most public, the most social, of events—at which they were extremely courteous to each other, with the graciousness normally reserved for strangers who *suspect* they will not get along, and who are accordingly all the more congenial. (Judging from the portrait that remained, Violet Odlin possessed a frail, faded, nervously intense kind of beauty, and her wedding dress with its hundreds of pearls and its eight-foot-long veil of Belgian lace had a waist so tiny—seventeen inches—that the young woman who had worn it must have been hardly larger than a child. Indeed, it was the only dress in the family that Christabel could wear for *her* wedding, and even then they had to squeeze her rather brutally into it.)

The tragedy of Samuel Bellefleur's "love match" was well known despite the Bellefleurs' attempts to keep it secret, and to this day a worried adult might wonder aloud whether, when a child was behaving badly, he or she might also *go over to the other side.* (The crude expression *take up with Negroes* was sometimes used as well.) Hiram's marriage to unhappy Eliza Perkins lasted hardly more than a year, but could not be said, even initially, to have been a love match; and though Della's ill-fated marriage to Stanton Pym *was* a love match, on her testimony at least, it came to an abrupt and tragic conclusion, albeit an accidental conclusion, after only a few months. And then there was Raoul, about whom no one dared speak above a whisper.

Most extraordinary of all, however, was the "love match" of poor Hepatica Bellefleur.

Hepatica lived a very long time ago, but her example was often raised when Bellefleur girls behaved in a headstrong manner. You know what happened to Hepatica—! their mothers said. And even the boldest of the girls grew sober.

Hepatica was a very pretty, and very spoiled, young girl of sixteen when she fell in love with the man who called himself Duane Doty Fox. (When, in subsequent years, Jeremiah became acquainted with relatives of the legitimate Duane Doty—the Wisconsin land speculator and circuit judge of some renown—they claimed to have never heard of "Duane Doty Fox." Which was unsurprising.)

Sunny, even-tempered, sometimes a little childish, Hepatica had long wavy hair in coloring rather like Yolande's, and a fondness for concocting, as often as the cook would allow, elaborate fanciful dishes of her own invention—a shellfish-and-whipped-cream mousse, an extremely sweet syllabub, a peanut-butter-and-pineapple tart that was a favorite of the children's to this very day; and of course, being a wealthy young Bellefleur heiress, and a strikingly pretty one as well, she had innumerable suitors, among them several very desirable young men (and some no longer young, precisely, but desirable just the same for various practical reasons): but without so much as asking her parents permission, she turned them all rudely down. I don't ever want to get married, she said, making a fastidious little moue; I don't want all that *fuss.*

But then, one warm April afternoon, while being driven home from the village (where she frequently visited with the rector's daughter—the only girl in the vicinity who was not too embarrassingly a social inferior) she happened to see, working with a small gang of laborers alongside the road, a most unusual young man. He was tall—he was shirtless—he wore a straw hat pulled low over his forehead—and as the Bellefleur two-seater passed he raised his head slowly, with the unhurried calm of a creature so wild, so totally undomesticated, that he had yet to discover pain at the hands of human beings: and stared openly at Hepatica in her yellow polka-dot frock and bonnet. No other man in the area would have dared look at her in quite that way; even small children, living in the vicinity of the castle, were cautioned not to *stare.*

But how silly he was, Hepatica thought, shirtless, gleaming with perspiration, his chest hair furry and frizzy—how wonderfully hilarious! (For it was extraordinary, the sight of a bare-chested man, particularly along the lakefront road—which was very nearly a private road of the Bellefleurs, though in theory it was open to anyone. Most unusual, Hepatica thought. *Most* strange.)

She saw too that he was handsome, though swarthy-skinned; and bearded (and she was not at all certain that she liked beards). For days afterward she kept seeing him at the side of the road, lowering his pickax to gaze at her, his face strong and broad and deeply tanned, his eyes very dark; dark but gleaming; *intensely* gleaming—or so she imagined. It did no good to chatter about him and ridicule him, to whoever would listen, for she kept thinking about him, thinking and thinking about him, and at the mere suggestion of a walk to the village, or even down to the lake, her heart fluttered so that she felt almost faint.

Where a more modest (or at least a more prudent) girl would have waited to encounter the young man again by accident, Hepatica, acting with a single-minded impetuosity more suitable, perhaps, in one of her brothers, made inquiries among the servants and the villagers, and soon learned that the young man, new to the area (he had just come down from Canada, it was believed, and had lived for a while previously in Wisconsin), was a blacksmith's assistant and a laborer-for-hire in the village; and his name was Duane Doty Fox.

Did he have any family? shameless Hepatica asked. Did he have a wife?

Evidently he had no one—no one at all. It wasn't even known where, exactly, he lived.

Ah, but didn't he live in the village? Hepatica asked.

He worked in the village but he lived, so far as anyone knew, up in the woods. A strange, quiet, unfriendly man . . . though he was said to be an excellent worker.

And so one fine spring day Hepatica walked to the village, accompanied by a servant girl whom she sent off on an errand of embarrassing flimsiness, and, quite alone, quite fearless, she strode directly to the blacksmith's shop (where her family never did business, since at that time the Bellefleurs employed their own blacksmith), and met with Duane Doty Fox. It isn't known what they talked of, at that first meeting—the conversation must have been awkward and strained—Hepatica *must* have been somewhat embarrassed—though perhaps (she was a marvelously inventive and imaginative child, and told lies with such a pretty flair that they never seemed serious) she simply prattled on about her favorite pony and his need for new horseshoes. She might have asked him about Canada, what sort of Indians and wild beasts lived there; or about Wisconsin; or what he thought of the new President; or any flibbertigibbet thing that flew into her head.

And so they met, and fell in love. Hepatica Bellefleur and the swarthy stranger known only as Duane Doty Fox: and it was a measure of Hepatica's precocious ingenuity that they contrived to meet some five or six times (always in the woods, or along a little-frequented stretch of Lake Noir; once on the banks of Bloody Run, high above the water) without arousing the family's suspicions. Just when the first of the gossip made its way to the manor, Hepatica, her eyes shining, brought Fox into the castle itself and introduced him—introduced him as her husband-to-be. There was her tiny white hand in his enormous grimy first—there was her curly wheat-colored hair beside his shoulder. It was not even a question of love, Hepatica said bluntly. It was a question of *need.* Neither could live without the other and that was that. . . .

The family objected, as one might expect. But Hepatica, perhaps telling the truth and perhaps not, simply whispered something in her mother's ear; something feverish and secret and unsurprising. And so the engagement took place. And then the wedding—a private wedding attended by only a few Bellefleurs, in the old manor chapel.

Are you happy? Hepatica's girl cousins asked enviously.

She had only to smile at them, showing her lovely white teeth, and they knew the answer. But there was something alarming (or so they liked to say, afterward) about the intensity of feeling in her. . . . It was over-wrought and exaggerated and unhealthy. Why, just to see that big dark brute squeeze his bride's hand in his, and smile his hesitant but unmistak-ably sensual smile . . . ! Just to be *near* the couple, and sense the unre-strained passion of their "love" . . .

The Bellefleurs were generous, however, and gave the couple a small farm up in the foothills, on Mink Creek, with the promise of assistance whenever Fox should request it, and the promise—unstated, but quite tangible—to Hepatica that she might return at any time. (For she wasn't the first Bellefleur to have married impetuously. And she might very well, like some of the others, wake one morning to a realization of her mistake.)

Now time passed: weeks and months and part of a year. And the young couple kept to themselves. Though frequently invited to the manor they never came. Hepatica's parents were heartbroken; and then angry; and bewildered; and again heartbroken; but what was to be done? They drove out to the farm as often as they dared (not being invited), and spent an empty hour or so with Hepatica, who looked and behaved much the same as usual, and insisted that she *adored* being an old-fashioned wife who did her own cooking and baking and housecleaning. (Though the house hardly looked clean. And the coffee cake she offered her parents, along with tea served in Sèvres cups already cracked, tasted lardy—not at all the sort of thing she had made at home.) Duane Doty Fox stayed out in the field, working. Or in the barn. Working. Shirtless, with his dirty straw hat set rakishly on his head, in manure-splattered boots. He did no more than wave a pawlike hand at his in-laws, ducking into a doorway, turning away out of shyness or indifference. How crude he was, their new son-in-law! How clumsy, how barely human!

And then one of Hepatica's uncles encountered Fox at a supply store beside the lake, and was astonished at the sight of him: for he hadn't remembered his niece's fiancée as *quite* so dark and hairy. And he was gruff as well: mumbled in so guttural a voice the storekeeper could hardly understand him. His muscular shoulders were somewhat stooped, and his neck was thick, and his beard was tangled and snarled. Worst of all, he barely responded to Hepatica's uncle's courteous greeting. A nasal sound that was part a grunt and part a snarl . . . and that was all.

Imagine, so primitive a man married into the Bellefleur family . . . !

During the long winter they kept to themselves, but soon after the first thaw Hepatica arrived at the manor, unaccompanied—she'd just ridden over for an afternoon's visit, she said, and didn't want anyone to make a fuss. Though she kept up a steady stream of chatter—charming and girlish and entertaining as always—she was obviously unhappy, and there were sad dark dents beneath her eyes. But to every question she replied in the same bright insouciant way, saying only that it was a pity

Duane couldn't be talked into coming along—but he was so shy, he was so *very* shy—he hoped they would understand.

(Was Hepatica pregnant? The question couldn't be asked, and she gave no hints. But she *was* distressed about something, despite her frivolous conversation.)

From time to time Bellefleur men encountered Fox in the area, and it was something of a joke, at first, how coarse and bearish he had become. Hepatica's cooking, perhaps? Or had he always inclined toward stoutness? His beard was no bushier than ever, perhaps, but now hair grew on his throat, and no doubt on his shoulders. There were tufts of thick hair on the backs of his hands. His eyes, which had been of ordinary size in the past, so far as anyone remembered, now looked small and close-set; even rather stupidly cruel. (Was he drinking? Was he drunk when they met him? He always brushed past or turned away, often without even a grunted hello.) They joked of "Fox," saying that he hadn't the comeliness of a red or even a gray fox; he hadn't a fox's intelligent grace. His hair resembled thick dark quills, heavy with oil. And his nose . . . his nose had become somewhat flattened, hadn't it . . . ?

Or were they imagining everything? (For the Bellefleurs, despite their affection for Hepatica, could not resist jests of a coarse nature; and such jests—as the men readily admitted—required a certain distortion of human reality.)

Hepatica came to visit her mother more and more frequently, and sometimes she began weeping as soon as she arrived; but she never explained what was wrong. Asked why she was crying she would say lightly, Oh, I just feel sad! or, I'm such a silly girl, wasn't I always a silly girl, don't take any notice of me!

But they noticed that she was thinner (and she had always been a slight, nervous little thing), and that she blinked her eyes rapidly while she spoke, and looked out the window frequently. There were bruises on her wrist and neck. There was an odd long wavering scratch on the back of her left hand. Oh, that's just a cat scratch! she said, laughing. Don't take any notice of it.

One day her mother asked her if she wouldn't like to move back to the manor? Her room was in readiness for her, unchanged; she could at least stay a few nights; and perhaps everything could be discussed. . . .

But there's nothing to be "discussed," she said listlessly. I love my husband and he loves me. There's nothing else.

He loves you—he truly loves you?

Oh, yes.

And you love him?

Well—yes.

You *do* love him?

Yes.

Hepatica—?

I said *yes.*

She spoke emphatically but with an air of bewilderment. As if she did not quite know what to say . . . only what ought to be said.

Leaving the manor she turned to her mother, and embraced her, and seemed about to burst into tears; but she restrained herself.

I don't *know,* Mamma, if anything is wrong. I've never been married before, the poor child whispered.

After that she stayed away for months. And when her father and one of his brothers drove up to see her, Fox met them in the driveway, and said, or seemed to say (for they could barely understand his slurred words) that Hepatica was "resting" and wasn't "receiving visitors."

Now it was clear that Fox had changed considerably. He could no longer be considered even remotely attractive. His teeth were tobacco-stained, he gave off a fetid, meaty odor, tufts of hair grew alarmingly on the backs of his hands and high on his cheeks, and his eyebrows, which had always been thick and glowering, had gone wild. His hair was greasy, tumbling to his massive, muscle-choked shoulders; his small cruel red-rimmed eyes glared like a beast's. He *was* a beast. It was suddenly quite clear—both Hepatica's father and her uncle realized the fact, at the same moment—quite clear, that Hepatica had married a beast.

A bear, it was.

A black bear. (Though he was several inches taller than the full-grown black bear. And his mouth hadn't yet lengthened into a snout.)

Unwittingly, the poor innocent girl had fallen in love with, and married, a *black bear.*

They went away, shaken. And returned home where they talked of nothing else. To convince the others (who did not really need convincing, of course) they imitated Hepatica's husband, stooping and grunting as he did, with their arms hanging loose, and their eyes murderously narrowed. They snarled that Hepatica was resting and not receiving visitors; they ran their hands violently through their hair, and fluffed out their beards. It was alarming, how successfully they imitated him—imitated a half-human bear.

For he *was* a black bear. No matter how improbable, how incredible, it might seem. A black bear who had cynically named himself "Fox"! . . . And what might they do, to rescue poor Hepatica?

("What do you think they did?" the Bellefleur children were asked. At first they did not reply—they stared into the fire, frowning—perhaps frightened—and then one of the girls said in a whisper: "Hunted him down, the nasty thing!")

So indeed they hunted him down; but not immediately.

Not immediately. For they had to be *certain.* And they didn't want to endanger Hepatica.

She did not return to the manor to visit, however, and as the weeks passed the Bellefleurs (who were obsessed with their girl's tragedy) grew more and more impassioned. Though Hepatica had seemed adamant about loving him, and even more adamant about his loving her, it was clear that something must be done: she couldn't remain married to a beast: she would have to be rescued.

In the end, not *quite* with her parents' knowledge, a group of young Bellefleur men and their friends rode out one night to the farm, their shotguns across their saddles. They dismounted a quarter-mile from the farmhouse, careful that the wind blew into their faces; they were far more cautious than if they had been hunting an ordinary bear. Even so, the Bear-Man must have sensed their approach, for when they burst into the house he was out of bed, staggering toward them, his teeth exposed in a hideous snarl that rose to a shriek. He was naked, of course—yet covered with thick greasy hair—everywhere, even on the backs of his toes —covered with thick dark greasy hair. They fired at him. But he kept coming. Swatting at them with his great clawed hands—managing to rake one of the men viciously in the cheek—catching another in the eye. Never had they heard such unearthly shrieking, they testified afterward.

In all, they emptied the contents of six double-barreled shotguns into him, two at exceedingly close range, before, it seemed, he finally died.

(And the cub, what of the cub?—what did they do with the cub?

There wasn't any cub, they swore.

But somehow it was disclosed, months or even years later, that there *had* been a cub; and that they had had to kill it as well. Though the young men involved in the raid always denied it.

There *was* no cub?

There was no cub.

And what of Hepatica?

She withdrew from the world afterward, and eventually entered a French house of the order of Our Lady of Mount Carmel—much to her parents' distress, for they were bitterly anti-Catholic.)

The Tutor

Somewhat reluctantly, yet not with the pouty self-pitying resistance her somber face seemed to declare (for though she didn't love him she didn't know she didn't love him, not knowing at that time what *love* should have been; and anyway since the burning of Johnny Doan on Germaine's first birthday she had such terrifying nightmares, she yearned to escape the castle), Christabel consented, meekly enough, to be wed to Edgar Holleran von Schaff III, the great-great-great-great-grandson of the Revolutionary hero Baron von Schaff. Edgar was a widower with two children, a wealthy man who owned, among other things, a chain of newspapers throughout the state. The first Mrs. von Schaff was the daughter of Bertram Lund, a U.S. Senator for many years; she had died while still in her twenties, in a tragic hunting accident at Silver Lake. Though Edgar's puffy, ruddy, creased moonish face was that of a man of middle age, he was in fact only thirty-eight years old. And he adored, as he frequently said, both in person and by hand-delivered letter, dear little Christabel.

Edgar had inherited, along with the newspapers, beautiful Schaff Hall at Silver Lake, some fifty miles from Bellefleur Manor, and the original 25,000 acres of fertile valley land deeded Baron von Schaff by the state, as payment for his services in the Revolutionary War. (The baron —whose nobility was questioned only by the envious—had been an officer in the Prussian Army, who emigrated to America at the request of General George Washington in order to train soldiers at Valley Forge. He later became major general and inspector general of the United States Army, where he served from 1777 to 1784. After the Revolution he became, like a number of other German professionals, a United States citizen; and in addition to the land given him in the Nautauga Valley he owned 30,000 acres in Virginia and 5,000 in eastern New Jersey—not the grandest of empires, but a highly respectable one.) Schaff Hall, a Greek revival mansion with some twenty-five rooms, and six Doric columns, and a superb view of Silver Lake, was erected by the baron's grandson, a contemporary of Raphael Bellefleur's, in 1850; it was said that forty yoke of oxen were required to haul the enormous limestone slab on the front portico. But on her first visit to Schaff Hall Christabel, gnawing at her thumb, was not impressed. The gilded wooden eagle over the front door looked, she said, as if termites had riddled it through, and the house *wasn't* anywhere near as big as Bellefleur Manor. "Don't be silly," Leah said, squeezing her daughter's hand, hard, in a little spasm of affection. "Don't be *deceived.*"

There were Bellefleurs, among them Della, who, not having seen Christabel for a while, were appalled that so young a child was even being considered for matrimony; but when they did see her—tall, lithe, self-possessed (though that was only an aspect of her terror), with her small shapely breasts and her uplifted chin—they were forced to agree, with Leah and Cornelia, that she was certainly mature enough to be wed. After all, many Bellefleur brides had been very young, and in every case—in nearly every case—the matches were excellent ones.

How strange, for Bromwell, grandmother Della said, Christabel's more than a head taller than he is, and while he looks like a little boy, still, no more than ten, she looks like a young woman of eighteen . . . ! Leah stared at her mother for several seconds, frowning. But why, Mamma, she said finally, *why* should it be strange for *Bromwell?* I don't understand you. . . . she had forgotten that Christable and Bromwell were twins.

Christable was required to meet with Edgar only three times, and always, to her relief, in the presence of others. Arrangements between the two families were made: papers signed, contracts sealed. The *fuss* she loathed took place somewhere beyond her exact awareness, which pleased her, though she came briefly alive at her bridal shower, cutting a wonderful six-tier angel food cake Edna had baked, with the special whipped frosting, vanilla threaded with apricot, Christabel loved: what *pleasure* it was, she thought suddenly, cutting cake for her girl cousins and friends . . . ! She had wished the lively little party, held in the remodeled Ivory Room, would never end.

Some weeks later she was married, snugly buttoned into great-great-grandmother Violet's wedding dress, with its magnificent long train and its hundreds of pearls and the lace veil that was, even to Christabel's skeptical eye, beautiful (though, clowning beforehand with her maids of honor, she draped it over her head and sucked it against her mouth and nose, claiming she couldn't breathe). Though "Edgar"—she did not call him that, did not call him anything, thought frequently of *him* as if *him* were a nebulous shapeless not exactly malevolent presence—though "Edgar" accompanied her back from the altar of the Lutheran church, his hand gripping hers somewhat less firmly than Leah had gripped it that morning, she was not required to speak with him, or even to acknowledge him in any *particular,* any *detailed* way. And the wedding party was a merry one. And the farewell, afterward, on the front walk of the manor, was very moving: hoydenish cynical Christabel actually burst into tears . . . !

Farewell, farewell. She hugged and kissed them all, one by one. Her mother, looking radiantly beautiful in a turquoise gown; her father, stooping to kiss her, and to accept her kiss; little Germaine in her white flower-girl dress (which, though somewhat stained, was still adorable); the new baby Cassandra, held wriggling and cooing in Lissa's arms; grandmother Cornelia in a curly new wig; grandfather Noel; grandmother Della, whose wrinkled prune of a face was wet with sudden, unacknowledged tears; uncle Hiram; cousin Vernon, whose thin-lipped melancholy grin made her cry all the more; aunt Lily; uncle Ewan; her cousins Vida and Albert and Raphael and Morna and Jasper and Louis and . . . And there was little Bromwell, blinking behind his glasses, extending a *hand* to her for a formal handshake . . . ! And Garth, and pretty Little Goldie; and aunt Aveline and uncle Denton; and Edna; and Lissa; and "the old man from the flood" who had been brought outside by great-grandmother Elvira; and of course great-grandmother Elvira herself, who had had her white hair puffed out for the occasion in a kind of pompadour, and whose frail fingers were surprisingly strong, gripping Christabel's wrist. (Since his rescue, the "old man from the flood"—who remained nameless because he could not recall his name, and the Bellefleurs were reluctant to assign him one since, as they supposed, they hadn't the right, and his own people would soon be stepping forward to claim him—had improved considerably, and was no longer in any danger, and capable, even, of playing games with the children (mainly Chinese checkers and Old Maid) and helping with little household tasks, when he felt strong enough. Dr. Jensen had given him injections of vitamin C and left behind a supply of iron tablets, and great-grandmother Elvira prepared for him, in the kitchen, allowing no one else to help, meals laced with special herbs, which were evidently quite beneficial, since the old man—who was a *very* old man, possibly older than Elvira—seemed to be gaining strength steadily. He was soft-spoken and gentle, and slept often, and caused no one any trouble. Though Elvira fussed in the kitchen, it was always a maid who brought the old man his meal, and Elvira did no more than peek in from time to time, from the doorway, making no response to the old man's hopeful, rather abashed, and perplexed greeting, when he was awake. Sometimes she complained of him, *that nuisance, that old fool,* but she was, in fact, the only person who remembered him from day to day.) And last of all tearful Christabel, squatting impulsively, so that her silk stockings broke out in a half-dozen runs and ladders, said farewell to the cats: to great-grandmother Elvira's Minerva, and to CeCi and Dexter-Margaret and George and Charley and Misty and Miranda and Wallace and Roo . . . and Troilus and Buddy and Muffin and Tristram and Yassou . . . and Mahalaleel, who bumped his large head against her as if nudging her, purring deep in his throat, pausing to lick, with his

sandpaperish tongue that was so wet and so *ticklish,* her stockinged knee:
beautiful haughty Mahalaleel himself, the ruff about his head plumped
out as if one of the children had just been brushing him, his frosted
bluish-gray coat gleaming in the sun. Christabel backed away, stumbling
in her high heels, weeping, "I'll never see you again! If I come back
everything will be different! I'll never see you again *like this. . . .*"

They called her a silly little goose, and Edgar took her arm, and
helped her into the gleaming black Mercedes, which, evidently, he was
going to drive himself.

Though the baron became a U.S. citizen in 1784 it was clear that he, and
his progeny, retained strong Teutonic memories. The Schaff collection,
old Mrs. Schaff told Christabel in a whisper, was a national treasure—
curious medieval weapons and shields; ancient panels; tapestries more
threadbare than those at Bellefleur Manor; sixteenth-century Flemish
stonewear; medieval and sixteenth-century stained glass panels; a seven-
teenth-century German bronze nest of weights; leather-bound books,
whole walls of them, in German; etchings, engravings, mezzotints; and of
course dark, time-stained oil paintings, one of which—*Folly, Cupid, Leda,
and Silenus,* attributed to van Miereveld—reminded homesick Christabel
of a large painting that had been hanging for years on the second-floor
landing of the east wing. Entire walls were muffled in the skins of animals.
Fireplaces were so festooned with furbelows and brass that they could not
be used. In every room, but concentrated in the Main Hall, were bald
eagles—wooden, pewter, wrought-iron, brass—some with arrows
clutched in their talons. It was said that the baron and his sons had
collected hundreds of Indian scalps (properly tanned and treated, of
course), but these were not in evidence.

Old Mrs. Schaff, a very short, cork-shaped woman, rose each morning at 6:30. She bathed, aided by a servant; read aloud from the Bible;
came downstairs promptly at 7:30 to lead the household staff in prayers;
breakfasted; then went upstairs again for a morning of letter writing,
sewing, mending, and further reading in the Bible. The main meal of the
day, to Christabel's amazement, was served at 2:00 P.M. It was a formal
occasion though only Edgar, Christabel, and Mrs. Schaff ordinarily dined.
(The kitchen, Mrs. Schaff pointedly told her new daughter-in-law, was
only for servants. It was in the basement. Food was prepared there by
persons Christabel never saw, and sent up by dumb waiter to the butler's
pantry above.)

Edgar's two little boys dined at noon and then again at 5:30, upstairs
in the nursery, with their tutor. The very first morning after her arrival
at Schaff Hall, Christabel, in a bright-flowered frock, with a yellow scarf
tied about her head, passed by the nursery just to peer inside . . . and saw,
to her surprise, and very much to her interest, the man who must have
been the boys' tutor: he was standing at an opened window, glasses in one
hand, rubbing the bridge of his nose and muttering to himself. He was

no age Christabel could determine. His ash-blond hair was ill-cut, falling unevenly across his collar; his jaw, clean-shaven, was strong but almost too square; the leather patch on the right elbow of his tweed jacket was hanging loose. He was quite solidly built, like a young ox, and more resembled a farmer's son than a tutor said to have been educated abroad, in England and Germany, and to have been employed by the very best families in the East.

Something about his stance, his air of lassitude and melancholy, touched Christabel to the heart. She stared, standing in the doorway, and halfway thought he looked familiar. That agreeably homely profile, those clumsily broad shoulders that made his coat strain into wrinkles across the back . . .

He turned, suddenly, and drew in his breath at the sight of her.

It was Demuth Hodge . . . !

Passion

It was as a consequence of an astonishing outburst of passion—remarkable in one so frail, and so customarily meek—that Garnet Hecht encountered Lord Dunraven, who was to bring so much guilt-ridden torment into her life.

She had arranged (her heart sinking at his weary *politeness*) to see her lover once again, after so many months of mutual renunciation: she did not like to think that she nearly pleaded with him, her tear-brimmed eyes if not her words begging O Gideon you must know how I love you, I have always loved you, I continue to love you despite the promise we made never again to see each other, the promise we made in order not to hurt Leah and your children. . . . (And had she not behaved nobly, surrendering her baby girl to the castle, to the Bellefleurs, guessing that this was the baby's father's unarticulated wish? How nobly, with what heartrending pain, only she herself knew. . . . Even good Mrs. Pym, who, alone among the Bellefleurs seemed to know, without having been told, of her liaison with Gideon, could not have guessed (for Garnet kept her sobbing to herself, and sometimes, in the pantry or the kitchen, thrust her fingers in her mouth to keep from moaning aloud at the double loss of her lover and her baby) at the depth of her suffering. Della frequently touched Garnet's shoulder and smiled sadly and spoke of her own terrible bereavement, at the hands of her own people, when she had been a young bride. "We must tell ourselves, Garnet—*This too will pass,*" Della said. "Every morning, every midday, every evening, when silly hopeful persons say their prayers, like children, we must say, calmly and clearly—*This too will pass.* For it will, my dear! Never doubt but that it will!")

While accompanying Mrs. Pym on a weeklong visit to the castle, shortly after the surprising occasion of Miss Christabel's marriage to Edgar Holleran von Schaff III, Garnet was able to draw aside (discreetly, though she trembled violently that they might be discovered even in so innocent a place as the nursery, where she was "visiting with" Cassandra) her lover Gideon; and to arrange for a secret meeting very late on the following night. "I will make no demands of you," she whispered. "But we *must* meet. One final time." Gideon, dressed for the outdoors, his dark beard newly trimmed (but it was, now, Garnet saw with a pang of love, threaded with gray—silver-gray), his somewhat prominent eyes darting quickly about behind her (touching upon, and veering off, the beautiful Cassandra napping on her stomach in the cradle), seemed at first incapable of speaking. He opened his mouth—smiled—the smile thinned—he blinked rapidly—cleared his throat—looked her full in the face—and, wincing, drew back an inch or two, as if involuntarily. She could see that, for Gideon as well as herself, even so casual a meeting was painful: it was likely that he suffered as she did, though of course he would never speak of such things. "I know, I know, this violates our promise," Garnet said quickly, half feeling pity for him (for herself, she had long abrogated pity, as unworthy of one who was loved by, and had borne a child for, Gideon Bellefleur), "but you must understand that I am desperate . . . I am so lonely . . . I'm afraid that something terrible will happen to me. . . . Ah, it was good, really, though your wife could not have known, that she came to take my baby away from me!" Garnet whispered.

"Don't talk like that, don't say such foolish things," Gideon said. "If you say them they are likely to become—"

She touched her fingers daringly to his lips. "Then we'll meet? Tomorrow? And you won't despise me? And you will come?"

He seized her hand and, hesitating a moment, kissed it; or anyway pressed it to his cold lips. Garnet was to feel the imprint of those lips against her hand (but it was the back of her hand, for he had, oddly, turned it at the very last instant) for many hours. Shamelessly, like a young girl new to love, and delirious with its promise, she had even kissed her own hand—hoping her foolishness would go unobserved.

"He does love me," she murmured aloud to her wan, indistinct reflection, as she plaited her hair for bed that night. "But his love makes our predicament all the more tragic. . . ."

And so they met, the following night. In the unused room on the third floor of the east wing where, so very long ago, in another lifetime, Garnet had gone, at Mrs. Pym's suggestion, to bring poor Gideon some nourishment. It was in the doorway of that room, in the shadowy corridor outside the room, that Garnet, staring as Gideon Bellefleur tore with ravenous appetite at the meat she had brought him, that she fell—plunged—was thrown, violently—in love. She had wanted to cry aloud O Gideon I love you, you must know, you cannot not know. . . . Perhaps (she sometimes wondered, reliving that night) she *had* cried aloud. . . .

Meeting *there* had been Garnet's idea. But if it struck her lover as foolishly sentimental, he gave no indication. (But then Gideon was so polite. So impassively courteous. Garnet had once overheard, out in the garden, one humid August afternoon, Leah herself shouting at him— What do you mean, showing that frosty insupportable gentlemanliness to *me*, to your own wife, who knows you inside and out!) Instead he merely nodded, and repeated the time she had said—1:00 A.M.—in a hurried and preoccupied manner.

Well before 1:00 A.M. Garnet slipped away, and climbed the drafty stairs to the third floor, daring only a small candle (whose flame flickered wildly, cupped behind her hand), for fear of being discovered. Bellefleur Manor, even during the day, was intimidating: there were corridors, and corners, and dark little niches, that looked as if no one ever visited them; and of course the sillier women, and even some of the men, among the domestic staff, freely complained of ghosts. But Garnet did not believe in ghosts. She found it difficult, at times, to believe in flesh-and-blood people—even in herself—certainly in the baby to whom she had given birth. . . . There were only the cruel stretch marks on her abdomen and a certain oversensitivity about her breasts, even after many months, to remind her of the arduous physical reality of her motherhood.

In preparation for the many houseguests who were to have stayed at Bellefleur Manor, for great-grandmother Elvira's birthday celebration, all the rooms had been cleaned; and in many—in *this* room, for instance— furniture had been reupholstered and new carpets laid. So Garnet's first impression was one of pleased surprise. The really quite filthy carpet upon which Gideon had slept was gone, and in its place lay what appeared to be an attractive thick-piled rug. There were chairs—a bureau—a large mirror—several small tables, inlaid with marble—and of course a bed— a double bed—a canopied bed with high pillows and a thick crimson cover. Blushing, Garnet saw by the flickering light (and perhaps she saw inaccurately, for the candle *did* flicker) a most embarrassing tapestry hanging just to the right of the bed: it showed a scantily clad couple, the woman as well as the man quite full-bodied, and vigorous, and impatient to make love, being surprised in a boudoir by—could it be?—a lascivious little Cupid leading, down a staircase, a horse—a horse with outlandish long eyelashes and a queer human expression. The lovers gaped with surprise: and indeed who would *not* have been surprised?

Garnet was staring at this strange tapestry (she could not decide if it was obscene, or merely playful; or both; but in any case it should be taken down and stored at the very back of a closet) when she heard a sound in the corridor. For some reason (had she doubted, even then, her lover's truthfulness?) her first thought was that someone other than Gideon was there. One or two of the male servants had expressed an interest in her—an interest, of course, fervently rebuffed—and there were tales of poor Hiram's sleepwalking, which had evidently flared up again after some months of quiescence; and innumerable cats, some of them quite large, roamed the castle freely at night. So she stood, cringing, the little candle cupped in her hand, a young woman who—despite her motherhood, despite her passion—looked hardly more than a child, staring at the empty doorway as if she had no idea who might appear.

And then of course Gideon *did* arrive, with a flashlight in hand—entering the room boldly, yet without haste. He murmured a greeting and reached out to take her hand (ah, how awkward she was!—Garnet jerked away because of the candle she was holding, not wanting it to be upset, and then of course it *was* upset; and her lover, swearing, had to scramble for it across the rug), and managed at last to kiss her on the forehead. Yet something was wrong. Garnet felt it, she *knew,* unmistakably.

Nevertheless she spoke, gripping his arm. She spoke, too rapidly, of her love for him, which had not ebbed, which had in fact increased—though, yes, she *knew* they had promised never to say such things again—never to torment themselves. But she had to break her vow: her life was so empty, so miserable, so futile. It was all the more intolerable, she told him, that his wife (who meant well—of course Leah always meant well) chattered about finding a "suitable" husband for her, and had even been making inquiries about eligible bachelors and widowers in the area. Couldn't he speak—discreetly, of course—to Leah? Didn't Leah realize how such remarks wounded Garnet? Didn't *he* realize? But that wasn't the primary cause of her unhappiness, as he must know. Even the surrender of Cassandra—which had nearly broken her heart—wasn't the primary cause.

And then, suddenly, desperately, she threw herself into his arms.

Gideon held her, rather awkwardly. He patted her back, he murmured words she could not interpret; he behaved, in short, exactly as Gideon Bellefleur—as nearly any Bellefleur, for that matter—might have behaved if, in public, quite suddenly, unpredictably, a grieving stranger had fairly collapsed in his arms.

Sobs wracked her body. She *knew*—knew from the very moment he entered the room, really—that he no longer loved her. (And the hairsbreadth of a thought which she hadn't quite had, about the handsome big bed—how that would return to haunt her, poor humiliated Garnet Hecht!) Still she could not keep herself from saying, "O I love you, I can't stop loving you, you are a prince among men, I *can't* stop loving you—please, Gideon—please don't abandon me! Haven't I given up my baby girl for *you,* for your sake—Haven't I doomed myself to a life of sorrow, knowing that my child will grow up apart from me—and even if she knows I am her mother, still—"

Gideon stepped back from her, blinking. He asked her to repeat what she had said.

"About Cassandra? Why, I—I—"

"You gave her up for *me?*" Gideon asked, baffled. "But what do you mean?—for *me?*"

"I—I naturally thought—"

"Leah told me that you had begged her to take the child: that you didn't want her: that the baby would interfere with your chances of getting married. What do you mean, now, by saying that you gave her up for *me?*"

He stared at her with such incredulity, with such an air of—of *unloving* alarm—that Garnet came close to swooning. She stammered, "I thought —I only thought—Leah and Hiram came to visit Mrs. Pym, you see, and —and— And somehow it came about— I don't remember clearly— I don't remember most things clearly, now— O Gideon I had thought *you* —you were behind it—sending them—her—to bring your own child back —to rear her as a Bellefleur—of course without letting Leah know— I had thought," Garnet whispered, "that it might even have been a test of—of —a test of my love for you—"

Gideon stepped back. He exhaled loudly—puffed out his cheeks and extended his lower lip and blew upward, so that his hair was stirred—in a gesture Ewan frequently made, to show half-amused disgust and bewilderment. ". . . but no not *really,*" he muttered.

"Gideon?" Garnet cried, reaching for him, stumbling toward him, "do you mean—do you mean—you didn't— As Cassandra's father you *didn't* especially want her—?"

He stepped back again, eluding her. As her fingers groped for his sleeve he brushed them half-consciously away. For a long moment he appeared unable to speak. A vein pulsed in his forehead, and another in his throat. ". . . so it was Leah . . . Leah's idea . . . she *knows* . . . must know . . . but why did she do it . . . to spite me, or . . . to spite you. . . . Or is there another reason . . ."

"Gideon," Garnet said, in a lower voice, "please tell me: you *didn't* ask her to bring the child back? You don't, even now, especially want her? As Cassandra's father you don't especially want her—?"

It was at this point that, quite suddenly, in a voice that hardly resembled his, Gideon said something that was to be as inexplicable—indeed, as unfathomable—in his own imagination as in Garnet's, and to cause him, in secret, great torment: he heard himself say sardonically, *"Am* I the father?"

For a long moment Garnet simply stared at him. She could not comprehend his words. Slowly, as if dazed, she brushed her damp hair out of her eyes—tried to speak—stood swaying—staring at him. It was only when his face contorted with shame, and guilt, and immediate sorrow, that she realized the terrible thing he had said. He exclaimed, "Oh, Garnet of course I didn't mean—" but already she had turned, and was running out of the room, her long hair streaming behind her.

He would have pursued her at once, and might have caught her, but in Garnet's shock she dropped the candle; and once again he had to scramble after it as it rolled, not yet entirely quenched, beneath the bed. "Dear fucking *God,* why is this happening," Gideon half-sobbed, his shoulder striking the bedframe (for he was a large man, and could not comfortably maneuver in that cramped space), "why am I plagued as I am, who is playing this vile trick, whom should I murder. . . . Jesus fucking

God!" he exclaimed, at last catching hold of the candle, and retrieving it. And with great passion he spat on the wick, though the meager flame had at last died. ". . . should have let it go," he murmured, "should have let everything go up in flames. . . ."

So Garnet fled, in a paroxysm of shame, hardly knowing what she did, which turn in the corridor to take, which stairway to descend. She fled, too stupefied even to weep, and somehow found herself in an unheated back hallway, and then at a door, throwing herself against a door, as dogs began to yip in a startled chorus. Gathering her cloak about her she ran across the lawn. Moonlight illuminated the long hill that dipped to the lake—illuminated the hill and not the surrounding woods—so that she had only one way to run. Now barefoot, her hair streaming, the skirt of her pretty silken gown beginning to rip, she ran, her eyes open and fixed. Somehow the cloak was torn off her shoulders—torn off and flung away. Still she ran, oblivious of her surroundings, knowing only that she *must* run, to flee the horror behind her, and to eradicate herself in the dark murmurous lake before her. Senseless words careened about her head: O Gideon I love you, I cannot live without you, I have always loved you and I will always love you— Please forgive me—

(An angel, transfixed by suffering! A crucifixion, Lord Dunraven was to think, afterward, in her lovely face! But how *terrifying* a sight she was, on that night, running like a madwoman, only partly clad, to drown herself in the frigid March waters of that ugliest of lakes!)

So Garnet fled; and would surely have drowned herself. Except, through the unlikeliest of coincidences (though not, upon reflection, any less likely, Lord Dunraven reasoned, than many another coincidence he had experienced in his lifetime, or had heard of in others' lives) there turned up the Bellefleur drive at that moment a carriage drawn by two superbly-matched teams of horses, carrying Eustace Beckett, Lord Dunraven, a distant relative of grandmother Cornelia's who had been invited, originally, for great-grandmother Elvira's birthday, but who had had regretfully to decline, though saying (with a graciousness that struck Cornelia as kindly rather than sincere) that he would like to visit his American cousin another time. A telegram announcing his arrival had been sent from New York, but had not, evidently, been delivered, for no one awaited him at the manor. As the carriage turned up the drive, and passed by the gate house, Lord Dunraven saw, to his astonishment, a ghostly figure running down the long, long hill—running barefoot, despite the cold—her hair flying behind her—her arms outstretched—and though the vision was a most alarming one (for Garnet *did* resemble a madwoman) Lord Dunraven had the presence of mind, and the courage, to shout for the driver to stop at once; and he leapt down; and pursued the girl to the very edge of the lake where, since his cries had made no impression upon her, he was forced to seize her bare arm, to prevent her from plunging in the water.

"No, no—you must not— My poor girl, you must not—" Lord Dunraven cried, out of breath. The girl tried to struggle free. She clawed at him, even slashed at him—quite harmlessly, as it turned out—with her teeth, and writhed with such demonic violence that her gown was torn nearly off her back, exposing the bare flesh. "I say you *must* not," Lord Dunraven grunted, holding her, at last, still, in the moment before she sank into blessed unconsciousness.

Another Carriage . . .

Another carriage, piled high with trunks, unceremoniously jammed with people, carried *her* away: so Jean-Pierre theorized, though in fact he could not see her: though he saw, quite clearly, her bewigged and vacant-eyed father.

The next day, outside a tavern, he joined a regiment bound for Fort Ticonderoga; and the night before leaving he dreamt, not of the girl, but of the ugly prison-castle his family inhabited for centuries, in the north of France: its monstrous walls eighty-five feet high and seven feet thick, the shallow green-scummed water of the moat giving off a most unpleasant stink.

Ticonderoga, Lake Champlain, Crown Point. . . . He left for the north without seeing a map. Henceforth he would not meet his fate passively: he would *forge* it.

The Noir Vulture

It was on a windless June day of heart-stopping beauty (only a very few clouds, diaphanous, subtle as milkweed fluff, were brushed against the china-blue sky) that Vernon Bellefleur, who had despaired for more than twenty years of being a poet (a genuine poet, in his own terms: everyone else referred to him, glibly, if not contemptuously, as The Poet), became, at last, quite suddenly, through an experience of obscene horror, a *poet*. And so he was to remain, for the rest of his exceptionally long life.

"A man's life of any worth," Vernon often intoned, "is a continual allegory. . . ."

But what is the nature, precisely, of this allegory? Are all men's lives allegorical, or only the few, the extraordinary few?

He liked to read to The People. To his family's field hands, or mill hands, good simple unquestioning sturdy folk, about whom the phrase *the salt of the earth* was not inappropriate: he liked to stand before them in his jacket that was too tight in the armpits, and buttoned crookedly, part of his beard caught up in the gay red scarf he knotted about his neck for such occasions, his voice rising with a dramatic intensity that stirred his listeners to a sympathy so profound it expressed itself in spasms of mirth. (But were *their* lives allegorical, their simple laborers' lives . . . ? Or might they require the transcendental services of the poet, of poesy, to transform them . . . ?) At any rate he read, though his knees trembled with the audacity of his undertaking (for he read out in the fields, standing atop a wagon; or on a window ledge in the Fort Hanna mill; even in crowded taverns on Friday evenings, where the tavern keeper, knowing he was a Bellefleur, commanded a modicum of attention for him), and tears jerked in the corners of his eyes, he read until his throat was hoarse, until his head reeled with exhaustion, until, glancing up, he saw that most of his audience had drifted away—for perhaps his thirty-eight-line sonnets on "Lara" were too painfully candid for them, or they found too difficult, too demanding, the words of certain other poets, lifelong heroes of Vernon's, whom he also read:

> Ah! who can e'er forget so fair a being?
>   Who can forget her half retiring sweets?
>   God! she is like a milk-white lamb that bleats
> For God's protection. Surely the All-seeing,
> Who joys to see us with his gifts agreeing,
>   Will never give him pinions, who intreats
>   Such innocence to ruin,—who vilely cheats
> A dove-like bosom. In truth there is no freeing
> One's thoughts from such a beauty; when I hear
>   A lay that once I saw her hand awake,
> Her form seems floating palpable, and near;
>   Had I e'er seen her from an arbour take
> A dewy flower, oft would that hand appear
>   And o'er my eyes the trembling moisture shake. . . .

Because he took little heed of such things, Vernon scarcely knew his own age. He was, he supposed, in his early thirties at the time of the great shock—the sight, to be repeatedly continuously in his mind's eye, whether he woke or slept, of an infant borne aloft in the talons of a gigantic vulturelike bird, and partly dismembered, and even *devoured*, in midair, before his helpless gaze; the last time anyone in the family (and that person had been Leah) thought to celebrate his birthday was a considerable number of years before, and he had been twenty-seven or twenty-eight at the time, he couldn't quite recall. Vernon will never grow up, Hiram once said, not caring that he spoke—with such unpaternal disdain!—within earshot of his son. But Vernon halfway thought that he had *always* been grownup. He hadn't had a childhood, had he?—hadn't it come to an abrupt, cruel end? But perhaps since his mother had abandoned him to the Bellefleurs, so many, many years ago, his childhood had been blighted from the start. He had been, he sometimes thought (though he didn't write about such sentiments because he believed poetry must be rhapsodic and hymnal and "beautiful"), a kind of changeling. . . . For though he was, by heredity, a Bellefleur, in his soul he most emphatically was *not* a Bellefleur.

So he frequently quarreled, not only with his father but with his uncle Noel and his aunt Cornelia, and his cousins Ewan and Gideon whom he had always, since boyhood, feared; for he knew himself an aspect of God, a fragment of God's consciousness, whose *bodily form* as well as his *family identity* was irrelevant. Once swaggering bullnecked Ewan asked him (in somewhat coarser language) if he had ever made love—"With a woman, that is"—and stared at him blandly, as if daring Vernon even to *sense* the insult of his words. Vernon's skin flared and prickled hotly, but he managed to reply, in his usual gentle voice, No, no, he hadn't, he supposed he had *not,* in the usual sense of the words.

"What other sense is there?" Ewan wanted to know.

He ignored such crudities, and forgave them, for he was, he supposed, something of a clownish figure; and anyway what choice had he? Sometimes in his wanderings back in the foothills, miles from home, when the towers of the castle were barely visible at the horizon, he allowed himself to think, warmly, that his poetry would someday be the means of his escape from those terrible soulless people—it would be the means of his power—his fame—his *revenge.* Ah, if he could only discover the *characteristica universalis*—the exact and universal language lodged deep in the human soul—what profound truths he would utter! Like Icarus he would construct wings to carry him free of this vast, beautiful, gloomy, overpowering corner of the world (which felt so often, in the mountains especially, or along the lakeshore, like an edge of the world); unlike Icarus he *would* escape, and live in triumph, for his wings would be the inviolable wings of poetry. At such times his heart beat painfully, and he yearned to seize hold of someone—anyone—even a stranger— and attempt to explain the rapture that swelled in his breast—which must be, he thought, like the rapture Christ experienced—Christ who yearned *only* to be the Saviour of pitiful fallen mankind, of the very people who failed to hear His words. Like a man trapped in a tomb, whose voice is not strong enough to penetrate the dense rock that has been rolled up against it, he yearned to explain himself, yet lacked the art.

Instead he stumbled, he stuttered, he groped, he annoyed and exasperated and embarrassed and bored other people, and made (ah, how frequently!) a contemptible fool of himself. One by one the children outgrew him. For a while each loved him—loved him very much—sought him out to tell little secrets to, to complain of the other adults' indifference or cruelty; gave him presents; climbed on his lap, kissed his prickly cheek, teased, even taunted him, played little tricks on him; but loved him. One by one, Yolande (sweet, pretty, strong-willed Yolande, who had broken his heart by running away without leaving, as he had truly thought she would, a message for *him*), Vida, Morna, Jasper, Albert, Bromwell, Christabel. . . . Garth had never liked him. Garth had always been faintly contemptuous of him, making rude razzing noises during lessons or during Vernon's readings. There was dreamy gentle dark-eyed Raphael, with his long pale slender hands, his white, almost clammish skin, Raphael who was so shy he had taken to avoiding, in recent years, not only his rowdy brothers and cousins and their friends, but Vernon himself. For a while Vernon and Raphael had been quite close. Vernon had liked to think of the boy as *his* son, a changeling of sorts, for wasn't it improbable —ludicrous—that beefy beery *Ewan* should be the boy's father? He had taken Raphael on hikes with him, he had shared with him certain beautiful moments—

> For I have learned
> To look on nature, not as in the hour
> Of thoughtless youth; but hearing oftentimes
> The still, sad music of humanity, . . .
>   And I have felt
> A presence that disturbs me with the joy
> Of elevated thoughts; a sense sublime
> Of something far more deeply interfused,
> Whose dwelling is the light of setting suns,
> And the blue sky, and in the mind of man:
> A motion and a spirit, that impels
> All thinking things, all objects of all thought,
> And rolls through all things . . .

—yet for some reason, when Raphael was about eleven years old, they became estranged. Of course it was all on the boy's side: Vernon had never ceased loving *him*. But the boy rose early and slipped away before breakfast, and spent all his time at the pond north of the cemetery (Mink Pond, it was called, though another pond, now dried up, had once been called Mink Pond), and when Vernon hiked out there to be with him he could feel how unwelcome he was: how, as he approached the pond's marshy reedy willow-choked bank, and caught sight of the boy lying stomach-down on his raft, staring into the water, he was clumsily violating the child's privacy, the child's very soul. It was, he thought, sadly, like tramping heedlessly on a bird's wing . . . Raphael lingered about the pond until after sunset, and then only reluctantly came home; even in the rain he played there; even on uncomfortably cold days. (What does he *do* for so many hours, Lily asked in exasperation, wondering if the boy needed a doctor's care, or simply a good spanking, and Vernon said, somewhat arrogantly, What do any of us *do*—?) But he had lost Raphael and would never reclaim him. Now there was only Germaine: Germaine, that sturdy red-cheeked beauty with the amazing, uncanny eyes, and Garnet's baby Cassandra, who was of course far too young, still, to appreciate Vernon's devotion. And someday, he supposed, he would lose Germaine and Cassandra too.

And then there was Leah.

Leah—"Lara"—his Muse—his inspiration—his folly.

Ewan had asked rudely if Vernon had ever performed the act of love with a woman; he had not asked if Vernon had ever *loved* a woman. Surely there was an important distinction. He had fallen in love with Gideon's young wife on the very day of the wedding, at the wedding party, as he gazed with longing at the dancers—at his cousin Gideon and Gideon's bride—magnificent Leah Pym—Leah from across the lake—Della Pym's daughter—one of the "poor" Bellefleurs. (Poor out of pride, it was said. For Della could certainly have lived in the castle had she wished.) He had loved her then and had been, over the years, content to love her at arm's length, like a courtier of old, reading in her presence (though not, alas, always with her attentive ear) poems of longing, his own and others', *With how sad steps O moon,* and "Greensleeves," and the tender, clumsy, assonance-heavy "Lara" sonnets; eager to do errands for her, to mind the children, to listen sympathetically as she complained of Cornelia's tyranny. But Leah was, in recent months, not always an inspiration. The gross but marvelous physicality of her pregnancy had somewhat unnerved him—he had discovered, then, that Leah in his imagination was sometimes lovelier than Leah in the flesh—but the Leah of the present was more extreme. Her glittering eyes disturbed him, and her fingers smudged with newsprint (for she read, each morning at breakfast, several papers), and her quick wit, her manner of addressing Hiram, even in Vernon's presence, in a language so studded with private allusions and financial terms and abbreviations of one kind or another that it constituted, nearly, a code—a code poor Vernon could not hope to decipher, and which caused him pain. And she was frequently imperious. Hoarse-voiced, and then shrill. Sending back the tea things because a single cup was cracked, or the tea wasn't hot enough, or there was an indentation —"Suspiciously like a thumbnail!"—in the icing on a piece of coffee cake. (Isn't she terrible, the servants whispered, sometimes in tears. Isn't she full of herself! And such was their distress that they frequently spoke in voices loud enough for Vernon to hear.)

Of course she was still beautiful. She would always be, Vernon knew, beautiful. Despite the fact that the soft plump placidity of her face had thinned slightly so that near-invisible lines showed about her eyes, ghost-lines, really, not seriously imprinted in the flesh, and visible only in harsh bright sunlight. . . . (She had lost a considerable amount of weight after her pregnancy, and continued to lose it. For she was always rushing from place to place—the state capitol, Vanderpoel, the Falls, Port Oriskany, Derby, Yewville, Powhatassie, even New York City—and even at home she rarely relaxed, as she had in the old days, in the walled garden or Violet's boudoir. Even sprawled exhausted in a chair she was thinking, thinking, planning, plotting, her mind turning and turning about like a windmill blade, giving off a nearly palpable heat. Vernon had actually glimpsed her, once, through the partly open door of Raphael's study, talking over *two* telephones, a receiver tightly couched against each of her hunched shoulders!) But Leah would always be a beautiful woman, Vernon told himself, sighing a lover's sigh of resignation, and he would always love her; and she would always belong to another man.

He wandered in the Lake Noir area, and in the foothills, gone sometimes for a week or ten days, tramping the fields and lanes and riverbanks in his muddy, leaking shoes, wearing on his head a cast-off rubber rainhat of Noel's, or a cast-off Irish hat of Ewan's he had found on the floor of a closet. With his straggly graying beard he looked decades older than he was, like a figure out of mythology, or out of the mountain mists, an incongruous red scarf tied about his neck, his trousers stained at the knee, his jackets sometimes baggy, sometimes tight, sometimes not even *his.* Aunt Matilde had knitted him a wonderful bulky sweater heavy as a coat, with generous-sized pockets for his books and papers and pens, and she had sewn on wooden buttons she'd carved herself, out of hickory wood; but one day he returned to the manor without it, shivering like a fool in the rain, and claimed that he could not—*could* not—remember what had happened to it. (A man who loses an article of clothing he is wearing, Hiram intoned, will eventually lose everything.)

So he wandered, always on foot. Eccentric, probably not "crazy" (for there were far crazier people in the hills), probably not dangerous. He was never to encounter, in his years of wandering, his cousin Emmanuel —by now an almost legendary, improbable figure, about whom the other Bellefleurs rarely spoke, as if they had forgotten he was a brother of Gideon's and Ewan's, and had come to think of him as remote in time, like Raphael's son Rodman, about whom so little was known: though presumably Emmanuel was still mapping the region, covering every acre on foot, and would one day return home in triumph. With his mismatched eyes (which always surprised and amused children, but sometimes made adults uneasy) and his untidy appearance and his "poesy" Vernon came to be famous in the region; of course he was also known as a Bellefleur, and given a wide berth. Farmers driving pick-up trucks along the country roads he traveled slowed courteously as they passed him, never offering him a ride (for to *offer* a Bellefleur anything might be interpreted as impertinence, coming from a social inferior, and everyone lived in dread of offending or insulting the Bellefleurs: Ewan had injured a number of men in fights, as had Gideon; and Raoul's temper had been legendary; Noel had been a hellion in his day; Hiram, in some ways the most sinister of the Bellefleurs, had exercised his kind of power decades ago by buying up, at dismayingly cheap prices, land belonging to farmers who had been forced into bankruptcy; and of course there had been Jean-Pierre II who had murdered eleven men one night, quite calmly and methodically, because of an "insult" he had overheard), though they were quick to stop if Vernon indicated he wanted a ride. And quick to allow him to sleep in their haylofts, or to help with farm chores (though he was almost comically clumsy) in exchange for meals. They liked Vernon—they liked *him* —however they may have felt about his family—and could forgive him his doggerel-poetry which he imagined, poor fool, would someday save the world. And if he spoke of a farmer's kindness, back at the castle, perhaps one of the harder-hearted Bellefleurs would overhear. . . .

Just as the Bellefleurs were sharply divided on the subject of religion— more specifically, on the subject of *God*—so were they divided on the related subject of the existence of Evil. Whether Evil "existed" or whether it only appeared to exist, from a necessarily limited point of view; whether it certainly *did* exist, and existed for a purpose (inevitably divine in scope if not in sentiment); whether there was no Evil, but a small galaxy of evils, each contending for its share of human flesh; whether Evil was simply the palpable absence of Good (thought to be the laziest of the arguments); whether, given a universe dominated by spirit, the only significant Evil could be spiritual; or, conversely, whether the only significant Evil could be material, given the fundamental material nature of the universe . . . so the Bellefleurs argued, sometimes quite passionately, sometimes with a lamentable lack of civility, and not only failed to convince one another but, by way of their very passion, closed their minds against those subtleties, however infrequent, which might have aided their intellectual growth. (Indeed, the spirit of contention was sometimes thought to be the essential curse of the Bellefleurs—for isn't it out of contention that all evils spring?)

Pious and good-natured, and stubborn, Vernon considered himself a henotheist, or perhaps a pantheist; what mattered, he reasoned, was not the *content* of one's belief but its *depth*. Since his God encompassed and swallowed up everything, every particle of matter—the filigree of synapses in that masterwork of cunning, the human brain; the speckled boxlike armor of the trunkfish; the screech of planing mills, Germaine's happy smile, his mother's tearful farewell, the splendor of Mount Blanc and the rank gloomy silence of Noir Swamp—since his God was identical with His creation, there could be nothing left over, no room for laborious theorizing. The pulses sang as pulses have always sung *Here I am, I am here by right, I exist, and the spirit of all creation through me,* and the wise man, and certainly the poet, echoes this song. (But there is a God of Destruction, too, Gideon said one day to Vernon, years ago, when members of the family still took Vernon seriously enough to quarrel with him, come and I will show you. . . . And dragged him away to the witchhobble-choked foot of Sugarloaf Hill where in angry boyish triumph he showed Vernon a partly eaten doe. The poor thing had been pregnant, evidently—her belly had been torn open by dogs—her throat so crudely slashed that she had bled to death—forced to watch (and her affrighted eyes, not yet picked clean by birds, were open and fixed) the horror of the dogs' greedy devouring jaws. She had died while witnessing the death of her fetus. And the dogs hadn't been especially hungry, Gideon said, look at all they've left. . . . Vernon gagged, and backed away; could not stop himself from vomiting, though he felt his cousin's excited contempt. But when he recovered he said, Gideon, the dogs must be nourished . . . we eat, and are eaten . . . don't despair. Gideon had stared at him. What do you mean, what do *you* mean, don't despair! Don't judge, Vernon whispered. Don't despair. But Gideon had looked at him uncomprehendingly, as, years later, the child Raphael was to look at him after having asked him a question about leeches. Don't despair, don't judge, don't set yourself apart from God so that you are forced to judge, Vernon implored Gideon, trying to take his angry cousin's arm. Don't touch me, Gideon said.)

The family was also divided, though not as decisively, on the subject of certain more immediate beliefs. Uncle Hiram did not believe in spirits, but his brother Noel did; most of the children believed in the giant snowman in the mountains, and in the Swamp Vulture, or Noir Vulture, as it was sometimes called (indeed, it was sometimes called the Bellefleur Vulture, by people in the area), and most of the adults—though certainly not *all* of the adults—did not. That there were Bellefleurs who claimed to have seen the enormous bird, up in the mountains, or circling the swamp, seemed to inspire, in the others, only amused contempt: All the more reason for knowing the thing is a hoax, Della once declared, if that pathological liar *Noel* claims to have seen it.

Bromwell maintained a scientific detachment, pointing out, pedantically, but quite correctly, that a *vulture* would not seize living prey, a *carrion-eater* would not kill and devour living things; hence the Noir Vulture, if it existed at all (and he had no opinion on that subject, and would never commit himself, even after that unfortunate June morning) was misnamed. But no one paid attention to him, for it seemed somehow pointless to quibble about a mere name, when the thing itself was such a horror.

Vernon would not have said he "believed" in the vulture, had he been asked, before the creature actually appeared in the walled garden (of all places!—of all secluded, private, *secret* places) since, to his knowledge, he had never seen such a bird, and he thought it wisest to minimize the children's fears. Yet when he caught sight of it with its naked, red head, its incongruously white feathers (tipped with black as if with a tar brush), and its curious pronged tail, he knew at once what it must be. . . . Even before he saw the baby gripped in its talons he began to shout. *Look! That thing! Stop it! Get a gun!*—for so Vernon's words were torn from him, at the mere sight of the hideous creature.

But of course there was nothing to be done. The baby was lost. As women's screams lifted from the garden the bird rose higher and higher, with a noisy muscular grace, already jabbing at the helpless prey in its claws—tearing and stabbing at it with its sharp beak—so that pieces of flesh and skeins of blood fell, it seemed almost lightly, back toward earth; like laundry flapping in the wind the Noir Vulture rose above the highest branches of the oak trees, an astonishing sight on that mildest of pale blue June days, bearing the baby away as if it were no more than a rabbit or chipmunk.

Vernon, who happened to be returning from a morning's hike down to the river, and who was approximately sixty feet from the southern wall of the garden (for he was approaching the manor from the rear) when the creature attacked, stood frozen on the path for an instant, simply staring. Then he began to shout. His cousins!—the boys!—weren't they always shooting off guns!—and now where *were* they?—but in the next moment he realized that the bird was carrying something away, and that it was something living—something human—

At first he thought it was Germaine. But it was too small to be Germaine.

Cassandra—?

So the Noir Vulture struck, taking advantage (taking advantage, it would seem, almost *rationally*) of Leah's absence from the garden: no more than a five-minute absence: for she needed to make a telephone call to undo the decision of an earlier telephone call, made impetuously at seven that morning. Five minutes' absence! Five minutes! That Lissa or another of the servants or one of the older children was not nearby, watching over the cradle, was something of an accident, for Germaine had been feeling feverish and prickly that morning, and had thrown such a tantrum at breakfast that the terrace was littered with shards of glass, and the child whisked away, up to the nursery; and after that Leah's nerves were such (so she explained, afterward, again and again) that she couldn't *bear* anyone in the garden with her, not even the least obtrusive of the servants. And she had wanted, for once, to be alone with Cassandra, and with her thoughts, which tumbled and cascaded and spilled in every direction on certain mornings, quite enchanting her. . . .

But she had been gone no more than five minutes: no more, certainly, than ten: how had that hellish creature *known?*

When she returned to the garden and saw the thing just rising from the cradle, its enormous wings beating the air, she began to scream at once, and ran forward, waving her arms as if the Noir Vulture were an ordinary bird to be frightened away. Then she saw the squirming bleeding baby in its talons, and cried out *Oh, Cassandra—no—* in the instant before she lost consciousness, and fell heavily to the stone terrace.

(Where Vernon, some minutes later, found her. Vernon, whose wild eyes and incoherent babble, whose ticlike grimace, were those of a man Leah had never before gazed upon.)

Kincardine Christ

Eight or ten miles north of Kincardine there was, suddenly, a giant putty-hued Christ stretched with unmuscular flatness upon His cross, angular, womanish, cartoon-crude, *weary*. The cross was made of two halved and unskinned logs. Three bloody teardrops moved down Christ's sunken cheeks.

The woman whom the driver of the car had acquired (not an hour previously, in the dim, smoky, overwarm recesses of Stan's Tropicana Lounge) reared back and squeezed his knee in girlish alarm, and laughed, though the sight of the thing could not have been entirely new to her. Didn't she live, after all, around here?

Not around *here*, exactly.

But your mother's people, you said . . .

Oh, they're from all over, they're scattered all over hell, she said irritably. She was straining to see the Christ as they passed, though she was lodged beside, had seated herself immediately beside, the man who drove the big cream-colored automobile. Jesus, she whispered. Then giggled clumsily at her mistake. Then giggled, blushing, at *that* lapse of taste. . . . The cross itself must have been about fifteen feet high. Christ was well over twelve feet tall. He gazed out through grape-hued melancholy eyes at the traffic on the highway, His back to the unpainted farmhouse, His dead-pale arms stretched out unnaturally wide. His hair was black—tar-black, crow's-wing-black. His ribs were prominent, perhaps He had been starved before being nailed to the cross, His legs were painfully thin, a child's legs, though very long. How silly a fate, the driver of the car thought briefly.

That funny kind of hat they gave him, there, the woman said. Her words trailed off.

The crown of thorns?

Oh, yeah—yes! The crown of thorns.

The woman had been pressing, perhaps consciously, her warm stocking-straining thigh against the driver's, and at the sight of the morose staring Christ she withdrew it slightly. She unknotted her scarf—a filmy powder blue, sprinkled with bits of stardust—and fastened it more securely about her hair. She cleared her throat. I suppose they're Catholic, she said. In that house back there.

In Stan's Tropicana Lounge, at 6:00 P.M. on a gauzy-hot July afternoon, there had been a noisy crowd despite the stagnant air: truckers bound for Port Oriskany five hundred miles to the west, men from the mills and the canning factory, farmhands, a few smalltime farmers, a number of very old men who sat quietly at the rear nursing glasses of tepid ale. Four or five unattached women, one of them Tina, who had finished with her job at Kresge's notions and baby clothes counter for the weekend. . . . Gay, teetering on her high heels, she fed coins into the new jukebox, which bubbled and glared with lights of many colors, and seemed, despite the slowness of its mechanical arm, incapable of making a mistake. Nickels were given her by the tall bearded heavy-lidded man in the stained white vest, a stranger, who had driven up (so everyone in the Tropicana knew, within seconds of his arrival) in a long low cream-colored automobile quite unlike anything they had ever seen.

He had a curled, sensual mouth, a very attractive mouth, inside that somewhat untidy beard. Tina, seated beside him at the bar, felt the weight of his interest, unmistakably the weight of his interest, though he said little, and appeared to be discomforted by the commotion around him. She leaned toward him, tapping her pretty painted fingernails against the bar, singing under her breath with the jukebox's shrill chorus *No not I, no not I, no no no no no not I.* . . .

When the music ended she slid from the bar stool, her skirt sticking (damn it, what a nuisance!) to her damp buttocks, and went to play the record once again, conscious of the man's gaze following her. *No not I.* . . .

Spider's legs, her mascara'd eyelashes. Black and stiff. Running in tears down her cheeks . . . perhaps down *his* . . . staining the pillow. And her ruby-dark lipstick smeared greasily everywhere: his mouth, his beard, his ears, his neck and chest and abdomen and thighs. . . .

No not I, she sang slyly, her skin glowing with high spirits, rocking from side to side so that her satin blouse strained against her plump shapely shoulders, *No not I, no no no no no not I. No no no, no no no, no no no not I* . . . *!*

That damn catchy tune! I think it's kind of cute, though. I love to sing. It's funny how you catch yourself singing, isn't it, when you're alone, or don't even know what you're doing.

You have, the man said with a smile, a pretty voice.

I've been fighting a cold all week.

. . . a pretty voice.

You know what those goddamn summer colds can be like.

Later, driving along the highway, driving very fast along the highway, he leaned over to unlock the glove compartment and took out a heavy pint-sized silver flask. A silver chain like the one Tina wore on her left ankle attached the cap to the flask. . . . You live around here, or your family is from around here, last name Varrell, you said?

Mother's side of the family. Out around Kittery. But they also live over there—in the mountains—spread out all over, y'know? Got cousins I never met, Tina laughed, and never want to meet.

She sipped daintily at the flask. If the bourbon struck her as especially fine she gave no indication.

My father's name was Donahauer. Jake. He got killed in the war—just didn't come back—was s'posed to be on some transport boat or something, but he *wasn't;* and that was that. My name, now, it's actually Schmidt. Tina Schmidt. You didn't know Al, I hope!

The name seemed to mean nothing to him. Or perhaps he hadn't heard.

Who?

Al Schmidt.

Your husband, you mean?

Ex-husband. Thank the good Lord.

She passed the flask to him and his fingers closed slowly about it, stroking her own.

In Stan's Tropicana Lounge, at the very end of the bar, his pale hair fading into long lazy diaphanous plumes of smoke, Nicholas Fuhr lifted a foam-ringed glass in a mock toast. Eying himself in the mirror, perhaps. Behind the disorder of the bottles and the fly-specks. . . . A barman's rag nearby, reeking. For of course there is always spillage: things smashed, liquids sprayed about. Beer, vomit, blood. Soaked rags. Shreds of clothing that resemble rags. Had he worn something on his head perhaps *that* would not have been injured; but there, in the Tropicana Lounge, lifting a glass gracefully as if he—as if they all—were whole, he appeared, again, unhurt.

At the sight of the car, parked in the weedy gravel lot, Tina's pulses leapt. Her eyes narrowed lustfully; but only for a moment. For she wasn't a silly greedy vulgar little half-assed *girl.*

She asked him a few questions about the car because not to ask would have seemed, maybe, unconvincing.

. . . German?

German. Yes.

I suppose, she said coquettishly, running the tip of her tongue lightly about her lips, stroking the fender (which burned, for the July sun was wicked), I suppose, she said, trying not to giggle, you're one of them men from the city . . . you know . . . from Port Oriskany. . . .

He looked toward her though not at her. His car keys in hand.

. . . like in the old days, you know . . . the speedboats on the lake . . . the seaplanes . . . running whiskey down from Canada. I saw one of the seaplanes once, at night. I halfway wanted to run on the beach, y'know, and wave my arms, and ask them to take me along . . . y'know, for the hell of it. . . . I was just a kid. I didn't know any better. Jesus, she said, shivering, smiling up at him, they would probably have mowed me down with machine-gun bullets.

You think I'm a gangster? the man in the vest asked.

His unlined face looked as though it had been baked, and was incapable of showing expression: but now he drew in a quick amused breath and the corners of his mouth curled.

A gangster from the city?

Oh, I know you wouldn't *say,* if you were, Tina cried gaily.

You think I run rum, at night? Across the lakes?

Oh, not *now,* they don't do that *now,* Tina laughed, as she brushed past him to climb inside the car. He held the door for her and it pleased him, her warm perfumy odor, lightly touched with an odor of sweat; it was something he had smelled many times before. But between women he could not, of course, remember it.

You think I'm a gangster from Port Oriskany. He laughed.

She settled herself gracefully inside the car, conscious of his admiring gaze. Almost primly tucked her narrow black skirt about her legs. Stockings, in this heat? And open-backed shoes with tiny black straps, bought just a few days ago. And the thin silver chain around her left ankle. And her toenails painted red.

I don't think anything, she cried gaily. I just like the smell of these seat covers—is it leather, real leather?—*white* leather? And the dashboard, here, made of some kind of fancy wood—

6:25 P.M. 6:32 P.M. His pulses leapt too—but sporadically, as if they obeyed an inner logic he could not control. Nicholas Fuhr, standing there. But of course it was not Nicholas. But then perhaps it *was.* His shadowed eyes in the mirror shifting to the side accusingly.

You made me kill Nicholas, Gideon had shouted at Leah.

I made you kill no one! You're insane! Leah shouted in return.

She slapped at him—he seized her by the upper arm—threw her across the bed. The old bed creaked in alarm at the weight of her, at the surprise of her. I loved Nick, you know I loved him, Leah sobbed. How can you accuse me of—

You didn't love him enough, did you! Gideon shouted. Don't love any of us enough, to keep us from dying!

But Gideon was not with Leah, Gideon was rarely with Leah, he was forcing himself to listen to a woman's high pleased giggly chatter. There was a flirtation of some kind going on: in the midst of it Gideon swallowed a good-sized mouthful of his father's finest bourbon and wondered that it had so little taste. But in the past several years this particular bourbon had begun to lose its potency too.

You think I'm a gangster? he said again, laughing.

Well—don't you know—*somebody's* likely to be! she said wittily.

You never did tell me your name, she said accusingly, nuzzling his ear.

My name, he said slowly. I'm not sure that I have a name.

What do your women call you?

My women?

Yes! You must have all kinds of women!

It was merry, it was gay and harmless, simply a flirtation.

I don't like anyone to call me by name, he said in the same slow bemused voice.

Well—are you married?

No.

Yes, you are, *yes,* you are—I can tell.

Not really.

Well, then what? Separated? Divorced?

No.

No—what?

No nothing.

She might have been nervous but she erupted in a peal of girlish laughter, as if he had said something extraordinarily funny. She beat on his thigh with her fist in a fierce little delighted gesture she had certainly used before, with other men. It *was* gay, it was merry and harmless, no one would be injured.

I bet you have a wife, sure enough, Tina said. And I bet she's beautiful.

Gideon said nothing. He pressed down on the accelerator.

Isn't she, eh? Beautiful? And rich too—rich too. I know you people. She laughed.

Do you? Do you know us? he asked.

I know your kind.

He glanced at her, his face stiffening. But then he decided to smile. For why *not* smile?—Nicholas had no right to accuse him, back in Stan's Tropicana Lounge. And perhaps Leah had told the truth: they were not guilty of killing anyone.

His tone changed, became formal, mock-formal: What do you say to the Nautauga House for dinner . . . ?

Ah, but she isn't dressed for a place like that! The very idea frightens her; sobers her. Then we'll take you somewhere first, he said vaguely, so that you can buy something. A half-hour should be enough, don't you think?

She laughed, still a little frightened. Wriggled her toes. (How quickly, how miraculously quickly, he was offering her things: clothes, expensive clothes, maybe perfume, jewelry. A summer fur? She'd seen, in a recent newspaper photograph, the "girl" of an alleged gangster, a skinny little pouty-faced thing with practically no breasts or hips, and *she* was wearing, for a Chicago courtroom appearance, a "summer fox boa.")

. . . But you don't know if you're going to like me yet, Rodman, she said, her voice dipping coarsely.

He murmured something she could not hear.

You're sweet, she said, linking her arm through his, and bringing her hand beside his on the steering wheel. *His* hand was immense—such a broad palm, such long wide strong fingers—she was sure they must be extremely strong.

She sang under her breath again. *No no no, no no no.* . . . Then began to tell him about her husband. Her ex-husband. You know, Rodman, she said, I like a man with a sense of humor. Willing to laugh at things, you know, not crying in his beer, taking it out on everybody else. Al went around with his head in a goddamn sack or something. I swear he did. My little girl—that's Audrey—maybe you'll meet Audrey sometime—was afraid of him, he had such a nasty temper. Got wounded in the war but nothing special, they gave him a purple heart like everybody else got, what the hell, it was all *he* was good for, getting himself shot in the leg, though actually it was his rear-end but he didn't like to say, he thought people'd laugh and they *did.* Audrey, y'know what she said, once, she was peeking out at him from a window, he was working on the car or something in the driveway, she came running to me and said, all excited, how funny it was, that Daddy's holes in his face were cut out right where his eyes were—Tina began to laugh. She laughed extravagantly, wheezing, gasping for breath. You ever heard anything so crazy? So funny? *Daddy's holes in his face are cut out right where his eyes are—*

He joined her, laughing. Uproariously laughing. As the heavy car sped along the highway. To the left, the sun was nowhere near the horizon but the sky, threaded with somber quizzical clouds, had begun to darken. There was a bruised, faintly resentful look to the air. But the clouds were too thin to be storm clouds.

North, into the mountains. But Nautauga Falls was in the other direction. So perhaps he should turn the car around.

He braked. And turned into a narrow dirt road, an old logging road. Drove a little too fast so that the big car rattled. The flask slipped out of Tina's hand and struck the dashboard, and bourbon splashed.

. . . driving too goddamn fast, she said, surprised.

Not for people in a hurry, he said.

At the mountainous rim, at the edge, of all he could see, there might be a place he could stand, to look back at what he was: but perhaps it was dangerous to go there. Men hacked their way to that place . . . and then did not return. They slipped over the edge, or stared down too long into the abyss; they couldn't remember where they had come from, still less why they had gone where they had. *There,* you forgot it was the rim, most likely. You didn't even think it might be the center of a circle because the idea of a circle wouldn't be there, for you to step into, the way you usually step into thoughts prepared beforehand.

Oh, look— That tree— There must have been a storm—

The road was impassable: a giant poplar lay at an angle across it.

All right, said the driver, get out. This is as far as we go, I want to see if I like you.

Tina was wiping at her skirt, which the bourbon had splashed.

You're in such a goddamn *hurry* all at once, she said sullenly.

But the color was up in her cheeks and her eyes were shining as she slid across the seat to get out his door. Grunting, giggling, trying to pull her skirt down. Embarrassed that her thighs, which showed for a moment, whitely, were so raddled and jellyish.

But he was staring off into the sky. Slowly he ran both hands through his stiff bushy hair. Broad-shouldered, tall, very tall, lean, handsome, but wearing that soiled white vest, and a pale blue shirt that looked as if he hadn't changed it for several days; and his beard needed trimming. They would stay at the Nautauga House, probably. Where (Tina knew, for a friend worked in the smoke shop off the lobby) there was a gentleman's barber. . . .

Now he turned to her, and was looking at her. For the first time, *at* her. She smoothed down her skirt, and staggered, her heels sinking in the sandy soil, and tried to smile.

All right, he said, as if not catching that smile, strip.

What?

Your clothes. Strip. Now. Before we go back. I want to see, he said softly, with an air of melancholy resignation, if I like you.

Reflections

Now the pond, Mink Pond, *his* pond, was at its prime: lush and glittering with reflections, trembling with ungovernable incalculable life: *his*.

How beautiful!—Is it possible to get closer?—Is there a path? So visitors cried, from the graveled walk. (But the banks were now overgrown with alder and water willow, cattails, pickerelweed, bulrushes, reeds, nameless tall grasses. So much water willow, and so suddenly— how, Raphael wondered, did it grow so fast this summer—sinewy stems with dozens of eager red roots, arching over the water and then sinking beneath the surface, to take hold of the muddy bottom. And growing, so ferociously, from everywhere on the pond's fertile circumference. From one day to the next Raphael's narrow, secret pathway had to be opened.)

Hello, Raphael—is that Raphael—? Raphael? Is he there? Raphael—?

Strangers' voices. Guests of the castle. (For there were visitors now all the time. But they rarely found their way to Raphael's pond.)

Reflections, at dusk, of a doe with her six-weeks' fawn. Stooping to drink. Cautious, yet rather noisy; splashing about; stepping on tussock sedges that sank slowly beneath their weight. The fawn's eyes were enormous but not greatly concerned with seeing. The doe's coat was a queer silvery-russet. As they drank spasmodic ripples radiated out, toward the pond's distant center.

Reflections, at midday, of dragonflies. The banks, the pond, the overhanging willow branches, alive with dragonflies: a frenzy of iridescent glitter, turquoise, onyx, reddish-yellow: their outsized monstrous heads: their pulsing wingbeats.

The pond in its maturity, in its prime. But in midsummer creatures lay about as if exhausted—frogs on tussocks, a snake on a sun-bleached rock—a snapping turtle, new to the pond and new to Raphael's eye, on a partly submerged log. Bright green algae, smelling of rot and sun. Far overhead but looking, in the pond's quivering brackish surface, as if it were only a few inches away, the pale gauzy-gray insubstantial sky was disturbed by whirligig beetles and fisher spiders and mud minnows.

Life, reflected in the pond, or sucked down into the pond and swallowed, given no reflection. Water snakes graceful and undulating, like bulrushes come to life; and silent. Silent too the innumerable yellow perch with their rows of minute dark stripes and their insatiable appetites.

Raphael—?

You don't love us, was Vida's sudden cry as, for no reason he could determine, she gave her brother a shove. Hurt and bewilderment in her voice, as well as anger. It was someone's birthday. Raphael was certain it had not been *his* birthday. . . . He slipped away, restless and bored with their foolish games. Musical chairs and "The Needle's Eye" and charades and tag and hide-and-go-seek and . . . It wasn't true, that he didn't love them. It was simply the case that he never thought of them.

The pond quivered and glittered and trembled with its secret spirits. He wanted to know them. He would know them. Sleeping things, scurrying things, spiders, crayfish, milfoil, pennywort, tadpoles, ugly black bullheads in the muddy shadows at the very bottom. Tiny, near-microscopic lice clinging to underwater grasses; bubbles, popping to the surface, stinking of decay like the body's gases; bubbles that revealed themselves not as air, as nothing, but as living globules, the size of fleas.

Reflections of swamp sparrows, red-winged blackbirds uneasily perched on cattails, wings thrashing about in the willow leaves. Once, through a maze of insect-riddled pickerelweed, the great white-winged bird with its skinned head and pointed beak, flying far overhead, so distant that the sound of its flapping wings could not be heard.

(The Noir Vulture, they called it. In their furious befuddled mourning. What a commotion they made, with their noisy tears, their grief, their anger! Gunshots sounded from the swamp, from the lakeshore, day after day; but they returned empty-handed. Raphael hid, and observed, and slipped away from the house as quietly as possible, and of course he was not asked to accompany the men into the swamp.)

Reflections of an eye, multiplied thousands—thousands upon thousands! —of times, in a single drop of water. Eyes reflecting eyes. The pond was, of course, more dizzyingly complex than a dragonfly's wings; more subtle than a bullfrog's papery shed skin; more slyly alive than the red midges. It was aware of him at all times, it lapped about his groping fingers, caressing, calculating, giving comfort. Eyes gazing into eyes gazing into eyes. Those long summer afternoons in which the very heat-haze seemed asleep, yet everything was alive, intensely alive, with thought. . . .

Reflections of flies, gnats, hummingbirds. Reflections of hungry pickerel, cast *upward* against the scummy pads of water lilies.

Reflections, too sudden and too bright (red, olive-red) of a cardinal and his mate, disturbing the tranquillity of Raphael's brooding.

If I could go down, if I could sink, if I could burrow my head into the dark warm mud, if my lungs were strong enough to endure pain . . .

Patience.

Stillness.

In the dim undersea of colored, dancing shadows, in the Rialto Theater, they had sat, a full row of them, delighted as small children with their new purchase. (Several downtown blocks of Rockland, to the west, in Eden County. Among the properties was an old movie theater with a sagging marquee and a vast, vaulted, cavernous foyer whose robin's-egg-blue ceiling was brushed with sequins that resembled fish scales.) They ate stale buttered popcorn—*their* popcorn—and devoured boxes of mints —and found it difficult to settle down, even when "The March of Time" showed such unspeakable sights. This was their property, Bellefleur property, the sandstone façade, the cheap plaster pillars, the worn, filthy "Oriental" rugs, the rows and rows of seats descending gradually to the stage; the faded scarlet curtains, fold upon fold of velvet; the ornate grimy molding at the ceiling; the screen with its criss-crossings of hair-thin cracks. What they did *not* own was the play of colored shadows on the screen, and so they settled back to watch: soon drawn, like the rest of the sparse audience, into the mysterious story set now in the cornfields of the Midwest, now in a tropical city, now in "Paris." There was a beautiful though hard-faced woman with platinum blond hair curled tightly under, too tightly under, so that she looked, to Raphael's skeptical eye, like a manikin. She wore gowns that clung to her breasts, even to her sloping pelvis. There was a girl, her younger sister, who appeared in only a few scenes, at the beginning of the movie and again at the end, when the woman returned to her hometown (though only briefly, because her mustached lover, her millionaire-pilot lover, pursued her across the continent), and this girl—with her frank pretty face and her shining wheat-colored hair and her soft melodious voice and her small smile—was so much more interesting than the woman, so much more attractive, that whenever she appeared on screen the audience's interest quickened; one could feel it, unmistakably. So small a role, and yet—wasn't that girl remarkable!

(But when Raphael leaned over to his mother, to say, Isn't that Yolande?—Lily pretended not to comprehend. Not even to hear. "Isn't that Yolande?" Raphael asked, raising his voice, and his family told him to be still—there were other people in the theater, after all. Afterward when the lights came on and the others left and the Bellefleurs remained sitting in their row, as if greatly moved, subdued by the screen's effortless miracles and its almost supernatural beauty, Raphael asked again about the girl—about Yolande—for certainly it *was* Yolande—and Lily said in a vague stunned voice, "No, it wasn't, I had that thought for a moment too but then I looked more closely, I suppose I'd know my own daughter if I saw her," and Vida snorted contemptuously, saying, *"That* actress is beautiful, and Yolande wasn't—she had an ugly nose," and Albert did no more than grunt in baffled amusement, and Leah said, squeezing Lily's hand, "Your daughter would be no more than fifteen, you know, and *that* girl—that young woman—was in her early twenties at least. She's probably been married and divorced a half-dozen times." Garth and Little Goldie, who had been sitting just across the aisle, holding hands and sharing a bag of peanuts and giggling, claimed not to have noticed the girl at all: a girl in the movie said to resemble poor Yolande . . . ? No, they hadn't noticed her at all.)

And of course there was no "Yolande Bellefleur" among the actors' names.

"What a silly idea, Raphael," Vida whispered, staring at him. "You're getting strange. I don't know if I *like* you."

Reflections darting through reflections. Faces swimming out of the movie projector's ghostly light, or taking shape out of the dark still water. (But there was not a single water, a single substance. Instead there were layers upon layers, currents entwined with currents, many waters, many spirits, unknowable.)

How is it possible, Raphael wondered, with a small stab of fear, that we recognize one another from day to day, even from hour to hour . . . ? Everything shifts, changes, grows fluid, transparent. He saw the photograph of a tall stocky frowning man in the newspaper, and did not realize until he read the caption that the man was his own father. Once, not long before dawn, when he crept down from his room without waking the others, and ran barefoot across the lawn, his heart lifting with an absurd hope (ah, to get there!—to get safely *there,* as quickly as possible!—to make certain the pond had not disappeared in the night, like one of his strange dreams), he happened to see, some distance away, in the swampy area adjacent to the pond, his great-aunt Veronica hurrying toward the house. Like a sleepwalker she made her way with her arms extended and her head upright. Coils of graying hair had fallen loose on her shoulders so that she resembled, in the mist-threaded light, a very young girl. It was no more than two or three minutes before dawn, and red-winged blackbirds were singing stridently; and back in the swamp an owl called. How odd, how very odd, that she should be hurrying back to the castle, from the undrained marshy area below the cemetery, that she should walk— glide—so gracefully along, making no sound whatsoever, and not noticing her nephew as he stood, one hand raised in a shy, tentative greeting, no more than thirty feet away. . . . Raphael noted that the fluffy-plumed reeds barely stirred with her passing.

Yet a minute later, gazing into the colorless waters of his pond, Raphael could ask himself whether he *had* seen her—whether he had seen anyone at all. The swamp was nearly hidden in mist. Coils of fog blew indolently along the ground, as if alive. And anyway weren't other people, members of his family as well as strangers projected flatly on a movie screen, unknowable from day to day, unrecognizable . . . ? Perhaps they were all bodiless as shadows, all images, all reflections.

Rising out of the quivering, agitated water into which he stepped, barefoot, was a face: the face of a young boy: a child's ancient water-dimmed face, nibbled by invisible currents. As if framing it tenderly between two hands the pond held it aloft. A stranger's face, it seemed. With that curious hopeful expression . . .

But perhaps Raphael was mistaken and the expression was not hopeful. Perhaps it *was* nothing at all: simply water, simply light. For if the dark waters were not there, the face would not exist either. It would vanish at once. It would never have been.

The Wicked Son

Even at the height of his fame and his power, in the very prime of his extraordinary life—even when it was quite plain that within a few years he could not fail to become a billionaire (for the first hops harvest of some four hundred acres had brought him profits far beyond his characteristically conservative estimation, and the second harvest, of more than five hundred acres, in a blessed conjunction with severe rainstorms that damaged plantations in Germany and Austria, and drove the world market price wonderfully high, brought him even greater profits), and he might exert his will more forcefully in politics (had he not *almost* convinced mistrustful Stephen Field that he was, despite his reputation for secrecy and stubbornness, and his unfortunate public manner, the very man for the office of governor during these troubled times)—even when the final additions to his magnificent estate were completed, the Roman bath with its priceless Italian tiles and the conservatory with its glass dome and the marble pagoda fronting the stables, and his hundreds of guests praised the manor in exalted language that would have embarrassed, had it been less than appropriate—even then, after a passage of time that, crowded with events as it was, should have exorcised the worst of his bitterness, Raphael Bellefleur often gave himself up to spasmodic outbursts of sheer rage, at the thought of his wicked son Samuel who had escaped him.

Of course Samuel had not "escaped" him. He was still in the castle, in the Turquoise Room, beneath his father's roof. And yet everyone behaved as if he had died, and Raphael went along with the fiction, for certainly the young man did not *exist* in the usual sense of the word.

Violet mourned the loss of her handsome young son but refused to discuss the matter with Raphael. We know what we know, she murmured, and of that we cannot speak.

Old Jedediah kept to himself as always, courteous, distant, his pale hazel eyes averted from Raphael's whenever they happened to meet. Unless Raphael imagined it, his aged father was *ashamed* on his account. To have lost a son like Samuel! A dashing young officer! And to have lost him in such a way—!

In the beginning, Samuel's young friends came frequently to visit. Raphael gave them food and drink but always excused himself from the drawing room; he could not bear to see the young men in their uniforms, none of them so tall and handsome and quick as Samuel had been. He overheard their murmurous conversation: Samuel would return, Samuel would reappear any day: and what stories he would tell! It was inconceivable that Samuel Bellefleur was dead. . . .

Of course he isn't dead, one of the lieutenants said. He simply chooses not to be with us.

Poor Lamentations of Jeremiah mourned the loss of his brother, going about in a melancholy daze, his inkwell eyes piteous to behold. Go away, go out of my sight, Raphael moaned, you must know you won't *do.* And the unhappy boy crept off to his room and locked the door.

Raphael would have liked to withdraw from the world for a spell, in order to properly mourn the loss of his son. And yet—he found himself unable to keep from thinking about the world. *The world. The world of time, and flesh, and power.* For wasn't the world always there, always in turmoil, no matter that one closed one's eyes to it? The sanctity of the Chautauqua mountains, the eerie mist-shrouded solitude of Bellefleur Manor, which seemed, to many a visitor from downstate, and to Mr. Lincoln himself (who had first visited it in the late fifties, when the nation's movement toward war began to violently accelerate), to place the castle out of time, and to give it an otherworldly, an almost legendary aura, was soon lost to Raphael: for, after all, *he* owned the estate, *he* knew all the blunders and heartbreaking miscalculations that had gone into its creation, *he* alone was responsible for its upkeep. Like the God of creation he could not reasonably take solace in his creation, for wasn't it—after all—*his?*

So he could not withdraw. He could not turn his restless darting insatiable intelligence away from the world, though of course this was precisely what Samuel had chosen to do. Only to Jedediah did Raphael dare say a few words, not of grief but of befuddled anger: Do you comprehend, Father, what the boy has done!—he has—he has—he has wantonly and with full deliberation *gone over to the other side, to the blacks.*

But white-haired Jedediah, distant as always, as if his soul abided still in the mountains, merely nodded vaguely and turned away. It was his affliction—or perhaps his pretense of an affliction—to be nearly deaf. Father, Raphael cried, his heart knotted in his chest, my son has gone over to the *blacks* . . . !

The Mud-Devourers

It was on the airless sultry eve of Germaine's second birthday, in the midst of a prolonged heat wave (of some twelve days' duration, with midday temperatures as high as 105 degrees, a record in the Chautauqua region) that Vernon Bellefleur, angular and impatient and bullying, in his "new" poetic voice, with his beard trimmed cruelly short so that it hardly resembled a beard and his long hair tied at the nape of his neck with a soiled red scarf, so antagonized a group of men at a Fort Hanna tavern that they turned upon him in drunken fury, and threw him into the Nautauga River to his death. Or so it must have been: for how could Vernon, his wrists and ankles bound with clothesline, Vernon who had, alone among the Bellefleur children, never learned to swim, prevent himself from drowning in those swift deep waters—?

The summer, the terrible heat, the busyness of the castle, comings and goings, the death of Cassandra, the surprise of Lord Dunraven's visit (and he had promised Cornelia that he would return, after his journey to the West Coast, to spend a few more days at the castle before leaving for England), Leah's and Hiram's and young Jasper's frequent trips to distant cities: too much, the older Bellefleurs murmured, simply too much was happening. There was the distressing change in Vernon, after the baby's funeral; there was Ewan's campaign for sheriff of the county, which he had begun lazily enough, with a cynical good humor, for certainly he didn't care—how could a Bellefleur *care* about such an office?—but which, as the weeks passed, came to seem more important. There was the problem of Gideon. (But, in Leah's presence, of course there was no "problem"—simply that he was frequently away, absent for days at a time.) There was the sharp disappointment of the rejection, from the governor's office, of Jean-Pierre's formal request for a pardon (and attached to the rejection was a hand-written, and entirely gratuitous, note to the effect that the "original sentence" was "lenient enough"—a remark that infuriated Leah, who vowed she would get her revenge on Grounsel someday.) There was the surprise of a peculiar (and not very literate) letter of many pages from the elderly Mrs. Schaff, addressed to Cornelia, complaining bitterly about her "headstrong" daughter-in-law who was "already exhibiting, at her tender age, the vices of her ancestors": Cornelia read certain selected passages to the family, who reacted with uproarious laughter, and then again with resentment, and still again with baffled rage. (Christabel, questioned by both her mother and Cornelia, claimed she hadn't any idea what old Mrs. Schaff meant. "Maybe because my knees hurt when we kneel for prayer, and sometimes I wriggle around, and once I snuck a rolled-up scarf to kneel on," Christabel said, tears in her eyes.) There was the surprise, which should have been a pleasant one though in fact it greatly disturbed the family, of young Bromwell's good fortune—but perhaps "good fortune" was the wrong term: he had published a thirty-page essay in a magazine no one had ever heard of, *The Journal for the Study of Time,* an essay whose meticulous graphs, charts, formulae, data, and vocabulary attested to an extraordinary intellect (a biographical note on Bromwell spoke of him as the youngest contributor in the publishing history of the magazine). The only member of the family who even attempted to read the essay was Hiram. "The boy certainly shows promise," he said evasively. "There's probably little reason for me to continue tutoring him in mathematics. . . ."

A more pleasant surprise was Lord Dunraven's extended visit. He was, he claimed, absolutely enchanted by the mountains and the wilderness land and the innumerable lakes: it struck him as astonishing that the Bellefleurs lived in so paradisaical a world, and lived in it so . . . so . . . unself-consciously, so *naturally.* Noel took him fishing along the north shore of Lake Noir (ah, that lake, that sinister lovely lake!—there was nothing like it in all of England, or even in the Scottish highlands), and there were frequently little fishing and hunting expeditions on higher ground, though it was observed that Cornelia's cousin, while in every respect in excellent health, and certainly, at the age of forty-two, in the prime of life, and certainly *enthusiastic,* tired more easily than the other men; once he fell asleep, or slipped into a stupefied unconsciousness, on the walking horse Noel had selected for him, and they had to secure him to the saddle and the horse's neck with rope. But he loved, he said repeatedly, the mountains—how high *were* the Chautauquas?—and the air was so fresh, the mountain lakes so beautiful—at least in the wilderness land the Bellefleurs showed him (for of course, elsewhere, there were ugly razed acres, and streams fouled by mills and factories, some of them owned by the Bellefleurs themselves). Noel answered vaguely, not quite knowing what he meant, that of course the mountains were beautiful but they had been, he thought, somewhat higher in the past, during his boyhood: he didn't know, maybe ten thousand feet or so, the highest peak . . . ? "Ah, there is nothing like that in my country," Lord Dunraven said, smiling sadly.

Lord Dunraven was of somewhat less than average height, at least by Bellefleur standards, but he carried himself well. His good-natured face was frequently illuminated by crinkling smiles that quite changed his appearance: he was capable of looking, even with the bushy graying hair that receded so sharply at his temples, like a much younger man. His cheeks seemed permanently windburned, with an attractive ruddy blush; his eyes were clear and kind; his manner, though highly studied and self-conscious, was graceful. If the Bellefleur children mocked him behind his back (Dunraven's accent, they thought, was hilarious) they nevertheless came to like him a great deal, and Germaine was especially fond of him. (Poor Germaine!—not only had she lost her baby sister Cassandra, but her father was rarely home, and now even cousin Vernon, who had always spent so much time with her, was never around.)

Lord Dunraven, Eustace Beckett, owned a large country estate in Sussex, and a town house in Belgravia; his fortune was modest by Bellefleur standards, but he had been his father's only heir, and lived comfortably. On the single occasion he managed to speak with Garnet, after the terrifying scene on the beach (about which no one knew, for of course Lord Dunraven respected the young woman's privacy, and her obvious sorrow) he explained to the unhappy girl that he was an "amateur" at life and sometimes felt, despite his age, and the frequency of deaths in his family, that he hadn't yet begun to live. And he smiled his tentative hopeful smile, and gazed upon her with such frank childlike tenderness, that Garnet turned away in confusion, and murmured an excuse—for she had to escape his presence—she could not *bear* his kindness, and the memory of that shameful scene on the beach. (After Garnet fled to Bushkill's Ferry Lord Dunraven made polite, casual inquiries about her, but of course no one told him about Cassandra; though they did allow him to know, obliquely, that the young woman's family background was somewhat common. Nevertheless Lord Dunraven wrote to Garnet, and even sent her flowers upon at least one occasion (so Della reported), and spoke of her with an unembarrassed warmth that indicated his ignorance of his own feelings. She had, he supposed, many admirers? . . . a girl of such quiet charm and beauty . . . a girl of such *delicacy*. Perhaps she was even spoken for? Well, said Cornelia flatly, *perhaps*.)

It was shortly after Lord Dunraven departed for his journey by train across the continent (and it rather amused the Bellefleurs that their English guest hadn't any notion of how wide the continent was, and couldn't seem to grasp its dimensions even when they were explained to him), that Vernon was brutally attacked by a group of Fort Hanna men one Saturday night, in a tavern in the very worst waterfront area of the city.

Everyone in the family remarked on how Vernon had changed, since the baby's death: after several days of lethargic depression, during which he had refused to eat, he emerged from his untidy room with his beard trimmed short, and his mismatched eyes glaring. The room stank of smoke—he had, he said, burnt all his papers—his old poems—notes for poems—even some of his books. All *that* was over.

He read them fragments of new poems, but his voice was so harsh and impatient, and the poems so jumbled—about the "fall" of God, the "divorce" between man and God, God's wickedness, God's ignorance, man's lonely lofty supremacy, man's duty to rebel, the stupor of the masses, the mud-devouring lot of the masses—that no one could follow, and the children, once embarrassed by their uncle's effusive goodness, were now embarrassed (and somewhat frightened) by his anger. At the very dinner honoring Lord Dunraven's departure, which Cornelia had planned with care, and which was held in the large dining room with its elegant murals, tapestries, and chandeliers, and the exquisite though rather heavy German furniture, Vernon distressed them all by insisting upon reading a poem-in-progress he had begun that afternoon, up in the cemetery. He stood at his place and read from scraps of paper that trembled in his hands, and then he looked up, fixing his gaze upon the ceiling, and recited from memory, all sorts of incoherent lines—some of them about the Noir Vulture, some of them about the baby's death, but many of them about unrelated things: God's betrayal of man, man's subservience, man's ignominious groveling nature, his selfishness, venality, cruelty, cowardice, and lack of pride. And some of the lines clearly alluded to a certain family who had, he said, exploited tenant farmers and servants and laborers, and the land, and *must* be stopped. . . .

"If that wasn't *poetry* the bastard was reciting," Ewan said, afterward, "I would have smashed his ugly face in."

In the days that followed the Bellefleurs learned, from a variety of sources, including a scandalized Della, that Vernon was wandering the countryside again—turning up at a Baptist church picnic in Contracoeur, at the old White Sulphur Springs Inn, in the village, in Bushkill's Ferry (where he evidently got hilariously drunk), as far away as Innisfail and Fort Hanna—eager to talk to anyone, young or old, who would listen. Where in the past he rarely drank, and then only shandygaffs (a drink beloved of many Bellefleur children, but only so long as they were children), now he tried to drink whatever other men were having—beer, ale, whiskey, gin—and paid for numerous rounds, as if he had been doing this sort of thing all his life. With his newly trimmed beard and his jabbing forefinger and a dramatic, harsh urgency to his voice he commanded attention as he had never commanded it before, though when his audience discerned the nature of his words—when they realized he was no longer exactly *nice,* and they couldn't either laugh at him comfortably, or like him—they grew uneasy. What had happened to Vernon Bellefleur, the "poet"! Even the word *love* evoked a cynical curling of his eyebrows.

In Contracoeur he harangued his bewildered listeners on the subject of their servile natures: if they gave their immortal souls up to that fiendish God, why naturally they would be soulless! On the rotting veranda of the White Sulphur Springs Inn he read in a trembling voice of man's contemptible failure to realize his destiny in the *flesh* and in *history,* and alarmed several of his listeners—elderly retired smalltime farmers and merchants—who, not hearing altogether correctly, believed he was reading off a proclamation of war. In the very village itself, so close to the manor, and almost completely owned by his family, he spoke sardonically of the Bellefleurs, and chided the villagers for their passivity. Why, for decades, in fact for centuries, had they endured their lowly positions?—why did they allow themselves to be exploited? They were slaves—they were parasites—they weren't *human.* To the Bellefleurs' tenant farmers he spoke in a similar vein, and did not appear to notice his listeners' resentment. At Innisfail and Fort Hanna he read lengthy impassioned sections from a poem-in-progress called "The Mud-Devourers," which evidently accused the masses of men of complying with their own degradation, and of being, in fact, grateful for it: Any compromise, he thundered, so long as it brings a cessation of conflict! It was no wonder God treated mankind as He did, grinding the masses of men beneath His heel and exacting from them all sorts of groveling pious declarations of love. . . .

The tenant farmers were slaves, and the mill and factory workers were slaves. Their eagerness to sell themselves (and to sell themselves cheaply) made them subhuman; yet they hadn't the dignity of animals, and none of the healthy instincts of animals. The workers, if organized, could bring the owners to their knees if they tried, but of course they were too cowardly to try: their initial attempts at unionizing, some years ago, were such ghastly bloody failures they shrank back from even *thinking* of such things. Sometimes he spoke directly, stabbing at the air with his bony forefinger; sometimes he read or recited his poetry, which was not at all "poetic," but punctuated with harsh, ugly, frequently shocking images—jaws devouring jaws, wormlike men crawling on their bellies, tides of ants rushing into a stream to be swept away, creatures who devoured filth and declared it manna, the Son of God as a babbling idiot. In Innisfail, at a volunteer firemen's picnic, he so outraged a small gang of mill workers that it was only through the intervention of an off-duty state trooper (a boyhood acquaintance of Ewan's) that he was taken forcibly away, and saved from a probable beating.

But there was no one to intervene, no one to save him, when, on the following Saturday night, at the Fort Hanna tavern near the old drawbridge, he somehow got into a quarrel with a number of young men. (One of them was said to be Hank Varrell, another was a Gittings boy—though, afterward, no eyewitnesses officially identified them, or were even willing to offer descriptions.) How Vernon managed to get to Fort Hanna when he had been sighted in the Falls earlier that day; why he sought out that particular tavern, frequented by men who worked at the Bellefleur mill, and who had, at one time, been under his "management"; why he insisted drunkenly upon addressing the men in the most intimate and provocative terms (he referred to them as *brothers* and *comrades*), no one knew. "He talked like a preacher," someone said. "He was so certain of himself—he was even *happy*—right up until the end."

That day the temperature had climbed above 100 degrees, and an airless stagnant heat seemed to radiate out of the earth itself. Though the tavern was on the Nautauga River, the river at this point was unspeakably filthy, and gave off a sulfurous stink that burnt the eyes. There had been a rumor for weeks, still unsubstantiated, that the mill might be closed down, and naturally the men were angry, and naturally they queried Vernon about it; but he denied that he was a Bellefleur, he denied that he knew anything, and insisted upon charging the men with their own predicament. *They* had destroyed the river, *they* had destroyed their own souls . . . ! "And I don't exempt myself from you," Vernon cried passionately. "I am of the same species as you! I too have devoured mud and called it manna!"

How the men managed to drag Vernon off, and to tie his hands and feet together with clothesline (clothesline stretched between two scrubby trees in a backyard adjacent to the tavern), without exciting the attention of anyone who might have called the police, how they managed to carry him up the steep, debris-cluttered hill to the road, and onto the bridge (which was fairly busy on a Saturday night), no one was able to explain. Evidently he put up a violent struggle, kicking and thrashing about, so that one of the young men suffered a badly cut lip, and another a cracked rib; evidently, at the very moment they dropped him over the side of the railing, he was screaming defiantly at them. It was said that he fell like a shot, sank, surfaced again some distance downstream, still screaming, wildly pumping his arms and legs, and, in the midst of a ferocious outcry, again disappeared from view. It was said that, afterward, as the young men ran away, wiping their hands, laughing, one called out to the others, "That's what we do to Bellefleurs!" and another, unidentified, said, "That's what we do to *poets.*"

Book Four
ONCE UPON A TIME...

Celestial Timepiece

Serendipity and *Felicity* and *All-Hallows-Eve* and *Wonder-Working Providence* and *Celestial Timepiece* were the names of the massive wool-and-feather-lined quilts Germaine's aunt Matilde made. The quilts grew slowly as Germaine watched, very slowly, square by square, as aunt Matilde talked with grandfather Noel and Germaine, her stubby fingers working constantly. Months passed, and years. *Glass Garden* and *Gyroscope* and *The Dance* (a dance of merry skeletons) and *The Bestiary* and *Noir Swamp* and *Angels*. They grew square by square, eventually spilling to the floor and hiding aunt Matilde's feet.

"Why do you take Germaine over there, to that woman's house," grandmother Cornelia asked irritably. "Matilde is hardly a good example, is she?"

"An example of what?" Noel asked.

"Leah doesn't like it," Cornelia said.

"Leah hasn't time to know about it," Noel said.

Yet they came often, to Raphael Bellefleur's "camp"—a half-dozen log cabins on the lake shore, many miles from Bellefleur Manor. Family legend had it that Matilde had moved there long ago out of sheer *spite*: she had failed to be a Bellefleur, had failed to attract a suitable husband, and so she simply withdrew into the woods. But grandfather Noel told Germaine that that wasn't true. Matilde had moved across the lake because—because she had wanted to.

"Can I live here too?" Germaine asked.

"We can visit," grandfather Noel said. "As often as we like."

Germaine rode her new pony Buttercup, and Noel rode his high-headed but lazy old stallion Fremont. And they did come *almost* as often as they liked.

Great-aunt Matilde was a large-boned woman who sang as she

worked, and had a habit of talking to herself. (Sometimes Germaine heard her: *Now where did I put that spoon, now what are you devils doing on that table!*) If she was lonely at the camp she never indicated it: on the contrary, she was the happiest Bellefleur Germaine knew. She never raised her voice and she never threw anything down in a rage and she never strode out of a room weeping. The telephone never rang—there was no telephone; letters came rarely; though the family strongly disapproved of Matilde they let her alone. (She was "strange," she was "headstrong," the Bellefleurs said. She was "stubborn" because she insisted upon her solitude, and making quilts and rugs for a living. Social gatherings did not interest her, not even weddings and funerals!—and she insisted upon wearing trousers and boots and jackets, and in the old days, as Lamentations of Jeremiah's daughter, she had even insisted upon working with the farm laborers; an eccentricity for which the female Bellefleurs never forgave her. She should have been born a man, they said contemptuously. She should have been born a dirt-poor farmer living on the side of a mountain; she doesn't deserve the name *Bellefleur*.)

But they let her alone, Perhaps they were afraid of her.

So she worked on her quilts, happy in her solitude, and grandfather Noel brought Germaine over to visit, and they spent wonderful long afternoons: Germaine was allowed to help Matilde sew, and Noel settled by the fire, his boots off and his stockinged feet twitching with pleasure, a pipe clamped between his teeth. He loved to gossip about the family—the schemes Leah had!—the woman was ingenious—and Ewan's behavior—and Hiram's problems—and what Elvira said to Cornelia—and what Lily's growing children were up to: the children were all growing up so *quickly*. Matilde laughed, but said little. She was deeply absorbed in her work. Noel complained of the swiftness of time's passing but Matilde could not agree. "Sometimes I think time hardly passes at all," Matilde said. "At this end of the lake, at least."

The quilts, the enormous wonderful quilts!—which Germaine would remember all her life.

Serendipity: six feet square, a maze of blue rags, so intricate you could stare and stare and stare into it.

Felicity: interlocking triangles of red, rosy-red, and white.

Wonder-Working Providence: a galaxy of opalescent moons.

Made for strangers, sold to strangers, who evidently paid a good price for them. ("Why can't we buy one of them," Germaine said to her grandfather, "why can't *we* take one of them home?")

Celestial Timepiece was the largest quilt, but Matilde was sewing it for herself—it wasn't to be sold: up close it resembled a crazy quilt because it was asymmetrical, with squares that contrasted not only in color and design but in texture as well. "Feel this square, now feel this one," Matilde said softly, taking Germaine's hand, "and now this one—do you see? Close your eyes." Coarse wool, fine wool, satins, laces, burlap, cotton, silk, brocade, hemp, tiny pleats. Germaine shut her eyes tight and touched the squares, seeing them with her fingertips, reading them. Do you understand? Matilde asked.

Noel complained that *Celestial Timepiece* made his eye jump. You had to stand far back to see its design, and even then it was too complicated—it gave him a headache. "Why don't you just sew some nice little satin comforter," he said. "Something small, something pretty."

"I do what I am doing," Matilde said curtly.

Sometimes, back in the castle, Germaine shut her eyes and called back Matilde's cabin. She saw the white leghorns picking in the dust, and the single dairy cow with the white face; and Foxy the red-orange cat, so much more gentle that the castle toms. (Mahalaleel's offspring were everywhere, underfoot, and though they were extraordinarily handsome cats even the females were short-tempered. You could not help petting them—they were so alluring—but you risked being scratched.) Matilde had a pet cardinal, kept in a wicker cage; he twittered and scolded like a tame bird. Germaine saw, in her mind's eye, his bright red feathers—his chunky orange beak. And the hollyhocks at the rear of the kitchen garden. And, in the washing shed, the wooden washtub with a "pounder"—a long tin tube, flared at the bottom. There was a stoneware churn with a wooden dasher. A spinning wheel. A loom, which Matilde used to weave her rugs, in yard-wide sections, out of balls of dyed rags. (Weaving was hard work, harder even than sewing quilts. It was especially difficult to get the correct number of balls for each stripe.) In the living room there was an aged wood-burning stove, made of iron; and Matilde's bed, a plain four-poster with white ruffled skirts, a cornhusk tick and feather bed on top, and one of Matilde's quilts for a counterpane. The high hard goosefeather pillows were covered with starched white cases edged with handmade lace. Germaine often napped on this bed, with Foxy curled up close beside her.

"Why can't we come to aunt Matilde's to live," Germaine asked querulously.

"You don't want to leave your father and your mother, do you?" grandfather Noel scolded. "What kind of talk is that!"

Germaine put a finger in her mouth, and then another; and then another. And sucked on them defiantly.

Nightshade

Superstitious Bellefleurs spoke of Nightshade as a *troll*
(as if anyone had the slightest notion of what a *troll* was!) but it is more
reasonable to assume, as Leah, Hiram, Jasper, Ewan, and other "reasonable" Bellefleurs did, that he was a *dwarf.* Not altogether an ordinary
dwarf of the kind one might find elsewhere—for surely Nightshade,
hunchbacked as he was, and with his wide, thin, near-lipless mouth that
stretched fully across his face—was unusual. For one thing he was dis-
tressingly ugly. If you wanted to like him, or simply to "take pity" on him,
his oversized but wizened face with its chiplike colorless eyes, and the
queer indentation on his forehead (as if, it was observed, someone struck
him long ago with the blunt edge of an ax), and that maddening unslack-
ening joyless wide smile, were so repulsive, you turned away in alarm,
your pulses racing; and the things Nightshade carried about in his numerous leather pouches and boxes (they were rumored to be bits of dried
animals but were probably only medicinal herbs, like boneset, heal-all,
henbit, dogbane, and, indeed, nightshade) gave off a sickish odor that
intensified in humid weather. Bromwell estimated that Nightshade would
have been about five feet tall had he been capable of standing upright:
but he was so badly deformed, his spine bent and his chest so caved in,
that he stood no more than four feet nine. Isn't he sad, people said when
they first saw him; isn't he pathetic, they murmured upon subsequent
sightings; isn't he *hideous,* isn't he *unspeakable,* they finally said, when
neither the poor thing nor Leah was within earshot. (It was to be one of
the most nagging of the Bellefleur mysteries, Nightshade's appeal for
Leah. For surely he came to acquire an extraordinary value in her imagination, during Germaine's third and fourth years, and a remarkable intimacy as well—an intimacy, alas, that, though it never overstepped the
affectionate but formal relationship of a woman and her favored manser-

vant, nevertheless provoked, in the ignorant, all sorts of cruel, foolish, spiteful, and obscene speculation.)

Nightshade came to dwell at Bellefleur Manor quite by accident—through, in fact, a series of accidents.

After the tragedy of the infant Cassandra's death, a number of Bellefleur men, joined, at various times, by friends and neighbors and visiting relatives (among them Dave Cinquefoil and Dabney Rush), sought, with shotguns and rifles and even a lightweight multiple-action gun of Ewan's, the Noir Vulture, which was believed to inhabit the deepest reaches of the swamp; but their expeditions were fruitless. They shot and killed, or shot and left for dead, any number of other creatures, in their understandable disappointment—deer, bobcats, beavers, skunks, hares, rabbits, raccoons, opossums, muskrats, rats, porcupines, snakes (copperheads, ring-necks, water moccasins), even turtles, and even bats; and a great variety of birds, primarily herons, hawks, eagles, and egrets, who somewhat resembled the deadly vulture—but they came away, exhausted and bitter, without the object of their hunt. Gideon, who had shown little interest in hunting, in recent years, was especially determined to kill the Noir Vulture, and led nearly all of the expeditions into the swamp; even when feverish from snakebite he insisted upon joining the other men. He never spoke of Cassandra, still less did he speak of Garnet, but he often spoke of the Noir Vulture and how he would hunt it down—how he wouldn't rest until it was killed. (Bromwell frequently told his father that there must be, of course, more than a single bird, though legend had it that only a single Noir Vulture existed—for how, otherwise, the primly courteous boy inquired, could the creature *reproduce* itself?) But each of the hunting expeditions ended in failure, and Gideon became increasingly bitter. He once suggested that the entire swamp—some sixty or seventy acres—be firebombed: couldn't Ewan (who had just been elected, by a narrow margin, sheriff of Nautauga County) acquire the necessary equipment . . . ? But Ewan laughed away the notion, which must have been a joke. We'll kill the thing eventually, he said. Don't worry, it won't escape *us*.

Yet the weeks passed, and the Noir Vulture was not even sighted, let alone shot.

By a happy coincidence there arrived at the manor, after an absence of many years (no one could quite remember how many, not even Cornelia), Gideon's brother Emmanuel, who had been exploring the Chautauquas in order to map them thoroughly: for even at the present time maps were crude and unreliable. Emmanuel reappeared in the kitchen one afternoon in his sheepskin jacket and hiking shoes, carrying a weathered knapsack, and asked the cook, in his softspoken, rather inflectionless voice, if he might have something to eat. The cook (newly hired, since the debacle of great-grandmother Elvira's birthday party) had no idea who he was but saw the Bellefleur nose (in Emmanuel it was a long straight beak of a nose, with unusually small nostrils), and was shrewd enough to serve him, quietly and without fuss. He was an extremely tall man, perhaps Gideon's height, with silvery brown hair that fell to his shoulders, and tanned, leathery skin that glinted with something metallic—salt, mica—and long, narrow, impassive eyes in which the dark iris floated like a tadpole, with a tadpole's tiny curl of a tail. It was difficult to say how old he might have been: his skin had so weathered that it looked ageless, timeless: he must have been about Gideon's and Ewan's ages but looked much older, and at the same time perversely younger. A servant ran to get his mother, and soon the whole household was alerted, and though most of them crowded into the kitchen Emmanuel continued to eat his beef stew, chewing each mouthful slowly, smiling and nodding in reply to excited questions.

It was evidently the case—much to his family's surprise—that he was *not* home for good; he planned to stay at the manor only a few weeks. The cartography project was not completed. He said, softly, in response to an exclamation of Noel's, that it was *far* from being completed, it would require years more of exploration. . . . Years more! Cornelia said, trying to take his hands in hers, as if to warm them, what on earth can you mean! Emmanuel pulled away, expressionless. If his face seemed to have an upward cast, a half-smiling air, it was because of his long, curling eyes; his lips were quite immobile. He explained quietly that the project he had set himself was a difficult, even a merciless one, and though he'd already covered many thousands of feet of parchment with his mapping and notations, he was really nowhere near finished for, for one thing, the land was always changing, streams were rerouting themselves, even the mountains were different from year to year (and even from day to day, he told the family, solemnly, they were eroding: Mount Blanc was now only about nine thousand feet high, and lost a fraction of an inch every hour), and a fastidious cartographer could take nothing for granted, though he had once charted, judiciously enough, all that he knew. But is that important, Noel broke in, laughing uneasily, I mean, you know, an inch here, an inch there—! Isn't it time you began to think, Emmanuel, about marrying—settling down—taking your place *here* with us— (It might have been at that precise moment that Emmanuel decided not to stay at the manor as long as he'd planned; but his face was impassive as he listened to his father's remarks. He was to leave home again on the morning of the fourth day of his visit, explaining to one of the servants that the manor was too warm for him to sleep comfortably, and the closeness of the ceilings oppressed him. And a certain gully at Lake Tear-of-the-Cloud nagged him, for he was convinced, suddenly, out of nowhere, that he had charted it incorrectly.)

But before he left he was able to answer Gideon's questions about the Noir Vulture. From out of his heavy oilskin knapsack he took a roll of parchment which he opened, carefully, spreading it on a table, explaining that this crude and really quite inadequate "map" was meant to cover the desolate swamp- and marshland to the south of Mount Chattaroy, which he had first investigated as a boy (indeed, hadn't Gideon accompanied him on one of his expeditions?), and again a few years ago, but without entirely satisfying himself that he knew it. However, he said, pointing with a forefinger (the nail of which curved wickedly, like an eagle's talon), I'm reasonably sure that the bird you want inhabits this region *here.* And he indicated an area of lakes and islands some twenty miles north of Bellefleur Manor.

Gideon stood leaning over the map, careful—for his brother seemed rather nervous—not to touch it. The intricate meandering lines were dizzying; he had never seen a map *quite* like this; and the few words that were included were obviously Indian names, no longer used, faded from memory. But he could, he thought, make his way to the Noir Vulture's habitat without difficulty. . . . Evidently they had underestimated its distance from the lake.

He straightened, smiling. He halfway wanted to seize his brother in his arms, and embrace him; but he mastered the impulse. That bird, that thing, that devilish son of a bitch, he laughed, won't escape *us.*

While the ignominious failure of the earlier expeditions had not dampened Gideon's ardor, but seemed, rather, to have increased it, the other men—Ewan in particular, who was busy with his new responsibilities—were somewhat discouraged; and the weather was growing chillier day by day. (After the terrible heatwave of late August a wall of cold air moved downward from the mountains, and brought a premature frost on the very first day of September.) So Gideon was able to cajole only Garth, Albert, Dave Cinquefoil, and a new friend named Benjamin (who shared Gideon's fascination with cars) into joining him on the hunt.

They took one of the pick-up trucks from the farm, and drove some fifteen miles north, along dirt roads and lanes and logging trails, until they were forced to give up and walk; at that very moment a light chill rain began to fall though the sky appeared cloudless. Gideon passed his flask of bourbon generously about but drank very little himself. He was almost desperately anxious to press forward. At first the others tried to keep up with him, then they gradually allowed themselves to fall behind. Garth was the only person who had actually sighted the Noir Vulture: he had seen it, or something closely resembling it, while hunting white-tailed deer as a boy of twelve. Albert had never seen it but believed fervently in it. Young Dave Cinquefoil and Benjamin Stone of course hadn't any idea what they were hunting—only that it had carried off and devoured an infant, and must be killed. Gideon had convinced himself that he had once seen the bird, many years ago, but the creature in his mind's eye was shimmering and indistinct, a fabulous bird composed of steaming vapors, with a glaring red eye and a daggerlike beak. It was a monster and must be killed. It had, after all, carried off a Bellefleur child . . . it had carried off *his* child.

His long desperate strides carried Gideon away from the others, but he took no notice. A dangerous way to hunt, but he took no notice. In the distance he heard a curious sound: at the very first it put him in mind of bowling (for he frequented the bars of certain roadside bowling alleys where, over the months, he had made interesting new acquaintances); then he thought it must be thunder, low and rumbling; then he wondered if it might be a waterfall. He was climbing a ridge, the marshy land to his right, and it was altogether likely that a small river or creek lay ahead. He *thought* there might be a waterfall—he believed he had once hunted this area, many years ago.

The thunderous sound rose and fell, and went silent. But it had come from somewhere close by. Gideon, panting, climbed the ridge as the sun began to shine with a sudden summery warmth. The swamp to his right gave off a rich brackish odor of decay and the tall pale oatlike grasses through which he plunged smelled of moisture and heat. He was suddenly very excited—he heard laughter ahead—he raised his gun and touched his trembling finger lightly against one of the triggers.

And then—and then, at the top of the grassy knoll, he found himself staring down in astonishment at a group of children. They were playing in a meadow. The grass was short, and extremely green; it was close-cropped enough to be pastureland, but Gideon was certain that this land wasn't used for grazing. The children were playing rowdily, shouting at one another, emitting high-pitched squeaking laughter. They were bowling—lawn bowling—it must have been a schoolhouse picnic—but why were they trespassing on Bellefleur land, and who were they?—and where was their teacher? The sound of the wooden balls (which were about the size of croquet balls) striking the clubs was disproportionately loud, as if the noise echoed in a small room, ricocheting off a low ceiling. Gideon flinched. The children's high-pitched laughter was also extremely loud. Though ordinarily Gideon liked children and even the idea of children it struck him suddenly that he didn't like *these* children and would take pleasure in running them off his land. . . .

So he descended the slope, shouting at them. They turned in amazement, their faces screwed up in angry, belligerent expressions, and he saw that they weren't children—they were midgets—some fifteen or twenty midgets—or were they (since their heads were oversized and their bodies misshapen, some of them quite grotesquely, with humps between their shoulders and crooked, caved-in chests) dwarves?—but why were they trespassing on *his* property—and where had they come from—

Gideon recklessly approached them, and though he saw, to his mild alarm, that they weren't backing away, that they were staring at him, in fact, with queer frozen expressions—grimaces so contorted they appeared to be involuntary, as if facial muscles had locked in spasms—eyes half-shut or screwed up in malevolent mocking winks—ugly little grins in which the preternaturally wide mouths were held shut and the thin, pale lips were stretched tight against the teeth—still he continued down the hill, slipping and sliding, though the safety lock wasn't on his gun and what he was doing was extremely unwise.

The force of the first wooden ball, striking him on the shoulder, was enough to nearly fell him; and in his pain and surprise he actually dropped the shotgun—but in another instant, acting before he had time to think, he snatched it up again. By then, however, the dwarves were upon him. Shouting and jabbering and squeaking, obviously furious despite their frozen screwed-up faces, they swarmed up the hill, like a pack of wild dogs, exactly like a pack of wild dogs, and one seized Gideon by the thigh and another climbed up him and seized his hair, knocking him over by the sheer weight of his body (which, though stunted and undersized, was remarkably heavy), and before Gideon had time to cry out he felt teeth sink in the fleshy part of his hand, and there was a terrible paralyzing kick to his groin, so that he nearly lost consciousness, and the high-pitched squeaking was exactly like that of shrews devouring prey—even other shrews—and even in the midst of his wild desperate struggling (for he *wanted,* ah, how he *wanted* to live) Gideon knew that they were going to kill him: these ugly misshapen creatures were going to kill *him,* Gideon Bellefleur—!

But of course it was not to be, for Garth had come up behind Gideon, and, at that unearthly sight, simply fired into the air; and the little men, terrified, scrambled off Gideon. Even in his consternation Garth was a cautious enough hunter to aim away from his uncle—he had time for only one more shot, so he turned to fire at a dwarf who had been jumping about at the edge of the commotion, tearing at his dark coarse hair with both hands, in a paroxysm of excitement. The buckshot tore into the hideous little creature's right arm and shoulder, and brought him down at once.

The other dwarves fled. Though panicked, they had prudence enough to snatch up their bowling balls and clubs, and not one was to be found afterward; but the meadow was so badly chewed up, it was not difficult to ascertain that a peculiar game of some kind had been played there. . . . By the time Albert, Dave, and Benjamin arrived, out of breath, the other dwarves had disappeared, and only the one Garth had shot remained. He was groaning and writhing about, bleeding from innumerable little wounds, his great misshapen head flailing from side to side, his clawlike fingers plucking at the grass. In silence the men gazed down upon him. They had never seen anything *quite* like him. . . . Not only was the creature hunchbacked, but his spine had curved so brutally that his jaw was mashed against his chest; he looked (the image flew into Gideon's mind, though he was staggering with pain and exhaustion) like a young April fern, coiled up, so tightly coiled up you would never think it might grow straight and flare out into its extraordinary beauty. . . . But, this creature, how ugly!—how repulsive! His shoulders appeared to be muscle-bound, and his neck was as thick as a man's thigh; his hair was coarse and shaggy and without luster as a horse's mane; there was an indentation on his forehead, a mark deep in the bone itself, and the skull had grown about it asymmetrically. As he whimpered and groaned and begged for mercy (for his queer gibberish, which sounded part Indian, part German, part English, was quite intelligible) he opened his mouth wide, as if grinning, and it is not an exaggeration to say that the mouth extended almost fully across his broad face, traversing the muscular cheeks. He flopped over onto his belly and began to crawl, dragging himself, toward a patch of higher grass and weeds, like a wounded turtle. The sight of his oily blood on the ground went to Albert's head; he drew out his long hunter's knife and begged permission from Gideon to cut the thing's throat. Just to put him out of his misery! Just to shut up that babbling! But Gideon said no, no, better not. . . . But didn't he lay *hands* on you, Albert said, didn't he *touch* you! And he ran over, fairly dancing with excitement, to the patch of weeds in which the dwarf lay, clutching frantically at the soil and grass, and seized hold of the dwarf's hair, and lifted his head in triumph. Gideon, please, he begged. Gideon. Gideon. Just this once. Ah, *Gideon* . . .

No, better not, Gideon said, adjusting his clothing, sucking at his wounded hand, after all the thing is *human*.

They called him Nightshade because it was a patch of purple nightshade he had dragged himself into, and they noted with what desperation, and what remarkable skill, he was crushing leaves and berries and mashing them against his wound. Within a few minutes the worst of the bleeding had stopped. And so efficacious was the nightshade juice that the creature did not afterward suffer any infection, and within a few weeks appeared to have totally forgotten his injury.

Long afterward Gideon was to regret not having allowed his nephew to slit Nightshade's throat: but, after all, how could he have foreseen the future, and how, in any case, could he take it upon himself to condemn even so repulsive a creature to death? Killing in the heat of a fight was merely killing, but killing in such a manner was murder. . . . No Bellefleur has ever committed murder, Gideon said.

So they brought the dwarf home, carrying him for five torturous miles from a maple limb held at either end by Garth and Albert (his ankles and wrists bound, he was unceremoniously slung from the pole, like a carcass), and then laying him in the back of the pick-up truck. He had long since lost consciousness: but each time they checked his feeble heartbeat (for, if he had died, it would be wisest just to dump him into a gully) they saw that he *was* alive, and would probably remain so. . . . What a *heavy* little bastard he is, they exclaimed.

Because Gideon had saved his life Nightshade was always craven before him, and would possibly have adored him—as he adored Leah— had he not sensed Gideon's nature, and prudently shied away from him whenever they happened to see each other. But at the very sight of Leah —Leah striding into the room—though her hair was disheveled and she looked somewhat drawn—not *quite* herself—a moan escaped from Nightshade's lips, and he flung himself to the floor, and kissed it, in honor of the woman he took to be mistress of Bellefleur Manor.

Leah stared at the hunchback, stepping back from his desperate furious kissing; she stared, her lips parted, and it was a long moment before she looked up to her husband, who was watching her with a small calm malicious smile. "What—what is this," Leah whispered, clearly frightened. "Who is—"

Gideon gave the dwarf a little shove with his foot, pressing the heel of his boot against the hump. "Can't you see? Can't you guess?" he said. The color had flooded back into his face and he looked quite triumphant. "He's come a long distance to serve you."

"But who is— I don't understand—" Leah said, drawing back.

"Why, it's another lover, can't you see!"

"Another lover . . ."

Leah looked at Gideon, her face furrowed and her lips puckered as if she were tasting something vile.

"Another—!" she whispered. "But I have none now—"

In time—in a very short time—Leah came to find Nightshade delightful, and took him on as a special servant, *her* servant, since he was so clearly infatuated with her. With his immense shaggy head and his small eyes and the ugly hump between his shoulders he was, as she said, a piteous sight —a pitiable sight—and it would be cruel for them to turn him away. And then he was remarkably strong. He could lift things, force things, unscrew caps, scramble with enviable agility up a stepladder to make a difficult repair; he could carry, single-handedly, a guest's entire luggage into the house, showing no indication of strain except the minute trembling of his legs. Leah outfitted him in livery, and from somewhere he acquired straps, belts, buckles, and little leather pouches, and wooden boxes, which gave to his costume a quaint, gnomish look. (Though he was certainly not a troll, as Leah said repeatedly, often in amused anger: Bromwell's official definition was *dwarf,* and *dwarf* it must be.)

He spoke rarely, and always with a fussy show of deference. Leah was *Miss Leah,* uttered in a half-swooning murmur, as he bowed before her, bent nearly double, a comical and somehow—or so Leah thought—a touching sight. He could play the mouth organ, and did simple magic tricks with buttons and coins, and even, when he was especially inspired, with kittens: making them disappear and reappear out of his sleeves or the shadowy interior of his jacket. (Sometimes, the children saw to their half-frightened astonishment, he made things—even kittens—appear when other things, unmistakably *other* things, had disappeared!—and it alarmed them, and kept them awake at night, worrying about the fate of the things that *had* disappeared.) Though he was so silent as to appear nearly mute, Leah had the idea that he was uncommonly intelligent, and that she could rely upon his judgment. His subservience was of course embarrassing—silly and annoying and distracting—but, in a way, flattering—and if he became too profuse in his adoration she had only to give him a playful kick, and he sobered at once. Despite his freakish appearance he was a remarkably *dignified* little man. . . . Leah liked him, she couldn't help herself. She pitied him, and was amused by him, and gratified by his loyalty to her, and she liked him very much, no matter how the other Bellefleurs—and even the children, and the servants—disapproved.

How odd it was, how annoying, how selfish, Leah thought, that they didn't care for poor Nightshade. Surely they must pity him?—surely they must be impressed by his indefatigable energy and good nature, and by his willingness (and his eagerness) to work at the castle for no salary, only for room and board? She could understand Gideon's contempt, for Gideon, she had always thought, was a severely limited person, as crippled imaginatively as Nightshade was crippled physically, and the sight of something *wrong* frightened him (she recalled what a whimpering coward he had been, at Germaine's birth, and how she had had to baby them both); but it was strange that the others disliked Nightshade too. Germaine shied away from him, and the older children, and grandmother Cornelia avoided looking at him, and it was said that the servants (led by the silly superstitious Edna, who would have to be replaced before long) whispered that he was a *troll.* . . . A troll, imagine, at Bellefleur, in these modern times! But it was unmistakable, the others' dislike of him, and Leah resolved not to give in to it: not to Germaine's silly fears, not to her sister-in-law's vague mumbled objections (for Lily didn't dare speak aloud in opposition to Leah: she was *such* a coward), not even to Gideon's disdain. In time, Leah thought, they will like him well enough, they'll like him as much as *I* do.

The first night great-aunt Veronica saw him, however, Leah couldn't help but be struck by something not only peculiar but, it seemed, *irrevocable* in the older woman's attitude. When Veronica descended the wide circular stairs, one beringed hand on the railing, the other grasping her heavy dark skirts in order to lift them slightly, to keep from tripping, she happened to see Nightshade (it was his first evening as Leah's "manservant," he was wearing his handsome little livery uniform) drawing a chair close to the fire for his mistress; and in that instant she froze, froze with one high-buttoned shoe uplifted, and her hand grasping the railing tightly. How very *queerly* aunt Veronica stared at Nightshade who, on account of his stooped-over posture, did not at first see her. It was only as he withdrew, backing out of the room, bowing, that he happened to lift his eyes to her . . . and, for a fraction of a moment, he too froze . . . and Leah, who would ordinarily have found all this amusing, caught a sense, a near-indefinable sense, of Veronica's and Nightshade's mutual alarm: not as if they knew each other, for it wasn't that simple, but that, instead, (and this is very difficult to explain), what they were was kin; what each *was* called out to, and drew back from, what the *other* was. (And afterward Veronica sat leadenly at her place at dinner, pretending to sip her consommé, pushing food around on her plate as if the very sight of it nauseated her (for there was the pretense, with Veronica, that she was —despite her generous heft—a finicky eater), swallowing a few mouthfuls of claret before excusing herself and hurrying back upstairs to "retire" early.)

Nor did the cats like him. Not Ginger and Tom, or Misty, or Tristram, or Minerva; least of all Mahalaleel, whom Nightshade tried to court, offering him fresh catnip (he carried various herbs wrapped in waxed paper carefully tied with string, in his several pouches and wooden boxes), but Mahalaleel kept his magisterial distance, and would not be tempted. Once Germaine came upon Nightshade in the dim, teakwood-lined reception room, stooped over more emphatically than usual, holding something in his gloved hand and calling *Kitty-kitty-kitty, here kitty-kitty-kitty!* in his high-pitched squeaking voice—and a moment later Mahalaleel, his back and tail bristling, bounded past the little man and ran out of the room. Nightshade paused, sniffed the herb in his hand, and followed along after the cat, calling *Here kitty, here kitty, kitty-kitty-kitty* in a tireless unoffended voice.

Automobiles

It was in a handsome two-seater Buick, canary-yellow, with rakish wire-spoked wheels, that Garth and Little Goldie eloped, and in a smart little fire-engine-red Fiat with a cream-colored convertible top and polished hubcaps (a gift from Schaff for her recent birthday) that Christabel and Demuth Hodge eloped one fine autumn morning, driving, for brief periods during their gay, reckless, euphoric flight, at speeds of a hundred miles per hour despite the winding mountain roads. It was a supercharged Auburn, chalk-white, with gray upholstery and exposed exhaust pipes, of gleaming chromium, another sporty two-seater, that carried away, into the labyrinthian shadows of an unnamed foreign city, possibly Rome, the beautiful young actress "Yvette Bonner" in a film called *Lost Love* which was seen, in secret, by a number of the younger Bellefleurs (who speculated not only upon the identity of the actress—for *was* she Yolande, or did she merely *seem* to be Yolande?—but upon the probability of her having, in real life as well as on film, the tantalizingly cerebral and *yet* erotic relationship with the young mustached Frenchman who, in *Lost Love,* drove her so boldly and noisily away).

Many years ago (and there were sepia-tinted photographs to prove it) great-grandfather Jeremiah, for all his ill-luck and despondency, nevertheless owned one of the first motorcars in the area, a gaily decorated Peugeot in which passengers (including great-grandmother Elvira in a richly flowered and wide-brimmed hat that tied firmly beneath the chin) sat facing one another. In styling the Peugeot closely resembled a horse-drawn carriage, open to the wind, with bicycle-sized wire wheels and a single headlight. (Its painted arabesques, which looked, even as reproduced in a poor photograph, extremely delicate and beautiful, put Germaine in mind of certain of great-aunt Matilde's quilts.) Noel and Hiram and Jean-Pierre shared, for a while, before their father's creditors claimed it, a wonderful little Peugeot Bébé: it seated only one person comfortably, was noisy and dangerous and almost comically gaudy (with a turquoise leather seat and turquoise trim about the wheels, contrasting with the rich russet wood of the wheels; and a black-and-gold-striped body; and four oversized brass lamps; and a brass horn that gave a loud ribald sound designed to terrify horses on the road), and had the distinction of being the only car of its kind in the entire state at that time. If Hiram, as an older man, never cared for motorcars and refused to learn to drive (and disliked even the family limousine though it was driven by a highly competent chauffeur) it was possibly because he still remembered the Peugeot Bébé with great affection, and was susceptible, from time to time, to black moods, pitch-black airless moods, reminiscent of the one he suffered after the car was sold at auction. (*Why love anything if you're going to lose it, why love anyone,* he frequently mused, *if there's a possibility you will lose her. . . .* And so he hadn't, it must be said, very *seriously* loved his young wife, nor had he much love for the unfortunate Vernon, whose death was as much an embarrassment to him (for he had *known* the boy would make a fool of himself!) as a source of paternal grief.)

It might have been Stanton Pym's Morris Bullnose, as much as his audacious attempt to marry, and to survive marrying, a Bellefleur heiress, that infuriated Della's family; for though the Bullnose was a small car, and cost considerably less than the family's cars at that time (a six-cylinder Napier and a Pierce-Arrow saloon car), its pert sporty air, and its brass fixtures, struck Della's brothers and cousins as impertinent and inappropriate for a junior officer of a Nautauga Falls bank. (After Stanton's death Della sold the car at once. Both Noel and a cousin named Lawrence offered to buy it from her—and to pay a respectable sum—but Della refused. *I would rather drive it into Lake Noir and sink along with it,* she said, *than sell it to either of you.*)

Great-aunt Veronica's fiancé Ragner Norst, who called himself a count and may in fact have been one, despite the Bellefleurs' doubts (for he had been, after all, or claimed to have been, an intimate friend of the famous Count Zborowski—the very Zborowski who owned so much property in New York, and entertained lavishly in Paris, and was killed in a freak accident while driving his splendid Mercedes in a ferocious race in the South of France) drove a most impressive Lancia Lambda, black as a hearse, stately, regal, with a *monocoque* body and independent front suspension—which the Bellefleurs envied, though they *suspected* Norst had acquired it secondhand: it had curious scratches on its doors, as well as its front fenders, and its thick gunmetal-gray cushions gave off an odor not unlike that of a stagnant pond, or a tomb.

For many years the Bellefleurs drove only one "good" car—a maroon Cadillac with steel-spoked wheels, one of the first of the Fleetwood Broughams (it had carpeted foot rests and adjustable swivel-type reading lamps and mahogany fixtures, among other things) and it was this car, rather badly in need of repainting, that Gideon was given as a wedding present, so that he might drive his young bride to their secret honeymoon hotel in style: but at that time Gideon, so enamored of horses, and in any case so enamored of Leah, hardly appreciated the automobile's 7030 c.c. V8 engine, which carried them along noiselessly though they drove, often without quite knowing it, at high speeds. After the ignominious loss of the plum-colored Pierce-Arrow at Paie-des-Sables, Gideon acquired, through his Port Oriskany friend Benjamin Stone (the son of the philanthropist Waltham Stone who had made his fortune in the production of washing machines), a number of remarkable cars—the magnificent Hispano-Suiza; rebuilt Aston-Martin; a bottle-green Bentley (which Lord Dunraven very much admired); and, somewhat later, at about the time of the migrant workers' strike, a white Rolls-Royce coupe with a virtually soundless engine—by far Gideon's favorite car, at least up until the time of his accident.

Rolls, of course, was the family's near-unanimous choice for their largest car; and so, as the Bellefleur fortune swelled, they acquired, at Leah's particular insistence, a six-seater Silver Ghost with every imaginable feature—leather upholstery, hand-painted panels, silver ashtrays, silver-framed mirrors, gold fittings, and thick fur (it was a novelty fur—Alaskan wolf), carpeting: a most impressive sight, and a fittingly impressive sight, to appear at the ugly portals of the Powhatassie State Correctional Facility to bear away poor meek ashen-faced Jean-Pierre II, who was at last deemed worthy of a pardon by the governor of the state. But it was not the Rolls, of course, Leah wished to take, as, accompanied by her manservant, Nightshade, and Germaine, and young Jasper (who was developing so rapidly, who seemed to know, now, as much about the estate's finances as Hiram himself, and nearly as much as Leah), she drove south in a fruitless and really quite ill-advised attempt to locate, and bring back, her erring daughter Christabel: for that purpose Leah drove her own car, an austere, practical Nash sedan which, she calculated, would never draw attention to itself or its occupants. But of course she never found Christabel and her lover Demuth, nor did the authorities ever find the Fiat, though Edgar had reported it missing at once. (What a generous gift it had been, that bright red coupe with its cream-colored top and its dazzlingly shiny hubcaps!—and all, as the elder Mrs. Schaff said bitterly, to provide a common whore with the means of flight from her husband and family; and who knows but that the Fiat hadn't *inspired* the little whore's love affair, as well as her escape from Schaff Hall?)

Over the years there had been, not in strict chronological order (for the Bellefleurs, reminiscing, quite shamelessly jumbled "chronological" order—indeed, to Germaine's way of thinking, they had a lofty *contempt* for it), a Packard limousine, and a Pierce-Arrow saloon car, and a green Stutz-Bearcat, and something called a Scripps-Booth (which no one seemed to remember); insurance records showed a Prosper-Lambert, evidently a French car, with acetylene gas lamps and seat covers of dyed kid. There was a Dodge, and a La Salle; there were several Fords including two Model-A's, which were among the hardiest of the Bellefleur cars. Interest in automobiles varied wildly among the Bellefleurs, and was not consistent, in any single individual, throughout a lifetime: though Ewan professed to have little genuine concern for what he drove, so long as it got him from place to place quickly and economically. He viewed with something like alarm his brother Gideon's sudden infatuation with cars, which seemed to him less plausible than Gideon's earlier infatuation with horses, if only because Gideon was now a fully mature man, and no longer an impulsive boy.

Ewan himself was content to drive a good, solid, handsome American car, a Packard, though he bought for his favorite mistress (the divorcée Rosalind Manx, who called herself a "singer-actress'), through Gideon's and Benjamin Stone's assistance, a showy blue Jaguar E-type with dyed rabbit-fur upholstery and silver fixtures, which was often seen tearing along even the narrowest of Nautauga Falls streets, evidently oblivious to (and immune from) traffic police. (Ewan would not have minded if Lily had learned to drive, though he didn't encourage it, and of course hadn't time to teach her himself: but he evidently expressed amused gratification when Albert, who had tried to teach his mother to drive Leah's Nash, pronounced her hopeless.) Albert himself owned a Chevrolet Caprice which was one day to sideswipe a tenant farmer's pick-up truck, injuring Albert and killing the farmer outright; Jasper drove a smart, practical Ford, with few frills, and Morna was to one day acquire, as *her* birthday present from a new husband, a handsome chocolate-brown Porsche. Bromwell was never to acquire a car, nor was he even to learn how to drive.

The oldest automobile the Bellefleurs owned, at about the time of Germaine's birth, was grandmother Della's black two-door Ford, a gift from a sympathetic uncle-in-law (one of Elvira's brothers) so that she might, if she wished, drive herself about: but of course Della never learned to drive, and the car remained, decade after decade, unused, its battery dead, swallows nesting in its cushions, in the old carriage house behind the red-brick house in Bushkill's Ferry. Leah, as a girl, had tried unsuccessfully to start it; she had nagged Della about getting it serviced, and in working order—for, if it worked, her boy friend Nicholas Fuhr had offered to give her lessons—and it might be fun, didn't Della think, if the two of them went for Sunday drives along the river, or southward out of the mountains on an overnight trip, for a change of scene?

"Whyever would you want a change of scene," Della asked irritably (for her tomboyish daughter had such a strident, aggressive voice), "aren't things troublesome enough *here?*"

So the old black Ford remained in the carriage house, graceless, unwanted, rusting in leprous patches, covered over with a film of dust and pigeon- and swallow-droppings—and so it remains, in fact, until this very day.

The Demon

           In the mountains, in those days long ago, Jedediah Bellefleur wandered, a penitent. And when he saw that a demon had come to dwell in Henofer's cabin, that the demon had pushed himself inside the old man's grizzled chest and now stared boldly out of the old man's eyes—boldly and *mockingly,* as if daring Jedediah to recognize him!—he knew that he must not suffer the creature to live.

I know you, he whispered, advancing upon him.

The demon blinked and stared. Henofer's face had undergone many changes, perhaps it was already the face of a dead man, astonishingly aged. Though Jedediah had lived on the other side of the mountain for only a year or two or three, in that period of time Henofer had become an old man, and it was possible that his infirmity allowed the demon to slip into his body.

Of course you know me, the demon said.

That isn't *his* voice, Jedediah said, smiling. You can't quite imitate *his* voice.

His—? Whose? What do you mean?

The old man. Henofer. You didn't know him, Jedediah said. So you can't imitate his voice. You can't deceive me.

What do you mean? the demon said. In a pretense of fear he began to stammer. I'm Mack—you know me—it's Mack, Mack Henofer—for God's sake, Jedediah, are you joking? But you never joke—

Jedediah looked around the clearing. There was Henofer's sway-backed horse, and his mule; his cowardly hound lay with his belly pressed flat against the ground and his ragged tail limply wagging, as if, having made peace with his master's murderer, he now wished to make peace with his master's avenger.

On a crude wooden rack by the doorway of Henofer's cabin there were several hides—bloodstained and ragged and unrecognizable—raccoons, foxes, beavers, squirrels, bobcats? The sight of them was a surprise.

I didn't know *you* could work the trap lines, Jedediah said, eying the creature with a sly smile.

Where Henofer would have laughed his wheezy blustery laugh, the demon, again pretending to be frightened, stared at Jedediah and moved his lips silently. A prayer to the Devil, perhaps, but Jedediah did not draw away.

You can't live on this mountain. This is a Holy Mountain, Jedediah said calmly. Henofer might have welcomed you—probably did—probably invited you to stay the night and drink with him and listen to his foul disgusting stories—yes?—but he never understood the nature of this mountain and he deserved to die. But *you:* you can't stay here. God will not tolerate it.

Henofer's lips parted in a queer gaping grin. It was not *Henofer's* smile but the demon's, and it bore no resemblance at all to the old man's.

You aren't well, Jedediah, the demon said. And then tried to offer him a drink—asked him to come inside that shanty, and have a drink—but God distressed him at that moment with a fit of coughing that left his blubbery lips wet with dark spittle.

Jedediah stood his ground, waiting. Though he harbored no fear of the Devil his insides were trembling and he had to fight the desire to join old Henofer in that wracking terrible cough.

The hound began to bay, its stump of a tail flopping about.

Jedediah wondered—Was there a demon, a dog-demon, coiled up inside that sorry creature?—would it too have to be destroyed? Or was the dog untouched, deemed by the Prince of Darkness as too lowly to be contaminated?

Though God refused still to show His face to Jedediah He made it known that Jedediah was the means by which His message would be broadcast. *The jaws devour, the jaws are devoured.* And again, louder, in a terrible bugle-blast of a voice: *The jaws devour, the jaws are devoured. So the Lord God has spoken.*

As penance for having raised his voice on the Holy Mountain Jedediah was to wander for an unfixed number of days, or weeks, or months —God would instruct him more specifically—and if his camp should be destroyed, if wild creatures should devour his vegetable garden and thieves break into his cabin and plunder it, and set fire to it, God's will be done. *The jaws devour, the jaws are devoured.*

There was a paradox in God's teaching. For though Jedediah had been chosen (and, again, it was difficult to discern God's wrath from His love) nevertheless he was forbidden to leave the mountains: he must, for instance, never leave the sight of Mount Blanc. When he lay down to sleep, having resisted sleep for as long as possible (for that too was part of God's instruction), he must face the mountain; and when he opened his eyes in the morning the mountain must be the first thing he saw—the first image to fill his stupefied consciousness. On those mornings when the great mountain was obscured by mist Jedediah lay paralyzed, blinking as if the entire world had vanished in his sleep.

He preached to the few people he encountered. Trappers like old Henofer; a party of hunters (how smartly dressed they were, how costly their shotguns and rifles and gear must have been!—they smiled upon Jedediah pityingly, yet with a kind of courteous patience; but their Indian guide—a tall big-stomached Mohawk who wore a white man's hat and carried a rifle heavy with silver ornamentation—fixed him with an unmistakable contemptuous stare); a settlement of four families on the south bank of the Nautauga, near a nameless crossroads (they frowned and grinned and jabbered at *him*, finally, in a foreign tongue, which he knew was not French, and which he could not hope to comprehend without God's grace). He approached a contingent of soldiers walking in loose columns along a dusty road, but they had no time for him, and their officer playfully—it may have been *seriously*—aimed his rifle at Jedediah's feet, and bade him begone into the woods before an "accident" took place. Nor had he any more luck with a group of men, working with oxen and mules, who appeared to be digging a canal from east to west, out of nowhere and into nowhere, a ludicrous blasphemy in the sight of God (for why build a canal when the mountains were so richly veined with lakes and rivers?—why disfigure God's landscape on a human, vainglorious whim?)—many of the men did not understand English, and even those who seemed to be speaking English did not understand Jedediah, and soon grew impatient with him, and drove him back into the woods with rocks and chunks of mud and obscene taunting shouts. All these humiliations Jedediah endured for God's sake, and in full expectation that God should someday soon reward him. For he was, after all, God's servant: all that had been Jedediah Bellefleur was swallowed up in God.

The jaws devour, the jaws are devoured. But the forces of darkness did not want this message taught. And so Jedediah was aware of God's enemies, and of his own father's spies, watching him from the shadows at the edges of clearings, from behind rocks, from inside crude rotting shelters that appeared to be abandoned but which he dared not approach, not even in the most ferocious of rainstorms. Sometimes it was unclear, which were God's enemies and which were his own: his father (whose name Jedediah had temporarily forgotten though he could see, in his troubled dreams, the wicked old man's face as vividly as if it floated before him) was perhaps an enemy of God, but then he had always seemed too caught up with the vanities of the world, too *busy*, to care enough about God to actively oppose him: or was this merely an aspect of the old sinner's cunning? It was true that he had repudiated Roman Catholicism when he repudiated his homeland, and his mother tongue, and set his face to the

West, and he had sloughed off this corrupt devil-ridden religion as easily as if he had done no more than wash his hands; and of course that must have pleased God. But he had erected no other belief in place of Catholicism, so far as Jedediah knew. He worshipped money. Political power, gambling, land speculation, horses, women, businesses of one kind or another—Henofer had told him many things, Jedediah remembered very little—but in the end only money, everything was transformed into money: money was his God. And was that God identical with Satan himself?

The old man, the wicked old man, wanted Jedediah to return to the flatland. So that he might marry, and propagate his kind; so that he might, like his brother Louis, bring sons into the world, to continue the Bellefleur name, and the Bellefleur worship of money. (Which was—or *was it?*—identical with the worship of Satan.) Sometimes, Jedediah rather wearily thought, the money-worshippers were too obsessed with their struggles to devour one another to think, even, of the Devil—they would have had no time for Mammon himself.

Still, there were enemies, enemies whose faces he never saw, but whose presences he sensed: at times, on windless nights, he could even hear their breathing. Shadows at the edges of clearings . . . shadows that came to life, stirring grouse and pheasants into terrified flight, sending rabbits across Jedediah's panicked field of vision. . . . Behind each of the larger pines a man might easily hide, if he were very cautious, and when Jedediah turned his back he might lean out to stare at him. These spies were probably in his father's pay. For it was not *logical,* Jedediah supposed, after long brooding, that mere strangers should care so much about him; and if there were devils (though could there, on the Holy Mountain, even in sight of the Holy Mountain, be devils?—would God permit such a blasphemy?), devils of course were bodiless, or so Jedediah understood, and would not need to hide behind trees or rocks.

That a devil might force himself *into* a man's body, and dwell inside that body, and wreak evil from within it—Jedediah hadn't comprehended at that time.

So he feared the presences, and traveled at night in order to confuse them, and hid during the day, as best he could (for sometimes he was overtaken by a painful hacking cough that seemed to be tearing his lungs out, and surely the creatures who spied upon him heard); and he tried to keep his heart alive with a constant prayer to God which his lips uttered at all times. *My God, my Lord and my God, blessed be Thy name, blessed be Thy kingdom, and Thy will, and Thine enemies ground underfoot. . . .*

One day, someone whispered in his ear, close against his ear, breathing warmly and tickling with her tongue, one day, Jedediah, you know what's going to happen?—they're going to jump at you from behind, and overpower you, no matter how you struggle and howl with rage, and they're going to carry you back down to home—hanging from a pole, maybe, like a gutted deer—and you'll wake up on a floor with them

standing around gaping and grinning at you—poking you with a foot—
Is *that* Jedediah Bellefleur who climbed into the sky looking for God—!
Why, isn't he a sight, now! Scrawny and puny and sick and lousy (for you
do have lice, that's a louse at this very moment crawling up the back of
your neck!) and worm-ridden too (for you *do,* you know, have worms—
you might not like to think of it, and you surely refuse to examine your
hard little bloody droppings, but even so, my boy, even so!)—*isn't* he a
sight—as if any self-respecting God would give a good goddamn for *him.*
And would any woman marry him? Have babies by him? Oh, what a joke!
God's been laughing up His sleeve for eighteen years now! And she
skittered away, shrieking with laughter, before Jedediah could lay hands
on her.

In his wanderings, before he came upon Mack Henofer's camp, and
saw what had happened there, Jedediah suffered many ugly sights. One
day he stepped out of the blazing tide of noon into the darkness of a forest
that rose out of marshy, spongy land, and saw a cannibal Indian seated
before a small fire, cross-legged, smoking a pipe, clothed in what appeared to be snakeskins—while all about him, in small tumbled-over
mounds, were the skulls and bones of human beings. They were human
bones, most assuredly they were human! And the snakeskins, Jedediah
saw to his terror, were not skins at all but living snakes: living snakes that
coiled and hissed about the brave's powerful naked body. (The snakes
appeared aware of Jedediah's intrusion, but the Indian—vacant-eyed,
expressionless, puffing soundlessly on his pipe—stared past him.) Long
after Jedediah fled that hellish vision, for days and weeks afterward, he
was to remember the horror of the heaped-up skulls and bones, and the
thick-bodied hissing snakes, and most of all the Indian's stony impassivity. . . . Hadn't Jedediah heard, as a boy, that the cannibals among the
Iroquois tribes had been exterminated, or converted to Christianity? And
how was it possible that the Indian should be clad in *living* snakes?

(The evil of the pagan Indians, Jedediah thought, was an evil that
came before the white man's—before the white man's evil, or his good.
It came before history itself. Perhaps even before God.)

And one day he saw a doe beset by dogs, farmers' dogs running loose
in a pack, snarling and yipping in a frenzy as they tore her apart—tore
at her immense swollen belly, where she carried a fetus that would have
been dropped in a week or two: he saw, and he fled, covering his ears,
his ceaseless prayer to God rising to an involuntary shout. *My Lord and
my God, my Lord and my God, have mercy. . . .*

And strangest of all he saw, suspended in a dark swamp pond,
fringed with rushes and cattails and water willow, a queer white floating
face: a stranger's face in which the eyes were so colorless as to be nearly
indistinct; and the chin, beardless, melted away into nothing. A human
face, yet with less substance than the skulls of the cannibal Indian. It was
strange, too, that the pond should be so lightless, so brackish, since it was
probably only a few feet deep, and fed by a fresh-running brook. But

Jedediah could not see its bottom. He saw only the ghostly floating face with its weak melting-away chin and its helpless smudged eyes, and he drew back in revulsion as well as in alarm.

And then one day, without intending it, he came upon Mack Henofer's campsite, and saw at once, in the first moment of the old man's shouted greeting and the dog's yipping, that Henofer had been plundered, his soul laid waste, his physical being taken over by a demon. How terrifying it was, to lift his eyes to Henofer's and to see, not Henofer's eyes at all, but those of a demon. . . .

"Jedediah! Jedediah Bellefleur! *Is* that you?"

He had known Henofer was a spy of his father's, a paid spy, but he had found it in his heart to forgive him; for vengeance is God's, after all. But now Henofer himself had been eradicated and what stared out at him from the old man's rheumy eyes was not even human.

"Jedediah Bellefleur," the demon crowed in triumph, before he understood that Jedediah had found him out, "aren't you a surprise on this side of the mountain!—aren't you a *sight!* Or is that even you, my boy? You look so different! My eyes, these days, they been giving me trouble —especially in the sun like this—Jedediah? Why don't you answer? You're thirsty, aren't you? Hungry? *Is* that you, looking so strange?"

He extended a broad dirty hand for Jedediah to shake, but Jedediah stood his ground. I know who you are, he whispered.

The Death
of Stanton Pym

In his smart little imported car, a two-seater Morris Bullnose with brass fixtures and aqua finish and aqua-and-orange spoked wheels, and its black convertible top rarely up, even in troubled weather (for he liked, the Bellefleurs saw, to be observed driving through Bellefleur Village on his way to the lakeshore road and the manor—Stanton Pym in a candy-striped sports coat and a pert straw hat with a red band, a bookkeeper's son and a canal digger's grandson courting in public the daughter of a man who, had he wished, might claim blood ties with one of France's oldest noble families), maneuvering the sporty car with a boyish self-consciousness along the graveled curves, as if confident he were being watched by envious eyes. Della's suitor appeared on Saturdays and Sundays and occasionally on Wednesday evenings to take her for long dusty drives around the lake, or to the Falls for dinner, or rowing on Silver Lake, or (on Wednesday evenings) to church services at the little white squat-steepled Methodist church on the Falls Road, or to the county fairgrounds where they might stroll hand in hand (so it was reported to the Bellefleurs) from one farm exhibit to another, and from one amusement to another, eating cotton candy and candied apples and hot buttered popcorn and drinking lemonade like any other young couple— except of course the match was doomed, and it was generally known that the suitor himself was doomed should he persist (but how *could* he, since he wasn't a stupid young man?) in the courtship.

The man who was to be Germaine's grandfather—her *other* grandfather—was, at the age of twenty-seven, already a bank officer in the First National Bank of Nautauga Falls. Apart from his natty dress (which of course was reserved for weekends) and his habit of repeating jokes judged to be only mildly amusing, he was a serious, even rather grave young man—wonderfully ambitious—bright and hard-working and wonderfully ambitious, as the bank's president told Noel Bellefleur one day. He had a talent for bank work and had specialized in mortgage loans. He *knew* a great deal. ". . . Is my financial situation part of what the young bastard knows?" Noel asked.

Of course it was clear that Stanton Pym was pursuing Della Bellefleur for her money and property—or for the promise of it, when she inherited; why otherwise would he have switched so readily, and, it seemed, so adroitly, from his courtship of the daughter of a Falls glove manufacturer to Della, when the glove manufacturer's business was sold at a loss?— though of course Stanton Pym withdrew from his pursuit of the girl long before the factory was actually sold, and before, even, rumors surfaced. It was simply the case, people said admiringly, that the bright young man *knew* a great deal.

At the First National Bank of Nautauga Falls Pym dressed in well-tailored and somber three-piece suits, and walked about with an almost military briskness and formality. If his grandfather had slaved in the pitiless midsummer sun to help build the Great Canal, and had died, of an undiagnosed internal hemorrhage, while lifting a shovel heavy with wet clay, at the age of forty-three; if his father had ruined his eyes and developed a hump between his shoulder blades, working a fourteen-hour day as an assistant bookkeeper for the largest textile mill in the region, and if he was dismissed after thirty years' service with no more than a token "pension"—exactly why, no one knew, though the dismissal might have had something to do with the man's failing eyesight and his perpetual melancholia—young Stanton seemed to know nothing of these indignities, and sometimes seemed, if questioned by people from his old neighborhood, to know nothing, with an almost charmingly innocent arrogance, of his family at all, living or dead. He gave his mother part of his salary, of course, and visited her as often as possible, but his new responsibilities—his new life—took up most of his time.

If, in the First National Bank with its sepulchral pretensions (though it was not the largest bank in Nautauga Falls it boasted a truly impressive neo-Georgian façade, and its floors, of simulated marble, were agreeably cold; it had cut- and frosted glass windows and, guarding the stairs to the vault, a pewter grille weighty as a medieval portcullis) young Stanton Pym dressed with admirable sobriety, and if he was careful to appear not only modest but self-effacing at the Methodist ceremonies he attended, at other times—Saturdays and Sundays in particular—he dressed in the latest men's styles and, had he been somewhat taller, and his eyes less close-set, he would have been one of the most striking of the "new" young men. (They sometimes appeared to be everywhere in those days —ambitious sons of farmers or even farmers' laborers—back from serving in the army, or back from a two-year course at business school, considerably taller than their parents, with firm frank handshakes and expectant smiles, and no intention whatsoever of living as their families had lived.)

Pym had no more than two or three outfits for each season, but by switching vests, wearing different shoes (sometimes white, sometimes white-and-brown, sometimes brown, sometimes black, depending upon the season and the time of day) and different neckties and hats, he was able to give the impression of being fashionable as any of the wealthier young men. (Far more "fashionable," after all, than the Bellefleurs—for young Noel and his many cousins cared more for horses, hunting, fishing, boating and other masculine preoccupations than they did for society.) In summer months he wore white as often as possible—white trousers, smartly creased; white shoes; the red-and-white-striped blazer; even white gloves—despite its impracticality (for he had, after all, an automobile to contend with—first a Model-T, which demanded a fair amount of tinkering and adjusting, and then the little English car, acquired second-hand from one of the bank's customers). It was in this jaunty summer costume that Della Bellefleur first saw him, on the boardwalk at White Sulphur Springs.

He was escorting the glove manufacturer's daughter, whom Della of course knew, but knew slightly, and without any great warmth. A slender young man, no more than Della's height, a year or two younger than she, perhaps, with pomaded dark hair parted precisely in the center of his head, and a small dark mustache, like a fuzzy caterpillar, riding his short upper lip. That Sunday, he even carried a cane with an ebony knob. Della and Stanton Pym exchanged no more than a half-dozen words upon that occasion, for there were so many other people close about, in his party and in her own, but Della sensed immediately—and was never to be shaken from her conviction, not thirty years after Pym's death—that Pym, *before* being introduced to her, *before* knowing she was one of the two Bellefleur heiresses, had stared at her with a curious startled intensity as if . . . as if he recognized her . . . or saw something in her face. . . . As if, in that first moment, on the crowded White Sulphur Springs boardwalk, he *knew*.

(Perhaps it was not love at first sight, Della was one day to tell Germaine, as she turned the pages of her old photograph album, because I don't believe such a phenomenon exists . . . and if it does, it's immoral. But there is such a thing as immediate regard. Immediate sympathy. And intelligent and fully conscious *awareness* of another's worth.)

At that time Della was twenty-nine years old. She was not a pretty woman, nor even—with her long nose and her prim censorious stare—a very attractive woman, but she carried herself proudly, and was known for her common sense and her reliability; her smile, when she smiled, *could* be appealing. It had been the family's intention for some years to marry her to a cousin-twice-removed who lived in the Falls with his widowed mother and spent his time speculating, fairly modestly, in real estate, but the match was stalemated by Della's and the cousin's silence on the subject. Do you actively dislike Elias, Della's mother and aunts interrogated her, is there anything about him that strikes you as unaccept-able . . . ? Or are you simply being stubborn? *Why* don't you say some-thing?

But Della said nothing, and though she and her cousin were brought together frequently, and encouraged to stroll about alone together, their "match" rested in a kind of apathetic equilibrium. They would be married someday—perhaps—but in the meantime there was no engagement. Della was spoken for, and no other suitors stepped forward, and the years passed, and though Della's mother and aunts discussed the situation tirelessly Della herself refused to discuss it at all. She quite liked her virginal status. She was *not* stubborn, as she frequently declared.

And then, suddenly, there was Stanton Pym.

How Pym knew about Della's conversion to Methodism, how he knew that she attended Wednesday evening services at the little country church (but not Sunday services: the family forbade *that*), how he managed to insinuate himself into her company there (for Della, being a Bellefleur, tended to hold herself somewhat apart from the others, even in her enthusiasm for their religion), how he managed to overcome her suspicions; no one knew. But suddenly they were "courting." They were said to be "sweet on each other." Noel learned that Pym went to the Methodist church only on Wednesdays, and that he had never been a serious churchgoer in the past; he learned that Pym had begun seeing Della only a week after withdrawing as a candidate for the hand of the glove manufacturer's daughter. He's after her, the Bellefleurs said, with an air of genuine surprise, he's actually *after* her. . . . Pym himself so misjudged Della's family's attitude toward him that he was always extend-ing his hand to the men when they happened to meet, smiling his perky little smile, commenting on the weather, telling jokes. (He very much enjoyed his own jokes and laughed richly at them, though never in the funereal recesses of the First National Bank.)

The family disapproved, quite vocally, but of course Della paid them no mind: she went out with Pym in the Morris Bullnose, delighted as a young girl, her flower-bedecked hat tied firmly beneath her chin. The two of them were seen on the amusement rides at the state fair, they were seen rowing at Silver Lake, at sunset, and dining together by candlelight in the Nautauga House; Della even admitted, after close questioning, to having been introduced to Stanton's mother. (Of course the mother is impossi-ble, Della said stiffly, she kept touching my arm and fawning on me and asking the most ridiculous questions—how many servants we had, how many rooms in the house, if it was true that my father had once been kidnapped—but, after all, Stanton is as critical of the poor woman as I am, and knows her faults thoroughly: and Stanton *isn't* anything like her. They are two quite separate and distinct persons.)

When it was pointed out to Della—now by Elvira, now by her broth-ers Noel and Hiram, even by her sister Matilde—that the young man was pursuing her only because she was an heiress, she simply waved the notion away as if it were completely absurd.

You don't know Stanton as I do, she said.

Stanton was of course to die an accidental death, as the witnesses and the coroner were to attest, yet long before the accident, long before the marriage, when he was warned of the possible dangers of marrying Della Bellefleur against her family's wishes, he waved the notion away as if it too were completely absurd. Della and I are in love, he said simply.

But the Bellefleurs—! Wasn't he afraid of *them?*

You don't understand, he would say, smiling. Della and I are in love. We know exactly what we are doing.

Though she was nearly thirty years old, and a fully mature woman, Della was sent away over the summer to visit with some of Elvira's relatives in another part of the state; and she and Pym were forbidden to see each other. They wrote letters faithfully but of course the letters were intercepted and opened, and their laconic, pious, possibly codified messages were read contemptuously aloud. It was noted that the words *engagement* and *marriage* were frequently used. And that they professed their *love* for each other: but always in a judicious, fairly formal manner. (The letters, at least, Della's family said, are not obscene.) While Della was away Pym suffered two unrelated accidents, both of them minor: the brakes of his automobile failed and he ran off the road, into a thicket of scrub pine; when he went to open his bedroom window one evening the window came loose, toppling over on him, and broken glass flew everywhere—cutting him, fortunately, only superficially. In telling Stanton Pym's story afterward, over the years, members of the Bellefleur family, with the exception, of course, of Della, usually emphasized the paradoxical fact that while Pym might very well have expected to be killed by Della's relatives, or at least badly beaten, he *did* die, in the end, an entirely accidental death—as if his fate were predetermined, and had nothing to do with Della at all.

Della returned at the end of the summer, and the couple became engaged at once. Pym was transferred to the new bank branch at Bushkill's Ferry, where he would be assistant manager, and he arranged to buy, with the aid of a considerable mortgage, an old but fairly attractive red-brick house with a clear view of the lake and, in the distance, Bellefleur Manor. If he encountered Bellefleur men on the street he always called out a hearty hello, and insisted upon shaking hands, no matter how coldly they eyed him; one day Lawrence, driving the handsome old gold-ornamented phaeton that had been his father's, on his way to see *his* fiancée, nearly had a serious accident when his team of matched horses reared up in a panic at the noisy approach of the Morris Bullnose—and rather than apologize for the horses' distress, Stanton Pym climbed out of his car and shook hands with Lawrence, amiably, as if it were all a lark; in fact he used the opportunity to tell Lawrence one of his jokes, which was especially inappropriate under the circumstances. (A man and a woman, on their honeymoon. The bridegroom's horse misbehaves. The bridegroom counts three, slowly, before whipping it. Next, the bridegroom's hound misbehaves. Again the bridegroom counts three, slowly, before whipping it. And then there is a disagreement between the bridegroom and his new bride: and slowly he begins to count, *One, two* . . .) Stanton exploded in childish laughter, throwing his head back so hard that his straw hat flew off. He was clearly in excellent spirits. He was clearly not in the least afraid of Lawrence. Before taking his leave he invited Lawrence to come visit him and Della after the wedding—for by then, as he said, with a parting smile, "Everything will be settled."

The wedding took place in late September, at the Methodist church, attended by only a few relatives. Della had a trust fund which paid a small but by no means contemptible dividend, and Stanton's new position at the bank was a highly promising one, and they *seemed,* according to visitors, happy enough: at any rate Elvira soon received word that Della was pregnant. Of course she could not stay away from her daughter, no matter how she disliked her son-in-law; and then, as time passed, she did not *really* dislike him all that much . . . though of course she disapproved of him . . . disapproved, at any rate, of the idea of him. For the young man himself, even with his foolish little mustache, was well mannered and cheerful and devoted to Della. Or so it seemed. So, indeed, it *seemed*— as Elvira declared to the others. But what else have we to go on? Shouldn't we perhaps begin to relent, since in the end we'll forgive them anyway?

So it came about that the young couple was invited to the castle, and a number of belated wedding presents were given them. Months before the baby was scheduled to be born Della was allowed to choose among the nursery's several antique cradles; Pym was invited to join the men for cards. (He always lost at cards with the Bellefleurs—but not *too* badly, so that while Della was vexed she had no reason to be seriously upset.) They were invited to spend several days at the castle during the Christmas holiday, when a number of other relatives and guests were to be there, and it certainly looked—it *looked*—as if the marriage were being tacitly accepted. (At no point did anyone take Pym aside, of course, and welcome him into the family; or even shake his hand with an expression of pleasure. But then the Bellefleurs were always reticent about their feelings. They would not have wanted to be called *sentimental.*)

It was on Christmas Eve that Pym was killed in a toboggan accident on Sugarloaf Hill. All that day there had been a fair amount of drinking and feasting (and Christmas Day promised a roast suckling pig, and champagne for breakfast), and perhaps Pym was simply unaccustomed to so much celebrating. It was believed that he and Della quarreled sometime during the afternoon, hidden away in their room on the third floor, but it wasn't known what they quarreled about. (Did Della object, suddenly, to her brothers' and cousins' interest in Pym? Was she jealous? For

her young husband's head was being turned, flattered by Noel and Lawrence in particular, and he seemed quite cheerfully willing to make a fool
of himself on ice skates, on the lake, and roughing about in the snow as
if he had been doing this sort of thing with the Bellefleurs all his life.)
    The Bellefleurs were betting on toboggan races with the Fuhrs and
the Renauds, and there was much good-natured horseplay out on the hill,
and more drinking. Beer, ale, Scotch, bourbon, straight gin, straight
vodka, and various brandies were being consumed. Della was to learn
afterward only that her husband had insisted upon taking part in the race
—had insisted that he knew how to handle a toboggan—though to her
knowledge he had never done anything of the sort before. That the men
would attempt Sugarloaf Hill on its steepest side, at night, with the moon
nearly obscured by clouds—that they would risk their necks in an absurd
bet (the winning toboggan was to collect only $200, to be divided up
between five or six men)—that they would plunge downward in the face
of a bitter northeast wind, with the temperature already minus five degrees: all this suggested drunkenness, swinish drunkenness.
    There were so many versions of what happened on the hill, some
overlapping and some flatly contradicting one another, that Della, in her
grief and fury, soon gave up attempting to sort out the truth from the lies.
She knew only that three toboggans raced—that poor Stanton, in a red
stocking-cap and muffler, doubtless quite drunk, had been in the fourth
position on the Bellefleur sled—that while in the lead the Bellefleur sled
struck an exposed rock and hurtled off to one side, toward a grove of
pines—the order was given to jump—and amid much shouting and
laughter the men did jump, happy to abandon the expensive toboggan
to its fate: but of course Stanton, who knew nothing of tobogganing, was
abandoned along with the sled, and killed outright when it smashed
against a pine. As quickly as that it happened—as quickly as it takes to
recount the incident—one moment the poor befuddled young man was
alive, and the next moment he was dead, thrown against a tree trunk like
a rag doll, his face so badly mutilated that several of the men, so drunk
they could barely stagger to where he lay, quarreled at first about who
it was.
    "But you know," one of them said finally, with inspired drunken
logic, "it must be what's-his-name—you know—the one with the mustache—*him*—Della's husband—because he's nowhere around here now,
and this one *here*, on the ground *here*, isn't any one of *us*—"
    They found the red stocking-cap some thirty feet from the body,
twisted about a tree limb.

    And so, grandmother Della said, stroking Germaine's cheek with her cool
dry hand that smelled of the harshest soap, you have only one grandfather: a Bellefleur grandfather.
    The little girl sat motionless, not drawing away from the old woman's
hand. For even to move, at such a moment, would be wrong.

. . . They wanted, of course, to kill the baby as well. They wanted me to miscarry. I was four months pregnant with your mother at the time and if they'd had the courage, grandmother Della said, shaking with laughter, sniffing, they would have invited *me* to ride the toboggan too. . . . But I didn't miscarry, despite the shock of losing Stanton. I was terribly ill for a long time, and I went to live with my sister Matilde, and then the baby was born, your mother Leah, and I wept that it wasn't a boy because I was somewhat out of my head at that time and I imagined that only a boy, a man, could take revenge on his father's murderers.

She closed the old photograph album. For a long moment she said nothing, and though Germaine ached to scramble off the sofa and run away, she remained sitting, her feet in their shining patent-leather shoes brought pertly together, her handknit red kneesocks exactly even. Finally grandmother Della sighed, and wiped at her nose with a rumpled hand-kerchief, and said in a half-amused tone meant to release her grand-daughter: But the one thing I did miscarry, thank God, was *God.* I never again believed in any of that barnyard manure from that Christmas Eve to this very day. For *that* I suppose I should thank the Bellefleurs!

Solitaire

In one of the manor's smallest and dampest rooms, on the second floor of the east wing, looking out upon a section of wall and part of a minaretlike tower with mock-battlemented turrets, the old man sat, backed into a corner, playing cards: slapping cards down on the table before him, one after another after another: studying, without expression, the message that finally lay flattened out before him, exposed and bereft of mystery. And then he snorted with contempt or impatience, and gathered the cards up, and shuffled them again.

Gradually, the children were told, their great-uncle Jean-Pierre would become adjusted to the "outside world," and to them; perhaps, in time, he would allow them into his room (but what a dreary room it was, with a low ceiling and dark-paneled walls and only one window!—and he had chosen it himself), and he would invite them to play cards with him; but at the present time they must respect his privacy and the dignity of his old age, and not spy on him through the keyhole, or jostle about in the corridor giggling like little fools.

Great-uncle Jean-Pierre was an old man, and he wasn't, after all, in perfect health. Sudden noises startled him. He could not bear the cats scurrying in the corridors—the sight of Nightshade, poor Nightshade, quite repulsed him—he hadn't any appetite for even the tastiest of the dishes his mother Elvira ordered for him (he preferred watery oatmeal, and the coarse white bread the servants ate, and he had a curious habit of sprinkling nearly everything—roast beef, potatoes, fresh lettuce and tomatoes—with sugar)—he hadn't (and this struck Leah as strangest of all) any *interest* in the family's affairs.

But then of course he wasn't well. He coughed, and sniffed, and spat angrily into his handkerchiefs, and complained of chest and stomach pains, and insomnia (for his bed was too soft, and the linen too scratchy-clean), and a sense of vertigo whenever he left his room, or even dared to look out the window. Bellefleur Manor was a horrific place—it was so inhumanly *large*—he hadn't remembered how large it was: ah, what a terror to contemplate! What sort of mind, driven by an unspeakable lust, had imagined it into being? The castle . . . the castle's grounds . . . the lightless choppy immensity of Lake Noir . . . the thousands upon thousands of acres of wilderness land . . . the mountains in the distance: a terror to contemplate: and beyond them, sprawling out on all sides, a greater horror, that entity glibly referred to as *the world*. What maddened mind, deranged by an unspeakable lust, had imagined all this into being . . . ?

Jean-Pierre II snorted with derision, and shuffled and cut and shuffled and dealt out his cards, one after another after another. He much preferred *his* game.

The Bloodstone

Because of a vow she had made as a young woman in her twenties, many years ago, after the second, or possibly the third, of her fiancés died (and one of the fiancés was a handsome thirty-year-old naval officer whose father owned a string of textile mills in the Mohawk Valley) great-aunt Veronica never emerged from her suite of rooms before sunset, and never wore anything but black. "Anyone as unhappy as I should hide away from the sun," she said. It was thought that she had imagined herself a beauty at one time—and perhaps she *had* been a beauty—and now she was in mourning not only for the two or three men who might have saved her from a perpetual virginity, but for her own youthful self: for the girlhood that must have seemed at one time inviolable, but which gradually eroded until nothing remained of it but the stubborn chaste irrelevant vow she had made, evidently before witnesses: "Anyone as unhappy as I should remain hidden away from people, so as not to upset them," she said boldly. "Ah, I *am* accursed!"

Because of the vow Germaine rarely saw her great-aunt, and then only in the winter months when the sun set early and Germaine's bedtime wasn't until well after dark. The surprise of great-aunt Veronica was her *ordinariness:* if the children hadn't known of her unhappy loves and her curious penitential vows they would have thought her far less interesting than their grandparents, and certainly far less interesting than their temperamental great-grandmother Elvira (shortly to become, at the age of 101, a bride again). Great-aunt Veronica was a plump, full-hipped and full-breasted woman of moderate height, with a placid sheep's face, smallish hazel eyes with innumerable blue tucks and pleats about them, a mouth that might have been charming except for its complacent set, and a fairly smooth, unlined skin that varied extremely in tone: sometimes it was quite pale, at other times mottled and flushed, especially about the cheeks, and at other times, still, it was ruddy, coarse, and heated, almost brick-red, as if she had been exercising violently in the sun. (Though of course she never exercised. It seemed to tire the poor woman even to walk *downstairs,* which she did with an air of listlessness that not even the promise of excellent claret and excellent food could dispel.)

Absolutely unexceptional were her pastimes: she did needlepoint, like the other old women, but would never have had the stamina or the imagination to create works of art like aunt Matilde; she played gin rummy from time to time, for modest stakes; she gossiped about relatives and neighbors, usually with an air of languid incredulity. She admired good china but had never built up a collection of her own. She could not tolerate anything but the finest linen against her skin (or so she liked to say), and of course she abhorred machine-made things, most of all machine-made lace. (All the Bellefleur women, even Leah, abhorred machine-made lace, no matter that the family had recently acquired a lace-manufacturing factory on the Alder River.) Her manners were mincing: she was *really* too much: sitting primly at the dining room table, night after night, sipping daintily at her wine, drinking a spoonful or two of soup, making a show of playing with her food as if the very notion of an appetite were abhorrent. (Indeed, it was a family joke of long standing that great-aunt Veronica gorged herself in her room, before coming downstairs for dinner, in order to preserve the myth of her girlish fastidiousness, decades after the myth had ceased to have any meaning—or anyone who might care to believe in it.) That Veronica had a dainty appetite was bluntly belied by her full, comfortable figure, and the suggestion of a second chin, and her obvious air of superb health. For a woman of her age—! people were always remarking, in wonderment. Though no one knew exactly how old she was. Bromwell had once calculated that she must be much older than grandmother Cornelia, which would have made her more than seventy, but everyone laughed him out of the room—one of the few instances in which the child was demonstrably mistaken. For great-aunt Veronica looked, even at her most torpid, no more than fifty; at her freshest she might have been as young as forty. Her small undistinguished eyes sometimes shone with an inexplicable emotion that might have been a pleasure in her own enigmatic being.

Upon occasion she wore open-necked gowns, which exposed her pale, rather lardish skin, and the beautiful dark-heart-shaped stone she wore about her neck on a thin gold chain. Asked about the stone she always gazed down upon it sorrowfully, and touched it, and said after a long painful moment that it was a bloodstone—a gift from the first man she had ever loved—the only man (she saw this now, so many decades after) she had ever loved. A deep green stone, flecked with red jasper, glowing and fading with variations in light, pulling heavily on the thin chain: a stone heart the size of a child's heart. *Is* it beautiful, *do* you think it's beautiful? she would ask, frowning, peering down at it so that her small pudgy chin creased against her chest. She couldn't, she declared, judge any longer, herself. For it had been so many, many years since Count Ragnar Norst had given her the bloodstone.

But of course it was beautiful, people said. If one liked bloodstones.

Norst introduced himself to Veronica Bellefleur at a charity ball in Manhattan, attended, it was said, by many persons of questionable background. Though Veronica, then a comely young woman of twenty-four who wore her red-blond hair braided and wound about her head like a crown, and who distinguished herself by her high tinkling spontaneous laughter, had, of course, a chaperone, and would not ordinarily have countenanced a stranger's approach—let alone a stranger's daring in actually taking her hand and raising it to his lips!—there was from the very first something so peremptory and at the same time so artless about his manner that she could not assert herself against it. In handsome though rather dated formal attire, with a very dark goatee and gleaming dark curls on either side of his forehead, Count Ragnar Norst identified himself ambiguously as the youngest son in a family of merchants who owned a shipping line that spanned the globe, doing trade in New Guinea and Patagonia and the Ivory Coast, and as a diplomatic attaché whose embassy was, of course, in Washington, and as a "poet-adventurer" whose only desire was to live each day to the fullest. Veronica's confused impression of Norst upon that occasion was a positive but troubled one —he *was* attractive, but how intensely, how *queerly,* he had smiled at her! And with what unwelcome intimacy he had kissed her hand, as if they were old, intimate friends. . . .

Yet she dreamt of him almost at once. So that when he reappeared in her life some weeks later, at a crowded reception at the home of Senator Payne, not far from Bellefleur Manor, she greeted him with an unthinking vivacity—actually held her hand out to him, as if they *were* old friends. It was not until he seized the hand and raised it to his warm lips and bowed over it that Veronica realized the audacity of her behavior, but by then it was too late, for Norst was chattering to her about any number of things—the weather, the beautiful mountain scenery, the "rustic" lakeside cottage he had rented for the summer at Lake Avernus (about twelve miles south of Lake Noir), his hopes for seeing her as frequently as possible. Veronica laughed her high scandalized laugh, and blushed, but Norst took no heed: he thought her, in his own words, "dreadfully charming." And so very American.

It soon came about that Norst was visiting Veronica at the castle, driving over for luncheon or high tea in his extraordinary black car—a Lancia Lambda, it was, a saloon model that stood high off the ground on wooden-spoked wheels, comfortably roomy enough so that Veronica's wide-brimmed hats were not in the slightest disturbed as she climbed in. He drove her along the Nautauga River, and down through the picturesque rolling countryside to Lake Avernus, which, already in those days, was beginning to be known as a resort area for well-to-do Manhattanites who hadn't the interest or the wealth to acquire a genuine Chautauqua camp of the sort Raphael Bellefleur had built on the northern shore of Lake Noir. On those long leisurely drives—which poor Veronica was to remember the rest of her life—the couple talked of innumerable casual things, laughing frequently (for surely, from the start, they were half in love), and though Norst questioned Veronica closely about *her* life, her daily life, as if every detail about her delighted him, he was conspicuously evasive in speaking of his own life: he had "duties" in regard to his family's shipping line which called him to New York often, he had "duties" in regard to the Swedish Embassy in Washington which called him there, often, and the rest of the time, well, the rest of the time was given over to . . . to his obligations to himself.

"For we have a grave responsibility, do we not, my dear Miss Bellefleur," he would say, squeezing her hand in excitement, "a responsibility entrusted to us at birth: the need, the *command* to fulfill ourselves, to develop our souls to their utmost? For this we need not only time and cunning, but courage, even audacity . . . and the sympathy of kindred souls."

Veronica was capable of intelligent skepticism in regard to innumerable domestic matters (dressmaker's and haberdashers' promises, for instance), and as a child of thirteen she had insolently repudiated the "God" of Unitarianism (for Veronica's branch of the family was solemnly experimenting with forms of Christianity they considered rational, since the irrational forms too embarrassing altogether); she was *not* a stupid young woman; and yet, in Norst's charismatic presence, she seemed to lose all her powers of judgment, and allowed his words to wash over her. . . . His voice was liquid and sensuous, the first genuinely *charming,* even *seductive,* voice the unfortunate young woman had ever experienced. Ah, it hardly mattered what he said! It hardly mattered: gossip about mutual acquaintances at Lake Avernus, gossip about state and federal politics, praise for the Bellefleur estate and farm, fulsome flattery directed toward Veronica herself (who, in the flush of giddiness attending her "love" for the count, was undeniably beautiful, and not at all innocent of the effect of her cruel wasp-waisted corsets on the snug-fitting silk gowns she wore). Veronica gazed upon Norst with a girlish fascination she did not even try to hide, and murmured in agreement, yes, yes, whatever he said, it *sounded* so utterly plausible.

It was a most unorthodox courtship. Norst would disappear suddenly, leaving behind only a few scribbled words of apology (but never of explanation) with a manservant; and then he would reappear, a day or twelve days later, never doubting but that Veronica would see him—as if she hadn't innumerable suitors who treated her more considerately. As if she hadn't, Veronica's parents and brother chided her, any *pride.* But there was Ragnar Norst in his aristocratic car, which gleamed like a hearse, and gave off a scent (which in time became quite sweet, in Veronica's opinion) of wax polish, leather, finely-veneered wood, and something mustily damp, like a bog made rich by centuries of decay. At all times he wore impeccably formal attire—frock coats, handsome silk cravats, dazzling-white cuffs with pearl, gold, onyx, and bloodstone cuff links, starched collars, plisséd shirts—and his pomaded hair with its twin curls was always perfect. Perhaps his skin was too swarthy, and his black eyes *too* black, and his moods too unpredictable (for if, one day, he was ebullient, gay, chattersome, and exhilarated, the next day he might be apathetic, or irritable, or melancholy, or so serious in his talk to Veronica of "the need to fulfill one's destiny" that the young woman turned aside in distress) . . . and in any case, as the Bellefleurs were beginning to say, more and more emphatically, there was something not altogether *clear* about him. Were the Norsts, indeed, an "ancient" Swedish family? Did they own a shipping line? But *which* shipping line? Was Norst associated with the Swedish Embassy under his own name, or under an incognito? Was "Norst" itself an incognito? It is quite possible, Veronica's brother Aaron said, even granting the man (which I don't) his identity, that he is involved in espionage of some sort. . . . It hasn't been our habit, after all, to trust foreigners.

Veronica tearfully agreed; yet, once in Norst's presence, she forgot everything. He was so *manly.* He could entertain her for hours with Swedish folksongs played on a curious little instrument that resembled a zither, and produced a keening and yet lulling, almost soporific, sound, a "music" so intimate that it played along her nerves and pulses, and left her quite drained. He told her of his many travels—to Patagonia, to the African interior, to Egypt, Mesopotamia, Jordan, India, New Guinea, Styria, the land of Ganz—and began to intimate, more and more explicitly, that she would soon accompany him, if she wished. And then he addressed her as no other man had ever addressed her, seizing her limp hand and raising it to his lips, kissing it passionately: murmuring shamelessly of "love" and "kindred souls" and "mutual destiny" and the need for lovers to "surrender" themselves completely to one another. He called her "dearest," "my dear Veronica," "my dear beautiful Veronica," and did not seem to notice her discomfort; he spoke in a tremulous voice of "rapture" and "passion"—that "unexplored country" which a "virgin like yourself" must one day traverse, but only in the company of a lover who had opened himself completely to her. There must be, he cautioned, no secrets between lovers—absolutely no corners or recesses of the soul kept in darkness—otherwise the raptures of love will be merely physical, and short-lived, and if the lovers *die* into each other they will *die* literally, and not be resurrected—did she understand? Ah, it was imperative that she understand! And he embraced her, fairly shuddering with emotion; and poor Veronica nearly fainted. (For no man had ever spoken to her like this, nor had anyone so abruptly, and so passionately, taken her in his arms.)

"But you shouldn't! That isn't nice! Oh—that isn't nice!" Veronica gasped. And, like a frightened child, she burst into peals of laughter. "That isn't—*nice*—"

That night she retired early, her head reeling as if she had drunk too much wine, and she was hardly conscious of pulling the bedcovers up before she slipped—sank—was pulled into—sleep. And in the morning she found the heart-shaped bloodstone on the pillow beside her!—simply lying on the pillow beside her. (She knew at once, of course, that it was a gift of Norst's, for two or three days earlier, as they dined in the Avernus Inn overlooking the magnificent lake, she had made a fuss over his cuff links—she'd never seen so richly dark a stone before, and found its scintillating depths quite fascinating. The family jewels she had inherited —a single sapphire, some modest-carated diamonds, a handful of opals, garnets, pearls—struck her suddenly as uninteresting. Norst's blood-stone cuff links might very well be, as he insisted gaily, inexpensive, even commonplace, but they exerted a fascination upon Veronica, who found it difficult to take her eyes off them during the meal.) And now—what a surprise! For several minutes she lay without moving, staring at the large stone, which was both green and red, and layered with darkness: *could* such a beautiful object be, indeed, commonplace?

He had gotten Veronica's maid to tiptoe into her room and lay the stone beside her, of course, and though the girl denied it—for her mistress was not so flummoxed by passion as to fail to wonder at the propriety of Norst's tipping (or bribing) a domestic servant—Veronica knew that this was the case: an audacious gesture, of which her family would angrily disapprove, but one which (ah, she couldn't help herself!) quite charmed her.

She slipped the bloodstone on a gold chain, and wore it about her neck that very day.

The more frequently Veronica saw Ragnar Norst, the less she felt she knew of him; it frightened her, and excited her, to realize that she would never *know* him at all. For one thing, his moods were so capricious. . . . He could start off on a walk with her in excellent high spirits, obviously filled to the brim with energy; fifteen minutes later he would be suddenly weary, and ask if Veronica wouldn't mind sitting on a bench for a while, and simply gazing, without speaking, at the landscape. Or perhaps he was sweetly melancholy, and kept staring mournfully into her eyes, as if he were yearning, starving, for something, for *her* . . . and then again, a few minutes later, he would be telling one of his lengthy, convoluted folk-tales, set in Sweden or Denmark or Norway, punctuated with bursts of laughter (for some of the tales, though sanctified by tradition, struck the blushing young woman as distinctly ribald—not really suited for her ears). He was at all times unusually perceptive, however: she felt that he was *seeing* and *hearing* and *thinking* with an almost preternatural clarity. At one unfortunate luncheon, high on the terrace in the walled garden, Veronica's brother Aaron—a 230-pounder with an exaggerated sense of his own powers of ratiocination, far more suited for hunting than for civilized discourse—began to interrogate Norst almost rudely about his background ("Ah, you claim there is *Persian* blood on your mother's side of the family?—indeed? And on your father's side, what sort of blood, do you think—?"), and it was quite remarkable to witness Norst's transformation: he seemed immediately to sense that a direct confrontation with this brute would be not only disastrous, but distasteful, and so he replied to Aaron's questions in a courteous, even humble manner, readily admitting when necessary that he *couldn't* altogether explain certain . . . certain discrepancies . . . no, he regretted that he *couldn't* account for . . . not altogether . . . not at the present time. Veronica had never witnessed a performance of such exquisite subtlety and tact; she gazed upon him adoringly, and did not even trouble to be angry with her boorish brother (he was five years her senior, and imagined that he knew more than she, and that a great deal of what he knew had to do with *her*), even though his questioning had brought droplets of perspiration to Norst's forehead.

And then, afterward, it struck her—Persian blood! But how marvelous! How enchanting! *Persian* blood: which accounted for his swarthy skin and his dark mesmerizing eyes. Little as she knew about Swedes she knew even less about Persians and found the combination totally enchanting. . . .

"That 'Count' is an impostor," Aaron said. "He doesn't even trouble himself to lie intelligently to us."

"Oh, what do you know!" Veronica laughed, waving him away. "You don't know Ragnar at all."

(Later it was revealed that Aaron had spoken with Senator Payne, and with two or three acquaintances in Washington, to see if Norst's visa couldn't be canceled—if Norst couldn't be, with a minimum of legal squabbling, simply deported back to Europe. But he must have had friends in high positions, or at any rate friends whose authority was greater than that of Aaron's contacts, for nothing came of the move; and when Ragnar Norst returned to Europe he did so solely at his own wish.)

And so Veronica Bellefleur fell in love with the mysterious Ragnar Norst, though she was not conscious of "falling in love" but only of becoming more and more obsessed with him—with the thought, the aura, of him, which pursued her in the unlikeliest of places, and was liable to call forth a blush to her cheeks at the least appropriate of times. Even before her illness she was susceptible to odd lethargic reveries during which his image haunted her; she would give her head a shake, as if to cast herself free of his spell. A warm lulling erotic daze overcame her. She sighed often, and her words trailed off into silence, quite maddening Aaron, who knew, no matter how she denied it, that she was in love with the count. "But that man is an impostor," Aaron said angrily. "Just as I'm sure that stone of yours, if you allowed me to have it examined, would prove to be a fake—!"

"You don't know Ragnar in the slightest," Veronica said, shivering.

Yet she herself was often disturbed by him. He insisted they meet in the evening, in clandestine places (in the boathouse; beside Bloody Run; at the very rear of the walled garden, where there was a little grove of evergreens in which, by day, the children sometimes played) no matter how such situations compromised her; he insisted upon speaking "frankly" no matter how his words distressed her. Once he seized both her hands in his and murmured in a voice that shook with emotion, "Someday, my dearest Veronica, this masquerade will end—someday you will be mine—my most precious possession—and I will be yours—and you will know then the reality of—of—of the passion which nearly suffocates me—" And indeed his breath became so labored it was nearly a sob, and his eyes glowed with an unspeakable lust, and after a terrible moment during which he stared into her eyes almost angrily he turned aside, throwing himself back against a railing, his arm upraised as if to shield himself from the sight of her. His chest rose and fell so violently that Veronica wondered for a terrible moment if he were having a seizure of some kind.

For several minutes afterward Norst remained leaning against the railing, his heavy-lidded eyes closed, as if he were suddenly drained of all strength. And afterward, escorting her back to the manor house, he said very little, and walked feebly, like an aged man; in parting he did no more than murmur a gentle, melancholy goodbye, and failed even to lift his gaze to hers. "But Ragnar," Veronica asked, bold with desperation, "are you angry with me?—why have you turned away from me?" Still he did not look her in the face. He sighed, and said in a weary voice, "My dear, perhaps it would be for the best—for *you,* I am thinking only of *you*— if we never met again."

That night she dreamt of him once again, far more vividly: she saw him more vividly, it seemed, than she had seen him in the flesh. He seized both her hands and squeezed them so hard she cried out in pain and surprise, and then he pulled her to him, to his breast, and closed her in his strong arms. She would have fainted, she would have fallen, had he not held her so tight. . . . He kissed her full on the lips, and then buried his face in her neck, and then, while the swooning girl tried with feeble hands to prevent him, he tore open her bodice and began to kiss her breasts, all the while holding her still, and murmuring lulling commanding words of love. It excited him all the more, that she was wearing the bloodstone around her neck (for indeed Veronica was wearing it in bed, beneath her nightgown). You must stop, Ragnar, she whispered, her face crimson with shame, you must stop, you must *stop*—

By day she only half-recalled her tempestuous dreams, though she was still under their spell. Strange emotions washed over her, and left her so drained of energy that her mother asked more than once if she were ill: she was by turns fearful, and disgusted, and wildly exhilarated, and ashamed, and defiant, and impatient (for when, *when,* would he see her again?—he'd left word with a servant that the embassy in Washington had called him), and delighted as a child (for she was certain he *would* see her again). Sometimes she ate ravenously, but most of the time she had no appetite at all—she simply sat at the dining room table, oblivious of the others, staring into space, sighing, her head aswim with languorous wraithlike images of her lover.

You must stop, Ragnar, a voice rose shrilly, you must, you must, you *must* stop before it's too late. . . .

And then a tragic accident befell poor Aaron, and it was Ragnar Norst himself who comforted the stricken young woman.

Unwisely, against his father's reiterated wishes, Aaron went out hunting alone in the woods above Bloody Run, accompanied only by one of his dogs. While crossing a white-water stream he evidently lost his footing, fell, and was carried hundreds of yards downstream, over a seven-foot falls, to his death in a swirling shallow rapids in which rocks and logs lay in manic profusion. The poor young man's throat was slashed by a protruding branch, and it was estimated that he must have bled to death, mercifully, in a matter of minutes. By the time the search party discovered him (he had been missing then two days) his body, so large, once so intimidating, was bled white, trapped in a tight little cove of froth-covered rocks and logs.

(Neither the dog nor the shotgun was ever recovered, which added to the mystery of the death.)

The stricken Veronica wept and wept, as much for the senselessness of Aaron's death as for the death itself: for to her there was no mystery, there was only the fact that she would never see Aaron again, never exchange words with him again. . . . No matter how they had quarreled they had loved each other very much.

How ugly that death was, and how *pointless!* If the headstrong young man had only listened to his father's words . . . No, Veronica could not bear it; she *would* not bear it. She wept for days on end and would allow no one to comfort her.

Until Ragnar Norst returned.

One morning he drove up the graveled lane in the stately black car (whose engine was overheated), and insisted that he be allowed to see Miss Veronica: for he had learned, in Washington, of Aaron's death, and he knew at once that Veronica must be comforted if she was to survive the crisis. She was so exquisite, so sensitive, the horror of a brute accidental death might undermine her health. . . .

The very sight of Norst enlivened her. But she took care, being a discreet young woman, to hide her feelings; and, indeed, a moment later, the memory of her brother's death swept over her once again, and she succumbed to a fresh attack of weeping. So Norst took her aside, and walked with her along the lake, at first saying nothing at all, and even urging her to cry; and then, when it seemed to him that she was somewhat stronger, he began to query her about death. About, that is, her fear of death.

Was it death itself that terrified her . . . or the accidental nature of that particular death? Was it *death* that so alarmed, or the fact that she would not (or so she assumed) ever see her brother again?

Above the choppy dark waters of Lake Noir they paused, to listen to waves lapping against the shore. It was nearly sundown. Veronica shuddered, for a faint chill breeze had arisen, and quite naturally, quite gracefully, Norst slipped his arm about her shoulders. He was breathing heavily. He gave off an air of excitement and exhilaration. But his voice was steady, steady and restrained, and Veronica gave no indication that she was aware of his emotion; indeed, she kept her gaze shyly averted. She wondered only if he was aware of the bloodstone she wore, hidden inside her shirtwaist. But of course he could hardly be aware of it . . . he could hardly know, under the circumstances. . . .

His arm tightened about her slender shoulders and he brought his mouth close to her ear. In a gentle, trembling voice he began to speak of death: death and love: death and love and lovers: and how, by the sacrament of death, lovers are united, and their profane love redeemed. Veronica's heart beat so powerfully she could barely concentrate on his words. She was aware of his nearness, his almost overwhelming nearness; she was terrified that he would kiss her, as he had in her dreams, and abuse her, ignoring her astonished cries. . . . "Veronica, my dearest," he said, cupping her chin in his hand, turning her face so that he might look into her eyes, "you must know that lovers who die together transcend the physical nature of the human condition . . . the tedious physical nature of the human condition. . . . You must know that a pure spiritual love redeems the grossness of the flesh. . . . So long as I am beside you, to guide you, to protect you, there is nothing to fear . . . nothing, nothing to fear . . . in this world or the next. I would *never* allow you to suffer, my dear girl, do you understand? . . . do you trust me?"

Her eyelids were suddenly heavy; she was nearly overcome by a sense of lassitude, vaguely erotic, that very much resembled the lassitude of her most secret dreams. Norst's voice was gentle, soothing, rhythmic as the waves of Lake Noir, beating against her, washing over her. . . . Ah, she could not have protested *had* he attempted to kiss her!

But he was speaking, still, of love. Of lovers who would "eagerly" die for each other. "I for you, my dear sweet girl, and you for me—if you love. me—and by that we are redeemed. It is so simple, and yet so profound! Do you see? Do you understand? Your brother's death offended you because it was an animal's death—brute, senseless, accidental, unshared —and with your sensitivity you crave meaning, and beauty, and a spiritual transcendence. You crave redemption, as I do. For by death in one another's arms, my love, we *are* redeemed . . . and all else is unadorned *unimagined* folly, from which you are perfectly justified to turn aside in horror. Do you understand, my love? Ah, but you will!—you *will.* Only have faith in me, my dearest Veronica."

Faintly she murmured that she did not understand. And she felt so suddenly exhausted, she must lay her head against his shoulder.

"Life and death both, if unadorned by love," Norst continued, in a rapid, low, excited voice, "are ignominious . . . mere folly . . . mere accident. They are indistinguishable when not enhanced by passion. For ordinary people, as you must have seen by now, are little more than aphids . . . rats . . . brute unthinking animals . . . quite beneath our contempt, really . . . unless of course they frustrate us . . . in which case they must be taken into account . . . taken into account and dealt with . . . ugly as that might seem. Do you see, my dear? Yes? No? You must trust me, and all will become clear. You must have faith in me, Veronica, for you know, don't you, that I love you, and that I have sworn to have you . . . from a time long past . . . a time you cannot remember and I, I can but dimly recall. . . . As for ordinary people, my dear, you must give them no thought . . . you will one day learn to deal with them as I do, only out of necessity . . . I will guide you, I will protect you, if only you will have faith. . . . And you *must* not fear death, for the death of lovers, dying into love, being born again through love, has nothing of the crudity of ordinary death about it: do you understand?"

She understood. Yet of course she did not understand. But her head was so heavy, her eyelids burned with the need to close, if only he would embrace her, if only he would whisper to her the words she so fervently wished to hear. . . . He had declared his love for her; she had heard it; she *had* heard it; yet he had not, yet, declared his wish to marry her; he had said nothing about speaking to her father, or . . .

Suddenly he drew away from her. He was quite agitated, and rubbed both hands vigorously against his eyes. "My dear Veronica," he said, in a different voice, "I must get you back home. What can I be thinking of, keeping you out here in this cold wind—!"

She opened her eyes wide in disbelief.

"I *must* get you home, you poor girl," Norst murmured.

That night Veronica felt feverish, and despite the drop in temperature she left her French doors open. And she experienced a dream that was by far the most alarming, and the most curiously exhilarating, of any dream she had yet experienced.

She was, and yet she was not, unconscious. She slept, but at the same time was quite aware of her bed, her surroundings, and the fact that she lay asleep, her long thick hair loose on her pillow, the bloodstone exposed on her breast. I am asleep, she thought clearly, as if her spirit floated above her body, how strange, how wonderful, I am lying there asleep and my lover is shortly to come to me, and no one will know. . . .

Almost at once Norst did appear. He must have climbed over the balcony railing, for a moment later he stood before the window, dressed as usual in his frock coat, his white shirt glaringly white in the darkness, his goatee and the savage little curls on either side of his forehead vividly defined. He was silent. He was expressionless. Somewhat taller than his daylight self—Veronica, paralyzed, unable even to make her eyelids flutter, estimated that he must be nearly seven feet tall—he stood for a long moment without moving, simply gazing upon her with an expression of—was it infinite longing, infinite sorrow?—was it yearning?—love?

Ragnar, she tried to whisper. My dear. My bridegroom.

She would have opened her arms to him, but she could not move; she lay paralyzed beneath the covers. Asleep and yet fully awake: conscious of her wild accelerated heartbeat and of *his* heartbeat as well. Ragnar, she whispered. I love you as I have never loved any other man. . . .

Then he was close beside her bed, without having seemed to move.

He was close beside her bed, stooping over her, and she tried to raise her arms to him—ah, how she wanted to slide her arms about his neck! —how she wanted to pull him to her! But she could not move, she could do no more than draw in her breath sharply as he stooped to kiss her. She saw his dark moist eyes drawing near, she saw his mouth, his parted lips, and felt his breath—his warm, ragged, rather meaty breath—she smelled his breath which was dank, and somewhat fetid—it put her dizzily in mind of the farm—the farm laborers hauling carcasses—hogs strung up by their hind legs—blood gushing from their slashed throats, into enormous tubs— She drew in his breath, which was sour with something dried and stale and old, very old, and in a swoon she began to laugh, every part of her was being tickled, tickled to delirium, to a delicious frantic delirium, and she did not mind his breath, she did not mind it at all, or his agitation, his impatience, his roughness, the grinding of his teeth against hers in a harsh kiss—she did not mind at all—not at all—she wanted to shout, and pound at him with her fists—she wanted to scream —to throw herself about the bed—to kick off the covers, which so exasperatingly pressed upon her—and she was so hot—slick with perspiration —she could smell her own body, her bodily heat—it was shameful, and yet delicious—it made her want to snort with laughter—it made her want to grab hold of her lover—seize him by the hair, by the hair, and pummel him, and press his head against her, his face against her breasts—like that —yes, exactly like that—she could not bear it, what he was doing to her —his lips, his tongue, his sudden hard teeth—she could not bear it—she would scream, she would go mad, snorting, shouting, tearing at him with her nails—My lover, my bridegroom, she would scream, my husband, my *soul*—

As the days and weeks passed, and Veronica sank ever more deeply into a state of languid, sweet melancholy, it was commonly believed that the shock of Aaron's death had plunged her into a "black mood" and that she would, in time, emerge from it. Yet Veronica rarely thought of her brother. Her imagination dwelt almost exclusively upon Ragnar Norst. Throughout the long, tiresome day she yearned for the night, when Norst came to her, unfailingly, and gathered her up passionately in his arms, and made her his bride. There was no need for him to speak of love any longer; what happened between them went beyond love. Indeed, the trivial notion of love—and marriage as well—now struck Veronica as uninteresting. That she had once hoped Ragnar Norst would ask her father for permission to marry her—! That she had once imagined him an ordinary man, and herself an ordinary woman—! Well, she had been a very innocent girl at the time.

Strange, wasn't it, people said, that the count had disappeared so suddenly. Evidently he had returned to Europe . . . ? And when would he return, had he said . . . ?

Veronica paid no attention. She knew that people whispered behind her back, wondering if she was unhappy; wondering if there was any sort of "understanding" between them. Would there be a marriage? Would there be a scandal? It did not trouble Veronica in the slightest, that her lover had left the country: for in her sleep he was magnificently present, and nothing else mattered.

During the day Veronica drifted about idly, thinking certain forbidden thoughts, recalling certain sharp, piercing, indefinable pleasures. She sang tuneless little songs under her breath, reminiscent of the songs Norst had sung. She tired easily, and liked to lie on a chaise longue wrapped in a shawl, gazing dreamily out toward the lake, watching the lakeshore drive. Sometimes Norst appeared to her though it wasn't night: she would blink, and see him standing there a few feet away, gazing at her with that shameless raw hunger, that embarrassing intensity she had not understood at the start. Graciously, languidly, she would lift her hand to him, and he would lean forward to raise it to his greedy lips . . . and then some clumsy heavy-footed fool of a servant would enter the room, and Norst would vanish.

"Oh, I hate you!" Veronica sometimes cried. "Why don't you all leave me alone!"

They began to worry about her. She was so listless, so pale, the color had gone out of her face and she looked positively waxen (though more beautiful than ever, Veronica thought, why don't you admit it—Ragnar's love has made me more beautiful than ever); she had no appetite for anything more than toast and fruit juice and an occasional pastry; she was absentminded, often didn't hear people speaking to her, seemed asleep with her eyes open, was obviously lost in grief for her poor dead brother. . . . Even when the doctor was examining her, listening to her heart with his silly instrument, she was daydreaming about her lover (who had appeared to her the night before, and who had promised to return the following night) and could not answer the questions put to her. She would have liked to explain: Her soul was swooning downward, gently downward, she was not at all unhappy, she was certainly not in mourning (in mourning for whom?—her boorish headstrong brother who had died such an ugly death?), everything was unfolding as it must, according to the destiny fate had determined for her. She would not resist, would not want to resist; nor did she want anyone else to interfere. Sometimes during the daylight hours she caught sight of a thin crescent moon, half-invisible in the pale sky, and the sight of it pierced her breast like her lover's kiss. She would lie down, suddenly dizzy, and let her head drop heavily back, and her eyes roll white in her skull. . . .

How sweet it was, this utterly unresisting melancholy: this sense of a downward spiral which was both the pathway her soul took, and her soul itself. The air grew heavy; it exerted pressure upon her; sometimes she found breathing difficult, and held her lungs still and empty for long moments at a time. She would have liked to explain to the nurse who now sat at the foot of her bed, or slept on a cot of her own just outside her door, that she was not at all unhappy. Others might be unhappy that she was leaving them but they were simply jealous, ignorant people who didn't understand her. They couldn't know how deeply she was loved, for instance; how Norst valued her; how he had promised to protect her.

There were times, however, when her dreams were confused and unpleasant, and Norst did not appear; or, if he did appear, his aspect was so greatly changed she could not recognize him. (Once he came in the shape of a gigantic yellow-eyed owl with ferocious ear tufts; another time he appeared in the shape of a monstrous stunted dwarf with a hump between his shoulder blades; still another time he was a tall, slender, eerily beautiful girl with Oriental eyes and a slow, sensuous smile—a smile Veronica could not bear to gaze upon, it was so knowing, so obscene.) On and on the dreams went, tumbling her about mercilessly, mocking her pleas for tenderness, for love, for her husband's embrace. When she woke from one of these dreams, often in the middle of the night, she would force herself to sit up, her head aching violently, and a flame of panic would touch her—for wasn't she seriously ill, wasn't she perhaps dying, couldn't something be done to stop the downward spiral of her soul? . . . Once, she heard her nurse groaning, thrashing about in the midst of her own nightmare.

And then two things happened: the nurse (an attractive woman in her mid-thirties who had been born in the village, and had trained in the Falls) grew gravely ill with a blood disorder, and Veronica herself, already weakened and anemic, caught a cold that passed into bronchitis and then into pneumonia in a matter of days. So she was hospitalized, and lapsed into a sort of stupor, during which busy dream-wraiths took care of her. They took excellent care of her: providing her with fresh, strong blood, and feeding her through tubes, so that she could not protest, and was thereby saved. In fact there was no question of dying, with so much skillful, professional activity on all sides; and in a week or two Veronica was not only fully conscious but even hungry. One of the Bellefleur maids shampooed her hair, which was still luxurious and beautiful; and she too was beautiful despite her pallor and the hollows around her eyes. One day she said, "I'm hungry," in a child's affronted voice, "I want to eat, I'm hungry, and I'm bored with lying here in bed. . . . I can't stand it a minute longer!"

So she was saved. Her lungs were well; the bouts of dizziness had vanished; her color was back. Upon admission to the hospital her doctors had discovered, high on her left breast, a curious fresh scratch or bite, that looked at the same time as if it were fairly old, which must have been made by one of the Bellefleur cats, hugged unwisely against Veronica's bosom. (For though the Bellefleurs had not nearly so many cats and kittens in those days, as they did in Germaine's time, there were at least six or ten of them in the household, and any one of them might have been responsible for Veronica's tiny wound.) Veronica herself knew nothing about it: she belonged to that generation of women who rarely, and then only reluctantly, gazed upon their naked bodies, and so it was a considerable surprise for her to learn that there was, on her breast, an odd little scratch or bite that had become mildly inflamed. Of course it was a very *minor* affair, her doctors assured her, and had nothing to do with her serious problems of anemia and pneumonia.

Indirectly she learned, to her astonishment and grief, that her nurse had died—the poor woman had died of acute anemia only a few days after having left Bellefleur Manor. Most extraordinary was the fact that, according to the woman's family, she had been in perfect health until she went into the employ of the Bellefleurs: she had *never,* they claimed, been anemic at all.

But Veronica had not died.

Now the disturbing, tumultuous dreams were over. A part of her life was over. She slept deeply and profoundly, safe in her hospital room, and when she woke in the morning she woke completely, well rested, elated, wanting at once to be on her feet. She was ecstatic with good health. In her luxurious cashmere robe she walked about the hospital wing, attended by her personal maid, and of course everyone fell in love with her: for she was radiant as an angel, and that long red-blond hair that fell loose on her shoulders—! She was merry and prankish as a child, she told silly little jokes, she even toyed, for a day or two, with the idea of becoming a nurse. How charming she would look, in her prim white uniform. . . . And then, perhaps, she would marry a doctor. And the two of them would be on the side of life.

Yes, that was it: she wanted to be *on the side of life.*

She was very happy, and begged to be discharged from the hospital, but her family was cautious (for, after all, Veronica's nurse *had* died—and she *had* seemed to be in good health), and her doctors wanted to keep her under observation for another several days. For there was something about her case that perplexed them.

"But I want to go home now," she said, pouting. "I'm *bored* with doing nothing, I hate being an invalid, having people look at me in that condescending pitying way. . . ."

And then one day, an odd thing happened. She was watching some teenaged boys playing football in a field adjacent to the hospital grounds, and though she wanted to admire them, and to applaud their physical dexterity and stamina, she found herself becoming increasingly depressed. They were so energetic, so vulgar . . . so filled with life. . . . Like aphids or rats. . . . There was no subtlety to them, no meaning; no beauty. She turned away in disgust.

She turned away, and began to weep uncontrollably. What had she lost! What had gone out of her life, when they had "saved" her here in the hospital! Her thin cheeks were growing rounded again and her dead-white skin was turning rosy but the mirror's image did not please her: she saw that it was uninteresting, banal, really quite vulgar. *She* was uninteresting now, and her lover, if he returned, if he ever happened to gaze upon her, would be sadly disappointed.

(But her lover: who was he? She could not clearly recall him. *Ragnar Norst.* But who was that, what did he mean to her? Where had he gone? The dreams had vanished, and Ragnar Norst had vanished, and something so profound had gone out of her life that she halfway felt, despite her heartiness, her relentless normality, that it was her very soul that had been taken from her. The hospital had seen to that: it had "saved" her.)

Still, she was grateful to be alive. And of course the family was delighted to have her back again. They thought, still, that she had succumbed to a severe black mood as a consequence of Aaron's death, and she could not tell them otherwise.

Yes, Veronica thought, a dozen times a day, I *am* grateful to be alive.

And then one afternoon as she was being driven to the Falls for tea with an elderly aunt, she saw the Lancia Lambda approaching—saw it appear around a turn in the road, blackly regal, imperious, bearing down upon her with the authority of an image out of a dream. She immediately rapped on the glass partition and told the chauffeur to stop.

So Norst braked, and stopped his car, and came over to see her. He was wearing white. His hair and goatee and eyes were as black as ever, and his smile rather more hesitant than she recalled. Her lover? Her husband? This stranger? . . . He had heard, he said in a nervous murmur, of her illness. Evidently she had been hospitalized, and had been *very* ill. As soon as he returned from Sweden he had come up to see her, and had taken rooms at the Lake Avernus Inn. What a delight it was to see her, like this, so suddenly, with no warning—to see her looking so supremely healthy, and as beautiful as ever—

He broke off, and took her hand, squeezing it hard. A flame seemed to pass over his vision. He trembled, his breathing grew rapid and shallow, she felt, keenly, the near-paroxysm of his desire for her, and in that instant she knew that she loved him, and had loved him all along. He managed to disguise his agitation by playfully pulling her glove down an inch or two, and kissing the back of her hand; but even this gesture became a passionate one. Exclaiming, Veronica snatched her hand away.

They stared at each other for several minutes, in silence. She saw that he was indeed the man who had come to her in her dreams—and that he fully recognized her as well. But what was there to *say?* He was staying at Lake Avernus, a mere twelve miles away; naturally they would see each other; they would, perhaps, resume their daylight courtship. It was harmless, and it gave them something to do during the long daylight hours. Norst was asking about her family, and about her health; and about her nights. Did she sleep well, now? Did she wake fully rested? And would she, just for tonight, wear the bloodstone to bed? . . . and leave the window of her room open? Just for tonight, he said.

She laughed, her face burning, and fully meant to say no; but somehow she did not say no.

She was gazing with a bemused smile at the teethmarks on the back of her hand, which were filling in slowly with blood.

The Proposal

Snow was falling for the first time that winter, out of a leaden sky, when, not a week after the scandalous surprise of the wedding of great-grandmother Elvira and the nameless old man from the flood (an event so resolutely private that most of the family was excluded from it, and only Cornelia, Noel, Hiram, and Della were in attendance—the four of them unified in their outraged opposition to the wedding, though, in deference to their mother's happiness, as well as to the irrefragable nature of her decision, they were absolutely silent: witnessed the brief ten-minute ceremony with blank, slack, stupefied faces)—and on the very same day that Garth and Little Goldie brought their baby to the manor house, to show him off for the first time (Little Garth was so tiny everyone who saw him supposed he must be premature, but in fact he was not: he was perfectly proportioned and healthy and *almost* beautiful, and had been born precisely on schedule)—when Germaine, in hiding because she had overheard part of a quarrel between her mother and father, and was very frightened, happened, quite by accident, and *quite* to her distress (it was not simply because of the fact that, being an unusually honest child, she disliked spying on adults, but she disliked being trapped as well), to overhear yet another private conversation: and was not able to escape until the participants, after an extremely emotional session of at least ten minutes, finally left the room.

The child had run into one of the downstairs drawing rooms to hide, not from her parents (for neither Leah nor Gideon had had the slightest awareness of her presence—they had been *that* coldly furious) but from the idea of her parents, and their quietly raised voices, and the air all jagged knives and icicles and protruding nails, and that sour black gagging taste at the back of the mouth; without knowing what she did she ran into the room now called, since its renovation that fall, the Peacock

Room (for Leah had had it papered in a sumptuous French silk wallpaper that showed, against an opalescent background, peacocks and egrets and other plumed, graceful birds in a style copied from a twelfth-century Chinese scroll), and threw herself down behind a love seat that faced the empty fireplace. There, she lay for some time, motionless, panting, prickling with unease. She did not know what her parents were quarreling about but she understood very well the light, deft, wounding, vicious nature of their banter, especially Leah's.

And then, suddenly, two people entered the room, engaged in an equally passionate conversation.

"But I've asked you—haven't I asked you—not to say such things," a woman said softly.

"But I cannot *not* say such things," a gentleman said at once.

Germaine did not recognize their voices. They were speaking in an undertone, and were clearly agitated. One of them—it must have been the woman—went to the fireplace to stand, and appeared to be leaning her forehead against the mantel, or against her arm which was stretched along the mantel; the other hesitated a respectful distance away.

"It's simply that I don't understand you," the gentleman said. "That you might ultimately refuse me—that you might even turn away in contempt—I can accept: but that you haven't the patience, or the kindness, or even the sense of—of humor—to hear me out—"

The woman laughed helplessly. "Ah, but *you* don't understand! You don't understand my circumstances!"

"I must beg your pardon, my dear, but I have made inquiries—discreet inquiries—"

"But no one would tell you, surely!"

"They have told me only that you're unhappy—that you're alone now in the world—a young woman of rare courage and character—but one who has suffered—"

"Suffered!" the woman laughed. "Is that what they say? Really?"

"They say that you've suffered a great deal, but choose never to speak of yourself."

"May I ask who this *they* is?"

There was the briefest hesitation. And then the gentleman said, in an imploring tone: "My dear, I really would rather not say."

"In that case please don't. I can't ask you to betray a confidence."

"You're not angry, I hope?"

"Why should I be angry?"

"At my making queries about you, behind your back."

"Well—!"

"What other course had I, my dear? As a stranger here—knowing that I must necessarily be cautious to whom I speak—for there are, you know, surely you know, a dizzying profusion of plots in this house—plots, calculations, aspirations, dreams—some of them, to my way of thinking, quite mad—as, I say, a stranger here, I was forced to make my way like a sleepwalker. For though I knew from that very first night exactly what my own dreams were, I could not speak my heart, for fear of deeply insulting someone or other—someone who had, let us say, her own plans for me."

"They want to marry you off?"

"I gather as much. But they seem somewhat confused—they haven't come to any mutual agreement—and so in the meantime I am relatively free. Except, of course, that I am," he said lightly, "anything but free."

The woman made a muffled sound like a sob. "But I've asked you not to say such things!"

"My dear, we have so little time, how can you deny me?—deny me, I mean, the only opportunity I may have to express myself? We are so rarely alone together, since you forbid it—"

"I know what's best," the woman said in a trembling voice. "Or do I mean—I know what is inevitable."

"But you won't have pity on me, not even to the point of—of facing me? Turning to me? No? But surely you know," he said in a low voice, "how I value you. How I worship you."

"Please—I will be forced to leave—"

"*Surely* you know, since that first night?"

"I prefer not to think of that first night. I am overcome with shame and humiliation, thinking of it."

"But my dear—"

"You injure me terribly, to bring it up!"

"You aren't being reasonable—"

"*You* aren't being reasonable," the woman said, greatly agitated. "In the guise of being my friend you are persecuting me far more cruelly than my enemies have persecuted me."

"Enemies! Have you enemies?"

The woman was silent, now pacing on the hearth a few yards away. Germaine could hear her gasping for breath. ". . . I've said too much," she whispered. "I dare not say any more."

"Surely you haven't enemies? People who actively wish you harm?"

"I'm afraid I must leave, please excuse me—"

"But you promised me this meeting, and we've only now begun—"

"I spoke unwisely. I'm forced now to change my mind."

"But to be so cruel—cruel not only to me but to yourself! I can see that you're tortured by something, you *do* want to turn to me, you *do* want to speak—isn't it so? My dear, won't you have faith in me?"

"This is impossible. No, really, I can't allow you to say such things under the circumstances."

"But what are the circumstances? You are a young, unattached woman; you appear to have no responsibilities or obligations to your family, so far as I know; and I," he said with a startling, bitter laugh, "am an unattached man, no longer young—except in experience."

"Please don't mock yourself."

"But how can I refrain from mocking myself, when it appears that I am, in your eyes, an object of mockery? Too contemptible even to hear out—even to humor."

"You misunderstand me," the woman said, weeping. "You—you simply don't know my circumstances."

"Then you must explain them to me!"

"Please. I really can't—I can't—I can't bear this," she said.

She wept, and the gentleman seemed about to approach her, and comfort her; but (and Germaine, cringing behind the love seat, could *feel* his misery) he dared not. After some minutes of silence, except for the woman's heartbroken sobbing, he said, "My dear, are you afraid that there is too great a discrepancy between our backgrounds? It's very difficult for me to express this—I lack fluency, and subtlety—but— Are you concerned that because you are alone in the world, and have no fortune, my people might object to—might object to our—"

The woman's sobs grew louder. Indeed, the poor thing seemed to lack all control. The gentleman continued to speak, in a voice that veered in pitch, and Germaine had the feeling (though she was by now pressing her fists against her ears, for it was all so *embarrassing*) that he was summoning all his courage to take the young woman in his arms—yet could not move. The two of them were a short distance away from the fireplace, now, in the far corner of the room.

"—might object to our marriage?"

The woman hissed something unintelligible.

"Ah, have I insulted you?" the gentleman cried in despair. "Simply by uttering the word *marriage*—? I had hoped it would not sound so despicable on my lips."

"I can't bear this!" the woman exclaimed.

There was then a scuffling sound, and a sharp surprised intake of breath, as if the woman had tried to brush past the gentleman; and he had acted upon instinct to prevent her.

Germaine's little heart was pounding with alarm and embarrassment. If they discovered her—! She was sitting on the floor with her back to the love seat, her knees drawn up tightly to her chin and her eyes shut. She did not, she did *not* want to hear them; she did not want to hear any of the adults in their private, secret, passionate conversations. (So much was said, and so much left unsaid. Her father's frequent absences from home; his expensive automobiles; a letter Leah had received from a girl . . . or was it from a young girl's mother. . . . Gideon saying to Leah, I don't make any claim upon you, why should you want, at this point, to make any claim upon *me,* and Leah saying coldly, you might at least think of the child and of how this is affecting her, and Gideon saying, with an air of genuine surprise, the child?—what child? Have we a child in common, still? And there were the hushed scandalized remarks, the week before, about great-grandmother Elvira and the old man from the flood: the old man who was evidently her "lover." But to allow the old fool to marry, at her age, and to marry that—that wretch! Hiram said dully. What might this mean about the estate? Will she want her will changed? And Noel saying, How dare you call our mother a fool! *You,* to call anyone a fool! I don't say the match is a felicitous one—I don't, in fact, say that *any* match is a felicitous one—but if Mother is happy, as she appears to be, marrying for the second time, at the age of—of, dear God, is it nearly 101?—we dare not oppose her. And the old man is, so far as I can judge, perfectly harmless—smiling and amiable and undemanding and— And senile! Hiram cried. His brain must have been soaking in the flood for days!—he simply *smiles* all the time, as if he knows we have to keep him for the rest of his life. And what if Mother dies first, and the estate falls into his hands, and *he* dies, and his heirs step forward? *What if we are evicted from our home? Displaced by brutes?* . . . And, earlier still, there were the low rapid exchanges between Ewan and Leah, about Vernon's death: Suppose you know perfectly well who killed him, but haven't any witnesses? Suppose you simply move in to take our revenge? Who would protest? Who would dare protest? But you'll have to be quick, when you do move. And don't be any more merciful than *they* were.)

So much said, and so much unsaid.

Now the woman's voice lifted bravely. "The circumstances are—the circumstances are simply that I am not worthy of you. And now you know, and must let me go."

"Not worthy of me!" The gentleman laughed. "How can you say such a thing, when I've declared my love for you—when I have practically begged you for the opportunity to declare it? My dear, my dearest, only stand still, and look me in the face—"

"But I can't! I can't!" she cried. "I *am* unworthy."

"What on earth can you mean?"

"I—I—I've been involved with another man," she said in a wild, choked voice.

For a moment there was silence. Then the gentleman said, evenly, "Why, yes, another man: of course, another man. I am saddened but hardly . . . I must admit, hardly surprised. For you are, after all, an extremely attractive young woman, and it stands to reason that . . . that . . ."

"The relationship was not a happy one," she murmured.

"Was he . . . Did he . . . Did he take advantage of you?"

"*Advantage!*" The woman laughed. "Perhaps it was I who took advantage of him!"

"What do you mean? Why do you look at me so strangely?"

"*'I* was the sinner, for I fell in love with a married man," she said angrily, "I fell in love, and pursued him, mad with love I could not let him alone, until at last—at last—"

"Yes?"

"But I've said enough! Already you must feel such contempt for me."

"My dear, your words wound me, but do I look as if I feel contempt?

Please! Don't turn aside! Do I look as if I feel anything for you other than love?"

"You're too good— You stand too far above me—"

"Please don't say such irresponsible things! When you are my wife, when all this is settled and behind us, and you realize the depth of my love, you'll see how inconsequential these feelings are. Set beside my love for you, my dearest—"

"But I tell you: *I am unworthy.*"

"But why? Simply because, as an inexperienced young girl, you fell in love unwisely? I suspect you were taken advantage of by this man you mention, this married man—I will not, of course, ask his identity— whether he is a member of this very household, as I am led to believe— I will *not* inquire, now or in the future—never—you have my word—you must trust me! But I cannot accept your harsh judgment, your condemnation of yourself. If, as an innocent young girl, you fell in love, and were deeply wounded—I can find in my heart only sympathy for you, and a desire to atone for that wretch's cruelty—"

"He isn't a wretch!" the woman cried. "He's a prince! He's not to be judged by us!"

"Then we must never speak of him again," the gentleman said slowly.

"Except for the fact," said the woman, "that I . . . I had a baby by him. A baby out of wedlock. Never acknowledged by its father, though all the world knew."

Germaine could hear the gentleman's labored breath.

"I see," he said quietly. "A baby."

"A baby, yes. Never acknowledged by its father."

"And so, and so. . . . You had a baby."

"Yes. That's right."

"And you loved its father. . . ."

"I loved its father. I love him still."

"A baby. . . ."

"A baby."

"Then I . . . I . . . Then I must love you both," the gentleman said, with an effort. "I must love the baby as I love its mother, without censure . . . without judgment. I am, my dear, fully capable of . . . of such a love . . . if only you will test me; if only you won't turn me away. This has been, as you can see, a considerable shock to me, but . . . but I believe I will recover . . . am already recovering. . . . If only . . . If . . . But I will, you see," he said, somewhat desperately, "I *will* love your baby as I love you, if only you give me the chance to prove myself!"

"Ah, but you don't understand," the woman whispered. "The baby is dead."

"Dead—!"

"The baby is dead. And I am lost, and should have been allowed, that night, to drown myself! If only you had let me go—if only you had had mercy on me!"

Suddenly she ran from the room, and the gentleman, stunned, called out after her, "But my dear— My poor darling— What have you said?"

He ran out after her, clumsily, panting.

"My dear— Oh, my dear— Please don't forsake me—"

Germaine, hidden behind the love seat, sat with her eyes shut tight and her fists pressed against her ears. She did not *want* to hear, she did not *want* to know.

Deep in her chest, in the lower part of her chest, that odd pulsating ache began, as if it were something that wanted violently to kick into life, to define itself. But she ignored it. She remained motionless, alone now in the room, hearing nothing. Her cheeks were damp with tears but she could not judge—were they tears of sorrow, or of rage? She did not *want* to be a witness to all that was forced upon her.

The Mirror

Preparing herself for her journey to Winterthur, where she was to sign a very important contract and to acquire a considerable amount of land, Leah studied her glowing reflection in the mirror and was well pleased with it. *Her* reflection, and *her* mirror: and even on one of her less triumphant mornings, when she woke confused and unrefreshed from a light, worrisome sleep, her mind already jangling and clattering like a trolley, the chaff of stray bits of quarrels blowing about her head, the mirror gave her back a calm, composed, and frankly—was there any need for modesty?—beautiful image. She turned from side to side, examining herself. Those magnificent eyes . . . the fleshy, full lips . . . the comely nose . . . the heavy red-brown hair, as lustrous now as it had been when she was a girl of sixteen. . . . She wore emerald earrings and a green cashmere suit with a sable collar, which Nightshade had selected for her (for the strange little man delighted in his mistress's clothes, her innumerable clothes, exactly as if he were a giddy young girl servant—and what did it matter, Leah said sharply to Gideon or Cornelia or Noel or anyone who presumed to criticize her, if he *was* somewhat repulsive, oughtn't they to look beyond physical appearances?); she slipped a gold bracelet watch, a parting gift from Mr. Tirpitz, around her wrist.

Germaine, she called out, absently, while gazing into the mirror, are you hiding in here?—where are you?

She had thought she'd seen, for a brief moment, the child's reflection in the mirror, behind her; but when she glanced around no one was there. A pale glowering winter light gave to the furnishings in the room—some of them familiar, some new—an inhospitable look.

Germaine? Are you playing a game with me?

But the child did not appear from behind the bed, or the desk, or the old armoire Leah had had moved upstairs from Violet's room, and since she rarely played games with anyone, let alone her mother on a busy morning, Leah concluded that she wasn't in the room: it was quite probable that the new girl, Helen, was still dressing her in the nursery. Perhaps one of the cats had darted beneath the bed.

Though it was a long journey by train to Winterthur, and a December blizzard was predicted, Germaine was to accompany Leah; for Leah would have been uneasy, for reasons she could not have articulated, if the child were left behind. Often, upon impulse, at the oddest times (when Germaine was being bathed, for instance, or when she was already asleep for the night, or when Leah was in the midst of an important telephone call), Leah felt the need, an almost physical need, to seek out her daughter, to hug her and stare into her eyes, to laugh, to kiss her, to ask, in a voice that never betrayed anxiety, What should I do next? What next? Germaine? At such times the child usually hugged her mother, wordlessly, and with a surprising strength; her slender arms could close like steel bands around Leah's neck, startling and delighting her. The *love* that passed between them—! But it was more than love, it was the passion of absolute sympathy: absolute identity: as if the same blood coursed through both their bodies, carrying with it the very same thoughts. Naturally the two-year-old never told Leah what to do, or even betrayed much intelligent awareness of Leah's actual words, but after a few minutes of hugging and kissing and whispering, during which Leah had no idea what she said, it might have been simply baby talk, she would invariably know what strategy to pursue: the idea, the perfectly formed conviction, would rise jubilant in her mind.

So Germaine *must* accompany her to Winterthur, to this extremely important meeting, despite Gideon's and Cornelia's objections; and of course Helen would be coming, and Nightshade, whom Leah was beginning to find indispensable; and at the last minute Jasper had been added to the party. (Hiram, of course, who had worked with Leah for months on these negotiations, had fully intended to go—but since his mother's wedding to that old derelict he had been sleeping poorly, plagued by bouts of sleepwalking; it would be too dangerous, he believed, to sleep in unfamiliar surroundings, even if a servant stayed up through the night to watch him. And he had to admit, he said with a wry laugh, that his nephew Jasper, though only nineteen, knew more than he in certain respects . . . the boy had business instincts as remarkable as Leah's.)

Leah took off the emerald earrings, and screwed on a pair of pearl earrings, tilting her head, noting with quiet pleasure how the winter light behind her outlined her figure (a superb figure, still, though she continued to lose weight, and her dressmaker was always busy) and, reflected in the mirror, illuminated her fine smooth pale skin. She was still a young woman, still young, though she had lived through so much . . . though she felt, at times, half-amused, as if she might be great-aunt Veronica's age. . . . Gideon, sullen Gideon, was graying: his wonderful black hair was turning salt-and-pepper: there were impatient, not very attractive, creases on his forehead. Of course he was still a handsome man. It hurt her, it angered her, to see how handsome he was, how little fools like two or three of their houseguests this past month, and of course servants like Helen, and that unfortunate Garnet Hecht, gazed upon him adoringly. They *were* fools, women were largely fools, and deserved whatever happened to them . . . whatever happened to them when they succumbed to men. . . . Since Gideon's little finger had been amputated, however, perhaps he would not seem so attractive; perhaps he would seem deformed; freakish; contemptible. (It was a measure of his absurd self-mocking stubbornness that the finger had had to be amputated at all. Gideon's hand had been infected from a bite of some kind, and though he must have felt pain for days, and noticed the angry red streaks reaching upward toward his heart, he had done nothing about it . . . claimed he was too busy to see Jensen. How angry Leah had been, how she had wanted to strike him with her fists, and claw at that dark imperious face! *You would let yourself rot away, wouldn't you, inch by inch, to spite me. . . .*)

But she hadn't attacked him. She had not even spoken to him about the finger. The *absurd,* the *ridiculous* finger. . . . It was an imperfectly kept secret that Gideon now slept in another bedchamber, at the far end of the corridor, though, for appearance's sake, or out of indifference, he kept most of his clothes in this room. Certainly the servants knew, for how could they fail to know, and anyway what did it matter: Gideon with his expensive automobiles (the Rolls coupe, Leah had learned to her dismay, had cost nearly as much as the family limousine, which seated eight people comfortably, in addition to the driver) and his lengthy unexplained absences (which Leah supposed had to do with business deals and investments of his own, for he and Ewan preferred to keep their money separate from the family, and were always alluding to matters no one else understood) and his imponderable inert spirit-paralyzing tarry-black moods (which Leah despised, for they were the purest form of self-indulgence): what did it matter, really?

The mirrored Leah raised her chin, untroubled. *She* did not care in the slightest about her husband; so one might gather from studying her impassive face. She looked, instead, as indeed she *was,* like a young woman about to embark upon yet another adventure—confident as a sleepwalker in the destiny opening before her.

That mirror, moved upstairs from Violet's drawing room when Leah had had her bedchamber expanded (a wall was knocked out, and a long modern plate-glass window took the place of the fussy old windows with their leaded mullions) to accommodate a spacious desk, as well as other new pieces of furniture, was one of the most handsome of the manor's antiques: it was about three feet by two, with a heavy ornate gold frame, inlaid with ivory and jade, in a girandole style. Leah had had it moved upstairs along with a somewhat crude but charming bas relief carving of the Bellefleur coat of arms, which hung now on the wall above her desk.

An antique mirror, evidently a favorite of Violet's: and, as it turned out, a most unusual mirror. For while it couldn't be trusted (for reasons of the light, evidently) to show everything that passed before it, as if finicky about its tastes, it certainly showed Leah at her most complete, her most characteristic. It was the only mirror she could rely upon. Dressing, preparing her hair, rehearsing certain facial mannerisms, gazing for long moments at a time into her mirrored eyes: so Leah communed not only with that expertly presented reflection, but with her own interior self, which was of course hidden from the scrutiny of others.

You know me! Ah, *don't* you know me! she laughed into the mirror, running her tongue hard over her front teeth, patting the back of her sleek, heavy coiffeur. If Nightshade were not present (for she often allowed him into her boudoir, he was so asexual, so harmless) she might even lean to the glass and brush it with her lips, innocently vain as a young girl before a ball.

No one else knows me as *you* know me, she whispered into the mirror.

It was quite true: for, on her way to her room on the eighteenth floor of the Winterthur Arms, after a highly gratifying afternoon during which another sizable chunk of the old empire was returned to them (piece by piece, slowly, it reasserted itself, Jean-Pierre's original property, though now it was, of course, not simply wilderness land but farms and orchards and mills and factories and villages, entire villages, and parts of cities as well), and Leah would be able to declare, in triumph, upon her return to Bellefleur, that they were now more than *half* their way to their goal— returning to her room undeniably tired but jubilant as well, and fairly gloating with her good fortune, feeling her strong heart beat with confidence, Leah happened to see, in the elevator's gold-flecked mirror, an image so clearly *not* herself that she laughed aloud, angrily, at the sight of it.

The broad, showy, vulgar mirror framed a woman of young middle age, with distinctly sallow skin, and querulous, even shrewish lines about her lipsticked mouth. The woman might have been handsome at one time; but now her eyes were shadowed, and her hair, though expertly and fussily arranged on her head, was dull and lusterless, and lacked body. She wore dangling earrings, evidently pearls, that, so close beside her skin, made it appear almost yellowish, and the fur collar of her jacket looked synthetic. How crude a mirror, and what an insult to the overcharged guests of the Winterthur Arms! Leah did no more than glance in it, absentmindedly patting the back of her head. The lighting in the elevator was poor and the quality of the mirror's glass was obviously inferior. . . .

No, only the antique mirror in her own room could be trusted.

Once Upon a Time...

Once upon a time, the children were told, a seventeen-year-old Indian boy was lynched not a mile away—hanged from a great oak on the lakeshore drive. The oak was called the Hanging Tree. But it was no longer there—it had been felled many years back.

Why was he hanged, the children asked.

Some men thought he had started a fire. A hay barn went up in flames, and people thought Indians had done it.

But did *he* do it?

Your great-uncle Louis thought he hadn't, probably.

Then what happened?—what happened to the Indians?

The boy was killed, and they dragged his body around the village for a while, and ended up with it at a riverside tavern. It might have gotten buried. As for the rest of the Indians—they ran away, as they always did. After a while, then, they came back.

Weren't they afraid?

Well—they came back.

Fredericka read aloud to her brother, punctuating her reading with sobs of angry despair, for men *were* animals, mankind as a whole *was* unregenerate, and only Christ's Word could redeem them: by lamplight on a sleeting January evening she read from Franklin's "A Narrative of the Late Massacres in Lancaster County of a Number of Indians, Friends of this Province, by Persons Unknown, with Some Observations on the Same," while Raphael sat with his fingers still, not drumming, on the desk top before him.

> ... These Indians were the remains of the tribe of the Six Nations, settled at Conestogo, and thence called Conestogo

Indians. On the first arrival of the English, messengers from this tribe came to welcome them, with presents of venison, corn, and skins; and the whole tribe entered into a treaty with the first proprietor, which was to last "as long as the sun should shine, or the waters run in the rivers."

This treaty has been since frequently renewed, and the chain brightened, as they express it, from time to time. It has never been violated, on their part or ours, until now. . . .

It has always been observed that Indians settled in the neighborhood of white people do not increase, but diminish continually. This tribe accordingly went on diminishing, till there remained in their town on the manor but twenty persons, viz., seven men, five women, and eight children, boys and girls. . . .

This little society continued the custom they had begun, when more numerous, of addressing every new governor, and every descendant of the first proprietor, welcoming him to the province. . . . They had accordingly sent up an address of this kind to our present governor, on his arrival; but the same was scarce delivered when the unfortunate catastrophe happened, which we are about to relate.

On Wednesday, the 14th of December, of 1763, fifty-seven men from some of our frontier townships, who had projected the destruction of this little commonwealth, came, all well mounted, and armed with fire-locks, hangers, and hatchets, having travelled through the country at night, to Conestogo manor. There they surrounded the small village of Indian huts, and just at break of day broke into them all at once. Only three men, two women, and a young boy were found at home, the rest being out among the neighboring white people, some to sell the baskets, brooms, and bowls they manufactured, and others on other occasions. These poor defenseless creatures were immediately fired upon, stabbed, and hatcheted to death! The good Shehaus, among the rest, cut to pieces in his bed. All of them were scalped and otherwise horribly mangled. Then their huts were set on fire, and most of them burnt down. Then the troop, pleased with their own conduct and bravery, but enraged that any of the poor Indians had escaped the massacre, rode off, in small parties. . . . Those cruel men again assembled themselves, and, hearing that the remaining fourteen Indians were in the workhouse at Lancaster, they suddenly appeared in that town, on the 27th of December. Fifty of them, armed as before, dismounting, went directly to the workhouse, and by violence broke open the door, and entered with the utmost fury in their countenances. When the poor wretches saw they had no protection nigh, nor could possibly escape, and being without the least weapon for defense, they divided into their little families, the children clinging to the parents; they fell on their knees, protested their innocence, declared their love to the English, and that in their whole lives they had never done them injury; and in this posture they all received the hatchet. . . . Men, women, and little children were every one inhumanly murdered in cold blood. . . .

The poor woman broke off, too moved to continue. After some minutes she asked, in a quavering voice, that Raphael join her in prayer —that they kneel together on the floor of his study, and beg God to forgive them their sins. The white race, she whispered, wades knee-deep in blood.

Raphael took off his pince-nez, sighing, and laid them on his desk, but did not kneel. He did not move from his chair. He said, before Fredericka could repeat her request, *Those* Indians have been dead a long time.

Louis's wife Germaine, now a woman of thirty-four, with a plump, ruddy, pretty face and hair that frizzed in humid weather, read, in her stumbling way (for she had never *entirely* learned to read) newspapers and magazines that came into the house, usually by way of her father-in-law, who traveled about so restlessly; and she always read Harlan Bellefleur's terse letters to Louis, for fear they might contain passages the children, or at any rate the fifteen-year-old Arlette, should not see. . . . For instance, in the Colorado Territory U.S. soldiers, led by Colonel J. M. Chivington, attacked a settlement of friendly Indians camped outside the walls of Fort Lyon, murdering six hundred of them in a day (most of them women and children), and mutilating and scalping them as well: some of the soldiers cut out the genitals of women and girls, and stretched them over their saddle bows, or wore them in their hats while riding in the ranks. . . .

Think if Arlette should happen to read of such a thing! Germaine said to her husband. Her full, broad cheeks had turned beet-red; her mouth was a tiny damp hook of consternation. Why, that shouldn't be talked about! That isn't—that isn't *nice,* she whispered.

One fine October day a flotilla of steamboats and canalboats appeared from the west, to celebrate the opening of the Great Canal. The Great Canal was nearly four hundred miles long and had taken eight years to complete, and all along its banks, on this day, crowds of cheering spectators awaited, and cannons were fired, and firecrackers were set off. In the villages and towns church bells rang as if it were a crazed Sunday.

The *Chancellor Livingston,* a steamboat, was the flagship of the squadron, and a fine trim ship it was—decked out in red, white, and blue streamers, and carrying the most fashionable of passengers. Another handsome ship was the *Washington,* carrying naval, military, and civil officers and their guests. There were, in addition, some twenty-nine sail-

ing ships, schooners, barks, canalboats, and sailboats, each receiving
cannon salutes from the forts they passed. A canalboat called the *Young
Lion of the West* was bedecked with flags and banners, and carried on
board, to the spectators' delight, two eagles, four raccoons, a fawn, a fox,
and two living wolves. The *Seneca Chief,* a barge drawn by four powerful
white horses, bore two fawns, two live eagles, a single brown bear, a
young moose, and two Senecan Indian youths in the costume of their
dusky nation.

Once upon a time, the children were told, there was a family named
Varrell.

Where did they come from, so many of them?

It was said they bred like rabbits, or aphids.

They must have sprung out of the earth, or maybe crawled out of the
Noir Swamp. The men were trappers, Indian traders, peddlers, farmers
on small scrubby good-for-nothing soil. . . . No, they were really trash.
White trash. They lived common-law back in the woods, and beat their
wives and children. They were notorious drunkards and bullies and law-
breakers. Horse theft, arson, tavern brawls, backwoods murders that
went uninvestigated. (If the Varrells killed people like themselves, or
killed one another, why would Chautauqua authorities intervene? Be-
sides, it would be dangerous to intervene.)

Even their moonshine, customers complained, was inferior. When it
wasn't outright poison.

Involved in the lynching of the Indian boy were Reuben, Wallace,
and Myron Varrell; their ages were forty-six, thirty-one, and twenty-two.
And there were other Varrells in the Lake Noir settlement—by some
estimates as many as twenty-five.

Where did they come from, so many of them, in a generation or two?
Men with hard flat faces, unkempt hair and beards, eyes the color of chill
swamp mist . . . ? Their crimes were of two types: one committed surreptitiously, often by night; the other committed boldly, even self-righteously,
in public, frequently with the help of others. Some of the Varrells had of
course been killed in brawls, and many of them had been badly beaten
(and even crippled: Louis Bellefleur had witnessed, from the street, the
drunken melee that erupted at a wedding party in a Fort Hanna hotel that
resulted in Henry Varrell's broken spine—Henry being young Myron's
father); a number were imprisoned at Powhatassie; but most of the time
they ran off unapprehended, and witnesses did not care to testify against
them. A Varrell girl had married into the family of a Bushkill's Ferry
justice of the peace, and Wallace, even with his record of arrests (for
fighting, arson, and petty theft) was a sheriff's deputy. . . . Reuben, who
dared to strike Louis's horse, and who shouted drunkenly for him to go
on home, had worked on the Great Canal and was said to be half-crazy
as a consequence of heatstroke suffered one sweltering August day. He
and his common-law wife had been arrested, but never tried, for the

malnutrition death of a ten-month-old baby. . . . So Reuben *should* have been in prison at the time of the lynching.

But where did they come from, so many of them? Breeding like rabbits or aphids? It seems they sprang from a single woman, a lumber-camp follower who passed herself off shamelessly as a cook. She lived right in the bunkhouse with the men. Migrated from camp to camp, from Paie-des-Sables to Contracoeur to Mount Kittery to the great pine forest east of Mount Chattaroy, season after season, bringing with her two or three squaws, a few white women, and a moronic baby-faced girl, grossly fat, who sucked her thumb and whimpered much of the time, when she wasn't eating or being employed by the men. Where, exactly, this string of diseased whores came from, whether the Varrell woman (who treated them sternly but not unkindly) had brought them to the mountains, to the lumber camps, or whether they had simply happened to meet there and to team up, for safety's sake, no one knew. The youngest and most attractive squaw, blind drunk on corn whiskey, tried to stab the foreman of the Paie-des-Sables camp to death, and did a fairly good job of it before his friends pulled her off; but in general the Varrell woman kept her girls under control. She was a tall, soft-bodied, good-natured woman with an agreeably ugly face and a nose that looked as if it had been broken. Already in her early thirties her stout legs were riddled with varicose veins, but as a girl, it was said, she had been *quite* attractive . . . at least to men in this part of the world, who might go for months without seeing a woman. She was foul-mouthed, blunt, frank, funny, and never wept. And never regretted anything.

She had one son, Reuben. And then another. And then another, and another, over a period of years. She left the lumber camps to live with a man; and then with another man; and then she wandered from town to town, living with her children when they were willing to take her in. In the end, it was said, she drank herself to death—and she wasn't that old, really: probably in her late fifties. But women wore out quickly in that part of the world. (Germaine, Louis's wife, believed she had once seen the old Varrell woman—that terrible creature—urinating in a public thorough-fare in Bushkill's Ferry. What a sight! How shameful, for everyone to see! Germaine had tugged at her daughter Arlette's arm, commanding her to hurry along, not to look back, but of course the willful girl *would* look, and even giggle in horror.)

It was commonly known, long before the lynching, that the Varrells resented Jean-Pierre because they believed he had "cheated" them of some land. (He had bought it from them. Had paid cash. Of course he hadn't paid much but then they hadn't expected much, had been in fact grateful for what they received.) They were jealous of him, as they were jealous of his son Louis, and of anyone in the area who appeared to be doing well—anyone who wasn't in debt, or struggling to pay off two mortgages. If it appeared that a Varrell might be establishing himself in town, like Silas with his partnership in the White Antelope Inn, it invariably happened that the business went bankrupt or suffered, uninsured, a fire loss; or simply died a gradual death that was no one's fault. The girl who had married into the justice of the peace's family soon left the mountains with her husband, to stake out a claim in Oregon, and was never seen or heard of again. Myron, who had served in the state militia, was rumored to have been promoted through the ranks—he was a first lieutenant, or a captain, or a major—but one day he merely appeared back home, a civilian again, discharged, with a wormlike little scar on his right cheek and $35 severance pay and no explanations. He worked intermittently as a farm laborer, sometimes alongside the Indian boy Charles Xavier, whom he had always disliked. An Indian with a name like that!—pretending to be a Catholic convert, of all the outrageous things! It was an insult, the Varrells thought, for a white man to work alongside an Onondagan half-breed.

Charles Xavier was short for his age, and considered mildly retarded (he was an orphan, abandoned at birth, found wrapped in some rags in a Fort Hanna alleyway on a stinging-cold March morning), though his small, sturdy shoulders and arms were well developed, and he could work long exhausting hours in the fields or orchards without complaint. He was valued as a farmhand but not especially liked, even by the farmers' wives who customarily took pity on him (for he *was* an orphan, and a Christian), since his narrow chin and dark scowling eyebrows and chronic silence gave him the reputation, possibly misleading, of being hostile even to friendly whites.

On the day of the opening of the Great Canal, which ran, for some miles, parallel to the wide, rough Nautauga River, when church bells were ringing in villages and towns, and firecrackers and Roman candles were being set off, and cannon discharged from atop the walls of the old forts, it happened, certainly not by accident, that a corncrib silo belonging to a farmer named Eakins, who lived just off the old Military Road, caught fire; and because volunteer firemen were all at the canal opening festivities, miles away, the silo blazed like mad, and a nearby storage barn also caught fire and was lost. Indians were blamed because Eakins had had difficulty with a gang of threshers, all Indians, he had hired not long before, and had been forced to fire (they had started out industriously, but soon lost energy and interest)—but those Indians, those particular Indians, had vanished.

It then happened, miles away at Lake Noir, that a hay barn belonging to a brother-in-law of the former Indian trader Rabin caught fire—and at once Indians were blamed. Charles Xavier happened to be hurrying along the muddy main street of the village, and though he belonged, or half-belonged, to a tribe of Indians who were considered "allies" (though pitifully few in number these Onondagans had fought on the side of the locals against the British, in the recent war) he was seized at once, by a group of men, and hauled into the White Antelope Inn, where he was questioned about the fire for approximately two hours. The more frightened the boy became, the more excited and angry his interrogators; the more he protested, not only his innocence, but his very knowledge of the fire (a fire which hadn't been, as everyone admitted, a very serious one), the more drunkenly ferocious the white men became. Old Rabin, Wallace, Myron, and a number of others, soon joined by Reuben, who was already drunk, and two or three of his friends; and men who drifted in off the street or who, having heard of Charles Xavier's "arrest," came running; and, just before the boy was hauled off to be hanged, the justice of the peace himself, a young-old man with a twitch beneath his left eye. His name was Wiley and since he had drifted over, years back, from Boston, he was considered a city man, and something of a cultured person, though the interests he pursued, in the Lake Noir area, were not very different, except in degree of intensity, from those pursued by most of the other male inhabitants. He drank, but hadn't the capacity of the others; he played cards, but not with much skill; he had courted a woman who was being courted, from the other side, so to speak, by Wallace Varrell, and had been forced to back away. It was rumored that he accepted bribes but that was probably not the case, usually: he was simply intimidated by the defendants who came before him, or by their numerous relatives. A murderer might be sent away to Powhatassie, or even hanged, but the men who had arrested him, the witnesses who testified against him, and the judge himself, were often not likely to survive. So while it was true, as Louis Bellefleur charged, that Wiley was a coward, he was not an altogether inexplicable coward. . . .

Those were hard times to live in, the children were told.

But weren't they exciting?—so the boys always asked. (For they knew, beforehand, what was coming: the lynching and burning of Charles Xavier; the angry public protesting of their great-uncle Louis; the "trouble" at the old loghouse in Bushkill's Ferry; the arrival, on a beautiful high-headed Costeña mare, of Louis's brother Harlan, who had disappeared out west almost twenty years before.) *Weren't* they exciting? the boys begged.

When word came to Louis that the Varrells and Rabin and their friends were interrogating poor Charles Xavier, and had, evidently, extracted a confession from him, Louis rode off at once for town—no matter that Germaine forbade him to go (for she knew, immediately, that the half-breed boy was doomed—Indian lives were cheap in the mountains, though not much cheaper than white men's lives), and his daughter Arlette threw a kind of tantrum, running alongside him as he trotted away on old Bonaparte, screaming for him to come back. At the age of fifteen Arlette was a head taller than her mother, and nearly as thick about the waist and hips; but her breasts were tiny and she often seemed, in jackets and pants and riding boots, as much a boy as her brothers. Her face was moon-shaped, a handsome golden tan, and she wore her dark hair—frizzy as her mother's—as short as possible, though it wasn't fashionable in those days for girls to wear their hair short. (Even her grandfather Jean-Pierre teased her, and complained to her mother. Didn't she *want,* after all, to be a woman?) While Louis saddled his old stallion Arlette shouted incoherently—she wanted him not to go, or maybe she wanted to accompany him—wouldn't he at least try to locate Jacob and Bernard, and *they* could accompany him— But Louis swatted her away, and did not trouble to reply. He couldn't bear hysterical women. He couldn't even listen to hysterical women.

Germaine, watching through a front window, saw her husband ride off, and her daughter, poor ungainly Arlette, standing for a while in the road, amid the puddles, bare-headed, somewhat stooped, her fingers twitching. She may have been crying: her back was to the house and Germaine couldn't see.

Of the three children, Arlette, the youngest, was the most difficult: they called her "high-strung." She endured her older brothers' teasing, and her grandfather's well-intentioned affectionate bullying; she obviously loved, and was deeply embarrassed by, her father (he was so loud and blustery, even in the close confines of the kitchen, on a snowy day, and of course he drank, and was always quarreling and even fighting, with his fists, with men like himself; and the queer half-frozen look of his face, paralyzed on one side, so that he never had more than *half* a smile, was excruciatingly embarrassing to Arlette); though she fought, alternately sardonic and tearful, with her mother, and seemed unable, since the age of thirteen, to bear her mother's mere *presence,* Germaine was inclined to think that it was just her age: it would pass: she was a good girl, not at all malicious, and in a few years, maybe after she married, or after she had her first baby, she would get over being so high-strung and come around to being . . . a sweet affectionate sensible daughter.

(But in the meantime, how difficult she was! The tantrum in the stable, and out on the road; plucking at her father's sleeve so that he had to swat her away; actually screaming at him, her face gone red and her eyes dilated, as if she had a *right,* an actual *right,* to behave like this with her father. She frequently exclaimed in disgust that she was ashamed of her grandfather—yes, he had made a great deal of money, and now he was famous for owning half of the *Nautauga Gazette* (where some of his own *pensées,* on horses, were appearing frequently), and everyone respected him, or at least feared him; but she couldn't forgive him for the Indian woman with whom he lived, when he was in the area, and whom he had actually brought home—to *their* home—several times, without apology. She couldn't forgive him for the way he favored his grandsons over her (though at the same time she couldn't have endured his "grandfatherly" attentions either, his teasing about her figure, or her hair that looked, on certain days, like a "pickaninny's.") It was probable that she admired her brothers, Jacob especially, for he most resembled their father, but they were frequently quarreling, like all brothers and sisters, and in any case neither Jacob nor Bernard had much time for her. She was most ashamed of her uncle Jedediah. She had never met him, of course, for he had gone off into the mountains before her birth, but she loved, with a disdainful fastidiousness, to ask Germaine and Louis about him. There were always stories about Jedediah, told at the country school-house, or brought home by Louis who, half-amused, half-contemptuous, repeated them, often with embellishments: sometimes Jedediah was sighted, ghostlike, in the mountains, clad in animal skins, with a long gray-white beard, and a cadaverous face, and "piercing" eyes. He was a prophet out of the Old Testament. Then again, he was quite simply loony —he didn't, as the saying went, deal with a full deck—but he wasn't any more crazy, probably, than most of the mountain hermits of local legend. At other times he was sighted, people claimed, upriver, at Powhatassie or as far away as Vanderpoel, again clad in fur (but these were fine furs— mink, or fox, or beaver—fashioned for him by an expert furrier), obvi-ously wealthy from his dealings in skins, on his way toward being another John Jacob Astor, perhaps: a handsome man in the prime of life, usually accompanied by a beautiful woman, who did no more than stare blankly, without recognition, at the scruffy Lake Noir men who gazed after him in the street, too awed to call out: Bellefleur! Aren't you a Bellefleur! . . . Then again he was a cranky, troublesome eccentric who never left the Mount Blanc area and whom no one (except Mack Henofer) had seen for years: it was he, surely, who was responsible for the sabotage of so many traplines that trappers now avoided his territory. He was raving mad, or then again he was simply mean-spirited; he lived with an Indian woman; or he lived alone on the side of a mountain no one could traverse. He subsisted on potatoes. He ate raccoons and squirrels raw. He was deathly sick. He was tall and muscular and in superb health. . . . But no one had seen him for years except Henofer, and now that Henofer was dead (he had been found, his body badly decomposed, at the bottom of a ravine near his cabin, his shotgun beside him, one barrel fired) it was likely that no one would ever see Jedediah again. It was even possible that he had died.)

Despite Louis's frantic intervention, and the audacity with which (not unarmed, for he was never unarmed in public: but he knew better than to show his pistol) he shouted at the men to release the Indian boy— despite his ill-advised courage in continuing to follow them on horseback, out to the edge of the village, when it was obvious that they were not only not going to be persuaded by him or by his threats but were positively goaded on by him, as by Charles Xavier's terror, and the presence of awed, excited witnesses—some of them women and children; and despite the fact that the men (Rabin, the Varrells, three or four others, and poor sweating grinning Wiley who was conducting, on horseback, a "trial," even to the point of attempting to cross-examine the bleeding, stupefied boy as he was dragged along behind Rabin's horse, barbed wire twined about his chest, pulled snug against his armpits) were all going to be guilty of murder—murder in the first degree, as Louis yelled: despite all this Charles Xavier was doomed, as Louis's wife had known he would be without leaving her kitchen. He was doomed, jabbering and sobbing with terror, as oblivious of Louis Bellefleur's attempt to save him as he was of Herbert Wiley's conducting of a somewhat truncated trial. The men, drunken and gleeful and so excited their hands trembled, and moisture darted out of the corners of their eyes, tossed the rope over the thick limb of the oak tree and brought the noose down around Charles Xavier's dark head just as Wiley, panting, pronounced the verdict: Guilty as charged! *Guilty as charged.*

There was a certain photograph in a certain book in Raphael Bellefleur's study which the children gazed upon, in silence, sometimes sticking their fingers in their mouths: for what was there to say, *what* was there to feel? It was not a photograph they cared to examine in one another's presence, for it was too shameful—too embarrassing—and someone was likely to burst into silly frightened laughter—and perhaps one of the adults would come running, or one of the ubiquitous servants. So they studied it in secret. Over the years. One by one, at odd times, tiptoeing into the library when no one was around, their faces flushed. Even Yolande had looked at it, aghast, and quickly closed the book and replaced it on the shelf, in its special place; even Christabel; and Bromwell (who might have had it in mind, or beneath the threshold of his mind, when he decided to turn away from the fleshiness of history to the cold purities of space); even young Raphael, who stared with his dark melancholy gravity and seemed not to judge, never to wish to judge, anything human. And in her time of course Germaine was shown the photograph, by one of aunt Aveline's children.

It showed, with surprising clarity, a group of some forty-six men circled about, but standing well back from, the flaming body of what had been, according to the caption, a "Negro youth." The men were, of course, all white, and they ranged in ages from about sixteen to sixty; there was a single child, peeping at the body as if he'd never seen anything so astonishing, so *bright.* A number of the men were staring at the blazing body (which was naked, very dark, partly obscured across its legs by burning boards and trash), some were staring at the camera. Most of the expressions were fairly serious though some were oddly bland, even bored, and others were quite jovial: a gentleman in the left foreground, with a showy zebra-stripe necktie and an umbrella, was grinning proudly for the camera, one hand upraised in a salute. The caption said *Lynching death of a Negro youth, Blawenburg, New York.* No date was given. No photographer's credit was given. The lynching must have taken place on a winter day because all the men wore jackets or coats, and hats—they all wore hats, without exception: fedoras, railroad caps, sailors' caps, even what appeared to be a bowler, dented at the crown. None of the men wore glasses. None of the men wore beards. It was a strange picture. Then again, if you studied it long enough, it was a very familiar picture. The blazing body was a blazing body but the men assembled about it were just men.

Mount Ellesmere

Bromwell, sent downstate to an expensive and allegedly prestigious boarding school for boys, began writing letters of complaint home almost as soon as classes started in late September. His instructors, he charged, were either well intentioned and ignorant, or deliberately malicious and ignorant. The studies he was forced to take were irrelevant, and presented in textbooks of an alarmingly simple-minded nature. The dining hall food might or might not be adequate—he hardly tasted it, not caring about food—but his living quarters were cramped and he was *forced* (that it was said to be for his own good made him all the more furious) to have a roommate, a rubber-faced, six-foot-tall illiterate whose only interests were football and pornographic magazines. The other boys— well, what was there to say about *boys?* Bromwell thought them not much more savage and infantile than his cousins, but it was difficult for him to avoid their company, as he had managed, since early childhood, to avoid the company of his cousins. For one thing, he had to room with that creature; he had to sit beside others in classes, in the dining hall, and at chapel; he had to participate in athletic activities, despite his delicate frame and his hypersensitivity and the fact that his glasses, though taped to his head, were always flying off. (But it was part of a boy's education, at New Hazelton Academy, that the body be challenged and subjected to stress as well as the mind. Yes, the headmaster knew, yes, he knew very well, he knew from painful personal experience—for he too had attended New Hazelton, many years ago, and he too had been physically weak, as he assured the angry, tearful Bromwell at each of their several meetings; sports *could* be difficult, but the lessons about life they imparted to a boy were invaluable. In later life Bromwell would agree, surely.) *I am surrounded by brutes and their slavish apologists,* Bromwell wrote home.

Part of the problem was that Bromwell was extremely young—only eleven and a half—and all the other boys were older by several years. (The boys' ages ranged from fourteen to eighteen; there was even a nineteen-year-old, a slack-jawed sadistic ox, who either could not manage to graduate, or did not wish to graduate.) Even for his age Bromwell was undersized, though his fair brown hair that looked, in certain lights, as if it were shading into silver, and his stern, rather censorious expression, and his glasses, gave him the air of a forty-year-old. Despite his physical size and the frequency of the other boys' bullying he could not seem to resist, especially in the classroom, murmuring sarcastic comments when they displayed their ignorance; he was not even able to keep to himself (though surely it would have been politic to do so) his amused incredulity as his instructors' blunders. But do you *want* to be so rigorously disliked by your peers, the headmaster asked, and Bromwell replied, after a moment, in a startled voice: Is being liked or not being liked important? Is it something other people think about . . . ? I must say, I have never considered it.

Everything about the school vexed him though he realized, as he said in his letters to Leah, that he couldn't remain at home: he *couldn't* endure those embarrassing tutorial sessions with uncle Hiram, and of course it was out of the question for him to attend the local school, or even the public school in Nautauga Falls. So he would try, he would try. . . . He would try to accommodate himself to the school's idiotic schedule (the boys were roused by clanging bells each weekday morning at 7:00 A.M. and were allowed to sleep until eight on weekends; "lights out" was at 10:30 P.M. every day except Fridays and Saturdays, when they might stay up until 11:30; if a boy did not march into the dining room with the others in his corridor, if he came in even a minute late, alone, he was turned away from his table; and of course they all had to attend—what primitive folly! —chapel).

No concessions were made to his repeated pleas that he be allowed to stay up as late as he wished, in the laboratory (which was shamefully inadequate) or the library (which was even more shamefully inadequate: the worst of it was, his own books were still in their crates, unpacked, in the school's damp basement, because there wasn't "enough room" for them elsewhere). He craved, with an almost physical desire, to stay up through the night . . . to know that his was the only consciousness, the only thinking consciousness, in the building . . . and as a consequence he lay awake until two or three in the morning, quite miserable, his mind beset by mathematical problems and astronomical speculations until he felt he might go mad.

Do you want me, Mother, he inquired politely, *to go mad? Is that part of your design?*

But Leah rarely answered his letters. She sent him his allowance, and usually scribbled a few words of a cheerful or innocuous nature (telling him nothing, even, about Christabel: the last news he had, she and her lover were being pursued by two separate teams of detectives, Schaff's and the family's, and had been traced to Mexico), making no reference to his queries.

He wrote to Gideon, and to grandfather Noel; he even wrote to his cousin Raphael, whom he *almost* missed—though he suspected that if he were back home, Raphael's moodiness would soon bore him. He complained that the athletic activities he was forced to endure were destroying him. During a recent basketball game, for instance, the boys had repeatedly thrown the basketball at *him,* right at his face, regardless of the fact that the referee was blowing his whistle like mad, and Bromwell's nose was dripping blood (his glasses, of course, had been knocked off immediately, and were—again—cracked); when at last, after great hesitation, he had ventured out to the end of the diving board, trembling with cold, a boy had rushed past him to dive into the pool, giving him a playful shove with the flat of his hand, and he'd fallen, sideways, to everyone's amusement, and so badly slapped his side, and filled his head with water, that he had nearly drowned. Yet these events were always called accidents, or instances of his classmates' high spirits. . . . Most distressing of all, Bromwell complained, was the fact that *Bellefleur* was so frequently whispered about. At the start of the term some of the older boys barged into his room, throwing themselves on his bed, eager to make friends; they had heard all sorts of things about his family, up there at Lake Noir, didn't the Bellefleurs own racing horses, weren't they mixed up in politics, weren't they wealthy, hadn't there been murderers in the family, and someone sent away to prison . . . ? Meeting Bromwell, then, had been a considerable disappointment.

(During the spring term news came of the Fort Hanna shootout, during which uncle Ewan and his deputies gunned down four men who were barricaded in a rooming house with rifles and a considerable amount of ammunition—but Bromwell met his classmates' respectful inquiries by claiming that he had never met Ewan Bellefleur, the popular sheriff of Nautauga County. He was a *distant* relative.)

It was shortly after the Fort Hanna incident, and after Bromwell had had to endure the ignominy of earning a grade of 55 on his American history exam (his grades in history were always poor, since he never studied), that he conceived of the idea of running away. The Bellefleurs had so wildly unrealistic a notion of his expenses at the school, and his pastimes, and the "treats" he might wish to buy for his friends, that several of them sent him allowances on a fairly regular basis, and there were frequently unexplained cash gifts from Leah and grandmother Della: so he had managed to acquire, without giving it any thought, more than $3,000. (Which he was shrewd enough to keep, not in his room, or even in the academy's safe, but in a bank in the village.)

He then wrote a highly formal letter to the Mount Ellesmere Institute for Advanced Study in Astronomy, which was located in a distant western state, expressing his hope that, despite his lack of official training and his age (which he did not give), they might allow him to study there. He received an application form, and an impersonal covering letter, so he filled out the form and mailed it back and, one Saturday morning in mid-May, without having heard from Mount Ellesmere, he simply left the New Hazelton Academy for Boys—arose at the usual time, breakfasted with the rest of the pack, and, wearing several layers of clothing (which his roommate thought was odd, but then Bromwell *was* odd), strolled down the school's brick driveway to the road and disappeared. Later, it was discovered that he had withdrawn all his money—a considerable sum —from a local bank, and that he had destroyed all his family's letters, and the few snapshots he'd brought with him to school. When last seen he was walking down the drive, his hands in his pockets; his lips were pursed, and he was whistling a cheerful, tuneless little air.

The Jaws Devour...

It was on a fair June morning that Leah woke with a headache and the curious words *The jaws devour, the jaws are devoured,* running through her mind. And then again on a July morning, very early, before dawn, waking with the thought that there was someone in the room with her, someone who meant harm, *The jaws devour, the jaws are devoured,* a hoarse phlegm-rattled mutter that was her own voice, but much altered. And again later in the month. No matter that her life was now a series of triumphs. No matter that the titanium—its quality as well as its astonishing quantity—now being extracted from the Mount Kittery mines would make it possible for the family to buy up the rest of Jean-Pierre's empire. The dull pulsing headache, the orangish parched taste at the back of her mouth, the sudden conviction that her arms and legs would not respond: that she would lie paralyzed in her bed until someone discovered her. . . . That morning in June, and two mornings in July, and then again in mid-August, before the busloads of migrant workers arrived and it was evident that, this year, the Bellefleurs would have trouble: the sensation of heaviness, despondency, too leaden to be panic, the sensation of grief, but grief, she wanted to shout, for what?—in Christ's name, *what?*

She was triumphant, she carried all before her, within a year or two her plans would be complete (though she was ready for a battle since certain property owners in the mountains, being nearly as wealthy as the Bellefleurs themselves, would not *willingly* agree to sell), on all sides she was admired, and feared, and of course envied; and disliked. But as Hiram told her, the Bellefleurs did not appear on this earth to be *liked,* but to fulfill their destiny. Old Jeremiah had been well liked, in a pitying contemptuous sort of way, and what good had that done him, or anyone? He hadn't even a place of rest in the family cemetery. . . .

She was triumphant, yet the moods came upon her with increasing frequency. Of course she recognized them as mere weaknesses, one of the manifestations of the silly Bellefleur curse, in which she did not really believe—not *really*—for how could she believe in what was almost the sanctity of despair, seeking its expression in a variety of unlikely (sometimes comically unlikely) forms? There was an old family tale of a Bellefleur woman who had simply retired to bed for the rest of her life: she hadn't even pretended, to herself and others, as most female invalids of that era had, that she was *ill*. And Della with her tiresome perpetual grief, which was so obviously nothing more, now, so many decades later, than a way of irritating the family; and Gideon with *his* selfish moods. . . . Well, it was clear to Leah that such behavior was contemptible. She would have roused that complacent old woman from her goosefeather pillows, and turned her out of her room: here, here is the world, it's *here*, you can't deny it! Over the years she had done her best to deflate Della's pretentious mourning, though with little effect: for Della was one of the most stubborn of the Bellefleurs, and would probably leap smiling into her grave knowing that she had managed, throughout the decades, to vex and annoy and sadden everyone who had known her. And then there was Gideon. Gideon with his black rages, his black despondency. Hidden from his admirers. Unguessed-at by his women. (For Leah conceded that he had, from time to time, though only casually, *women:* very much in the plural. But so long as no one in the family knew that she knew, or suspected, so long as Gideon himself didn't know, she was, in a sense, still innocent of her husband's infidelity—a kind of virgin—a defiant and righteous virgin who would one day, at her leisure, have her revenge. But then she sometimes toyed with the idea of a reconciliation. For of course she could win her husband back, if she wished. Whenever she wished. She hadn't any doubt but that he loved *her*, beneath, or beyond, or simultaneous with, his numerous adulteries. Perhaps she *would* summon him back to her bed someday. If she wished.)

The jaws devour, the jaws are . . .

So Leah fell, day by day, into despair. She knew very well that it was absurd, it was quite senseless, yet she could not help herself; she woke earlier and earlier in the morning, no longer with her old sense of impatience, but with a sense, leaden and horrible, of infinite *patience . . .* her limbs so heavy she could barely move them, her head weighed down, her eyelids burning as if she'd spent the night, in secret, in tears. It was mid-August. It was late August. Eight busloads of migrant workers, jabbering their strange, sibilant, malicious tongue, were threatening to go on strike: or the foreman who now represented them (for the old foreman, the one the Bellefleurs had always dealt with, was gone—rumor had it he had been killed earlier in the season) was threatening to go on strike: and the acres and acres of peaches, pears, and apples from the Bellefleur orchards would be lost, falling rotten from the trees, to lie in mounds, food for yellow-jackets, flies, birds, worms. Ewan and Gideon and Noel and Hiram and Jasper were greatly upset, and every day, nearly every hour, something was happening; but Leah, a damp cloth over her eyes, lay on her chaise longue in her darkened bedchamber, too weak to move, too indifferent to care, hearing only a hoarse sluggish voice, *The jaws devour, the jaws are devoured,* a voice she did not recognize and in which she had no interest, any more than she had, now, in the Bellefleur fruit harvest or the Bellefleur fortune.

Water going down a drain. Counterclockwise, did it move? Ever more quickly and quickly as it ran out. A sucking gurgling sound. Not at all disturbing. Restful. Restful as the compost heap the gardener kept, just outside the garden wall. Restful as old Raphael's mausoleum. (But sometimes it angered her, even in her lethargy, to realize that Raphael too had been betrayed by his workers. His employees. *After* the poor man had begun improving their living quarters along the edge of the swamp, *after* he had allowed himself to become convinced by a visiting Manhattan physician that it was his responsibility, as their employer, to provide better sanitary conditions for them, and to treat, or attempt to treat—for there were so many!—those who were suffering from that mysterious intestinal ailment: *after* he had actually made a number of improvements, why then the reporters had swarmed into the village, eager to "expose" him, under instructions from their editors, who were in turn under instructions from newspaper publishers who wanted, for crude political reasons, to ruin Raphael Bellefleur's chances for election. The injustice! The irony! And there was nothing he could do, no way to suppress the fact that thirteen people had died, among them a number of very young children (who were, as the gloating reporters insisted in story after story, working in the hop fields in 102-degree heat alongside their parents)— no way to erase from the minds of the sensation-greedy masses the charges that were laid against him in the public press. And now, and now, Leah thought wearily, that ugly tale was repeating itself, and the family would be helpless, the fruit would rot and thousands upon thousands of dollars would be lost, the workers were being led by a madman, a common criminal, but nothing could be done . . . the Bellefleurs would not only lose their fruit crop but they would be, throughout the Valley, possibly throughout the state, held up to ridicule in the press, and "pitied" by their competitors. Leah *would* have been angrier but she was so tired: so simply, helplessly, shamelessly tired.)

The jaws devour . . .

Those words, which rose in her mind at unpredictable times, frequently brought with them a wraithlike image of Vernon's face: she wondered if he had written them, if they were from one of his long, baffling, exasperating poems. And in that instant, suddenly, she missed him. She missed him very much. So many winters ago, in the downstairs drawing room, knowing that he adored her, smiling and laughing and touching his arm, teasing, making *him* smile, making *him* boyishly happy. . . . Pretending to listen to his recitations. But sometimes listening (for the poems were not *always* incoherent, there were snatches of beauty here and there, and melodic sounds), making an effort to listen. If only she hadn't been so distracted . . . ! She could not remember, now, what had distracted her. And now Vernon was dead. *They* had killed him. That they were now dead themselves as a consequence of Ewan's shrewdness (he had known that to take Vernon's murderers alive would be a blunder, since no witnesses would come forward to testify, and even if they did, and Varrell and Gittings and the others were convicted, some indifferent judge might hand down to them a light sentence, and they might have been paroled in a few years)—that justice had been done, revenge taken —did not soothe her. She missed Vernon. Somehow it had happened that she had not mourned him. One day he was with them, the next day gone: killed by drunken idiots on a Saturday night, thrown bound by his ankles and wrists into the river!—one day she had taken him for granted, as everyone did, and the next day he was gone forever. She hadn't had time, then, to mourn him; or even to think much about him. She had wanted of course to destroy his murderers, and she had been fairly certain that they *would* be destroyed, in a matter of months; but she hadn't had time to dwell upon Vernon himself. And now those strange, haunting, unpleasant words reminded her of him. And she almost wept—she *wanted* to weep—lying motionless on her chaise longue.

Vernon, who had loved her, was dead: and the young woman he had loved, with such passionate shyness, was dead.

Thoughts of Vernon pulled her toward thoughts of her daughter Christabel, whom she had lost; and now there was Bromwell (though a week ago a picture postcard showing mesquite and cactus in flower, addressed merely to "The Bellefleurs," arrived with an enigmatic little message on it and Bromwell's initials: he hoped he had not caused them any worry, he said, but his flight had been necessary, and everything was *quite* fine in his life); and Gideon, of course; Gideon who had deserted her bed after Germaine's birth; Gideon who failed to love her sufficiently. She wanted to weep, and indeed her face constricted, and her mouth opened in a soundless wail; but there were no tears. She hadn't wept, Leah thought, for years.

Gideon, dancing about so clumsily to that tune, how did it go, *the needle's eye, the needle's eye,* staring into her face, speechless with emotion, Gideon so tender, so absurd, crimson-faced, his silly nose bleeding so that he ran out of the room and the children laughed. . . . He had been such a fool, even as a boy.

Hiram wanted to talk with her about Gideon. But her eyelids were so heavy, she yearned only to fall asleep. . . . What does it matter, she whispered, her lips dry and cracked, what does it matter, let him make a fool of himself negotiating with those people, let him give them everything they ask and we'll go bankrupt and everyone will laugh at us, what does it matter, she said, her voice so feeble Hiram could barely hear.

Leah, he said.

Yes.

Leah, is it this strike that has upset you?

I'm not upset.

Are you worried about the crop?—are you worried they might set fire to the barns?

Your voice is too loud, she whispered.

Are you worried they might incite the other workers—

Leave me alone, my head aches, your voice is too loud, she whispered.

So he went away; and she dragged herself up, and managed to dress without glancing in her mirror, and actually went downstairs; and ate what someone gave her; and allowed them to fuss over her, and to tell her about the strikers' demands—higher hourly wages, better living quarters, better food, legal contracts, attorneys on both sides, but primarily higher wages, *much* higher wages—as she sat with her head balanced on her neck on her shoulders so precariously, so very precariously, her head brittle as crockery on her neck that had no strength on her shoulders that yearned to slump forward as water yearns to circle, faster and faster, the drain through which it is plunging.

So she made an appearance downstairs. So she could do it, whenever she liked. Did that satisfy them? Did that answer their anxious questions? She wanted to yawn, and swat them away like flies, and say that everything comes to an end: life ends: there was no point in continuing with the charade.

Then, moving carefully as an elderly woman, she went back upstairs.

She had not cried, and would not.

There was a triumph in that, that she hadn't weakened; that she felt, really, only indifference. It was pure, it was virginal, her supreme indifference. . . . Hiram and the others might think she was despondent because of the strike, but in fact, as they must have known, Leah had begun to sink into her black mood weeks before. She sank three feet, and rose two; she sank eleven feet, and rose eight; one day she sank thirty feet and did not rise at all. On her chaise longue with a damp cloth over her eyes, too tired even to scream at Germaine, or Nightshade, or whoever it was rattling at the doorknob pleading to be let in, she simply floated, bodiless, at the bottom of a great dark pool of water. She was the drowned Vernon, she was Violet, she was Jeremiah who had been swept away in a flood. What remained of *Leah* cared to protest nothing.

And there had been much, that summer, to protest. For somehow it had happened, no one knew exactly how, that the castle was overrun with children. . . . They were all Bellefleurs, the nieces and nephews of distant relatives; cousins many times removed; strangers with the name *Bellefleur* who had arrived at Lake Noir for the summer, evidently at Leah's (or Cornelia's, or Aveline's, or Ewan's, or Hiram's) invitation. If you can't come yourselves, send your children . . . they will love the lake and the woods and the mountains. . . . So there were, at different times, nine children, and then twelve, and then fifteen. Of course the servants complained bitterly. Edna wept because she was insulted by them, and the kitchen servants wept because the kitchen was a shambles, the groundsmen were furious, the groom complained that Germaine's pony was being mistreated, Nightshade was hurt (though of course he didn't let on) by their whispers and giggles; and grandmother Cornelia discovered that several of the visitors had dusky skins and very black eyes, black moist wicked eyes, could they possibly be *Bellefleurs,* with that sort of blood in them . . . ! One July day when Leah felt reasonably well she had been walking restlessly in the garden when she came upon two children scrambling over each other on the ground, beneath low-hanging evergreen boughs, and she saw to her astonishment that one of them was her nephew Louis, Aveline's boy, and the other was a girl she had never seen before: a ferret-faced insolent little wench with dark blue eyes and a defiant Bellefleur nose: and both the children were half-naked. What on earth are you doing! Children your age! Get out of here—get out! Leah shouted and clapped her hands, with as much fury as if she'd come upon one of the cats sharpening his claws on a piece of antique furniture.

But the adults were no better. The adults were worse. Ostensibly to celebrate the success of the Mount Kittery mines, Ewan had thrown open the castle on July 4, and a great crowd of people—invited and uninvited —arrived, and swarmed over the grounds, and gobbled up and drank everything in sight. (Hams, roasts, lobster, caviar, every conceivable sort of salad, fresh-baked breads and rolls and pastries, fruit and cheese, and of course whiskey, bourbon, gin, vodka, wines, brandies, beer and ale on draft. . . .) Not two weeks later Ewan had another party, a somewhat smaller one, on the lake; and every Friday night now his guests arrived, already merry and braying with drink, men from the sheriff's department, Nautauga Falls policemen, business friends and acquaintances, smalltime gamblers, the owners of bowling alleys and taverns and roadside restaurants, and their women, all their women, in various stages of intoxication. Ewan had paid a lighting contractor to set up, on the dock, an ingenious mechanism that flashed out onto the dark water all sorts of colored designs: crescent moons, snakes, human silhouettes. There was usually a small band, and dancing, far into the night, and in the morning the beach was littered with sleeping couples and other debris, among which dogs and cats and even, at times, mice and rats prowled boldly. As Leah's despondency deepened and she spent more and more of her time upstairs, Ewan's parties became increasingly noisy, and the behavior of his guests—and Ewan's behavior as well—became increasingly blatant. Lily never attended these parties, of course, claiming that she disliked the loud music and the behavior of the guests, but everyone knew that Ewan didn't want her, and simply ordered her to remain in her room. Some of the older children attended these parties, unsupervised. There was a brawl between Dabney Rush, a seventeen-year-old Bellefleur from—

where was it?—somewhere in the Midwest—and a man said to be a smalltime bookie out of Port Oriskany, allegedly over the favors of a photographer's model from the Falls; the boy's face had required thirty-two stitches, but even then he had refused to go home. Some of the parties, begun on Friday night, spilled over onto Saturday, and Saturday night, and broke up late Sunday afternoon, but what could anyone do? Gideon was absent, or indifferent; or perhaps he attended the parties himself; so far as Leah knew, he never challenged his brother. Grandfather Noel and grandmother Cornelia looked the other way, as did Hiram, murmuring, But Ewan feels he has to repay the people who put him into office . . . and he has so many new friends now . . . he was always a gregarious young man. . . . Most astonishing of all, some of Ewan's guests had asked if they might see Jean-Pierre II, about whom so much was whispered, and the old man consented to appear, in person, down at the lake, smiling a loose, frightened smile, his dead-white skin glaring in the shadows, his eyes darting from side to side. He had even dressed for the occasion in an old loose-fitting frock coat. Ah, is that *him* . . . ? Is that the one . . . ? So Ewan's guests whispered, drawing back in awe.

Leah was angry, but tired; she was very angry, or would have been, if she hadn't been so tired; so the weeks passed. *The jaws devour, the jaws are devoured.* . . . In a listless twilight sleep she heard, at a distance, the clarinets and drums and isolated squeals, and wondered idly who they were, those guests of Ewan's, possessed of such gaiety, such zest. . . . It exhausted her even to listen to them.

Vernon.

And Christabel.

And Bromwell.

And Gideon.

And that baby of Garnet's. That baby. Leah turned her back for a half-moment and the great flapping jabbing bird had appeared: and afterward, on the flagstones, there were coin-sized splotches of blood.

So many decades earlier, her own father. Killed as a prank on Christmas Eve. She had heard the story so frequently she half-thought she had witnessed the death. On Sugarloaf Hill. But which tree?

Nicholas Fuhr. Atop Sugarloaf Hill, gazing down at the stunted evergreens. The elfin forest, it was called. They had embraced. They had kissed. Many times. Her hands flat on his chest she had pushed him away, trembling. The memory of his mouth: so warm, damp, loving, *living.* He might have been her lover, and not Gideon. But she had not loved him, finally; she had not even met him on Sugarloaf Hill. Another girl met him, perhaps. Other girls. Women. There were so many . . . so many women. . . . Nicholas, Gideon, Ewan, and their friends, and their innumerable women. Months ago, or was it only weeks ago, Leah had received a letter from an Invemere woman who claimed that her nineteen-year-old daughter had had an abortion and nearly died, nearly bled to death, right in her room, upstairs in her room, and of course it was Gideon's fault though the girl refused to admit it: would rather die than implicate her lover. Her lover who didn't love her. But what is that to me, Leah wondered, studying the letter—filled with misspellings, grammatical errors, odd stilted phrases—what is it, even, to Gideon, if he doesn't love her? Probably he doesn't remember.

She didn't even regret not having gone to Sugarloaf Hill, that day. Nothing would have been changed, probably.

The doorknob rattled and it was her little girl, her sweet Germaine, begging to be allowed in. Or was it her servant Nightshade. If only, Miss Leah, you will allow me to serve you . . . if only you will allow . . . She turned her head aside and did not hear and in a while the noises ceased. *The jaws, the jaws devour.* But what is that to me, she thought. She wanted to cry. But could not. She *wanted* to mourn. But how? And why? What good did it do, exactly? What was the point? She was too practical, too efficient. She was dry-eyed, her skull floated on a dark featureless sea, she was very tired.

Even when they came to her, unlocking her door with a forbidden key, even when they whispered that Gideon had had an accident out on the highway, she could not weep. She found it difficult, even, to open her eyes. What is that to me, the hoarse parched voice wished to say, but hadn't the strength.

The Strike

Sam, the new foreman, the spokesman for the workers, was a nut-brown youngish man with a small, slick head and a spidery body. He was several inches shorter than Gideon but carried himself so erectly, his head flung back, that it appeared he was staring at Gideon from his own level. Sam's smile was constant. His teeth flashed, as if with surprise. The Bellefleurs deliberated: was that smile ingratiating, or was it mocking?

He means well, they murmured.

He doesn't at all mean well: he's a rabble-rouser.

He speaks with surprising clarity, when you consider . . .

If this were the old days there would be no problem.

They say he has studied law. . . .

He has glanced through *magazines and books,* he has a stack of *newspapers* at the rear of the bus, that's all he has "studied."

He is in contact with a union downstate.

He doesn't care about the others—he's only promoting himself.

Some of the ideas aren't unreasonable. . . .

Demands, not ideas. They're demands.

It wouldn't cost much to put in new floors. Cement floors. To clean‘ out that well. . . .

It's true, the septic tank *is* near the well, it must be leaking after all these years. . . .

Why does he smile so much? Is that a smile?

He's frightened of us.

He's frightened of Gideon.

No, he's mocking us. You can see it, the way his shoulders swing. The way his mustache twitches. . . . Then he goes off, putting his arms around his lieutenants, and they roar with laughter, they don't even trouble to disguise their hostility, can't you see it?

I don't mind the cement floors, or the well, grandfather Noel said slowly, sucking at his unlit pipe, I don't even mind fixing up the latrines (in this weather, when the wind blows from that direction, I think I can smell them—or is that my imagination?—across all that distance!), or even buying new mattresses or whatever. Or even giving them more food. Food costs nothing, after all. *That* kind of food. What I mind, grandfather Noel said, his voice rising, is giving them more money. Because that will escalate season by season.

And they want a contract.

We could pick the fruit ourselves.

All these children running around, let them work for a change: they might be diverted, they might think it was exciting, picking fruit.

The workers aren't on strike yet. I don't think they will strike.

"Sam" says—if I can imitate the little bastard's accent—"Sam" says they don't *want* to strike, striking is like *war,* it's a *desperate measure*—it's only resorted to when negotiations fail.

Meanwhile the fruit is ripening. It's beginning to rot.

It isn't beginning to rot!

It's *almost* beginning to rot.

Won't they starve, if they don't start work and aren't fed?

They brought along their own food. In cans and boxes.

But that won't last.

They're prepared for a wait.

They prepared for this, coming up here. Sam prepared them.

In the old days there wouldn't be any problem. . . .

They killed what-was-his-name, Barker. Of course they killed him. Somewhere along the road. This new one, Sam, must have killed him.

We don't know that he's actually dead. . . .

With Barker, there was never any trouble.

He was reasonable, he knew his way around.

If they killed him Ewan should arrest them. He should start an investigation.

It isn't in his jurisdiction, is it. Another state.

If he arrested Sam and took him away, we could deal with the rest of them ourselves. Hiram could assemble them and make a speech. . . .

I don't know, Hiram said uneasily, that I would exactly want to do that. Because, after all, Sam isn't the only one.

He's the leader. They've elected him.

There are those two or three others, I don't know their names, he calls them his lieutenants; and there must be eight, nine, ten other men helping to organize this. . . . I have their names somewhere. It's reliable information. Because not all the workers, of course, like Sam, some of them are worried, as they should be, they've been picking for us year after year and they know what to expect, but with these new ideas, going out on strike, going out on strike after having traveled a thousand miles on those rattle-trap buses, well, naturally they're frightened. So they come to me, on the sly. They give me information. I'm fairly sure it's reliable but the problem is, everything changes so swiftly, maybe there are twenty-five men directly supporting Sam by now, or maybe some of the others have dropped away, it just goes on and on, how many hours have we been discussing this—

Striking is like *war,* it's a *desperate measure,* nobody *wants* to strike because *everybody* suffers—but if the owners aren't *reasonable*—if they aren't *fair-minded*—

The hellish thing is, they arrived late. The telegram said they were unavoidably delayed but I suspected fraud at once—*unavoidably delayed,* what kind of language is that for fruit pickers!

Sam picked it out, leafing through one of his magazines.

I didn't think they were behaving normally, when they first arrived. Wouldn't look me in the eye. I'm out there in my overalls bare-headed in the sun, shaking hands and welcoming them back, making a fool of myself, ice water for everyone, noon meal ready, and they told me Barker wasn't with them any longer, they mumbled and giggled and wouldn't look me in the eye, then this cocky little bantam in the crimson shirt comes up to me, I'd noticed him watching me, whispering with his friends, he comes up and introduces himself, he's Sam, he's their elected representative, doesn't even want to use the word foreman, he sticks out his hand and forces me to shake it . . . *he* sticks out *his* hand. . . . Crimson shirt, crinkly little mustache, hairs growing out of his nostrils and ears. I don't suppose Ewan could arrest him?

Not until there's violence. Until the fighting begins.

Is there going to be fighting?

Oh, they'll attack our own workers—they'll set fire to the barns— what the hell, they know we can't stop them—they can sense the attitude you are all taking. Nothing escapes someone like Sam.

I think you are exaggerating. For one thing—

The negotiations are a ruse. What they really want is to bring us to our knees. The Bellefleurs, on our knees. They want to see us beg. Because they know they've got us: the fruit is ripe, the fruit is going to rot, we can't handle things the way we used to.

Remove Sam, and they'd be as docile as ever.

It's more than Sam, as I pointed out. It isn't just Sam. There are even *women,* for Christ's sake, who are angry about the situation. That jabbering, that shouting you hear—

I don't hear anything.

But it isn't just Sam. They want him to speak for them. It isn't just Sam.

You exaggerate everything.

You exaggerate.

There was a sound from the doorway, and they all glanced around to see, peering into the smoky room, old Jean-Pierre himself. He looked somewhat dazed; he was wearing a badly soiled silk dressing gown that hung loose on his emaciated body. Noel stood quickly, to offer his brother a chair, but the old man remained motionless, blinking.

Is there trouble? he whispered, clutching at the neck of his robe. Are we in danger?

Jean-Pierre, don't be distressed. There isn't any trouble, there isn't any danger, nothing we can't handle. Don't upset yourself.

Fire? Someone is going to set a fire? To the castle? To us? Why? What will happen? What can we do?

There *isn't* any trouble, Noel said, patting his brother's shoulder. We have everything under control.

Jean-Pierre's jaw trembled almost convulsively, and his clawlike fingers shook. His rheumy eyes darted from place to place but came to rest on no one, as if there were no one in the room he recognized.

Danger . . . ? he whispered. Here in Bellefleur Manor?

And then, to everyone's surprise, the negotiations went fairly well.

Sam and two of his lieutenants came to the coachman's lodge, and from 4:30 until well past midnight the situation was discussed: the demands for better living quarters, for better sanitation, for better food and drinking water, a legal contract, attorneys on both sides and a legal contract; and of course more money. One by one the points were contested and one by one they were conceded. It was only on the issue of money that they seriously disagreed: for Sam claimed that his people wanted a 200 percent increase in their hourly wage, and the Bellefleurs claimed that this was a lie.

That would break us, Noel said. You know that would break us.

Certainly it wouldn't! Not *Bellefleur,* said Sam with a quick warm flashing smile.

So they argued, and occasionally raised their voices, and one of the Bellefleurs left the table snorting with disgust, and Sam himself, lightheaded with exhilaration, or audacity, or from having gone too long without eating, pounded on the table so hard his fake-gold ring left a mark on its gleaming surface. I will pay for this, he said wildly, I will buy a new table. . . . Don't be absurd, one of the Bellefleurs said.

By 12:45 they had agreed on 160 percent. Which was very high. Which, Noel kept intoning, with as much grief as if it were true, will break us.

So they agreed, and shook hands, and Sam said he would call for a vote among his people in the morning, though he was absolutely certain the result would be positive (and then, he said with his leaping glinting smile, we can at last get to work—which is after all why we came); and the Bellefleurs promised to have their attorney on hand, and to arrange for another attorney, a presumably disinterested party, to represent the workers. By 1:00 A.M. Sam and his lieutenants had left, and the Bellefleurs went to the main house to drink themselves to sleep. Gideon, though he drank the most, was awake the longest, until nearly 5:00 A.M.

He contemplated his maimed right hand. Was that the correct term, *maimed?* The little finger was missing; it was decidedly missing; one's eye kept worrying the empty space, knowing something was wrong. There was ugly scar tissue where the dwarf had bitten him. It had been healing, like an ordinary scab, and should have simply flaked away, but for some reason it had turned into a substantial scar. It seemed, Gideon sometimes thought, as if it were growing.

Still, it was fascinating. What perverse little miracles the body could provide. . . .

Then in the morning Sam, with a mock-apologetic smile, announced that his people had vetoed the offer of a wage increase.

They had accepted, of course, the other offers; which were in fact their own demands; but they had refused the offer of 160 percent, and had instructed Sam to tell the Bellefleurs they would go no lower than 185 percent.

Vetoed the offer, Noel said faintly, and Hiram said in a jerky, incredulous voice, Vetoed! . . . that offer! Those scrubs and derelicts and whores and halfwits. . . .

Not only did they want higher wages, Sam said, his darkly tanned hands clasped before him, but they wanted several more things: free medical service on demand, insurance policies, private lavatories *in* the barracks and not outside, and ice water available in the orchards. He had had, he said with a droll smile, to talk them out of demanding a percentage of the Bellefleur's profits—their net profits. They had been noisy about it, but he had overcome their wishes, as he'd overcome what he considered to be trivial demands (for telephones, stoves with ovens, refrigerators, swimming privileges in Lake Noir, the use of the Bellefleurs' boats); but I was able to do so, he said, only by promising them that next year's contract would include such things.

Next year's contract! Noel said, pressing his hand to his chest.

—for after all, as I explained to them, raising my voice to them, Sam said, we have come here to *pick fruit,* and the fruit will soon rot or the birds will get it. Those lovely pears and peaches . . . and even the apples, too, are getting ripe. Not an hour to lose, when there are so many acres! I was very stern with them, Sam said.

Hiram staggered so that Jasper had to catch him in his arms. A percentage of the profits, Hiram whispered. The net profits. . . .

This will break us, Noel said. It has already broken us.

Gideon stood over Sam. He said, Now you know you're lying: you don't really expect us to believe this.

Sam pretended to cringe, grinning up at him.

You *know* this is absurd, Gideon said.

They are excited, they've been drinking, they have a will of their own, Sam said with a shrug of the shoulders.

It's your will, it isn't theirs—

See for yourself! Go and ask them yourself, if you know so much!

A percentage of the profits, Hiram whispered. The net profits. . . .

We don't believe that vote, said Jasper. We challenge that vote.

Then you'll see! Sam said. He waved his arms about, and his smile widened and contracted without ever deepening. He gave off a tart odor, wine and heat and sweat. The people have their own will, I am not their leader but only their spokesman, *I* can't control them—I am the last person you should blame!

Gideon seized him by the shoulders and walked him to the door and shoved him out. Liar, Gideon said, extortionist.

Sam's knees buckled and he nearly pitched forward into the drive. But he regained his balance, and straightened, and made a flurried little obscene gesture at Gideon.

Extortionist, Gideon said.

Bellefleur, Sam muttered, walking away without haste.

But it seemed that the workers were in earnest, and some of them believed that the strike had already begun; a small gang of children ran wild in the pear orchard, knocking pears off trees with clubs, trampling them underfoot, throwing them at one another. There were high shrill shrieks and outbursts of laughter and many of the workers, even those as young as twelve or thirteen, appeared to be half-intoxicated by nine in the morning.

They're going to destroy us, Noel said.

It would only be the fruit harvest, wouldn't it, Cornelia said. But she was white-faced, and sat huddled in her chair, an unconvincing wig slightly askew on her head. It needed a firm brushing: it looked as if mice were nesting in it.

The first loss will be the fruit, Noel said tonelessly, and then the wheat, and then the others, and the dairy farm too, and the property in Rockland, and the Falls, and the gypsum mine is a demonstrable failure, and the titanium may run out . . . or the miners will go on strike . . . yes, surely, they will go on strike . . . when they hear . . . when . . . when they hear of . . . when they hear of our humiliation.

If only Leah were well, Cornelia whispered.

Leah! Noel said. He blinked stupidly, as if, for some queer old-man reason, he had already given her up for dead.

When they heard of the workers' astonishing decision, the young people announced at once that *they* would pick the fruit. Let the buses load up and haul those fools away, those lazy sons of bitches, the Bellefleurs would pick their own fruit, it was obviously such easy work.

Garth was most enthusiastic, but there were a number of others, many of them city children, houseguests for the summer, who crowded about him shouting with excitement. Nearly all the servants volunteered, as well, except of course for those who were too old; even Nightshade, despite his hump and his caved-in chest (which would, one might think, make reaching up to pick fruit a torture) seemed eager to begin. With rabble it is important to hold fast and never to surrender, not even an inch, he said excitedly, to whoever would listen.

So the young people led the way, trooping off into the orchards, not bothering with sun hats or gloves, making a game of it, whistling and singing and feinting at one another with the ladders as if they were battering rams. Their zeal was such, as they shouted up and down the rows of trees, and tossed fruit at one another, and climbed up into perilous positions high in the creaking limbs, that it was a full forty-five minutes (and the sun, though still far from noon, was blistering hot) before the first of them weakened: a Cinquefoil girl with a chubby high-colored skin that had gone alarmingly white. Oh, I think I'm going to faint, she murmured, dropping her quart basket of peaches so that it bounced on the rungs of her ladder.

And then rather quickly Vida grew faint (for it *was* terribly warm, and the sun beat so mercilessly through the leaves); and the younger Rush boy, who had overheated himself by scrambling up and down ladders, grabbing at ankles in play; and one of the kitchen girls, though she looked hearty and tireless as a young ox. They dropped their containers and let the peaches roll where they would, while the others jeered. Aren't they lazy! Look at them! Aren't they *soft!*

But the sun was ferocious and no one was accustomed to such strangely hard work, for hadn't picking fruit from a tree seemed easy, but then you were always reaching overhead, and your shoulder began to ache so quickly, and your hand, and then your legs, and sweat ran down your sides in trickles, and odd black blotches floated in the sunshine, and soon—and soon only Garth and Nightshade and a half-dozen of the domestic help remained in the orchard, grimly picking, hand over hand, as the sun climbed toward noon—and then only Garth and Nightshade remained—and then suddenly, at about three o'clock, Garth was seized by a terrible spell of vomiting, and that was the end for Garth. Nightshade would have probably continued to pick until dusk except for a misstep as he climbed his ladder, so that his right foot slipped forward and his left backward, and with a high-pitched terrified cry the poor little man fell into his ladder face-first and brought both ladder and container (and it was three-quarters filled with peaches) down on top of him. So that was the end of the picking for Nightshade.

What a disappointment it was, to see how little fruit they had picked ...! When the bushel baskets were emptied into one another, and lined up, there couldn't have been more than three dozen of them; and much of the fruit, as Gideon saw, examining it, had been bruised.

Folly, thought Gideon. He straightened, the small of his back aching, and stared for a long moment into the massed foliage of the orchard, where so many hundreds, so many thousands, of ripe peaches hung. Folly, he thought, staring sightless at the sky.

He fled Bellefleur. He drove off in his dirt-splattered white Rolls coupe, accelerating at every turn, leaning over to rummage through the glove compartment for his flask. Though of course it was dangerous, though of course he could hear there was something wrong with the engine, something alarmingly wrong, but what folly, he thought, as the wind rushed against his face and whipped his hair back.

The vibrating in the engine became a knocking. How crudely they had tampered with the automobile, Gideon thought contemptuously. He pressed down on the accelerator. In a moment the highway would straighten and he could speed along it at a hundred miles an hour, at 110, all the way to Innisfail. The knocking was a heart gone wild. Desperate and baffled. He took no pity, but continued to accelerate.

He had wanted to take his little daughter with him, just for a ride. He saw her so rarely. He loved her, but saw her rarely. She held back shyly as if intimidated by his manner (he was boisterous, uncharacteristically cheerful) but would surely have consented to ride with him, had Lily not said, with surprising bluntness: No. You drive too fast. We know about you. You're a marked man, like my husband. *Leave the child alone.*

(Because Germaine's mother was ill Lily was taking care of her. Feeding her peanut-butter cookies, and sourdough bread with plum jam. They were making shell jewelry. Stringing pretty pale blue and cream-colored shells on lengths of twine, to make necklaces; one of them was going to be a birthday present for Germaine. Did he know her birthday was coming up in a few days . . . ? No, he hadn't known.)

Still, Gideon said aloud, she *is* my daughter. I had a right to her, if I insisted.

He was taking the turn onto the old Military Road when something happened: it was as if he'd driven over an enormous sheet of metal; there was such a crashing deafening sound. His foot flew to the brake and the automobile began to skid, the rear wheels yearned to change places with the front, then he was rushing through a shallow ditch, then into some bushes, through the bushes and into a barbed-wire fence, through the fence, heaving and bucking, into a cornfield. He was thrown against the windshield, then against the door, and the door came open, so he found himself finally, after many confused minutes, on the ground, in the corn-field, dripping blood into the dirt. He groped about for Germaine. For his little girl. Where was she?—had she been thrown clear? (For he thought, irrationally, that the car would explode.)

Germaine? Germaine? Germaine?

The Harvest

And then, quite abruptly, on the eve of Germaine's third birthday (a still, airless, humid night of oddly varying temperatures, unillumined by any moon or stars) an event took place that altered everything: the strike was averted; the fruit pickers returned to work (docilely, near-silently, and for their last year's wage); a bumper crop of peaches, pears, and apples was harvested; and Leah, after weeks of despondency, of being someone other than *Leah,* was wakened from her trance.

And all because of Jean-Pierre II.

When grandmother Cornelia, happening to glance out an upstairs window early in the morning (just before seven: the poor woman rarely slept later), saw her elderly, infirm brother-in-law making his way unsteadily toward the house, on a graveled walk that paralleled, at a distance of some twenty yards, the garden wall, she knew at once—without having seen, yet, the stained hog-butchering knife he carried close against his body—that something had happened. For he had, to her knowledge, never left the castle before. (No one had dared tell her of his appearance at Ewan's party.) And there was something about the mere sight of him, down there, in the early morning, italicized by his black frock coat and his starkly white hair against the damp green of the lawn, that struck her as unnatural.

She hurried immediately to Noel, and roused him from his heavy slumber. (For he had drunk himself to sleep, the night before—sick with worry about the hospitalized Gideon, and about the rotting fruit.)

"You'd better go downstairs. I think. At once. I *think.* I can't tell you why," she whispered, pulling at him, thrusting his eyeglasses at him, "but I think . . . I'm afraid . . . , Your brother Jean-Pierre . . ."

"What? Jean-Pierre? Is he ill?" Noel cried.

"Yes, I think he must be," Cornelia said.

Hiram too saw him, from *his* bedroom window: for Hiram had been unable to sleep except in patches during the long airless night. His brain had churned with images of mounds of rotting fruit, and the spectacle of his family's public humiliation (there would be another auction, strangers would tramp mud through the downstairs rooms of the castle, this time even the buildings would be sold—and for a mocking pittance), and the horror of his only son's death, which he had not had time, yet, to completely grasp. (Thrown by the family's lifelong enemies into a filthy river, his wrists and ankles bound, like a dog!) And now with Gideon hospitalized in the Falls, with multiple fractures and a concussion . . .

In his underclothes, not yet shaven, Hiram peered out the window and adjusted his glasses as the dark figure hobbled into sight. At first he believed it must be a sleepwalker, a fellow sufferer: for the man made his way with such vague groping steps, his head tilted back as if he were making no attempt to see the ground at his feet. (And indeed he walked blindly. Now on the graveled path, now on the grass, now stumbling through the narrow border of phlox and coral bells.) It was some minutes before Hiram recognized his brother Jean-Pierre. And then, like Cornelia, he knew something had happened.

"I hope he didn't . . . That fool . . . !"

Young Jasper saw the old man, alerted by the nervous whimperings of his dog, who slept at the foot of his bed; and great-grandmother Elvira, who arose each morning promptly at six, and fussed about preparing, for her bridegroom (whom she had begun to refer to, secretly, silently, as "Jeremiah," though to his face she called him only "You") a breakfast of fresh peaches and cream, and honey toast, and good strong black coffee; and Lily saw him, going to the window to see what it was, down on the lawn, that so drew the interest of her little niece Germaine (for the child had crept out of bed, her curls atangle, her pudgy fingers stuck in her mouth, and now she knelt on the velvet window seat and stared and stared at her great-uncle who was making his way to the rear of the house, his head flung nobly back, something glinting in his hand); Raphael may have seen him, for the boy slept lightly, and was uneasy these days because his pond—lovely Mink Pond—had been invaded by the fruit pickers' children, who loved to splash and belly-dive and paddle in it, meaning no harm, of course, intending no serious harm, but trampling down the cattails and the flowering rushes nevertheless, and tearing out by the roots the lovely waxed water lilies; of course Raphael had avoided the pond for days, and could not hope to return until the intruders were banished, or went, at last, to work in the orchards. And some of the servants must have seen him. The kitchen help, and Edna, and Walton; though of course they were to say nothing, and immediately averted their eyes, when they recognized both Jean-Pierre II and what he carried in his right hand, half-hidden alongside his leg. Nightshade, however, sighting the old man from a distance, had both the wit and the audacity to hurry upstairs to his mistress's chambers: for *she,* he knew, must be told.

"Miss Leah! Miss Leah! Arouse yourself! Come quickly! Mr. Jean-Pierre has made his move!"

So the hunched-over little man whimpered and whined, rattling his lady's doorknob in a frenzy of concern, until, at last, after many minutes, after *many* minutes, during which he alternately begged and commanded her, and punctuated his words with spasmodic sobs, the door was unlocked: the door was actually unlocked: and a slack-faced blinking Leah stood before him.

(She had wakened from her hideous trance. Or had been awakened. And was soon to forget, with merciful completeness, its claustrophobic calm, its sickly peace. She would never suffer such an uncharacteristic episode again. Interpreting it, afterward, she would say, frowning, so that those sharp, rather poignant lines appeared between her anxious brows, that her "black mood" had been nothing more than premonitory. It had no reference to her, to her own life, certainly not to the Bellefleur affairs as a whole; it had reference only to Jean-Pierre's extraordinary behavior that August night. She had sensed something would happen—she had, somehow, known it would happen—but had been powerless to prevent it—like Germaine—for Germaine, too, "saw" things yet could not prevent them or even comprehend them—and so she had fallen into a black pit of a mood, quite helpless: but then of course she had been freed. Once the horror had taken place, once it was *there,* in the world, quite naturally she was freed.)

During that night, or, more precisely, from about 2:00 A.M. until after six, Jean-Pierre II had managed, despite his palsied hands and his weak legs and the difficulties he must have confronted, wandering in the starless dark, in an unfamiliar corner of the estate, to slash the throats not only of Sam and his lieutenants, and the dozen or so men who most vehemently supported him, but some eight other people, seven men and one woman. (It was generally thought, afterward, that he had slashed the woman's throat in error, having mistaken her—she was hefty, a light down grew on her face—for a man.)

In a faint feeble voice that trailed off Jean-Pierre said only that the workers were evil . . . they weren't penitent . . . they had to be dealt with immediately . . . they had to be prevented from further insulting their betters.

He had surrendered the hog-butchering knife at once to grandfather Noel, amiably. It was a wicked long instrument with a slight curve, and it seemed to have been recently sharpened. But it was, of course, badly stained and scarified, from all the use to which the old gentleman had put it. Noel took it soberly, a handkerchief protecting his hand.

"We must, I suppose," he said, licking his lips, "wake Ewan."

So one of them—it was Jasper, barefoot, bare-chested, wearing only white summer trousers—ran upstairs to Ewan's apartment. And rapped loudly on the door. (For, since Ewan did not arrive at his office in the Falls until 10:00 A.M., he generally slept until eight, and did not like his sleep disturbed.)

When Jasper told Ewan what had happened, and that they had calculated, from the old man's incoherent murmurings, that anywhere from five or six to twenty or more people had been murdered, Ewan's great shaggy head shot forward from his shoulders, and his sleep-groggy eyes, threaded with blood, opened and narrowed and opened again in a matter of seconds.

He asked Jasper to repeat what he'd said. *How* many . . . ?

Then he said, his chest heaving with a sigh, "I *thought* that's what you said, my boy."

It was as Nightshade had said: Jean-Pierre II had made his move.

Book Five
REVENGE

The Clavichord

Contrary to rumor, and to her husband's embittered and reiterated conviction, it was not the Hayes Whittier episode that plunged Violet Bellefleur into a dreamy melancholy that ended with her taking her own life (for so the expression went: one "took" one's own life, as if one were "taking" another person's fur muff or an undeserved extra slice of fruitcake) one chilly September night; it was not even the neurasthenia brought on, or exacerbated, by her numerous pregnancies and miscarriages. Nor was it the unfortunate woman's perversity. ("Perversity" being her husband's term. Raphael came to employ it more and more frequently as the years passed, for it helped to explain, and to condemn, his sister Fredericka's passion for an imbecilic Protestant sect; his brother Arthur's inexplicable willingness to die—as indeed he did, at Charlestown, while attempting to kidnap John Brown's corpse so that it might be spirited away to the North where partisans planned on reviving it with a galvanic battery; the behavior of his sons Samuel and Rodman; the political climate of the era; and the oscillations of the world market for hops, which, when it favored him, was "healthy," and when it failed to favor him was "perverse.")

Nor was it love. Not love in any commonplace sense. For love between a man and a woman not related by blood would necessarily have to be erotic; and there was no provision, in Violet's world, for erotic love outside marriage. And she was of course married. She was extremely married. She would not have thought, as a young girl in her parents' home in Warwick, that one could be so *extremely* married.

Tamás too was married—or had been. Though he looked so young, and had so naïve, so uninstructed a manner. They said his wife had run away from him after their ship from Liverpool landed in New York (they had come to Liverpool from London, to London from Paris, to Paris from

Budapest, where they had both been born); then again they said his wife had refused to sail with him, and had stayed behind. In one version overheard by Violet (who never, really *never,* eavesdropped on anyone, let alone her domestic help) the young woman had betrayed him with other men because she was ashamed of his "stammer." In another version, no less plausible, his "stammer" had been caused by her betrayal. Violet noted, without caring to interpret the fact, that in her presence Tamás's difficulties with speech were such that he appeared to be on the verge of strangulation, and went an alarming beet-red; so it was no wonder that he soon ceased to speak at all, and, if it was necessary to communicate with her about the clavichord he had been hired to build, he left notes, or inquiries with the servants. He never had the opportunity to speak with Raphael, nor did he see him more than two or three times, always at a distance, for of course Raphael had not directly hired him. It is probable to assume that the shy young man with his prominent Adam's apple and his tight-fitting clothes and, of course, the embarrassing stammer (though Violet's personal physician, Dr. Sheeler, believed it was a speech impediment) would have been terrified of the master of Bellefleur Manor. That he, Tamás, presumed to entertain certain feelings—certain unmistakable feelings—for the master's young wife: that he dared simply to *think* of her as he worked lovingly on the clavichord: all this would have been as outrageous to Tamás as to Raphael Bellefleur himself.

It was by way of Truman Geddes, the Republican congressman, and the man who shot, in Raphael's company and on Raphael's land, the last moose in the Chautauquas (in 1860—though of course no one knew at the time that was to be the *last* moose, or even one of the last), that Tamás came to Bellefleur Manor to build the clavichord for Violet. She had expressed, half-seriously, a desire for a musical instrument that might be "easy" to play. So Truman turned to Raphael and said that *his* wife and girls were enjoying themselves immensely pounding away at a curious tinkling instrument that was hardly more than a keyboard and strings, called, he thought, a *clavichord.* It was a pretty little thing, a work of art, built for them by a Hungarian boy who was in the hire of a Nautauga Falls cabinetmaker. Truman said he wouldn't dare sit down at the instrument, himself, because it was too delicate: it was a woman's thing. And, for all its beauty, it hadn't cost overmuch.

So Tamás was brought to Bellefleur Manor, to build a clavichord for Violet, and to add drawers, shelves, and cabinets here and there in the castle, in rooms Raphael considered still incomplete. When he first saw Violet Bellefleur he thought she was one of the household staff—if not a maid, perhaps a governess—for the young woman wore a plain gray shirtwaist with leg-of-mutton sleeves and a long skirt, and a pocketwatch on a chain about her neck, and her manner seemed shy, even childlike. She was slight; her face was almost too narrow, especially about the chin, to be considered pretty; her eyes were intense, and frequently showed a thin crescent of white above the iris. That she was indefinably, perhaps hopelessly, *ill* seemed somehow obvious, though in Tamás's presence (indeed, in the presence of any of the servants) she carried herself with a beautiful precision, and her voice, though low, never shook. It was rare to see her with her children, though they were grown and could not have taxed her strength. After Tamás learned that the mistress of Bellefleur Manor was a deeply spiritual person he believed he could see, in her face, perhaps even radiating about her hair (which was a quite ordinary brown, though fine and lustrous, worn in a fashionable French twist in which pearls, amber beads, and occasionally even lilies of the valley were twined) an aura of grace, of otherworldliness, quite unlike anything he had ever seen before, except in paintings by Botticelli or certain anonymous German artists of the medieval period.

"The mistress is always sickly," the housekeeper told him, with a droll smile, "and we know what *that* means."

"What—·what does it mean?" Tamás asked.

"Oh, well, we *know.*"

"Yes, but what?"

"Ladies who are always complaining of headaches and breathlessness—who wish to be allowed their private beds—"

Tamás turned abruptly away. And said, after a moment, in a voice so strengthened by anger that his stutter had virtually disappeared, "I refuse to listen to backstairs gossip."

And the housekeeper, of course, had been properly silenced.

It was not to be a very defined love story, perhaps not a love story at all.

For *love* was not an issue. Between Violet and the young Hungarian *love* was not an issue since it was not a thought; it wasn't a thought since it had not been expressed as a word.

Violet must surely have sensed, in the young man's presence (she often visited his workshop at the rear of the coachman's lodge) that something—something was amiss. Something was unbalanced, and highly exciting. That he rarely spoke to her made the situation all the more peculiar. Of course he was polite, as courteous as anyone of her own social class, though he avoided her eye, and in showing her the plans he had drawn up for the instrument he stood well away from her, some four or five feet. It was as if something might suddenly happen: a strong breeze was about to fling a glass door inward, and smash it; a spider or a roach (for, unfortunately, even magnificent Bellefleur Manor had roaches) was about to declare itself, scuttling across an antique tapestry. Violet must surely have sensed Tamás's agitation but she gave no sign, visiting him in her plain shirtwaist dresses, bringing with her a scent of lily of the valley. She enjoyed watching his skillful hands (which were not slender, as she had imagined—had she been dreaming of them?—but strong, a peasant's hands, with square-tipped fingers and short blunt nails); she observed the instrument's slow construction with a strange subdued pleasure. Of course there were other musical instruments in the castle, many others, including a handsome grand piano, at which she might play the half-dozen salon pieces she knew; but the clavichord was to be *hers*. Tamás had asked her to choose the kinds of wood she wanted (cherry-wood primarily, and birch for the inside; and the graceful curved legs of the instrument and its matching bench were to be covered in strips of veneered oak) and he had expressed, in his difficult way, great pleasure at her preference for a keyboard made of walnut rather than ivory. It would be most unusual, most unique. And would she like ivory, gold, and jet ornamentation . . . ? It seemed to please him immensely, and to excite him, when she told him he must do as he wished—that she knew very little, and wanted only what he wanted.

She came to his workshop, silhouetted in the sun-filled doorway, her slender figure outlined, her hair shining. Because Tamás was so silent, Violet, despite her customary reserve, felt inclined to chatter. She spoke to him about her love for small, meticulously crafted things made by artists like himself—European-born—with a respect for beauty—and knowledge of the sanctity of beauty. She spoke to him, not minding that he answered her only in inarticulate grunts, of her girlhood in the country —her father's modest estate—the music lessons she and her sisters had been given, despite the expense—her amateur's enthusiasm for Scarlatti, Bach, Couperin, Mozart, the nocturnes of John Field, and the "easier" pieces of Chopin. It was a pity, she said, that he had never taken music lessons himself, for obviously he had such a love, such a feeling, for the instrument he was building. . . . How fragile it appeared, how delicate, and yet she knew it would be extraordinarily strong for its size. A beautiful thing. A miracle, really, that anyone could create it with his hands: mere *human* hands!

Stooped over his workbench the young Hungarian paused, not quite looking at Violet, and murmured something that sounded like an assent. His thin lips stretched in a shy, unsmiling grimace, but he was obviously deeply moved.

So the days passed, and the weeks. And one day Violet suggested that the clavichord—which was now nearly completed—be moved to her drawing room, and that Tamás continue his work there, so that he could best judge the instrument's tone and strength in the place in which it would be played. She was so very eager, she said, to see it there. . . .

Tamás straightened, as if in alarm. Though his narrow, lately rather pale face showed nothing. He nodded, after a moment; of course he would oblige; this request too must have pleased him, for a slow deep blush spread from his face down to his neck. A tiny screwdriver slipped from his hands and fell in the pile of wood shavings at his feet.

Now the clavichord was nearly finished, placed in the shallow bay window overlooking the walled garden where, illuminated by sunlight passing through antique glass with its subtle distortions and near-microscopic bubbles, it took on an unearthly, almost a ferocious beauty. How the cherrywood gleamed! And the walnut keys! And the gold and jet! Tamás accepted the many compliments uttered in his presence with a wordless, chastely polite bow of his head; if it was sometimes suggested, by the insensitive housekeeper, or one or another of the domestic staff, that he was certainly taking a *long* time with that dainty little thing, he turned away, and made no reply. Indeed, he had all but given up speech in recent weeks. And despite the skill of his hands, and his ability to work tirelessly for long hours (for as many, at times, as twelve, without a break), he was obviously not altogether well. His skin had grown translucent, and appeared to glow, as if with heat; he had lost a shocking amount of weight, so that his clothes hung loose on his tall, stooped frame; when he was not actually working on the clavichord his hands were observed to tremble. The kitchen staff joked that he hadn't any appetite and they thought they knew exactly why.

He arose at dawn, and went immediately to the drawing room, where, in the light that flooded from the southeast, the clavichord gleamed with its extraordinary beauty. It stood no more than three and a half feet high, and the bench would necessarily be a low one, and as delicately beautiful as he could make it, set upon graceful curved legs that were to give the impression of being covered, but very subtly, in grapevines, all of veneered oak. A prodigious amount of work. . . . And it had struck him the other day, covertly noting his mistress's small hands, and estimating that she probably had a reach of no more than a seventh, that the entire keyboard would have to be done over: each key would have to be reduced in size, and beveled, so that she might have (he grew suddenly ambitious, even bold) a reach of a tenth. Weeks of meticulous toil, yet necessary.

When he conveyed this message to Violet, by way of a carefully-composed letter, she surprised him by glancing up, at him, in alarm. And saying, very nearly in a stammer of her own: "But—but—but I thought, Tamás, that my clavichord was nearly finished—I had thought it might be completed this very week—"

He shook his head impatiently, blushing.

She stared at him. For a moment she could not think what to say: the young Hungarian, who was always so docile, so amiable, stooped over his work with such concentration that one realized it was an unearthly, a sacred task, now looked defiantly angry. His Adam's apple jerked, he swallowed and licked his dry lips, his high pale forehead gleamed with perspiration. He shook his head. No, no, no. No. No.

"But I—I'm only an amateur musician—I play for my own pleasure," Violet said, clasping her hands before her as if imploring him, "and of course I haven't any genuine talent—only a love for—for the sound—for the *activity*—for the purity of—of— If I can't reach a note I simply skip it or jump to it, you know, and it really doesn't make any difference—*really* it doesn't— Why, I hardly intend to play for anyone other than myself. Not even close friends, or—"

Tamás began to speak, but his words were strangled, and his eyes protruded alarmingly out of their dark shadowed sockets; so he merely shook his head again, stern as a schoolmaster whose pupils have disobeyed.

"But Tamás, the clavichord is so beautiful—I'm so eager to play it —And how will I explain to my husband, who thinks it's nearly—"

Tamás withdrew the letter from her trembling fingers, and wrote in a stiff, unusually large hand: MUST BE PERFECT. NO COMPROMISE. OTHERWISE—SMASHED WITH THE AX!!!

So Violet acquiesced, and did not tell Raphael. And the labor of creating the new keyboard was begun.

The weeks passed. The new, small keyboard appeared, and was as beautiful, perhaps more beautiful, than the other; and after each of the keys was set into place, and strung, Tamás asked Violet to sit at the instrument and play it, so that he could determine precisely where the metal wedges must go. Violet had thought that a professional tuner would be employed, and murmured her surprise, her pleased surprise, that Tamás could tune the instrument himself. He had, evidently, perfect pitch.

She ran her fingers over the keys, self-consciously. Of course this wasn't a piano keyboard and, unless she pressed down emphatically, no note would sound, or it would arise muffled and indistinct. So she played a scale or two, with girlish enthusiasm, and uneven speed, while Tamás fussed with the metal wedges. "It's lovely," Violet said, "isn't it lovely! I can't thank you enough—" But Tamás took no heed of her chatter. He was adjusting the strings with such concentration that a bead of sweat ran to the very tip of his thin, waxen-pale nose, and hovered there for a long moment before dropping off.

He listened to her rather hesitant playing from various corners of the elegant room, and even from the doorway, and the corridor. He was grave, intense, perhaps somewhat feverish. (Because he ate so rarely, and had lost so much weight, his breath had, unfortunately, turned sour; but Violet tried to take no notice.) Sometimes he hurried to her, to strike a note himself. He pressed his long blunt finger down, and held it on the key, with such pressure that all the blood ran out of the finger's tip, and a rosy half-moon appeared beneath the nail. At such moments Violet shivered in the heat of his intensity: she could feel it, she could feel it radiating from him, frightening her, exciting her as she could not recall having been excited before. She did not know if she felt disappointment, or relief, when Tamás muttered, hardly opening his mouth, "Not right. Not *right.*"

He took to prowling about the house at night, making his way through the servants' wing into the Great Hall, and into the drawing room. There, he drew the heavy velvet drapes (as if fearing the night watchman or the gate-house keeper or one of the dogs would see the light, and expose him), and worked, undisturbed for hours, on the clavichord. One morning Violet herself, still in her dressing gown, discovered him, and was astonished to see how pale the poor young man had grown, and how *strange:* he must have weighed little more than a hundred pounds, and his hair was plastered to his damp forehead, and his thin lips were tightly pursed as if he were resisting the impulse to scream. His hooded, rather weary eyes flashed to her, and he attempted a wan smile: but clearly he was unwell.

"Tamás," Violet cried, "why are you doing this? Why are you destroying yourself!"

He turned away, though not discourteously, and, with a tiny screwdriver, proceeded to adjust something on the inside of the clavichord.

That morning, Violet insisted upon feeding him bouillon, toast, and bacon rind, which she brought to her drawing room herself, on a silver tray; she made certain the door was closed behind her so that no inquisitive servant could peer in. Tamás ate, though reluctantly. It was clear that he ate only to please her; he kept glancing at the clavichord (which looked, in the brilliant morning light, more beautiful than ever), and his fingers involuntarily twitched. Violet asked him what was wrong—why was he so often unhappy—melancholy—was it thoughts of his homeland? —his wife? (She spoke in a near-whisper, trembling with her own audacity. But Tamás seemed not to care, or even to hear. Homeland? Wife? Unhappy? He merely shrugged his shoulders, and his eyes drifted back to the clavichord.)

"Ah, but it *is* beautiful!" Violet cried. She rose, unsteady, and went to the clavichord, and struck a bold chord, using all her fingers. And struck it again, her heartbeat crazy and light as a butterfly's. *"Isn't* it beautiful, *haven't* you produced a wonder!" she whispered, in triumph.

When she looked back at Tamás he was gazing at her, and at the clavichord, with an expression of simple, mute adoration. Droplets of perspiration, or tears, ran down his thin cheeks, and he was, she could see, perfectly at peace. He fairly glowed with a still, calm, inviolable ecstasy.

It was on a fine, clear, sunny May morning that Violet entered her drawing room to see the clavichord finished. She knew Tamás had finished it because he had laid, on the bench, the green brocaded cushion Violet intended to use.

"Ah, how lovely," Violet said, approaching the instrument. She depressed a note and it sounded, remote, but bell-like, with an indescribably sweet tone.

She sat, and played a scale or two, and part of a simplified rondo, really a children's piece, which she knew by heart. It seemed to her that the clavichord's tone was even more beautiful than she remembered. What had Tamás done with it, overnight . . . ? She leaned forward to inhale the odor of the fine polished wood, and could not resist touching her cheek against it. A master craftsman had fashioned this exquisite instrument for *her*. He had thought enough of her taste to allow her to choose the woods, and the ornamentation; he had made a keyboard scaled to *her* delicate hands. Not one of Raphael's costly gifts (the sable opera cloak, the new phaeton, the diamonds, pearls, and rubies, even the manor house itself) meant as much to her as Tamás's clavichord which wasn't, strictly speaking (for of course Raphael was paying for it) a "gift" from the young Hungarian at all. . . .

In her satin dressing gown with the kimonolike sash Violet sat at the little instrument, playing her pieces one by one. Tamás would enter the room at any moment. She could imagine him making his way along the servants' hall . . . into the Great Hall . . . pausing at the door of the drawing room, his hand on the knob, listening to this delicate, simplified mazurka . . . a haunting dancelike tune written by Chopin at a very young age. It was not quite suitable for the clavichord, nor were Violet's little fingers agile enough, but the tone, the tone! . . . it was so exquisitely beautiful that tears started into Violet's eyes.

When the young Hungarian entered the room Violet was going to rise from the bench, and hold her arms out to him. For a long wordless moment they would stare at each other. And then he would close the door gently behind him, and . . .

Her fingers were so clumsy, she exclaimed aloud. Ah, how frustrating, to be unworthy of this exquisite thing! But she would practice. She would honor it as Tamás had honored it, knowing the clavichord was something from another world, only entrusted, in a manner of speaking, to her. One day she would play not only her simple girlhood pieces but ambitious, brilliant, heartstopping pieces by Scarlatti and Couperin and Bach and Mozart, perhaps she would even have a kind of salon, and invite intelligent, cultured men and women—not Raphael's acquaintances, not his contemptible political associates!—and Tamás would be the guest of honor—he might live at the manor as long as he wished—he would become famous throughout the state—a builder of clavichords and harpsichords—a master craftsman whose instruments were extremely costly but, as everyone acclaimed, more than worth their price: *he* had built, everyone would say, Violet Bellefleur's clavichord, and there was never a more lovely, a more indescribably beautiful thing. . . .

Violet broke off her playing, having heard something odd. She turned but there was no one in the room. Her own portrait, painted some years earlier by a flattering society portraitist, was, in its position above the marble fireplace, the natural place for her glance to alight; but she looked away at once, vexed and obscurely ashamed of its sleek, pretty, falsely rosy tones—what had Tamás thought, working for so many months in this room, forced to see, whenever he glanced around, *that* conventionalized image!—Tamás who was himself so superb an artist? He must have been secretly contemptuous not just of that portrait, and of Raphael's matching portrait (which hung in the Great Hall), but of most of the Bellefleur acquisitions.

I realize now what I must do, Violet would say to the young man when he appeared, having grasped the principle of beauty embodied in your work: I will have to remake this room, to suit it. To make a kind of shrine for it. Beginning of course with the removal of that insipid portrait—!

(But perhaps he would recoil in surprise. Not wanting the painting to be discarded. He would ask, shyly, if it might be given to him. To hang in his room. But where was his room? In the servants' wing. What a fuss there might be. . . . Too much whispering and speculation. . . . And if Raphael learned . . . But of course he would learn, at once. . . .)

Violet saw by the clock on the mantel that it was getting late, nearly midmorning. Where was Tamás? He was usually hard at work by now. In another minute or two a solicitous servant would rap gently on the door and ask Violet if she wanted her morning coffee, and if Tamás then appeared, why the moment would be quite botched. . . .

Perhaps he was ill? He had looked so worn, so exhausted, the day before. In fact for a number of days. He had refused even to drink the hot bouillon she had brought him yesterday, though she had thought that might have developed into a routine, a small pleasant ritual.

Tamás?

Are you ill?

Aren't you coming?

By and by a servant did knock, and Violet sent her away, irritably, to find Tamás. It was *very* late. What could he be thinking of! It was inconsiderate of him, it was rather cruel, to so deliberately keep her waiting, since he knew very well she would be seated at the clavichord, like a child with a new toy. Unlike Tamás, Violet thought, to be affectedly modest.

But Tamás was not in his room. Nor could they find him anywhere.

"What do you mean," Violet said in dismay, rising from the bench, "have you *looked*? Of course you haven't looked everywhere!"

So they searched the house, each of the floors and the basement; they searched the grounds and the outbuildings; they inquired of all the servants, and the groundsmen and the farmhands and even the itinerant help housed down by the swamp; and they reported to Miss Violet that Tamás was nowhere to be found. The bed in his little room was neatly made as always, and his clothing and toiletries appeared to be undisturbed.

"But surely there is a note?" Violet said, stricken. "He— We— My husband— The clavichord has not even been paid for—"

They searched for him in the woods, using hounds, for he had been distracted for so long (except when working at the clavichord) that it was altogether possible he had wandered away and was lost. But they could not find him; the dogs could not even locate his scent. Violet wired the Nautauga Falls cabinetmaker for whom Tamás had worked, but the man had no knowledge of him; he claimed not to have heard from Tamás for nearly a year.

"How could you do this to me!" Violet whispered. Her heart

pounded so strangely, she thought she would faint. She was so angry, and so frightened, and so *vexed,* like a child who has lost her closest playmate: and there stood the clavichord in the window, the lovely matchless clavichord, meant to be shared, meant to be exclaimed over in *his* presence, and played for *him:* and he was gone.

Gone, as it turned out, forever.

From this time afterward Violet lived sunk within herself, and only appeared to come to life, albeit fitfully, while seated at the clavichord. Years and years and years were to pass, and Tamás was not to be found, nor did anyone receive word of him. Raphael thought the entire incident was extremely suspicious. He had never heard of a workingman or tradesman or carpenter or whatever the young fool called himself who had declined to present his bill, and it upset him, for years, that services done for *him* should remain unpaid: that wasn't the Bellefleur way of doing business.

Violet played the clavichord, at first for brief periods of an hour or less, then for two, three, four, and even five hours at a stretch. She refused to accompany her husband on his most ambitious campaign journey about the state, and Raphael afterward blamed her, quite unreasonably, for his poor showing. It was not uncommon for the mistress of Bellefleur Manor to descend to her drawing room immediately upon rising, and, in her dressing gown, with her hair all atumble down her back, quite indifferent to the demands of the household, and even, frequently, to the presence of household guests, seat herself at the clavichord and play for hours, the door locked behind her. Once, discovering the door unlocked, her son Jeremiah, then an ostensibly grown man, entered the room shyly, and stood listening for some twenty or thirty minutes to his mother's frantic, feverish playing, in which he could discern from time to time (but with difficulty, for Jeremiah had never been musically inclined, and had received no training) sudden queer sounds—airy, light, muted, faint—of unutterable beauty. The clavichord was not an easy instrument to play, Jeremiah judged by his mother's exertions, and the frequently flat, tinny notes she struck, it seemed at times hardly more than a glorified lyre or guitar, but from somewhere there arose, unpredictably, with eerie force, a voice—an almost human voice—or perhaps it was the echo of a voice —frail and all but inaudible—thin with pain, and distance, and loss. It *is* lovely, Jeremiah thought. And understood, or almost understood, his mother's devotion.

Once, in Jeremiah's presence, Violet stopped playing suddenly. Her arms fell loose, and her head sank forward onto her bosom. Jeremiah wondered if he dared approach her; she appeared to be sobbing soundlessly. But when he whispered, "Mother?" she turned to him with a look of chagrin and anger, and denounced him for spying on her. *"You* wouldn't understand, any of you," she said, closing the keyboard roughly, "he was an artist, he completed his task and scorned to ask for payment, how could any of *you* understand! His art is defiled by your mere presence."

Raphael, of course, was less patient with his wife. He engaged Dr. Wystan Sheeler to treat her, for it seemed to him altogether obvious that Violet was suffering from a nervous disorder of some kind (was it brain fever? anemia? a female complaint to which no medical name might be given?). When Dr. Sheeler failed to cure her, or even to satisfactorily diagnose her malady, Raphael ordered him from the house—and it was to be some years before the celebrated physician forgave him, and returned, at Raphael's plea, to treat Raphael himself.

Why did she hide herself away on the loveliest of summer days, to play that wretched instrument? Why did she ignore her houseguests, her husband, even her lonely, aimless son? Raphael charged her with—with —he knew not what—he knew not how to express it. That she was *unfaithful* to him, and gloated in her behavior, seemed to him obvious, and yet —and yet—he had no proof—and in more rational moments wondered precisely what he meant. He dared not accuse her, for of course she would deny it, she might even (since in recent years his demure young bride had hardened somewhat) laugh contemptuously at him. Unfaithful! Unfaithful to him! In the privacy of her own drawing room! Alone! With her clavichord—with her *clavichord!* Yes, she might very well laugh, and he would be defenseless against her scorn.

In the end, shortly before Violet walked into Lake Noir and drowned herself, "taking her own life" in the least obtrusive of ways (for the body was never found though the lake was dredged), the clavichord was irreparably damaged.

Standing one morning outside the drawing room door Raphael had been convinced he heard a stranger's voice inside the room—beneath, or behind, or arising within the music. He threw open the door and rushed inside and though he found no one—no one beside a terrified Violet— he was so infuriated, so frustrated, he brought his fist down hard on the top of the clavichord, and cracked the fine wood. Several strings broke —a high, faint, incredulous shriek sounded from inside the instrument— and though it was repaired afterward (indeed, Raphael was thoroughly ashamed, and baffled that he should so wantonly damage his own goods) the clavichord was never quite the same again. Its tone was flat and tinny and dead though of course it remained, and was, still, in Germaine's time, an exquisitely beautiful piece of furniture.

God's Face

High in the mountains the seasons sped swiftly. Now the planet tipped north, now south. Now aurora borealis flooded the night sky and pitched into drunkenness all who gazed upon it; now all light was sucked back into nothing and the world was black—black—utterly and wordlessly black, as if eclipsed by the deep mire of man's sin.

How many seasons?—how many years?

Jedediah tried to count them on his fingers, which ached with cold. But as he passed from *five* to *six* his mind fluttered and died.

Clouds drifted idly downward out of the night sky, below the icy peaks of the mountains, down, downward, below the timberline. As mists rose from secret steaming rivers. The bowels of the earth, hidden from sight. In all this, Jedediah noted, there was a willful absence, for God refused to show His face. Though his servant Jedediah had been kneeling in expectation for many seasons.

God, you would not force me to beg. . . . You would not force me to grovel. . . .

Aurora borealis, seen always for the first time. A stilled frenzy of light. What had its beauty, its unfathomable incalculable beauties, Jedediah wondered spitefully, to do with God? Did God, indeed, dwell in that beauty? In that "sky"?

The northern lights faded. Eventually the pitch-dark night returned, and obliterated all memory. Spirits, hidden by the mists, roamed freely. Did as they chose. Mocking, jeering, fondling one another's bodies. The most intimate caresses. The most obscene whispers.

Was God there, Jedediah wondered. In that? In those creatures?

He had climbed back into the sky, after months of wandering as a penitent. All that he had seen—the men and women he had encountered, and had tried to convince of God's love—the actions God had forced him to take, often against his own wishes: all closed over now, and was obliterated, for the Holy Mountain had nothing to do with the flatland. Memory sank. The past closed over. Only Jedediah remained. And God.

Sin, Jedediah saw, tugged more powerfully at God than love. Sin demanded that God show His face while love, mere love, begged.

Sin. Love. God.

But as he was God's servant he could not commit sin. God gave him no freedom. He wondered, kneeling, in his night-long vigil, if he was then incapable of love.

Even his fury for the demon who had ousted Henofer's soul from his body swiftly died. For Henofer, no doubt, had complied in that obscenity. He was not to be pitied. The demon, cast out of his body, had probably slipped away under cover of the ravine's shadows, and the turbulence of the stream. It would push its way into another body and soon be at home. The smugness of evil, Jedediah thought. While I kneel on this ledge. Begging. My joints are stiff and my bones ache and there are such sharp stinging pains in my belly that I want only to double up, to grovel in Your sight. . . . Which would please You, wouldn't it!

. . . Because for thy sake I have borne reproach; shame hath covered my face. I am become a stranger unto my brethren, and an alien unto my father's children. . . . O God, in the multitude of thy mercy hear me, in the truth of thy salvation. Deliver me out of the mire, and let me not sink: let me be delivered from them that hate me, and out of the deep waters. Let not the waterflood overflow me, neither let the deep swallow me up, and let not the pit shut her mouth upon me. . . . And hide not thy face; for I am in trouble; hear me speedily. Draw night unto my soul, and redeem it. . . .

Hide not thy face.
Hide not thy face.

It was shortly after Jedediah's return to his cabin on Mount Blanc (which he saw, without emotion, had been left untouched—his enemies were too clever to step unwittingly into the traps he had fashioned for them), in a weatherless calm that belonged as easily to late winter as to late fall, that he took upon himself the task, the great task, the fearful task, the task for which he had come to the mountains so very long ago, despite the ridicule of his family: to look upon God's face.

To know, to love, and to serve. But before all these, to *look.*

So he knelt on his ledge in a muttered frenzy of prayer so passionate the mountain spirits did not dare approach him, not even to jab him under the arms or between the legs, or to blow into his ears; he knelt, and clasped his hands before him, and bowed his head, as one must. And he prayed and waited, and prayed, and waited, and again he prayed, throughout the night, and waited, waited, praying all the while, as indeed he had been praying for years, without counting the seasons, without knowing the seasons, praying and waiting, waiting and praying, praying, for he was Jedediah, waiting, always waiting, patient for too long, humble in prayer, humble in waiting, God's servant, God's child, an emaciated bearded hollow-eyed creature whose breath stank and whose body was crusted over with a film of grime that only a hard-bristled brush might erase.

That night, that terrible night, Jedediah knelt on his ledge on his mountain and whispered to God to show His face, for it was the last time he would grovel before His indifference: and his voice rose as if dislodged from him, as queer needle-sharp pains passed through his stomach and abdomen, leaving him chilled, then perspiring, then chilled so suddenly and so thoroughly his body shook. *O God my God,* he whimpered, bent forward, steadying himself with both hands on the rock until the pain subsided. Then he began again, speaking in a normal voice. Quickly and rationally. As if nothing were amiss. As if conversing, merely conversing, with God. With God Who was Himself rational, and Who listened with infinite patience and concentration.

Then suddenly the pain returned, but now it was one, then two, then three fist-sized rocks edging sideways, to the left, through his guts.

He could not believe the pain. It soared beyond what one could measure. A cry was torn from his lips but it was a cry of sheer surprise, for the pain itself could not be uttered.

O my God—

Swift as a knife blade something pierced his belly, slicing down through his abdomen, the very pit of his abdomen, which had come alive with agony. It writhed, it coiled, it had come alive, furiously alive, as Jedediah clutched at himself, staring sightless at what would have been the sky. He could not, he could not believe, he could not believe the pain, he was now whimpering like a child, as something bubbled and swelled to bursting, swelling larger and larger, to bursting, in his guts. What was happening—! What must he do—! His numbed fingers tore at his frayed belt and at the buttons of his trousers, and he managed to lower his trousers, despite the agony that had doubled him nearly in two, for it was quite simply an attack—an attack of the flu—a sudden diarrhea—a storm erupting in his body that had nothing to do with *him.*

O God, help—

He had lowered his trousers just in time: his insides voided themselves hotly, splattering on the sacred rock, and the stench that arose nearly overpowered him.

Squatting, he hobbled away, his trousers caught about his ankles, his body covered with a thin fine stinging film of sweat. He could not believe, he could not *believe* . . . The agony in his belly bubbled again, and swelled, swelled to the size of a watermelon, and he began to groan as much in terror of it (for it was alive—it was not him, it was alive) as in pain. Gaseous balls pushed their way through his intestines until once again his insides gave way, and the storm was unleashed: more violent, more pitiless, than the first.

His face was afire. The pores stung with tiny flames. Every quill of hair arose, in astonishment. *God,* he begged, *what is happening—*

He tried to rise, to straighten, so that he might flee this despoiled place. But a convulsion ran through him. He clutched at his belly, falling forward. And on his hands and knees, his trousers still caught about his ankles, he crawled a few yards . . . until another convulsion ran through him, rattling the teeth in his head. He was chilled, he was freezing, yet at the same time a furious flame passed over him, and his mouth was suddenly so dry he could not swallow. Foul air was released: so very foul, so inestimably foul, that his lungs closed; he could not breathe.

His guts were livid with pain. Coils and writhings. He squatted, his head clenched between his hands, and rocked back and forth in his agony, waiting. But though he was sick, unutterably sick, the poison would not pass from him. *God, God,* he begged, but nothing at all happened: he merely waited, his outspread fingers pressed against his burning cheeks. He was a child, an infant, an animal stunned with pain.

Nothing mattered now except voiding himself: emptying his guts of the lavalike mass packed inside him.

Tears ran down his face. His body too wept—his torso, his thighs. Something hellish had sprung into life inside his very being and he could not, he could not free himself of it, he was subordinate to it, humiliated, craven, waiting half-naked to be delivered. He would have uttered God's name except the suffering was such, so suddenly, that he could not grasp any word: language dissolved into sheer animal sounds. He wept, he whimpered, he cried aloud. He rocked on his poor shriveled haunches.

Now his entire body ached. Now his soul fled his body, affrighted. His torso was slick with sweat, his thighs and bony hips, his slender, hard, tensed legs. He must free himself and yet he could not. The bubbling swelling pain grew larger, there was a terrible pressure inside him, yet he could not defecate, he could not free himself, he had no control.

Then, suddenly, the pressure rose until it forced itself out of him, erupting with a vicious unearthly heat. And again the sacred rock was splattered with his sick, watery, abominable feces.

Scalding-hot, and a hideous odor. He had never known such an odor in his lifetime.

Panting, he crawled away. He crawled blindly. The pressure had subsided, his bowels felt empty, suddenly his fever was gone and he shivered with cold, his teeth chattered with cold, he had wanted to return to his cabin but the cabin was behind him, he was crawling instead to a narrow stream that trickled down from the mountain, so that he might wash—so that he might cleanse himself.

He plunged his hands and face into the icy-cold water.

Now the cold shook him, now the cold passed through him, so that his entire body was wracked with shivering. He must get to his cabin. He must get there, and sleep, in the safety of his cabin, by his fire, and in the morning he would be restored to himself, and his soul would have returned to his body. . . .

He gathered strength. And tried to stand erect. Slowly. Shakily. But a faint tinge of pain, or was it merely the expectation of pain, frightened him, and he froze, bent, crouched low as an animal. Ah, God no, no, it could not be happening *again*.

But it happened again. Another diarrhetic spasm. Another ferocious loosening of his bowels, so that the scalding watery excrement ran down his thighs and legs. Then there were great soft chunks. Coils, streams. So sick. So sick. The stench was overwhelming, he felt faint, he was in danger of fainting. . . . Swift excruciating knife blades of pain. So that his body twisted as if desperate to escape. But it could not escape for the hell was within it.

His eyeballs went blind. His mind was an utter blank. Not a thought remained, not an image, not the feeblest of desires. He had become sheer sensation, an animal crouched on the mountainside, given over wholly to the flesh. Where *Jedediah* had been now only streams and coils of scalding excrement remained.

And so the night passed. The interminable night.

Hour upon hour. The spasms in his belly, followed by bouts of faintness and shivering, when he lay on the ground, too weak to crawl back to his shelter. Then another spasm, another explosive liquid-hot attack: his bowels rumbling with a foul gaseous thunder: his body wracked with pain. Hour upon hour upon hour. No end to it. No mercy. During periods of relative lucidity his mind called forth appalling images of food: food devoured and digested: devoured and digested and turned to excrement, to be voided with rage. He had imagined, these past years, that he had fasted; he had brought his body's humiliating needs under the dominion of his will; but in reality he had gorged like any animal. He had stuffed himself, ravenously, wishing to turn everything into food to be digested in *his* entrails. And now he must suffer for it.

. . . Another sudden contraction of the bowels. A lightning-flash of pain. And though he would have believed, had he been capable of thinking, that his poor writhing body was by this time purged, there was another, still another, explosive outpour . . .

He gagged. He wept. He hid his face.

Such pain. Such sickness. Horror. Stench. Helplessness. Shame. Hour upon hour. *Jedediah* who was no more than this, all along. He saw that his entire lifetime, not simply these years on the mountain, had been nothing more than an organism's process, an ongoing ceaseless remorseless insatiable process—the gluttonous ingorging of food, the digesting of food, the voiding of food, writhing, seething, bubbling with its own ferocious life, not *his,* nothing human, nothing with a name, to which, nevertheless, the name *Jedediah* had been given. What a mockery, that endless stream of food and excrement, given a human name! So much was packed up inside him. Hellish. Burning. And were there worms in his guts, were there thin white slugs crawling dazed in the liquid shit he had voided all across the mountainside . . . ?

He had not the courage to look. Though of course he *had* looked, without seeing. And the excrement was alive with them. Of course. The excrement *was* them, as it was himself.

So the night passed, and the attacks came upon him, hour upon hour, without mercy. Until his pelvic bones jutted through his skin and his belly and abdomen were hollow and a thin, cold, morning breeze sifted through his pain-wracked head. There was not a word left, not a syllable, not a sound! The organism that was himself had not died, nor was it living.

So God showed His face to His servant Jedediah, and forever afterward kept His distance.

The Autumn Pond

Whether on account of the extraordinary dryness of the season (for everywhere farmers lamented, and day by day the pine woods grew more brittle and more susceptible to fire), or whether it had something to do with the fruit pickers' children romping and splashing and tearing in their brief delirium (for they had, Raphael discovered to his horror, not only torn out water lilies and cattails and marsh marigold: they had also littered the pond's banks with the carcasses of hundreds of bullfrogs, which they had evidently caught by hand and dashed against tree trunks, or against one another); or whether, as rumor had it throughout the Valley, secret mining operations in the Mount Kittery area were having a deleterious effect upon streams in the foothills, including Mink Creek, which fed into Mink Pond; or whether it was simply the case that the pond was aging, and must, like all aging, dying ponds, begin to contract upon itself, choked with more and more vegetation (and he saw, baffled more than dismayed, how willows now grew nearly everywhere—they had marched across the pond and met in the middle and struggled for dominion of the rich mucky bottom, crowding out even the bulrushes), so that only small shallow regions of open water remained, hardly more than puddles, cut off from one another with creatures trapped inside them—a few pickerel, a water snake, the last largemouth bass, which must have weighed twenty pounds, but was beginning now to turn belly-up, and would die within a few days: or whether this was simply Raphael's punishment for having loved something so much, so much more than his family: he did not know. But the pond was obviously dying.

His birch raft, partly dismantleed by the strangers' children, lay shipwrecked on a little island of bulrushes; as he approached, barefoot, his feet sinking in the warm squishy black mud, several bullfrogs croaked in alarm and leapt away, and a single black duck flew up, flapping its wings in terror.

But you needn't be frightened of *me,* Raphael wanted to cry.

He sat cross-legged on his raft, gripping his ankles. For a long time he surveyed his little kingdom and the emotion he felt was bewilderment rather than dismay.

Bewilderment shading into fear.

For of course the pond was dying.

But: but still there was life. Life remained. Life on all sides.

Diving beetles and water striders and water scorpions and dragon-flies and snails and slugs and loosestrife and floating pondweed and wild celery and fanwort and mud minnows and mushrooms looking solid and resilient as if they were made of rubber, though they would crumble at the gentlest touch. Richer than ever were the tussock sedges, and the trillium with its shiny red berries, and the spongy bright mosses that had no names. There would always be plankton, algae, scum, there would always be, Raphael reasoned, leeches.

He inclined his head sharply—had he heard a sound? a small voice?

The pond's voice?

He listened for a long time, trembling. Many years ago—he could not have fathomed how many, in human time—but perhaps it was only the week before last, in the pond's time—that voice, refined to pure sound, had soothed him and buoyed him up and saved his life. The Doan boy —had that been his name?—ugly name!—*Doan*—but now all the Doans were gone—gone, scattered, their shanty of a house razed, the barns and outbuildings gone—the Doan boy had tried to kill Raphael but he hadn't succeeded: and on that day, at that hour, the pond had made itself manifest to him. It took him into its depths, it embraced him, whispered his name which was not *Raphael,* which had nothing to do with *Raphael* or *Bellefleur.*

Come here, come here to me, I will take you in, I will give you new life. . . .

In recent years Raphael's mother Lily had become "religious." (So the mocking Bellefleurs spoke of the change in Lily—"She's become 'religious.' And can't you guess why!") She had tried to take the children to church with her but of course Albert had refused, laughing, and Vida went no more than twice, claiming that it was all so slow and dull and the boys her age not at all interesting, and the girls frankly insipid; and Raphael too had refused, in his shy, stubborn, speechless way. But Christ offers us everlasting life, Lily said, vexed and frowning, her voice doubt-ful. Raphael, don't you want—aren't you afraid not to want—*everlasting life?*

But the pond spoke more clearly. Because it did not use human words at all.

Come to me, come here to me, I will take you in, I will give you new life. . . .

In a trance Raphael stretched out upon his raft. Ah how rich, how voluptuous, the odor of decay! He inhaled it deeply. He could not get enough of it. For months, perhaps even for years, he had been smelling this rich ripe rotting odor, this swampy stench, without knowing what it was. Only that it was different from the odor of fresh water. Fresh water and sunlight and wind. Mink Creek's white-water rapids a few miles away, which he had seen years ago. (But perhaps Mink Creek too was drying up? Perhaps—so the rumors flew—the Mount Kittery mining operations had killed it?)

Raphael did not know. The world beyond the pond, stretching out on all sides of the pond, had no interest for him. It existed; or perhaps it did not exist; he could not know. It was not *his.*

Decay . . . rot . . . decomposing logs and aquatic plants . . . fish floating belly-up . . . a certain queer beauty to their placidity. (And he saw now that the bass had died. Perhaps it had been dead for days.) For a long while he had been smelling the odor of decomposition without knowing what it was, and he had grown accustomed to its richness, its suggestion of night, a secret nighttime maintained in the day, in defiance of the sun's rude health. The sun had one sort of knowledge but the pond had another. *Come to me, come here to me, sink into me, I will take you in, I will protect you, I will give you new life. . . .*

The Rats

Multitiered and ambitious were plans for the expansion of the Bellefleur empire that autumn, and numerous too were the unexpected plums fate tossed into the family's lap—for instance, quite without intending it (for she *was* still a young girl) Morna caught the eye of Governor Horehound's eldest son, at a charity ball at the governor's mansion, and the young man was ardently courting her; and one fine October day the Bellefleurs received word that Edgar Schaff had died suddenly of heart failure in Mexico City, and that his fortune, including Schaff Hall, was to fall to his wife, under the terms of his generous will (for the poor distraught man had never altered the will, despite Christabel's disappointing behavior, as if he had believed he might, after all, persuade his straying wife to return home with him).

(The difficulty here was, as Leah pointed out, that Christabel was still in hiding, presumably with her lover Demuth, and even the Bellefleur-hired detectives couldn't find her. They too had traced her to the Mexican border—but then they couldn't find her. How could the Bellefleurs get hold of the Schaff estate, if Christabel didn't come forth to claim it in person? And the Schaffs, of course, headed by that dragon of a matriarch, had lost no time with grief, and were already contesting the will. For Schaff, intoxicated with a passion more befitting a far younger bridegroom, had left Christabel everything—the newspapers; the investments; the estate; Baron Schaff's priceless antiques, memorabilia, and special collections; and some 60,000 acres of strategically located wilderness land.)

And Ewan, after the temporary setback in August, when he had had to arrest his own uncle for murder, was now more popular than ever: a series of blitzkrieg gambling raids throughout the county, including a highly publicized one at Paie-des-Sables (where, it was disclosed, half-breed Indians were coolly cheating naïve white boys of their entire life savings and even their automobiles and farm equipment) had netted for the county extraordinary sums of money and even a considerable supply of guns, rifles, ammunition, and explosives, which would be put to good use. And Gideon, though he had recovered rather slowly from his accident, had roused himself into action by selling off the rest of his cars, and negotiating with the owner of a fair-sized airport in Invemere (some seventy-five miles northeast of Lake Noir) for a partnership of some kind: a procedure that worried the more conservative members of the family, who gravely distrusted airplanes, but pleased Leah immensely.

There were important changes being made at the Bellefleur farms, under Noel's supervision: the old barns were razed and new barns with smart aluminum roofs were built; there were automated silos, bulk tanks, hundreds of arc lights; henhouses operated by batteries in which as many as 100,000 Rhode Island reds lived out their lives in tiny cages, fed special grain to increase both their capacity for egg-laying and the size of their eggs; under the dry-lot system, dairy cows now lived *their* entire lives in concrete enclosures, receiving feed (mainly alfalfa) from an overhead conveyor. Despite the enormous cost of the investments in this new equipment the family would be saving, year by year, the burdensome cost of their hundreds of unreliable tenant farmers and farmhands—under a near-automated system only a few "farmers" need be retained; and Albert had expressed an eagerness to oversee the entire operation. "If only we could get rid of the *smell* of those creatures too." Aveline was heard to say. She meant of course the animals.

Naturally there were minor frustrations, for things did not *always* go well. There was, Leah knew, a certain perversity in the fabric of the world. She and Lily had groomed Vida, sweet little Vida, for the eye of the governor's son, but he had preferred Morna, and now Aveline was queening it over them; Leah's plans for a handsome new camp on the fifty-acre site across the lake, where aunt Matilde lived in willful squalor, were temporarily stalled—but only temporarily—by the crazy old woman's refusal to move; and Garth, Little Goldie, and their infant son had left the stone cottage in the village, shortly after the "difficulties" with the fruit pickers (for so the events of late August came to be known within the family), to live in another part of the country. Garth claimed that he wanted a farm of his own, in Iowa or Nebraska; he and Little Goldie wanted to live somewhere where no one knew the name *Bellefleur*.

("All right, then, but don't you come begging back here, don't you come crawling back to *me!*" Ewan said. He was so deeply wounded by Garth's decision to move away that he would not even shake hands with him, on that last day; he refused even to glance at Little Garth, though Little Goldie held the squirming infant up to his grandfather for a goodbye kiss. "Don't you come back here, my boy, because we aren't going to let you in! Is that understood?" Ewan cried. Garth merely nodded, forthrightly, as he backed away. He and Little Goldie had traded in the yellow Buick for a small van, which was now packed with their household items.)

So there were minor disappointments, minor frustrations. But in general, even the pessimistic Hiram had to agree, things were going very well indeed: for quite apart from the Schaff windfall they now owned slightly more than three-quarters of the original property, and the rest was certain to be theirs within a few years.

"But we must concentrate on what we're doing," Leah said frequently. "We mustn't allow ourselves to become distracted."

Governor Horehound and his family and part of his entourage were invited to the castle for a week of hunting, as soon as deer season opened; and less than a week before the visit Nightshade approached Leah with a proposal. "As you know, Miss Leah," he said humbly, "there is the matter of the rats."

"The what?"

"The rats, ma'am."

"The rats?"

"The rats, yes, ma'am. That live in the walls and the attic and the cellar and the outbuildings."

Leah stared at her manservant. In recent months she had become so accustomed to the little man that she rarely noticed him—and now it alarmed her, the clever wizened face with its eyes like glass chips, and the dull shallow indentation on the forehead. Odd too was the wide lipless smile that appeared to stretch from ear to ear. Though Nightshade was not exactly smiling; one could not call it a smile. The children complained that he carried in one of his pouches a "made-up" animal, a mandibulate, fashioned out of bits of dried mice, beetles, newts, snakes, bullfrogs, baby birds, turtles, and other creatures, which he used to frighten them, though he always denied that was his intention. The thing was about the size of Nightshade's fist (which was big as Ewan's), and it gave off a queer sickish odor that was exactly like Nightshade's odor.

Leah sent the children away, annoyed with their silly tales. She doubted very much that Nightshade had created his own dried animal, still less that he used it to frighten the children. And it wasn't true that he smelled. She noticed nothing. In fact, in recent weeks it seemed to Leah that the poor hunched-over man had grown an inch or two taller; or, at any rate, his severely stooped posture had begun to correct itself. The good food he received in the castle, and the pleasant surroundings, and, perhaps, her frequent small kindnesses to him were having a salutary effect.

And now he came to her with a strange proposal: that she allow him to brew a concoction that would rid the castle once and for all of its rats. "Before Governor Horehound and his people arrive, Miss Leah," he said softly.

"But we don't have any rats," Leah said. "Oh, perhaps there are a few—I suppose there are, in the outbuildings especially—in the old barns —and maybe in the cellar. And mice: I suppose there are mice."

Nightshade nodded gravely. "Yes. There are mice."

"But there aren't enough, are there, to matter? If there were, we could call in a professional exterminator. But of course we have the cats."

Nightshade's lips twitched but he said nothing.

"Yet you say there are rats?" Leah said, growing somewhat irritated.

"Yes, Miss Leah. A concentration of rats."

"And how do you know this? Have you seen them?"

"I am capable of certain judgments, ma'am."

"Well—I would have thought our cats—"

Nightshade chuckled softly. "Not *your* cats, Miss Leah," he said, "not *these* rats."

So he brewed a special concoction of poison, with an arsenic base, on the kitchen stove. Two gallon-sized kettles were filled and allowed to simmer for several hours, until most of the liquid had evaporated. This particular poison, he assured everyone, attracted only rodents—and poisoned only rodents. Cats and dogs would not touch it, nor would children, under ordinary circumstances, be drawn to it. There was no danger whatsoever: *only* rodents would die.

"But we don't have that many rodents," grandmother Cornelia said stiffly. "I grant you there are field mice that turn up sometimes in the cellar . . . and of course in the barns. . . . And a rat or two, wood rats, I believe they are, nasty things, but not a problem, really. I *don't* see that we require a mass extermination."

"It does seem rather excessive," uncle Hiram said.

"But now that Nightshade has made the poison," grandfather Noel said, with a peculiar smile, "of course we must allow him to use it. Otherwise it will only go to waste."

So very early the next morning, before most of the family had awakened, Nightshade crept about the castle and the outbuildings, sprinkling his poison crystals (which were a dazzling white) in every conceivable corner. He then filled buckets and pans with water, and carried them into the larger rooms of the castle, on all three floors; and he carried several heavy tubs of water into the cellar; and arranged others outside, in the shrubbery, among the ornamental trees in the garden, on the back steps. His furrowed, pasty-pale forehead was soon beaded with sweat, and his lipless smile was more pronounced than ever. As he toiled, the castle's cats scurried away before him, or leapt onto high places, from which they watched him with bright narrowed eyes. One and then another of the dogs began to howl, but faintly, almost timidly. He took no notice of these creatures but arranged buckets, pans, pots, tubs, and even troughs of water, grunting as he worked.

He then sat back to wait.

But there was little waiting: within a half-hour the rats appeared.

From out of cellars, walls, closets, cupboards, from out of drawers, from out of haylofts, from beneath floorboards, from inside overstuffed cushions and pillows, from out of the larder, from out of Raphael's leather-bound library, came the rats—squeaking, clawing, their eyes glittering, mad with thirst. Some were more than a foot long, some were pink hairless babies. All ran, scuttling crazily, tumbling over one another, scrambling, screeching, their toenails clicking on the floors, their whiskers abristle. How thirsty they were! Desperate with thirst! Mad! Maddened! They fought one another viciously to get to the water, and plunged headfirst into it, and in their maniacal eagerness to drink some of them were actually drowned. What a screeching and a squeaking! No one had ever heard anything like it before.

Streams of rats and mice and shrews, jostling one another blindly, thumping about inside walls until, finding a hole or a soft spot, they pushed through with their heads, and forced their way out, and ran to the water. . . . The Bellefleurs, astonished, climbed atop furniture, even crouched on the dining room table of the Great Hall, staring at the writhing jabbering creatures. So many! Who would have thought there were so many! And how violently thirsty they were, how greedily they drank, drank and drank and drank, as if their thirst could never be quenched! No one had ever seen anything remotely like it before.

And then, after a brief time, the convulsions began.

The living bodies bloated, second by second, balloonlike, and soon they were flinging themselves about, rolling over and over, screaming and clawing and slashing. They writhed, they foamed at the mouth. Their legs paddled crazily. Their high-pitched squeals grew ever more frantic until the Bellefleurs, panicked, had to press their hands over their ears to keep from screaming themselves.

How strange a sight, how hideously fascinating, the creatures' swollen bodies! Stomachs bloated white, the skin stretched to bursting; legs flailing about as if they were drowning; stiffening tails. Death leapt invisibly from one to the other, touching a whiskered chin here, a balloon-stomach there, until, after some time, after many minutes of agony, the last of the beasts lay still. Now their tongues protruded, and were also bloated; and very pink. In death the larger of the creatures resembled human infants.

Nightshade, wearing thigh-high fishing boots, walked among them gingerly, picking them up one by one by their tails and putting them in gunnysacks. If a rat was not yet *entirely* dead Nightshade stepped on its belly, pressing down firmly, with immediate results. (Some of the Bellefleurs hid their eyes. Others gazed upon the horror as if they could not turn aside. A few had grown deathly ill, but were incapable of vomiting: they merely stared, helpless, too weak to move.) Though Nightshade worked quickly and efficiently, and though not one of the rodents resisted him, or crawled away to hide, the task took him a considerable period of time.

Each of the gunnysacks held between fifty to one hundred rodents, depending upon their size. (The Norway rats were, of course, enormous, but the shrews were smaller than mice.) And there were thirty-seven sacks all told.

Thirty-seven sacks!

Leah said, when Nightshade approached her, bowing, rather pale from his day-long exertions, that she would have liked him to have *warned* the family; of course they had had no idea so many rodents lived in the castle. It was rather upsetting, she said, in a voice that faltered, it was rather upsetting . . . for the older Bellefleurs especially. All that scrambling and squeaking and jabbering, and those hideous, agonizing deaths! It had been quite repulsive, really. "If only you had warned us, Nightshade," Leah said.

Nightshade bowed even lower. After a long moment he dared raise his eyes to the hem of her skirt. "But Miss Leah is not displeased, is she?" he whispered.

"Oh—well— *Displeased!*" She halfway laughed.

"Perhaps I acted imprudently," Nightshade murmured, "but the rats *are* dead. As you have seen."

"Yes. Indeed. As I have seen."

"And so—Miss Leah is not displeased with me?"

"I suppose not. I suppose you've done a good job."

"A good job?"

"—excellent job," Leah said faintly. For a moment she felt nauseous: the walls and ceiling reeled, and a rich dark dank odor wafted to her from the hunched-over little man. "Still," she said, "we were all so taken unawares—we would have thought, you know, that our cats—"

"Ah, well," said Nightshade with a sudden wide smile, stretching from ear to ear, "*your* cats—! Not, you know, with *these* rats."

The thirty-seven gunnysacks, filled to bursting and smartly tied with rope, soon disappeared. What Nightshade did with them no one knew, nor did Leah want to ask.

The Spirit of Lake Noir

Once upon a time, the children were told in whispers, a terrible thing happened. It would have been a terrible thing had it happened to anyone; but it happened to *us*.

On an October night in the year 1825, in the settlement beginning to be known as Bushkill's Ferry—

But should the children be told, generation after generation?

Is anything gained? What is gained?

What is lost?

But they must be told!

But why must they be told, if it terrifies them?—if it makes the young ones whimper in their sleep, and the older ones restless with thoughts of revenge?

—in the settlement known as Bushkill's Ferry, in the old log-and-brick house Jean-Pierre and Louis had built, six persons were murdered in cold blood, without warning: Jean-Pierre and his forty-year-old Onondagan mistress, Antoinette; and Louis (then forty-six) and his three children, Jacob, Bernard, and Arlette. Louis's two dogs—a mongrel retriever and a collie with one clouded eye—were also killed, with clubs, and for some inexplicable reason (the killers later blamed the Lake Noir air) the retriever was crudely decapitated with a hunting knife. And then the house, sprinkled with gasoline, was set afire.

The five horses in the stable were spared.

It was on account of the fire—the murderers' fatal blunder—that Louis's wife Germaine was saved: she had been left for dead, and the fire naturally attracted neighbors, who broke in and rescued her. (An accident, really, that they located her at all, for she was lying where she'd fallen, against the bedroom wall, between the wall and the bloodsoaked bed where Louis's badly mutilated body lay.)

So Germaine survived. Despite her injuries (deep cuts and lacerations on her face and torso, a broken collarbone, a cracked pelvis, a slight concussion), and the unspeakable terror she must have endured. As soon as she regained consciousness she cried out the names of the murderers —those five of the eight or nine she had recognized, despite their burlap masks and women's clothing: the Indian trader Rabin, and the Varrells; Reuben, Wallace, Myron, and Silas. She was able not only to identify the men but to give testimony against them at their trial.

She was thirty-four years old at the time of the massacre, and she was to live, as another Bellefleur's wife, for twenty-two more years. Unless she was pointed out (*That woman, you see, there, that woman is Germaine Bellefleur, her husband and three children were murdered before her eyes. . . .*) no one would have guessed that the stout, rosy-cheeked, graying woman had lived through such an ordeal: she seemed so ready to *smile*. Indeed, perhaps she smiled too frequently. Sudden noises always frightened her, of course, and she became hysterical if a dog's baying continued for too long. But she appeared quite normal. She even had other children, three other children, as if to replace the ones she had lost. God sent you these children, it's a sign from God, two boys and a girl, wasn't it two boys and a girl you lost, people whispered, but Germaine did not reply. She did not say with a contemptuous laugh, What a fool you are, to talk of God! —my husband and I saw to these babies, and nobody else. She did not say, You dare not speak of my dead children, or of me; you know nothing about us. She nodded slowly as if thinking, and smiled her pleasant shadowless smile. There was an attractive brown mole beside her left eye.

Do you forgive those who have sinned against you? the minister asked.

Yes, said Germaine. And added in a low voice: Since they are all dead.

But should the children be told, generation after generation?
Vernon, a child of seven, held his ears. Did not want to hear.
But they must be told! They must understand the secret workings of the world —the fact that, once someone has injured you, he will never forgive you.

There were, nevertheless, Bellefleurs who winced at the very mention of the name *Varrell*, not because they wanted vengeance (for the time for that was long past: weren't most of the Varrells dead, and those who remained scattered and impoverished, mere white trash), but because they were ashamed of being linked to such primitive behavior. The old Lake Noir settlement—hunters and trappers and traders and lumber-camp workers—a single muddy street in which stray dogs prowled, and were shot for sport by men on horseback—kegs of corn-mash whiskey— the taverns—the drunken fistfights—the frequent stabbings and shoot-ings—arson—crude bullying animal-men who were (so Raphael realized, years later) *almost* not to be blamed for their violent behavior since most of them, it seemed, were mentally impaired: they had the intelligence of eleven- or twelve-year-olds.

In England, where Raphael was to search for five months before finding, in a quiet country village, the eighteen-year-old Violet Odlin, people frequently asked him about the "blood feuds" of his native country. Was it true, they inquired, that families warred against one another until, one by one, all their members were destroyed? Raphael answered stiffly that such behavior was eccentric even in the West—even in the Far West—where civilization had not yet firmly established itself. But most of the citizens of my native country, Raphael said, in an inflectionless voice from which all traces of a Chautauquan accent had been eradicated, are not, of course, *native* to the country.

Vernon held his ears though the other boys mocked him. And afterward he dreamt he was in his closet, in the dark, and someone was searching for him, heavy-footed, speaking his name in a sly voice, Vernon, little Vernon, where are you, where are you, under your bedclothes? under your bed? or are you hiding in your closet? He had coiled upon himself to make himself as small as possible. And he *was* small—about the size of a cat. Are you in your closet, is that where you are?—so the voice ran on, and suddenly there was a terrible sound, as the prongs of a pitchfork came crashing through the door. And he screamed and screamed in his sleep and woke, screaming. (Though Arlette had not been stabbed to death in her closet. They had dragged her out, and she was to die, in fact, the most merciful of the deaths, in the kitchen of the old house.)

But the other boys, their faces dark with blood, prematurely adult in their anger, wanted to hear—wanted to hear—wanted to hear everything. And then they interrupted one another, shouting. Why hadn't great-uncle Louis known this would happen! Why hadn't he killed them first! Reuben and Wallace and Myron and Silas, and Rabin and his brother-in-law too, and Wiley, the "peace officer," and the others—whoever they were— Why hadn't he guessed what they would do, and killed them first, in secret? Hadn't he a shotgun near his bed? Why did he believe, even for a confused half-minute, that there was a lawman among that party, with a warrant for his arrest? (There were things for which Louis Bellefleur was not altogether blameless. Fines, for instance, which he had refused to pay, just as his father had refused to answer a certain summons issued by the justice of the county court at Nautauga Falls, having to do with suspected fraud—since the heavily mortgaged Chattaroy Hall, at White Sulphur Springs, had burnt down not long before, insured for $200,000.) Why had the poor man *almost* raised his hands so that his wrists might be shackled—hadn't he seen, despite his grogginess and the confusion of the moment (but it was thought too that he might be blind in his right eye, since the eyelid was always somewhat lowered, and the entire right side of his face was paralyzed) that the men who had broken into his house and into his bedroom, at two in the morning, were wearing masks, and women's clothing?—and thigh-high rubber boots?

He had put up a ferocious struggle, the boys were told. Though at once his attackers took out their knives, and one appeared in the doorway with the pitchfork (Louis's own pitchfork), and of course he was doomed.

But why hadn't he killed them all *first!* the boys cried.

At first Germaine said that the men had all worn women's clothing. Then she changed her mind—she thought maybe they hadn't—only three or four of them—coarse feed-meal skirts that fell just below their knees, revealing their boots. And had they *all* worn masks, burlap masks, with crude holes for eyes? She thought they had—or some of them—yes, they had—all of them—*all* of them. Because she hadn't seen any faces. Their faces had all been hidden.

She told her story so many times, certain details dropped away, and others suddenly appeared, she stammered and went silent and began again, and wept, and lay back fainting on the pillows, and even those who knew very well what had happened at the Bellefleur home that night (and knew, even, who the unidentified men were) began to say that maybe she had made it up. Made up, that is, the murderers' identities.

Here is a theory: complete strangers might very well have ridden up to the Bellefleur house under cover of darkness, having been attracted by its spruce-lined drive and its size (for it was by far the largest private home in Bushkill's Ferry at that time), or by old Jean-Pierre's reputation (by now *The Almanack of Riches,* though shamelessly derived from Franklin's *Almanack,* had gone into its sixtieth printing; and the fire at the White Sulphur Springs spa had acquired a certain statewide notoriety; and Jean-Pierre's oscillating fortunes at horse racing were a matter of common knowledge)—complete strangers, perhaps men from the city, might very well have committed the murders, intending to rob the family and changing their minds at the last minute; and Louis's wife, so brutally beaten, and terrified, might have *imagined* she could recognize voices. . . .

But she insisted. She knew who they were: she knew. Though she was to repeat her disjointed story innumerable times, sometimes forgetting certain details, remembering others, though she was often to break down in the middle of it, she never wavered in her identification of the five men. Reuben and Wallace and Myron and Silas Varrell, and old Rabin, whose hatred for her father-in-law went back at least thirty years: those were the murderers. She knew.

Night after night at the White Antelope Inn they had gathered, drinking, talking of what must be done to Louis and his father. And one night in October they made their move.

Eight or nine of them, led by Reuben Varrell.

(Wiley had not ridden out with them, nor had he willingly given the handcuffs to them, though, of course, afterward, he was to say nothing about the incident. The handcuffs *were* his—that is, they had been taken from his office—but he claimed to have no idea how the murderers had acquired them.)

Dressed in their playful, outlandish costumes—young Myron had even stuck a woman's bonnet on his head, tied beneath his chin—they rode the mile and a half to the Bellefleur house and, carrying knives and mallets and shotguns (which they planned not to use unless forced, on account of the noise), they kicked open the unlocked front door, and rushed to the two downstairs bedrooms.

In one of them lay Louis and Germaine, asleep. In the other lay Jean-Pierre and Antoinette.

They shouted: You're under arrest! We're officers of the law! Don't move!

In Louis's room one of the murderers lit a kerosene lamp, and the others hauled Louis out of bed. It was their plan, their initial plan, to handcuff both Louis and the old man, and take them away to kill them; and dump their bodies in the lake, weighted, so that they would never be found. But somehow—somehow it happened—there was so much screaming from Germaine and the squaw—and the dogs were barking and snarling crazily—and of course the two boys ran downstairs from their bedroom under the eaves, one of them carrying a two-by-four: somehow it happened that they began stabbing Louis almost immediately. And Jean-Pierre was never even dragged out of his bed. He had no time to reach for the pistol he kept beneath his pillow, nor had the Indian woman time, as Germaine did, to crawl from the bed and try, with piteous clumsiness, to hide under it. With steel hunting knives and ten-pound mallets they struck both Jean-Pierre and the woman innumerable times, and killed them in a matter of seconds.

Louis fought like an enraged bull. Wounded, bleeding from a dozen places, half his face frozen and the other half twisted into a violent grimace, he lunged from side to side, striking his attackers, shouting for help. It was then that one of the masked men, bellowing drunkenly, rushed upon him with the pitchfork.

Louis's body, recovered from the fire, would show evidence of having been stabbed more than sixty times.

Seventeen-year-old Bernard was killed in a corner of the kitchen, where he had fled; the huskier Jacob, grown as tall as his father, put up more of a struggle, swinging the two-by-four until it was wrenched from him, and then turning, as blood gushed from a cruel wound in his throat, to throw himself out the window—but they seized him from behind, and threw him to the floor, and with shrieks and war whoops (for the blood lust was upon them, they could not stop themselves) they stabbed the boy to death.

The dogs, of course, had been killed.

The cat, it was thought, escaped: a burly long-haired gray tom, with one badly frayed ear and a sagging belly.

And Germaine: with one blow of his mallet Reuben Varrell struck her on the collar bone, having aimed for her face, and his brother Wallace seized her by her long braided hair and pummeled her against the wall. When blood gushed from her nose and mouth, and she fell heavily to the floor, it was thought—it must have been thought, though in the commotion no one was capable of thinking—that she was dead. For they left her, they forgot her. They ran from the room, whooping and laughing, colliding with one another, wiping their bloody hands on one another, in a stampede to escape.

The killings had taken only a few minutes.

Five persons, in a little more than five minutes. And the retriever, and the half-blind collie.

And then one of them said: But isn't there a girl—?

But should the children be told? Should they be told everything?

In order to understand the secret workings of the world—

In order to understand what it means to be a Bellefleur—

They stared, white-faced. Some of them, like Vernon, pressed their hands over their ears.

Some of them whispered, But why didn't they kill *them* first!

One of the girls—it might have been Yolande, long ago—took hold of both her pigtails and tugged at them, crying angrily: Oh, why didn't *she* have a knife! She could have killed one of them, at least!

Afterward, riding away, riding back to the village, exhausted, sober, drained of their exuberance, the murderers were to think that spirits had driven them to their frenzy. They had not intended to kill the women, or even the sons (though of course, if they had thought about it, calmly and sanely, they would have known Jacob and Bernard must die)—they had not intended, certainly, to kill Arlette. For she was the closest friend of Rabin's brother-in-law's sixteen-year-old daughter, and often visited the girl at home.

But the air of Lake Noir, the heavy damp evil air, the whisperings and proddings of nighttime spirits, the shouting and screaming and war whooping: the men had lost control of themselves, they hadn't been able to stop until everyone was dead. Until all the Bellefleurs lay lifeless, smashed and bleeding.

The Indians had always feared the Spirit of Lake Noir, as an angel of mischief and death. It was that spirit—for it hadn't been they, themselves—who had worked them up to their ecstasy of killing.

They rode away, beating at their horses' flanks. One of them retched dryly, another was whimpering to himself. Reuben kept saying, over and over, in a low dazed emphatic voice: Nobody will know, nobody will know, nobody will know.

Behind them the house was burning. They had sprinkled gasoline throughout the downstairs rooms and tossed down matches. Within a few minutes the flames would leap through the roof and the walls—and all the evidence, they reasoned, would be destroyed.

But who had done it—!

The Spirit of the Lake.

Though they detested the squaw, and thought it brazen of old Jean-Pierre to be living so openly with her (she was an attractive woman, not beautiful, not especially Indian-looking, nearly four decades younger than Jean-Pierre), as everyone in the village did, they had not intended to kill her. Or Germaine, or the sons. Or the girl Arlette. And someone had even cut off the dog's head. Why, amid all that confusion, had one of them taken the time to cut off a dog's head . . . ?

(No one would admit to it. Most likely Myron was responsible, for he had been observed killing the dogs; but he denied having cut off the retriever's head. I wouldn't do such a crazy thing, he said sullenly.)

Arlette had hidden in her closet beneath the eaves. She had known—she had known at once—not only that her family was to be killed, but who the murderers were, and why they had come. Near-fainting, she crawled from her bed in the dark to hide in the closet; and it was there the men found her, crouched, so terrified she had lost control of her bowels and soiled herself.

They shrieked and yodeled, pretending to be Indians, and dragged her out of the closet, and tore off her flannel nightgown, and for some reason—perhaps they intended to take her away with them on horseback, or out of the house that stank now of death—they carried her downstairs. The sight of the naked, struggling, terrified young girl, the reek of her panic, excited them all the more: in high-pitched whining begging voices they shouted what they would now do to *her*.

But Silas Varrell, waiting downstairs, rushed at them. That's enough, this is enough! he cried. He shoved one of his brothers away, and with a single blow of his mallet he smashed Arlette's skull.

Now the house was silent.

Now the house was silent except for the murderers' ragged heaving breaths.

. . . four, five, six. Six of them dead. And so much blood. And they *had* intended only two.

Query

Query: Poems by Vernon Bellefleur.

"What on earth—!"

"What is *this*—"

"Who put this here?"

They discovered the slender volume in Raphael's library one morning, a book of poems by someone with their name!—the name, in fact, of one of the recently deceased members of the family. The book had an attractive nubby oatmeal-colored binding with stiff grayish pages and fine, delicate type whose ink looked already faded. How odd, how very odd, and who was the prankster who had slyly laid the book atop a cabinet in the library?

"This," Noel said slowly, paging through the book, "is *very* odd."

Cornelia peered over his shoulder. "Do the poems rhyme? I don't think they *rhyme.*"

They passed the book around, turning pages quickly and suspiciously, pausing to read a line here and there with a growing sense of unrest. For was it possible . . . ? Was it possible that Vernon had not drowned, after all, but had managed to escape the Varrells . . . ? And now he would expose the Bellefleurs to the world; now nothing could stop him from telling their most intimate secrets.

What was most disturbing, the poems made little sense. There were strange unfamiliar words embedded in them, ungiving as chips of mica, and sentences did not tamely complete themselves but trailed off into nowhere—into nothing. Lily said uncertainly, "But some of the poems are beautiful, aren't they . . . ?"

No one answered her. Cornelia said, "It's like code! Riddles! Nasty things you can't understand without breaking your head over!"

Ewan seized the book and flipped the pages angrily. "Do you suppose it is possible," he said in a low dangerous voice to his father, "that our Vernon did *not* drown after all. . . ."

"Impossible," Noel said curtly, taking the book from him and shutting it with a snap.

It was never to be determined, though all the children and servants were interrogated, who had put the book on the cabinet: who had acquired this preposterous *Query* by a preposterous *Vernon Bellefleur*. For of course the name was a forgery. Or, even if it were legitimate, and did belong to the poet, the poet was not *their* Vernon. "Why, that poor fool went mental at the end," Aveline said, "preaching against his family the way he did. How could he find a publisher, raving mad as he was? This can't be him."

"Better yet," Ewan said, "how could he save himself from drowning? He couldn't even *swim* as a boy."

"We could trace him," Gideon said disdainfully, "through the publisher or the printer. If we chose to."

"But there's no address given! Only the name of the press, Anubis, and doesn't that sound as much an imposture as "Vernon Bellefleur" itself?" Jasper said. (For he was one of the leading suspects—he traveled often to the city, by himself, on business errands for Leah—and he wanted to dissociate himself from the volume altogether.)

It was thought finally that Christabel or Bromwell, those rebellious unhappy children, might have sent the book through the mail, simply to stir up trouble. For of course Vernon was dead. Their Vernon was dead.

Query remained on the cabinet top for nearly two weeks. No one cared to tell Hiram about it, yet no one (for such was the impish nature of the Bellefleurs) wanted to spare him the experience of discovering it. Every day Noel and Cornelia whispered together: Has Hiram read the thing yet? Has he gone into the library, has he picked it up?

Cornelia was convinced that the author *was* Vernon. Her beloved nephew Vernon, whom she had somehow, unaccountably, paid no attention to during his lifetime. "And I just know those poems are about *us,* in some hideous code we can't read!" she said, pressing her beringed hand against her bosom. "He was always so strange, even before he turned against us."

"Don't be absurd, old woman," Noel said. *"That* Vernon is gone."

"But he always had talent—! Whatever talent is. He was always—oh, you know—he was always so—so spirited, so hopeful— The way he used to tag around after Leah—"

"The words that came out of his mouth were *incomprehensible!"* Noel said angrily. "Do you call that talent—?"

But he was not really angry. In the past several months—since the "difficulties" with the fruit pickers, and his brother Jean-Pierre's abrupt and unceremonious return to Powhatassie (where the old man was now ensconced, for therapeutic purposes, about which the Bellefleurs were in unanimous agreement, in the Wystan Sheeler Memorial Wing of the prison)—he had acquired a slapdash, almost hearty air, and looked more than ever like a cocky old bantam, restless for a fight. The family's amazing financial successes struck him as unreal, and he could not see, as Leah so frequently and so teasingly insisted, that they had something to do with Germaine: he had lived so long with failure, he could not put much faith in the present. Success was a pair of $200 Spanish-styled boots, failure was the old filth-softened pair of slippers he wore about the house. The one fitted tightly, the other was sprawling and splayed as his old feet themselves. There was no question which he preferred.

"We are millionaires once again," his wife sometimes whispered, silly as a girl. "And Leah promises more—even more!"

Noel grunted a reply, discourteously.

He liked to turn family conversations around to problems, like the mysterious "Vernon Bellefleur" whose book of poems they had been privileged to read. Or the inexplicable leaks in the new slate roof which had cost them—ah, God!—so many thousands of dollars. Half the new trees in the garden were dying of a mysterious black spot blight, had they noticed? And what of the rebellious old couple (great-grandmother Elvira and the old man from the flood, her absurd bridegroom, who had begun to strut about like a member of the family, turning his foolish paternal smile on anyone who approached) and their plans to move across the lake—? They were openly defying Leah; they insisted upon going to live with great-aunt Matilde to spend their "twilight years," as they called them, in solitude; and naturally this would prevent Leah from tearing down the old camp and rebuilding it according to her and her architect's elaborate plans. You see, you see, Noel liked to chuckle, things are *always* going against the grain—!

No one dared give the book to Hiram, directly. But one evening, having returned from a three-day business trip to Winterthur, he came upon it while riffling through an accumulation of financial newspapers and journals and odd bits of mail.

Query. Poems by Vernon Bellefleur.

No one was present in uncle Hiram's room to observe his face as he snatched the book up; no one was present to observe with what urgency he began to read. A nerve twitched in his right cheek as he leafed quickly through the book, pausing here and there, murmuring a line of verse aloud. *What was this—! How had anyone dared—!*

Trembling, Hiram forced himself to return to the beginning, and read the poems in order.

Whether, in the end, he believed the poet to be his son, or an impostor, or, simply, a stranger with the improbable name of "Vernon Bellefleur"—no one knew. Nor was it known (for no one, not even Noel, dared ask) what he thought of the poems, whether he found their gnomic queries provocative or maddening. It *was* common knowledge that the book, a dozen of its handsome pages torn out and a dozen more mutilated, and the spine broken, was discarded along with the accumulation of newspapers, journals, and nuisance mail, and burnt in the incinerator by one of the servants.

Air

Insatiable Gideon Bellefleur!

It was not known (for he himself would have scorned to keep a tally) how many women Gideon Bellefleur loved in his lifetime, and loved, shall it be said, successfully; still less was it known how many women loved *him*. (And loved without hope, in defiance of fate, even when it had become common knowledge throughout the region how cruelly Gideon behaved.) But it was known to a few persons at the Invemere airport, among them the former bomber pilot Tzara, who was to be Gideon's flight instructor, that the last woman he loved was the tall, aloof, mysterious "Mrs. Rache" who, dressed in tight-fitting men's trousers and a khaki jacket, appeared at the airport every week or ten days to take up, alone, the airport's single Hawker Tempest, a surplus fighter from the last war. The Tempest was the little airport's prize: for it boasted a 2,000 horsepower engine. And it was this feisty plane the Rache woman rented!

Gideon fell in love with her one chilly November afternoon when he happened to see her striding into the hangar, roughly tucking her colorless brown hair into her helmet, her narrow shoulders hunched forward in an attitude of impatience, her back to him. She wore, as always, a man's trousers. And a drab khaki-colored jacket or shirt. And her pilot's helmet, with the amber goggles snugly in place. Gideon stared after her, losing the thread of the conversation he was having with Tzara. Quickly and helplessly his eye took in the compact strength of her buttocks and thighs, the long, lean stretch of her back, the graceless movement of her elbows as she tucked in her hair, eager to get to her plane. When Gideon did not reply to a question of Tzara's but continued to stare into the hangar, Tzara said, with a sad smile, That's the Rache woman. And that's all I can tell you. We don't even know exactly where she flies.

Before that Gideon had loved Benjamin Stone's wife, and before that a nineteen-year-old beauty named Hester, and before that . . . But the affairs had ended badly. Abruptly, and badly. There were tears and pro- testations and occasionally threats of suicide, and always self-pitying lita- nies: How did I fail you, Gideon, what did I do wrong, why won't you look at me, why has everything changed. . . . Fatiguing, and predictable, and even at times silly, once Gideon's feeling for a woman died (and it might die overnight—it might die in an hour), these sad litanies: and the tear- glistening cheeks and the mournful does' eyes and the lips that, no longer eagerly kissed, always appeared faintly repellent. How did I fail you, Gideon, the women asked, sometimes "bravely," sometimes in raw shameless gasping voices that might have been the voices of children; why have you stopped loving me, what did I do wrong, won't you give me another chance, what has happened. . . .

Gideon's natural good manners prevented him from thrusting them away, or shouting at them to have some pride (for, like most of his family, he detested people who wept in public, or who broke down in situations clearly inhospitable to their tears); he had often to restrain himself from taking an abandoned mistress in his arms, and covering her face with kisses merely to soothe her, knowing how such an action would only prolong the woman's agony. He had encountered women who, knowing love had died, would have eagerly and desperately settled for pity—that most despicable of emotions!—and it was his strategy, his necessary strategy, to behave as coolly and judiciously as possible with them, though never without courtesy, until they grasped the fact that he would never love them again: that the extraordinary "feeling" they had evoked in him simply did not exist any longer.

Why, he wondered, sometimes irritably, *did* they love him?—why with such passion?

How much simpler his life would have been, he often thought, if he'd been born with a different face! His cousin Vernon's, for instance. Or a different manner, a different *presence.*

In the months since his accident Gideon had begun to think about his life, though thinking, and certainly brooding, were quite alien to his character. The notion of *thinking,* of withdrawing oneself from action in order to systematically *think,* struck him as not only unmanly but implaus- ible: for how could one force oneself to think, merely *think,* when the world awaited! But since his hospitalization Gideon had begun to con- template his life, and though he never turned his thoughts onto his family or his marriage or, in fact, anything connected with the castle, he fre- quently considered the many women with whom he had been involved over the years.

He had loved them, each of them, so *much* at the time. He had loved them painfully and recklessly and desperately. One after another after another . . . His need for them had been raw and intense, almost frighten- ingly intense; his sexual appetite at such times was insatiable. And far

from alarming women this appetite seemed to evoke in them a corresponding hunger . . . or was it merely a helpless yearning . . . a wish, at
bottom childish and doomed, to maintain that appetite even as they fed
it, and to maintain their sense of themselves as beautiful, desirable
women capable of a man's prodigious desire. That there were so many
ugly rumors about Gideon Bellefleur throughout the land, that he was (so
it was whispered) responsible for more than one young woman's death,
seemed to deter other women not at all: he sometimes thought his reputation aided him. Though how perverse, how absurd, how *doomed* it all
was—! His mother-in-law, the insidious spiteful Della, once muttered in
his unwilling ear that after poor Garnet, every woman will deserve him,
and though he hadn't, of course, acknowledged the old woman's words
with more than a curt bow of his head, he was coming to see their gradual
truth. For didn't these women *deserve* their fate, bound up as it was with
their endless capacity for self-delusion . . . ?

And then there was Gideon himself: handsome, still, in a manner of
speaking, but no longer the Gideon of old.

He eyed himself without sentiment, even with a kind of sardonic
gratification. For his skin was now sallow, even somewhat jaundiced—
even, in certain lights, somewhat bronzed—and it was drawn tightly
across his cheekbones, which were cruelly prominent. Hospitalized, he
had had to endure the humiliation of endless examinations, and they had
shaved his skull more than once, so that the hair grew out unevenly, in
coarse gunmetal-gray clumps through which he could barely force a
brush. He was now beardless, for the first time in many years. His angular
jutting chin promised no tenderness, nor did his curved, sensual mouth,
with its look of impatience. His eyes were darkly shadowed and striking,
perhaps more striking than before, but he had, hadn't he (so he amused
himself, *thinking* as he eyed the stranger in the mirror), the gaunt watch-
fulness of a long-legged sharp-billed aquatic bird of prey . . . ! Flesh had
melted away from him, not only at his belly and waist, but at his chest and
shoulders and upper arms as well, so that he simply wasn't as muscular,
as strong, as he had been; and he wondered—was it his imagination, or
had he actually lost an inch or two in height? His frame seemed to be
settling down, settling into itself. And of course he had a permanent limp,
a rather appealing slight limp, as a consequence of his smashed right
kneecap.

Gideon Bellefleur, so much changed! Yet he saw clearly that it *was*
Gideon Bellefleur. And he was still handsome, even with that gaunt
hungry stare, and the cold, rather reptilian smile he could not, it seemed,
control. Women were struck by him, they were attracted to him, they
succumbed (after a siege that might be absurdly protracted, or absurdly
abbreviated) to his demands, and this was "love," this was a "love affair,"
always profoundly exciting at the start. Perhaps if he shaved his head
again, Gideon thought, and went about with a convict's mean, sour,

ravenous look, women would then fear him . . . ? Or would it have little effect?

The only woman in the land who could never be brought to feel desire, let alone love, for him was Leah. And so he was free, wasn't he, he was wonderfully free, fairly drunken with freedom, and quite guiltless! The world was all before him, to explore as he wished. And hadn't his own mother-in-law predicted that each of his women, after Garnet, would deserve her fate?

Still, he fell in love with the Rache woman, whose first name no one— not even Gideon—ever learned.

Even before happening to notice her at the little airport north of Invemere Gideon had been mildly interested in private planes; it was a slight prickling of an interest, strong one day, somewhat abated the next, unpredictable. The previous spring he had arranged for an extensive and costly crop-dusting operation out of the Invemere airport, and he had found himself boyishly impressed with the aging pilot Tzara's performance. Flying with such lordly brazenness low across the fields of wheat and alfalfa—pulling back and rearing, rising, at the very final moment, to avoid a line of trees—bringing the battered old Cessna high, with an appearance of effortlessness—checking speed and dropping—and then again rising—the single constant-speed propeller whirring invisibly—the low-slung wings and prominent tail now colorless, now glaring with sunlight as if afire: how masterful Tzara was! As Gideon sat in his air-conditioned automobile, with the windows rolled up tight, Tzara had flown over the road, quite low over the automobile, and waved at him. He had, it seemed, winked. Or so Gideon thought.

And in that instant it seemed to Gideon that Tzara—who was in his late fifties, if not older, and had flown more than two hundred bombing missions in the war-before-last—possessed a freedom that went beyond anything Gideon had ever known. The speed, the mastery!—the daring! The courage! Tzara in the compact little plane, skimming low over the Bellefleur fields, with clouds of white powder billowing out behind him, Tzara in his frayed helmet and goggles, hired by the hour, a servant, in a sense, of Gideon's, nevertheless soared above Gideon, and knew secrets Gideon did not know.

The plane's agility, even hampered as it was by the 1,800-pound chemical hopper tank, made Gideon's automobile seem tiresomely earthbound.

After the accident he had come to feel a certain revulsion for cars. Not for the cars themselves—for he admired, still, their appearance—so much as for the fact that, in a car, one was forced to drive along a road. A narrow strip of pavement; or, worse, a dirt or gravel road. How predictable it was, how *earthbound.* His fastest car had taken him 125 miles per hour along the highway to Innisfail, late at night or very early in the morning, but even the Cessna crop-duster could fly at 151 miles per hour, and there was an open-cockpit Fairchild at the airport that could go much faster. And there was, of course, the Hawker Tempest with its compact body and comparatively brief and low-slung wings, and its dazzling bold red-and-black fuselage. . . .

Who is that woman, Gideon wanted to know, the one who takes up the fighter? How does she know how to handle it? Did she get her license here? Don't you know *anything* about her?

Only that her name was Rache. But not even that: only that she was married to a man named Rache, whom they never saw.

Tall, lean, flat-bodied. With the hips of a young boy. Always, in the instant before Gideon (who had taken to hanging about the airport) managed to see her, pulling the plastic goggles down over her eyes, tucking her hair impatiently into the helmet. A strong jaw, pursed lips, a handsome deeply tanned skin. Her profile, Gideon saw, almost with resentment, was aristocratic: the nose not unlike his own. He judged her age to be thirty, thirty-two. . . . She was not exactly young, she was certainly not a girl, and he was tired, ah, how he was tired, of the trembling bleating inconsolable passions of girls! Perhaps, he thought one day, having nearly confronted her as she strode toward her plane, she was even older. Whatever age she was would please him. *She* would please him, simply by glancing his way.

He stood on the runway, shading his eyes, watching her taxi the plane out, steeling himself against the propeller's passing roar and the possibility—which was of course only a frail possibility—that she might suddenly lose control of the plane, just at takeoff, and nose-dive into that clump of poplars. He stood on the cinder runway, shivering in his lightweight clothes, watching the Hawker Tempest until it was well out of sight—rising and rising and rising, and banking to the left, to the west, toward the mountains. Sometimes he waited for her to return, though she was always gone a considerable period of time, and it halfway embarrassed him, that she should see him there, waiting, so flat-footed and earthbound and hopeful. Waiting for her. Waiting for something.

He had come to feel a certain revulsion for the earth itself.

He had been thrown against it so carelessly, as if he were nothing more substantial than a rag doll. Knocked against the windshield of the Rolls, tossed against the door and against the stubbled cornfield—dripping blood into the August dust—crying Germaine, Germaine! My God, what have I done to you! (And, later, in the hospital in Nautauga Falls, waking delirious from the anesthesia, he had continued to call for her. Why did he think, everyone wondered, he had carried his three-year-old daughter off, to speed with him along the Innisfail road?)

A certain revulsion for the earth, and for himself. Tricked as he had been, by the men who had tampered with his car. (Yet had he been *tricked*, knowing very well that they had tampered with it?) . . . A revulsion for

Gideon. Walking on the earth. Walking on the earth as one must, so long as one lived. And now he limped, now his right knee ached, he was beginning to resemble his father whom he had, he scarcely knew when, stopped loving.

Germaine . . . ?

Far from home, in nameless towns, often with nameless women beside him, Gideon woke uttering that name. *Germaine, is it time? Is it time for all of us to die?*

Insatiable Gideon!

Fascinated now with the air, and with planes. *What is air, and how do we climb into it? How do we escape the earth?*

Falling in love with the Rache woman, who either ignored him or returned his greeting with a curt nod. His blood going heavy and sullen with love for her: his breath going shallow.

Cessnas and Fairchilds and Beechcrafts and Stinsons and Piper Cubs and other small light planes, taxiing along the bumpy runway and lifting above the poplars and banking into the wind and rising, rising . . .

He came to love the odor of gasoline and oil. And the hush, the fear, the almost palpable fear (for the plane *might* crash in the instant its wheels touched earth) as Tzara returned with one of his student pilots. Shall I take lessons? Shall I make a fool of myself? Why the hell not!

Prowling about the grimy little airport, whistling tunelessly. Making casual conversation with the mechanics, who never flew, who had no interest in flying, but who had certain opinions—offered cautiously enough—about the Rache woman. (Her original pilot's license, they said, had been issued in Germany.) Feeding coins to the cigarette machine and smoking those stale cigarettes; chewing, simply because his hunger leapt upon him, chocolate bars tasting of wax, from the vending machine in the manager's office. Gideon in love, insatiable Gideon in love. When the Hawker Tempest taxied out the runway and lifted into the sky and began its slow ascent Gideon felt his soul drawn after it, thinner and thinner, until nothing remained in the cold glowering air but the wind sock's sullen flapping noise. It was the noise, he knew, of his own heartbeat.

Insatiable Gideon Bellefleur, a gaunt shivering figure at the Invemere airport, obviously homeless.

Though Tzara knew the Bellefleurs were buying the airport, he never spoke of the transaction to Gideon; when he spoke, and he spoke rarely, it was only about flying, and about the weather.

He took Gideon up for the first time in a Curtiss biplane with faded yellow wings, one of his own planes. Gideon climbed into the cockpit, his eyes filling with tears behind the amber-tinted goggles. Of course his life was being changed. It would never be the same again. His heart rocked in his chest as if he were a small child, and genuinely frightened.

What is air, and how do we climb into it? How do we escape the earth?

The old plane taxied down the runway, bouncing and vibrating, and lifted, at the last minute (for the line of scrawny poplars had been rushing back with dismaying speed), and Gideon's breath was torn from him and he exclaimed aloud with a child's delight and terror: ah, how wonderful! how uncanny! they were in the air now! they were flying! Absurdly, he could not stop trembling. His jaws clenched, his breath came in shudders. As if it were secretly attached to the earth the pit of his stomach sank as the plane rose.

Now the earth fell away. It was only a surface, falling away. As Gideon stared in amazement the sky swung downward and opened majestically. The poplars were gone. The weedy field adjacent to the runway was gone. Now they were flying, wind-buffeted and rattling crazily, above a forest. And now above a field. In the near distance the Powhatassie River wound narrowly through winter fields, glittering snakelike as he had never seen it before. Tzara carried them above it, and it was gone, fallen away behind them. Fields, forests, rectangles of farmland, houses and barns and silos and outbuildings, grazing animals in snow-stubbled fields, ever smaller, ever more miniature as they climbed into the air: how queer, how marvelous, how uncanny! Of course it was perfectly commonplace, planes were perfectly commonplace, Gideon knew he had nothing to fear, and yet he could not stop trembling, and he could not stop a mad sunny smile from raying across his face. At last! Such joy! Such freedom! His heart soaring! His spirit rising above the earth!

This is it, isn't it! he shouted to Tzara, who could not, of course, hear.

The Joyful Wedding

Many were the impassioned cross-Atlantic wires, and the tear-splotched letters in reply; many were the tasteful, modest gifts Lord Dunraven sent to his shy beloved (on Michaelmas eve an antique ring with a single pink pearl, on Christmas Day a Japanese shawl shot through with bright purples and greens, on Twelfth Night a tiny German music box inlaid with tortoiseshell and hammered silver—which poor Garnet felt she could not accept, and yet could not bring herself to return for fear of hurting her suitor's feelings). When Lord Dunraven returned to America shortly after the New Year, and was, of course, a houseguest of the Bellefleurs, there were many weeks of letters delivered by hand to Garnet, in Mrs. Pym's house in Bushkill's Ferry, and weeks of ostensibly secret meetings in that house (with Della, of course, close by in an adjoining room, as a kind of chaperone), weeks of sleepless nights, increasingly impassioned pleas from Lord Dunraven's side, gradually weakening defenses from Garnet's: until at last, to everyone's astonishment, not least to Lord Dunraven's own, Garnet agreed to be his bride.

"I cannot say—I cannot *know*—if I will ever come to feel such love for you, as you declare you feel for me," Garnet wept in his arms, "but —but—if you truly do not think me unworthy—if you *truly* do not hold me in secret contempt for having given my heart and soul to another man —and ah! how unwisely— If it's as you declare, that my hand in marriage will make you happy, will save you from despair, then—then—then I cannot refuse you, for you are, Lord Dunraven, as everyone exclaims, the kindest of men—the most generous, the most considerate—"

Garnet's words brought to Lord Dunraven's ruddy face an even deeper blush, and for a moment it appeared that he did not comprehend —did not *dare* comprehend the import of what he heard. But then, whispering only, "Ah, my dear! my beloved Garnet!" he tightened his embrace and pressed upon her anxious lips a warm, passionate, husbandly kiss.

Garnet Hecht, the parentless servant girl, the step-granddaughter of old Jonathan Hecht, impoverished, barely educated, and, since the shame of her affair with Gideon Bellefleur and the birth of her illegitimate child, a figure of contemptuous pity in the Lake Noir area—Garnet Hecht to be Lord Dunraven's bride! To be the bride of that finest of gentlemen, and to live on his country estate in England for the rest of her life!

It was really, as everyone said, most extraordinary.

Extraordinary, said Leah. Our unhappy little Garnet to be *Lady Dunraven.*

Of course there was a great deal of excited talk. And yet, oddly, very little of it was mean-spirited. For it seemed quite clear to the Bellefleurs, even to Leah, that Garnet *had* resisted Lord Dunraven's proposals; she *had* attempted to break off communication with him more than once; it was certainly not the case that she had seduced him, and cajoled him into marriage. She had, they felt, behaved honorably. Though Garnet was not a Bellefleur she had exhibited a Bellefleur's integrity—it was a pity, really, that they couldn't claim her for one of their own.

Grandmother Cornelia offered to throw the castle open for the wedding: for it looked as if, if Morna were actually going to marry Governor Horehound's son (and *that* courtship was a stormy one), the wedding party would be held at the governor's mansion, and not at Bellefleur Manor. And it was not to be until June, if indeed it took place at all. "You really must allow us," grandmother Cornelia told the shy couple, "to do all we can. The renovations in the west wing are nearly complete—we've made over the entire third floor into a particularly lovely guest suite and of course it would make an ideal bridal suite—so spacious, so private—"

But in the end Della insisted, and of course no one dared oppose her, that the wedding party be held at *her* house. Garnet and Lord Dunraven would be married at the Anglican church in Bushkill's Ferry, and there would be, afterward, a *small* gathering at her house. "Garnet has been, as everyone knows, the dearest of daughters to me," Della said, her lips twisting as if she were trying not to cry, "and I will miss her—I will miss her terribly. But I want only her happiness. And this marriage has come to her from heaven. It has come to her from what must be *called* heaven."

So the wedding and the party would be held across the lake. But the date presented a problem. For Lord Dunraven naturally wished to be married as quickly as possible (he had waited so long, so very long, for his beloved's consent, and he was not a young man; and he was anxious, as well, to return to his homeland), but Jonathan Hecht was now critically ill, and it was feared he might die at any time. Dr. Jensen held out no hope. And, indeed, the cadaverous old man *looked* deathly. Cornelia and Della discussed the situation for hours. If they went ahead and planned the wedding for early March, as Lord Dunraven seemed to want, it was probable that Jonathan would just have died—and the wedding would have to be postponed. But if they waited for Jonathan to die—that was, of course, out of the question, in execrable taste. The most strategic thing would be to have the wedding immediately, but this too was out of the question—the haste would only provoke unseemly gossip, and ruin plans for a meaningful celebration.

In the end they scheduled the wedding for the first Saturday in March, before the start of Lent.

And so it took place on that day, without a single difficulty. There were fears that at the last minute Garnet might change her mind—for she *did* continue to worry about the propriety of the marriage, and whether she deserved Lord Dunraven's love: but she held fast to her decision, and exchanged her wedding vows in a clear, firm voice. Never had a bride, everyone exclaimed afterward, looked so exquisitely beautiful. And never had a wedding been so joyful.

The little church was tastefully decorated with lilies, white roses, and white and pink carnations; the bridegroom, his silvery-gray hair brushed back smartly from his temples, had never looked more handsome; and the bride—ah, the bride: her slender hips and small, high breasts were shown to advantage in a simple white dress with a smocked bodice, and she wore, on her thick honey-blond hair, which was parted in the center of her head to fall in two gentle curving wings over her temples, a veil of Flemish lace that had been Della's bridal veil. She carried herself proudly —there was no fear, as some of the less charitable Bellefleurs said, that she would slink guiltily up the aisle, or burst into tears at the crucial moment. Her skin appeared creamy, and flawless (the subtle ravages of the past two years had quite disappeared); her neck was nobly columnar; the erect grace of her carriage suggested that she *was,* even at this time, Lady Dunraven. The only testimony of her nervousness was the trembling of her bridal bouquet of white and pink carnations.

Quite apart from the beauty of the bride, and the love that showed so clearly on the bridegroom's face, the wedding was remarkable for another reason: not only had old Jonathan Hecht managed not to die and disrupt the plans, he had, through what must have been a preternatural effort, forced himself up out of his sickbed, and, in the wheelchair he had not been able to use for five or six years, he attended the wedding—and gave the bride away.

"What a feat! What a surprise!" grandfather Noel said, gripping the old man's arm afterward. "You go your own way, don't you, eh?—like all of us!"

Noel was the liveliest, and the loudest, of the wedding guests. He declared he didn't mind making a fool of himself, and went about kissing the women, and insisting upon dancing with the bride, almost as if she were his daughter. "Lady Dunraven, is it? Lady Dunraven? Yes? Right?" he said, winking, and hugging the blushing young woman until Cornelia came to take him away. "You go your own way like all of us! I see that now! I'm beginning to see that now!" he crowed.

And so Garnet and Lord Dunraven were wed at last, and soon sailed for England, where they were to live out the rest of their lives in contentment: for the joyful wedding *did* prognosticate a joyful marriage. The following January they were to send a wire, never received, announcing the birth of a son; but in general, after they left for England, communications between them and the Bellefleurs were but feebly maintained. "It's true, it's true," Della said with a sad smile, "we all must go our own way."

And yet:

A scant two days before the wedding Garnet sought out her lover Gideon, and spoke passionately with him, in secret, for three-quarters of an hour.

She wanted, she said, simply to say goodbye to him. For, as he must know, she would be married on Saturday, and would leave for England shortly afterward. Her life was taking a turn she could not have anticipated. "Between us . . . between you and me . . . so much has passed," she said with difficulty, "that it is almost as if . . . almost as if we *had* been married, and had suffered together the loss of our child. And so . . . And so I wanted to say goodbye to you, in private."

Deeply moved, Gideon took the young woman's hand and brought it to his lips. He murmured something about her pretty engagement ring —the small pink pearl in the antique setting—which he had not seen before.

"Yes," Garnet said vaguely, "yes, it's very pretty—Lord Dunraven is so fine a man, I scarcely—I scarcely—" and, staring at her lover's gaunt, melancholy face (for he too had suffered, perhaps more cruelly than she), she lost the thread of her words.

After a pause Gideon released her hand. He wished her happiness in her marriage, and in her new homeland. Was it likely she would ever return to America?

Garnet didn't think so. Lord Dunraven frequently expressed a wish to "settle down," after the draining turbulence of the past year; for he was, evidently, accustomed to a far quieter life. "He is by nature a gentle person," Garnet said. "Unlike . . . unlike you. And your family."

"A fine man," Gideon said slowly. "Who deserves happiness."

"Yes, a fine man. An exceptionally . . . fine man," Garnet said in a hollow voice.

They stood for a while in silence. In another part of the house a piano's treble notes were struck merrily, and children shouted with laughter; there was a comfortable odor of wood smoke from one of the fireplaces; the door to this room, not firmly closed, was nudged open by one of the cats—by Mahalaleel himself, resplendent in his thick ruffed winter coat. He mewed inquisitively and trotted forward, quite as if he and Gideon were on friendly terms. His tawny eyes, in the lamplight, glowed with a covert intelligence, and his enormous silver plume of a tail was carried high.

"Well—" Garnet said. She paused, blinking rapidly. "I had only meant to— I thought, since between now and Saturday—"

Gideon nodded gravely. "Yes, there is a great deal to be done, I should imagine. You'll be very busy."

"Mrs. Pym tells me—she tells me you've bought an airport, in Invemere, is it? And you're learning to fly a plane—"

"Yes," Gideon said.

"But isn't—isn't that sort of thing dangerous?"

"Dangerous?" Gideon said. He had stooped to rub the great cat's head, and seemed distracted. "But—but a man must challenge himself, you know. Only in motion is there life."

"And your wife doesn't object?" Garnet said in a small, quavering, reckless voice.

"My wife?" Gideon said strangely.

"Yes. She doesn't object? For of course it must be—it *must* be dangerous."

Gideon laughed, straightening. Garnet could not interpret his tone.

"Only in motion is there life," Garnet said. "I will remember that."

She turned upon her lover a bright, melancholy smile, which so dazzled him that he looked away.

"I suppose," Garnet whispered, "we must leave each other now. I suppose—"

Mahalaleel rubbed against her legs, mewing in his throaty, guttural voice, but when Garnet stooped to pet him he eased away, and leapt onto the back of a chair, and then onto the mantel. A crystal vase wobbled and nearly fell, brushed by the cat's tail.

"I suppose we must," Gideon said.

His manner was subdued, almost somber. Did he want to weep, did he want to cry aloud, as she did? In recent months he had taken on the look of a mourner. But despite his thin, lined cheeks, and his shadowed eyes, and the almost cruel turn of his lips, he was still an extremely handsome man. With a pang of gratified alarm Garnet saw that she was doomed to carry this man's image with her, in the secrecy of her heart, for the rest of her life.

"If, at the very last moment," she said suddenly, her heart kicking in her chest, "if—even on the church steps— Or, after the ceremony, when we are about to drive away— If, you know, you made a sign to me — Only just raise your hand as if you were— As if it were accidental— Ah, even at the very last moment, Gideon, you know I would return to you!"

Now the restless cat leapt from the mantel to a table, and, in so doing, *did* knock the vase down; and caused it to break in a dozen large, wickedly curved pieces.

As the newlyweds were about to climb into the Bellefleur limousine, as they waved goodbye to the assembled well-wishers on the steps of Della's house, Gideon, standing at the rear, in his long heavy muskrat coat (for the March winds were ferociously cold), a matching fur hat atop his head, felt a sudden itching in his ear—and, without thinking, raised his hand to scratch it—*began* to raise his hand, to scratch it—and then froze. For he saw how the bride stared at him.

She was waving farewell giddily. Her pretty little white-gloved hands flew about, and her lovely hair was being blown by the wind, when, suddenly, seeing him about to make a gesture, she paused—paused and stared—stared at him with an expression in which hope, terror, and incredulity were mingled.

But Gideon had *not* scratched his ear. Wisely, prudently, he lowered his hand. He could tolerate the itching in his ear, he reasoned, despite its violence, until the limousine was well out of sight on the Falls road.

The Skin-Drum

How strange! Whyever did he do it? Whyever did he sink into such cynicism, such despair? Imagine, the great Raphael Bellefleur willing himself to be, immediately following his death (which of course he had brought about by fairly starving himself, and taking not a one of the drugs prescribed for him by Wystan Sheeler), *skinned,* and his hide treated, and stretched across a Civil War cavalry drum that was to be, according to the terms of his will, kept "forever and at all times" on the first floor landing of the circular stairs leading up from the Great Hall of Bellefleur Manor! The man who had built the castle was to be preserved within it, in a matter of speaking, made into a drum, and the drum was to be (again, according to the will, though this clause was never obeyed) sounded each day to announce meals, the arrival of guests, and other special events. . . . What perversity, people said, laughing and shuddering. But then, you know, he wasn't even *insane:* he didn't have that excuse.

Properly played, the Skin-Drum of great-great-grandfather Raphael gave out a smart, brisk, magisterial tattoo which had the power to penetrate every corner of the castle. Hearing it (for sometimes the children played with it, risking severe punishment) the family shivered and stared off into space. *That,* they could not help but think, even those Bellefleurs who scorned superstitions, is old Raphael, living still.

The Skin-Drum was often disappointing, at first. For when the children showed it to their cousins or friends they frequently withheld the most significant information about it: that it was made of the hide of a human being. So it presented itself as a Civil War drum, in quite good condition, with brass fittings, and faded red velvet ribbons, not strikingly different from drums the children might have seen elsewhere. Here, why don't you play it, one of the Bellefleur children might say, handing over the sticks —see what it sounds like.

One of the visitors (in fact it was Dave Cinquefoil, a few days before the mysterious death of the Doan boy) seized the drumsticks and, holding the drum awkwardly between his knees, as if he were riding a horse, hammered wildly away, giggling, and became so intoxicated with the sound (for it almost seemed, judging from the rat-tat-tat he was producing, that the boy had a natural talent for the drum) that he found it difficult to stop. Grinning, giggling, gasping for breath, he sat on the landing and drummed away with the sticks, his hands and arms moving so quickly they were hardly more than blurs, his face wet with perspiration and his eyes glittering, while the Bellefleur boys tried to stop him, appalled at the racket, for they hadn't, certainly, thought their cousin would have such an enthusiasm for the thing! From everywhere in the castle people appeared, holding their ears—even the shyest of the servants—even the youngest of the children—and still, and still, Dave hadn't wanted to stop—until finally Albert wrenched the sticks away from him, shouting, frightened, *For Christ's sake that's enough!*

Afterward, they told Dave that the drum was actually made out of the skin of their great-great-grandfather Raphael—who was of course Dave's great-great-grandfather as well. He had stared at them, his mouth slack, and smiled a queer loose smile, and said, finally, wiping his face, that he had guessed it: maybe he'd heard the story from his own parents, maybe he'd heard about it at the castle, but he didn't think so, he really thought he'd guessed it, while playing the thing. Not Raphael Bellefleur's exact identity, of course. But that the drum was fashioned out of a human being's hide, and that the person had been a Bellefleur. Yes, Dave said, laughing uneasily, I guessed it right away. *He* was the one who made me keep going.

It was generally known that old Raphael's physician, the renowned Wystan Sheeler, had tried to dissuade him from the "drum fancy" (for so Dr. Sheeler called it, in an effort, perhaps, to undermine its power over the sick man's mind)—he had pointed out that such a whimsical, indeed capricious, action would have the inevitable effect of eclipsing the many significant things Raphael had done in his lifetime. He *had,* after all, built Bellefleur Manor. There was nothing quite like it in the Chautauquas— poor Hans Dietrich's castle had come nowhere near it in grandeur or ambition, and the medieval-Gothic monstrosity erected downriver by the brother of the "grain baron" Donoghue was, at best, a hunting and fishing lodge. Raphael had been, hadn't he, one of the founders of the Republican Party, at least in this part of the North, and he had built his hops empire up from nothing, meeting, in his prime, weekly payrolls involving more than three hundred workers. . . . Everyone knew that he had entertained royally: Supreme Court justices, among them the formidable Stephen Field, had been houseguests at the castle, and the brewery king Keeley, and the senators Kloepmaister and Fox, and the visiting Prince of Wales, and Secretary of State Seward, and Secretary of War Schofield, and the Attorneys General Speed, Stanbery, Hoar, and Taft, and Nathan Goff after he stepped down from his position as Secretary of the Navy, and of course there were briefer visits from Schuyler Colfax when he was Vice President, and Hamilton Fish just after the notorious *Virginius* episode, and even, for an afternoon, James Garfield when he was campaigning for the Presidency. Chester Arthur had been scheduled to spend a weekend at Bellefleur, but his wife's illness, at the last moment, detained him in Washington; Ulysses Grant had accepted an invitation but failed to appear; and of course there was the mysterious "Abraham Lincoln" who had sought refuge at Bellefleur, where he was to spend the rest of his days.

(Dr. Sheeler had never spoken with this individual, for Raphael kept him sequestered, for the most part, but he *had* caught several fairly direct glimpses of him—and it was true that the aged man resembled the late President. Gaunt, hollow-cheeked, with a melancholy visage, and an obviously intelligent face, and a beard not unlike Lincoln's: but he was much shorter than Lincoln had been, probably not more than five feet six, and so of course he wasn't Lincoln; could not possibly have been Lincoln; and why Raphael persisted with the folly, or truly believed that it was not folly, Dr. Sheeler could not determine. Perhaps, in his premature dotage, poor Bellefleur had so *wanted* to have been a significant political figure, or, failing that, an intimate acquaintance of a significant political figure, that he had invented an Abraham Lincoln of his own . . . ? On what was to be his deathbed Raphael "confided" in Dr. Sheeler: while President of the United States Lincoln had been near to collapse, near, even, to suicide, overcome with attacks of panic and guilt and horror arising from the thousands upon thousands of deaths the Union had suffered, and he had been quite sickened by the behavior and arrogance of Secretary of War Cameron, and of course by the meanness of Congress, and the turbulence of the country at large, even in those areas in which there was no active fighting, and (though he admitted it to no one at the time) he knew he had done wrong by imprisoning so many civilians in Indiana and elsewhere, simply because they had been suspected of proslavery sentiment, he *knew* he had behaved wickedly, and must be punished. So, aided by Raphael Bellefleur, whom he had recognized as a soulmate, the aggrieved man devised a scheme whereby an actor would be hired to "kill" him in a public place, and after his "death" an expertly constructed wax corpse would lie in state for thousands of mourners to view, and Lincoln himself, freed of his mortality, would retire to the paradise of the Chautauquas, as Raphael's permanent guest. All this came about flawlessly, Raphael insisted, and Lincoln spent his final years in near-seclusion on the estate, wandering in the woods, contemplating the lake and mountains, reading Plato, Plutarch, Gibbon, Shakespeare, Fielding, and Sterne, and playing, on long ice-locked winter evenings, chess and backgammon with his host, who was himself becoming a recluse. It wasn't long after Lincoln's "assassination," Raphael told Dr. Sheeler, that he halfway wished he might arrange for his own death in so bloodless and yet irrevocable a fashion.)

But why did Raphael want to mock his own dignity, and desecrate his body, by insisting that his heirs have him skinned and made into a *drum*? Dr. Sheeler simply did not understand.

Raphael considered the question politely. In his final years he moved slowly, with a patrician studiedness; his every action, even so small and ostensibly casual an action as the lifting of a teacup, was measured and ironic, and imparted an air of tension to anyone who watched. If the tone of the first three-quarters of his life was zeal, the tone of the last quarter was irony. "Are you asking," he said finally, "why I have chosen a *drum* above other instruments . . . ? If so, I can only say that it was the first idea that flew into my mind. Because we have, you see, a cavalry drum on hand."

Dr. Sheeler chose to ignore his patient's exquisitely modulated sarcasm. He said, softly, "I meant, Mr. Bellefleur, why do you wish to mock yourself by mutilating your body in that fashion? I can think of no precedent for such an extraordinary act."

"*Is* it mockery?" the old man asked, knitting his brows. "I had thought, rather, it was a kind of immortality."

"Ah, immortality! Being stretched across a crude musical instrument, which your heirs will be instructed to play several times a day!— it's at the very least," Dr. Sheeler said, "a most unusual notion."

"I have provided for the conventional resting place, I've designed a handsome mausoleum, to be fashioned of white Italian marble, with graceful Corinthian columns, and charming androgynous angels with tinted marble eyes, and Anubis himself to stand guard," Raphael said, drawling out his words. "Unfortunately there is no one to share it with me. Mrs. Bellefleur, as you know, did away with herself in a most mysterious fashion; and my sons Rodman and Samuel have quite, quite vanished. And it isn't likely, I suspect, that they will be found—even after my death I doubt that they will step forward. Lamentations is my only heir, and you see what *he* has become."

"He's a steadfast, generous young man."

"He's a fool. And his wife Elvira: you're aware, of course, that she has returned to her parents' home, temporarily, as she insists, in order to have her baby there, claiming that the atmosphere of the manor is disturbing . . . ? I doubt that that headstrong young woman will return here while I am still living."

"She loves you, but it's quite possible that she *does* find the atmosphere disturbing. This new notion of yours—"

"Loves me!" Raphael said contemptuously. "Of course she doesn't love me. Nor does my son. Nor do I especially want them to. It's on account of *that*, you see, that my wishes must be carried out to the letter."

"That—?" Dr. Sheeler asked, baffled.

"That," Raphael said with finality.

After years of estrangement Dr. Sheeler was summoned back to Bellefleur, to treat Raphael (who had aged considerably since his third defeat at the polls) for "sluggish circulation," sleeplessness, and chronic depression. It was clear to Dr. Sheeler that his patient had given up on life, even as he made languid, drawling requests for the proper medicines to treat his condition. He often wandered about the walled garden in the rain, or tramped slowly along the lake shore, leaning heavily on his cane, his pince-nez, secured by an elastic band, swinging free of his face. He no longer troubled to change his linen often, or even to shave; his eyebrows had become grizzled; he muttered aloud to himself, gnashing his teeth, reliving old battles.

Three times he had run for the office of governor, and three times he had lost! And the third defeat had been the most humiliating. So many thousands of dollars wasted . . . so much of his spirit, his strength, his idealism. . . . There had been, of course, savage editorials against him. There had been clownish cartoons, vile caricatures. Libelous "exposés" by journalist hacks: HOGS TREATED BETTER THAN BELLEFLEUR HOPS PICKERS. And: BELLEFLEUR LABORERS DYING LIKE FLIES. Midway in his campaign he had rushed home to initiate a clean-up of the barracks, which *were* somewhat unclean, but it was too late, the influenza was already raging; and then the summer was so unusually wet; and the following summer as well, when he couldn't get enough pickers to work in the fields, and the hops ripened prematurely and began to rot. . . . Thousands upon thousands of dollars, rotting. The green jungles, acres of green, vines snaking from left to right around the supporting poles, a sea of leafy green, lush and overlush, rotting in the moist sunlight. *And how everyone had rejoiced, knowing he was broken.*

Hayes Whittier too had betrayed him. Hayes's tubercular son had died, finally—the camp on Lake Noir had not saved him—but it wasn't on account of the son's death that Hayes had turned against him, and may even (stories differed, of course) have spoken publicly against him, during the last days of his doomed campaign. Hayes had been in love with Violet. Or had behaved as if he were. Struck, as he called it, by something "haunted" in her face. (Her morbid attachment to that halfwitted Hungarian carpenter whose name Raphael had forgotten, perhaps!) It had seemed to Raphael that Hayes's sentimental passion for Violet had increased as his son's strength ebbed. He gazed upon her with moony vacant eyes. He was eager to accompany her to receptions and dinners and even, upon occasion, to a lavish society funeral in Vanderpoel—his lovesick manner rather comically at odds with his portly bulk and his mussed muttonchop whiskers and his formidable wife (the granite-bosomed Hortense Frier, the bishop's daughter), and his reputation as one of the shrewdest and most audacious leaders of the Republican Party.

That he had betrayed other men, out of necessity, as he claimed, and driven at least one of them (Hugh Boutwell, after his bid for senator) to a premature grave, had seemed to Raphael proof of the man's authority: he had never dreamt Hayes might turn against *him.*

Take me with you to Washington, Violet had begged, on that crucial April morning (the day before, as Raphael rather irrelevantly recalled, Palm Sunday), I can't bear to stay at Bellefleur while you're gone, and Raphael, vexed at his wife's sudden foolishness, said irritably, My dear, I am only going to be absent for two days! The ride in the carriage would exhaust you, and then we would be returning immediately—it *isn't,* you must know, a pleasure jaunt. Then tell our houseguests to postpone their visit, Violet said. Certainly not, Raphael said, staring at her through his pince-nez, can I have heard you correctly? Tell our houseguests—! But, said Violet, the Whittiers are so—so— *Both* Whittiers, said Raphael enigmatically, you are speaking of—? She had paced about the room like an actress signaling distraction, she had even managed to pull strands of her hair loose, and seemed to her husband willful and not at all charming: for she *would* misunderstand his very faith, his husband's inviolable faith, in her. That *she* might even think that *he* might even think her capable of succumbing to Hayes Whittier's importunate attentions—! It was foul, it was unspeakable. Raphael seized her lavender parasol, that silly beribboned French thing, and kicked it across the room. Madame, he cried in a high wounded voice, you defile the very air of our home, with the sort of sentiments I cannot help but intuit, and reject with all that is in me!

Much later, the Washington trip not only completed but its meager fruits forgotten, when Raphael had occasion to dine with Hayes and several other gentlemen in Manhattan, he noted Hayes's palpable coolness, his forced "good manners," and deduced—with relief, with gratification—that his husbandly faith in Violet's virtue had not been misplaced: *certainly* she had never been that big-bellied bewhiskered creature's mistress, even for a night: the very idea was obscene. And how is Mrs. Bellefleur, Hayes asked over brandy and cigars, rather belatedly, not quite meeting Raphael's eye, and Raphael said curtly, Violet is well.

"Perhaps you want to defile yourself," Wystan Sheeler said cautiously, "because you feel, without quite articulating it, guilt over your wife's—"

"Not at all," Raphael said. "Rather, it is *she* who must feel guilt, and shame as well. For didn't she betray me?—didn't she betray her wedding vows, by taking her own life so wantonly?"

"The guilt of which I speak," Dr. Sheeler said, "is not a conscious guilt. It is not an *examined* guilt. It is, instead—"

"*She* is ashamed, like the others," Raphael said in a flat weary voice.

"Such guilt is, instead—"

Raphael began to laugh suddenly. Propped up against pillows, sweating out a severe attack of the flu that had come upon him, as nearly as his physician could deduce, as a consequence of an unwise midnight walk along the lakeshore, in a driving rain, the aging man looked both abstracted and painfully *knowing.* He screwed up one side of his face and all but winked at the alarmed Dr. Sheeler. "Forgive me," he said, gasping for breath, "but I was forced to think of—of—my grandfather Jean-Pierre —of whom, as you know, I rarely think—for I never knew him, he was dead before my birth—long dead—and if he had not died, he and the others, those unhappy others, *I* would not have been born, and so—! And so—there are inevitably things of which one does *not* think if one wishes to remain sane—until such time as—as they are thrust into the open— But I was saying— I seem to have lost the thread of what I was saying—"

Dr. Sheeler lay his hand against the fevered man's forehead, and attempted to calm him. "We were speaking only of a theoretical matter," Dr. Sheeler said gently, "and perhaps this is not the time. . . ."

"Guilt," Raphael said, thrusting his physician's hand away, "my wife's or mine, or whatever you are proposing. Guilt and shame and— and all the rest. And suddenly I found myself thinking of one of the old crook's schemes: the selling of 'elk' manure over in the Eden Valley. Special Arctic manure, the highest quality of manure, twenty-five wagons of it, I seem to recall, sold at $75 a wagonload to some idiot farmers . . . ! And they bought it, they bought it," Raphael said, beginning to laugh again, wheezing with laughter. Tears spilled from his narrow stone-colored eyes. "Elk manure. The old crazy crook. No wonder he died as he did, as he *had* to. . . . And Louis and . . . and the others. . . . For if they hadn't died *I* would not have seen the light of day: I and Fredericka and Arthur. And so. And so, Dr. Sheeler, you see," he said, laughing so that his caved-in chest began to heave, "there is, at the bottom, elk manure. Your theories—my guilt—hers—theirs—anyone's: *elk manure.* The very finest high-grade Arctic nitrogen-rich *elk manure.*"

Dr. Sheeler drew back from the sick man's bed, and stared rather coldly at him. After a long pause, during which Raphael continued to laugh with an abandon ill-fitting his condition, and his stature, the good physician said, "Mr. Bellefleur, I fail to understand the basis of your mirth."

But Raphael, dying, laughed all the harder.

And so the famous Raphael Bellefleur *did* die, for it was, evidently, one of the grimmest aspects of the Bellefleur Curse that one had to die . . . whether in old age or in youth, whether willingly and eagerly, or with revulsion: no escaping it, one simply *had* to die.

In sickbeds or in the beds of strangers. In the lake, that eerie dark-hued lake; or on horseback; or in flaming blazing "accidents"; or as a consequence of a simple household misstep—slipping down the stairs of the Great Hall, for instance, or being infected by a cat's scratch. Bellefleurs tend to die interesting deaths, Gideon once observed, many years before *his* death; but his observation was not necessarily accurate.

Raphael's, for instance, was not a particularly interesting death.

Heart failure as a consequence of severe influenza: and then of course he was simply an old man: prematurely aged. He died, not in his comfortable canopied bed, but on the floor of Violet's drawing room, which had been preserved exactly as she had left it on the night of her suicide. (How the sickly old man had dragged himself there no one could guess. He had seemed, the day before, totally without strength.) He died in Violet's room very late one June night and was found by a servant the next morning, face down on the carpet, beside the clavichord. The green brocaded cover had been pulled off the bench, but the keyboard remained closed.

Of course he was mourned throughout the state, and even his old enemies, and the numerous men who had mocked and ridiculed him behind his back, were appalled at his passing. Raphael Bellefleur, who had built that monstrous castle, dead—! Dead like anyone else!

The aged Hayes Whittier, confined to a wheelchair in his Georgetown mansion, was said to have burst into tears when the news was told him.

"It's the end of our great era," he said. "America will never see anything *quite* like it again." (Though Whittier's *Memoirs,* published posthumously, were disappointingly circumspect about his private life, even as they were boldly frank about his public life, it is possible to deduce from the tone of melancholy resignation with which he spoke of "the beautiful Englishwoman" with her "haunted" face who was mistress of Bellefleur Manor that he had never been Violet's lover.)

So the great man died, he who had been, in his prime, many times a millionaire: and his single heir Lamentations of Jeremiah had not the audacity to disobey the terms of his will. The body *was* skinned, and the skin treated, and stretched across the frame of a cavalry drum, to be kept for many decades in its appointed place on the first-floor landing of the Great Hall. The drum was judged a fairly handsome instrument, as such things go. It had not, for instance, the graceful beauty of Violet's clavichord—but it was attractive in its own way.

Only a very few times was the Skin-Drum used as Raphael had wished, played, upon significant occasions (the birth of Jean-Pierre II, the stroke of midnight of New Year's Eve of 1900, the anniversary of Raphael's death), by a uniformed servant, a sort of butler-handyman, who had been, in the Civil War, a drummer boy. After this servant's departure from the castle Jeremiah himself attempted the task, his teeth chattering, the sticks slipping repeatedly from his numbed fingers; and that was it. No one wanted to play the Skin-Drum, still less did anyone want to hear it. For it gave out an astonishingly penetrating sound not easily forgotten.

Instead, as Raphael could not have foreseen, the Skin-Drum became invisible.

Of course it was there on the landing, it was always there, but no one saw it, even the servant girl who routinely dusted it did not see it, and only when Leah prepared the castle for the celebration of great-grand-mother Elvira's hundredth birthday did anyone realize what it was: and then, suddenly, it was looked upon with horror, disgust, and embarrassment: and of course someone (quite possibly Leah) hauled it away for "safekeeping."

And in a closet, or in the attic, or in the darkest regions of the cellar, the Skin-Drum was to remain, for as long as Bellefleur Manor stood.

The Traitorous Child

Now in that final summer there began, at first in secret and then quite openly, a contest between Germaine's mother and father: over her, for her, with *her* as the prize.

Which of us do you love? Leah whispered, gripping her tight by the shoulders. You must choose! *Choose.*

And Gideon, in secret, squatting down before her, gripping her too (though less painfully) by the shoulders: Would you like to come flying with me, Germaine, sometime soon? In one of the smaller planes? In one of the Cubs? You would love it, you wouldn't be at all frightened. Just you and your daddy, for an hour, to Mount Blanc and back, so you could see all the rivers and lakes and this house, even, from the sky, and nobody here would ever know—!

The contest was invisible. Yet you could feel it. A teeter-totter's motion: first one side and then the other and then the other again, and then the *other*. For all that one had the other demanded. And then again the other demanded. And then again . . .

Which was very strange, like a dream that wouldn't end but went on rumbling and rolling no matter how you tried to wake up. Which was very ugly. And made the little girl (who was, in June of that year, exactly three years and ten months old) run away and hide in the long narrow dark closet in the nursery, where old cast-off clothes and toys were kept; or down at the bottom of the garden, behind the new hedgerow.

She stuck her fingers in her mouth: first one, then two, then three. She learned to be cautious. For once, on the terrace, pretending to read the newspaper over her mother's shoulder, she *did* begin to read out loud, shouting and giggling, suddenly very excited, and Leah turned to her in astonishment—astonishment not *altogether* pleased.

My God, Leah exclaimed, you know how to read. . . . You know how to *read*.

Germaine backed away, bumping into one of the wrought-iron chairs in her excitement. Her face had gone very warm.

But who taught you? Leah asked.

Germaine, sticking a finger in her mouth, did not reply.

Someone must have taught you, Leah said. Was it Uncle Hiram? Was it Lissa? Vida? Raphael? Was it your father?

Germaine shook her head, suddenly mute. She stood, stubborn and shy, with two fingers in her mouth, her head bowed, peering at amazed half-angry Leah, with nothing at all to say for herself.

You didn't teach yourself, did you, Leah said, rummaging through Bromwell's old books? All those old books in the nursery? You *couldn't* have taught yourself.

Germaine blinked, watching her mother closely.

Or did *I* teach you, without knowing it? These mornings on the terrace, going through the newspapers . . . Leah contemplated the little girl, perplexed. She fumbled for her cigarillos and shook one out onto her palm: though smoking made her cough, and she had vowed to give it up soon. Why don't you answer, why do you look so guilty, Leah asked. It *wasn't* your father, was it? As if he'd have the time!

So she learned to be cautious.

Skin and Bones, they call him, Leah whispered. The women. The girls he chases. *Skin and Bones.* And some of them, the younger girls, even call him *Old Skin and Bones.* Think of it—! Gideon Bellefleur who thinks so highly of himself!

Early on the day of Morna's wedding, when everyone had been up since dawn, and the house was in a turmoil. When Leah sent one of the maids away, in tears, because the clumsy girl couldn't make Leah's chignon look the way it was supposed to look.

She couldn't decide whether Germaine should wear a yellow satin frock with a bow at the collar (which would match her own yellow satin gown), or a dotted-swiss with long white ribbons. She couldn't decide whether Germaine's corkscrew curls should be left as they were, hanging down the poor child's back (for the little girl, of course, detested those curls), or brushed out quickly, and her hair swept up in imitation of her mother's, fastened with gold barrettes, a sprig of lily of the valley pinned in place.

Do you know—they laugh at him behind his back, and call him Old Skin and Bones! Leah said. But of course you mustn't tell anyone. You mustn't even ask me about it. I suppose I shouldn't have told you—you will have so debased—disappointed—so *sad* a memory of your high-and-mighty father—

And at breakfast, at their hurried breakfast, Leah had leaned over to kiss Germaine, but really to whisper in her ear (*almost* within Gideon's hearing), *Old Skin and Bones!*

But why was that?

Because he was so thin now.

And why was he so thin?

The automobile accident, the concussion, the quarrels, not eating right, drinking too much, staying away for so long, and now this business, this crazy selfish business, of flying planes. . . . And I wouldn't be surprised (so people whispered) if there was another woman involved. Up there in Invemere. Another, another, *another* woman.

Old Skin and Bones: with his yellowish hawkish hollowed-out face: so restless most of the time he couldn't sit still, couldn't even sit down, because his mind was taxiing down the runway and lifting into the sky, always lifting, lifting into the sky, and his heart leapt at the thought of it, pursuing the Hawker Tempest, following it to its secret destination somewhere north of Lake Tear-of-the-Cloud. Restless most of the time, and sleepless too, so that a quart of bourbon a day wasn't unusual, simply so that he could *sleep* after the excitement of the sky; but then again, then again, there were days when he was too drained of spirit even to rise from bed and dress himself, and at eleven or eleven-thirty his mother would rap timidly on his door, saying Gideon? Gideon? Are you all right? This is Cornelia, are you *all right?*

"What I object to," Gideon said, on their way to Morna's wedding, seated, the three of them, in the back seat of the smaller Rolls limousine, with the glass partition firmly shut, "what I particularly object to is your obsessiveness. Your morbid obsessiveness with the child."

"What on earth are you saying—!" Leah laughed.

"Your *interest* in her."

"She's only a three-year-old, she needs her mother, it isn't uncommon for mothers and daughters to be inseparable," Leah said, looking out the window. "And you, after all, have no time for her."

"You weren't like this with Christabel."

"Who? Ah, Christabel! But she and Bromwell had each other, it was an entirely different thing," Leah said quickly. "They were twins, and—and—it seems so long ago."

"You fawn over her and bully her," Gideon said, "as you did this morning at breakfast, and according to my parents you do constantly, never letting her out of your sight. As if she were much younger. As if she were a baby."

"She's only three years old! Aren't you, sweetheart?"

Germaine, seated between her parents, pretended to be very interested in her coloring book. With purple, orange, green, and scarlet crayons she was coloring in a rainbow of her own design, which curved through the not-very-interesting drawing of a farmhouse and barn she was meant to color. In the yellow satin frock with the big bow at the collar, and her smart new patent-leather shoes, she was somewhat uncomfortable, but forced herself to sit still; for otherwise Leah would scold.

"She's almost four. She's very mature for her age," Gideon said. "She *isn't* a baby."

"But you know nothing about children, do you," Leah said. *"You—!"*

"I am not thinking of myself," Gideon said evenly, "I am thinking only of *her."*

"You think of no one except yourself."

"That isn't true."

"Even your other—your other— Your other *interests,"* Leah said, with a small stiff smile, still turned away from her husband, "are ways of thinking about yourself."

"We won't discuss that now," Gideon said.

"We won't discuss it at all: I'm not interested."

"It isn't just my objection," Gideon said, "but my parents' as well, and even Ewan said he noticed—"

"Ewan—!" Leah said. "He's home even less than you are."

"And Lily, and Aveline—"

"Ah, the Bellefleurs are siding against me!" Leah laughed. "The redoubtable Lake Noir Bellefleurs!"

"And Della too."

"Della! But that's a lie," Leah said angrily.

"According to my mother—"

"According to your mother! Don't they have anything else to do, those absurd old women, but sit around and gossip about me?"

"You upset Germaine with your constant attention, your constant fussing, even the way you sometimes look at her," Gideon said, still in an even voice, "I've seen it myself: it would frighten *me."*

Leah made an impatient snorting sound. *"You.* It would frighten *you."*

"I don't mean to suggest that she doesn't love you. Of course she loves you. She's a wonderfully sweet little girl, she *does* love you, but at the same time . . . at the same time, Leah . . . don't you really know what I mean?"

"No."

"You don't *really?"*

"No. I told you no."

"Your obsessiveness, your morbidity . . ."

"Obsessiveness! Morbidity! You've gotten light-headed from flying, haven't you, up there in the sky with nobody around, so you can think your selfish cruel thoughts with no interruptions! Of course her mother has had to love her: her father has no feeling for her at all."

"Leah, that's ridiculous. Please."

"Well—should we ask her?"

"Leah."

"She's sitting right here pretending not to be listening, isn't she! Should we ask her whether her father loves her?—or whether her mother isn't *the only person in the world who loves her.*"

But Germaine did not look up. She was shading in the rainbow now with a bright scarlet crayon.

"Suppose you had to choose, Germaine," Leah said softly. "Between your father and your mother."

"Leah, please—"

"Germaine," Leah said, touching the child's shoulder, "are you listening?—do you understand? Suppose, just for the fun of it, you had to choose. Between your father and me."

But the little girl did not look to left or right. She remained bent over her coloring book, her lower lip caught in her teeth.

"Let her alone, Leah," Gideon said, reaching across to take Leah's yellow-gloved hand. "You really know better. This isn't like you."

"But it's just in play, it's just for fun," Leah said, pulling her hand out of his. "Children love to play: they invent the most outlandish things: they invent entire worlds! Which *you* wouldn't know, because you've cut yourself off from your children. So Germaine, just tell us, nod your head one side or the other, which of us you'd choose. If you had to. If you were going to live with one of us or the other for the rest of your life."

"Leah, really," Gideon said uneasily, "this is what I mean by—"

"Germaine? Why are you pretending not to hear?"

But the little girl did *not* hear.

She continued coloring, and when the scarlet crayon snapped in two she simply used the larger of the pieces, and kept on coloring, without glancing up.

Now the rainbow was wide, now the rainbow was immense, crowding the house and the barn and the earth out.

"You're upsetting her," Gideon said. "This is exactly what I mean."

"*You* began it, and now you're frightened," Leah whispered. "You're frightened she might not choose *you.*"

"But there's no need for her to choose— It's false, it's melodramatic—"

"Who are you to speak of something being *false!*" Leah laughed. "You of all people!"

"It was a mistake for me to speak to you," Gideon said angrily. "You clearly don't have Germaine's well-being in mind."

"But I do! Indeed I do! I am giving her the right to choose, at this moment, I am giving her a privilege few children have: and what is your decision, Germaine? Just nod your head right or left—"

"Stop, Leah. You must know you're upsetting her."

"Germaine?"

"If you want, I'll have the driver stop and let me out. I can ride with my parents, I'll be happy to leave you alone—"

"*Germaine? Why do you pretend not to hear?*"

Leah bent low, peering into the child's face. She saw with what willfulness her daughter stared at the coloring book, and would *not* look up.

"Aren't you bad! Aren't you bad, to pretend not to hear!" Leah said. "It's as if you were lying to me. It's exactly like lying . . ."

But the little girl did *not* hear.

She selected another crayon, a very dirty white crayon, and began to shade over the rainbow, in quick rough slovenly strokes.

Later, when they were alone, Leah stooped and gripped Germaine's shoulders tight. For a long moment she said nothing, she was so angry. The faint lines on her forehead had become creases; her skin was blotched with indignation. Germaine could see without wanting to see how her mother's hair had thinned: her scalp was faintly visible, and the skull looked oddly, crudely layered, as if the bone were growing irregularly, in planes that did not quite meet. She was a haggard woman, and not at all beautiful, even in her yellow gown, with strands of pearls about her neck. . . .

"Selfish Germaine!" Leah was saying, giving her a shake. "Selfish! Nasty! *Traitorous!* Aren't you? You know you are!"

The Vanished Pond

Where, everyone wondered, was poor Raphael . . . ?

The undersized child with his pale, clammy skin, and that furtive expression tinged with a melancholy irony, the son of Ewan's who could not possibly *be*, Ewan thought, his son, or the son of any Bellefleur, was seen less and less frequently that summer until, finally, one morning, it was discovered that he had simply vanished.

Raphael, they called, Raphael . . . ?

Where are you hiding?

At family gatherings Raphael had always been distracted and reluctant, and he was so frequently absent (he hadn't, for instance, gone to Morna's wedding) that it was several days before anyone actually *missed* him. And then only because one of the upstairs maids reported to Lily that his bed hadn't been slept in for three nights running.

They went in search of him to Mink Pond, of course. Albert led the way, shouting his name. . . . But where was Mink Pond? It seemed, oddly, that Mink Pond too had vanished.

By midsummer the pond had shrunk to a half-dozen shallow puddles, grown over with grasses and willow shrubs; by late summer, when Raphael was discovered missing, nothing remained but a marshy area. It was a meadow, really. Part of the large grassy meadow below the cemetery.

Where was Mink Pond, the Bellefleurs asked in astonishment.

A low-lying marshy ground, where bright mustard grew, and lush green grasses, and willow trees. It gave off a rich pleasant odor of damp and decay, even in the bright sunshine.

We must be standing in it, they said. Standing on it. Where it once was.

But looking down they saw nothing: only a meadow.

Raphael, they cried. Raphael. . . . Where have you gone? Why are you hiding from us?

Their feet sank in the spongy earth, and their shoes were soon wet and muddy. How cold, their surprised wriggling toes . . . ! Germaine ran and chattered and giggled and slipped and fell but immediately scrambled to her feet again. Then they saw that she wasn't giggling: she had begun to cry. Her face was contorted.

Raphael! Raphael! Raphael!

In Lily's arms she hid her face, and pointed toward the ground.

Raphael—*there.*

After a search of many hours, up along Mink Creek (which had narrowed to a trickle of peculiar rust-tinged water that smelled flat and metallic) and back through the cemetery into the woods, and a mile or two into the hills, they returned to Mink Pond again—to what had been Mink Pond —and saw that their footprints were covered over, in rich green grass.

Raphael? Raphael?

Was there a pond here, really, one of the visiting cousins asked.

It was here. Or maybe over there.

Here, below the cemetery.

By those willows.

No—by that stump. Where the redwings are roosting.

A pond? Here? But when? How long ago?

Only a week ago!

No, a month ago.

Last year.

They wandered about, calling Raphael's name, though they knew it was hopeless. He had been so slight-bodied, so furtive and pale, no one had known him well, none of the children had liked him, Lily wept to think she hadn't loved him enough—not *enough*—and now he had gone to live beneath the earth (for, after Germaine's hysterical outburst, Lily was never to be placated, or argued out of her absurd conviction) and would not heed her cries.

Raphael, she called, where have you gone? Why are you hiding from us?

Ewan, hearing about the pond, and his little niece's words, went out to investigate. But the pond of course was gone: there *was* no pond.

He stamped about, a thickset, muscular man, graying, ruddy-faced, somewhat short of breath. His stomach strained against the attractive blue-gray material of his officer's shirt; his booted heels came down hard in the moist soil. Long ago he had shaved off his beard (for it displeased his mistress Rosalind) but now an irregular patch of gray stubble covered his jaw and a good deal of his cheeks.

It was absurd, this business about the pond. There had never been a pond here. Ewan remembered quite clearly a pond over back of the apple orchard, in which he and his brothers had played as children—*that* pond still remained, probably—but he hadn't the energy to search for it.

Nor, curiously, had he the energy to search for Raphael. After losing Yolande, and then Garth . . .

He stared down at the moist marshy earth beneath his feet. It was just a meadow, good grazing land, rich with grass, probably fertile beneath. If it were fifty years ago they would plow it up and plant it, possibly in winter wheat; but now everything was changed; now. . . . He could not remember what he had been thinking.

For a long while Leah's and Gideon's strange little girl (about whom her grandmother Cornelia said with a mysterious smile, Ah, but Germaine isn't as odd as she *might* be!) refused to walk on the lawn, even in the walled garden where she had always played. She wept, she began to scream hysterically, if someone tried to lead her out; the graveled walks were all right but the lawns terrified her. If it was absolutely necessary that she cross a lawn, why then Nightshade (who did not at all mind the task, and reddened, like a proud papa, with pleasure) had to carry her.

But aren't you a silly, willful girl, Leah scolded. And all because of some nonsense about your cousin Raphael. . . .

The little girl frequently began to cry at the very mention of that name, and so the others, even Leah, soon stopped pronouncing it in her presence. And very soon they stopped pronouncing it at all: for, it seemed, young Raphael had simply vanished: there *was* no Raphael.

The Purple Orchid

It was shortly after the agreement with International Steel, involving the mineral-rich land around Mount Kittery, that Leah's manservant Nightshade, grown conspicuously taller (though in fact the droll little man was simply straightening: his spine, while still misshapen, twisted queerly to one side, was gradually becoming erect) brought his mistress, one morning, a florist's box containing a single purple orchid of exquisite loveliness. It was also somewhat oversized, being about a foot in diameter.

But what is it? Leah cried, staring.

If you will allow me, Miss Leah, Nightshade murmured, taking the flower out.

An *orchid,* Leah whispered. Is that thing an *orchid.*

A very beautiful orchid, Nightshade said. He spoke with sudden passion, as if *he* had sent the mysterious flower. (In fact there was no envelope, no card, attached. And the delivery man had had no idea, of course, who was responsible.)

A *very* beautiful orchid, Nightshade said. As you can see.

Leah stared at it. She took it from him. It was odorless, and weighed nothing. And it *was* beautiful: purple and lavender and creamy-lavender, and a rich midnight-blue purple; and a purple so dark, so glistening-dark, it appeared to be black.

Leah stared at it for so long that her servant, waiting at her elbow, became uneasy. Miss Leah, he said gently, shall I bring a vase—? Or would you like to wear it in your hair?

Leah, holding the orchid, did not hear.

Though it is a large flower, Nightshade said, in his deep, guttural, passionate voice, I believe it would look most charming . . . *most* charming

. . . in Miss Leah's hair. I could, you know, fix it there myself. You needn't call one of the girls. Miss Leah . . . ?

Without thinking Leah began to shred the delicate fluted petals with her thumbnail. How lovely the colors were—purple and lavender and a creamy-pale lavender that was almost white—and a rich, rich midnight-blue; and a glistening-dark purple that might have been black. How delicate, how airily delicate, the white pistil, the dark trembling stamens, which protruded so far, and dissolved into dust on her fingers! Seven stamens on seven thin stalks: soon broken and crumbled away to nothing.

Ah, Leah cried, what am I doing—!

For without thinking she had quite destroyed the lovely flower.

Take the silly thing away and throw it in the garbage, she said, a minute or two later, and don't interrupt me again this morning, Nightshade. You *really* know better.

Revenge

Once upon a time, the children were told, a man rode through the main street of Nautauga Falls attired in such handsome clothes, and mounted upon a horse of such exceptional grace and beauty, that all who happened to gaze upon him were stopped in their tracks, and spoke of the sight for years afterward. He was a deeply tanned man of indeterminate age, no longer young, in a suede suit that closely fitted his tall, slender body, with a high-crowned wide-brimmed black wool hat, and a black string tie, and smart lemon-yellow gloves, and leather boots with a pronounced heel: quite clearly a stranger, from another part of the country. And what a *handsome* man he was, everyone agreed.

Did they know he was Harlan Bellefleur, come to revenge his family's deaths? Did they recognize his Bellefleur profile, no matter that he wore a Western hat, and no longer spoke like a native of the Chautauquas?

In any case they sent him to Lake Noir, to the Varrells. And not a single hand was raised against him when, the following day, he shot down in cold blood (for so the greedy newspapers termed it, *cold blood*) four of the five men who had been accused by his sister-in-law of having murdered his father, his brother, and his brother's children.

There, that's done, Harlan was reported to have said, with a disdainful smile, when the last of the Varrells, Silas, lay dead. With a meticulous sense of style (for indeed he was being watched, indeed there were numerous witnesses) he then turned to walk away.

That, the children were told, was revenge. Not just the acts, the murders, themselves: but the style as well.

Nothing is quite so profound as revenge, they were told. Nothing quite so exquisite. When Harlan Bellefleur rode into town and hunted down his family's murderers and shot them one by one, like dogs—!

The taste of it. Of revenge. Honey-rich in the mouth, it was. Unmistakable. The lurching of your heart, the powerful intoxicating waves of blood coursing through your veins, a raw clamorous yearning tide of blood. . . . Unmistakable.

(But how ugly, revenge. The very thought of it. Animals tearing at one another. The first blow, and then the next, and the next, and the next: the sickening quaver of the knees, that tarry-black taste at the back of the mouth. . . . So Vernon Bellefleur thought, alone amid the excited children. He must have been a child, among them; at any rate he was in disguise as a child. Then. In those blurred interminable days long ago. Revenge, the others whispered, laughing aloud with the sheer nervousness of certain thoughts. Ah—revenge! If only we had lived *then*.)

But how *exquisite* it was, really. There was nothing like it. No human experience, not even the experience of passionate erotic love, could match it. For in love (so the more articulate Bellefleurs speculated) there is never, there can be never, anything more than the sense, however compelling, that one is fulfilling *oneself;* but in revenge there is the sense that one is fulfilling the entire universe. Justice is being done by one's violent act. Justice is being exacted *against the wishes of mankind.*

For revenge, though it is a species of justice, always runs counter to the prevailing wishes of mankind. It makes war against what is fixed. It is always revolutionary. It cannot exert itself but must *be* exerted; and exerted only through violence, by a selfless individual who is willing to die in the service of his mission.

Thus Harlan Bellefleur, hawk-faced Indian-red Harlan Bellefleur in his black Stetson, on his sleek brownish-gray Costeña mare, riding into Nautauga Falls one fine May morning in 1826. . . .

(*Vengeance is mine, sayeth the Lord.* So Fredericka insisted, arguing with Arthur. For John Brown *was* a murderer, wasn't he, no matter that he imagined himself in the service of the Lord? And Harlan Bellefleur as well. A murderer in the face of the Almighty.)

Dr. Wystan Sheeler could not have known, nor could Raphael Bellefleur have explained (lacking, as he did, any sense of the interior life—which he would have considered merely weakness), but, some seven decades after Harlan appeared on his high-stepping mare, Raphael was to subside into that cynical, dispirited melancholy, and order himself skinned for a drum, partly as a consequence of certain events that had happened before his birth.

What rage he felt, and what shame—! Though without exactly *feeling* anything. For Raphael had no conscious memory of having been told (by neighbors?—by classmates?—certainly not by his parents, who never spoke of the past) about the Bushkill's Ferry massacre and the trial and

Harlan's sudden reappearance; he had, indeed, very little conscious memory of himself as a child.

(Though he *must*, he knew, have been a child—at least for a while.)

These were the things to be contemplated, over the years, at the periphery of his highly active life: the massacre, and the rescue of Germaine from the burning house, and the arrest of old Rabin and the Varrells, and the hearing, the indictment, the trial itself. . . .

Above all, this: his mother's humiliation.

His mother Germaine, slow-speaking and easily confused, in the courtroom day after day, that late winter of 1826, before hundreds of curious staring strangers. Her humiliation there was more grievous, in a way, than the massacre itself, which was over so quickly. (It never ceased to astonish: six persons killed in a matter of minutes. So quickly!)

His mother Germaine, in a shapeless black dress, twisting and pleating her skirt as she spoke. . . .

Raphael wondered: Did she look over to the defendants' table, did she look upon them, her family's murderers . . . ? No doubt she would have found them, in the stark light from the courtroom's high windows, quite ordinary men; diminished as much by their surroundings as by their guilt. Or did she keep her gaze stonily averted throughout the many days of the trial. . . .

Yes, I recognized them, yes, I knew them, my husband's and my children's murderers. Yes, they are in this courtroom.

The county courthouse at Nautauga Falls boasted a sandstone façade and four "Greek" columns; it overlooked a handsome square, and the old county jail, at the square's opposite end. The courthouse was, for its time, a spacious building, and accommodated more than two hundred spectators for what was known variously as the Bellefleur trial, and the Varrell trial, and the Lake Noir trial. (The Lake Noir district with its innumerable unsolved crimes—theft, arson, murder—had been notorious from the time of its first settlement in the mid-1700's; and though the Bellefleur murders were considered excessive, and particularly hideous because of the fact that children were involved, the public, and the downstate newspaper reporters, tended to see them as representative of the region's lawlessness—brutal, barbaric, but unsurprising.)

Crowded into the courtroom's pewlike seats were friends and neighbors of the Bellefleurs, and friends and neighbors and relatives of the Varrells, and others from the area who had not precisely chosen sides; and innumerable strangers—some having come to the Falls in horse-drawn wagons, others in handsome carriages. The poor had brought their own food and ate it outside in the square, despite the cold; wealthier parties were staying at the Nautauga House and the Gould Inn, or drove downtown from their estates on the Lakeshore Boulevard, curious to see the Bellefleur woman and the men, the dreadful men, who had murdered her husband and children. (Some of the well-to-do spectators had known, in their time, old Jean-Pierre Bellefleur, though few of them would have admitted it.) That a woman should be a witness to such horror, and yet survive. . . .

Poor Germaine Bellefleur.

That *wretched* woman.

Newspaper sketches of Germaine Bellefleur showed a dark-eyed, staring, profoundly somber woman in her mid- or late thirties, with a somewhat thick jaw, and premature creases bracketing her mouth. She was not, opinion had it, pretty. Perhaps at one time, but not now: decidedly not now: wasn't there even something stubborn and bulldoglike about the set of her mouth, and her eyes' narrowed expression? Called to the witness stand, seated in the chair on its high platform, she looked smaller of build than she was, and her voice, faltering, had a nasal, sexless ring; it was decidedly unmelodic, and cost her sympathy. As she answered the prosecutor's interminable questions, and, afterward, the defense attorney's interminable badgering questions, it was observed how she twisted and pleated the skirt of her unflattering dress, and stared at the floor, as if *she* were the guilty party. . . . (The newspaper reporters were disappointed not only in Mrs. Bellefleur's appearance, which lacked feminine grace, but in her testimony as well: it was so obviously *rehearsed.* For of course Mrs. Bellefleur, as well as the murderers themselves, and most of the witnesses, would not have dared speak in such a place, before a judge and jurors and so many spectators, without having memorized, like school children, their every word—with the consequence, as one correspondent for a Vanderpoel paper said wittily, that everyone, Mrs. Bellefleur as well as the accused murderers, and their neighbors, struck outside observers as belonging to one large dull-witted family, with the intellectual skills and manners of brain-damaged sheep. How graceless they all were!)

Backcountry people. Hill people. "Poor whites." (Despite the fact of the Bellefleurs' vast property holdings, and Jean-Pierre's numerous investments.) There was old Rabin with his sunken cheeks and near-toothless gums, his face wrinkled as a prune, and *so* ugly; and the Varrell men in the first suits and neckties they had ever worn—Reuben and Wallace and Silas, looking sick—and the boy Myron, who looked, now, not much older than seventeen, gazing about the courtroom with a vacuous half-smile. Old Rabin and the Varrells and Mrs. Bellefleur: weren't they all Lake Noir people, weren't Lake Noir people always involved in feuds, weren't they all uncivilized, and hopeless . . . ?

A life, several lives, reduced to a single hour.

The terrible exhausting *concentration* of meaning: as if Germaine's life had stopped, on that October night, along with the others' lives. As if nothing existed apart from that time: not an hour, really, but considerably less than an hour.

Will you please recount for the court, as clearly as you can, omitting no details, exactly what happened on the night of . . .

The silence of the courtroom. Silence, interrupted frequently by waves of whispers. Ladies turned to one another, raising their gloved hands to shield their faces, and their words. Germaine broke off, confused. What she had said, what she was yet to say, what she had already said so many times, tangled together, like ribbons, like an unwisely long thread, and should she stop, should she snip the thread at once and begin again, or should she continue. . . .

Please tell us, Mrs. Bellefleur, as clearly as you can, omitting no details . . .

And so, again. Again. The halting procession of words. The sudden panicked realization that something had been forgotten: and should she pause, and return, stammering and blushing (for she knew very well, how could she fail to know, how pitying and contemptuous certain persons were of her, facing her hour after hour, how they *judged* her), or should she continue, repeating one thing after another, *And then in the next room I could hear them with Bernard, I could hear Bernard scream,* one set of words after another, as if she were crossing a turbulent stream on stepping-stones that threatened to overturn beneath her weight. She *must* keep going. She couldn't stop. And yet—

And you are absolutely certain, Mrs. Bellefleur, that you recognized the murderers' voices. . . .

And again, again, the names: the names that were like stepping-stones too: Rabin and Wallace and Reuben and Silas and Myron. (And though it occurred to her while she lay convalescing in a neighbor's home that she knew, really, who one and possibly two of the others were, she could hear again their voices and recognize them, or almost recognize them, yes she really *knew,* she *knew,* it was advised that she restrict herself to her original story, for the defense would surely interrogate her about "remembering" so many days after the fact.)

The defendants at their table: coarse-faced, sullen, baffled men, three of them with whiskers that covered half their faces, the youngest, Myron, vacant-eyed, smiling at the judge and the jurors and the sheriff's men as if they were old friends. (The Varrells' attorney wisely kept Myron off the witness stand, for he would probably have confessed had he remembered the crimes. Myron, it was said, didn't deal with a full deck now, and it might have been as a consequence of his amiable calfishness that, some months after the trial, he was to drown in a canoe accident on Silver Lake, in unremarkable weather.)

Boldly and defiantly and with an incredulous little laugh deep in his throat the Varrells' attorney (twenty-eight years old, an Innisfail boy with political ambitions) moved that the case be dismissed because of lack of evidence: for of course his clients had alibis, relatives and neighbors and drinking companions had from the very first supplied detailed stories of the men's whereabouts on that night (absurdly detailed stories which newspaper reporters thought further proof of Lake Noir ignorance—a curious combination of naïveté and brutality), and in any case there was no proof, there was absolutely no proof, merely a confused and spiteful woman's accusation. . . . How, the young man asked Mrs. Bellefleur, drawling her name as if he thought it somehow extraordinary, could she possibly ask the court to believe that in the confusion of the moment she could have recognized anyone? When, by her own testimony, the murderers were wearing masks?

Certainly there was no proof. Not even circumstantial evidence. And his clients had alibis. Each of them could account thoroughly for that night, for every hour of that night. It was a single woman's word against the word of dozens of others, each of whom had sworn on the Bible to tell the truth.

And you ask us to believe, the young man drawled, smiling as he looked about the courtroom, at the twelve men in the jury box, and the judge, and the spectators crowded into the rows of seats, *you ask us to take seriously, Mrs. Bellefleur, an accusation that by your own account must be judged as frankly dubious . . .*

As if sharing his clients' guilt the attorney was edgy, bold, arrogant, even indignant. He had learned a trick of smiling very faintly just *after* he made a statement he considered outrageous: smiling faintly, with his head lifted in mute astonishment. *And you ask us . . . And you ask the court . . .* He must have taken elocution lessons, he projected his thin, reedy voice with such confidence; and his small portly body with its melonlike belly was always perfectly erect.

His questions then fastened upon Jean-Pierre and Louis. But especially Jean-Pierre. The Onondagan woman Antoinette who had died along with the others—what was her relationship, if any, to the family? Wasn't she, the attorney asked with a mocking hesitancy, a particular friend of Jean-Pierre Bellefleur's . . . an *intimate* friend . . . who had shared the Bellefleurs' household for years . . . ? At first Germaine did not reply; she stared at the floor, and her face appeared to thicken. Then she said in a slow voice that the woman kept to her part of the house. They rarely spoke. They rarely saw each other. . . . In a louder voice, somewhat bitterly, Germaine said that of course she hadn't approved, not with the children, but what could she do . . . what could anyone do . . . that was the old man's way . . . he did what he wanted . . . and even Louis wouldn't stand up to him . . . though she hadn't asked him to, because . . . because he would have been angry . . . because he always took his father's side against anyone.

Might the killings, the attorney asked, have had anything to do with the Onondagan woman? With the fact that she was living common-law with Jean-Pierre Bellefleur . . .

Germaine, hunched forward, appeared to be thinking. But she did not reply.

Mrs. Bellefleur, isn't it possible that . . .

Baffled, the creases deepening beside her mouth, Germaine shook her head slowly. She seemed not to comprehend the line of questioning.

A young Onondagan woman, your elderly father-in-law with his innumerable . . . his innumerable, shall we say, former business associates . . .

And then there were questions about Jean-Pierre's various activities since his years in Congress. The many acres of wilderness land he had accumulated, under several names (a fact that appeared to surprise Germaine, who stared at the attorney in bewilderment), his part-ownership of Chattaroy Hall and the coach line from Nautauga Falls to White Sulphur Springs and the *Gazette* and the steamboat and the Mount Horn logging company that had filed for bankruptcy and . . . and hadn't there been a large fertilizer sale . . . a hoax . . . reputedly Arctic elk manure . . . many wagonloads of . . . And during Jean-Pierre Bellefleur's last term in Congress hadn't there been the sensational exposé of La Compagnie de New York . . .

So the questions came, one after another. Germaine tried to answer. *I don't know,* she said haltingly, shamefully, *I don't know, I don't remember, they never talked about business, I don't know.* . . . And then abruptly she was being interrogated about the night of the murders again, and the masks. Hadn't she been terrified, hadn't she been confused, wasn't it even the case that, according to her own admission, she had been unconscious most of the time the men were in the house . . . ? *How,* if the men had been masked, had she recognized their faces?

And she hadn't been a witness to the others' deaths. Only to Louis's. In the other wing of the house Jean-Pierre Bellefleur and the Onondagan woman had been killed, quite some distance away; and in the parlor and kitchen the children. So she hadn't witnessed those murders. She couldn't possibly have known what was happening. Or who the murderers were. She claimed to have recognized voices but how could she possibly have recognized voices. . . . The murders had been committed, the young man claimed, in a high ringing voice, by strangers. It was quite plausible that they were thieves, attracted to the Bellefleur home because of its size and the reputation of old Jean-Pierre; or that they were Indians, furious at the Onondagan woman for her relationship with the notorious Jean-Pierre; or that they were—and this was *most* likely—enemies of Jean-Pierre's who wished him dead for reasons having to do with his discreditable business practices. Mrs. Bellefleur in her deranged state may have convinced herself that she heard familiar voices . . . or she may even have wanted (for reasons it would be indelicate to explore) to accuse the Varrells and Rabin because of the long-standing enmity between her family and them. . . .

Germaine interrupted. *I know who they were,* she said. *I know. I was there. I heard them. I know them! I know!* And then, rising, before the sheriff's men hurried forward to restrain her, she began to scream: *They did it!*

Them! Them there! Sitting over there! You know it and everybody knows it! They killed my husband and children! They killed six people! I know! I was there! I know!

A light snow was falling very early on the May morning when Harlan Bellefleur managed to shoot and kill, within an hour and forty-five minutes, four of the accused murderers; the fifth, young Myron, was spared because in trying to escape from Harlan he not only turned his back to run but fell to his hands and knees and began to crawl, desperate as a maddened animal. And so Harlan, acting out of a sense of revulsion rather than pity, raised the barrel of his silver-handled pistol skyward, and did not fire.

Old Rabin was shot just once, in the chest, as he opened the door to his shanty on the north shore of Olden Lake, in answer to Harlan's loud knocking; Wallace and Reuben were killed on the main street of the village known at that time as Lake Noir; Silas was shot in the darkened back room of the White Antelope Inn, where he appeared to be awaiting Harlan (for by then—by midmorning—he had heard, of course, that Bellefleur was on his way), simply sitting hunched over in a cane-backed chair, weaponless. Harlan, euphoric from the morning's activity, and followed by a small gang of admiring townsmen who urged him on, *Now Silas, Silas is next!*, kicked open the tavern door and strode into the building as if he knew beforehand that Varrell, this particular Varrell, would put up no struggle. Pity for the moronic Myron had weakened him but he would have no pity for Silas, cowering there in the dark, his breath audible at a distance of some yards, through a closed door.

So you were found Not Guilty, Harlan laughed. And raised the pistol and fired point-blank into the man's face.

Unknown to Gideon . . .

Unknown to Gideon, who was to become, as the summer deepened, more and more obsessed with flying (for now he had his pilot's license, and had bought, at Tzara's encouragement, a handsome high-winged cream-colored Dragonfly with a 450-horsepower engine that could cruise at exceptionally low speeds), unknown to Gideon, Old Skin and Bones (for so the young women affectionately called him—though they still feared him, somewhat), whose three or four hours of nightly sleep were titillated by lurching visions of the Invemere runway which he *must* bring his craft down to, in safety, despite the fact that the dream-plane rushed with such violence through the air and threatened at any moment to disintegrate, so that he woke grinding his teeth, on the very edge of screaming: unknown to Gideon, who imagined his fascination with the air to be, like his fascination with the Rache woman, quite unique —*really* quite unique in the history of his family—there were two distant cousins, as unknown to each other as they were to Gideon, who had, in their time (a time long past) lived out *their* devotion to flying.

One assisted the elderly Octave Chanute in the late 1890's, at his work camp on Lake Michigan, experimenting with gliders and eventually with biplanes; it was young Meredith Bellefleur, in fact, who built the first biplane with a compressed-air motor, with the glider as its foundation, and Bellefleur whom Chanute most praised. Hungry for more praise and evidently quite young, still (little is known of Meredith Bellefleur other than the fact that he moved away from his family at the age of seventeen, to "make his own way" in the world), Bellefleur then volunteered to fly one of the old man's riskiest gliders, partly for the glory of it, partly because the contraption was so beautiful (it had ten wings, each seven feet long, rather like a crane's wings, and a small kitelike wing directly over the pilot's head, all painted a brilliant fearless red): but he was at the mercy of insidious wind currents that blew him, jerkily, in spasms, farther and farther out over the lake, until finally he was out of sight. . . . Octave Chanute mourned the loss of Bellefleur as he might have mourned the loss of his own son. The body was never found, nor was the prodigious glider's wreckage washed ashore. I can't help but think, Chanute frequently said, afterward, that young Meredith died happily. For to die like that . . . to die like that is surely a privilege.

Equally privileged was another young Bellefleur man, from the Port Oriskany Bellefleurs, who were, in the words of the Lake Noir Bellefleurs, never anything more than "middle-class"—they owned a block or two of Port Oriskany, and had something to do with lake freighting, and their marriages were undistinguished. This boy, Justin, spent his summers in Hammondsport, working with Glenn Curtiss; the passion there was to build upon the Wright brothers' invention, to surpass it, in as brief a time as possible, for of course there would be a great deal of money involved in airplanes—the future itself was contained in airplanes—and whoever built the most efficient and most practical model would be as wealthy, eventually, as Thomas Edison and Henry Ford themselves. Curtiss's company turned out an early version of the June Bug in 1907, a charming little craft with a 40-horsepower engine and a chain-driven pusher propeller, capable of flying as fast as 35 miles per hour. Justin, then nineteen years old, was to fly the plane in the First International Aviation Meet in Reims the following year but an inexplicable accident—he had *appeared* to have taken off smoothly, into a firm, stable wind—resulted in his premature death. (Falling from a height of no more than forty feet, young Justin might have survived; but he suffered vicious lacerations from the propeller, which seemed to have gone berserk as the little craft crashed to earth.)

In addition to the cousins Meredith and Justin, about whom so little was known by the Lake Noir Bellefleurs, there was a story—possibly legendary—about Hiram's wife Eliza being carried off in a trim little seaplane, a surplus Navy vehicle, very early one morning before the household was awake: but whether the pilot was the woman's lover, or whether he had, for totally incidental reasons, landed his plane on the lake in order to make a minor repair, and was then waved ashore by the distraught woman—no one knew. At any rate she did disappear, leaving behind her little boy Vernon, who was to mourn her forever. (Unless—and this *is* possible—Vernon was to meet with her in later years, far beyond the boundaries of the Bellefleur empire, and of this chronicle.)

Unknown to Gideon too was the fact that Leah had been making surreptitious inquiries about the obscure Mrs. Rache for weeks (*Who is this new "love" of Gideon's? Old Skin and Bones, wouldn't you think he might act his age! Who is the bitch's husband? Do they have money? Where do they live? Does she love Gideon? What does she think of him?—of us?*), but quite without success. Tzara would give out no information, and the airport's mechanics knew nothing about her other than the fact (so frequently repeated,

Leah grew cynically amused) that she wore tight-fitting trousers, men's trousers with a zipper in front, and a tan leather jacket that came only to her waist, and goggles, and a leather helmet into which she heedlessly tucked her hair as she strode out to her favorite plane. So far as anyone knew she had never exchanged more than a half-dozen words with Gideon, who introduced himself to her one July afternoon as the airport's new owner. (Startled at his voice, which came at her unexpected, and sounded—for poor Gideon's voice *had* changed—both strident and thin, she had paused, and turned, but only from the waist, peering at him over her shoulder, her eyes narrowed behind the tinted lenses as if she fully expected to meet, in the shadow of the hangar, a stranger's lustful stare: and in response to Gideon's words she offered nothing of herself, not even a smile to acknowledge his hopeful smile, but asked only what the afternoon's weather would be—was the wind going to change?—would there be a break in the cloud floor?)

Sometimes in the Dragonfly, sometimes in a cream-and-red Stinson voyager, sometimes in a handsome Wittman Tailwind W-8 with a continental engine, Gideon raced with his newly acquired flying friends out of the Invemere airport, toward the Powhatassie, or westward into the Chautauquas (which were not nearly so dangerous to navigate as they appeared, for the highest peak, Mount Blanc, was only about 3,000 feet high), or southwest toward the great lurid oval of Lake Noir, or due south to Nautauga Falls where, if they liked, they might land at the Falls airport and spend an hour or two at the Bristol Brigand, a pub close by. Gideon enjoyed his new friends though he did not much believe in them. Perhaps he sensed that his life was running out—perhaps he sensed that he was being borne along by a quick, sullen, capricious wind that cared not at all for *him*—but he did not credit his friends (Alvin and Pete and Clay and Haggarty) with much substance. Two were former bomber pilots, and had flown many missions, and had survived, and a third—Pete—had even survived a crash-landing in a cornfield east of Silver Lake. They were excellent drinking companions; they loved to tell tales about flying, and to give Gideon pointers (for, in their boisterous company, he appeared somewhat subdued, and despite his emaciated frame and pouched eyes he appeared comparatively youthful) not only on flying but on life as well —even on women. (That Rache woman! Wasn't she something! Ugly as hell! *Ugly*, yes! But, still—*still*.)

They drank, and returned to their planes, and taxied out the runway, and plunged into the sky, reckless and euphoric. Life was so simple, so extraordinarily *clear* as soon as one lifted into the air: it was only the earth that gave trouble.

On July 4 Gideon and Alvin managed to fly their planes *beneath* the eight-span Powhatassie Bridge within sixty seconds of each other, and with only about four feet to spare; the other pilots, approaching the bridge, lost their courage, or frankly panicked, and flew over it to forfeit their bets. (The bets were small—$100, $150—and meant nothing to Gideon; but he had to be careful not to insult his friends.) On another occasion Gideon, Alvin, and Haggarty managed to "thread the needle" between two immense elms a quarter-mile beyond the Invemere airport, though Gideon was the only one to repeat the trick. How childlike they were, how sweetly exhilarated they felt! Life was so easy, so uncomplicated, there really was nothing to it, so long as one stayed in the air. . . . Another time, in mid-August, the men raced one another to Katama Pass nine hundred miles to the north, where the brother-in-law of one of them owned a fishing lodge. They were able to land, though not gracefully, on a stretch of unpaved highway.

So Gideon had his friends, in whom he did not altogether believe.

And he had Mrs. Rache: Mrs. Rache of whom he thought a great deal, but never with pleasure. (He had offered the woman, tauntingly, the Hawker Tempest. As a gift. Would you like it? Why then take it! You're the only one who flies it out of this airport. . . . He had offered her the airplane but she hadn't known how to respond. Reluctantly she turned to him, her hands on her hips, turning to stare at him, to assess him. She did not fear him as a woman might fear a man. She feared him, he saw, with a pang of excitement, as one man might fear another man—not knowing whether the offer was serious, or meant in jest. It would involve, after all—wouldn't it?—property worth thousands of dollars.)

Of course he tried to follow the Hawker Tempest. From time to time. Unobtrusively. When the mood was on him. He did not expect to keep the plane in sight for long, though it always alarmed him how quickly the fighter *did* disappear, banking to the west, climbing to 2,500 feet and then to 3,000 and higher. The Hawker Tempest had a 2,000-horsepower engine and could be flown hundreds of miles in a brief period of time, but Gideon had no idea where the woman took it, or even if she brought it to earth. He himself leveled out at about 2,000 feet and cruised at 145 miles per hour westward into the Chautauquas, his excitement gradually waning (for the Rache woman was simply too fast for him). He had no destination and no sense of urgency; he hardly had a sense of being Gideon Bellefleur (and, yes, he knew he was frequently called Old Skin and Bones, and he did not really mind); once he was off the runway, once he cleared that line of sickly poplars he had acquired along with the mortgaged airport, nothing earthly mattered. Nothing weighed upon him seriously—certainly not his sentimental lust for a woman whose face he had never seen.

Alone. Alone and floating. Buoyed up by the ocean-currents of air, moving effortlessly, languidly. At seven to eight hundred feet his sense of the earth was already dissolved; he floated free, and even the window-rattling forward motion appeared to diminish. The takeoff and the initial climb were headlong plunges but once he was secure in the sky he felt the earth shift below him, quite harmless. Even the engine, throttled back to cruising speed, was quiet, hardly more obtrusive than his own heartbeat.

Now what was the world and its claim upon him in this exhilarating sea of the invisible, this vertiginous wave-upon-wave of air upon which he floated, weightless, indeed, bodiless, flying not into the future—which did not, of course, exist in the sky—but into the obliteration of time itself? He directed his trim yellow lightweight plane away from time, away from history, away from the person he had evidently been for so many years: trapped inside a certain skeleton, defined by a certain face. Gideon, Gideon!—a woman called. Ah, what yearning in her voice! Was the woman Leah, was she his wife Leah, whom he loved so deeply, with so little sentiment, that there was rarely any need for him to think of *her* at all? Or was the woman a stranger? A stranger, calling him to her, forward to her?

Gideon, Gideon—

Though the plane moved at 145 miles per hour and was buffeted about by the shifting air currents Gideon experienced no speed. Nor was there speed below: only the slow orderly placid almost indifferent and relentless progression of fields and intersecting roads and houses and barns and curved streams and lakes and forests that belonged to the earth, and consequently to time. Gideon floated above it. The emptiness of the air was fascinating because it was an emptiness with great strength. It upheld him, and bore his plane, cresting and falling upon unseen waves that must have been (so Gideon surmised) astonishingly beautiful. Though of course he could not see them. If he narrowed his eyes it sometimes seemed . . . it sometimes seemed that he could *almost* see . . . but perhaps he was deluded. The vast gravity-less space that upheld him must always remain invisible.

Alone. Alone and floating, drifting. In absolute solitude. Above the mist-shrouded mountains, through languid strips of cloud, now at 4,000 feet, slowly and lazily climbing, so that not only the checkerboard of fields below faded from sight but the vision of the runway which had so haunted Gideon during the first several weeks of his training had vanished as well: obliterated by the immensity of the sky, which took in everything, swallowed up everything, without a ripple.

At such times, in such isolation, Gideon experienced without emotion certain flashes of memory. Though perhaps they were not memories so much as mere spasms of thought. He heard, or almost heard, voices. But he did not answer them. Sometimes two spoke at once: Tzara instructed him to give the trim crank a turn or two, Noel boasted half-drunkenly of the Rosengarten property, the very last jigsaw puzzle piece, some 1,500 acres of devastated pine forest the Bellefleurs were soon to acquire. (And this would be the final purchase. It would regain for them all of Jean-Pierre's lost empire.) Leah spoke, taunting him, using words he had never heard from her—your bitches, your sluts, *aren't* they fortunate to have you as a lover!—and then pleading with him, and complaining of the most petty things (for it quite infuriated her, that great-grandmother Elvira and her elderly husband *had* moved across the lake to aunt Matilde's, and now they would refuse to be dislodged, the three of them, and Leah's plans for a handsome new camp would have to be postponed until the old people died—but when would that be, Leah cried, your people live so long!). There was Ewan wanting to talk with him about the children. Their children. Ewan uncharacteristically grave. Half-drunk, of course, and smelling of ale when he belched, as he frequently did, but grave: distressed. Not only Albert's accident with the new Chevrolet—that little fucker, Ewan groaned, he must have been going over ninety when he sideswiped the truck—*over ninety* on that dirt road!—but the others as well. For Albert wasn't seriously hurt, Albert would recover, he would recover and buy another car, but what of Garth who had moved away and betrayed his family, what of Raphael whom no one had loved, what of Yolande . . . ? And what of Gideon's own children?

The voices, the faces. Gideon did not resist them, nor did he accept them. He never answered their accusations. He never sympathized. . . . There was his little girl Germaine gazing upon him with an odd sullen weariness. In recent months she had lost something of her spirit: her eyes were no longer so bright, her movements so quick: she was, Gideon halfway supposed, no longer a child. An unfamiliar face, floating close beside him. But of course it wasn't unfamiliar. It was *his*—his child's.

But do you believe that, Gideon?—so Leah mocked bitterly. That she is yours? That she is anyone's?

(For Leah, impulsive queenly Leah, had begun to notice the child's change as well. Evidently Germaine shrank from her with increasing frequency, would not allow Leah to stare into her eyes, was rebellious and willful, and burst into foolish tears at the slightest provocation. She can't help me any longer, Leah said dumbly, she won't help me, I don't know what to do, I don't know what is happening. . . .)

But she *was* a child, still. Not yet four years old.

Faces, voices, the wave-upon-wave of the air, bucking slightly now that he had again leveled, at an altitude of 4,500. Beneath him nothing existed. Colorless banks of mist, said to be cloud. A chill wind from the right —the north—and soon he must turn 180 degrees—turn and bank carefully—holding his position firm as the waves of air, grown suddenly more violent, sought to throw him about. But he would not return just yet. He had—hadn't he?—a great deal of time. The fuel tanks had been full at takeoff. He had all the time he required. Gideon, the voice cried plaintively, and then, mischievously, Old Skin and Bones!

He smiled, slightly. He surprised himself, smiling. But of course he was utterly alone in the cockpit and not even Tzara was beside him any longer. Gideon, the woman cried, Gideon don't you love me, Old Skin and Bones don't you love me, don't you understand who I am . . . ?

He turned quickly to her, and caught only a glimpse of her gloating shadowy face. But he *did* know who she was.

The Jaws . . .

One after another the two-year notes were signed, with most of the estate as collateral. The mines were depleted: the timberlands which had seemed inexhaustible were razed: though the Bellefleur farms produced more wheat, alfalfa, soybeans, and corn, and far more fruit, than their competitors in the Valley, the market was poor and would continue to be poor because of extraordinary harvests everywhere in North America: and so Lamentations of Jeremiah, baptized Felix (but long ago, long ago, in happier times) grew desperate.

He *must* have grown desperate, his sons reasoned, for why otherwise would he have consented to enter into a partnership with Horace Steadman of all people—Horace whom the Steadmans themselves mistrusted?

"He's essentially an innocent man," Noel said slowly.

"He's innocent, yes. And extraordinarily ignorant," said Hiram.

"You shouldn't say such things about our father, it isn't proper," said Noel irritably. And then, with an impatient gesture: "It isn't good luck."

In their father's presence they said little, for though Jeremiah's reserved, rather shy manner, coupled with the lurid white scar on his forehead (his only "badge of honor," to use his curious expression, from the war of his young manhood, in which so many of his contemporaries died), gave him an air of vulnerability, they were restrained by a natural Bellefleur reticence: natural, at any rate, between father and sons. After the debacle, after Steadman's flight to Cuba, each accused the other of having humored the old man.

Young Jean-Pierre, dabbing after-shave cologne on his smooth white skin, offered no opinion whatsoever. His sensibilities had been so shattered by his father's failure—so Elvira was to charge, hysterically—that he *hadn't* any opinion. And he couldn't possibly have acted of his own free will that terrible night at Innisfail, no matter what the jurors charged.

The night he was swept away in the flood, poor Jeremiah had been goaded, against his own nature, into drinking far more than he ordinarily allotted himself. For as the raindrops thickened and began to pelt the windows, as the afternoon prematurely darkened, he found himself thinking of the silver foxes he and Steadman had raised—the 2,300 silver foxes he and Steadman had bred, giddy with expectation, quite certain that they would become millionaires within two or three years. (For so they'd been convinced, by the silver-fox breeder who had sold them the original foxes.) And then, and then . . . And then, incredibly, one terrible night, the creatures had somehow broken through their close-meshed wire fences to tear one another to pieces. Jeremiah, even in wartime, had never seen anything like it. He had *never* seen anything like it. Why, the creatures were cannibals, they were monsters, they appeared to have devoured, or attempted to devour, their own offspring—! Acres of carcasses. Bloody strips of flesh, and muscle fibers, and the ravens and grackles and shrikes picking at their eyes, a sight too hellish to be borne. Jaws devouring jaws . . . And then, the next day, to learn that Horace had taken what remained of the money (hardly more than $500, in Jeremiah's vague estimation) and fled to Cuba with his fifteen-year-old mulatto mistress, about whom everyone had known except Jeremiah. . . !

"You've failed once again and this time you have humiliated us all," his wife Elvira screamed. She hit at him with her small fists, and her face looked wizened, and he was struck by the realization that though she might never love him again he would continue to love her, for he had pledged himself to her, for as much as they shared of eternity. *Her* detesting *him* did not free him from his pledge. "When your father was living I couldn't bear to be in the same room with him," Elvira wept, "because of his thinking, his terrible tireless *thinking*, but now that you have taken his place, now that you have so inadequately taken his place, ah, how I wish he were still here! *He* would have known Steadman for the villain he is, and *he* would have known better than to breed those hideous cannibals!"

"But they didn't *appear* to be cannibals," Jeremiah protested softly, backing away from his wife's blows. "You yourself said, dear, didn't you say, they were so beautiful, they possessed so unearthly a—"

"And now there will be an auction, won't there! A public auction! Of our things! Of your father's precious things! And all the world will trample our gardens and lawns, and track mud onto our lovely carpets, and everywhere people will laugh at us, and talk will surface once again of the curse—"

Jeremiah, backed against a fireplace, tried to take hold of his wife's wrists; but though she was a small woman, and her wrists were touchingly slender, he could not hold them still. "But there is no curse, dear Elvira—"

"No curse! You, of all people, to claim that there's no curse!"

"The very notion of a curse on the family is a profanation, a blasphemy—"

"How else to explain these catastrophes?" Elvira cried, turning away from him to hide her face in her hands. "From the very start . . ."

"But we haven't been accursed," Jeremiah said, smiling foolishly. "It's entirely possible to interpret our history as being a history of—of blessedness."

Elvira stumbled away, sobbing. She wept as though her heart would break: and Jeremiah was never to forget the pathos of the moment. For he had of course failed her, and he was quite conscious of having failed his father as well (whose presence filled the castle at certain troubled times, and whose skin, on that ugly drum, quivered slightly whenever Jeremiah passed near, whether in rage or in simple hope that he might draw his hand along it, it was impossible to know—for naturally Jeremiah did *not* touch it, or linger on the stairway landing), and of course his children, his innocent children, whose inheritance was dissolving away to nothing.

The catastrophe of the silver foxes; and the necessity to sign yet another of the two-year notes (for the extension of credit out of the largest Vanderpoel bank); and the necessity, at last, anticipated for so long, of auctioning off certain of their treasures. (And the paintings and statues and various art objects *were* treasures, as the appraisers declared: a pity that buyers found them not to their taste, and worth, on the auction block, in the remorseless clarity of a midsummer sun, less than one-third of their estimated price.)

Not long afterward Lamentations of Jeremiah rushed out into a rainstorm, thinking that he would save his horses—no matter that Elvira begged him to stay inside, and Noel himself attempted to keep him there by force. He *wanted*, he *yearned* . . . It was an almost physical craving, that he rush out of the relative comfort of his father's house and into the violent storm, imagining that he heard the horses' screams, and that only *he* could save them from the rising waters. "Jeremiah! Jeremiah!" Elvira cried, trying to follow him through the knee-high muck, until he outdistanced her, shielded by the dark. Ah, how badly he *wanted*, he *yearned*, he *must* . . .

Swept away, the current sucking his feet out from under him, knocking his head against an uprooted tree stump, swept away in the raging storm (in intensity hardly different from the storm that ruined Leah's plans for great-grandmother Elvira's hundredth birthday celebration), he had time only to realize, before his consciousness was extinguished, that it was his pony Barbary he had been seeking out in the flooded stable: Barbary, his lovely gray-and-white dappled Shetland pony with the large shining eyes and the long thick almost woollike hair, Barbary the companion of his childhood, the companion of his innocent days as Felix. Yet still he *wanted* to plunge into the storm, he *yearned* to submit himself to it, as if only so violent a baptism, far from the rude claims of *Bellefleur* and *blood*, could exorcize his memory of the foxes and their hideous bloody jaws. *I am not one of you, as you see*, the drowning man pleaded.

The Assassination
of the Sheriff
# of Nautauga County

That final summer it did seem as if Germaine was losing her "powers"—she had no foreknowledge, evidently, of her great-uncle Hiram's death, and apart from a queer lethargy that gave to her small pretty face a somewhat leaden tone, and several sleepless nights preceding her fourth birthday, she seemed to have no clear sense of the impending catastrophe itself: the destruction of Bellefleur Manor and the deaths of so many members of her family.

On the morning of her uncle Ewan's assassination, for instance, she exhibited no signs of distress. She had even, it seemed, slept very well the night before, and woke in an excellent mood. At the breakfast table on the terrace Leah watched her daughter covertly, listening as the child prattled on to one of the servants about a silly little dream she had had, or was it a dream one of the kittens (according to Germaine) had had— kittens with wings who could fly, and if they wished they could paddle on the lake, and everything was buttercup-yellow, and someone was passing around cupcakes with strawberry icing—and it occurred to her that her daughter was a perfectly ordinary child.

Bright, and pretty, and somewhat willful at times, and given to spells of bad temper like all children; and of course she was somewhat large for her age. But, really, any stranger would consider her nothing more than a normal child: which is to say an *ordinary* child. Her eyes which had once seemed to hold an amazing light within them now seemed to Leah merely a child's eyes. And her rate of growth, so prodigious in the first two years, had certainly slowed, so that she was probably only an inch or two taller than the average four-year-old. It was true that she was unusually quick: she had taught herself to read somehow, and to do simple arithmetic, and she could, when she wished, reply to adult queries in an eerily adult manner. But her quickness, her intelligence, no longer struck Leah as exceptional. Set beside Bromwell, for instance . . .

Sensing her thoughts the child turned shyly toward her. The charming little story of kittens and flying and cupcakes died away, and the servant girl returned to the house, and for a moment mother and daughter regarded each other, wordless, unsmiling, with a certain caution. Germaine's eyes *were* pretty, Leah thought, that pale tawny-green, nothing like Gideon's eyes, or her own; and thickly-lashed. And usually bright with curiosity. But there was, she saw with a pang of dismay, nothing remarkable about them.

Uneasily, the child lowered her head while keeping her gaze fixed, still, upon her mother. It was a familiar mannerism, and seemed to Leah falsely and coyly submissive: an appeal to be loved, an appeal not to be scolded, when of course there was no likelihood she *would* be scolded (though the inane babble about the dream had been irritating), and of course she *was* loved.

Didn't she know, didn't the exasperating child know, how very passionately she was loved . . . ?

There must have been something in Leah's face that disturbed Germaine, for Germaine continued to gaze at her, lowering her head still more, and now bringing her fingers to her mouth to suck. Though this was a habit Leah angrily forbade.

"Germaine, really," Leah whispered.

The walled garden was absolutely still: no birds sang, there was no movement in the leaves, the placid filmy sky overhead showed no motion, as if the sky were nothing more extraordinary than an inverted teacup with here and there a fine hairlike crack. All the world hung suspended on this August morning while Leah and her peculiar little girl stared at each other in a silence that grew more strained as the seconds passed.

Then the creases between Leah's eyebrows deepened, and without knowing what she did she knocked the folded *Financial Gazette* off the table, and said, half-sobbing: "But what am I to do without you! What will I do with the rest of my life! And now I'm so close to—to—completing what I started— You can't desert me now, you *can't* betray me!"

Some eighteen hours later, in the bedroom of Rosalind Max's twentieth-floor apartment in the new Nautauga Tower, Ewan was surprised in his sleep by gunfire, and could not defend himself against an unknown assassin who shot, at a distance of less than ten feet, seven bullets into his helpless body. Five passed through his chest, one through his right shoulder, and one lodged in the very top of his skull. Rosalind, who happened by a propitious accident to be in the bathroom at the time, and hid there in terror during the shooting, emerged to see her burly lover sprawled sideways at the very head of the bed, completely still, and covered with blood.

Just as Germaine's pleasant little dream foretold nothing of the violence her unfortunate uncle was to experience, so did Ewan's own dreams foretell nothing. He slept, as always, deeply, in a near-stupor, his breath rattling as he both inhaled and exhaled; one could not imagine, observing so utterly blissful a sleep, that the sleeper might be much troubled by anything so immaterial as dreams, or thoughts of any kind. Which was, indeed, the case. If Ewan dreamt he forgot his dreams promptly upon waking. It could not be said, even by those who loved him, that he was one of the more intelligent Bellefleurs, but he felt nevertheless an almost patrician contempt for the superstitions of certain family members. Don't regale me with such backcountry crap, he frequently said, jocularly or angrily, depending upon his mood. He was most disrespectful to his wife, whose fears—fears "for your life," since he became sheriff—bored him. (As Lily herself bored him. If she had been jealous of Rosalind, Ewan complained to Gideon and his friends, if she had shown some healthy angry curiosity, why then he might not have minded: but her long mournful face, her sighs and tears and foolish "premonitions" about his safety merely antagonized him. Of course he loved her—all Bellefleur marriages were strong ones—but the more she grieved, the more he stayed away from home: and when he *did* come home he often flew into a rage, and knocked the silly woman against the wall. Why do you test my love for you! he shouted into her dazed face.)

Ewan was a thick-bodied ruddy-faced man in the prime of life when he met Rosalind Max in a Falls nightclub, and introduced himself to her despite the fact that she was in the company of a political rival whom Ewan knew to be contemptible. He soon dropped his other women, and he and Rosalind were seen about town two or three or four times a week, a striking couple, not exactly attractive, though of course Rosalind *was* harshly and defiantly pretty (she spent an hour or more spreading onto her full, solid face a patina of bright make-up that left her skin glowing and poreless, and her dyed red hair was flamboyantly and blatantly artificial, razor-cut to give a gypsy effect; her lips were a flawless scarlet). It was commonly known about town that Ewan was crazy about her, though comically suspicious as well, and that, over a period of months, he had given her a number of costly gifts: the eye-striking blue Jaguar E-model with the dyed rabbit-fur upholstery and silver fixtures and a built-in telephone, and an emerald ring said to be a family heirloom (which the careless Rosalind promptly lost while sailing with a friend on the river), and a freezer stocked with filet mignon, and an ankle-length sable coat, and a twenty-five-foot sailboat with purple and green sails, and any number of smaller items. The penthouse apartment in the new apartment building overlooking the river was, of course, in Ewan's name; but then the building itself was owned by his family. The more uneasy he was about her, the more generous he became.

"Of course I don't really love her," he told Gideon once or twice, when the brothers still confided in each other, "she's a—" and he uttered a word at once so obscene and so clinical that Gideon didn't know whether to be disgusted, or amused. And Ewan frequently said, too, that he couldn't possibly love her: she wasn't worthy of his name.

Nevertheless he gave her the apartment with its magnificent view of the river and the Falls and Manitou Island to the east, and he gave her the innumerable costly gifts, like any lover, like any befuddled excited lover, and he even arranged—exactly why, Rosalind did not know—for each of them to sit for a portrait, to be painted by an artist who moved about the fringes of Nautauga Falls society, and who had painted, for absurdly high fees, portraits of a U.S. senator from the area, and the mayor of Nautauga Falls, and the millionaire owner of the racetrack, and several society women, wives of businessmen and philanthropists, whom Ewan dismissed as far less attractive than his flame-haired Rosalind. The portraits had been completed by Christmas of the preceding year, and were hanging, at the time of the assassination, in the living room of the apartment: Rosalind's was theatrical, rather stiff, but conventionally glamorous; Ewan's showed a beefy, jowled, arrogantly handsome man of middle age, with eyes narrowed in merriment, or perhaps in meanness, and the soft pudgy flesh of his chin creased against his collar. It was *almost* an insult, that portrait, and indeed Rosalind had had to plead with Ewan not to attack the artist physically, but if one studied it long enough to become somehow attractive, even charming. The oddest thing about it was (as everyone attested who examined it long enough) that the portrait-ist had, whether knowingly or not (he claimed not) created a dull almost imperceptible aura about Ewan's head so that it looked as if the notorious sheriff of Nautauga County had a *halo.* Which was, of course, vastly amusing to Ewan and Rosalind and their circle, and rather mysterious. For the halo wasn't always there. But then again, if one peered closely and was patient, it reappeared.

From the first evening of their acquaintance Rosalind's independence excited Ewan: here was a woman who didn't want to be married, not even to a Bellefleur. She was a part-time singer in nightclubs in the city, and an occasional photographer's model, and she had done, she said, "thea-ter." (From the age of seventeen to twenty-one when, she said mysteri-ously, her life had been rudely altered, she had acted in supporting roles at the Vanderpoel Opera House, where comedies, musicals, and melo-dramas were sometimes performed; but of course Ewan had never seen her there.) Naked one night except for a frothy ostrich boa wound about her waist, Rosalind had high-stepped about the bedroom clapping her hands and singing in a hoarse, rowdy, utterly delightful voice, "When the Boys Come Home," the concluding number, she said, of one of her most successful musicals. Ewan had stared, bewitched. It was obvious that he *did* love her.

But he was suspicious. At times he felt sick with dread that she had betrayed him—was betraying him at that very moment—and nothing would do but that he had to telephone her, or send a man over on some contrived pretext (bringing her a dozen white roses, or a chocolate mousse, her favorite dessert, from the city's prestige restaurant in the Nautauga House); once he had ordered the police helicopter flown back to town from some dreary backwoods logging community where a tedious murder investigation was underway, and it had landed, creating quite a disturbance, on the penthouse terrace. (That day, a gentleman in a trench coat was observed leaving Rosalind's apartment hurriedly, but when Ewan questioned Rosalind she explained quite convincingly that she'd woken with a miserable toothache, and had called her dentist over for an emergency consultation.) Another time, Ewwan observed at the racetrack that his mistress's bets—for $25, $40, all small sums—were placed on quirky horses with 100–1 and 85–3 odds, and that these horses *won;* but Rosalind explained that she'd overheard her hairdresser chatting with a woman patron, and remembered the names of the horses mentioned, and, of course, she just had good luck. She wasn't a close friend of anyone connected with the racetrack, she said, and as for jockeys —jockeys repulsed her physically. Which Ewan believed, after some deliberation. His jealousy was such that he imagined lovers of Rosalind's crouched in closets, or hiding in shower stalls, when he entered the apartment unannounced; he *did* find outsized footprints in the pink marble bathtub, and hairs not Rosalind's or his own on her silk-covered pillows, and his stock of ale, kept in the apartment's second refrigerator, was often decimated; but he was sensible enough to doubt his own suspicions, and at any rate Rosalind always joked and teased him into a good mood. You spend all your time chasing criminals, she said, naturally you're suspicious. But you mustn't let it color your vision of human nature, Ewan. After all—! We pass this way but once.

Though Ewan enjoyed the city's nightlife, and felt quite wonderfully flattered by being seen in the company of gorgeous Rosalind Max, he liked best, as he told Gideon, spending a long period of time—twelve hours, eighteen hours—locked up in the penthouse with his mistress, with a generous supply of liquor, ale, salted peanuts, frozen pizzas, and doughnuts (glazed, powdered, cinnamon, apple, cherry, whipped-cream) from the city's most popular bakery, Sweet's. He and Rosalind made love, and drank, and ate, and made love again, and drank, and made love, and fixed themselves enormous meals out of the freezer and refrigerator, and drank and ate doughnuts, and slept awhile, and woke to make love, and poured themselves more drinks, and finished off the rest of the doughnuts . . . and so the weekend went; at such times they consumed more than two dozen Sweet's doughnuts, and an unfathomed quantity of other food and drink. I don't love her, she's a notorious bitch, Ewan complained with a wry smile, but, you know, I can't think of a better way to spend my time. . . . Then you're very fortunate, Gideon said curtly, and broke off the conversation. (The brothers had been growing apart for years, and after Gideon's accident, and his acquisition of the Invemere airport, they rarely spoke; it happened that they were rarely home at the same time, and when they were they tended to avoid each other.)

It was 3:00 A.M., Sunday morning, when, after a protracted bout of lovemaking, eating, and drinking, Ewan had fallen into his stuporous sleep, and was snoring loudly (indeed, Rosalind was to say that she owed her life to her lover's snoring—it had kept her awake—she'd decided to take a bubble-bath—and happened to be in the bathroom, sunk in the luxurious hot water, when the assassin broke into the apartment and into the bedroom and began firing at poor Ewan); and he never woke up again —never, that is, as Ewan Bellefleur, the sheriff of Nautauga County.

How quickly it happened! A stranger bursting into the room—firing seven shots from an automatic pistol—Ewan bleeding onto the silken pillows and sheets—Rosalind hiding terrified in the bathroom. And then everything went quiet again.

How quickly, how irreparably . . . And after it appeared that the murderer had gone Rosalind came out, shaking, knowing what she would find in the bed, and yet screaming when she saw it: her poor naked helpless lover, her dead lover, his body riddled with bullets, the very top of his skull penetrated. He was dead, yet his fingers still twitched.

He was dead, he must have been dead, shot at such close range: yet his eyelids fluttered. So she screamed and screamed.

But of course Ewan did not die, and it was a measure of his neurosurgeon's skill, as well as the resiliency of his own constitution, that he recovered as quickly as he did: a mere five weeks in the hospital, two in the intensive-care unit. And then he moved to a convalescent home on Manitou Island, chosen by the Bellefleurs for its proximity to the manor, as well as the excellence of its professional staff.

Ewan did not die, and yet—and yet it could not be said that he had survived. Not the Ewan Bellefleur whom everyone had known.

Some forty-eight hours after the shooting, when Ewan first regained consciousness in the intensive-care ward, his eyes rolled, and his pale lips moved, and he tried to grasp the hand of the attending nurse—and his initial words, but dimly grasped, had to do with blood and baptism. He then lost consciousness again, and remained in a comalike state for another two days, and when he again awoke, this time permanently, it was observed at once by Noel and Cornelia—the only people allowed to see him at that time, for Lily had collapsed and was inconsolable—that *this* Ewan did not appear to be *their* Ewan.

He recognized them, and seemed to be unusually clear-minded about the ward, the hospital, the delicate operation performed on his brain, and the circumstances of what he called his "misfortune." But he spoke in a near-whisper, and his manner was contrite, even chastened; it alarmed his parents that he said not a single word about the attempted murder—he knew that someone had tried to kill him, certainly, but he showed no anger, no bitterness, not even any curiosity about the assassin's identity. (The assassin was never to be found, though the sheriff's office and the city police launched an extensive investigation. If only Rosalind had caught a glimpse of the man—! But of course she had not, nor had anyone in the building, including the doorman in attendance downstairs, seen him; and the gun—a quite ordinary .45 Colt automatic, found twenty floors below in the alley—proved to be untraceable.)

From the first, then, Noel and Cornelia had known something was gravely wrong. Of course they were grateful that their son had survived: how many men, even with the bodily constitution of a bull, like Ewan, could have survived five bullets in the chest (miraculously, they had passed through him, striking no vital organ), a cruel shoulder wound, and a bullet lodged in his skull . . . ? And he had lost so much blood, and had arrived in the emergency ward in an advanced state of shock. But the Ewan who regained consciousness, the Ewan who held their hands and comforted *them,* and spoke gently (and apologetically) to his wife, and wept with delight to see Vida and Albert, and was so courteous with the nurses . . . this Ewan was no one they knew.

He was soft-spoken, he was contrite, he blushed with shame over the circumstances of his "misfortune" (for he was never able to bring himself to do anything more than allude to Rosalind, and the penthouse apartment, and his life of "error"); only while in the convalescent home, when he was free to walk, with a cane, about the sloping lawns, in the company of one or two members of his family, did he bring up—and then hesitantly, apologetically—the experience he had had, and the necessity, now, for changing his life.

Of course, he said quietly, he would resign his office. Had already resigned, in fact. Knowing what he did about life—about the nature of sin —about the baptism of blood—and Our Saviour's overseeing of every moment of our lives—he could not continue with his worldly occupation; even the very memory of it filled him with dismay. (That he had actually carried a handgun! That he had gloried in his rifles, automatics, shotguns! His soul was aggrieved.) Since he had no secrets from them or from anyone he was willing to show them the letter he had written to his former mistress, breaking off all further relations with her, and signing over the apartment to her for as long as she wished to have it—though he could not resist begging her to consider the self-defeating sinfulness of her ways, which might one day drag her down to Hell. His parents and his wife prudently disclaimed their right to read the letter, and it was sent by registered mail to Rosalind Max, who never replied. (Though of course she kept the apartment, and the car, and the rest of the gifts, including even the twin portraits.)

As time passed and he mended and grew strong Ewan was willing to talk more openly, and with a great deal of spirit, about his "baptism." Evidently he had died, or almost died, and at the very moment of death, as he was about to pass over into the other world, Jesus Christ Himself had appeared, and called out sternly to him, for it wasn't time yet for him to die, how could he die when he hadn't fulfilled his task on earth!—and he had better kneel, and submit to baptism. So Christ Himself had baptized Ewan, and with Ewan's own blood. (He had touched Ewan's chest wounds, had even poked a forefinger near his heart, in order to bloody his hands for the baptism.) They were together a long, long time, Ewan on his knees, Christ standing before him, instructing him, not so much in the sinfulness of his past life—for Ewan knew very well, now, the scales had fallen from his eyes and he *knew*—as in the life ahead, which would be extremely difficult. He would meet resistance, especially from those he loved; especially from his family. (Even Lily, though "religious," did not *really* believe.) But he must have courage. He must never slacken, he must forever remember the circumstances of his baptism, and Christ's love, and though the world might mock him he must only go forward to meet his destiny and fulfill himself on earth.

They stared at him, speechless. Their faces lengthened with grief. Ah, Ewan! What has happened to Ewan! *Their* Ewan . . .

Lily wept, and collapsed again. She moaned in her delirium that that whore had murdered her husband: why didn't the police arrest her and throw her in jail! *Of course* Rosalind Max had done the shooting herself. . . . everyone in Nautauga Falls knew that.

Noel and Cornelia and Leah and Hiram had no idea what to think. Ewan *wasn't* demented and yet he wasn't sane; his brain evidently had *not* been damaged, and yet . . . Gideon visited with him only once, and came away shaking: with distress or rage, no one knew. Ewan had seized his brother's hands and pleaded with him to accept Jesus Christ as his personal Saviour, and to accompany him, Ewan, on his pilgrimage to Eben-Ezer in the western corner of the state; he had pleaded with Gideon to cast off his worldly pursuits and devote himself to the Lord, before it was too late. For somehow it had come about—no one knew exactly how, nor could anyone at the Manitou clinic explain—that Ewan had met with a certain Brother Metz, who claimed to be a direct descendant of the German "saint" Christian Metz, who had founded the sect known locally as "True Inspiration" a century ago. The stooped, bearded, eagle-nosed old man *had* appeared at the clinic, and he and Ewan had spent several hours together in earnest discussion, on the veranda, but where he had come from . . . how he had known about Ewan . . . was to remain forever a mystery.

With tears in his eyes Ewan announced to his family that he would not be returning to Bellefleur Manor.

He had, he said, relinquished all his worldly goods, with the exception of $10,000, which he had given to Brother Metz's community at Eben-Ezer; as soon as he was formally discharged from Manitou he was to journey, on foot, to the community, where he would live for the rest of his days. He might in time become a minister in the True Inspiration church, when Brother Metz deemed him worthy, but of course he had no plans, he had no ambition, whatever the Lord wanted of him would come to pass, and in that would reside his happiness. . . .

He would *not*, he promised, harangue his family about their misguided lives. The pursuit of money, the pursuit of power—the mad desire to amass the wilderness empire old Jean-Pierre had once owned, which had brought him to his doom—! No, he would not harangue; that was not the way of True Inspiration. One lived one's life as a model of Christian virtue, just as Christ had lived His faultless life. So Ewan explained, gently. There would be no preaching except to those who wanted to believe.

His fellow policemen and his many acquaintances in the Falls assumed he was joking, until, one by one, they visited him. And came away, like Gideon, appalled. For Ewan Bellefleur *wasn't* demented and yet he wasn't sane. . . . Most baffling of all was his lack of interest in revenge. He didn't appear to care about the progress of the investigation; he adroitly changed the subject when one of his lieutenants named certain names, suspects among Ewan's numerous enemies in the county. Nor would he suggest names himself. (As for the theory that poor distraught Rosalind had had anything to do with the attempted assassination . . . Ewan simply shut his eyes and shook his head, smiling.) His associates were shocked at the change in him, and though they discussed it in detail, for weeks and months (indeed, the conversion of Ewan Bellefleur provided material for debate among people who barely knew him) they were never able to decide: was he mildly insane, had the bullet damaged his brain, or was he far healthier than he'd ever been before, in his entire life . . . ? But it did seem perverse, even repulsive, they thought, that a former sheriff should have so little interest in apprehending a dangerous criminal.

Vengeance is mine, sayeth the Lord, Ewan whispered.

Pretty Vida in her white high-heeled pumps, her jaws moving surreptitiously as she chewed gum (her mother and grandmother thought such a habit, in a young lady, insufferably vulgar), sat in the tearoom of the Manitou clinic with its mirrors and ferns and fleur-de-lis wallpaper, asking Albert repeatedly if he could understand what was going on, if he *really* believed that strange, frightening man was their father. And Albert, baffled, resentful, restless, lit matches and dropped them burning into the ashtray and said with a shrug of his shoulders, It's him all right, it's him bullying us in a new way.

But I can't *believe* it, Vida whispered.

It's him, Albert said, wiping at his eyes. The old fucker.

And one morning in late summer, wearing a plain, inexpensive brown suit, tieless, with the collar of his white shirt worn on the outside of his lapels, and carrying a small canvas valise, Ewan Bellefleur checked out of the convalescent home unattended, and set out on his journey westward to Eben-Ezer (now called, in these fallen times, Ebenezer) some five hundred miles away. He was going on foot, like a pilgrim.

Most of the staff saw him off. A number of the nurses wept, for Ewan had been the best-loved patient they had had in years; several staff members vowed that they would come visit him, and in the meantime they would pray for their own enlightenment. Though red-faced and still somewhat stocky, with a broad, muscular chest that strained proudly against his shirt front, and small bright eyes encased in a galaxy of wrinkles, Ewan nevertheless exuded a remarkably boyish enthusiasm. About his gray hair, they claimed, a frail, pale, almost invisible aura radiated; or so it seemed, in the confused excitement of his departure.

The Brood of Night

It was a fear commonly shared by the Bellefleurs that great-uncle Hiram, afflicted as he was by a sleepwalking malady that admitted of no cure (from the age of eleven he had been subjected to every sort of treatment: strapped in his bed, forced to swallow pills, powders, and foul-tasting medicines, led through exhausting and humiliating exercises, pleaded with, "talked to," forced to undergo, at White Sulphur Springs, a vigorous regimen of hydropathy under the direction of the famous society physician Langdon Keene—his "bodily poisons" were flushed away by enemas, wet packs, long soaks in the odorous waters, submission to waterfalls and cascades and other forms of "ex-omosis," and all, alas, to no avail)—it was a fear certainly shared by Hiram himself—that he would one day succumb to a disastrous accident while groping about in his uncanny somnambulist's stupor: but in fact the unfortunate man was to die fully awake, in the daytime, of a curious but *evidently* quite serious infection that grew out of a minor, nearly imperceptible scratch on his upper lip. It seems to have been the case, so far as anyone could judge, that his death at the age of sixty-eight had nothing at all to do with his history of noctambulism.

But how strange, how bewildering, his mother Elvira said (for she had, over the tumultuous decades, worried more than anyone else about Hiram's affliction, which she saw to be a direct response to the child's shame at his father's financial blundering), how *absurd,* the elderly woman said, half-angrily, when they told her about his sudden death. "There's no logic to it, no necessity, he simply died of anything at all—" she laughed—"when we had worried ourselves sick over him for almost sixty years. . . . No, I don't like it. I *don't* like it. Sixty years of carrying on like an idiot during the night and undoing the sense he made during the day and then to die of an infection that might have happened to *anyone.*

There's no necessity to it, there's something vulgar about it, I forbid you to tell me anything more!"

And though her elderly husband, known vaguely among the Bellefleurs as the "old-man-from-the-flood," and great-aunt Matilde (with whom the couple now lived, on the remote north shore of Lake Noir), grieved for her son's surprising death, great-grandmother Elvira remained tearless and resentful, and *really* would not allow anyone to bring up the subject of Hiram and the last week of his life.

"There's something hopelessly vulgar about accidental death," the old woman said.

Even as a boy Hiram had been serious and hard-working, and he was, he suspected, often compared favorably with his shallow brothers Noel (who spent all his time with horses, as if mere *animals* could occupy the intelligent energies of an adult male) and Jean-Pierre (who, long before the fiasco at Innisfail, was a grave disappointment to the family); at the age of eleven he was already astute in business matters, and could not only discuss the various aspects of the Bellefleur holdings, including the troubling tenant farms, with the family's accountants, attorneys, and managers, but challenge these gentlemen when it seemed to him they were mistaken. It was, in a sense, in defiance of his obvious talent that he chose to study classics at Princeton, where he was, surprisingly, an only mediocre student; and no one ever quite understood why he left law school so abruptly, in the spring of his first year, in order to return to Bellefleur. As a boy he had lightly mocked his family and their eccentricities, and spoke as if he wanted nothing more than to dwell hundreds—perhaps thousands—of miles away, in a "center of civilization" remote from the Chautauquas; but living away from the manor for even a few months greatly distressed him, and the bouts of sleepwalking grew so frequent (he was once discovered by a night watchman crawling on all fours on the ice-encrusted roof of Witherspoon Hall, at Princeton, and again stumbling into the waters of Lake Carnegie; he was quite seriously injured when, at about eleven o'clock in the evening, he walked, clad in pajamas and bathrobe, directly into the path of a horse-drawn carriage on muddy Nassau Street)—and the daytime anxiety so acute—that the family speculated he might simply be homesick, despite his angry disavowals. (For all his life, up until the very eve of his death, great-uncle Hiram was infuriated by anyone's theories concerning him: his gray, intelligent, normally contemplative eyes narrowed, and his jowls quivered with rage, at the very suspicion that anyone, even a loved one, might be forming an opinion about him. "*I* am the only person qualified to know about myself," he said.)

It had always been remarked, how *peculiar* Hiram's transformation was: for while during the day he was alert, quick-witted, and characteristically abrasive (a mere game of checkers, for instance, inspired him, even in the presence of children, to a pitiless intensity, and he was not a

good-natured loser)—while during the day he missed nothing, handi-
capped though he was by his clouded right eye—as soon as he fell asleep
he was entirely at the mercy of whims and muscular twitches and wisps
of fey, cruel dreams, and often attempted, in his noctambulism, to destroy
by shredding or fire the numerous papers, ledgers, journals, and leather-
bound books he kept in his room. (It was one of the shameful secrets of
the poor man's life, confided only to his brother Noel, and then after
much agonizing, and a spirited vow by Noel that he would never, *never*
tell anyone, that both his children—his son Esau who had lived only a few
months, and his son Vernon—had been conceived, evidently, *while he was
asleep.* Poor Eliza Perkins, his bride, the eldest daughter of a moderately
wealthy spice importer in Manhattan, had had to endure not only her
conscious husband's fumbling, awkward, embarrassed intercourse, which
so often ended in sweaty failure, but her unconscious husband's intercourse as well—more successful from a physiological point of view,
though no less dismaying in other respects. It was not known whether
Eliza confided in anyone, or that she quite grasped the situation: she had
been, at the time Hiram brought her to fabled Bellefleur Manor to live,
an extremely innocent, even rather charmingly ignorant, girl of nineteen.)

During the day great-uncle Hiram was always impeccably dressed,
and carried his high, round little stomach with a rigid propriety. He
contemplated with a grudging approval his balding skull, and his still-
dark curly sideburns; he had always been pleased with his long, soft,
"sensitive" fingers (to which he applied, every morning, an odorless
cream lotion manufactured in France). His drawing-room manners were,
as everyone attested, superb. When angered he spoke with an icy, cutting
delicacy, and though his sleek pink skin flushed even more darkly, he
never lost his temper. It would be common, it would be vulgar, he said,
to show one's feelings in public; or even in certain rooms of the house.

He was one of the Bellefleurs who professed to "believe" in God,
though the nature of Hiram's God was highly nubilous. A comically
limited God, in many ways less powerful than man, and certainly less
powerful than history: a God who might have been omnipotent at one
time, at the dawn of creation, but who was now sadly worn out, a kind
of invalid, easing toward His eventual extinction. (It seemed to Vernon,
who believed, for a while, most passionately in God, that his difficult
father had hit upon a belief calculated to offend both the God-fearing
Bellefleurs and the God-deniers.) Nothing was more amusing, or more
provoking, than to hear great-uncle Hiram interrupting his relatives'
remarks with long, elegant monologues punctuated with Greek and Latin
quotations, ranging over the entirety of religions and religious thought
—now Augustine was ridiculed, now Moses, now the Gospels, now John
Calvin, now Luther, now the entire Popish church, now the cow-worship-
ping Hindus, now the arrogant, confused, self-promoting Son of God
Himself. At such times he spoke in fastidious sentences, even in para-

graphs, with an air of detachment and irony, and even those who disagreed violently with him were forced to admire his wit.

But he worried, he brooded: for it sometimes seemed to him that his
appearance, proper as it was, did not *entirely* suggest the distinguished,
cerebral, highly contemplative person he knew he was. His wartime injury, resulting in the loss of much of the vision in his right eye, might have
added to his air of distinction, he felt, if only he could find exactly the
right pair of eyeglasses. . . .

Thus Hiram Bellefleur during the day.

But during the night: ah, how alarming the transformation!

Those who glimpsed him in his somnambulist's trance were appalled
at his appearance. Hiram at night resembled only scantily the Hiram of
the day: the muscles of his face were either slack and sagging, or screwed
up into extraordinary twitching grimaces. His eyes rolled. Sometimes
they remained closed (for, after all, he *was* asleep); sometimes they
showed pale trembling crescents; sometimes they were wide open, their
gaze unfocused. He stumbled and staggered and groped about, often as
if he were about to wake up, and were orienting himself to his surroundings; but he never did wake up until he injured himself, or someone
prevented him, in time, and shook him awake. (Though it was dangerous
to do so. For the childish, impish Hiram, asleep, threw his arms about and
kicked and even butted with his head, exactly like a two-year-old in a
tantrum. And there were times when the shock of being awakened on the
edge of a roof, or on the abutment of a bridge, or in a freezing rain, or,
more recently, while attempting to hug to his breast the furious yowling
Mahalaleel, so affected him that he was in danger of a heart attack.)

The caprices of noctambulism! Dr. Langdon Keene himself, physician to the notorious Jay Gould (who suffered from a somewhat milder
form of the disorder than poor Hiram), made a study of Hiram's body
fluids, and forced the young man—he was seventeen at the time, and
extremely prone to depression—to drink several quarts of water a day,
even when he wasn't a patient at the White Sulphur Springs spa. But the
sleepwalking did not cease: on the contrary, the demands of Hiram's
bloated kidneys gave to his shrewd nighttime manuevering an especial
grace (born perhaps out of desperation), so that he was able to slip by
the servant who attended him, like a wraith, and descend the great circular stairs of the manor, his arms extended, one foot unerringly placed
below the other, in absolute silence, and make his way out to the well
some two hundred yards to the east of the house, where only the hysterical barking of the dogs prevented him from urinating over the fieldstone
side of the well, and into the family's drinking water. Upon another
occasion the young man—who professed a loathing of horses—made his
way asleep into the stable, and attempted to climb on the back of an
unbroken colt of Noel's, awaking only when the frantic young horse leapt
about in the stall and struck at Hiram with his hooves. He might, one
would think, have been grievously injured: but apart from a few bruises

and a bloodied nose, and of course the trauma to his system caused by
the abrupt awakening, he was unhurt. Dr. Keene thought that aspect of
his young patient's noctambulism particularly interesting—for whether
Hiram slipped and tumbled down a flight of stairs into the cellar, or
waded out into the swamp in brackish snake-infested water that came to
his knees, or walked unheeding through an octagonal stained-glass window, or fell some forty feet from the balcony of one of the Moorish
minarets, or, as a young officer in the army, wandered toward the enemy's
trenches in total obliviousness of the gunshots and fiery explosions on all
sides of him, he was, relatively, time after time, *unhurt.* "He should have
died many times by now," the physician said, rather tactlessly, while
discussing Hiram's case with his parents. "In a sense, you might consider
the remainder of his life a gift."

"Yes," said Elvira impatiently. "But he still must *live* it, you
know—!"

(One of the most unsettling of Hiram's nocturnal adventures, which he
was to tell no one about, not even Noel, took place three weeks after his
young wife Eliza had disgraced herself by running away. Though as a
precaution against sleepwalking he had not only strapped himself into
bed, and rigged a system of bells attached to wires which would sound
an alarm if he blundered into them, but had posted a reliable servant boy
in the corridor outside his room as well, he nevertheless found himself
—woke suddenly to find himself, confused and terrified—some twenty or
more feet out onto the ice of Lake Noir. It was only mid-November; the
ice was extremely thin; indeed, he could hear it cracking and sighing on
all sides. Petrified with horror he dared not move, but looked about him
like a madman, seeing only the cold glittering ice and the moon reflected
haphazardly in it and, at a seemingly great distance, the dark shoreline.
The castle itself was hidden in shadows. It took the distraught man a
minute or two to absorb the circumstances of his situation, and its danger;
he was so panicked that he did not even feel, clad in his woollen night-
shirt, the idle ferocity of winds that blew from the mountains, sending the
fairly mild temperature (it was about 32 degrees Fahrenheit) down some
fifteen or twenty degrees. Sweat broke out through every pore of his
body. As the ice cracked beneath his paralyzed feet he looked down, and
saw, quite suddenly, a figure standing below the ice, exactly where he
stood—a figure who was upside down, and whose feet were evidently
pressed against his. Though at other times the waters of Lake Noir were
disturbingly dark, and its ice near-opaque, as if heavy with minerals, on
this occasion the ice appeared to be translucent, and Hiram could stare
down to the very bottom of the lake some forty or more feet below. The
presence of the shadowy figure—it was a man, he saw, a stranger—quite
unnerved him, for what was he doing there?—how on earth had he come
to be there, beneath the crust of ice, upside down, in the bleak silence
of a November night? Sweating, trembling, Hiram dared not move, but

stood with his bare feet pressed against the stranger's feet (and were they too bare?—he could not quite see), hearing the irritated cracking of the ice on all sides. The figure was motionless, as if paralyzed or frozen in place. And a few feet away another figure stood, upside down, shadowy as the first, unmoving. And there was another . . . somewhat smaller of stature, a child or a woman . . . and still another . . . and as Hiram's eyes adjusted to the gloom [here, even his clouded eye possessed a penetrating vision] he saw to his astonishment that there was a considerable crowd of reversed figures, some of them moving but most fixed in place, their feet against the thin crust of ice, their heads nearly lost in shadow. He wanted to cry aloud in terror: for who were they, these upside-down silent people, these doomed people, these strangers! *Who on earth were they and why did they dwell in the Bellefleurs' private lake?*)

And yet, in the end, so far as anyone could discern, Hiram's death at the age of sixty-eight appeared to have nothing at all to do with his somnambulism.

He had returned from the factory town of Belleview, a two-mile stretch along the Alder River which the Bellefleurs owned, and had built up within the past several years, and, exhausted, his eyes and nostrils still smarting from the chemical stench (the paper mill was by far the most virulent-smelling of the factories, it really left him quite sick), his head reeling from the offensive sights he'd seen (for the mill workers' living quarters, whether in the barrackslike apartment buildings the Bellefleurs had erected, or in their own ramshackle wood-frame dwellings which marred nearly every hill and knoll, were *really* unfit for human habitation, and threw Hiram into a frenzy of doubt about the worth of human nature itself en masse), he lay down fully clothed except for his shoes atop his massive brass bed, and slipped into an uneasy vexing sleep that had to do with Leah's unreasonableness and the ferret-faced impudence of one of the mill managers and his sister Matilde who was so eccentric, up there on the north shore sewing her outlandish incomprehensible savage quilts, and his son Vernon who appeared, in this waking-dream, not *altogether* dead (which seemed to Hiram's way of thinking something of a betrayal of the family name) . . . and suddenly, suddenly, it must have been because of family concern, over the weeks, about Gideon's behavior, his monomania for flying (the willful young man—for to Hiram he would always be "young"—had bought still another airplane, at considerable expense, merely for his own private pleasure) . . . suddenly Hiram was seeing again, and hearing, the insolent engine of that sporty little seaplane, painted in camouflage spots, pontooned, with a single whirring propeller, as it taxied bouncing along the choppy surface of the lake, and rose into the air, shakily at first, and then with a rakish confidence, bearing Eliza Bellefleur away from the embrace of her lawful husband. . . .

No, no, *no,* Hiram muttered, grinding his teeth, trying to force him-

self awake, no, you don't, not again, not for a second time, leaving me
to the humiliation . . . the shame . . . the loneliness night after night.
. . . But he could not manage to wake up. It was about five-thirty in the
afternoon, the sun shone vigorously through his latticed windows, down
on the lawn the children were noisy and a dog was barking foolishly, yet
he could not quite force himself awake; and suddenly his tearful bride was
back in his bed, in his arms, and he was trying desperately to think of
something—anything—to say to her, to explain himself, or to apologize,
but her panicked odor disturbed him, her wet dark warm intimate odor,
he could not think of a single word to say, not even in his own defense,
it exasperated and maddened him that the woman wept so frequently,
and turned herself from him in shame—in modesty—though of course he
did somewhat despise her, for certain bodily weaknesses she could not
control, and were, indeed, part of being female—as he surely understood
—and did not truly blame her—except—if only they were downstairs in
the drawing room or the Great Hall or at the dinner table, fully and
formally clothed, with witnesses to hear and appreciate his remarks!—
but, alas, they were, as it seemed they *forever* were, trapped in that bed
that stank of panting futile exertion, and he could not think of a word,
not a single saving word, to utter.

Then, abruptly, he woke.

He did awake. And lay there, in his vested suit, with his pocket watch
ticking confidently away, his toes in calf-high black silk stockings twitching with exasperation. But the odor was still in the room with him. That
wet dark warm furry intimate odor, with its slight scent of blood. Yes,
blood. It *was* blood. How odd, how very odd, how disgustingly odd, the
dream-stench was still in the room with him; it was, in fact, in his very bed.

"What—!"

He exclaimed angrily, having pulled back the covers to see an astonishing sight: one of the ginger cats lying on her side in the bed, four
hairless, blind kittens nursing and mewing and kneading her belly with
their tiny paws.

A mother cat had burrowed her way into *his* bed, to give birth to her
kittens! And she had made a mess, a repulsive mess, damp bloodstains
and bits of skin or flesh. . . .

"How dare you, how *dare* you," Hiram cried, shrinking away from the
creature, until his back pressed hard against the headboard, and the
entire bed shook with the intensity of his disgust.

That afternoon, he rang at once for a servant, and angrily ordered the
woman to drive away the cat and her kittens, and to clean up the mess
in his bed. And he stalked out of the room, fairly quivering with outrage.
What *could* the fools who ran the household be thinking, to allow a
mother cat to give birth to her kittens in *his* room, in *his* very bed! It was
unspeakable.

He complained at great length to whoever would listen—Noel, Cornelia, Lily, even, later in the day, aunt Veronica; Leah had no time for him

(she was vexed and rattled from a two-hour telephone conversation with their Vanderpoel broker), but instructed her manservant to take care of the situation. By which, she said sternly, looking Nightshade full in the face (for he was now as tall as she, though his posture was always craven in her presence), by which I do *not* mean you should put the kittens to death.

For they were so clearly Mahalaleel's kittens, they would grow up to be beautiful creatures: they *must* be allowed to live.

So Nightshade and two or three of the young visiting cousins set up a comfortable bed for the cat, in a corner of a supply-room adjacent to the kitchen. It was an ordinary cardboard box set on its side, with soft rags for the mother cat to lie on, and bowls of fresh water, milk, and chicken scraps nearby. Since the blind kittens were sensitive to light, the room would have to be kept fairly dark; and of course the mother cat's privacy would have to be respected. No one should peek in on her—at least not very often. Nor should the kittens (so darling!—tiny and near-hairless as baby rats) be handled since they were so extremely delicate.

The new bed was established, and though the mother cat—a pretty silky marmalade with striking white paws and a white mask in which her greenish eyes glowed—was hostile at first, and clearly disoriented, she seemed, after a few hours, to have adjusted.

And so Hiram quite naturally forgot about the incident. For he had so much to think about, so very much to think about, the negotiations for that final 1,500-acre block of land had hit a snag, and there might very well be a walk-out at Belleview, and a similar workers' uprising at Innisfail. . . . He was away on business for the weekend, and when he returned, hurriedly preceding the servant who carried his suitcase, he threw open the door of his room and was struck at once by the odor: an odor so intense, in a way so sly, that he was nauseated. His eyes fairly started from his head, he looked from side to side, resisting the impulse to gag, while the idiotic servant carried his suitcase into his dressing room as if nothing were amiss. The cat! Her smell hadn't been eradicated! Though he had expressly ordered the maids to clean the bed, even to change the mattress, and to air out the room thoroughly . . .

"That smell, Harold," he said.

The servant turned politely to him, raising his eyebrows. Quite clearly the fool was pretending not to notice. "Sir . . . ?"

"That *smell*. How can I be expected to remain in this room, how in God's name can I be expected to sleep in that bed, with this horrific *smell*. . . . I had asked the pack of you, as you must recall, to clean out my room."

"Sir?" the servant said, blinking slowly. His parchment-colored forehead crinkled into a row of perfunctory wrinkles, but his calm level mocking gaze remained unchanged.

Hiram, his heart thudding, made an exasperated gesture as if he wished to brush the fool out of the way; but he went instead to the bed, and flung back the covers.

And there—again—incredibly—*there*—the silky ginger cat lay on her side, sleepily licking one of the tiny kittens (who was mewing and paddling the air frantically) while the other three, their bluish-orangish-gray skin rippling with the intensity of their hunger, nursed at their mother's teats.

"This is—this is insufferable—" Hiram cried.

So great was the mother cat's audacity, she merely gazed at Hiram, and continued her rough washing as though nothing were amiss.

"I tell you, Harold," Hiram said, in a shrill voice, *"this is insufferable."*

He lunged for the cats—the mother cat hissed, and appeared to lunge at *him*—in a blind rage he snatched up one of the ratlike things, repulsive as it was with its swollen little belly that looked as if it might burst, and a dribble of watery excrement running down its hind legs— and threw it against the wall. Where it struck with a surprising cracklike noise, and fell, dead, to the floor.

"Get them out of here! Get them out of here! Every last one of them!" he shouted, clapping his hands, as the frightened servant stared. "And clean the bed! Change the mattress! At once! I command you! All of you! Under threat of dismissal! Change the mattress and clean the room and air everything out, at once, at once!"

So, indeed, his command was obeyed. A flurry of servants, both men and women, changed not only the mattress of his bed but the bed itself, having located, at grandmother Cornelia's instructions, a handsome bed with a brass headstand in one of the attic storerooms; they changed the carpet, and the heavy velvet draperies, and threw open all the windows so that a fine clean breeze aired the room completely out, and gave it an odor of sun-warmed grass, and the indefinable scent of the mountains. *Now,* said Cornelia in an undertone, surveying the servants' work with approval, that absurd old man should be satisfied.

And so, cautiously, he was.

"And has that disgusting creature been done away with?" he asked, "and those even more disgusting kittens?"

They assured him (not altogether truthfully: for the mother cat and her kittens had been moved to one of the barns, cardboard box, rags, bowls of food and all) that of course she had been done away with, and would never bother him again.

"It really is—was—insufferable," he muttered.

But then one afternoon, not three days later, Hiram returned to his room after a lengthy midday meal, and saw, as he approached his end of the corridor, something trotting along . . . something trotting along, head slightly lowered . . . cat-sized . . . and at the door to his room the thing nudged the door open (for evidently it had been left ajar) and slipped inside.

It can't be, he thought wildly. *It cannot be.*

They had killed the cat and her kittens according to his instructions, but surely that was the cat, once again, carrying a kitten (for he had caught a dim glimpse of something in her jaws) by the scruff of its neck. . . .

He began to shout. He ran into the room, and saw a hellish sight: the very same ginger cat with the white mask and white paws and greenish eyes, a squirming kitten in her teeth, just lowering the kitten to his bed. She had made a kind of nest for herself by burrowing beneath the covers, and had managed to pull back the heavy brocaded spread. What was most hellish was the fact that there were *three* kittens already nestled there, in addition to the one she was just bringing. All four were mewing piteously, and paddling the air with their tiny paws.

"This cannot be! I refuse to acknowledge it!" Hiram cried.

Even in his consternation he was clear-minded enough to realize that of course the household staff, and even his sister-in-law, had lied to him: humored him: as if he were a ridiculous old man. Which added considerably to his rage. And this time the ginger cat quite insolently confronted him, refusing to be driven away by his shouts and handclapping. Her pretty ears were laid back, her eyes narrowed, she crouched just in front of her brood to protect them, and hissed, and growled deep in her throat. And when the infuriated Hiram lunged toward her to seize her by the throat she slashed out, so quickly her movement was no more than a blur, and caught him with a single claw on his upper lip.

"How *dare* you— How *dare* you—" Hiram sobbed, scrambling away.

That claw, that single claw (it was in fact a dewclaw), was so remarkably sharp, far sharper and more treacherous than a needle, that Hiram was quite astonished; and the sight and taste of his own blood demoralized him (though there wasn't much blood, really—the scratch was a minor one.)

"Oh, how dare you—all of you—how dare—how *dare* you—" the poor man wept.

They found him, sobbing inconsolably. He was sitting in a corner of his darkened room, in a rocking chair, bent over, his eyeglasses fallen to the carpet. I'm going to die, he whispered. She has scratched me, she has drawn my blood, and infected me, I'm going to die, he said, grasping feebly at his brother's arm. Noel told him not to be a fool, why didn't they turn on some lights, for God's sake, what was this?—and when they lit the lamps they saw the ginger cat curled in Hiram's bed, the kittens sleeping beside her, perfectly content. The cat blinked drowsily at them but made no movement to escape.

"No one has ever died of a tiny cat scratch," Noel said, laughing.

Brown Lucy

Brown Lucy, Lucy Varrell, drunken and hilarious, naked, her great ungainly breasts leaking milk, milk for *his* baby (a son, not yet named: she had managed to beat poor clothespin-lipped Hilda by two or three weeks, and did not even mind—for such was her savage good nature, and one of the reasons Jean-Pierre could not stay away from her —that he boasted to whoever would listen), straddling him in her upstairs room at the Fort Hanna House, riding him, slapping him playfully but hard up and down his sides, against his quivering thighs, until, suddenly delirious, he began to shout. A dribble of watery milk across his face, her uncombed grease-stiffened hair cascading against his eyes and mouth. *Don't! Don't! Stop! Oh, Sarah—*

At the land commission office at Fort Hanna there was excited, gloating talk of the *bankruptcy,* and the *imprisonment,* of Alexander Macomb himself.

In his elegant gentleman's attire the son-in-law of Roger Osborne, one Jean-Pierre Bellefleur, arrived to negotiate for the purchase of certain wilderness lands; but once in Fort Hanna, and having journeyed as far north as the trading settlement at Paie-des-Sables, he was possessed of a notion to buy up everything he could, or, to the contrary, sell the holdings he had already bought from Macomb's agent in New York, and return to the city at once.

The wilderness! The mountains! The broad flat Nautauga River! . . . In Manhattan his father-in-law, though infirm, had spoken with zest of the riches of the north—the uncut pine, the firs—and, seated in the dark-paneled library of the Broadway town house, he had insisted that Macomb's extravagant purchase of the ten townships (townships formed after the destitute Oneida Indians were forced to cede their land to the state) was a brilliant move: for within two years Macomb had resold the land, at considerable profit, to other speculators: and the way was now cleared for . . .

But now Macomb was bankrupt, people said. And jailed.

Here, in Fort Hanna, the Northern Missionary Society contended with the loose brawling community of trappers and traders and ex-soldiers and whores like Brown Lucy who (so rumor had it, but the rumor was false) had acquired fortunes. Brown Lucy and Erasmus Goodheart and a former secretary of Aschthor—John Jacob Astor—and other members of the "criminal element" Roger Osborne feared might corrupt his immature son-in-law.

Goodheart, for instance. Drinking with Goodheart at Fort Hanna House. The man claimed to be part Algonquin, part Seneca, part Dutch, and part Irish. He looked no more Indian than Jean-Pierre. He had been, evidently, Lucy's lover. In a manner of speaking. He was one of those who spread the rumor, perhaps not maliciously, that Lucy had a small fortune hidden away—it added to her value, her charm. (The first sight Jean-Pierre had of the woman was a discouraging one: she was big, and the bigness appeared to be muscle, except for the large, flimsily-corseted breasts; she was much younger than he had anticipated, and good-looking in a harsh jocular way. He would, he saw, have to compete for her attentions.)

When Jean-Pierre first arrived in the north country the wilderness frightened him except when he had downed a certain number of drinks. His first tumbler at midday, the best he could acquire in this wretched part of the world, sipped like wine. *My dear Hilda,* he wrote, *Each day is a tumult of new impressions & new knowledge . . . I scarcely know what to think. . . . The wilderness land awakes in us (I must say us because we seem all equally afflicted, except for the Indians who remain, and the elderly or infirm or mysteriously dispirited),a sense of . . . a sense . . .* He crumpled the letter and began again, irritated at his task, for not only did he resent having to write to *her* (whom he did not love) but he gravely resented the fact that it was so devilishly difficult to express what he felt (when in conversation he was glibly skillful, and could make anyone understand his meaning or at least acquiesce to it). *My dear Hilda, The air is intoxicating, I lie awake as demons cavort in my skull, drawing me in one direction and then in another . . . enticing me to this, or to that. . . . The wilderness land is alive. I did not grasp that earlier. Nor does your father understand, with his prattle of . . . his smug prattle of . . .* He pushed the stiff sheet of paper aside, and poured another inch or two of whiskey into his glass. Gently, like the brushing of a lover's eyelashes against one's cheek, the image of the girl Sarah touched him: touched his overheated skin. He had not thought she would follow him *here,* so far from the place he had last glimpsed her. By now she was settled in England, by now she might even be married, it was not a preposterous thought, he had lost her forever, he had made a fool of himself, married to a washboard-plain woman whom he did not love but who was too sweet, too self-effacing, for him to dislike with pleasure. And then too there was the dowry. And the father-in-law's generosity. (*Was* Osborne senile, or somewhat rattled by the drugs his physician fed him; or was he simply anxious to keep Jean-Pierre happy?) *My dear Hilda,* Jean-Pierre wrote, in a sudden frenzy, *There is only one principle here as elsewhere, but here it is naked & one cannot be deceived: the lust for acquisition: furs & timber: timber & furs: game: to snatch from this domain all it might yield greedy as men who have gone for days without eating suddenly ushered into a banquet hall & left to their own devices. One stuffs oneself, it is a frenzy, the lust to lay hands on everything, to beat out others, for the others are enemies. At the banquet there is so much food! There is in fact a surplus of food! But we are all the more ravenous, we cannot contain ourselves, we fear there won't be enough to go around and so we must gobble up everything on the table. . . .*

But Hilda would not understand. Would be frightened at his passion, and show the letter to her father.

My dear Hilda, he wrote, his hand more controlled, *I shall never voluntarily leave this wilderness paradise.*

Many months later Brown Lucy rolled from bed, and padded out barefoot into the back room, and returned a minute later with a pail of fish heads and tails and guts which she dumped atop her lover.

"That's for your *Sarah!* Your precious *Sarah!*" she screamed.

Half-awake he tried to protect himself but the shock was paralyzing: to hear *her* name uttered aloud, when he had carried it with him for so long, in secret. . . .

"But how did you know," he said, wiping frantically at himself, "you filthy bitch, goddamn you!—how did you know?"

"And Sarah isn't the name of the one in New York, is she!" the woman shouted. She rushed at him, her breasts swinging, and he turned aside and lost his balance and fell back across the bed, into the remains of the fish. (*His* fish, brook trout, which she had cleaned for him.) "Liar. Bastard."

"But how did you *know?*" Jean-Pierre cried in a daze.

So it went, months and years. One must surmise.

There was, as well, sinewy yellow-eyed Goodheart, with his scarred forehead and rotting teeth and a lurid cascade of tattoos on both arms, telling Jean-Pierre, when they were alone, and drinking far into the night, of the old days at Johnson Hall, when Sir William was his majesty's General Agent for Indian Affairs. Before the old man died of apoplexy in 1774. Before his sons inherited his estate, and his position, and everything went bad. The tribes of the Six Nations had gathered at Johnson Hall every summer for their games, and there were days and days of celebrating, and more food than anyone could eat, provided by the Crown. But Jean-Pierre had difficulty envisioning those days.

Lucy had told Jean-Pierre that Goodheart, despite his beard and natty clothes and his modest local fame as a cardplayer (his winnings were always small, as if he were eager not to incur wrath; but they were consistent) had been born of a slave family: both his mother and grandmother were household slaves of Sir William's. But he never alluded to his own past; he joked freely of the relative worthlessness of Indians as slaves.

It was commonly known, for instance, that they were capable of dying at will. Their spirits could depart at any time from their bodies, leaving behind bodies which might absorb *any* punishment. Sir William's oldest son John, after the old man's death, had once ordered an Onondagan slave, a man in his mid-thirties, flogged to pieces . . . literally to pieces, to shreds, for "willfulness and sloth." Indian slaves always sold for far less than Negroes. And there were so many more of them.

Goodheart accompanied Jean-Pierre by steamboat down the wide fast-flowing Nautauga, and down the Alder, where he might view the despoiled mansions of the great landowners who had fled north in 1776. There were tales, he said, that Sir John had buried much of his treasure in an iron chest somewhere on his property, before fleeing to Canada with his family and his Scottish tenants and a dozen of his most valuable slaves.

Sometime later, Jean-Pierre bought the Johnson property, which brought with it more than 60,000 acres of land. It had been confiscated by the state, and sold to Macomb, and sold again after Macomb's bankruptcy. Gradually the frenzy grew: in one month he bought 48,000 acres west of treacherous Lake Noir, where no one lived, and 119,000 acres of impenetrable wilderness land around Mount Horn. The following year he was to acquire, at seven and a half pence an acre, 460,000 acres north of the tiny settlement of White Sulphur Springs.

And so it went. Months, and years. Long ago. Though Jean-Pierre supervised the digging up of the Johnson property—the extensive lawns, and the overgrown formal garden—he never found the legendary treasure. He halfway suspected that Goodheart had lied to him but it was for other reasons that he had Goodheart jailed at Fort Hanna, in 1781, the year of Harlan's birth.

Trespassing and poaching on his land, he charged. He couldn't allow it.

By then Brown Lucy too had disappeared. He had paid her off, had given generous bonuses for the sons (were there three of them, or four), had sent her up to Paie-des-Sables to live, where her sagging breasts and belly and her forlorn, savage face wouldn't depress him.

And Hilda too, eventually, must be banished. For like Brown Lucy she came between Jean-Pierre and his love: though his love was nothing more than a fleeting image, a moon-pale child's face glimpsed at the rarest, the least anticipated, of moments.

"*Sarah!* What do you mean by *Sarah!* I'll give you *Sarah,* you hogshit son of a bitch!" the woman stormed above him, overturning the pail of fish guts on his head.

When they came to get him, so many decades later, in the farthest bedroom of the house he and Louis had built, he had no time to think of any of the women: he had no time to think at all. Nor could he interpret their taunts, their furious jeers, as they dragged him and Antoinette out of bed. Why were they so angry!—why did they want to kill *him!*

But he had no time, even, for that thought.

"*Bellefleur—!*" came the cry, drunken and murderous.

Bellefleur.

The Broken Promise

On the eve of Germaine's fourth birthday a uniformed messenger arrived at Bellefleur Manor to deliver a document containing such upsetting news that Leah, to whom it was addressed, grew faint, and staggered, and would have fallen into a swoon had not Nightshade, alert as always at his mistress's side, stepped forward. "Ah, how could she!— how could she! How could such a thing happen!" Leah cried. The household was all in a commotion but Nightshade retained his calm: murmuring solicitously, as if comforting an animal or a very small child, he tore open one of the leather pouches he carried about his person, and released, with admirable alacrity, a bluish, highly astringent mist that cleared Leah's head at once. Her small, rather narrow, rather colorless gray-blue eyes opened wide and staring.

She threw herself down in a chair, and tossed the heavy document —it was a parchment sheet, at least twelve inches long—at her father-in-law, who was insisting noisily that *he* be shown whatever it was. But she continued to moan, in a low voice that writhed with anger and helplessness and sheer incredulity, "How could she! My own daughter! Lost to all shame, and now *this*! They are betraying us one by one, they must be stopped! How *could* she, a daughter of mine!"

For, it seemed, the wanton Christabel had been made Demuth Hodge's lawful wife in a civil ceremony in, of all places, Port Oriskany (so close to home!—and the detectives' last report, filed months ago, with a list of extraordinary expenditures, placed them in Guadalajara, Mexico); and she had, in a handwritten letter to old Mrs. Schaff, forfeited her claim to the inheritance—all of Edgar's fortune, all of the property, Schaff Hall, and the many thousands of acres of precious land. Old Mrs. Schaff, acting, perhaps, out of a venomous desire to prostrate poor Leah, had

had the letter duplicated on stiff legal-sized stationery, and it was this ugly document Leah had received.

"Nightshade, how *could* she," Leah whispered, grasping the creature's wrist with a desperate familiarity that did not go unnoticed among the Bellefleurs, "Christabel whom I loved so dearly, Christabel who was so precious to us all!"

A false rumor started among the domestic help that Leah had wept: had actually been seen weeping. But it was soon contradicted by the housekeeper and several of the maids who had been present, for of course Leah had not wept, despite her perturbation. She *never* wept, so far as anyone knew. Not as a young woman, not as a girl, not even as a child had she wept; and though everyone had supposed her especially close to Hiram, despite their occasional differences of opinion, it was observed that she remained tearless at the old man's funeral.

Because of Hiram's sudden death the entire household, of course, was thrown into mourning: or at the very least (for the Bellefleurs were magnificently pragmatic people) into the *semblance* of mourning. Naturally there could be no formal birthday celebration in Germaine's honor. Leah promised a secret party, maybe, upstairs in her boudoir-office, with a birthday cake and a few presents, but the revelation of Christabel's spiteful act was so upsetting that Leah forgot about the party, and called instead an emergency meeting of the family council, including the family's various managers, financial advisers, accountants, and attorneys.

If Germaine was disappointed she did not show it, for she had become accustomed to playing by herself for hours, hidden away in the most remote rooms of the castle, with no one but the gentler cats for her playmates. (The toms, of course, were too rough: their lazy pawing might turn in a moment into kicking and scratching and serious biting, and since uncle Hiram's death there was naturally great concern about infection as well. Mahalaleel alone among the male cats would have been a trustworthy pet for Germaine, since he was exceptionally fond of her, and always sheathed his claws when she petted him, but of late, for the past few weeks, he hadn't been sighted anywhere in the vicinity of the castle; and it was feared that, at last, he had disappeared, as mysteriously as he had appeared so long ago.)

So Germaine played with her favorite cats, talking and chattering to them, or she read aloud to them, as best she could, from old books she discovered in out-of-the-way places, crammed between the cushions of old sofas, stacked untidily in closets that stank of dust and mice, or hidden beneath fur boas and scraps of yellowed lace in bureau drawers that opened only with difficulty—and what odd books they were, how heavy their ancient leather bindings made them!—heavy, weighted with age and sorrow, and yet captivating, even on sunny mornings when of course she *should* have been playing outside. In later years Germaine would recall these volumes with disturbing clarity, for though she had not been capable of understanding more than a few sentences here and there she had pored over the books at length, turning the stiff yellowed pages reverently, reading aloud in a shy, faltering whisper. *Belphegor* of Machiavelli, *Heaven and Hell* of Swedenborg, *The Subterranean Voyage of Nicholas Klimm* of Holberg, the *Chiromancy* of Robert Flud, the *Journals* of Jean D'Indaginé, and of De La Chambre, *The Journey Into the Blue Distance* of Tieck, *The City of the Sun* of Campanella, the *Confessions* of Augustine, and of the Dominican Emyric de Gironne, Hadas's *Nocturne,* Bonham's *Doppelgänger,* Sir Gaston Camille Charles Maspero's *Egyptian Mythology*. . . . The old books, despite the costliness of their bindings, looked as if they had never been read, or even opened; they must have been acquired in bulk by one of the child's great-great-great-grandfathers, along with works of art and pieces of antique furniture.

Occasionally she climbed the stairs into the tower her brother Bromwell had once claimed for his own, and standing at one of the windows she peered for long minutes into the sky, waiting to see a plane. She had pleaded with her father to take her flying one day soon—for her birthday, perhaps—she wanted no other present—nothing else would please her. When he wasn't home, which was frequently, she begged her grandmother Cornelia or her grandfather Noel or whoever would listen. (Not Leah. Leah would *not* listen if Germaine brought up the subject of a plane ride.) But it's too dangerous, her grandparents said. It isn't for little girls. It isn't for any of *us*—except your father.

If she sighted a plane in the distance she climbed atop the windowsill, and waited to see if it would come closer. She knew that her father and his pilot friends did wild, playful things in the air, for she had overheard her mother's complaints (they were maniacs, they were insane, flying between the spans of a bridge on a bet, making emergency landings in fields or on roads or, in the winter, on frozen rivers and lakes); it was quite possible, she thought, that he would fly to her, he would circle close to the tower, and somehow, somehow, she didn't know how, he would pull her up into the plane with him, and they would fly off together, and no one would ever know where she had gone. . . .

But though she frequently sighted planes they rarely came near the castle, and when they did they were, evidently, strangers' planes: they simply flew overhead, the noise of their engines growing louder and louder and louder, and then fading, rapidly, until they were out of sight, and she remained behind, crouched on the sill, staring, her hand still upraised.

Daddy . . . ? she whispered.

Then on the eve of her birthday Gideon relented.

He relented, and promised her a ride the next day. Just the two of them—in the cream-colored Dragonfly—and it would be *very* nice.

But Leah protested. He was being ridiculous, she said.

Gideon did not reply.

He was being selfish, he was trying to come between her and her daughter—

But Germaine began to cry. For she wanted nothing more than to go for a plane ride with her father; she wanted no other birthday present.

Germaine, Leah began.

But Gideon arose, and walked from the room without looking back.

And Germaine ran after him, ignoring her mother.

Daddy! Daddy, wait! she cried.

—but he only wants to come between us, Leah protested. He doesn't love you.

Her voice was a hoarse frightened whisper. She clutched at her daughter, who struggled at first to free herself, and then quieted, suddenly, when she saw how agitated her mother was. And anyway her father had left. And anyway (so she told herself fiercely) he hadn't retracted his promise.

But he doesn't love you, Leah said, squatting so that she could look Germaine in the face. You must know that. You *must* know. He doesn't love any of us, he only loves—he only loves, now, his planes and—and the sky—and whatever he finds there—

If Germaine slept poorly on the night before the catastrophe it was not, as one might surmise, that she anticipated the destruction of the castle, and the deaths of her parents: it was simply because she both dreaded and yearned for the morning, when her father would take her into the sky as he had promised—but then again perhaps he wouldn't, perhaps he *would* retract his promise—ah, what might happen! She was only four years old, she was small and helpless and frightened and so exhilarated she woke every half-hour, her bedclothes tangled in her legs and her pillow crushed in the oddest ways. The spittle-stained panda who slept with her found himself unaccountably on the nursery floor where his young mistress impetuously tossed him, waking from a nasty little dream in which her father *did* retract his promise and fly away without her.

In the morning, very early, she ran in her summer nightgown out into the hall, and called out *Daddy, Daddy*— and at once he appeared, as if he had been waiting for her (thought she knew of course he hadn't—probably he had been planning to slip away in secret); and he wished her a happy birthday, and kissed her, and told her yes, yes, of course, he hadn't forgotten, he certainly planned on taking her for a ride, but she had to get dressed first, and she would have to have a little breakfast, wouldn't she, and then they would see about the ride.

He hadn't changed his mind? He hadn't forgotten?

He wore a white suit with a dark shirt, open at the neck, and Germaine thought she had never seen anything so dazzling white, and so beautiful. The coat hung loose on him—the shoulders drooped slightly —but it was a very handsome coat and she wanted to hide her face against it, and say Why don't we take Mamma too, why don't we ask Mamma, then she wouldn't be so angry, maybe, she wouldn't hate us both so much—

But he sent her off to breakfast.

And appeared downstairs in a half-hour, to take her to Invemere. Wearing the white suit with the dark blue shirt, and a white hat with a deep crest in its crown and a band of braided leather that looked so smart, so handsome, she laughed aloud at the sight of it and clapped her hands and said that *she* wanted a hat just like that. Leah lit one of her long cigarettes and brusquely waved the smoke away and coughed that tight quick cough of hers, but said nothing. How strange it was, but how wonderful, that this morning Leah didn't seem to care! The airplane ride, and Germaine's birthday: and she didn't seem to care. But then so many people were coming later that day. The attorneys, the advisers, the managers, the tax men . . .

Gideon took Germaine's hand, and at the doorway he paused, and lifted his white hat in a little farewell gesture. Which Leah didn't notice. He asked if she *would* like to join them.

"Don't be ridiculous," she said. "Go on, go away, take her away, do what you want."

She stubbed her cigarette out in a saucer, and the saucer rattled noisily against the table. And when she looked up again her husand and her daughter were gone.

She seized the little silver bell, and rang impatiently for Nightshade.

Driving along the lake Gideon spoke gaily of his Dragonfly and how Germaine would like it. We'll have to wear parachutes, he said. In case of trouble. I'll have to strap yours on you and give you some instructions though of course nothing will happen. . . . Your Daddy knows how to fly as if he has been flying all his life.

He gave her his wristwatch to examine. It was a new watch with a wide leather band which she had never seen before. The face was so complex—there were so many numerals and moving hands, black, red, and even white lines—she could not tell the time, though she had learned to tell time perfectly well on the castle's numerous clocks.

Can you see the red hand moving? Gideon asked. That's the second hand.

She studied it, and did see it moving. But the black hand moved too slowly. And there was a small white hand that moved too slowly also.

So they drove along on a hot August morning and the dust billowed up behind them and Germaine was studying the watch so intently, she did not notice that her father had stopped his idle cheerful talk, and had turned off the lakeshore road. The car bumped and bounced along the narrow lane that led to aunt Matilde's house.

At once she knew. She knew, and let the watch fall, and said in an aggrieved voice: But this isn't the way to the airport! This isn't the way!

Hush, said Gideon.

Daddy, this isn't the way!

He drove faster, without glancing at her. She kicked at the seat, and knocked the watch onto the floor, not caring if it broke; she began to sob that she hated him, she loved Mamma and hated him, Mamma was right about him, he didn't love any of them, Mamma was right, Mamma knew everything! But though she thrashed about and cried until her face was wet and overheated, and even the front of her polka-dot jumper was damp, he did not stop the car, nor did he even try to comfort her. And of course he didn't say he was sorry for lying.

Why did you promise, Daddy! she screamed. Oh, I hate you—I hate you and wish you were dead—

And she did not even care that aunt Matilde and great-grandmother Elvira and the smiling old man were so pleased to see her. She didn't *care,* she was still sobbing and hiccuping, there was the tame red cardinal in his wicker cage, in the sun, making his high questioning chip-chip-chip sound, there were the white leghorns and the white long-tailed rooster with the bright red comb, but she didn't care, she drew away from aunt Matilde's hug, even Foxy the red cat, hiding around the corner of the house and finally venturing forth, seeing who it was, even Foxy couldn't distract her, for she knew she had been betrayed: her father had broken his promise to her, and on her birthday of all days.

The old people wanted him to stay but he had no time for them.

Let me make you some breakfast, aunt Matilde said. I know you haven't eaten. Eggs, buckwheat pancakes, sausages, muffins—blueberry muffins, Gideon—don't you have time for us, really?

But of course he hadn't time.

Ah, Gideon, look at you—! Aunt Matilde sighed. So thin—!

He stooped to kiss Germaine goodbye but she turned half-aside in disgust.

She was such an outraged, poker-faced little lady, he couldn't help laughing at her. It's because of the wind, he said, the wind isn't right, it's coming from the mountains too hard, it would knock our little plane out of the sky. Germaine? Do you understand? Another day, when it's calmer, I'll take you up. We can fly right over Lake Noir and see the castle and the farm and you'll be able to see Buttercup out in the pasture, and wave to him, all right? Another day. But not today.

Why not today! Germaine screamed at him.

He waved his hat at them as he backed away, smiling. But it was nothing more than the shadow of a smile, just as his eyes weren't anything more than the shadows of eyes, and of course she knew.

She knew, she knew. And would not even glance at the watch he left behind for her—the big ugly watch with all the confusing numerals and lines.

He got in the car and backed it around and drove away, and even waved at them out the window, but he was already gone, she wouldn't wave back, she stood there staring at him, panting, no tears left, the salty tears already drying on her cheeks, and when the car was out of sight down the narrow lane she wouldn't let the old people comfort her because she knew she would never see him again, and it would do no good to cry, to scream, to throw the watch down into the dust and stamp on it: she knew.

Another time, another time, great-grandmother Elvira whispered, touching Germaine's hair with her stiff chill fingers.

A Still Water

In a strange land where the sky has disappeared and the sun has gone dark and the rocky inhospitable soil beneath our feet has vanished, on the borders of Chymerie . . . on the borders of the deathly-dark lake . . . beneath the waters of the deathly-dark lake . . . the god of sleep, they say, has made his house.

For there are, according to the immense monograph *A Hypothesis Concerning Anti-Matter,* by Professor Bromwell G. Bellefleur, slits in the fabric of time, "portals" linking this dimension with a mirror-image universe composed of identical (and yet unrelated, opposed, totally distinct) beings.

How may they be identical, and at the same time "unrelated, opposed, and totally distinct"?

The god of sleep, a corpulent god, a most greedy god, has made his house where the sun has no dominion, eclipsed by the brute matter of the earth. There, no man may know aright the point between the day and the night. In that place a still water abides . . . a still, lightless, bitter-cold water which runs upon the small stones and gives great appetite for sleep.

A Hypothesis Concerning Anti-Matter. Eight hundred dense pages long, filled with Bellefleur's small, chaste, rigorous handwriting, and hundreds of equations, and graphs, and sketches, and impatient desperate doodles, which mimic the work's somber thesis. Prefaced with an enigmatic and loosely translated remark of Heraclitus, on the nature of time: or, rather, on the nature of our conception of time.

Those who read *A Hypothesis Concerning Anti-Matter* and were not acquainted with the brilliant young man who wrote it feared for his sanity; those who knew Bromwell were disturbed but not at all surprised. And of course they did not fear for his sanity, for who among them was half so sane as that boy-genius who had never grown up . . . ?

(For Bromwell had changed only superficially from the boy who walked so briskly away from New Hazleton Academy for Boys long ago. A "child" of no more than four feet nine inches, with a wise, lined face, and thick wire-rimmed glasses, and thinned-out hair that looks blond in some lights and silver-gray in others. There is a rumor among his associates at Mount Ellesmere, and among his disciples, and even among his many rivals and enemies (for of course he has enemies, though he knows none of them by name), that he has a twin: but who, or what, might this "twin" be—! Of course no one has ever seen Bromwell's twin, nor does anyone know whether the twin is a male or a female.)

Over the long years, as he labored on the *Hypothesis,* Bromwell chose to live on the most meager of part-time salaries, supplemented at times by grants and fellowships, not so much confident in the ultimate worth of his research as indifferent to his circumstances and surroundings. If he never grew past the height of four feet nine, observers claimed, it was primarily because he didn't *try.* And of course he ate poorly, and slept little, and worked himself to the brink of collapse—and may even, on one or two occasions, have crossed over into that murky indefinable terrain known to the impoverished of imagination as madness. But he soon righted himself, and returned. For *there* was not his kingdom, *there* his splendid mind had no dominion.

He was condemned, as he saw from the start, to sanity. His rejection of the remorseless claims of blood was but one aspect of his sanity. Even when word came to him of the destruction by fire of Bellefleur Manor and the deaths of both his parents, and, indeed, of most of his family, he showed nothing more than the startled concern a sensitive person might feel for any catastrophe—he might mourn, but he could not truthfully weep.

He had proven, in his massive study, that the future as well as the past is contained in the sky—and so of course there is no death. But there is no pathway to that other dimension, whether it is called "future" or "past." Only by way of miraculous, unwilled slits in the fabric of time that link this dimension with a mirror-image universe of anti-matter can one pass freely into that other world. But of course they are unwilled.

The author of *A Hypothesis Concerning Anti-Matter* maintained a most unusual equilibrium of mood: neither blissful nor melancholy as his fame spread. For since he had proven that the future as well as the past exists, and exists at all times, he had of course proven that he himself existed, and that everything about him existed, and had from the beginning of "time," quite without justification.

Nevertheless he sometimes dreamt of the god of sleep who swallowed them up one by one by one. In that dark place where the sun has no dominion, and a still water abides . . . a still, lightless, bitter-cold water which runs upon the small stones and gives great appetite for sleep. And sometimes he even dreamt, oddly, that the water (but the water was only a metaphor!) had frozen, and those who clung to its surface, upside down, were trapped beneath the ice, their heads lost in the chill shadow, the soles of their feet pressed against the ice. After news came of the destruction of Bellefleur Manor he had this hideous dream, several times. And then, gradually, it faded.

The Destruction
of Bellefleur Manor

And so it came to pass, on the fourth birthday of the youngest Bellefleur child, that the renowned castle and all who dwelled within it both as masters and as servants (and all—a considerable number of persons—who were attending the family council that afternoon, summoned by Leah: attorneys and brokers and financial advisers and accountants and managers of a dozen businesses and factories and mills) were destroyed in a horrific explosion when Gideon Bellefleur crashed his plane into the very center of the castle: a quite deliberate, premeditated act, of unspeakable malice, and certainly not accidental, as Gideon's flying associates were to claim. For how could the destruction of Bellefleur Manor and the deaths of so many innocent people have been an accident, when the plane that dived into the house was evidently carrying explosives, and when it was directed so unerringly, so unfalteringly, into its target . . . ?

(And how ironic was the fact that Gideon's brother Raoul had just arrived at the castle, summoned by a telegram of Leah's—Raoul who had not visited Bellefleur for decades, and who had refused his parents' invitations and summonses and even their frequent pleas. Raoul, about whom so much was whispered, living a decidedly peculiar life down in Kincardine. . . . But so appalled was the family by his behavior, so stricken were they, that they *never* spoke of him; and Germaine was never to learn the smallest detail about him.)

(Ironic too was the fact that Della was at Bellefleur Manor that week, partly to console her brother for the loss of Hiram—who assuredly was dead, and had been buried, though Noel complained of hearing him bumping and stumbling about the corridors late at night, afflicted still with his sleepwalking mania. Ironic also, that young Morna and her husband Armour Horehound were there, visiting aunt Aveline; and Dave

Cinquefoil and his bride Stella Zundert; and a Bellefleur from Mason Falls, Ohio, whom no one had ever met before, but with whom Leah had evidently been corresponding, about the possibility of the Bellefleur corporation acquiring a steel mill there; and there were several others, relatives or acquaintances of relatives, visiting the castle on that unlucky day. Only great-grandmother Elvira and her husband, and great-aunt Matilde, and of course Germaine herself, of the Lake Noir Bellefleurs, survived. Most of the household cats and dogs, with the probable exception of Mahalaleel, who had been missing for some time, were, of course, also destroyed.)

So powerful was the blast, so great the assault upon the earth, that the ground of nearby Bellefleur Village heaved and cracked, and the windows of most of the houses were shattered, and dogs set up a mad forlorn clamor; and Lake Noir rose darkly and pitched itself against its shores, as if it were the end of the world; and the tranquillity of mountain villages as far away as Gerardia Pass and Mount Chattaroy and Shaheen was shaken. The inhabitants of Bushkill's Ferry who rushed from their homes to watch the holocaust across the lake—seven miles wide at that point—were seized with a collective panic, and stared, rigid as paralytics, at the flaming castle, convinced that the end of the world *had* come. (There were those who claimed afterward to have heard, across that great distance, the unbearable screams of the dying, and even to have smelled the hideous blackly-sweet stench of burning flesh. . . .)

Though Bellefleur Manor had appeared to be centuries old, it was, in fact, only about 130 years old. And of course it was never rebuilt since there was no one to rebuild it, or at any rate no one who wished to rebuild it, or had the financial resources to do so: the ruins remain to this day, on the southeastern shore of remote Lake Noir, some thirty-five miles north of the Nautauga River. Weeds and saplings and scrub pine grow there freely, amid the rubble, and every year the earth reaches up a little higher to reclaim it. The place, children say, is *not* haunted.

Shortly after he became the Rache woman's lover Gideon arranged for instructions in the Hawker Tempest with his former teacher Tzara, despite Tzara's superstitious dislike for the plane (he had had, he told Gideon passionately, his fill of bombers in the war: it seemed to him that former warplanes stank of death though they were always miles away from the ghastly deaths they unleashed); and after only seven or eight hours in the air he felt confident, or very nearly confident, that he could manage it alone. It rode the air differently, of course, than any of the lighter planes: one could feel something crude and monstrous about it. While the other planes inspired affection and even love the Hawker Tempest inspired only grim respect.

And there was the matter, too, of the Rache woman's intangible presence, which acted keenly upon Gideon's somewhat overwrought senses.

(For he was very much aware of her, once in the cockpit, with the Plexiglas roof closed and secured. Gideon now owned the plane but he could not help thinking, each time he climbed into it, that he was trespassing; he was violating the woman's innermost being; and he was enjoying it immensely, with an exhilaration he had not felt since the early days of his love for Leah. Tzara never mentioned the Rache woman, though Gideon suspected that he knew she was now Gideon's mistress. He was confident, however, that only he could discern her scent amid the rough odors of metal and gasoline and leather—a scent that lifted from her hair as she shook it impatiently loose; a scent that arose, salty and gritty, from between her small hard breasts with their puckered nipples that looked always as if they were outraged; the scent of her belly and thighs. . . . *How many women have you had before me!* she said with mock bitterness. And Gideon said: *But you will be the last.*)

How fierce the Hawker Tempest was, even when it floated, comparatively noiselessly, at the highest of altitudes! Fierce and urgent and combative and never playful, like the other planes. With its more powerful engine and its greater weight it did not simply ride, it thrust itself forward, like a swimmer, always forward, penetrating the harsh northerly winds as effortlessly as it penetrated the shimmering hot currents of a thermal day. It quivered with strength, it began to look, to Gideon's eye, absurdly crippled on the ground, with its canvas top pulled snug over it like a blindfold on a horse. The red and black of its fuselage seemed to him a muted shout. Such an airplane *must* be freed from the spell of gravity, it *must* be taken into the air as often as possible: so Gideon came to think, exactly, perhaps, as the Rache woman had come to think. When Tzara told him in an offhanded manner that he really should stay away from the Tempest for a few weeks, since the feel of such a plane could become addictive, and could spoil the other planes for him, it was already too late. *There it is,* Gideon thought, when he arrived at the airport each day, *that's the one, it will be only a matter of time now.*

After leaving Germaine at aunt Matilde's Gideon drove directly to the airport, and arrived at midmorning. He was observed in a loose-fitting white suit, wearing a sporty Western-looking white hat no one had seen before, with what appeared to be a band of braided leather. (The hat was later discovered in Gideon's office, left behind, for of course he had worn a helmet and goggles in the plane.) He spoke to Tzara and one or two of the mechanics; he avoided talking with his friend Pete, who arrived at the airport at 10:30, and took up a Wittfield 500; he opened mail, dictated a few letters to the office's only secretary, spoke briefly on the telephone; strolled out along the edge of the runway, in the oil-flecked weeds, his hands in his pockets, his head flung back. (Like all pilots Gideon now studied the air. He knew that the vast ocean of air that stretched invisibly above him, from horizon to horizon, was far more significant than the land. He knew that his human life was conducted on the floor of that invisible sea and that he might redeem himself only by rising free of the land, from time to time, however briefly, however vainly. So nothing mattered quite so much as the texture of the day: were there clouds, and what kinds of cloud; was it warm; was it cold; was there humidity, and haze; was it clear; above all what was the *wind*—that feeble word intended to explain and to predict so much, in fact everything, that was not the earth! He could see and hear and taste the wind, he could feel it on every exposed part of his body; his fingertips twitched with a secret and ineffable knowledge of its mystery.

So his employees observed him, strolling along the runway. Old Skin and Bones, he was. With his limp, and his maimed right hand. With his hot glaring half-crazy eye for women, which was, as the women discovered to their chagrin, really a sign of his vast indifference, his contempt. Old Skin and Bones. Shrunken inside his clothes. His cheekbones prominent, his nose jutting. Elbows and knees jerky. Restless. He could not sit still, could not bear to remain behind his desk, was always pacing, so the secretary complained, imagining he was staring at her when he passed behind her desk, though in fact he had no awareness of her—no interest, of late, in any woman except Mrs. Rache. Gideon Bellefleur. *The* Gideon Bellefleur about whom so much was whispered. His automobiles, and before that, long ago, when he was a young man, his Thoroughbred horses: hadn't he once owned a magnificent albino stallion, hadn't he once ridden it to victory in a race that had brought his family hundreds of thousands of dollars in illegal bets? Or was that, perhaps, another Bellefleur?—his father, or grandfather? There were so many Bellefleurs, people said, but perhaps most of them had never existed. They were just stories, tales, anecdotes set in the mountains, which no one quite believed and yet could not quite disregard. . . .

Though Gideon, of course, certainly existed. At least until the day he committed suicide by diving his airplane into Bellefleur Manor.

He left his rakish white hat in his office, and strapped on a pilot's helmet with amber goggles. His figure was quick and spare, and he walked, observers noted, with an unusually pronounced limp. He had told Tzara he might take the Tempest up for an hour or so but he didn't check with Tzara beforehand, and the perfunctory flight notes he had made—pencil scrawls, nearly unintelligible—were left behind on his desk. Quickly he checked the airplane: the oil, the sparkplugs, the fuel line connections, the propeller, the wings (which he caressed somewhat more hastily than usual, as if not caring what dents or cracks or other imperfections he might discover), the tires, the brakes, the generator belt, the gasoline. And all was well. Not in perfect condition, for the Hawker Tempest was an old plane, rather battered from the War; it was said to have survived more than one crash-landing, and more than one pilot. But it would do, Gideon thought. It was just the thing for him.

With a sudden burst of energy Gideon hauled himself up onto the wing, and into the second cockpit; and there, crouched down in the first cockpit, hugging the two-by-four box on her lap, was Mrs. Rache, awaiting him. She was twisted about, gazing at him over her shoulder. A slow smile, a wordless greeting, passed between them.

So she had come, as she'd promised! She had been waiting for him all along. But discreetly out of sight.

Gideon did not lean into the cockpit to kiss her; he smiled upon her with a lover's lordly yet somewhat dazed smile. She had come, she was his, and the box was on her lap: so it would take place, as they had planned. . . . He did not kiss her, knowing she would draw away in displeasure (for she detested any public show of affection or intimacy, or even friendship), but he could not resist reaching down to squeeze her gloved hand. Her fingers were hard and strong, returning the pressure. It excited him to see that she wore khaki trousers and a long-sleeved man's shirt and a badly scruffed leather vest, and the helmet with the amber goggles that resembled his own. Every tuft, every tendril of hair had been tucked severely into the helmet; her darkly tanned face looked, in the glare of the August sun on the fuselage and wings, almost featureless. *My love,* he whispered.

She had come, she was his! And the box she had promised was on her lap.

Trembling with excitement he climbed inside and settled into place and fastened his seat belt. No parachute—no time for a parachute!—and of course *she* had not troubled with one either. He smiled at the control panel. He primed the engine and started it and listened carefully to hear how it sounded, and he watched the controls as the oil pressure came up, and all was well, all was as it should be. He released the brake. He began to move—it began to move—taxiing somewhat jerkily out along the runway. The engine grew ever louder and more powerful. Daddy, screamed the heartbroken little girl, why did you lie—! But the sound of the engine drowned her out as the air-speed needle leapt off its peg and started around the dial. The control wheel vibrated in his hands.

Farewell to Tzara, who had, perhaps unwisely (for he had sensed from the first the melancholy drift of Gideon's mind), taught Gideon to fly so well; farewell to the mortgaged airport which would soon be bankrupt and abandoned, its runway overgrown with weeds. Farewell to the twelve or fifteen brave little planes spaced about in the grass, awaiting their turns in the air; farewell to the frayed weathercock, and to those who witnessed the fighter's takeoff into a glowering hazy-humid sky in which, at an altitude of less than 1,000 feet, the contours of the land would probably be lost. Farewell to the earth itself: Gideon's pride was such that he hoped never to set foot upon it again.

The runway flew beneath. The propeller's blades disappeared in a blur of speed. The wind, the wind, suddenly the wind came alive, and beat against the plane, but Gideon held it steady and all was well. Sixty miles an hour, sixty-five. The wind wanted now to seize the plane beneath its wings and lift it into the air, perhaps to overturn it, but Gideon held it steady, and near the end of the runway he eased the wheel back and the nosewheel left the ground and they were in the air—they had left the ground, and were in the air—three inches, eight inches, a foot, two feet in the air—in the air and rising—rising—to clear that line of poplar trees—

Now they were safe in the air, and rising steadily: climbing eight feet a second, ten feet a second: and Gideon's hands instinctively maneuvered them through the bumps and pockets of air. The great ocean was invisible, but it was quite solid. One must be extremely skillful to manage it. Three hundred feet, three hundred seventy-five, and climbing, climbing steadily, at six hundred feet he banked to the right, at eight hundred he began a long sweeping climb out and away from the airport, turning toward the south.

All was well: within a half-hour the ordeal would be completed.

He climbed to 2,500 feet, then to 3,000 feet. The ground was invisible. The heat-haze lay everywhere, thinning out only as the plane rose. And then over Lake Noir, over the cooler air of Lake Noir. The noisy plane plunged through shreds of cloud and opened suddenly into patches of clear blazing sunshine and then reentered the clouds again, at 3,500 feet. Gideon felt in the engine's throb and in the fine vibration of the wheel that all was well.

Stray blasts of wind. Voices, faces. Some tore at the windshield as if wishing to open it and pull him out to his death. But of course their frantic fingers were powerless: *he* was in the cockpit, and in control. Others drifted alongside the plane, clutching playfully at the wings, their long hair streaming. Gideon! Gideon! Old Skin and Bones!

He did no more than glance at them, amused. He wondered what *she* thought of them.

An uneventful and fairly smooth passage across the lake, despite its legendary dangers. (Its waters were so cold near the center, pilots said, that planes were tugged downward—tugged downward as if someone were pulling at them. But not Gideon, not today.) Thirty-five minutes from the Invemere airport, on a southwesterly slant across the lake, flying at a moderate speed, for of course there was no hurry: and then they broke through the heat-haze and saw the immense stone castle, glowing a queer pink-gray, a contorted and unnatural sight rising out of the green land.

How oddly it had been constructed, Bellefleur Manor, with its innumerable walls and towers and turrets and minarets, like a castle composed in a feverish sleep, when the imagination leapt over itself, mad to outdo itself, growing ever more frantic and greedy. . . . Gideon had of course seen it from the air in the past; he had spied upon the place of his birth, the place of his ancestors, many times; but on this warmly glowering August day he seemed to see it for the first time, as the destiny to which he had been drawn all his life, as the roaring plane was drawn, descending now from 4,000 feet and beginning to bank, to circle, deftly, shrewdly, with infinite patience (for hadn't he, really, forever?—forever in which to calibrate his own doom, and his release?), now only minutes from the explosion and the conflagration.

In the whitely-hazy August sunshine the castle took on a variety of seductive colors: dove-gray, an ethereal feathery pink, a faint luminous green shading into mauve shading once again into gray. Yet it was stone: a place of massive stone: and he saw that it *was* his destiny, just as this moment, this last long dive, was his destiny, which he would not have wished to deny. He was Gideon Bellefleur, after all. He had been born for this.

Behind the amber goggles his gaze was unwavering.

Here. Now. At last.

And so—

The Angel

One spring day there came to Jedediah a young man with
straight, lank white-blond hair and Indian features—a curious combination indeed—who introduced himself, stuttering slightly, as "Charles
Xavier's brother." When Jedediah told him that he had no knowledge of
"Charles Xavier" the young man looked confused, smiled, squatted on
his heels in the dirt, and appeared to be thinking; for some minutes he
said nothing, making marks with both forefingers in the soft, pliant earth;
then he gazed up at Jedediah with his pale stone-colored eyes and said
again, softly, that he was "Charles Xavier's brother" come to bring Jedediah back with him.

Back? Back where?

Home, said the young man, smiling faintly.

But my home is here, Jedediah said.

Home. Down below.

With my family, you mean—! Jedediah said contemptuously.

The young half-breed shook his head slowly, and gazed upon Jedediah with a look of pity. You have no family, he said.

No family?

No family. Your brothers are dead, your father is dead, your nephews
and your niece are dead: you have no family.

Jedediah stared at him. He had been clearing underbrush all that
morning, working shirtless in the May sun, and the exertion, though
satisfying to his body, nevertheless made his head ring; he could not be
certain he had heard correctly.

No family—? The Bellefleurs—?

Dead. Murdered. And your brother Harlan came to revenge them,
and was shot down at their grave, where he'd gone to mourn them—he

was shot down rushing at the sheriff, which is the way he must have wanted to die.

Harlan? Revenge? I don't understand, Jedediah said faintly.

The young man pulled something out of his vest—a soiled gentleman's glove, lemon-yellow. He held it reverently, and explained that it was Harlan's glove: after Harlan had been carried away he'd found it by one of the muddy graves. Did Jedediah want it? Everything else had been confiscated—you would have thought Harlan's possessions might have been given to Germaine, but they were confiscated: the handsome black hat, the Mexican boots, the silver-handled pistol, the magnificent Peruvian mare with the long, long mane and tail and the hooves (so everyone said, and Charles Xavier's brother had seen for himself) that glittered like quartz or rock crystal. Everything confiscated! Stolen! And the widow bereft! Of course she had the satisfaction of knowing that four of the murderers had been shot down by Harlan. . . .

I don't understand, Jedediah said. His knees buckled; he sat heavily on the ground. I . . . You are telling me . . . My family has been murdered . . . ? My father, my brother . . .

Your father and your brother Louis and your nephews and your fifteen-year-old niece, the young man said in a soft incantatory voice, and now your brother Harlan. Four of the murderers were shot down, as they deserved to be, by your brother Harlan; but the others remain living. Everyone in the community knows who they are. I will tell you their names when it is time for you to act.

Jedediah buried his face in his hands. My father, my brother, he whispered, my brothers, my nephews and my niece and . . .

No, said the young man gently, they didn't kill your brother's wife. She survives, a most unhappy woman. Of course you know her well. And she knows you: she awaits you.

Jedediah had begun to weep. My father, my brothers . . . Will I never see them again . . . !

You will never see them again, the young man said.

Dead? *Murdered?*

It was your choice, Jedediah, to escape them, and to live on Mount Blanc for twenty years; it was not God's will but your own.

Twenty years! Jedediah said. He lowered his hands to stare at the young man. But I haven't been gone twenty years.

Twenty years. It is now 1826. It is the year of Our Lord 1826.

The date meant nothing to Jedediah, who continued to stare at the young man's pale hard rather insolent eyes. What are you telling me! he whispered. What lies! You have come here to—to—

He looked about wildly. Had he no weapon? Only the ax, dropped a short distance away; and a hand saw with a rusted blade. And perhaps the sinister young Indian was armed—

Your sister-in-law Germaine awaits you, the young man said evenly, watching Jedediah with the same pitying expression. You must return and marry her: you must continue the Bellefleur line: and you must exact revenge on your enemies.

Germaine—? Marry—? I— I—

She has not sent me here, no one has sent me here, the young man said, holding the soiled yellow glove out to Jedediah, who was too confused to take it. I act out of a deep love and respect for your family, because I am Charles Xavier's only surviving brother.

Germaine—? She is waiting—? For *me?* But there is Louis—

Louis is dead. Murdered before the poor woman's eyes, along with his father and his children. And his father's mistress as well—but of *that* you needn't know, at this time.

I am to return and marry her, and continue the family line, and—

And to exact revenge upon your enemies.

Revenge? But how do you mean—

Revenge. Of the sort your brother Harlan exacted. An eye for an eye, a tooth for a tooth. As it is written.

But I don't believe in such things, Jedediah whispered. I don't believe in bloodshed.

In what, then, asked the young man, with a subtly ironic curve of his lips, do you believe?

I believe in—I believe— I believe in this mountain, Jedediah said, and in myself, my body—my blood and bones and flesh— I believe in the work I do, in this field I've been clearing— In the wild geese that are flying overhead at this very moment: do you hear them?

You believe in nothing, the young man said flatly. You live on your mountain in your selfish solitude and you believe in nothing, and the nothing in which you believe makes you perfectly happy.

Jedediah pulled at his beard, staring at the young man's harsh Indian features. But I did once believe—I did once believe in God, like everyone else, he said, uncertainly, I *did* believe, once, but it passed away from me —I was purged of my madness—and—and then—

And then you believed in nothing, and you believe in nothing now, said the young man, except your mountain; and, of course, your perfect happiness.

Is it wrong, then, to be happy, Jedediah whispered.

For twenty years you have hidden on your mountain, the young man said, again holding the glove out to Jedediah, pretending that God had called you here. For twenty years you have wallowed in the most selfish sin.

But I don't believe in sin! Jedediah cried. I have been purged of that —of all of that—

And now your sister-in-law awaits you. Down below. The same woman—*almost* the same woman—whom you fled twenty years ago.

She awaits me—? Germaine—? Jedediah said doubtfully.

Germaine. None other. Germaine whom you love, and must marry, as quickly as possible.

Marry—?

As quickly as possible.

But my brother—

Louis is dead.

The children, the babies—

They are dead.

But there *is* no God, Jedediah said wildly, and no one can deceive me: I know what I know.

You know *only* what you know.

But they're dead? And Harlan too?

Harlan too.

Harlan came back for revenge, and—?

He killed four of the murderers, and was shot down himself. He acted with great courage.

But the family is *all* dead, even my father—?

All dead. Murdered in their sleep. Murdered by people who want the Bellefleur line to become extinct.

Ah—extinct! Jedediah whispered.

Extinct. An ugly word, isn't it?

And only Germaine survived?

Only Germaine. And you.

Only Germaine, Jedediah whispered, seeing again the sixteen-year-old's rosy face, the dark bright eyes, the mole beside the—was it the left eye?—the left eye. Only Germaine, he said, and me.

The young half-breed straightened, rising above Jedediah, who was too weak to stand. He held out the glove to Jedediah a third time, and now, gropingly, as if he were only barely conscious of what he did, Jedediah accepted it from him.

Only Germaine, he repeated, blinking at the glove. And me.

How vividly he saw the girl's pretty little face, so darkly-bright, and her eyes so lovely! Twenty years were as nothing: he had *not* been gone twenty years. He looked up at the strange young man, with those harsh Indian features and that lank blond hair that fell to his shoulders, and that queer intimate stare that would, in another time, have maddened him to fury (for of course Jedediah would have believed the stranger was a devil, or at the very least one of the deceitful mountain spirits) and perhaps even to violence: but now, this morning, he did not know, he simply did not know, and wanted to weep with the sorrow of his own ignorance.

Well—she awaits you. Down below. And the others—the murderers —*they* await you too, the young man said.

He was preparing to walk away.

Jedediah scrambled to his feet, panting. But I—I—I don't believe in the shedding of blood—

Do you believe, then, at least, said the young man impatiently, in *marriage?*—in *children?* In your Bellefleur blood?

He was backing away. His expression was no longer pitying; Jedediah thought instead that it showed anger, a half-amused anger; but he was backing away, he was preparing to leave, and Jedediah was too weak to pursue him.

I—I—I don't know what I believe, Jedediah sobbed. I wanted only happiness—solitude—my own soul uncontaminated—

The young man made a dismissive gesture, whether of resignation or disgust Jedediah could not tell. Jedediah had fallen back onto his haunches again, his head ringing, his vision splotched, as if he were about to collapse from heat exhaustion. But he hadn't been working in the sun that long, he was certain he hadn't been working more than an hour or two. . . .

When Jedediah's belief in God had been purged from him the previous year his belief in spirits and devils had been purged as well, and since that day he no longer feared visitors: there had been times, surprising times, when Jedediah had actually welcomed visitors to his cabin: but perhaps, he now thought, burying his overheated face in his hands, he had been mistaken. This insolent stranger had brought him such ugly news. . . .

I don't know, he whispered, I don't know what I believe— I wanted only solitude, and—

The young girl's face arose again in his mind's eye, and he saw that she was smiling shyly; she held an infant to her breast, she was nursing an infant so very small, it must have been less than a month old! He stared, astonished. Whose infant was it? Twenty years were as nothing: surely the half-breed had been mistaken, had miscalculated: Jedediah had *not* been parted from Germaine for twenty years.

The young Indian had gone. Jedediah was alone in the half-acre of stumps and underbrush, sitting on the damp ground. It was unwise to sit like this but he felt too weak, too confused, to stand. And what was this he held, clutched in his trembling fingers—a gentleman's finely-stitched glove, a most impractical lemon-yellow, made of dyed suede cloth now badly soiled?

He stared at it. Harlan's glove. So the young man had said. But perhaps he lied? Perhaps he lied about Germaine as well? But here was the glove: *here* was the glove: it was incontestably real, as real as Mount Blanc itself.

His father—dead?

His brother, his nephews and niece?

And Germaine waiting for him?

And the burden of revenge?

I don't know what to believe, Jedediah cried aloud, clutching the glove in his hand.